It's his dut...
de...

It's a choice b...

DETERMINED TO PROTECT, FORBIDDEN TO LOVE

Three of your favourite authors bring you
three pulse-racing romances

DETERMINED TO PROTECT, FORBIDDEN TO LOVE

BEVERLY BARTON

JOYCE SULLIVAN

CARLA CASSIDY

MILLS & BOON

DETERMINED TO PROTECT, FORBIDDEN TO LOVE
© Harlequin Books S.A. 2009.

First published in Great Britain 2009
Harlequin Mills & Boon Limited,
Eton House, 18-24 Paradise Road, Richmond, Surrey TW9 1SR

The publisher acknowledges the copyright holders of the individual works, which have already been published in the UK in single, separate volumes, as follows:

Ramirez's Woman © Beverly Beaver 2005
Her Royal Bodyguard © Joyce David 2004
Protecting the Princess © Carla Bracale 2005

ISBN: 978 0 263 87166 1

64-1109

Printed and bound in Spain
by Litografia Rosés S.A., Barcelona

RAMIREZ'S WOMAN

BY
BEVERLY BARTON

Beverly Barton wrote her first book at the age of nine. After marriage to her own "hero" and the births of her daughter and son, Beverly chose to be a full-time homemaker, aka wife, mother, friend and volunteer. This author of over thirty-five books is a member of Romance Writers of America and helped found the Heart of Dixie chapter. She has won numerous awards and appears on many bestseller lists.

For my brilliant editor and dear friend,
Leslie Wainger

Prologue

Look at him, the smug, arrogant bastard. And that's what Miguel Ramirez is—a bastard. The son of a whore. What makes him think he's good enough to run for the highest office in the land? The leader of Mocorito has always been a member of the ruling class, an aristocrat, with the blood of royals running through his veins. Yes, it was true that Ramirez's father was the descendant of the last Mocoritian king, but Ramirez had been born out of wedlock, his mother a poor peasant girl who had grown up in the ghetto of the nation's capital, Nava. And Ramirez himself had lived in that same squalor until he was nearly grown. The stench of his plebeian upbringing could not be sanitized by his suave good looks, his beguiling charm or his American education at Harvard.

When Ramirez had qualified to run for office, the opposition had laughed, believing he had no chance of winning. But as the weeks and months went by and it became evident that the Nationalist Party candidate had become the unsung hero of the populace, the opposing party stopped laughing and began plotting. They had dug into Ramirez's past and found not even an inkling of a scandal. And in today's political climate, the fact that he'd been born poor and to an unwed mother only made him all the more appealing because he had overcome the handicaps of his childhood. The man had become a lawyer, who, for the past eight years, had worked tirelessly for the downtrodden and needy citizens of his country, endearing himself to them.

El Presidente, Hector Padilla, had been told that there was only one way to deal with Miguel Cesar Ramirez. Eliminate the son of a bitch. And do it soon. But make sure the assassin could never be traced back to the Federalist Party.

Miguel believed he had been born for this—to be a political force for good in Mocorito. It was past time to oust the corrupt Federalist Party and give power back to the people. His people. His mother's people. The majority vote was his. All the recent polls showed him winning by a landslide if the election were held today. He could think of nothing that would alter the outcome. In less than two months, he, Miguel Cesar Ramirez, the man of the people, would be elected president of Mocorito. The dream of a lifetime was on the verge of coming true.

As he approached the podium, flanked by his staunchest supporters and good friends, Roberto Aznar and Emilio Lopez, the cheering crowd went wild, shouting his name again and again—Presidente Ramirez, Presidente Ramirez.

Smiling, holding up his hands as if to embrace his public as he stood before them in the central downtown square in the heart of Nava, Miguel basked in the pleasure of being loved by his people. His relationship with the people was symbiotic. He loved them, fought for them, gave them his best. And in return, they would bestow upon him the great honor of allowing him to serve them as their leader.

After a good five minutes of trying to quiet the crowd so that he could speak, Miguel finally managed to calm them enough to begin his speech. Not words written by another, not false sentiments and fake promises. But words from his heart. A love letter to his supporters.

"Good people of Nava, now is the time for change," he told them.

The shouts and applause filled the square, drowning out Miguel's next words. But he didn't care. If this speech took him two hours instead of twenty minutes, what difference did it make? There was no place on earth he'd rather be than where he was this very minute.

Suddenly, Miguel heard an odd sound, then the earsplitting screams of frightened people. A spray of bullets ripped across the podium's wooden floor. Emilio knocked Miguel down and fell on top of him, protecting Miguel with his own body.

"Stay down," Emilio told him.

"Has anyone been hit?" Miguel asked.

"I do not know," Emilio replied.

Within minutes, silence prevailed on this warm Autumn afternoon. Eerie, unnatural quiet. Miguel shoved Emilio up and off him, then glanced around and noted the thinning crowd as people fled. On the podium behind him, two of his supporters lay covered with blood. Major Rodolfo and Jose Gomez.

Roberto rushed forward and helped Miguel to his feet. "Are you all right?"

Miguel shook his head. "I am fine, but how are Rodolfo and Jose? How could this have happened?"

"It was an attempt on your life," Emilio said. "We must take you away from here to safety. We can wait in the car until the police arrive."

"Not until we help Rodolfo and—"

"Only our blessed Father in Heaven can help them now," Roberto said. "They are both dead."

Crossing himself, Miguel whispered a hasty, heartfelt prayer.

"We must go. Now!" Emilio grabbed Miguel's arm.

Knowing at this point that his best course of action was to take cover and wait for the police, he allowed his friends to guard him as they crossed the square to reach the big black limousine waiting for them.

Carlos hopped out and opened the back door. "Are you all right, Señor Ramirez?" the chauffeur asked, true concern evident in his voice and his facial expressions.

Miguel patted him on the back. "I am fine, Carlos."

Once inside the limo, Emilio said, "The Federalists were behind this assassination attempt. I would stake my life on it. There is no other explanation."

"We cannot make accusations without proof," Roberto cautioned. "If it was the Federalists, then we will find the proof and tell the people. But it could have been a disgruntled citizen, someone out to kill a politician."

Shaken and angry, Miguel agreed with his two best friends. "Emilio is right. I believe the Federalists sent someone to kill me because they fear that Hector Padilla cannot win reelection. But, you, too, are right, Roberto. We cannot make accusations without proof."

"From now on, you must have a bodyguard with you at all times," Emilio said. "I tried to tell you from the very beginning that you would not be safe without protection."

"How can I parade around with a bodyguard at my side when my opponent has never resorted to using armed men to protect him?" Miguel balked at the thought of showing any weakness. "Padilla has made a point of telling the people that under his leadership, the president has no need for bodyguards as El Presidente of old had, back in the days when the government leadership changed at the drop of a hat and dictators and presidents alike were murdered on a regular basis."

"Miguel is right. He can show no sign of weakness. The Federalists would use it against him," Roberto said. "We must find another way to protect him, one that does not require a bodyguard."

"By not taking heed, you will not only put Miguel's life at risk, but jeopardize our party's chance to take power. We will lose the opportunity for a representative of the people to govern this country." Emilio glowered at Roberto.

"Do not argue, my friends," Miguel said. "I believe I know a solution to our problem."

Both men turned to Miguel, their expressions questioning.

"I was lucky today, but I may not be so lucky a second time. Two good men were killed because they were with me. I cannot show weakness by hiring an armed bodyguard, some burly man who will remind the people of the past. But if a beautiful young woman were in my company, day and night, no one would suspect her of being my protector. They would simply say how fortunate Miguel is to have such a lovely companion. If necessary, we can even pass her off as my fiancée, so as not to upset the female voters."

"Are you suggesting we hire a female bodyguard?" Roberto asked.

"That is a brilliant idea," Emilio said.

"There are no female bodyguards in Mocorito." Roberto threw up his hands in exasperation.

"But I am quite certain that there are female bodyguards in America," Miguel told them. "We will simply contact Will Pierce and ask him to arrange for one to be brought here as soon as possible."

"The CIA cannot send one of their agents here," Roberto said. "The Americans must appear to have no interest in this election. If they provide you with a—"

"I am sure Will can arrange something through an independent agency." Miguel narrowed his gaze thoughtfully. "I will suggest he find me a tall, elegant blonde. Everyone knows that I have a weakness for blondes."

Chapter 1

J. J. Blair zipped in and out of Atlanta traffic on her glacier-white Harley, loving the feel of riding the big, roaring brute. For a woman who was five-two and weighed a hundred and seven pounds soaking wet, the FXD/FXDI Super Glide Custom was big, even though it was actually one of the smaller motorcycles that Harley Davidson built. However, it fit her and her needs to perfection. She never felt more herself, more free and in control than when astride her customized hog. It had taken her three years to put aside enough money to pay cash for this sweet baby—a cool fifteen thousand, once she added all the extras. Two months ago, after purchasing her dream machine, she'd sold her old reliable FXR, the bike she'd bought used six years ago when she'd run away from her old life in Mobile, Alabama.

Having worked off her last case for the Dundee Private Security and Investigation Agency only four days ago, she had thought she might have a full week to kick back and relax. But Daisy Holbrook, the office manager, had phoned her late yesterday evening to inform her that their boss, Sawyer McNamara, needed her to show up for a meeting first thing in the morning.

All Daisy had said was, "The job is in Mocorito, so I figure since you and Dom speak Spanish fluently, you two will be assigned to this case."

"Know any details?" J.J. had asked.

"Nope."

J.J. did speak Spanish fluently, as well as French and some Italian. She also knew a little German, Japanese and Russian, but not enough to do more than order a meal or ask where the restroom was. Her father, Rudd Blair, had been a career soldier, so, as a kid, she'd lived all over, at least until her parents had divorced when she was eleven. Her teachers had been amazed at how adept she'd been at picking up foreign languages. But her mother Lenora had said fiddlesticks, her people, the Ashfords of Mobile, were all brilliant and Jennifer Joy was half Ashford, wasn't she?

As J.J. drove into the underground garage of the building that housed the Dundee Agency, which leased the entire sixth floor, she tried to remember what she knew about Mocorito.

Mocorito was a small island nation off the coast of South America, the population a mixture of races, but the strong Spanish influence of the earliest settlers dominated the country. Okay, so she remembered that much from either high school social studies or from having read something more recently. She wasn't sure which. One thing for sure—her father had never been stationed there.

After removing her shiny purple helmet and shaking loose her black curls, she unzipped her purple leather jacket and headed for the bank of elevators.

Hadn't she heard something on the ten o'clock news last night about Mocorito? She'd been in the kitchen making herself a cup of hot cocoa while the news was on and had returned to the living room just in time to catch the last snippets of the story. The presidential election was coming up in a few weeks and somebody had taken a potshot at one of the candidates. Yeah, that's what it was. Some guy named Romero or Rodriguez. No, no. Ramirez. That was it.

As the elevator zoomed upward, J.J. groaned. Surely that incident didn't have anything to do with this new Dundee assignment. After all, why would a South American presidential candidate hire a security firm based in the U.S.?

When the elevator stopped on the sixth floor, J.J. exited straight into the heart of the Dundee Agency, where she had been employed for the past three years. After leaving Mobile over six years ago, she'd traveled around the country on her FXR for a couple of years, picking up odd jobs here and there and trying to figure out who she was and what she wanted to do when she grew up. Then four years ago she'd wound up in Atlanta. Back in the South. But not the South in which her mother had been reared as one of the privileged Ashfords of Mobile, with hot and cold running servants, membership in all the exclusive clubs and an air of snobbery acquired over generations. No, Atlanta was part of the new South, having shed the past like a snake shedding dead skin.

She had worked for nearly a year at a local martial arts studio, where she'd finally acquired her black belt. Although she'd enjoyed that job, it hadn't been challenging enough for her. When she'd met an Amazonian redhead in a coffee shop near her apartment and discovered that the lady—Lucie Evans—worked for a private security and investigation agency based in Atlanta, she'd made inquiries about employment. Lucie had set up an interview for her the very next week, and, as luck would have it, one of their agents had just resigned.

J.J. had taken to the world of private security like a duck to water. Being trained in the martial arts and having served in the army as a second lieutenant after graduation from college had helped her zip through the six-week training course that Dundee required. Being one of only three women agents at Dundee, she had expected some ribbing, maybe even harassment from the men, but what she'd gotten was acceptance and camaraderie. Even the CEO, Sawyer McNamara, had told her that her looks were deceiving, that she had shown everyone during her training sessions that she was more than qualified for the job despite being a petite bombshell. Sawyer's comment had come shortly after she'd equaled his impressive shooting on the firing range. Her father had taught her how to use a gun when she was twelve and over the years, she had practiced relentlessly to perfect her skills.

Daisy Holbrook, the office manager, also known as Ms. Efficiency, glanced up from her desk located in a glass cubicle in the center hub of the office complex and smiled at J.J.

"Morning," Daisy said. "Love the purple jacket. Is it new?"

J.J. did a feminine twirl. "I splurged on this and a pair of boots to match." She lifted her jean-clad leg high enough for Daisy, who leaned over her desk, to see the supple leather boots.

"Don't you look good enough to eat," a deep masculine voice commented. "Like a delicious purple grape."

Laughing, both J.J. and Daisy turned to face Domingo Shea, Dundee's Latin lover. Some women might take his remark as a sexist comment, but J.J. knew Dom well enough to take what he'd said as the compliment he'd meant it to be. Dom and she were friends, comrades-in-arms and drinking buddies who often played cards with several other agents on a fairly regular basis.

"Well, good morning to you, too, Mr. Tall, Dark and Politically Incorrect." J.J. grinned at the drop-dead-gorgeous Texas heartthrob. Dom was one of those men who took your breath away because he was so good-looking. Jet-black hair that he'd been wearing a bit long and shaggy lately only added to his macho appeal. And when he gazed at a woman with those sharp black eyes, more often than not she melted into a puddle at his feet. Then there was that body. God almighty, what a bod. Six-three, muscular and lean.

"Are you here for the meeting this morning?" Dom asked.

J.J. nodded.

"Vic's coming in, too, for the same meeting," Daisy told them. "It seems he knows people in Mocorito from back in his spook days."

J.J. glanced at the clock on the wall behind Daisy's desk. "We're a little early. Is Sawyer here yet?"

"He's in his office with the door closed," Dom said. "He's holed up in there with Lucie. Some little disagreement concerning her expense account on her last assignment."

J.J. groaned. "There's no such thing as a little disagreement between Lucie and Sawyer."

"No, with those two, it's always all-out warfare." Dom glanced down the hall toward the CEO's office, which was behind the glass-enclosed office of his private secretary. "Who's the guy sitting there in Ms. Davidson's office? Somebody waiting for Sawyer?"

"His name is Will Pierce. I figure he's alphabet soup," Daisy said. "FBI, CIA, DEA. Take your pick."

"Six of one, half a dozen of the other." Dom, a former navy SEAL, knew as well as J.J. and Daisy that a good percentage of the Dundee staff, past and present, had come from various government agencies.

"A new agent?" J.J. looked at Daisy.

Ms. Efficiency shook her head. "We're fully staffed at present and not looking to hire, unless Mr. Dundee decides he wants to expand the business."

"Any chance of that happening?" Dom asked.

"How would I know?" Daisy smiled coquettishly, deepening the cheek dimples in her heart-shaped face.

Dom leaned his six-three frame over the office manager's desk. "Because, Daisy, my darling, you know everything there is to know around here. Don't you realize we're all aware of that fact that you're the one who really runs the Dundee Agency and not Sawyer."

Daisy giggled. "That silver tongue of yours must come from a combination of Latin charm and Irish blarney."

Before Dom got a chance for a response, Sawyer's office door flew open and Lucie Evans stormed out, tromped through Ms. Davidson's office and came barreling down the hall, hellfire in her smoky brown eyes.

"That man infuriates me!" Lucie paused at Daisy's cubicle.

"Like that's a news flash," Dom said under his breath.

"What's he done now?" Daisy asked sympathetically.

Lucie took a deep breath, then let it out with a loud, exasperated whoosh. "Nothing he hasn't done before and nothing he won't do again. He's questioning a twenty-dollar charge on my expense account. It's ridiculous and I told him so. I'm sick and tired of this crap. I have half a mind to quit."

Dom laughed. "Now, Lucie, you and I both know that you are not going to quit, because that's exactly what Sawyer wants you to do and you'd walk over hot coals to keep from letting him have his way, now wouldn't you?"

Lucie huffed. "Yes, you're right. I wouldn't give him the satisfaction of quitting."

"Besides, you enjoy making his life miserable far too much to quit and leave the man in peace," Daisy added.

Lucie smiled, glanced at her friends, and then laughed.

Vic Noble joined the others. "Did I just miss a good joke?" he asked.

Lucie leaned over and kissed Vic on the cheek. "Why can't Sawyer be a sweetheart like you?"

Vic chuckled quietly. "You two been at it again, huh?"

"Considering you're ex-CIA, you wouldn't happen to know a discreet assassin I could hire to eliminate a certain pain in the ass, would you?"

"You don't want Sawyer dead," Vic told her. "You'd miss tormenting the man far too much."

A roar of good-natured laughter rose up inside and around Daisy's cubicle.

The laughter died the minute a deep, authoritarian voice called

loudly from down the hall. "Dom. J.J. Vic." Standing outside his
current secretary's office—the boss went through secretaries on
the average of two a year—Sawyer McNamara motioned for
them with a commanding flick of his big hand. Dressed to the
nines like a model out of *GQ,* he looked like a wealthy businessman. But those who knew him well understood that beneath that
handsome, stylish facade beat the heart of a deadly warrior.

"The master calls," Lucie said. "You'd better run or he'll
threaten to send y'all to obedience school, along with me."

Everyone chuckled, but quickly left Lucie with Daisy and
headed down the hall toward the boss's office. Once the three of
them were inside, Sawyer closed the door and made introductions

"Will, these are the three agents I've chosen for the job,"
Sawyer told their visitor. "Vic Noble is a former CIA contract
agent." Vic nodded. "Dom Shea is a former navy SEAL." Dom
smiled. "And this is J.J. Blair. She's an expert marksman and is
proficient in the martial arts. Dom and J.J. both speak Spanish
like natives."

Mr. Pierce studied the threesome for a full minute, then nodded. "I'm Will Pierce, with the CIA." His gaze met with Vic's
for a split second. "You may or may not know that yesterday afternoon, someone tried to assassinate Miguel Cesar Ramirez, the
Nationalist Party candidate for president of Mocorito. Unoffi-
cially, the United States government wants to see Ramirez
elected. He's a new breed of Mocoritian. A man of the people,
but educated in the U.S. He graduated from Harvard Law School
and has numerous American friends."

"Our interest in this election wouldn't have anything to do
with the fact that Mocorito is in possession of more oil than any
other country in the western hemisphere, would it?" Vic asked.

Will pinned Vic with his pensive glare. "I don't think I need
to answer that question, do I?"

"Señor Ramirez needs a full-time bodyguard," Sawyer said.
"That's where the Dundee Agency comes in."

J.J. narrowed her gaze as she focused on her boss. "Why doesn't he already have bodyguards?"

"Neither the presiding president nor his opponent have bodyguards," Pierce explained. "In the past, before Mocorito was a democracy, the leader—either a president or a dictator or at one time the king—was always surrounded by a contingent of armed guards. President Padilla refuses to have bodyguards in order to show that he has nothing to fear from his people because they love him so much. Ramirez can hardly surround himself with guards and take the chance that he'll be perceived as either weak or afraid."

"Why send us? Why not U.S. undercover agents?" J.J. asked.

"We can't send in any of our people," Pierce said. "If it ever came out that we were backing Ramirez…well, let's just say, we don't want that to happen. And Ramirez has refused a regular bodyguard. The only way he'll agree to having twenty-four-seven protection is if the bodyguard is female and is willing to pose as his lady friend."

J.J.'s mouth gaped open. "Are you saying that I'm supposed to pose as this guy's latest paramour? Are we talking putting on a show for the public only or are we talking about being lovey-dovey in private, too?"

Will Pierce frowned. All eyes turned to Sawyer.

"Only Señor Ramirez, Mr. Pierce and Ramirez's two closest confidantes will know the truth," Sawyer said. "As far as everyone else is concerned—and that includes family, friends, supporters and any servants working in the house—you will be Ramirez's girlfriend."

"His lover, you mean?" J.J. glared at Sawyer.

"If you aren't comfortable in that role, then Señor Ramirez might be willing to present you to everyone as his fiancée," Pierce said.

"Oh, that makes me feel a whole heap of a lot better." J.J. bristled at the thought of having to fight off some Latin Romeo with whom she'd be forced to share a bedroom for the next few weeks.

Dom chuckled. "You can take care of yourself and we all know it. Just lay down some ground rules with this Ramirez guy first thing. If he steps over the line, show him a few of your best moves. You can kick his butt. You've proved you're capable of downing a guy twice your size."

"The election is in four-and-a-half weeks," Pierce said. "Ramirez is the front-runner. We can't allow anything to go wrong."

"While I'm playing kissy-kissy with the future el presidente, where will Dom and Vic be?"

"Vic will be working undercover to help find out who tried to assassinate Ramirez." Pierce glanced at Dom. "Mr. Shea will pose as a distant American relative who has come to Mocorito to cheer on his cousin in his bid for the presidency."

"Dom will be close by if you need him," Sawyer told her. "He'll be living in the same house and his job will be to find out if there's anyone inside Ramirez's organization who can't be trusted." He pinned her with his imposing glare. "J.J., your sole duty will be to protect Miguel Ramirez. Do whatever you have to do to keep him alive and do it without seeming to do it. You understand?"

She nodded. "Cling to Ramirez's arm, bat my eyelashes at him, giggle and smile and act all feminine, but if anyone tries to harm him, stop them without making it obvious that I'm actually a trained bodyguard who just saved the future president's life."

"You'll fly to Caracas by Dundee jet, then go first class into Nava, the capital city," Sawyer explained. "Arrangements have already been made for J.J. and Dom to fly together. Vic will go in separately. Dom, you and Vic go home, pack your bags and meet back here by noon." He turned to J.J. "You go shopping. Buy whatever you need to look totally feminine. Daytime wear, a couple of evening gowns, sportswear and…" Sawyer cleared his throat. "Some negligees, underwear…"

"Say no more." J.J. held up her hand in a stop gesture. "I get the idea."

"When y'all come back into the office, I'll brief you, as a group, on what your roles will be. J.J., you and Dom will use your own names. Our government will do whatever is necessary to make sure any inquiries about one or all of you are handled through proper channels."

Understanding that they'd just been dismissed, Vic, Dom and J.J. headed for the door. Being the last of the threesome to exit, J.J. paused before leaving and asked, "What's my budget for this wardrobe I'm supposed to buy during the next few hours?"

She had asked Sawyer, but it was Will Pierce who answered. "Spend whatever you think is necessary, Ms. Blair. And get whatever you feel you'll need to adequately do your job."

Miguel's home in Nava had once belonged to his father's cousin, Count Porfirio Fernandez, an extremely wealthy old man who had died unmarried and childless. Cesar Fernandez had inherited his uncle's home, various properties throughout Mocorito and his millions. In turn, he had deeded the house to his illegitimate son and set up a trust fund for the child he hadn't known existed until the boy was thirteen. Cesar had never acknowledged Miguel as his own flesh and blood, not legally or in any public way. He had taken care of him financially and sent him to the best schools, educating him in America, as generations of Fernandez men had been educated. But Miguel and his father had met only twice. The first time had been a brief visit at his father's office in downtown Nava when Miguel was eighteen and leaving for Harvard. It was an unemotional exchange, with little said except an admonishment from his father to do well in his studies. Then, three years ago, when Cesar lay on his deathbed, Miguel had been called to the old man's home. It was only then, on the day his father died, that Cesar's legitimate son and daughter had learned of their half-brother's existence. And it was only then that Cesar had mentioned Miguel's mother.

"Luz Ramirez was a very pretty girl, if I remember correctly,"

Cesar had said. "You have her golden-brown eyes, but the rest of you is pure Fernandez."

That was the closest his father had come to acknowledging him.

By anyone's standards, Miguel was wealthy, but although he lived in this beautiful old home and used his trust fund for the upkeep and to pay the servants required to maintain the house and grounds, he had left the bulk of his fortune untouched. Occasionally he used the money to help others, whenever he saw a desperate need. Since returning to Mocorito after law school, he had worked tirelessly for the poor and downtrodden in his country, providing the general public with legal assistance, something few citizens could afford under Hector Padilla's reign.

Often he felt guilty for living so well, surrounded by luxury, here in this magnificent old home, but, God help him, since moving in eight years ago, he had grown to love every square foot of the palatial two-story mansion. This was a home meant to be shared with a wife and filled with the laughter of many children. He intended to marry someday, had hoped that by now he would have met the perfect woman, a lady who would not only love him, but love his dream for Mocorito's future.

Perhaps the lady with whom he planned to dine tonight would turn out to be that person. Emilio's wife, Dolores, was hosting a small, intimate dinner party for six, here in Miguel's home. After yesterday's assassination attempt, Dolores had suggested canceling the dinner, but Miguel had insisted that they proceed as planned. So, Emilio, Dolores and Roberto, as well as Miguel's old and dear friend, Dr. Juan Esteban, and the lovely Zita Fuentes were due to arrive at any moment.

He had met Zita at a political rally several weeks ago, where she had pledged her support to his campaign. Since Zita was a wealthy widow, her support meant more than lip service. She had made a sizable donation that had helped pay for the television ads running day and night now that the election was a little over a month away. Zita was the type of woman who would make a traditional first lady: cultured, demure and subservient to her husband's wishes. Having been married very young to a millionaire industrialist, she had been trained to be the perfect wife for a professional.

He couldn't say that it had been love at first sight for him, but he had been quite attracted to the lady. Black-eyed and auburn-haired, the tall, slender Zita possessed an appealing air of elegance and sophistication. However, now that the U.S. government had arranged to send him a female bodyguard who would pose as his girlfriend, he could hardly begin courting Zita Fuentes. But after the election was over, and his fake relationship with the Dundee agent had ended, he would initiate his plan to woo the alluring widow. He only hoped that making his affair with another woman so public wouldn't ruin his chances with Zita.

"Miguel," a sweet, feminine voice called his name from the open French doors leading from the house to the patio where Miguel stood enjoying the serenity of the enclosed garden.

He smiled and turned to greet a very pregnant Dolores Lopez, his second cousin, who was as dear to him as any sister could be. "You look lovely tonight."

She tsked-tsked and shook her head. "You are wonderful to lie to me. I know I look more and more like a hippopotamus every day."

Emilio, only a few inches taller than his five-six wife, came up behind her and slipped his arm around her waist. He patted her protruding belly. "But you are my little hippopotamus and the prettiest mother-to-be in the world."

She turned and kissed her husband on the cheek, then focused on Miguel. "We are the first to arrive, are we not? I would not want to neglect my duties as your hostess. But you really should have a wife, Miguel. When you are elected president, you will need a first lady."

"I believe Miguel can handle his own love life," Emilio said, always eager to defend the man who had been his best friend since the two were boys.

"I'm not so sure of that." Dolores walked over and kissed Miguel on both cheeks. "He is thirty-five and still unmarried."

Miguel slipped his arm around his cousin's shoulders and hugged her to his side. "I promise you that as soon as this election is over, I will get down to the serious business of finding myself a wife."

"A wife for you and a first lady for Mocorito," a gruff male voice called from behind them.

All three acknowledged Miguel's good friend, Roberto Aznar, who joined them on the patio. Roberto, a staunch Nationalist, was Miguel's campaign fund-raiser, and Emilio was the campaign manager, overseeing every detail of their quest to win the election.

"I will leave you men to talk politics," Dolores said. "I need to speak to Ramona to make sure dinner will be ready at precisely seven-thirty." As she headed toward the open French doors, she asked Miguel, "Did the florist deliver the arrangements I ordered?"

"Yes, yes," Miguel replied. "The flowers are perfect, the dinner table is perfect and we all know that Ramona's meal will also be perfect."

"But of course," Dolores said. "However, I simply must see to everything myself."

Once Dolores disappeared inside the house, Emilio spoke quietly, as if he were afraid his wife would overhear. "I do not like keeping secrets from Dolores. This business of an American bodyguard posing as your lady friend is something we should tell my wife. Otherwise, she'll worry herself sick that you're involved with some American floozy."

"The fewer people who know, the better," Roberto said. "I am very fond of Dolores, but you know as well as I do that she cannot keep a secret. If we tell her, we might as well tell the world and that would defeat the purpose of having a female bodyguard in the first place."

Miguel clamped his hand down on Emilio's shoulder. "In this case, Roberto is right. As much as I love Dolores, I can't trust her with this information. It would be bad enough if the public were to discover I had a bodyguard, but think how the voters would react to learn that I have a woman guarding me."

"I know, I know," Miguel replied. "But once this woman from the Dundee Agency shows up, Dolores will make it her business to become acquainted with her. She guards your back like a fierce mama tiger."

Dom and J.J. took a taxi from the airport to Miguel Ramirez's home in the oldest and one of the most prestigious neighborhoods of Nava. Huge brick and stucco mansions lay behind iron gates, every impressive structure and sprawling lawn well- maintained. Only the very rich and powerful could afford to live here.

"I thought this Ramirez guy came from humble beginnings," J.J. whispered to Dom, speaking quietly on the off chance the cabdriver understood English. "These are rich folks' homes."

"He inherited the place from a relative," Dom said. "Didn't you read the bio on Ramirez that Daisy gave you?"

"I didn't have time to do more than skim it before we left. It took me four hours of intensive shopping to find a suitable ward- robe for this assignment." She adjusted the neckline on the sim- ple beige crepe-knit dress she'd worn on the plane. "I must have missed the part about him living in a palace."

The cabby turned off the street onto a brick driveway that led to a breathtaking two-story, white stucco house, with a red-tiled roof and a veranda that appeared to span the circumference of the mansion.

Speaking in Spanish, the cabby said, "Is Señor Ramirez ex- pecting you? If not, you will not be able to get in to see him with- out passing inspection."

"Miguel is my cousin," Dom replied. "I live in Miami and when he was visiting there this past spring, he invited me to come for a visit."

"A cousin, you say." The cabby's mouth opened in a wide,

friendly smile as he parked the car and turned around to look at Dom and then at J.J. "This lovely lady, she is your wife?"

"No, she's a friend of mine and of Miguel's," Dom said. "Her family has entrusted me with her care while we are visiting here."

The cabby looked J.J. over thoroughly, then nodded. "It is good that her father did not allow her to travel alone. Too many young women are acting like men these days, ruining their reputations and making them unsuitable for marriage."

J.J. had to bite her tongue to keep from making a comment, but when her eyes widened and she clenched her teeth, Dom grinned, knowing full well that she was more than a little irritated.

After they got out of the cab, Dom helped the driver take their suitcases to the veranda, then he tipped the guy generously. "We'll just leave our luggage here for now," Dom said. "Thanks."

As the cabby drove away, Dom rang the doorbell. "Get ready for the performance of your life."

"My playing a lovesick fool will require an Academy-award-winning performance."

A heavyset, middle-aged woman opened the door. Without any expression on her slightly wrinkled, makeup-free face, she sized up the two guests.

"I am Domingo Shea," he said in Spanish. "I am Señor Ramirez's cousin from Miami. And this—" he indicated with a sweep of his hand "—is Señorita Jennifer Blair."

"You are expected?" the woman asked.

"Yes, I believe he's expecting us tomorrow," Dom told her. "But we were able to get away earlier than anticipated. I do hope our early arrival will not be an inconvenience."

"Please, come inside and I will announce you."

Dom and J.J. waited in the massive, marble-floored foyer. Overhead a huge chandelier shimmered with what appeared to be a hundred tiny lights, all reflecting off the crystal gems. A wide, spiral, marble staircase led from the foyer to the second level, the wrought-iron banisters circling the open landing.

"This is some place," Dom said. "I can't imagine any presidential mansion being more impressive."

"Actually, it reminds me a little of my Grandmother Ashford's place in Mobile."

"Poor little rich girl."

"My mother is rich. My stepfather is rich. Me, I'm just an ordinary woman who works for a living."

Moments turned to minutes as they waited. And waited. And waited. After a good ten minutes had passed, a tall attractive man, with thick salt-and-pepper hair and a thin, dark moustache, appeared and greeted them. J.J. guessed his age to be somewhere around forty. Mentally reviewing the photos she'd been shown of the people closest to Ramirez, she realized that this was Roberto Aznar.

"You have arrived a day early." Aznar seemed genuinely agitated.

"I hope that won't be a problem."

"No. No problem. I'm sure the servants can prepare your rooms tonight. I'll ask Ramona to see that your bags are taken upstairs and if you'd like to freshen up—"

"We'd like to see Miguel," Dom said.

"Yes, well…you see, he has guests. He's giving a small dinner party for—"

"Wonderful." J.J. sighed. "I'm starving. You know how airline food is. Like cardboard, even in first class. Please, be a dear and lead us to the dining room." J.J. slipped her arm through Roberto's, much to his astonishment. "Besides, I know Miguel will be thrilled to see us. I'm sure he's missed me as much as I've missed him."

Dom followed as Roberto led J.J. down the hall and into the dining room. The table sat twenty, but this evening the guests were placed at the far end of the table, the two men and two women flanking the head of the table where Miguel Ramirez presided.

When Roberto entered, bringing J.J. with him and Dom coming in behind them, Ramirez rose from his chair.

Impressive, J.J. thought. The man's photographs didn't do him justice. He was one-hundred-percent male, from his wide shoulders to his lean hips and long legs. He was handsome without being pretty. His bronze skin was a shade darker than Dom's, but he had the same blue-black hair, only his was cut conservatively short and neatly styled. But it was his unique golden-brown eyes that captured J.J.'s attention. Large, expressive eyes, the color of dusty topaz.

"Your cousin Dom has arrived a day early," Roberto said. "And look who he has brought with him."

Ramirez hesitated for a moment as he studied J.J. Then he smiled, scooted back his chair and walked hurriedly around the table and straight to her. He opened his arms in an expression of welcome, then reached down and grasped both of her hands in his.

"*Querida,* it is so good to see you again." He kissed first one hand and then the other. "Please, come in and let me introduce you to everyone."

They stood there in the dining room, just beyond the threshold and stared at each other, his gaze locked on her face. J.J.'s heart skipped a beat. Uh-oh, that wasn't a good sign. As a general rule, most men didn't have this effect on her, but when one did, that meant she was in trouble. She had hoped the man she would be protecting wouldn't set off a frenzy of crazed butterflies in her belly. So much for hoping. The little buggers were doing a Saint Vitus dance in her stomach right now.

He led J.J. farther into the room, then paused while the others stared at her.

A very pregnant, black-haired woman glanced from J.J. to Miguel. "Who are these people?"

Dom spoke up first. "I'm Miguel's cousin, Domingo Shea, from Miami."

"And this is Jennifer." Miguel's voice embraced her name. "She is—"

"I am Miguel's fiancée," J.J. said, deciding on the spur of the moment that she did not intend to spend the next month being treated like a mistress. Then she turned and looked Miguel right in the eyes, daring him to contradict her. "That is, if your proposal is still good and you still want me." She batted her eyelashes.

His eyes widened in surprise, but, barely missing a beat, he replied. "Of course, I still want you, *querida*. More than ever."

Chapter 2

The lady was not what he'd been expecting. No six-foot Viking goddess. No cool, sophisticated Grace Kelly blonde. Not even a hard-as-nails, pro-wrestler-type female with a killer look in her eyes. No, Jennifer Blair was none of those things. What she was was a petite, raven-haired beauty with an hourglass figure and the most striking blue-violet eyes Miguel had ever seen. And the way she'd taken charge of the moment—accepting a fictitious marriage proposal in front of an audience—told him she expected to run the show. Call him old-fashioned, call him a macho pig, but he preferred his women to defer to him in all things. And that included his female bodyguard. Miguel chuckled to himself as he held the lady's small, delicate hands. She didn't look as if she could swat a fly, let alone protect a man more than twice her size.

"*Querida*, let me introduce you to everyone." Miguel slipped his arm around her tiny waist and led her farther into the room. Without glancing back, he said, "Come along, Dom."

Dolores glowered at J.J., so much so that he felt his cousin's hostility as if it were a viable thing. "You asked this woman to marry you and you have told no one here about her? I find that very strange."

Emilio cleared his throat, then said hastily. "Miguel told me about Miss Blair, but he swore me to secrecy. Otherwise, you know I would have told you."

"Dolores, don't be upset with Emilio," Miguel said, falling hurriedly into the act that he would have to perpetuate for the next few weeks. "I met Jennifer on my trip to Miami. She is a friend of Dom's and he introduced us. We had a whirlwind romance and I—" The words caught in his throat. Lying about loving a woman was something he'd never done. "We fell in love and I asked her to marry me. But we agreed that she would wait to give me an answer, that we would put some time and distance between us to make sure what we felt was…real love."

Skewering J.J. with her cynical gaze, Dolores came toward her. Dolores knew Miguel the way a sister knows her brother, so convincing her that he was in love with this American woman would not be easy.

"You have decided that you love Miguel and wish to be his wife?" Dolores asked.

"Yes, that's right," J.J. replied, keeping her phony smile in place.

Emilio wrapped his arm around his wife's shoulders and hugged her to him. "Then congratulations are in order, are they not? We should ask Ramona to bring in champagne….er…uh…and sparkling cider for you, my sweet."

"I did not know we had a cousin in Miami." Naturally, the ever-skeptical Dolores was not convinced that J.J. and Dom were genuine. His cousin's feminine instincts had warned her that something wasn't quite right about the situation, that something was rotten in Nava tonight.

"He is my cousin, not yours." When Miguel tightened his hold around J.J.'s waist, he realized that his actions had told her that he was tense, that already the lies were bothering him. "He is from the other side of the family. The son of one of Papá Tomas's cousins."

"Hmm…" Dolores glanced from Dom to J.J. "Have you had dinner?"

A collective sigh permeated the room. Miguel loosened his tenacious hold about J.J.'s waist. Dolores's cordiality did not mean she had accepted these strangers on face value, but it did mean she was giving them the benefit of the doubt and would allow them to prove themselves to her.

"As a matter of fact, we haven't." Dom went around the room, shaking hands and making nice. When he paused by the chair where the elegant redhead sat, the woman stopped glaring daggers at J.J. and smiled at Dom.

"And who is this enchanting creature?" Dom asked.

Not waiting for a proper introduction, she spoke for herself, "I am Zita Fuentes and am I delighted to make your acquaintance, Señor Shea." She cut Miguel to the quick with a withering glare.

"If you all will entertain Dom, I need a moment alone with Jennifer." Not giving anyone a chance to halt him by word or action, Miguel grasped J.J.'s arm and all but dragged her out of the dining room.

Once outside in the hall, she jerked free and stopped dead still. "Do not ever pull that Me-Tarzan-You-Jane routine with me again."

Totally exasperated with this woman, Miguel groaned. "Lower your voice. Sound carries in this old house, especially in the hallways."

She looked him square in the eye and said softly, "Then let's go somewhere more private. We should set up the ground rules for this charade immediately. That way, we'll both know where we stand and what to expect from the other person."

"Agreed. Come with me."

He did not touch her again; instead he allowed her to fall into step beside him as he led her away from the dining room. A few minutes later, he opened the massive double doors to the mahogany-paneled library with bookcases on three sides that reached to the top of the fourteen-foot ceiling.

"Would you care to sit, Ms. Blair?" He indicated one of the two leather chairs flanking the fireplace, in which a warm blaze emitted delicious heat on this unseasonably cool October evening. Here in Mocorito the temperatures seldom dropped below the high sixties.

"I'll stand." She tilted her chin defiantly.

Wonderful, Miguel thought. He was dealing with a hot-headed little feminist. How was it possible that a woman could look like a beautiful young Elizabeth Taylor and be a ball-bashing women's libber? He had encountered numerous women such as this during the years he had spent in the United States, but none had been as lovely as Ms. Blair. And none had been assigned to him as his bodyguard; nor had they played the part of his fiancée for several weeks.

"Suit yourself," Miguel told her.

"I usually do."

Miguel huffed.

"First thing you should know is that there will be no sex between us while we're playing lovers." She crossed her arms over her ample chest, as if it to make a point.

Point duly noted. And her large, full breasts were duly noted, also. "Of course," he replied. "No sex."

"In public, I will play the part of a dutiful, obedient fiancée, a woman totally besotted with you. But in private, I will be myself. Understand?"

"Yes, I understand. And I will do the same. In public, I will be your adoring future husband."

"In matters of your security, my word is law," she told him. "You will make that clear to Emilio Lopez and Roberto Aznar. Neither they nor you will question my authority in that area."

"I assumed Mr. Shea would—"

"Dom is here to do an internal investigation and to act as my backup. I am completely in charge of you."

Miguel groaned silently as the image of this lovely creature dominating him in a very intimate way flashed through his mind, sending arousal signals to his lower anatomy. Willing his traitorous body under control, he nodded, then said, "I am not accustomed to taking orders from a woman."

"Well, 'el presidente,' you'd better get used to taking orders from this woman." She tapped herself in the middle of her chest. "Because until you take the oath of office and we unearth the people behind the plot to kill you, I'm going to be your worst nightmare."

Bristling at her derogatory use of the title, he glowered at her. "Meaning?"

She smiled. "Meaning you're going to obey me, not the other way around. When I say jump, you ask, how high?"

Enough of this nonsense, he told himself. Who did this arrogant, cocksure woman think she was? Miguel Cesar Ramirez had spent his life proving to himself and the world around him that he was a man of integrity and self-assurance, a leader and not a follower. He was on the verge of being elected the president of Mocorito, a country where the majority of women knew their place.

"You overstep your authority, Ms. Blair. You have not been assigned to this job to issue me orders. You are here to watch over me, to ensure my safety, and even to take a bullet for me, if necessary."

She didn't so much as flinch nor did she blush with embarrassment as most females would do. "I haven't been here thirty minutes and already we seem to be at odds over the ground rules. And I had so hoped that your being educated in the United States would have prepared you to deal with a woman as an equal. I will play the subservient female in public, but in private, I am in command. Take it or leave it, Señor Ramirez."

He surveyed her from the top of her head to the tips of her toes. "Your ego is bigger than you are."

"Don't let my size fool you. You know the old saying, don't you?" She grinned mockingly.

He lifted an inquisitive eyebrow.

"Dynamite comes in small packages," she said.

"In your case, I do not doubt it for a moment." And he did not doubt that under the right circumstances, his little American bodyguard would be as hot as a firecracker in bed. In his bed. He would truly enjoy setting her off and seeing the sparks fly.

"Then we understand each other? I'm the boss."

"If you need to think of yourself in those terms, then by all means, do so," he told her.

"Are we at an impasse?"

"If by that you mean it is apparent that neither of us is willing to back down from our position, then yes, Señorita Blair, we are definitely at an impasse."

She heaved a deep sigh, apparently as aggravated with him as he was with her. "We're in a no-win situation. I suppose you realize that. We're stuck with each other, whether we like it or not. There is no way another female agent can come in and pose as your fiancée now."

"Ah, yes, my fiancée. Who gave you permission to announce yourself as my fiancée?"

"I was told that you were willing to pass me off as your fiancée, if the circumstances warranted it." She shrugged. "I felt it was necessary. There's no way I'm going to pretend to be your mistress for weeks on end. Not here in this male-dominated country where mistresses are second-class citizens."

He could not deny the truth of her statement. Mistresses *were* treated as second-class citizens, a fact he knew only too well. His sweet, caring mother had been treated like dirt beneath the feet of the ladies and gentlemen of Mocorito because she had borne her lover's child out of wedlock.

"I had assumed that being an American woman, you would not mind being thought of as my mistress, but apparently I was wrong."

"You were dead wrong."

He studied her closely, forcing himself to break away from those hypnotic violet eyes. She wore a simple dress of some non-wrinkling fabric in a shade of cream, a complimentary shade to her pale olive complexion. The garment was not too tight, but it draped her body like a well-fitting glove. Until this moment he had not truly taken in her appearance, other than to note that she was beautiful, in a sexy, earthy way. Her short black hair curled about her face in soft waves, enticing a man to run his fingers through the silky locks. Her lips were full and painted hot pink, bringing to mind a set of other moist feminine lips. His body reacted in a natural way, warning him that arousal was imminent.

He glanced away, took a deep breath and then turned his back on her. He could not allow himself to continue reacting to her in such a carnal way. "Unless my life is in danger, in public you will be the demure, adoring fiancée. Any disagreements we will keep private, between the two of us. Agreed?"

"I suppose I can live with those terms," she told him, her lips twitching in a barely restrained smile.

"Agreed?" he demanded harshly.

"Agreed, agreed."

He glowered at her. "I will tell my guests that you were tired and wished to have dinner in your room tonight. They will understand."

She laughed.

Damn the woman.

"I take it that I'm being dismissed and sent off to the attic for being a bad girl?"

"Your room is far from an attic. It is the master suite. Ramona will bring you a dinner tray and unpack your suitcases and attend to any of your needs. If you require a personal maid while you are here, I will provide you with one."

"You're giving me the master suite? How kind of you to give up your personal quarters—"

"I give up nothing," he told her. "As my fiancée, you will share my suite and my bed. Since you are an American and assumed not to be a virgin, it will be expected."

"Hold up just a minute there, 'el presidente.' Sharing your suite is okay. As your bodyguard, I will need to be close to you, but—"

"Feel free to sleep on the floor, if you wish, as long as none of the servants are aware that you are doing so."

Tilting her chin so that she could look him directly in the eyes, she said, "Believe me, sleeping on the floor will be preferable to sharing your bed."

A scrapper to the bitter end, Miguel thought. Such passion. "You, Señorita Blair, are in a minority. Most of the women I've known would much prefer to share my bed."

"You'll find that I'm not like most women."

"I have already discovered that fact."

She gave him a sharp nod. "Very well. I'll go quietly upstairs to *our* room for the evening, but beginning tomorrow morning, I'll be stuck to your side like glue, twenty-four-seven."

He bowed graciously, then smiled at her. "I look forward to every moment. Now, if you will excuse me, I'll send Ramona to see you to *our* room, then she'll bring your dinner up on a tray. And I'll see that Paco takes care of your and Mr. Shea's luggage."

"Perhaps you should call us Dom and Jennifer, even in private," she told him. "It will help you become accustomed to our names. After all, you wouldn't want to slip up and call your cousin Mr. Shea or your beloved fiancée, Ms. Blair."

"Point taken…Jennifer. Or would you prefer that I call you *querida?*"

"You choose, depending on your mood."

If he called her what his present mood dictated, his grandmother would come down from heaven and wash his mouth out with soap, as she had done when he was a child and had dared to use foul language in her presence.

* * *

With Señorita Blair—Jennifer—ensconced in his suite upstairs and his "cousin" Dom regaling his friends with a completely fictitious story of how Miguel had contacted him on his most recent trip to Miami, Miguel breathed a sigh of relief as he rejoined the others in the dining room.

"You've missed dessert," Dolores told him, then eyed him inquiringly. "Or perhaps you consider time alone with your future wife sweeter than any of Ramona's delicious pastries?"

"Well put, little sister," Miguel said, but his gaze connected with Zita's. Her expression told him that she was displeased, that she had come here tonight expecting this to be the first evening of many they would share. He could hardly tell her that he, too, had wanted the same. But those plans had been altered by circumstances beyond his control. First and foremost, his loyalty and dedication belonged to the people of Mocorito. Any personal happiness had to come second.

He turned to Roberto. "My dear friend, will you please see Señora Fuentes home? I'm afraid the sudden arrival of my darling Jennifer and Cousin Domingo must, of necessity, bring our evening to an early close."

"Of course, Miguel, I would be delighted to escort the *señora* home." Roberto walked over and held out his hand to Zita, who smiled graciously and rose to her feet.

"I shall say good night, also," Dr. Esteban said. "I have early rounds at St. Augustine's in the morning and will be rising before dawn."

"Juan, thank you for coming tonight." Miguel shook hands with his old friend, a man who shared his hopes and dreams for a true democracy in Mocorito.

"You must bring your lovely fiancée to dine with Aunt Josephina and me one evening soon, before the two of you are flooded with invitations," Juan said. "Everyone in Nava will be eager to meet Señorita Blair."

"And naturally, I would be honored to receive an invitation to your engagement party," Zita told him as Roberto led her past Miguel.

"Of course. How very gracious of you, my dear Zita." Miguel was not sure she would ever forgive him for this farce, even if he explained everything to her when the danger had passed and he had been elected president. It was possible that this evening's events had destroyed any possible future he might have had with the charming young widow.

"Since all of you are making it an early evening, I think I'll do the same," Dom said. "If you will have someone show me to my room, I'll call it a night."

"I have sent Paco for your and Jennifer's bags," Miguel said. "Once he has delivered Jennifer's luggage, I'll have him show you upstairs."

"In the meantime, why don't you walk Emilio and me to the door?" Dolores said to her cousin.

Miguel would have preferred to avoid being drilled by Dolores. But better to get it over with tonight and hope he could persuade her of his sincerity. His little cousin knew him too well and even if he swore to her on his mother's grave, she would still have some doubts. Whenever she was around, he would have to be doubly careful because she would watch him with Jennifer Blair as a hawk watches a chicken.

They had no sooner exited the dining room than Dolores checked to make sure Roberto and Zita were not within earshot, then she began the inquisition.

"She does not look pregnant, your fiancée," Dolores said. "So why are you marrying this woman you barely know? An American woman! Is she Catholic? Is she willing to give up her United States citizenship? Do you truly love her or is it just great sex that has you acting like a fool?"

Emilio mumbled under his breath, evoking God to take pity

on them—he and Miguel. "Dolores, *querida,* have faith in Miguel. Everything he does, he does for the right reasons."

Halting before reaching the foyer, she snapped her head around and glared at her husband. "Exactly what does that mean?"

Miguel put his arm around her shoulders. "It means that I am engaged to be married to a woman who will be sharing my life these next few weeks as she stands at my side and helps me win the presidency. Jennifer has come to me to help me, not harm me in any way. She understands the duties she must perform as my fiancée and she will not fail me. I trust her with my life."

Dolores studied Miguel contemplatively. "Do you have any objection to my spending time with her? To our becoming better acquainted?"

"None whatsoever," Miguel replied. "As long as you treat her with the respect she deserves as my future wife."

"Do you love her?"

"Would I ever ask a woman to marry me if I did not love her?"

Dolores sighed, then reached up and caressed his cheek. "Then I pray that she loves you as much as you do her."

Emilio emitted a nervous chuckle. "As far as you are concerned, no woman would ever be good enough for Miguel."

"Perhaps that is true," she agreed.

"Come, come. We must go and get you to bed, little mother. You need your rest." Emilio hovered over his wife, petting and soothing her as best he could.

Miguel stood on the veranda and watched his guests leave. First Roberto and Zita, then Juan Esteban and finally Emilio and Dolores. The evening had not gone as he had hoped due to the unexpected arrival of his American guests.

"Lovely evening," Dom Shea came up beside Miguel.

"It was."

"Sorry that we stormed in on you without warning, but our orders were to get here as quickly as possible."

"Will Pierce's idea, no doubt."

Dom glanced all around, then asked in English, "Do your servants speak English?"

"No, they do not," Miguel replied.

"Then I suggest that whenever we need to talk concerning private matters here in your home, that you, J.J. and I speak English."

"J.J.?"

"Her name is Jennifer," Dom replied. "But no one calls her that."

Miguel nodded. "Was she the only female agent available?"

Dom chuckled. "She's a handful, isn't she? But she's good at her job. You'll be in safe hands with her." Dom took a deep breath of fresh evening air. "To answer your question, no she wasn't the only female Dundee agent available, but she was the best-qualified for this assignment. As you must have noticed, she speaks fluent Spanish."

"Yes, her command of the language is excellent."

"You should know from the years you spent in the U.S. that American women are not like Mocoritian women. And J.J. is a breed apart. You look at her and you see sultry sex kitten, but I suspect you've already learned that in her case looks can really be deceiving."

"That, Mr. Shea, er, Dom, is the understatement of the century."

"May I give you some advice on how to handle J.J.?"

Miguel turned and looked at Domingo. The two of them being of almost equal height, they stood eye-to-eye. "I would appreciate any advice you can give me."

"Don't try to boss her around. She hates that. Let her think something is her idea, not yours. Make suggestions, but ask her opinion. Allow her to believe that she is totally in charge."

Miguel smiled. "You know her well, do you? There is a personal relationship between the two of you?"

"I've worked with J.J. for three years. I like and respect her. We're friends. Nothing more, nothing less. But I should warn you that if you do anything to hurt her, you'll have at least half a dozen of Dundee's best men coming after you."

"I certainly do not want that."

Miguel and Dom stood on the veranda for several more minutes, not speaking, then Dom broke the silence. "We need to discuss something you probably prefer not to talk about at all."

"And that would be?"

"The loyalty of your friends, closest supporters and household employees. My job is to make sure there are no traitors in your camp."

"I trust my friends and employees completely, as I do the supporters I have known for many years."

"But you don't have any objections to my digging around in their lives, do you? I will do it as discreetly as possible."

"Is that really necessary?"

"Someone tried to shoot you yesterday, Señor Ramirez," Dom said. "And behind the shooter is the person who hired him. That person wants to see you dead."

"We are relatively certain that the Federalist Party was behind the assassination attempt, which means Hector Padilla was part of the plot."

"That may be true, but I doubt President Padilla actually hired the rifleman who fired at you. We need to find the person or persons who paid the assassin. Often, behind something like this, you'll find a small group of people, not just one person."

"You will discover that none of my friends, supporters or employees are involved," Miguel said with total assurance. "But I give you permission to do the job Will Pierce hired you to do."

"Hmm…"

"What?"

"Another bit of advice."

"Yes?"

"When you speak to J.J., try not to use those exact words."

"What words?"

"Don't ever say to her that you give her your permission to do something. That would be like waving a red flag in front of a bull."

Miguel snorted. "Other than the fact she speaks Spanish fluently, what possible reason could your superior have thought she was the ideal person to pose as my girlfriend?"

"Your fiancée, not your girlfriend."

"Yes, she chose to become my fiancée instantly, without consulting me. That is a case in point of why she is unsuitable."

"She really ticked you off, didn't she?"

"Let us just say that I would prefer facing a mountain lion without a weapon than having to deal with your J.J."

"She's not my J.J. She's your J.J., Señor Ramirez, at least for the next few weeks."

"¡Que Dios me ayude!" Miguel said aloud, then repeated the prayer to himself. God help me!

Chapter 3

Miguel's bedroom suite comprised three rooms—bedroom, sitting room and bath—and a massive walk-in-closet that had probably, at one time, been a small nursery. A huge round iron chandelier hung in the middle of the ten-foot-high ceiling, crossed with weathered wooden beams. The stucco walls possessed a soft gold patina, as did the cast-stone fireplace, which was flanked by sets of double French doors. A plush coral velvet sofa hugged one wall. Round tables and nail-head-trimmed chairs in taupe leather served as bookends for the marble-topped decorative-iron coffee table in front of the sofa. Across the room, two rich gold arm chairs sat like fat mushrooms growing out of the antique Persian rug.

Luxurious was the first word that came to mind.

Paco had deposited J.J.'s bags in the closet and told her that Ramona would see to the unpacking in the morning. That had been at least twenty minutes ago and it had taken her every second of that time to explore the rooms she would be sharing with

Miguel for the next few weeks. It wasn't that she hadn't known luxury before—she had when she'd lived with her mother and Raymond, her stepfather, in their twenty-room mansion in Mobile. But this was no antebellum mansion, although she suspected it was as old, if not older than many of the homes built pre War Between the States.

The French doors led to a large balcony that overlooked the courtyard gardens. J.J. had stood out there for several minutes, breathing in the cool night air and thinking about how she would handle her first night with the future president of Mocorito. If she weren't terribly attracted to him on a purely physical level, it might be easier to share these intimate quarters without her mind wandering from the job at hand to considering what it would be like to actually be engaged to this man.

She would never—not in a million years—marry a man like Miguel Cesar Ramirez, a male chauvinist from the old school of male superiority. But the very thing that she disliked about him the most was what also attracted her to him. That powerful male essence that declared to one and all that he was king of the hill, master of all he surveyed. Her father had been that kind of man. *Was* that kind of man. Rudd Blair was a career soldier, having moved up the ranks over the years. The last she'd heard, he was a general and his son, eighteen-year-old Rudd, Jr., had just graduated from military school. She had spent her entire life trying to earn the privilege of being what her half-brother became the moment he was born—the apple of their father's eye. Hell, she'd even joined the army after college graduation in the hopes that her becoming a soldier would please her father as much as it pissed off her genteel, Southern-belle mother. But it hadn't mattered to Daddy Dearest that she had graduated top in her class or that she'd excelled in her duties as a second lieutenant. As far as Rudd was concerned, J.J. was nothing more than a female offspring who should get married and do her best to produce some grandsons for him.

Okay, so it was unfair to compare Miguel to her father, despite the fact that they were probably cut from the same prejudiced cloth. She figured that over the next few weeks, she would learn to dislike Miguel intensely for reasons that had nothing to do with her past history with her father.

A soft rapping at the door drew J.J.'s eyes in that direction. "*¿Sí?*" she asked.

"I have your dinner, *señorita*," a woman's voice called from the other side of the door.

Ramona, no doubt. "Please, come in." J.J. rushed across the room to open the door.

Carrying a small silver tray covered with a white linen cloth, Ramona entered the room, walked over and placed the tray on the coffee table and turned to J.J. "If you require anything else, *señorita*—"

"No, thank you. Not tonight."

Ramona nodded, then turned and left the sitting room. The woman had been neither friendly nor unfriendly. J.J. wasn't certain how she should interact with the servants in Miguel's house. The servants who worked for her mother were treated well, but were thought of as socially inferior, and one never associated with them on a personal level. However, her mother was especially fond of her old nanny; Aunt Bess, as everyone in the Ashford family referred to the woman, was now eighty-six and living in an assisted-living facility paid for by Lenore Ashford Whitney.

J.J. hated barriers of any kind—social, economic, race or religion. And sex. Her mother had been a snob, her father sexist. She prided herself on being neither. That was one reason she could not allow herself to judge Miguel without getting to know him better. He deserved to be judged on his merits and flaws alone and not on some preconceived idea J.J. had of him.

Wondering what Ramona had brought for her to eat, J.J. removed the white linen cloth from the silver tray. Cheese, bread, grapes, wine and some sort of cake that looked sinfully rich. She grabbed the grapes and nibbled on them as she strolled into the bedroom. This room intrigued her, and for more than one reason. She had no intention of this area becoming a battleground tonight or in the nights ahead.

What makes me think he's going to try something? she asked herself.

The answer came immediately. He's a man, isn't he?

But I don't think he likes me any more than I like him.

Maybe not, but that unnerving charge of awareness you felt wasn't a one-sided thing. That sensation of I-want-to-rip-your-clothes-off-and-have-you-here-and-now tore through his gut just like it did yours.

She'd seen that look in his eyes. Had he seen it in hers? If so, he would make his first move tonight.

The bedroom was as large as the sitting room, but where the latter had been decorated in warm, earthy shades, the decor in this room reflected peace, tranquility and age-old charm. Everything in the room, from bed linens to lamp shades, reflected the simple elegance and color scheme of the ivory stucco walls. Color came from the rich glow of the dark wooden floors, accent pieces, and dark wooden bedside tables. The king-size bed was modern in size and structure, but an intricately carved wooden arch made a dramatic antique headboard.

The bed was large enough that she could actually lie beside Miguel and never touch him. Yeah, sure, like she was going to take the chance that he wouldn't touch her.

Scanning the twenty-by-twenty room, J.J. sought and found an alternative place for her to sleep. A large, comfy chaise lounge, covered in ivory damask, sprawled languidly in front of the floor-to-ceiling windows. All she needed to make the chaise her bed was a pillow and a blanket. Both items would be easy to discard come morning, to keep the servants unaware that she had not shared a bed with Miguel.

Finishing off the grapes, J.J. returned to the sitting room and hurriedly ate part of the cheese and bread, then lifted the glass of wine and carried it with her as she headed for the bathroom. Would she have time for a leisurely soak in the massive marble tub before Miguel came upstairs for the night? Nope. Better not risk it. A quick shower would have to suffice.

She entered the walk-in closet, set her glass on top of a high-boy to her left, then bent over and opened one of her suitcases. Without giving much thought as to which peignoir set to wear, she yanked up a lavender silk gown and matching robe from the large bag. She hurriedly turned around and grabbed her wineglass on the way back into the bedroom. When she entered the bath-room and hung the gown and robe over the vanity chair, she sighed as the light hit the almost iridescent silk. At home she slept in pajamas in the winter and an oversize T-shirt in the summer. Since it was rare that a man ever saw her in her sleepwear, she didn't own anything really sexy, certainly nothing like the items she had purchased with her corporate charge card.

Stop it, right this minute, she warned herself. She could not—would not—allow herself to wonder what Miguel would think or how he would react when he saw her in the ultrafemi-nine lavender peignoir set. Besides, if she timed things just right, she'd be asleep on the chaise by the time he came up for the night and she could either rise early and be out of the bed-room before he got up or she could sleep late and let him be the first to leave.

He had been expecting a telephone call about Miguel's secret bodyguard, but not tonight. His contact—the spy with Ramirez's camp—had told him the Dundee agent would arrive tomorrow.

"His American bodyguards arrived early. They came tonight instead of in the morning as we'd been expecting."

"Did you say two bodyguards? I thought there would be only the woman." He swirled the liquor in the crystal tumbler, sniffed the aroma and took a sip.

"Yes, there are two," said the quiet voice at the other end of the line. "One male and one female. They are telling everyone that the man is Miguel's cousin from Miami and the woman is Miguel's fiancée."

"Fiancée? I thought she was to pose as his mistress." He did not like it when plans changed—especially when the change was not in his favor.

"That was the original plan, but this American woman accepted his proposal there in front of everyone present tonight."

"Then our plan to use the woman against him will have to be altered." He set aside his glass, placing it atop a stone coaster on his desk. "A mistress can easily be discredited. A fiancée is a different matter. If the voters believe he plans to marry this woman, they will view her in a different light."

"If we cannot use the woman against him, we must find another way. I do not want Miguel killed, only frightened enough to withdraw from the presidential race."

Personally, he would prefer Ramirez dead and buried, but if they killed him, the people would see him as a martyr and possibly revolt. That was the last thing he and his party wanted. Besides, this traitor who had proved so useful to him was not the only Federalist who did not want to resort to murdering Ramirez. Some of them had no stomach for fighting dirty, for doing whatever it took to win. And some of those weak men already thought of him as a bloodthirsty tyrant.

"We tried scaring Miguel with the assassination attempt, but he simply hired a bodyguard, using his contact with that American CIA agent to hire her. If only we had some type of proof that Miguel has sold out to the Americans—"

"We have discussed this before, as you well know. If we could prove this to be a fact, it could well work against us instead of for us. A vast majority of the people here in Mocorito see the U.S. as an ally, a friend who will help us."

"Then perhaps we could reveal that the woman and man liv-

ing in Miguel's home are actually American bodyguards, that he
has lied to the people. That could make them turn against him."

"Putting out such a rumor will be easy enough, but proving
it is a different matter. Unless you can prove your claims, trying
to discredit Ramirez could harm us instead of him. The people
adore him, unfortunately. They see him as their hero."

A very unpleasant thought suddenly crossed his mind. Once
he had learned that the Dundee Private Security and Investigation Agency would be involved, he had made it his business to
find out everything he could about them. The private bodyguard
for Miguel did not worry him. But the fact that another agent had
come with her did concern him. What if there were others? What
if they were mounting an investigation? "Are the two American
bodyguards who arrived tonight, the only two?"

"What?"

"Are there others? Perhaps working undercover?"

"If there are, I don't know of them."

"Find out."

"But how?"

"You will think of a way."

Dolores traipsed through the house in her bare feet, stopping
outside the door to her husband's study when she heard him
speaking in a low, quiet voice. She knocked on the closed door,
then entered. Emilio jerked around and stared at her, his eyes
wide, his hand clutching the telephone receiver.

"Who are you talking to this late at night?" she asked.

He covered the mouthpiece with his hand and replied, "Roberto. We are discussing how to handle the announcement of Miguel's engagement." He removed his hand and said into the
telephone, "We will discuss this matter further in the morning."
He hung up the phone and held open his arms for Dolores.

She went to him, allowing him to envelop her in his gentle,
loving embrace. There had never been another man for her. Only

Emilio. Since they were children together—she, Emilio and Miguel—she had loved Emilio and had always known that someday she would become his wife. Their road to happiness had taken many years and numerous detours, but in the end, she had been blessed with all she desired. She had been Emilio's wife for two years and now she was carrying his child. His son.

"You must be tired, *querida*." Emilio rubbed her back with wide, circular motions.

"You should rest more and not do so much work on Miguel's campaign. And now that he has a fiancée, you must allow her to take over the duties as his hostess."

"What do you know about this woman, this Señorita Blair?"

Emilio shrugged. "Only that Miguel met her on his last trip to Miami and asked her to marry him."

"It is not like Miguel to keep such important news from me."

"Perhaps he wanted to wait to see if she would accept his proposal."

"Hmm…perhaps."

Emilio turned her around and urged her into movement. "Come to bed with me."

She smiled at her husband. "And we will make love?"

"I would like nothing more, but if you are too tired—"

She stopped him with a kiss, one that quickly became passionate. His strong, smooth hands moved over her shoulders and across her heavy breasts. When he flicked her tight nipples with his thumbs, she moaned deep in her throat.

"Did I hurt you, my love?"

"No, no, you didn't hurt me."

Hand-in-hand, desire burning inside them, they rushed to their bedroom and closed the door. Within minutes, Dolores no longer thought about Miguel and his mysterious American fiancée or about Emilio's late-night phone call from Roberto.

Josephina Esteban Santiago did not sleep well. Her arthritic hips often woke her in the night and once awake, her overactive brain would not allow her to fall peacefully back to sleep. Since she often woke several times during the night, she usually went to bed early and stayed in bed late. The financial support of a loving nephew afforded her certain luxuries in her old age. Not that she was impoverished. Her late husband had left her comfortable, but she had used a great deal of her money to send Juan to medical school. She was so proud of him, her brother's only child, a boy she and her late husband Xavier had taken into their home shortly after his parents were killed in a car crash when he was nine.

As Josephina crept along the semidark hallway toward the kitchen, she thought she heard voices coming from the parlor. Surely not at this late hour. It was nearly midnight. But she paused and listened. Yes, that was Juan's voice. She would recognize it anywhere. Not meaning to eavesdrop, she turned and continued toward the kitchen, but before she reached her destination, Juan called out to her.

"Is that you, Aunt Josephina?"

"Yes, dear. I am sorry to have bothered you. I am going to the kitchen to prepare some warm milk. That often helps me sleep."

"I'll come with you and we will drink warm milk together," he told her as he came out of the parlor.

"You're up rather late, aren't you, dear?" She patted his cheek when he drew near enough for her to touch him. "Did Miguel's dinner party last this long?"

"No, it actually ended a bit early," Juan told her, then leaned down to kiss her cheek. "You heard me speaking on the telephone, didn't you?"

"Yes, I heard you speaking to someone, but I couldn't hear what you were saying."

"I was on the phone with St. Augustine's. I wanted to check on a patient whose condition greatly concerns me."

"You are such a good man. Such a conscientious doctor."

"You thought I was on the telephone with her, didn't you?" A frown marred Juan's handsome face. Handsome to her, although perhaps not to everyone. His wide, flat nose and high cheekbones revealed his mother's Indian heritage, while his height had been inherited from the Esteban family, who could trace their roots all the way back to Spain. What her nephew lacked in good looks, he made up for in brains and talent.

"It is none of my business to whom you speak," Josephina told him. "But you know how I feel about her. She is a woman betrothed to another man, yet she seeks you out time and again. If anyone discovers that—"

He grasped her hands in his and held tightly. "We are friends, Aunt Josephina. Only friends. She is very unhappy and needs to talk to someone she can trust. I am her doctor."

"And she tells you she does not want to marry this man because she does not love him. What nonsense. In my day, we married for better reasons than love."

"There is no better reason," Juan said, a wistful tone to his voice.

"You may be only friends with her, but you love her, do you not?"

"Come along and let me prepare us both some warm milk."

Josephina allowed him to change the subject momentarily as he led her into the kitchen and aided her in sitting at the table.

"If she does not marry this man, her family will disown her, especially if they discover she has feelings for you and learn that you are one of Miguel's dearest friends." Josephina cradled her stiff, aching hands in her lap. Arthritis was such a curse. "Have you told Miguel that you are friends with his sister?"

"His half-sister," Juan corrected. "And no, I have not mentioned my friendship with Seina to Miguel. There is no love lost between Miguel and Cesar Fernandez's family. Seina knows that Miguel is my friend. She has no animosity toward Miguel, not the way her brother and mother do."

"Be careful, my dear boy, that Seina Fernandez does not use you in any way."

"What are you implying?"

"As you say, there is no love lost between Miguel and his late father's family. It is no secret that the Fernandez family support the reelection of Hector Padilla. If they could use you against Miguel, they would."

"I would never allow that to happen."

"I hope not. Miguel is a good friend and he is the people's hope for the future of Mocorito."

Roberto Aznar hung up the telephone and turned off the light. The lady waited for him. He would be a fool to leave her, not after such a warm invitation to stay the night, to share her bed. Perhaps she had made the offer only because she was angry with Miguel, but he was not a man who would turn down a beautiful woman just because she wished he were another man. The loving would be just as good for him regardless of who Zita Fuentes pretended was between her spread thighs. It wasn't as if he would be betraying Miguel. After all, Zita and Miguel had not had even one date and now that Miguel had a phony fiancée ensconced in his home, in his bedroom, it was highly unlikely that Zita would forgive him, even if the truth about the American woman came to light. Besides, after the election, when he was assigned a choice government position, he would be on a more equal footing, at least socially, with women such as Señora Fuentes. Who knew, without Miguel as a rival for Zita's affections, she might consider him as potential husband material. What a delectable thought—having access to the lady's millions, as well as having her in his bed every night.

"*Querido,* why are you keeping me waiting?" Zita called from the head of the stairs. "I thought you had to make only one phone call."

Taking the steps two at a time, he rushed upstairs and into the welcoming arms of the luscious and naked widow.

Miguel stayed up past midnight, deliberately giving Señorita Blair enough time to eat, bathe and go to sleep. He did not want another confrontation with her tonight.

Standing outside the door to his bedroom suite, he hesitated, wondering if, when he went inside, he would find her asleep in his bed. Would she be curled up in the middle of the down mattress topper, sleeping like a little black kitten, purring softly as she breathed in and out, her breasts rising and falling with each heartbeat?

He could not continue doing this to himself. Yes, she was a highly desirable woman and yes, they would be together day and night, possibly for weeks. But an affair was out of the question.

Why was it out of the question?

She was a woman; he was a man. Neither of them was married or otherwise attached. Why shouldn't they consider an affair?

Miguel opened the door quietly and eased into the semidark room. Only the moonlight floating through the double set of French doors on either side of the fireplace illuminated the sitting room. Scanning the area, halfway expecting to find her asleep on the sofa, he moved toward the bedroom when he did not see her.

The bedroom was slightly darker, but enough light came through the floor-to-ceiling windows for him to make his way into the room without tripping over anything. Within minutes his eyes had adjusted to the dark and he noted that his bed had been untouched, except for a missing pillow. As he made his way across the room, heading for the closet, he paused and searched for her. She lay on the chaise lounge, a cotton blanket covering her from the waist down, leaving her bare shoulders and neck visible.

Was she asleep? Should he call her name? Or should he do the wise thing and ignore her? But how did a red-blooded man ignore the fact that a scantily clad woman was in his bedroom, sleeping only a few feet away from him?

Miguel entered the closet, flipped on the overhead light, then closed the door halfway. After finding his robe, he searched through the highboy for a pair of pajamas. He owned several, but seldom wore them, preferring to sleep in the raw.

Chuckling silently to himself, he wondered what Señorita Blair would think if she woke in the morning to find him lying naked in his bed? Being an American woman who had probably been with many men, he doubted she would be the least bit shocked.

Just how many men had there been in Jennifer's life? Two or three? A dozen? Two dozen? She looked young, no more than her late twenties, but American girls became sexually active in their teens, so it was possible that she'd had numerous lovers.

Why should he care how many lovers his make-believe fiancée had had? It wasn't as if he was actually going to marry this woman, or that she would be the mother of his children.

After rifling through every drawer in the highboy, he finally found two pairs of pajamas, one set silk and one cotton. He chose the black silk, which had been a gift from a lady friend a number of years ago. He'd never worn them. Hurriedly, he removed his shoes and socks, then slipped out of his slacks and dress shirt. He laid them out for Ramona, who would take care of the items in the morning. Wearing only his black cotton briefs, he hung the robe and pajamas over his arm and walked back through the bedroom and into the bath, forcing himself not to glance toward the chaise.

If he were spending the night making love to his phony fiancée, he would take the time to shave. He possessed one of those heavy black beards that required him to shave twice a day if he didn't want to go to bed with thick, prickly stubble, which women apparently hated. But tonight, he would be sleeping alone, as he did more often than not. Although he had known his fair share of women since reaching manhood, he had never been a Don Juan, and he had not indulged in what the Americans referred to as a one-night stand since his college days at Harvard.

Wearing the black silk pajamas and carrying the robe, he made his way back into the bedroom and went straight to his bed. While turning down the covers, he hazarded a quick glance toward the chaise. She had turned over, her back to him, and the cotton blanket lay on the floor beside her.

Don't go over there, he cautioned himself. If she becomes chilly, she'll wake, find the blanket and pull it up and over herself again.

But before he had finished the thought, he was halfway across the room. As he approached the chaise, he slowed his movements. Standing over her, he glanced down and wished he hadn't. She had turned in her sleep and her lavender silk gown had ridden up and twisted around her, revealing her calves and lower thighs. The material stretched tightly across her hips and derriere. Nicely rounded hips and full, tight derriere. A perfect upside-down-heart-shaped butt.

Miguel swallowed.

Her short, curly hair shimmered a rich ebony against the white pillow beneath her head. Her lavender gown was cut low in the back, almost to her waist, giving him a view of her smooth, satiny skin. His fingers itched to reach out and touch her.

Whatever you do, do not touch her.

Leaning over, he picked up the cotton blanket, spread it out and laid it over her from bare feet to slender neck. She stirred and mumbled the moment the blanket came into contact with her skin. Her eyelashes fluttered.

He held his breath, praying she wouldn't wake and find him standing over her. When she curled up in the blanket and sighed contentedly, he backed away from her, then practically ran to his bed. After crawling in and drawing the covers up over his chest, he lay there and stared up at the ceiling.

In the distance he heard St. Angela's church bell announce one o'clock. It was already early morning and he had an incredibly busy day ahead. Instead of lying here with an erection thinking of Jennifer Blair, he should be sleeping. He would need his rest for the hectic schedule facing him, not only tomorrow, but in the weeks to come.

After tossing and turning for what seemed like forever, he sat up in bed, unbuttoned his pajama top and removed it. Lying back down, he settled against the cool, soft sheets. He liked the feel of his naked skin against the luxurious cotton. But despite being more comfortable half-naked, he remained awake, longing for sleep that wouldn't come. Sometime after he heard the church bells strike twice, Miguel finally dozed off to sleep, his last thought of the woman lying only a few feet from him.

She woke before dawn and needed to go to the bathroom, but she didn't want to traipse across the bedroom and risk waking Miguel. She lay there until she couldn't wait a minute longer, then she tossed back the cotton blanket, slipped off the chaise and stood up on her bare feet. Tiptoeing across the room, she cast a quick glance at the large body lying sprawled in the middle of the king-size bed.

Ignore him. Pretend he isn't there.

She rushed to the bathroom, closed the door as quietly as possible, then, without turning on a light, she felt her way to the commode. Afterward, she washed and dried her hands in the dark, feeling for the soap and the towel and finding them without knocking anything over and causing a disturbance.

As she made her way back across the room, she found herself walking toward the bed instead of the chaise. She stood at the side of the bed and looked at Miguel, his body clearly visible in the moonlight. He lay flat on his back, his arms sprawled out on either side of his body and one leg bent at the knee. His chest was muscular and sprinkled with curly black hair that tapered into a thin line and disappeared into his pajama bottoms. Those black-satin bottoms rode low on his hips, low enough to reveal his navel. His long arms were large and well-muscled. He possessed the body of a man in his prime.

J.J. sucked in a deep breath, then released it slowly. Everything feminine within her reacted to all that was masculine in him.

This wouldn't do. No, sirree. She never—ever—got involved with a client, no matter what. But she had never been instantly attracted to a client—no, make that any man—the way she was to Miguel Ramirez. It didn't make sense to her. He was far from the first gorgeous man she'd ever met. And he wasn't the first whose blatant machismo reminded her of her father, whom she had adored as a young girl. Whatever it was about this man that attracted her so, she had to deal with it now and move past it.

Suddenly, Miguel rolled over onto his side and whispered one word as his big hand caressed the empty space beside him.

"Querida..."

She all but ran back to the chaise, snuggled into a ball and wrapped herself in the cotton blanket. Okay, so maybe she'd wait until later today to face her fears and find a way to vanquish them.

Chapter 4

J.J. woke with a start. Sunlight flooded the room, telling her that it was well past dawn and that she had overslept. Without thinking, she tossed back the cotton blanket and slid to the edge of the chaise lounge as she sat up and stretched.

"Good morning," Miguel said.

J.J. froze. Oh, God. In her early-morning haze, she had forgotten all about him.

Daring a glance in the direction of his deep voice, which came from the sitting room, she saw him standing in the doorway. Fully clothed in a lightweight charcoal-gray pinstriped suit, pale gray shirt and burgundy tie, he looked like a successful businessman—or a political candidate dressed for success. And here she was, his bodyguard, wearing a flimsy fluff of lavender silk that clung to every curve and bared way too much flesh. Reaching behind her in as nonchalant a way as possible, she felt around on the back of the chaise for her matching robe. It wasn't there. Damn, it was probably lying on the floor.

"What time is it?" she asked.

"Seven-fifteen," he replied as he walked into the bedroom.

No, don't, she wanted to shout. Go away. Don't come any closer. But instead she squared her shoulders and offered him a half-hearted smile.

"Give me fifteen minutes and I'll be ready to go."

He came closer and closer. Her heart caught in her throat. Although she wasn't naked, she felt as vulnerable as if she were. She had shared a bedroom with a client before, but she'd always slept in more appropriate attire—usually baggy sweat pants and T-shirt. And she'd never had a client who struck every female chord within her.

When Miguel walked past her, she let out a deep breath, but that relieved sigh was short-lived. From the corner of her eye, she saw him bend over and reach down for something, then suddenly he came up behind her and draped her sheer silk robe over her shoulders. When his big hands grazed her naked shoulders, she gasped.

He ran his hands across her shoulders, slowly, sensuously. She shuddered.

"While you dress and prepare yourself for the day, I'll put away the blanket and return the pillow to my bed," he told her as he gave her upper arms a gentle squeeze. "We cannot have Ramona or the other girls thinking we have had a lover's quarrel on your first night here, can we?"

J.J. swallowed. "No, we certainly do not want that."

She pulled away from him and hurried to the closet. Before closing the door, she peeked back into the bedroom. Miguel folded the blanket and placed it in the intricately carved walnut cabinet on the far side of the room, then he picked up the pillow and tossed it onto his bed.

Stop wasting time staring at the man, she told herself. If he knew he had her rattled, she'd lose the upper hand with him. And that was something she couldn't allow to happen. Let a man like

Miguel—like her father and all macho chauvinists—know they had any kind of hold over you and they would use it against you. She'd learned that the only way to deal with such a man was to show him that not only did he not intimidate her, but that his blatant masculinity had no effect on her whatsoever. Let the airheaded, silly women who needed a big, strong man to lean on feed those men's huge egos.

After closing the door, J.J. sorted through her choice of clothes. Damn, she had no idea what was on today's agenda and since she was not officially acting as Miguel's bodyguard, she could hardly wear her standard outfit of slacks, button-down shirt and jacket. Oh, no, on this assignment, she had to dress as if she were the candidate's fiancée and she'd have to carry her weapon—which Miguel was supposed to furnish—in a handbag. How inconvenient was that? The extra time it would take her to open the bag and get her hands on the gun could mean the difference between life and death for her or for Miguel.

What insanity! That a man's ego might cost him his life didn't make sense to her. That had been one of the things she'd never understood about her father. And no matter how much she had adored him—idolized him, really—she'd been forced to face a hard truth. Rudd Blair was one of those men to whom the birth of a female child was a disappointment.

J.J. cracked the door and peered out into the bedroom. Her gaze settled on Miguel's wide shoulders. Forcing herself not to do a quick survey, she cleared her throat and called to him.

"What is on today's agenda? How should I dress?"

Keeping his back to her, he replied, "We will attend a sort of pep rally this morning at the Nationalist headquarters, then I have a television interview at noon, followed by lunch with a group of supporters at the country club. Domingo will go with us for the rally, but then he will return here. This afternoon, I will be followed by a news crew as I tour St. Augustine's pediatric ward. We will end the day with a dinner held in my honor at the home of one of my most famous and influential supporters, Anton Casimiro. Of course we will return here to change before going to dinner."

"*The* Anton Casimiro, the famous opera tenor from Argentina?"

"Yes, that Anton Casimiro."

"I had no idea he was living in Mocorito."

"He keeps a penthouse in downtown Nava," Miguel told her. "Anton's mother was born here in Nava and he has cousins in the city."

"Oh." Switching gears, returning to her original concerns about how to dress for the day, she asked, "Then will a simple suit be appropriate for today?"

"Yes, I should think that would be quite appropriate."

J.J. closed the door and rummaged through her clothes, each outfit covered with a protective plastic bag. She had packed shoes and purses in another suitcase and jewelry in a smaller overnight case. The clothes she had chosen for this assignment reflected her mother Lenore's tastes. Simple elegance. Understated, yet fashionable.

With all the necessary paraphernalia in hand, she trekked back into the bedroom and felt a great sense of relief when she found the room empty. The door to the sitting area was closed, so she assumed Miguel had done the gentlemanly thing and given her some privacy.

She'd taken a shower last night, so a quick sponge bath this morning should suffice. And being blessed with curly hair, which she kept cut fairly short, all she needed to do was brush the curls into place. Although she often didn't wear any makeup, today she would. Lipstick. Blush. A bit of eye shadow. Just enough, but not too much. Makeup should always look natural, or so her mother had told her numerous times.

Before she stripped, she made sure the door was locked, then she bathed, brushed her teeth and put on her underwear. She hated pantyhose with a passion, so when forced to wear a dress or suit, she preferred wearing a garter belt and stockings. Yesterday she'd worn pantyhose on the flight from Atlanta to Caracas on the Dundee jet and from Caracas to Nava on a commercial flight. After peeling them off and tossing them away, she'd been doubly glad that she'd packed a couple of garter belts and a dozen pair of stockings in various shades to wear for the rest of the time she was in Mocorito.

Although she'd heard that men loved to see women in garter belts and stockings, she had never chosen to perform in that particular attire for any man. She wore them to please herself, not to satisfy some drooling male who treated women as nothing more than sex objects.

Out of the blue, an unwanted image flashed through her mind. Miguel in his pajama bottoms sitting in his bed, his back propped against the elaborately carved headboard, watching her as she removed her clothes, down to her bra, panties, garter belt and stockings. A foreboding shudder rippled up her spine. It would be a cold day in hell before she'd strip for any man, and that included Miguel Ramirez!

"Dr. Esteban, I am not sure what to do." Juan's nurse, Carmen, caught him between patients. "Señorita Fernandez insists on seeing you. She is waiting in your private office."

"When did she arrive?"

"About five minutes ago, Carmen replied. "I told her you were very busy this morning and in the middle of doing rounds here at the hospital, but she said she would wait however long it takes."

Juan patted Carmen's back. "I will see her now. It must be important or she would not have come here to the hospital so early this morning."

As they walked together down the corridor toward the elevator, Carmen caught him by the arm to slow his pace. He paused and looked at her questioningly. Carmen had been with him since he finished his residency here at St. Augustine's and became a member of the staff. She was round and plump, with gray hair and expressive hazel-brown eyes that often revealed the emotions stirring in her compassionate heart.

"It is not my place to advise you in personal matters, but…" Carmen lowered her voice as they entered the elevator. Once the doors closed and they were alone, she continued. "Señorita Fernandez belongs to a very powerful family and if her brother were to find out that—"

"I don't need you to warn me," Juan said. "Aunt Josephina spoke to me only last night about the dangers of becoming involved with Seina."

"Did you listen to your aunt? No, you did not. If you had taken heed to her warning, you would have told me to explain to the *señorita* that you could not see her today."

The elevator doors opened on the ground floor where Juan's office was located. He held the door for Carmen, then together they walked down the corridor. When they neared his private office, he paused and turned to her.

"Go to the cafeteria and bring back some coffee for us…in about fifteen minutes," Juan told her.

"It is not wise for you to be alone with her."

"Please, do as I ask."

Huffing indignantly, she glowered at him. "I will return in fifteen minutes. And I will not knock on the door." She didn't look back as she walked away hurriedly.

Juan heaved a deep sigh as he grasped the doorknob. No one needed to tell him the foolishness of being in love with Seina Fernandez. He knew that there could be no future for them. Even if she were not engaged to another man, one chosen by her family, Seina and he could never marry. Not unless she broke all ties to her family and gave up her inheritance. He was not a poor man, but he could never give her the kind of lifestyle into which she had been born.

Garnering his courage, praying for the strength to do what was right for Seina, he opened the door and entered his private office. The moment she saw him, she sprung from her chair and rushed toward him. Despite his best efforts to remain aloof, he found himself opening his arms to her and holding her with gentle strength as she wrapped her arms around his waist and laid her head on his shoulder.

"Mother has made plans for my engagement party," Seina said. "In three weeks. She and Lorenzo's mother have set the date for our wedding. It will be six months from the night our families officially announce our engagement."

"You knew this day would come." Juan tightened his hold on her.

She lifted her head and stared pleadingly at him with her huge black eyes. "We must find a way to be together. I do not love Lorenzo. I love you. I want to be your wife. Please, Juan, please, do not tell me that marrying another man is what is best for me. You cannot want me to be Lorenzo's wife."

Juan grasped her shoulders and held her away from him. "I die inside thinking of him touching you, kissing you, making love to you."

"Oh, Juan…"

He shook her gently. "But I will not allow you to lose everything to be with me. In time you would come to hate me."

"I would never—"

He shook her again, then released her. They stood there staring at each other. Tears gathered in Seina's eyes. Juan swallowed the emotions threatening to choke him.

"I should never have allowed this to happen. That first time, when you came to see me as a patient and we felt an instant attraction, I should have sent you to another doctor that very day."

"But you didn't because you felt as I did. You knew we were meant to be together."

He shook his head. "We are not together and we never can be."

"You want me. I know you do." Tension etched frown lines in her lovely face.

"I would never dishonor you." Juan looked at the floor, knowing he dared not look at her. She was temptation personified.

"Then you are willing to send me to another man still a virgin, knowing he will take from me what I long to give you."

Juan's stomach muscles clenched into knots. "You must not say such things."

"I say only what is in my heart. If…if I cannot be with you, my life is not worth living."

He snapped his head up and looked directly into her eyes. Tears streamed down her cheeks. *"Querida…"*

"I shall kill myself."

"No, Seina, you must not say such a thing. You must not even think it."

Suddenly the door opened and, unannounced, Carmen walked in carrying two cups. "I apologize for interrupting you, Dr. Esteban, but I knew you would want your coffee before returning upstairs to finish your rounds."

Juan glared at his nurse. "Please, place the coffee on my desk. Señorita Fernandez and I have not completed our—"

"No, no, I do not want to keep you from caring for your patients," Seina said.

"Thank you for being so understanding, *señorita.*" Carmen placed the coffee on the desk. "If you would like, I can see you out. Do you have a car waiting or did you drive yourself?"

With her gaze downcast, Seina replied shyly, "I do not drive. A friend brought me. She is waiting for me in the parking lot."

"Seina…Señorita Fernandez…" Juan looked at her longingly. He knew it was best for both of them if she left, if they never saw each other again. But a man in love seldom chose what was in his best interests. "We will speak again."

"When?" she asked hopefully.

"Soon."

* * *

Gala Hernandez waited in the parking lot of St. Augustine's Hospital for her dearest friend. When Seina had telephoned her early this morning and pleaded with her to drive her here to see Dr. Esteban, she had done everything she could to dissuade Seina. Not only was her friend's secret relationship with the doctor dangerous for Seina, but it also put Gala in a no-win situation. She had made some foolish mistakes several years ago and had it not been for Diego, Seina's older brother, intervening on her behalf with the police, she would now be serving time in prison for drug use. Diego had not only protected her, he had sent her through a rehabilitation program and kept the whole thing in strictest confidence. And not once since then had Diego ever asked anything of her—until a few weeks ago.

"I know that Seina is slipping around seeing Juan Esteban," Diego had told Gala. "I will, of course, put a stop to that relationship, when the time is right. But for now, it may be of use to me. To us."

"I don't understand. I thought that if you found out, you'd be furious."

"I am displeased, but I trust you to keep me informed of what is happening with my sister and Dr. Esteban. If you think she is on the verge of sleeping with this man—"

"Seina is still a virgin. I swear she is."

"Good. I know that you two share everything. She tells you what she is feeling, what she is doing. You know more about her than either I or our mother, and that is why I want you to report to me every time she sees Esteban. I want to know every word she says about him. I want to know what they talk about, who they discuss."

"You think they discuss Miguel Ramirez?"

"It is possible. Especially if you were to encourage Seina to ask Esteban about his good friend. Encourage her to learn more about her half-brother. She is curious about him, and she has said that she believes we should get to know him. I'm afraid my little sister has a soft heart. Use your powers of persuasion to gain whatever information you can."

Unlike his younger sister, Diego Fernandez did not have a soft heart. Handsome, charming and powerful, he could be a good friend. Unless you opposed him. Then he was ruthless. He hated his half-brother and would do anything to keep him from winning the presidency. She didn't know for sure, but she suspected that he was somehow involved in the recent assassination attempt on Miguel Ramirez's life.

The morning sun grew warmer by the minute. Even with the top down on her small sports car, Gala had begun to perspire. Seina had promised her she would be gone only a brief time, but she'd already been inside the hospital for nearly thirty minutes.

As she kept watch on the side entrance to the hospital, Gala's cell phone rang. She knew before answering who the caller was.

"Hello."

"Is she still with Dr. Esteban?" Diego asked.

"Yes."

"I want a report the moment you take her home."

"Very well."

"And I have an assignment for you."

"What sort of assignment?" Gala asked, her stomach tightening with apprehension. She could not refuse Diego. Her life was in his hands. He could, even now, see that she went to prison. If that happened, not only would her life be ruined, but her parents would be brokenhearted and disgraced.

"There is a luncheon at the Nava country club this afternoon in honor of Miguel Ramirez. I want you to attend. I've arranged for your name to be on the guest list."

"But everyone knows that Seina and I are close friends."

"Yes, I know. You will, however, publicly disagree with our family's politics. And you can even imply that my sister secretly

supports her half-brother, although she cannot publicly commit
to him."

"What purpose will this—"

"You are a beautiful woman, Gala. Ingratiate yourself to whatever man you can within the Ramirez camp, perhaps even Ramirez himself. I want you trailing the Nationalist candidate.
Become a camp follower. Keep your eyes and ears open. I am
especially interested in any information about Ramirez's new fiancée, Señorita Blair."

"You ask too much, Diego. It is bad enough that you have
made me betray my best friend, but now you want me to work
as a spy for the Federalists."

"Of course, you have a choice."

Gala swallowed the fear lodged in her throat. "I will do as
you ask."

"Good. You have made the right choice. I am good to my
friends, as you already know."

"I have to go now. I see Seina," she lied.

"Ask her about her visit with Esteban, then take her home. If
she gives you any interesting information, call me. Otherwise,
show up at the country club at one-thirty, then I will contact you
this evening."

Miguel shook hands with everyone on staff at the television
station directly following his fifteen-minute interview on the
noon news. Afterward, with his fake fiancée at his side, he spoke
at length to the huge audience crammed into the small audito-
rium at the station. He noticed the way she not only kept watch
over him, but continuously surveyed the area around them. Everyone seemed as interested in meeting Jennifer as they were in him.
But who could blame them? The woman even intrigued him.

The television station was owned by a member of the Nationalist Party who provided Miguel with a weekly interview as well
as numerous free one-minute ads that ran often during each

twenty-four-hour period. When the reporter doing the interview had asked about Miguel's fiancée, he had been given little choice but to bring her on camera and introduce her to the people of Mocorito. His lovely Jennifer had surprised him. The ease with which she appeared on camera, a warm smile in place and her hand clasping his the whole time, told him that she had done this type of thing before today. She was what the Americans referred to as "a natural."

When asked how she felt about her future husband being a candidate for president, she had replied without missing a beat, "I am very proud of Miguel and support him without reservation. I will do everything within my power to help him become el presidente because I know in my heart how much he loves Mocorito and all the people of this wonderful country."

"Thank you, J.J. I am a fortunate man to have found such a loving and caring helpmate," he had said as he'd gazed lovingly at her.

He had deliberately referred to her as J.J., the nickname that Domingo Shea had told him everyone close to her used. For half a second, she'd reacted, her eyebrows lifting ever so slightly, but then she had simply smiled and continued looking at him as if he were the sun and moon and stars to her.

If he had not known better, he would have believed every sweet word out of her mouth. The lady had been quite convincing, all that he could have asked for in a fiancée. Not only had she shown her support by word and deed, she had presented herself as a fashionable yet conservatively dressed lady. The simple purple suit she wore was accented with pearl earrings and necklace. Her shoes and handbag were a rich, dark purple leather. Everything about her whispered aristocratic sophistication. Understated and elegant.

After the interview ended, he told her in a quiet voice, yet loud enough for everyone around them to hear, "You were perfect."

"Thank you, Miguel."

She gazed at him with those incredible blue-violet eyes and he found himself unable to resist the urge to kiss her. Only at the last minute, with Roberto clearing his throat behind them, did Miguel manage to restrain himself and simply brush her cheek with a tiny peck.

"Miguel, my friend," Mario Lamas, the TV station's owner clamped his hand down on Miguel's shoulder. "The phones have been ringing off the hook. Your lady is a huge success. The people love her." Mario turned to Jennifer, took her hand and kissed it. "You, my dear Señorita Blair, are a definite asset in this election. You must accompany Miguel everywhere from now until election day."

"I plan to do just that, isn't that right, *querido?*" Jennifer slipped her hand into Miguel's. A subtle yet effective sign of affection.

"Absolutely." Miguel confirmed her statement.

"I don't mean to rush you," Roberto said, "but if we are to arrive at the country club at one-thirty, we must leave now."

"Yes, yes, go, go," Mario told them, waving his hands expressively. "And next week, you and your lady will come back here for another interview. Each week until the night before the election, you will speak to the people for an hour. Yes?"

"Yes. Thank you, Mario."

Miguel shook Mario's hand before slipping his arm around Jennifer's waist and, following Roberto, escorting her outside to the waiting limousine. Roberto waited until they were safely ensconced in the back of the limo before he slid inside with them and closed the door.

Knowing what was next on Miguel's schedule, Carlos shifted into Drive and headed the car away from the downtown television station and onto the main thoroughfare that would take them a few miles out of the city limits to Ebano, a suburb of Nava, where many of the up-and-coming middle-class and upper-middle-class citizens lived. Dolores and Emilio had purchased a home in Ebano only six months ago and Juan Esteban lived there with his aunt in one of the older sections of the area that had been updated in recent years.

Once inside the limousine, Miguel had expected Jennifer to move as far away from him as possible. But she didn't. She remained at his side, although several inches separated them.

"You put on quite a performance, Señorita Blair," Roberto said, an odd tone to his voice.

Miguel glowered at him.

"You object, Roberto?" she asked, using his first name, as she would have done had she truly been Miguel's fiancée. "I would think you would approve of the fine acting job I did. We don't want the people to suspect that I'm not only a fraud, but that I am Miguel's bodyguard."

"I apologize if it appeared I was criticizing," Roberto said.

"It sounded that way to me, too," Miguel told him.

"Then I apologize to both of you. I meant it as a compliment, although I admit I was surprised that an American woman, especially one trained as a bodyguard, could so effectively present herself as a lady of breeding."

Jennifer's laughter stopped Miguel from chastising his friend. Undoubtedly she found Roberto's comment amusing.

"You can thank my mother for that aspect of my personality. You see Lenore Ashford Whitney is a lady of breeding and nothing would please her more than to know I am capable of presenting myself as a carbon copy of her when the situation calls for it."

Miguel studied her closely. Those seductive blue-lavender eyes. That mane of shiny black curls. The pouty pink lips. The oval-shaped face, the tiny nose and the translucent, creamy complexion. If he allowed himself the luxury, he could easily fall under her spell. And if other matters were not far more important in his life, he would set about seducing the beautiful Jennifer.

Suddenly, without any warning, a loud bang reverberated through the limousine. The car bounced, then skidded off the road, onto the shoulder and crashed into the ditch. The wreck happened so quickly that there was no time to think, only to react. As the limo came to a jarring halt, Miguel reached out and grabbed a tumbling J.J. seconds before his left shoulder slammed painfully against the crushed back door.

Chapter 5

"Phase one has begun," he told his comrade. "I just received a phone call telling me that Miguel Ramirez's limousine has wrecked. It seems a tire blew out and the vehicle is now in a ditch."

Hector Padilla smiled broadly, the corners of his thick black mustache lifting. "Perhaps if Miguel is not afraid for himself, he will soon realize that those near and dear to him are in danger. Since we have no proof his fiancée is a fraud, we can't use that against him. Not yet. And now that she has appeared on television with him, the people seemed to be quite taken with her."

"If Miguel truly cares more for others than himself, then convincing him that the lives of others are in danger because of him could be more effective than trying again to eliminate him."

"With the American bodyguards on duty around the clock, it will be more difficult to strike Miguel himself, so your plan to show him how vulnerable others are was quite brilliant."

"Thank you, Hector. You know there is no one in Mocorito who wishes to see you reelected more than I do."

Hector laughed. "Despite our being friends, I am no fool. What you want, more than anything else, is to see Miguel Ramirez defeated."

"The man does not deserve to be president. He is an upstart. The bastard son of a whore, a man with delusions of grandeur."

Placing his hand on his good friend's shoulder, Hector asked, "And when is the next incident set to occur?"

"There will be a minor incident at the luncheon, if Ramirez makes it to the country club. I have arranged for an unpleasant surprise for his guests. But tonight, at Anton Casimiro's party, we have something more significant planned."

J.J. found herself on top of Miguel after the crash. Everything had happened so quickly that it took her a couple of seconds to get her bearings. The first thing that struck her was her awkward position—her body intimately pressed against Miguel's and his arms securely holding her, one hand cupping her hip.

"What the hell happened?" Miguel spoke first.

"I believe a tire blew out, Señor Ramirez," Carlos said.

"Is everyone all right?" Roberto asked. "Miguel? Señorita Blair?"

"I am unharmed," Miguel replied. He ran his hands over J.J. with gentle familiarity, as if the two were actually a couple. "How are you, Jennifer?"

Looking him square in the eyes, she lifted herself up and off him. Then when she had firmly planted her behind in the seat beside him, she responded. "None the worse for wear."

"I think perhaps we should call a wrecker," Miguel said.

"Good idea." J.J. scooted across the seat and opened the door. "Everyone stay put. I'm going to check the tires, see if one of them did blow out and try to determine the cause."

"Do you suspect foul play?" Roberto asked.

"I assume this limousine is kept in excellent condition," J.J. said. "That being the case, the odds that a tire just blew out are slim to none. I'll bet money that someone using a long-range, high-powered rifle shot the tire."

"If that is the case, then why aim at the tire and not at me?" Miguel asked.

"These windows are tinted." J.J. swirled an index finger around, indicating the darkened windows. "Firing into the vehicle could have resulted in a death, but not necessarily your death."

J.J. hopped out of the car and onto the rocky, uneven ground. Immediately the heels of her shoes dug into the soft, sandy soil. Damn! On any other assignment, she'd be wearing a pair of sensible shoes, but here she was dressed to the nines and forced to climb out of the ditch in two-and-a-half-inch heels. After briefly inspecting all four tires and taking a closer look at the one flat tire, she surmised that her theory about a rifle shot blowing the tire had been correct.

But something didn't add up here. Carlos had been driving the speed limit, which wasn't much more than a slow crawl in afternoon traffic. Why would anyone shoot out a tire and cause a minor accident that was unlikely to result in any major damage to the occupants of the limo? If Miguel was the target, why not shoot at him while he was entering or exiting the television station? Unless "they" knew he was being protected by a bodyguard, who might have taken the bullet in his place. How was it possible that Miguel's enemies knew she was his bodyguard and not his fiancée? She had been told that only Miguel and his two closest associates knew the truth. Roberto was here with them, but that didn't rule him out as a suspect, did it? And Emilio was family. However, family had been known to betray family.

Of course, her theory that Miguel's enemies knew who she really was and why she was posing as Miguel's fiancée was only that—a theory.

As J.J. mulled over the possible scenarios and scanned the area, trying to figure out from which direction the bullet had come, she suddenly noticed that dozens of cars had stopped on the highway and people were heading in their direction. She cursed under her breath.

A rapid barrage of questions flew in her direction. Insistent, concerned questions that demanded answers.

"Is Señor Ramirez all right?"

"Is there anything I can do to help?"

"Has an ambulance been called?"

Before J.J. could respond, Miguel did exactly what she'd told him not to do. He emerged from the limousine, climbed out of the ditch and came straight to her. Putting his arm around her waist, he faced the crowd of concerned citizens.

"We are all well," Miguel told them in his most charming, yet authoritarian voice. "J.J. and I appreciate your concern. Our limousine had a flat tire and my driver was unable to stop the car from going into the ditch. We have called a wrecker, so everything is under control. I am afraid we are causing a traffic jam, so I want all of you to return to your cars and clear the roadway."

One by one, the people returned to their vehicles, all except an elderly man who approached Miguel. J.J. moved to stand between them, but Miguel held her to his side. She glowered at him and whispered, "Let me do my job."

"I know this man." Miguel held out his hand to the silver-haired gentleman. "Uncle Tito, how good to see you. What brought you into the city today?"

"I am returning from a doctor's visit," Tito replied. "Señor Miguel. You are not harmed? You and your lady?"

Miguel shook hands with the old man. "We are fine." He tightened his hold on J.J.'s waist. "Jennifer, I would like to introduce you to an old family friend, Tito Lopez. He is Emilio's great-uncle. Uncle Tito, this is my fiancée, Señorita Jennifer Blair."

Tito's wrinkled face brightened. He nodded and smiled at her cordially. "It is my great pleasure to meet Miguel's lady." He looked to Miguel. "You are on your way to the club for a luncheon, are you not? Our little mother, Dolores, is hosting the event today. It is all she has talked about for weeks now. You cannot disappoint her. Please, allow me to drive you and the *señorita* to Ebano."

"Thank you, Uncle Tito. We would be honored to have you drive us."

J.J. grabbed Miguel's arm and whispered, "I don't think this is a good idea."

"Nonsense," he replied in a hushed voice so that only she could hear. "I trust Uncle Tito implicitly."

Groaning, J.J. accepted defeat, knowing that without creating an unpleasant scene—which would probably accomplish nothing—she had little choice but to go along with what Miguel wanted.

By the time they arrived at the Ebano Country Club, only ten minutes late, everyone there had heard about the accident, which was the story Miguel had told Roberto to issue to the media. Dolores met them at the entrance, tears glistening in her large, dark eyes. She waddled toward them the minute they exited Uncle Tito's old car.

"Tell me that you are unharmed." Dolores threw her arms around Miguel and hugged him as closely as her round belly would allow.

"I am fine." He held her away from him, far enough to kiss her first on one cheek and then the other. "Jennifer and I are both unharmed. It was only a flat tire. I left Roberto with Carlos to wait for the wrecker."

"Only a flat tire?" Dolores looked at J.J. "Is he telling me the truth?"

Miguel put his arms around Dolores's shoulders and then J.J.'s. "Come along, ladies. We have kept our guests waiting long enough."

Dolores did not protest, but she glanced in J.J.'s direction, the look in her eyes telling J.J. that the two of them would talk later.

When they entered the main dining room of the Ebano Country Club, the hundred-plus women assembled rose to their feet and applauded. J.J. found herself immediately swept up in the moment, becoming a part of the enthusiasm, reluctantly seeing Miguel through his admirers' eyes. Their adoration was real, almost worshipful. How could this many women admire and support a man unless he had numerous redeeming qualities? Had she misjudged him? Or had he simply enchanted his female followers with his good looks and charm? Surely this many women weren't all susceptible to such superficial qualities. But then again the Mocoritian women were different from American women. They were more old-fashioned, more accustomed to men ruling the roost, so to speak.

The group consisted of women of various ages, ranging from the early twenties to elderly ladies with white hair. But, to a woman, they looked at Miguel as if he could walk on water. No wonder he possessed such an air of confidence, even cockiness. This kind of adoration could easily go to a man's head.

When they reached the raised podium where Miguel's table had been placed, J.J. noted there were five chairs and five place settings. Two women were already seated at the table. One she instantly recognized—Zita Fuentes, the auburn-haired beauty who had been at Miguel's home when J.J. and Dom arrived last night. The lovely widow watched J.J., not Miguel, her dark eyes studying J.J. as if she were a specimen under a microscope.

Sizing up the competition? Was Señora Fuentes more than a friend and political supporter? Did she see J.J. as a rival?

Reaching down to grasp J.J.'s hand, Miguel paused and spoke to Señora Fuentes. Nothing more than a cordial hello and thank you for being here today. J.J. sensed an odd tension between the two and knew she had guessed correctly. If there wasn't something intimate between these two, then one or both of them wished there was.

Miguel led J.J. to the other side of the table where an elderly woman, rather regal in appearance, sat. When they drew nearer, a warm smile appeared instantly on her weathered face.

"Dear Aunt Josephina." Miguel leaned down and kissed the woman on the cheek.

She grasped his hand and looked directly at J.J. "And this must be your fiancée. Introduce us, dear boy."

"Aunt Josephina, may I introduce my betrothed, Señorita Jennifer Blair." He lifted J.J.'s hand to his lips and kissed it. "*Querida,* this is my friend, Juan Esteban's aunt, Señora Josephina Esteban y de la Romero viuda Santiago."

"I am delighted to meet you." Josephina inspected J.J. closely. "You have done well, Miguel. She is lovely." The good doctor's aunt concentrated her sharp gaze on J.J.'s face. "I assume you are madly in love with our Miguel, as we all are. He is irresistible, is he not?"

"Yes, Señora Santiago, I am madly in love with him and I found him irresistible the moment we first met."

Nodding approval, Aunt Josephina laughed. "You are a brave woman to marry such a beloved man. You know you will have to share him with his people for the rest of your lives."

"I'm not jealous of Miguel's love for his people." J.J. said what she thought this old woman would want to hear. "Knowing how deeply he cares for his country, for his people, only makes me love him all the more."

"Ah-ha! Now, I know why you have chosen this rare gem to be the first lady of Mocorito." Aunt Josephina reached out and grasped J.J.'s hand. "Take good care of him, dear child. He is the hope for the future of this country. Give him many fine sons."

J.J. had to struggle to keep her smile in place. This dear old lady had no idea that her last comment had struck a nerve in J.J., reminding her that men like Miguel—and men like her own father—wanted sons. Appreciated sons. Loved sons.

Miguel wrapped his arm around J.J.'s shoulders again. "Every man wants a son, Aunt Josephina, but I want a daughter, also."

"Of course you would want a daughter, wouldn't you?" Josephina smiled. "Jennifer, my dear, if you give him a daughter, beware. A little girl will wrap this one around her little finger."

J.J. felt as if a huge boulder had been lifted from her chest and she was able to breathe freely again. She had never expected Miguel to express any desire for a daughter or that this old woman who seemed to know him so well would believe Miguel could be beguiled by a little girl of his own.

"Sit down, sit down." Dolores motioned to them. "I will introduce you and then you must introduce Jennifer as you did on the newscast earlier today."

The next hour seemed surreal to J.J. from the second round of unrestrained applause for Miguel, to his glowing introduction of her as his fiancée. Because he appeared to be besotted with her, his loyal supporters accepted her wholeheartedly. She couldn't help wondering how their breakup, after the election, would affect his popularity with his constituents. The best thing for him to do would be to lay all the blame at her feet, to accuse her of not being the woman he'd thought she was, of running off and leaving him when he needed her most. If he did that, he'd probably have women coming out of the woodwork eager and willing to offer him comfort.

Although everyone had been exceptionally nice to her, J.J. felt uneasy. With her stomach muscles tied in knots and her mind swirling with unexplained apprehension, she nibbled at her delicious lunch. Call it a sixth sense or just gut instinct, but she had the strangest feeling that something was wrong—or soon would be. But nothing seemed out of place. She did her best not to be obvious as she surveyed the dining room, the women in attendance and the numerous waiters and waitresses. This entire event was a security agent's nightmare. But without a staff of agents and a client willing to accept his vulnerability, there was little she could do except stick to Miguel like glue.

As she picked at her dessert, some elaborate chocolate concoction, and listened while Miguel made small talk with the others at their table, a sick feeling hit her in the pit of her belly. Like an animal whose hackles had risen, she sensed danger.

Then it happened.

Someone screamed.

J.J.'s first thought was to protect Miguel.

She shot out of her chair and prepared to hurl herself at him and knock him out of his chair and onto the floor. However, he grabbed her and pulled her down into his lap, as if he intended to protect her, not the other way around.

"Wait." He spoke only that one word.

Another scream echoed from the back of the room. And then another.

"Snakes!" several women cried out.

"There are snakes crawling around on the floor," Dolores cried. "Look. See them. There."

"My God!" Josephina gasped. "Are they poisonous snakes? Does anyone know?"

"There must be at least a dozen of them," Zita Fuentes said. "Someone must do something immediately."

Before she could stop him, Miguel came up out of his chair and planted J.J. on the floor, then barreled off the podium and into the audience. Standing quickly, J.J. jumped off the podium right behind him, landing haphazardly on her high heels. She almost smacked into his back when he stopped abruptly to study one of the slithering creatures near his feet.

With women screaming, some climbing on their chairs, a few already on top of the tables and others trying to escape through the nearest exits, which seemed blocked by even more snakes, Miguel picked up one of the reptiles.

Smiling as he held the cold-blooded creature in his hand, Miguel called out in a loud, clear voice. "They are not poisonous. Please stay calm. These are hognose snakes. They're harmless."

"They're not poisonous?" J.J. eased out from behind him and, avoiding the snake he still held, came to his side.

He shook his head. "Completely harmless, but they seemed to have served their purpose." He glanced around at the panicked women. "Someone released these snakes to make a point."

"To show you how vulnerable you are, how easily they can get to you," J.J. said. "The same reason they shot out the tire earlier today. Scare tactics."

The country club's manager and male members of the staff rushed into the dining room. When they saw the snakes slithering around on the floor, several men balked, but when Miguel assured them the reptiles were harmless, they set about capturing the creatures. Miguel handed over his captive to the manager.

In her peripheral vision, J.J. caught a glimpse of a tall, slender brunette in a striking hot-pink dress as she bent down and grasped one of the snakes and handed it to a waiter. Only after the fact did J.J. realize that Miguel had seen the incident, and now the attractive woman was smiling at him as she walked toward him.

"A fearless woman," Miguel said to her as she approached them.

"Señor Ramirez…" She held out her slender, well-manicured hand to Miguel. "What a shame that someone had to play such a dreadful prank and ruin the luncheon for everyone."

Miguel kissed the woman's hand. She batted her long eyelashes at him and smiled coyly.

"A day is never ruined when I make the acquaintance of such a lovely and brave lady. I am afraid you have me at a disadvantage," Miguel said. "You know who I am, but I do not know who you are."

"I am Gala Hernandez."

"It is my pleasure, *señorita*. It is *señorita*, is it not?"

She giggled. The silly woman actually giggled. J.J. glared at her.

"I'm Jennifer Blair, Miguel's fiancée." J.J. stuck out her hand.

Gala glanced at J.J.'s hand, but quickly returned her attention to Miguel. "I must tell you, before someone else does, that I have ties to the enemy camp."

Miguel lifted an inquisitive eyebrow.

J.J. tensed.

"Your sister…your half-sister, Seina, is my oldest and dearest friend."

Getting close enough to brush her shoulder against Miguel's, she lowered her voice to a whisper, making it difficult for J.J. to hear what she was saying. So J.J. pressed up against Miguel's other side.

"Your sister secretly supports your bid for the presidency," Gala told him. "She does not dare speak publicly on your behalf. I am certain you can understand. So, she has sent me in her place."

Miguel eyed the woman suspiciously. Good for him, J.J. thought. At least he's not buying her story hook, line and sinker. For all they knew, Gala Hernandez could be a spy for the enemy camp.

"Please tell Seina that I appreciate her support and when I am president, I hope that she will be able to publicly acknowledge me as her brother."

"I am sure that is her heartfelt wish," Gala said.

"Miguel, *querido*…" J.J. tugged on his arm. "I do not mean to take you away from a new convert, but you really should make a statement to the ladies who are still here, then we need to contact Roberto and Carlos to make arrangements for a car to pick us up. We're due at St. Augustine's in less than an hour."

"Oh, please, allow me to drive you back to Nava," Gala said. "It would be my honor."

J.J. groaned internally. Bad idea, she wanted to shout, but kept quiet. Surely, Miguel would decline the woman's offer.

"How very kind of you, Señorita Hernandez. Thank you. But I am sure my driver has arranged for another car and will soon arrive to pick us up."

J.J. breathed a sigh of relief and looked at Miguel with new respect.

* * *

A crew of news people had followed Jennifer and him as Juan introduced them to the children at St. Augustine's. His lovely fake fiancée had shown genuine compassion and caring for the residents of the pediatric ward and somehow he had not been the least surprised to find that the lady had quite a way with children. The little ones had responded to her warm smile and gentle touch.

After returning home, both of them weary from the events of the long day, J.J. had gone upstairs to his bedroom suite and was now soaking in his marble bathtub. But he was not alone. Per J.J.'s instructions, Domingo Shea stayed at his side.

"Whenever I can't be with you, Dom will be. After all, he is supposed to be your cousin and there's no reason for anyone to be suspicious when he's often with you."

Miguel had called in Emilio and Roberto to discuss the two possibly unrelated incidents that had plagued him today. A rifleman shooting out one of the limousine tires and someone releasing a dozen hognose snakes at the Ebano Country Club luncheon. Neither had been life-threatening, although each had been momentarily unnerving.

"What information do you have for us about the limousine?" Miguel asked Roberto. "You kept the incident confidential, as I asked."

"We took the car to a trusted auto shop," Roberto replied. "The tire has been replaced and some of our people are running a check on the bullet. Señorita Blair was correct about the tire being shot by a rifle."

"For what purpose?" Miguel glanced from one man to the other.

"To scare you?" Roberto suggested.

"To make a point," Dom said.

"And that point is what? That they could take a shot at me anytime they choose and there's nothing I can do about it. We already knew that."

"Dolores was very upset by what happened at the club," Emilio told them. "If shooting out the tire on the limo was to scare you, to make a point, what did they hope to accomplish by letting a dozen hognose snakes loose in the dining room during your luncheon?"

"Once again, to make a point," Dom said.

"And perhaps to make a laughingstock of you," Emilio added.

"No, there is more to it than their wanting to show me that they can reach out and touch me at their will. The assassination attempt already proved that is possible." Miguel feared the real reason was far more frightening, but he hesitated voicing his thoughts aloud.

"You can't have overlooked the obvious," Dom said as his gaze connected with Miguel's, the two men sharing a silent acknowledgment.

"And that would be?" Roberto asked.

"They already know that I am willing to put my life on the line, that they cannot frighten me into withdrawing my candidacy," Miguel said. "But what if, now, they want to see if I'm willing to risk the lives of others?"

"You can't mean that you think—" Emilio's eyes widened in shock.

"I think only that it is a possibility." Miguel grimaced. He prayed he was wrong. What if he had to choose between the presidency and the safety of the people he loved? What would he do if he was forced to make that kind of decision?

Chapter 6

J.J. had intended to soak in the tub for no more than ten minutes. But she had stayed twenty before reluctantly getting out, drying off and putting on her silk robe. Now, she had to choose the proper attire for tonight's dinner party. Miguel had told her that it was not a formal affair, that he wouldn't be wearing a tuxedo, only a suit and tie and suggested she wear something suitable for a cocktail party. As she stood inside the huge walk-in closet, flipping through her choices that hung alongside Miguel's numerous suits, she thought about today's events. While she'd been soaking in the tub, she had deliberately erased all thoughts from her mind, concentrating on total relaxation. If the blown tire and the fiasco with the snakes were any indication of how tonight's dinner party would play out, then she had to be prepared for just about anything. It appeared that Miguel's enemies were trying a new tactic.

Perhaps the first assassination attempt had been solely to frighten him into withdrawing from the race—which it hadn't—

and now they were showing him they could get to anyone at any-time, could easily harm his friends and family. That was the most reasonable explanation for what had happened today. But what if they also knew Miguel now had a bodyguard, posing as his fiancée? There would be no way they could prove such an accusation, even if they knew it for a fact. And if they knew the truth about J.J., that meant someone very close to Miguel had leaked the information. She felt certain that if she mentioned her suspicions to Miguel, he would defend Emilio and Roberto with every breath in him. Being a loyal man himself—and she instinctively felt this—Miguel would trust his two closest friends, would never question their allegiance to him. But she would and did question their loyalty. After all, it was her job, wasn't it, to distrust everyone associated with Miguel?

"Jennifer?" Miguel called to her from the bedroom.

Her heart lurched halfway out of her chest. Damn, she had to stop reacting like an idiot every time he got near her.

"I'm in the dressing room, choosing something to wear to tonight's dinner party."

"Before you choose, come out here, please. I have something for you, something that may help you make a final decision about your attire for Anton's party."

Taking a deep, get-hold-of-yourself-girl breath, J.J. tightened the belt on her robe, opened the dressing-room door and walked into the bedroom. Miguel had removed his jacket and tie and undone the first three buttons of his shirt, thus revealing a peek of the dark curling hair on his chest. She was so engrossed in his handsome face, his charming smile and his to-die-for body that at first she didn't notice the jeweler's case he held in his hand.

"What's that?" she asked.

"A gift from Nava Jewelers," he replied. "An engagement gift for you."

"You—you bought me a gift?" She froze half a room away from him, unable to make her feet move any farther.

"It would be expected," he told her.

"When did you have time to—"

"I telephoned them this morning and placed a specific order."
He held out the large jeweler's case."

Move feet, damn you, move! Taking slow, deliberate steps,
she made her way across the room and when she neared him, she
held out her hands and accepted the gift. When she opened the
case, she noted that there were three smaller cases nestled inside,
one obviously a ring box. Her heart did a nervous pitter-patter.
Several years ago, she had sworn to herself that if she ever did
find a man she wanted to marry, she would tell him that if he wore
a wedding band, she would, but that she did not want a fancy engagement ring. She'd been engaged once, had worn her fiancé's
one-carat diamond solitary for several months before coming to
her senses and breaking things off with the man her mother had
chosen for her.

J.J. flipped open the lid on the ring box. Her mouth gaped as
she gasped silently. Oh, my God! The center jewel was an oval-
cut amethyst, at least four carats, and was surrounded by small
half-carat diamonds. A ring that size should have been gaudy and
ostentatious . But it wasn't. It was exquisite, like a ring belonging
to a princess.

"Miguel, this is…"

"You don't like it?"

She glanced up at him. "No, I mean yes, of course, I like it.
It's exquisite."

"It will be expected," he told her by way of an explanation.

"Yes, certainly. I understand."

"Here, let me help you." He reached out and removed the ring
from its velvet bed. While she held the large case in her right
hand, he took her left hand, held it up and slipped the ring on her
third finger. "Ah, a perfect fit. And the perfect ring for you. If
only there was a touch more blue in the gem, it would match your
beautiful eyes."

Oh, please, don't say something like that to me. She might not be a silly, gullible woman, easily influenced by flattery, but she was discovering that she wasn't completely immune to Miguel's Latin charm.

"That's a good line," she told him. "Very convincing. It's something you must tell people when they aah and ooh over the ring."

"Yes, you are correct. If I repeat that line, everyone will be convinced that I adore you." He snapped open the lids on the other two boxes within the jeweler's case. "The necklace and earrings are an engagement present. Everyone will expect to see you wearing them tonight and for every special occasion from now until our wedding."

The earrings and necklace were diamonds. Breathtakingly beautiful diamonds, the settings simple and classic.

"I am told that diamonds, like pearls, go with anything a woman chooses to wear," he said.

"Yes, you're right. That's exactly what my mother always said. A woman can wear pearls or diamonds with a designer gown or with a pair of blue jeans."

"Later, when you are dressed for the evening—" His eyes raked over her silk robe, lingering on her pebble-hard nipples "—if you need my help with the catch on the necklace, let me know." His gaze locked with hers.

A tingling sensation spiraled out from her central core and radiated through her body. No wonder the man was such a successful politician. He possessed an overabundance of charisma.

"I…yes, thank you."

They stood there and stared at each other for what seemed like endless minutes. Finally Miguel broke the silence.

"Ramona has unpacked and put away your things satisfactorily?" he asked.

"Oh, yes. Yes, thank you."

"Will you require a maid to help you prepare for this evening?"

"Huh?"

He smiled, apparently amused with her puzzlement.

"An unnecessary question, I'm sure. I cannot imagine you would want someone to assist you in dressing."

"Oh, no. You're right about that." She chuckled softly. "Even my mother doesn't have a lady's maid."

"Most of the younger women in Mocorito do not use lady's maids, either, only the older ladies, such as my father's wife and her kind."

J.J. caught just a hint of resentment in his voice, a subtle trace of ridicule. "You're not old-fashioned about everything, are you?"

He eyed her questioningly. "You consider me old-fashioned?" He shook his head. "The people of Mocorito think of me as a very modern man, even a liberal to some degree."

"You—a liberal?" J.J. laughed out loud.

"And what do you find so amusing about that?"

"In America you would be considered an old-fashioned, conservative, male chauvinist. But surely you know that since you went to college at Harvard."

"But we are not in America, my dear J.J. We are in Mocorito and only in the past twenty years have women been allowed to vote. And only the younger generation of women have been allowed the freedom of choosing their husbands, although some, such as my half-sister, are trapped by the old traditions imposed on them by their parents and grandparents. One of the things I want to change, when I am president, is women's rights."

J.J.'s mouth fell open in astonishment. "You're kidding me?"

"I assure you that I am not."

She stared at him, searching his face for the truth. Why should he lie to her? "I thought you didn't approve of aggressive, pushy women? Aren't you the man who is passing me off as his fiancée because he doesn't want anyone to know that he has a female bodyguard? Aren't I suppose to be demure and ladylike at all times?"

"This is like asking me if I am a man. Yes, I prefer my women gentle and accommodating and I would like a wife who would allow me to, as you Americans say, wear the pants in the family. Men, like countries, do not change overnight. We change gradually. Mocorito will never be like America, but we can be a country where our women have equal rights. Who knows, perhaps one day my daughter or granddaughter will be president of Mocorito."

"Who are you and what have you done with Miguel Ramirez?" she asked jokingly.

Before she realized what he intended to do, he reached out and caressed her cheek with the back of his hand. A non-threatening gesture. A gentle touch, yet all the more seductive because of the gentleness. He brought his hand down the side of her neck and held it there. Her pulse throbbed against his fingertips.

"I suspect that I do not know you any better than you do me, *señorita*." He held her captive with his hypnotic gaze. "We have preconceived ideas of who the other is and in reality, we are strangers who do not know what is in each other's heart."

She couldn't speak, but managed to nod agreement with what he'd said.

Miguel removed his hand, but kept his gaze locked with hers. "If you have a little black dress in your wardrobe, wear that tonight…with the diamonds I gave you."

He turned and walked toward the bathroom.

"Miguel," she called after him.

He paused and glanced over his shoulder. "Yes?"

"You do realize that there is a good chance that something else could be planned for tonight, another incident in the same vein as the blown tire and the snakes at the luncheon."

"Yes, of course. But I am unafraid. I have a bodyguard to protect me."

With that said, he went into the bathroom and shut the door. Momentarily dazed, J.J. stood there, uncertain whether she should laugh or tell him to go to hell.

Why was it that she had such conflicting emotions where this man was concerned? One minute she found herself as susceptible to his charm as any other woman and the next minute she wanted to kick his butt for being such a…a man! What was it about Miguel that affected her so strongly? It wasn't as if she hadn't known her share of swaggering males with egos the size of Texas. She'd been a soldier's daughter and had learned first-hand what being a he-man was all about, learned from the master himself—Rudd Blair. And from the age of twelve, when she'd blossomed into a bosomy girl who had inherited her mother's beauty, but none of her Southern-belle femininity, she'd been fighting off male advances. To her mother's dismay, J.J. had spent more time trying to earn her father's approval by acting like one of the guys than she had in learning the art of being a femme fatale.

No matter how attracted she was to Miguel, she was not going to give in to her baser instincts. She had managed to stay in charge of every relationship in her life—except the one with her father—and there was no way in hell she would allow this South American Romeo to seduce her.

Even if you want to be seduced? an inner voice asked.

After answering his cell phone, Dom Shea walked outside into the center courtyard of Miguel's home. The lush, tropical garden surrounded him as he sat on the stone bench several feet away from the house.

"Are you alone?" Vic Noble asked. "Can you talk?"

"I'm alone, but even if one of the servants overhears my end of the conversation, they won't know what I was saying. None of them speak English."

"Are you sure?"

"I asked Ramirez. He should know."

"He should, but… Does he know that his good friend, Dr. Juan Esteban, has been having secret rendezvous with his half-sister, Seina Fernandez?"

"Hmm… Interesting. If he knows, he hasn't mentioned it to me or to J.J."

"He should be told," Vic said. "It's possible that the half-sister is using Dr. Esteban to gain inside information. Or it's possible that the good doctor is a traitor."

"Have you checked out Emilio Lopez and Roberto Aznar? On the surface, each man seems to be devoted to Ramirez, but—"

"Lopez has been Ramirez's best friend since they were boys and now they're family. I've found out nothing, at least not yet, that would implicate either Lopez or Aznar. But my sources tell me that the Federalists know J.J. is Miguel's bodyguard."

"That means there is a traitor in Ramirez's camp," Dom replied. "Someone close."

"Find out if he or Lopez or Aznar has told anyone else about J.J.'s true identity. If they haven't, then either there's a leak on our end—meaning the CIA—or one of Ramirez's best friends has sold him out."

"What does Will Pierce think?"

"I haven't made contract with Pierce since we arrived in Mocorito. We're supposed to meet up tomorrow. But I already know what he'll say. He'll assure me that none of his people have leaked the info because our government sending Dundee agents into Mocorito was top-secret and on a strictly need-to-know basis."

"Have you come up with anything on the shooter? Any names? Any links to the Federalists?

"I have a few names and I'll be checking them out, one by one. But so far, that's it. My guess is any ties between the shooter and the Federalist Party are invisible. Proving a connection will more than likely be impossible."

"We had a couple of odd incidents today." Dom explained about the blown tire and the snakes.

"Kid stuff. Especially the snakes. That was more of a prank than anything else. What's your take on it?"

"I'm holding off judgment until after we see how tonight's dinner party at Anton Casimiro's penthouse goes. J.J. and I will be on alert, but not knowing for sure what sort of game our opponents are playing puts us at a disadvantage."

"Are you going to the party?"

"Yes, Ramirez invited me."

"Y'all won't know whether to expect a potentially dangerous attack or another prank of some sort."

"The only thing we can do is make sure Ramirez is safe."

"Yep, that's your job." Vic chuckled. "How's our J.J. handling playing the dutiful, subservient fiancée?"

"If I didn't know better, I'd swear she's taken to it like a duck to water."

"You're kidding!"

"Hey, Ramirez is good-looking, charming, rich and powerful. That's a combination that any woman would find hard to resist."

"J.J. isn't just any woman," Vic reminded him. "Her hobby seems to be cutting men down to size, even guys like Ramirez."

"I'd say in this case, the odds are fifty-fifty as to who will wind up cutting the other down to size."

J.J. surprised him. He had been certain when he'd asked her to wear a little black dress this evening, she would deliberately choose the exact opposite. If he'd bet on her actions, he would have lost.

She stood at the top of the stairs looking like a beautiful princess. His princess. No, not a princess, a first lady. El presidente's lady. He and Dom Shea watched her as she descended the stairs, her Dundee partner apparently as entranced by her as Miguel was.

Luscious red lipstick stained her full, pouty lips, making her creamy skin appear even lighter than it was. Her dress was black, a classic style, with a rounded neckline that showed just a hint of décolletage and a hem that stopped an inch below her knees and showed off her shapely calves encased in black silk stockings. The dress fit her as if it had been molded to her body, yet was not skintight. She had brushed her short, curly hair behind her ears to show off the diamond earrings. The delicate diamond necklace sparkled around her slender neck.

It was at that moment that Miguel knew he had never seen anything more beautiful in his entire life. Jennifer was truly beauty personified. He wanted her with a desperate passion.

And he would have her!

"Good evening." She glanced from Dom to Miguel, then as if sensing the desire raging inside him, she turned her gaze back on her fellow Dundee agent.

"What did you do, rob a jewelry store?" Dom stared at her diamonds.

She touched the shimmering necklace. "I'm wearing engagement gifts from my fiancée." She wiggled her ring finger in front of him.

Dom let out a long, low whistle. "Aren't you a lucky girl."

"I'm pretending to be."

Miguel cleared his throat. The easy camaraderie between Dom Shea and Jennifer bothered him. Admit the truth, he thought to himself. You are jealous of Dom. Of any man who is her friend.

Ignoring Miguel completely, J.J. asked Dom in English, "I assume you're carrying a weapon, right? The gun Miguel provided for me is in my handbag."

"You are both expecting something unpleasant to happen tonight?" Miguel asked, also in English.

"Possibly," Dom replied.

"Probably," J.J. added.

"I will be among friends and supporters. I doubt Anton will have invited anyone who would attempt—"

"You were surrounded by admirers at the Ebano Country Club today and yet somehow, someway, a dozen snakes were released in the dining room and created havoc," J.J. quickly reminded him.

"Then you expect another silly prank?" Miguel asked.

"We don't know what to expect," Dom said.

"Before we leave, let me remind you that if anything does happen, I'm your bodyguard," J.J. told him. "It's my job to protect you, not the other way around. Do you understand?"

"Yes, I understand. But as a man, it is simply my nature automatically to protect a woman."

"Don't think of me as a woman," she told him. "Think of me only as your protector."

"I will try, Señorita Blair, but it will not be easy."

When J.J. caught a glimpse, in her peripheral vision, of Dom grinning, she cast him a don't-you-dare-laugh glare.

"Shall we go?" J.J. slipped her arm through Miguel's.

Dom followed them outside to the limousine. Carlos stood by the open door, waiting for them. J.J. steeled her nerves as she slid into the limo. She didn't know which concerned her most—her irrational attraction to Miguel or not knowing what might happen at tonight's dinner party.

Anton Casimiro's penthouse apartment in downtown Nava was large and lavishly decorated with the best money could buy. Tonight, the crowd gathered here were all avid supporters of Miguel Ramirez, many devout Nationalists and others simply new converts to the party because of their admiration for the beguiling Ramirez.

How Diego had managed to acquire an invitation for her tonight, Gala did not know. And she dared not ask. She was here on an assignment, one Diego expected her to carry out without fail. All she knew was that she had an accomplice who would actually do the deed, but she carried the means of accomplishing that deed in her purse.

"You will carry this purse tonight." Diego had handed her the designer, one-of-a-kind, cobalt-blue leather handbag, etched with a floral design in burgundy thread. "You will leave your purse wherever the other ladies leave their bags. After that, you are free to enjoy yourself. Flirt with Ramirez. If you can draw him away from his fiancée, all the better. It would be amusing if you could place him in a compromising situation."

"That should not pose a problem. He was very attentive when I met him at the country club today."

"Be careful not to give yourself away." Diego had grasped her chin and clamped his fingers harshly into her cheeks. "Ramirez is no fool. If he smells a trap, he will run. Or he will turn on you."

She knew what she had to do. She had already left her purse with the other ladies' purses and was now free to search for amusement. If she could not seduce Miguel, then she would turn her attention to someone in his group of close confidantes. Emilio Lopez perhaps. With his wife fat as a cow at present, he should be easily seduced. If not, there was always Roberto Aznar. There was a smoldering sensuality about the man that intrigued her.

As she made her way through the crowd milling about drinking and nibbling on hors d' oeuvres, she heard someone shout, "He's here."

Standing on tiptoe for a better view of the foyer, Gala Hernandez frowned the moment she saw the way Miguel's fiancée clung to his arm, her gaze glued to him with rapt attention. Miguel looking at her adoringly. Jennifer Blair might be beautiful, but how talented was she in the bedroom? Gala did not know any man who could resist the promise of oral sex. As soon as she could get near enough to Miguel, she knew exactly what she would whisper in his ear.

Chapter 7

Having acquired a guest list for this evening's event, J.J. knew before she arrived that this would be a buffet-style dinner instead of the sit-down meal she had hoped it would be. A sit-down dinner usually limited the number to twenty or less, whereas with a buffet, the guest list could swell to fifty or more. From the wall-to-wall people she saw when they first entered Anton Casimiro's spacious penthouse apartment in the heart of Nava, J.J. surmised that there were already a good fifty people in the huge living room/dining room combined. There had been no way she and Dom could check out the apartment beforehand, which they would have done on any normal assignment. And with a crowd this size, they would have used at least two more agents disguised as guests to mix and mingle. Although a part of her mind was immersed in her role of playing Miguel's fiancée, the protector side of her personality told her to stay alert, to be vigilant and prepared for anything.

Dom came up behind her and spoke quietly into her ear. "You

stay with Miguel. I'll start mingling and look things over. My gut tells me that we're in for a surprise, and probably not a pleasant one, before the evening ends."

She nodded and smiled. And kept her hand securely in Miguel's. She had no intention of letting him out of her sight, not even for a minute. In a crowd this size, it would be easy to become separated. And that's all an assassin would need—one unguarded moment.

As they entered the lounge, heads turned. Hushed whispers blended with the chatter, laughter and tinkling of wineglasses. Dom eased away from them and made his way practically unobserved into the crowd. Suddenly a hefty, bearded man wearing a flamboyant orange silk shirt burst through the crowd and, with arms outstretched, came zooming toward them. Thankful that she knew what their host looked like, J.J. tried to relax when Anton Casimiro encompassed both Miguel and her in a bear hug. When he pulled back, laughing, his dark eyes twinkling with mischief, Anton sized J.J. up and then grabbed her hand. After kissing her hand, he held it and while looking right at her, spoke to Miguel.

"You lucky devil, you," Anton said. "Your fiancée is the most delectable creature I have ever seen." He kissed her hand again, then told her, "If he ever disappoints you in any way, come to me, lovely lady, and I will be very good to you."

Accepting Anton's flirting in the good-natured way she was sure he had intended it, J.J. responded in kind. "I will certainly keep your offer in mind, *señor.*" She cuddled closer to Miguel. "But I know, in my heart, that Miguel will never disappoint me. In any way." She winked at Anton.

The world-famous tenor laughed boisterously. "Come, come. Everyone is eager to see you. Both of you."

When Anton led them from the edge of the foyer and into the lounge, the other guests applauded and several called out his name in a resounding cheer.

"You must say a few words," Anton suggested.

Keeping his arm around J.J.'s waist, Miguel held up his other arm, signaling the guests to end their exuberant welcome. But only after he began speaking did the round of applause and cheering cease.

"Thank you, one and all, for being here tonight." He gazed lovingly at J.J. "Jennifer and I look forward to speaking personally to everyone. But this is a dinner party, not a political rally. Let's eat and drink and enjoy one another's company."

J.J. saw the woman halfway across the room, her gaze riveted to Miguel. Damn, how had she finagled an invitation? Her name wasn't on the guest list. Undoubtedly she had persuaded some man—any man—to bring her here tonight as his date. If J.J. thought that Gala Fernandez's interest in Miguel was only personal, she wouldn't be as concerned. But all her instincts and training told her that there was more to Señorita Fernandez's sudden appearances in Miguel's life than met the eye. Although she'd been giddy and flirtatious this afternoon at the country club, the lady had also seemed slightly nervous. And tonight, as Gala gazed at Miguel, J.J. thought she saw something more than desire in the woman's expression. But she wasn't certain if that barely concealed emotion was fear, anger or concern.

When a waiter approached with a tray of champagne flutes, J.J. accepted a glass, as did Miguel. But before either could take the first sip, several people cornered them and immediately gushed and gooed over Miguel. They were true fans, pledging their allegiance to the Nationalist Party and promising their full support for Miguel, not only with their votes, but with their checkbooks.

While Miguel made small talk with his admirers, J.J. stayed right at his side, commenting occasionally when she thought it appropriate, always keeping in mind that she was playing the part of the demure, steadfast helpmate. In fact, while Miguel charmed the guests, she was worrying about the wine, the food and the catering staff. Emilio and Roberto had assured Miguel that the guest list, the caterers and the musicians for Anton's party had been thoroughly checked out and, to-a-person, no one posed a threat. No one had any ties whatsoever to the Federalists Party.

No one except Gala Hernandez, who had not been on the guest list.

How easy it would be to poison Miguel's drink or his food. And even though Anton had promised that each musician and caterer would be inspected before entering his apartment, it might be possible for one of the hired help for tonight's shindig to manage to smuggle in a weapon.

What about the guests themselves? J.J. asked herself as she continued smiling graciously while Miguel shmoozed with his constituents. Gala probably wasn't the only person here who had finagled her way in, coming along as the date of an invited guest. However, considering that the woman wore a skintight red dress, J.J. doubted there was a concealed weapon on her.

Glancing over the throng of celebrators, J.J. searched for anyone who looked the least bit suspicious. As her gaze surveyed the room, she noticed Dom mixing and mingling, doing just what she was doing—hoping to spot potential trouble. Preventing a disaster of any kind would have been so much easier if the Dundee agency was in charge. Having to placate Miguel's ego and allow Emilio and Roberto to make decisions they were not trained to make undermined the Dundee agents' efficiency. Having to do things Miguel's way made their job ten times more difficult.

J.J. recognized only a few people. Roberto had escorted Señora Fuentes and the two seemed quite chummy where they stood in the corner, sipping champagne and gazing into each other's eyes. Across the room, seated on one of the three sofas, Josephina Santiago appeared deep in conversation with her nephew, Juan Esteban. Here and there, J.J. saw a vaguely familiar face, a few women she'd met at the country club earlier today and some people from campaign headquarters this morning. Emilio had phoned to tell them he and Dolores would not attend tonight since Dolores was still quite shaken by the snake prank at the club.

For a man who knew his life was in danger, Miguel appeared calm, cool and collected. Was he really not concerned about his own welfare or did he think he was invincible? Perhaps neither. He was a man with a mission that apparently meant more to him than anything else on earth. Even more than his own life?

When Gala Fernandez walked straight toward them, J.J. tensed. She tried to tell herself that the knot in her gut was there because she didn't trust Gala, that she feared the woman was dangerous. But when Gala smiled at Miguel and placed her hand on his arm, J.J. realized she was jealous. The idea hit her like a bolt from the blue. She did not want this woman—or any other woman—touching Miguel in a familiar way.

This is totally unacceptable, she warned herself. It was only natural to feel protective of a client, but what she felt went way beyond the norm. She felt not only protective, but possessive. The inner primitive female inside her was screaming, Hands off, bitch, he's my man.

"Good evening, Miguel." Gala all but purred as she ran her hand down his arm. "I am utterly delighted to see you twice in one day." She ran the tip of her tongue over her lips.

Oh, get real, J.J. thought. How obvious could a woman be? She'd practically propositioned Miguel—and with his fiancée clinging to his arm. And clinging was just what J.J. was doing. Realizing she was holding on a little too tightly, she loosened her grasp.

"Señorita Hernandez, you look lovely tonight." Miguel's arm around J.J.'s waist tautened, drawing her closer. "Almost as lovely as my beautiful Jennifer." As if it were the most natural action in the world, he leaned down and kissed J.J.'s temple.

Skyrockets went off in her belly, surprising her. No, actually shocking her. Good grief, she had to get a grip. What was wrong with her? Feeling jealousy over a man she barely knew. Going weak in the knees because he kissed her forehead.

Gala's smile vanished for a moment, but she recovered quickly and replaced the genuine smile with a phony one. "You are a very fortunate woman, Señorita Blair, to have such a devoted fiancé."

"I am the lucky one." Miguel lifted J.J.'s hand and held it over his heart.

"If you will excuse me, I see my date is looking for me." Gala quietly slipped away and hurried over to a short, stout man in his midforties, someone she had apparently taken advantage of in order for her to attend tonight's dinner party. Poor fool. He probably had no idea what a sucker he was.

"You laid it on a little thick, didn't you?" J.J. removed her hand from Miguel's.

"I beg your pardon?"

When those golden-brown eyes of his settled on her face, a troop of fluttering butterflies danced maddingly in her stomach.

"Does Gala Fernandez frighten you so much that you felt it necessary to fawn over me to warn her off?"

Miguel chuckled. "My dear Jennifer, the lovely and sexy Gala wants me very badly." J.J.'s mouth dropped open. "The only thing is I'm not sure whether she wants to make love to me or to kill me."

J.J. let out a relieved sigh. "Then you don't trust her anymore than I do, do you?"

"No, I do not trust her. She is trying much too hard to insinuate herself into my life. Of course, it is possible that she finds me so irresistible that—"

J.J. playfully poked Miguel in the ribs with her elbow.

"What?" he asked guilelessly. "You doubt that a woman could find me irresistible?"

"Oh, no, I don't doubt it for a moment. You can be charming and attentive and make a woman feel as if she's the only woman in the world. In a moment of utter weakness, she just might find you completely irresistible."

Leaning close—too close—his nose grazing her cheek, he whispered, "If only you were that woman, *querida*."

While her heart beat ninety-to-nothing and tingling warmth spread up her neck to flush her cheeks, J.J. struggled to think of just the right response. But she was saved by Roberto and Zita's appearance.

"Would you mind terribly if we left early?" Roberto asked.

"No, of course not," Miguel replied. "Is everything all right?"

Zita Fuentes slipped her arm around Roberto's waist. "Everything is perfectly fine. But I have a slight headache and Roberto has kindly offered to take me home."

Yeah, right, she had a headache. Surely Miguel didn't buy that old excuse. It was obvious that these two wanted to go somewhere to be alone. Although they weren't making a public spectacle of themselves, it was apparent they could barely keep their hands off each other.

"Wait here," Roberto said to his date. "I'll get your purse and wrap and then we'll leave."

J.J. wondered if she should say something to Zita, something to soothe the awkward moment. After all, Miguel had to realize that one of his best friends was going to take this woman home and make love to her. If Miguel had feelings for Zita or she for him, one or both of them must be slightly embarrassed and perhaps even upset.

"I was surprised that Señor Casimiro has a jazz ensemble here tonight." J.J. said the first thing that popped into her head. The cool jazz number the group was playing right now had caught her attention. The alto sax moaned the melody of "The Good Life" as the piano, bass and drums played softly in the background.

"Anton loves jazz," Miguel replied. "He plays the piano and sometimes sits in with the group. He has very eclectic tastes in almost everything, especially in music."

Suddenly Zita's gaze zeroed in on J.J.'s left hand. Her eyes widened, her mouth opened into a perfect oval of surprise. "Your ring is lovely." She looked at Miguel. "You chose it for her, of course."

"Of course." Miguel looked like a man who'd been caught doing something he shouldn't be doing.

"I don't know what is keeping Roberto." Zita glanced around the room, avoiding direct eye contact with either Miguel or J.J.

Poor woman, J.J. thought. She's in love with Miguel and it's breaking her heart seeing him engaged to someone else. But the question that plagued J.J. was—did Miguel love Zita? If he did, wouldn't he have shared the truth with her, that his engagement to J.J. was not real?

"It appears he has been waylaid by someone near the buffet table," Miguel said. "If you'd like, I can go rescue him."

When Miguel turned, intending to go toward the buffet table, J.J. clasped his arm, momentarily halting him. He gave her a puzzled glance, then sighed and nodded when he apparently remembered her cautioning him not to leave her side this evening.

"No, that won't be necessary," Zita said. "I will go and wait for him in the foyer, away from all this noise." She rubbed her right temple. "I am afraid my headache has become worse."

"I'm so sorry," Miguel said sincerely.

"Perhaps Señor Casimiro has some aspirin or—" J.J. offered.

"I'll be all right, thank you." Zita all but ran away from them.

J.J. glared at Miguel.

"Why are you looking at me as if I were an ax murderer?" Miguel asked.

"Just how involved are you with Señora Fuentes?"

"Lower your voice, please. We don't want anyone overhearing you. You sound very much like a jealous woman."

J.J. huffed. She was not jealous. She had simply asked a logical question. "It's obvious the lady is upset that you're engaged," J.J. said quietly. "I think I have a right to know—"

"Zita and I are not lovers," Miguel said. "We have not even dated."

"But?"

"But I had given some thought to courting her and I believe she found the idea quite agreeable."

"Are you in love with her?" Oh, God! She couldn't believe she'd asked him that.

Grasping her around the waist, he pulled her close and whispered, "Retract your claws, little she-cat. Your jealousy is showing."

J.J. gasped aloud, which made Miguel laugh. Several people near them turned to see what was going on.

Miguel shrugged and laughed again as he faced those inquisitive stares. "I am afraid I said something that caught my fiancée off guard and embarrassed her. You know how young ladies can be when we men are too blunt-spoken."

The devil! The charming, smooth-talking devil.

Forcing herself to smile at the onlookers, she didn't withdraw when Miguel led her toward the balcony, where several other couples were dancing or gazing up at the moon. She balked when they reached the double set of open French doors.

"You might consider the possibility that I'll be tempted to toss you over the balcony railing if we go out there," J.J. said for his ears only.

"I will take my chances. I very much want to hold you in my arms right now. Besides, if we don't dance at least one dance, everyone will wonder why not."

"I'm hungry," she said. "Why don't we eat first, then dance?"

As if she hadn't spoken, he led her out onto the balcony and pulled her into his arms. "First we dance. We can eat later."

"Of course, *querido*. Whatever you say. After all, you're my lord and master and I would never want to do anything to displease you," J.J. told him in English, a phony smile plastered on her face.

"Quite a few people in Mocorito speak English. We wouldn't

want anyone here tonight to realize you were speaking to me in such a sarcastic manner."

J.J. kept quiet as Miguel led her into the dance. She didn't protest when he pulled her so close that her breasts pressed against his chest. Being this close to him was hypnotic. Like all his other attributes, Miguel's dancing was flawless. As the music wove itself around them and their bodies moved slowly and rhythmically under the starry, tropical sky, it was all J.J. could do to keep her wits about her. This was like a scene from some old forties movie—an American heiress being wooed by a South American playboy. Only Miguel wasn't actually a playboy and although she would someday inherit several Ashford millions, she wasn't a true heiress, not in the traditional sense.

When one tune ended, another began almost immediately, which probably explained why Miguel didn't release her. The moment the music started again, a bluesy rendition of "You Don't Know What Love Is," he reached down and tilted her chin with his crooked index finger. Standing there in his arms, she looked up at him.

Be still my heart.

When had she ever been this foolish? Not even as a teenager had she fallen so hard and so fast for a guy.

"After this dance, we can go through the buffet line," he told her. "I would rather take you home early, but since I...we are the guests of honor, we can hardly be one of the first couples to leave, can we?"

She managed to nod her head, temporarily rendered mute by the surge of passion heating her from the inside out. She had to put a stop to her raging hormones and do it ASAP. This guy was good. Damn good. He knew just what to say and do to seduce a woman, to make her feel as if she was special. But she knew better. She meant nothing to Miguel. For goodness sake, she was his bodyguard. Letting herself fall under his spell could prove dangerous for both of them.

All he wants is for you to be his latest conquest. One more notch on his bedpost. Once he's had you—

What the hell was she thinking? No way was she going to give in to temptation.

"Why don't we cut this dance short?" J.J. suggested. "I really am starving and that boiled shrimp looked delicious."

He eased her out of his arms, but grabbed her hand when she started to walk away. She paused and fell into step beside him as they left the balcony.

"You may have my share of the shrimp and cocktail sauce," Miguel told her. "I do not like shrimp. I made myself sick on shrimp as a teenager and have avoided eating it ever since."

"I did that with popcorn when I was a kid and I was twenty before I could stand the smell of the stuff."

Miguel squeezed her hand as they entered the buffet line of half a dozen people. "You realize that we are sharing confidences, stories of our childhoods." He smiled. "It is what lovers do to become better acquainted."

"We are—" She'd been about to say, "we are not lovers," but he squeezed her hand really hard, warning her to be careful what she said. "We are becoming better acquainted every minute we're together."

Miguel lifted a plate and handed it to J.J., then picked up one for himself. The people ahead of them in line offered to let them prepare their plates first, but she and Miguel declined simultaneously.

Then, just as J.J. reached out to the platter of boiled shrimp, someone called out loudly, "Do not eat anything else! Five people have become very sick in the past few minutes."

J.J. froze to the spot for a half second, then she stood on tiptoe so that she could discern the identity of the speaker. Dr. Juan Esteban made his way through the shocked crowd, coming directly toward them. She scanned the room, searching for Dom. Standing head and shoulders above three-fourths of the men and women there, he was easy to spot. Her gaze locked with Dom's and a silent understanding passed between them. What if someone poisoned the food?

"I have called for an ambulance," Dr. Esteban told Miguel. "Five people have become deathly sick—vomiting and diarrhea—in the past few minutes. One of the ladies has fainted."

"Could it be food poisoning?" Miguel asked.

"That would be my first guess. Have you eaten anything? You or Señorita Blair?"

"No, we haven't eaten a bite." J.J. put her plate down on the buffet table, then grabbed Miguel's plate and put it atop hers.

"I must go with those who are sick to the hospital. There could be others," Juan said. "In case there are, I will send another ambulance to be on standby."

"What is wrong?" Anton Casimiro approached them, a concerned frown wrinkling his forehead and creasing his plump cheeks.

"We fear food poisoning," Miguel said. "Several people have become violently ill."

"That cannot be!" Anton's round face turned beet-red. "I have used these caterers before and never has anything like this happened."

"It isn't your fault," Miguel assured his friend.

"It is probably only one dish," Juan said. "Otherwise everyone who has eaten would be ill and everyone is not."

"All the food should be left right where it is," J.J. told them. "Each dish will have to be analyzed to find out which one was either spoiled or tampered with on purpose."

Anton's eyes widened in shock. "Are you suggesting someone deliberately poisoned a specific dish? Whatever would make you think such a thing, *señorita?*"

"Jennifer is a great fan of murder-mystery novels," Miguel hurried to explain.

"Murder?" Anton gasped.

Off in the distance the sound of sirens shrilled loud and clear.

"The ambulance should arrive any moment." Juan turned and rushed back into the bedroom to see about his patients.

"I believe it might be a good idea to explain to everyone what has happened," Dom Shea said as he came up beside Miguel. "If we could figure out which dish is the culprit, we could narrow down those who might yet become ill."

"I will make an announcement," Anton said. "This is my home, my party…"

While Anton spoke to his guests, Dom asked Miguel, "Do you have a favorite food?"

"What?"

"Did your host ask about a favorite food he could provide for you tonight?"

"No." Miguel shook his head.

"Would he or the caterers, or anyone for that matter, know you would be sure to eat one thing in particular tonight?"

"I can think of nothing. I enjoy a wide variety of food, but there is nothing on the buffet table tonight that is a particular favorite."

"But there is something that is not a favorite," J.J. said. "How many people know you hate shrimp and won't touch a bite of it?"

"What?" Miguel and Dom asked.

"If you were not the target—"

Dom cursed under his breath. "It makes sense, after the other two incidents today."

"What are you talking about? How does not poisoning me, but poisoning others make sense?" By the time the words were out of his mouth, realization dawned on Miguel. "Mother of God! They are striking out at my friends and supporters, at the very people I would do anything to protect."

"They're showing you how vulnerable your people are," Dom said.

"If you won't withdraw from the presidential race out of fear for your own life, then perhaps you will do it to protect others," J.J. told Miguel.

"Before we run with this theory and know for sure that's what's going on, we need to have the shrimp and the cocktail sauce tested," Dom said. "Tonight, if possible. I'll make a phone call and have someone come and pick up the remaining shrimp and sauce."

Miguel nodded. "I should go to the hospital and check on those who were stricken. If any one of them were to die… To put myself in danger is one thing, but to put others in danger…"

"This isn't your fault," J.J. told him. "Stop beating yourself up about it. And whatever you do, don't make any decisions about your candidacy tonight. If you think your supporters would want you to withdraw from the race to protect them, then you aren't thinking straight."

"You two go on to the hospital and find out how seriously ill the poison victims are," Dom said. "My guess is that the intent was not to kill anyone, only to make quite a few people sick. Enough to send a warning message."

J.J. hated the pained expression on Miguel's face. This was a man who cared for others, cared deeply. Right now, he was feeling guilty, taking the blame for what had happened upon himself. She couldn't let him do that. She wasn't sure why it was so important to her to support and encourage Miguel, but it was.

She slipped her arm through his. "I'll call down and have Carlos bring the car around, then we'll go straight to St. Augustine's. And once we find out that everyone is going to be all right, I'm taking you straight home." She turned to Dom. "You'll stay here and guard the food, especially the shrimp and sauce, until the proper person takes samples of everything."

"Yes, ma'am." Dom grinned.

"She is rather bossy, is she not?" Miguel said, then looked at J.J. appreciatively. "It is good for a man to have a fiancée who can take care of him when the situation calls for it. Feel free, *querida,* to continue issuing me orders tonight. I believe you know better than I do what is best for me."

Moisture glistened in J.J.'s eyes. Damn him! He'd done it again. Said just the right thing to touch her heart and make her want to wrap her arms around him.

Chapter 8

J.J. and Miguel waited at the hospital for news about the people who had taken ill at Anton's dinner party. When all was said and done there were fifteen altogether. Eight men and seven women. Within an hour after she and Miguel arrived at the hospital, both Emilio and Roberto appeared. Dom had telephoned Emilio and he in turn had contacted Roberto. The two men had approached Miguel with different opinions on what he should do and how he should handle the situation.

"You must make a statement to the press immediately," Roberto had said.

"No, no, that is the wrong thing to do," Emilio had told them. "Wait until Juan tells us what the situation is, if anyone has died or if everyone will survive."

"You must make it clear to the people of Mocorito tonight that you will not be intimidated, that nothing can convince you to remove yourself from the presidential race." Roberto had glowered at Emilio, as if daring Emilio to contradict him.

Without blinking an eye, Emilio had shot back, "He cannot do that. It would send the wrong message. What if the people believe Miguel is not concerned for the welfare of those closest to him, that he is willing to risk other people's lives?"

While the two had argued, J.J. had persuaded Miguel to walk to the chapel with her. She supposed that eventually Roberto and Emilio would realize Miguel wasn't still there listening to them squabble, but she really didn't care. All that mattered right now was helping Miguel, doing whatever she could to relieve the stress he felt and ease the guilt eating away at him.

Though the small hospital chapel was devoid of the niceties of a real church, the small statue of the Madonna on one side of the altar and the large painting of Jesus on the cross hanging behind the altar gave the sparsely decorated room a spiritual feel. She wasn't Catholic, but she had attended services several times with various Catholic friends. She had been raised a Protestant, her father Baptist, her mother Presbyterian. It had always seemed to her that there was something profoundly reverent about a church, no matter what the denomination.

She sat beside Miguel on the first bench in a single row of six wooden benches. After he had lit candles for Juan's patients, he had taken a seat and closed his eyes. J.J. knew he was praying and that fact touched her deeply. After quite some time, she reached over and clasped his hand. He opened his eyes and looked at her.

"What would you do?" he asked.

"What would I do if I were you? Is that what you are asking me?"

"Yes."

"I would wait. I would not make any hasty decisions. We don't have all the facts."

"And if the worst happens, if someone dies and we know for certain someone poisoned the shrimp or the sauce?" He took a deep breath, then released it slowly.

"If our worst fears are confirmed, then you must decide what you are most afraid of on a personal level—of innocent people being killed or of the Federalist Party maintaining power and slowing the progress of Mocorito, possibly even taking your country back in time instead of forward."

"The many or the few," he said sadly. "You do not mince words, do you, Jennifer?"

"One of my many faults," she admitted, then said in English, "I call 'em like I see 'em."

He frowned. "Do I have the right to sacrifice others for a cause I believe in with my whole heart?"

It was a difficult question. One to which she had no answer. What would she do, if she were in Miguel's shoes? What if a family member's life or the life of a friend hung in the balance, and she alone had the power to decide their fate?

"You can give the people the right to choose for themselves." She paused, then looked him right in the eye. "I would definitely wait until I had all the facts, then if what we suspect is true, I would take this information to the people it concerns the most. Put their fate in their own hands. Speak with your family, closest friends and most avid supporters first and ask them what they want you to do. Then, if and when circumstances warrant it, go directly to the people in a radio or television broadcast."

The corners of his lips lifted in a half-hearted smile. "You are a very wise woman for one so young."

"Thank you." Everything in her longed to comfort Miguel. It was all she could do to stop herself from wrapping her arms around him and telling him she would make everything all right for him.

When the closed chapel door opened, J.J. shifted in her seat so she could glance over her shoulder. She nudged Miguel. "It's Dr. Esteban."

Miguel shot to his feet, still clasping her hand and inadvertently dragging her up with him. "Please, tell me you have good news."

"I have good news," Juan said. "Several of the patients are severely dehydrated and they will all be sore from the retching, but it appears all fifteen will recover completely. Probably by tomorrow morning."

"Thank God." Miguel grabbed J.J. and hugged her fiercely.

She threw her arms around his neck and laughed when he lifted her off her feet.

"Take him home, Señorita Blair," Juan said. "See to it that he gets a good night's rest."

"Yes, thank you, doctor, I'll do just that."

Juan nodded. "I must return to my patients."

"I will call first thing tomorrow to check on everyone," Miguel said as he set J.J. back on her feet.

"Come on, let's follow doctor's orders." J.J. tugged on Miguel's hand.

Just as they exited the chapel and had walked no more than ten feet, Dom came around the corner.

"Emilio told me he thought I could find you two in the chapel," Dom said.

"Have you heard the good news?" J.J. asked.

"Yes, just before I showed up, Dr. Esteban had informed Emilio and Roberto that everyone was going to live."

"Do you have any news for us about the food?" Miguel asked.

Dom shook his head. "It will be tomorrow sometime before we know anything for sure. Will Pierce will call me as soon as his people know anything. They took samples of all the food at Casimiro's buffet table before the police arrived."

"Good. Good." Miguel clenched his jaw.

"You don't trust the police?" J.J. asked.

"Some of them, I do. But many of the higher-ranking officials here in Nava are loyal to Padilla. They are, how do you say it in America? On his payroll."

"Then one of your first official acts as president should be to clean house in the police department here in the capital city." J.J. glanced at Dom. "Are there any reporters downstairs?"

"Hordes," Dom replied. "That's why I had Carlos take the limo around to the back entrance to wait for us."

"Shouldn't I make some kind of statement tonight?" Miguel asked.

"Let Emilio or Roberto make it for you," J.J. said. "Have them say that you are well and greatly relieved that all those who got food poisoning at the dinner party are going to be all right. Leave it at that. For now."

Miguel put his arm around her shoulders. "You are quite adept at public relations, *querida*. You would make a most admirable first lady."

Dom lifted his eyebrows speculatively, the expression on his face clearly asking if there was something intimate going on between her and Miguel. She chose to pretend she hadn't noticed that inquiring look.

"What are you doing here?"

Diego was furious. She knew he would be, but she did not give a damn. Within a few minutes of learning that fifteen people had been poisoned at Anton Casimiro's dinner party, Gala had begun feeling guilty. Although she hadn't known that the vial hidden in her designer handbag had been filled with poison, she had suspected as much. What she hadn't suspected was that whoever had retrieved the vial from her purse had used it to doctor one of the food items at the buffet table. She had assumed it would be used in Miguel Ramirez's champagne. Not caring what political party ruled Mocorito, what did it matter to her if Diego and his friends eliminated the Nationalist Party's candidate? But poisoning fifteen people was something else. If they had died, it would have been mass murder.

"I came to tell you that I will not do any more of your dirty work." Gala glared at Diego. Even though she was still afraid of him and the power he held over her, the liquor she had consumed before coming to his home had infused her with false bravado.

"Lower your voice." He grabbed her arm and pulled her with him into the front parlor. After flipping on a lamp, he shoved her into the nearest chair and came down over her, bracing his hands on either armrest. "My mother and sister are upstairs asleep and several of the servants are still up and stirring in the back of the house."

"You should have told me that you planned to poison innocent people. I would never have helped you do such a despicable thing."

Diego laughed, then put his face up to hers. "No one died from the poison. Killing innocent people was not our goal. We simply wanted, once again, to show Miguel that he cannot protect his friends, family and supporters."

"And if convincing him that your people can harm those he cares about does not stop him, what will you do then?" she asked. "You should kill him. Hire another assassin. Don't harm innocent people."

"We do not want Ramirez dead," Diego told her. "Killing him would be a last resort. If he is killed, the people could turn him into a martyr and revolt. No, we cannot risk that. What we want is for Ramirez to withdraw from the presidential election."

"Why did you wait until only weeks before the election to—"

"Not until recently did we realize there was a chance he could win," Diego replied. He grabbed her by the shoulders and shook her. "Go home and sober up. And do not ever come back here telling me that you will no longer obey my orders. Have you forgotten that I could send you to prison, just like that?" He snapped his fingers.

"No, I have not forgotten." Tears sprang into her eyes.

He released his painful hold on her shoulders and yanked her to her feet. Their gazes connected for a brief moment and she thought she saw a hint of sympathy in his eyes. God, was she losing her mind? There was no sympathy, no compassion in Diego Fernandez. At least not for her.

He tickled her under her chin. She gasped.

"Be a good girl and do as you are told," Diego said. "I do not want to see you in prison. There are far better places for a beautiful woman such as you."

She shivered at his touch and hated herself for actually being aroused. There had been a time when she had thought herself in love with Diego. Years ago when she had been just a girl, she had admired her best friend's big brother from afar.

"If you please me, I will see that you become the mistress of someone very rich and powerful, perhaps one of Hector's ministers."

His words were like a slap in the face. What had she expected? Diego would never see her as she had once been—an innocent. A virgin, like Seina. No, he knew about her drug addiction years ago and about the men she had given herself to in order to support her habit.

"I am willing to do almost anything you ask," Gala said. "But please, Diego, don't make me a part of harming innocent people. Even I must draw the line somewhere."

He grabbed her arm and escorted her out into the foyer and through the front door. When they stood on the portico, he forced her to face him.

"Did you have any luck with enticing Ramirez? Perhaps you will be of more use to us if you can become his lover."

She started to tell Diego that there was no chance of Miguel Ramirez being unfaithful to his fiancée, that the man seemed hopelessly in love with the American woman.

"We spoke tonight at the party," Gala said. "And flirted a little." She had flirted; he had not. "A second meeting might prove more productive. A meeting where there are no snakes and no poison."

Diego laughed. "Go home, Gala, and tomorrow we will figure out a way for you to come in contact with Ramirez again."

A true friend would not have allowed her to drive herself

home. After all, she had had much too much to drink. She wasn't exactly falling-down drunk, but she was far from sober. However, Diego wasn't a true friend. He wasn't a friend at all. He was a master manipulator who had no qualms about using her.

Gala managed to open her car door and get inside, but it took her several tries to stick the key into the ignition switch. Finally, she got the car started, then pulled out of the driveway and into the street. Less than two blocks from the Fernandez mansion, she heard the screeching of brakes and horns honking. Her last coherent thought was, "Did I run through that stop sign?" Then suddenly she felt a jarring impact as another vehicle broadsided her.

Seina Fernandez hid in the dark, in a secluded nook at the back of the entrance hall. Trembling, her heart hammering inside her ears, she held her breath as Diego closed the front door and locked it. After he walked up the stairs, she crept out from her hiding place just enough to look up so that she could see if he had gone to his room. Then and only then did she release her breath.

Only a few minutes ago, she had come downstairs to ask Conchita to prepare her some warm milk because she had found it impossible to fall asleep tonight. After an argument with her mother over her upcoming engagement party, she had been heartsick and longed to go to Juan for comfort. But what excuse could she have given for leaving the house so late in the evening? Slipping away to see Juan was much easier during the day. Since neither her mother nor Diego suspected she was seeing another man, they did not keep close tabs on her during the daytime.

Her life was already plagued by problems she could not solve alone. And now? Dear God in heaven, what would she do now that she had heard what her brother had done? What he had forced poor Gala to do? She had never meant to eavesdrop, had had no idea to whom Diego was speaking so harshly when she passed by the front parlor.

Why, oh why, had she not gone on to the kitchen instead of stopping to listen, wondering who Diego's late-night visitor was? How could she deal with this information, with the knowledge that her brother was involved in the plot to destroy Miguel? She had known, since their father's death, that Diego despised their half-brother, but she had never dreamed he was capable of such despicable acts. This was not the Diego she knew and had loved all her life. Yes, he could be domineering and controlling, as their father had been, but never cruel, never dangerous.

How could Diego have involved her best friend Gala in his murderous plots? He was actually blackmailing Gala, using her past drug use against her. There had to be some way she could help her friend, some way she could stop Diego. If she went to him and talked to him? No, that would accomplish nothing. If Diego's hatred had taken him over the edge into obsession, talk would not be enough to convince him how very wrong he was.

And speaking to their mother would be useless. She adored Diego so much that she would support him in whatever he chose to do, even if he killed Miguel with his bare hands. Perhaps she could not blame her mother for hating her husband's illegitimate son. Perhaps she would feel the same if her husband had betrayed her. But try as she might, she could not hate Miguel. In truth, she admired him.

Should she go to Juan and tell him what she knew? He could then go to Miguel and warn him. But if she did that, would she not be betraying Diego? Would she not be choosing one brother over the other?

Dear God, what must I do? Please, help me make the right decision. I do not want to betray those I love, but how can I stand by and do nothing?

Miguel, J.J. and Dom arrived at Miguel's home in the early-morning hours. Ramona met them at the door, concern in her weary, dark eyes. Miguel did his best to reassure his housekeeper that all was well, but knowing him as she did, she saw through his false optimism. He wanted to believe that today's three incidents were the beginning and the end of his enemy's scare tactics, but he knew better. Hector Padilla and his corrupt Federalist Party were running scared. Since all the independent polls showed Miguel winning the election by a wide margin, the opposition party had only one choice—either kill him or force him to drop out of the race. If they killed him, the people might turn him into a martyr and rebel against Padilla and his kind. The more Miguel thought about it—and he had been thinking of little else these past few hours—the more he realized that the best course of action for his enemies was to force him to withdraw his candidacy.

"Good night," Dom said as he paused outside his bedroom door. "Try to get some rest. Both of you."

"Good night." J.J. looked at Dom. "If you hear anything—"

"I will let you know the minute I get a call about the lab results."

J.J. nodded, then she grasped Miguel's hand and led him down the hall to his bedroom suite on the other side of the house. She opened the door and turned on several lamps while he trudged to the liquor cabinet.

"Would you like a drink?" he asked.

"No, thanks, but you go ahead. I'm going to clean all this makeup off my face, sponge off and put on my pajamas."

He nodded, then lifted a bottle of whiskey and poured himself half a glass. The liquor sailed down his throat, warming his esophagus on the way down, then hit his belly like a hot coal. He coughed a couple of times, then took another swig. His head ached, his stomach churned and his conscience nagged at him. How was it that a man with good intentions, with his heart in the right place, could cause harm to others? All Miguel had ever wanted was to make life better for the people of his country. Having grown up in poverty, the bastard son of a woman thought of as a whore, seeing daily the plight of people forgotten by their government, he had known, even as a child, that someday he would change things for the better.

After finishing off his drink and feeling the effects as a warming sensation that settled in his belly and took the edge off his nerves, Miguel sat down on the side of his bed and removed his shoes and socks. Just as he took off his jacket and tie, J.J. emerged from the bathroom. He took one look at her and became instantly aroused. She wore her lavender silk robe, loosely belted at the waist. As she walked across the room, she unintentionally revealed one calf and thigh and he caught a glimpse of the sexy black lace garter belt to which her black silk stockings were attached.

He swallowed hard.

The whiskey had helped a little. Sex would help a lot. Nothing relieved a man's tension better than sex. Fast, furious, hot and wild sex.

With J.J.

Miguel closed his eyes and tried to erase the picture of her branded in his mind. But instead, his imagination went to work. He could see her coming toward him, removing her robe and standing in front of him wearing only her stockings, garter belt, bikini panties and bra. When she began stripping, removing her bra first, Miguel opened his eyes and cursed softly.

J.J. was nowhere in sight. She had disappeared into the walk-in closet. Miguel sighed heavily, then stood, removed his shirt and added it to the haphazard pile of clothing he had tossed on the floor. What he needed was another drink.

Lifting his arms over his head, he stretched his taut muscles. He thought he heard a soft gasp and when he lowered his arms and glanced over his shoulder, he saw J.J., in a pair of ivory satin pajamas, standing several feet away, staring at him. She came toward him, her hands outstretched.

"What should I do with these?" she asked, holding out the diamond earrings and necklace she had worn to Anton's party.

"Put them wherever you want," he told her. "You'll be wearing them again in the days ahead." He glanced down at the engagement ring he'd given her. "Don't take that ring off. Keep it on day and night. It is a bad omen for a woman to remove her engagement ring before the wedding."

J.J. simply nodded. No arguments. No reminders that their engagement was not real and that there would never be a wedding. She turned quickly and went back into the closet. While she was gone, Miguel poured himself another drink. If he couldn't get laid, he'd get drunk. A stupid thing to do, maybe. But right now, for a few hours, he did not want to be a pillar of strength, the savior of Mocorito. All he wanted was to stop thinking, stop worrying, to cease to feel anything.

When she returned to the bedroom, J.J. paused several feet away from him and cleared her throat. With the second glass of whiskey in his hand, he turned to her.

"Is there something you want?" he asked.

"Isn't that your second drink?"

"Yes, it is."

"Do you think you should be drinking so much?"

"Yes, I think I should."

"Miguel…" She took several tentative steps in his direction. He held up a restraining hand. "No, do not."

"Do not what?"

"Do not come any closer."

At first she didn't say anything, just stood there and stared at him. Then she turned around and walked over to his bed. His heartbeat accelerated. She turned down the covers. His sex hardened painfully. She reached out and grabbed one of the feather pillows. His mind screamed. *Damn, damn, damn!*

"You should go to bed and try to sleep," she told him as she went to the armoire, opened it and removed a cotton blanket. "But if you would like to talk—"

"I believe we have already said all there is to say, have we not?" He brought the glass to his lips and downed a sizable amount of whiskey. He coughed, then blew out a hot breath.

"Miguel, please don't drink any more."

He grinned. "Do you have another remedy that will work better than liquor?"

She frowned. "On top of all your other problems, if you drink much more, you will wake up with a horrible headache."

"I already have a headache," he told her. "As a matter of fact, I have two headaches."

She stared at him, her frown deepening. "I think you've already had too much to drink."

Bossy American female! If she had no intention of giving him what he really needed, then to hell with her. He didn't need her. Didn't want her. Could do just fine without her.

Liar!

In an act of childish defiance, Miguel lifted the liquor bottle and filled the glass to the rim, then he saluted her with the glass and took another hefty swig.

She whirled around and marched over to the chaise lounge, placed the pillow at the top, then lay down and pulled the cotton blanket up to her neck.

Ignore her, he told himself. She has dismissed you completely.

With the glass held tightly in his slightly unsteady hand, Miguel opened the French doors and walked out onto the balcony overlooking the courtyard. The breeze was cooler than usual, a hint of rain in the air. A million and one thoughts raced through his mind, swirling about, tormenting him, driving him mad. He threw the glass over the balcony. Whiskey flew in every direction, some splattering on his naked chest. The glass hit the rocks below and shattered into pieces.

Miguel clutched the wrought-iron railing, then closed his eyes and prayed. He asked for guidance, for the ability to choose the correct path. And he begged for an hour or two of relief. If only he could stop thinking, stop worrying, stop caring so damn much.

He felt her presence behind him before he heard her soft footsteps or smelled the faint, lingering scent of her perfume. Why
could she not leave him alone? Did she not know that her presence alone was driving him mad?

Her small hand touched his back. He tensed, every muscle in
his body going stiff. As stiff as his sex.

"Miguel?"

He turned and faced her, but before she could say or do anything, he grabbed her, yanked her into his arms and kissed her.
His mouth took hers with a hungry passion, the taste of her far
sweeter than he had imagined. She neither fought him nor coop-
erated, but let him ravage her mouth as he ran his hands over her
lush body. Then just as he ended the kiss and started to lift his
head, she moaned softly and her mouth responded, kissing him
back. Eager and greedy. Wild with need.

Chapter 9

J.J.'s bones dissolved into liquid and her body heated to the boiling point as she and Miguel shared a kiss to end all kisses. Fourth of July fireworks. Hurricane waves crashing against the shore. The thunder of her own heartbeat deafened her as electrical shock waves heated her blood. She couldn't get close enough to him, couldn't meld her body to his as tightly as she longed to do. Only the intimate joining of lovemaking could come close to uniting them in the way she needed to be part of him.

She had been in love once…or thought she had been. And she'd had great sex…or thought she had. But nothing J.J. had ever experienced came anywhere close to what she was feeling now. She had never known what real, honest-to-goodness yearning was until this very moment. Yearning so powerful that it obliterated everything else, reducing her to a purely emotional creature.

As she kept kissing him, tasting him, devouring him as he was her, she rubbed her hands over his shoulders and back, longing for the feel of his naked flesh beneath her fingertips. Rational thought was slipping away fast. If she didn't hang on, didn't force herself immediately to think about what she was doing, she would be lost.

But I want him, an inner voice pleaded. I want him more than I've ever wanted anything or anyone.

She couldn't give herself to him. She could not surrender to the weakness overwhelming her. This wasn't love. This was lust. Primitive animal magnetism, drawing two young, healthy primates together.

All right, so this was nothing more than uncontrollable passion. What was wrong with that? Just because she'd never had sex with a man she didn't care for deeply, why couldn't this be the first time?

J.J. pulled away, ending the ravaging kiss, but Miguel moaned and sought her mouth again, his hands cupping her hips and holding her mound against his erection. Her damp femininity throbbed. Wanting. Needing.

"No, please," she spoke the words against his demanding mouth. "We can't. I can't."

He kissed her again before easing his lips to her jaw and then down her neck, ending up by burrowing his head against her shoulder. When the tip of his tongue flicked repeatedly against her collarbone, she sighed.

"No, Miguel, this isn't fair."

Either not hearing her or completely ignoring her protest, he lowered his head to her left breast. Her entire body tensed with anticipation. His mouth covered the areola through the satin material of her pajama top and sucked until her nipple tightened into a pebble-hard point. While he suckled her greedily, she cupped the back of his head and held him in place at her breast. Spirals of desire spread out from her breasts and connected with the core of her body.

As the last coherent thought floated through her mind—put

a stop to this now while you still can—Miguel dropped to his knees in front of her and kissed a damp path from her breast, over her midriff and across her navel. He paused, slid her pajama bottoms down a couple of inches, stuck his tongue into her navel and laved the small, deep indentation.

J.J. unraveled completely when his big hands grasped her hips and eased her pajamas farther down her hips.

Oh, mercy, mercy. She wanted this. Oh, how she wanted it. But she couldn't let him do it. Could she?

"Miguel?" his name was nothing more than a pleading whisper.

"Yes, *querida?*" His hands paused in their task.

"We can't do this. You know we can't. We met only yesterday. We're strangers. This is all wrong. You know it is." There, she had been sensible and called a halt to this madness.

He nuzzled her mound through the thin satin barrier. "If it's so wrong, why does it feel so right?"

"Because we're acting and reacting from an adrenaline rush," she told him, as she caressed the back of his head. "Danger, fear, intense emotions all combined to heighten our senses. Wanting sex to diffuse tension is the most natural thing in the world."

"I agree." He kissed her mound. She trembled. "The sex would be good. It would be very good for both of us."

"I don't doubt that for a minute, but—"

He made his way up her body, inch by inch, his hot breath searing her through the satin and his big hands working their way up and over her buttocks. When he rose to his full height, he looked down at her, his golden eyes smoldering.

"You are not a virgin?" he asked.

"No, but that doesn't mean—"

"You have been with other men, why not with me?"

"I don't love you. I don't even know you."

He cradled her buttocks with his palms and pressed her firmly against his pulsating sex. "What better way to become acquainted than to make love? I promise that you will not be disappointed. I have been told I am an excellent lover."

"Ah—! What a macho, male, he-man thing to say." His words had been like a bucket of cold water dumped on her head. She shoved against his chest until he released her. "Just when I was beginning to like you, you have to go and be a….a…a man!"

Miguel chuckled. "*Sí, señorita,* I am indeed a man. A man who very much wants to make love to you."

"You want sex," she told him, avoiding eye contact. "Any woman would do."

Frowning, his gaze narrowed as he glared at her. "You do not truly believe that, do you? If sex with any woman was all I wanted, there are dozens of women I could have. I could pick up the telephone and make a call and any one of them would come to me now, in the middle of the night. But I do not want any of those women. I want you."

J.J. stiffened her spine. She believed him. About the dozens of willing women and about him wanting only her. "I'm your bodyguard. My job is to guard you and protect you, to keep you alive during the election campaign. Having sex with you would be unprofessional."

"What are you so afraid of, Jennifer?" Although he no longer touched her, he caressed her with his seductive gaze.

She swallowed, then looked up at him. "The truth?"

"Yes, the truth."

"I'm afraid that I'll become fond of you, that I'll care for you, and I'll get my heart broken."

"*Querida.*" He held his hand out, as if he intended to touch her.

She moved backward, just out of his reach. "I do not have casual, meaningless affairs. The only relationship you and I have now or will ever have is a farce. I'm your pretend fiancée. And that's all."

He dropped his hand to his side. His defeated expression told her that she had finally gotten through to him. "You should go in to bed now," he told her. "I will stay out here for a while longer."

"Will you be all right?" That's it, Jennifer Joy, fawn over the man. Didn't you just tell him that you weren't in love with him, that you didn't care for him except as a client?

He turned his back to her and looked down at the dark garden below, illuminated only by the moonlight. "I will be fine. Go to bed."

Reluctantly, wondering if she was a fool for rejecting a man she so desperately wanted, J.J. went back into the bedroom. She looked down at the chaise and then over to the huge king-size bed. Images of Miguel and her sharing that bed, the two of them naked, thrashing about, making love, flashed through her mind. She groaned as she lay down and pulled the cotton blanket up over her.

How long would Miguel stay outside? Would she still be awake when he went to bed? She closed her eyes and tried to think of anything other than the tall, dark, handsome man standing alone on the balcony. But despite her best efforts to erase all thoughts of him, he filled her mind. And her own traitorous body reminded her of the pleasure his mouth and hands had given her.

Miguel had made certain that he was showered, shaved and dressed before J.J. awoke. He had been exceptionally quiet, trying to not disturb her. He knew she had spent restless hours tossing and turning on the chaise lounge, just as he had in the massive king-size bed. He had finally fallen asleep sometime shortly before dawn and rested for a couple of hours. When he'd left his bedroom suite, J.J. had been awake, but she'd been pretending to be asleep. He understood that she was as reluctant as he to discuss what had transpired between them in the early hours of this morning.

He would leave things as they were. For now. In the clear light of day, he could think more clearly, more rationally. Having a love affair with his American bodyguard might give him immense physical pleasure, but at what price, not only to him, but to her? Was his life not already complicated enough without adding an ill-fated romance to the mix?

When he entered the dining room, Ramona, who was busy overseeing the dishes being brought into the room by the kitchen help, spoke to him.

"Good morning, Señor Ramirez." He could tell that she wanted to ask him something, possibly question him about the dinner party last night.

"Have you heard about what happened at Anton Casimiro's party?" Miguel asked. "About some of his guests having food poisoning?"

"Yes, *señor*. It is in the newspaper, on the radio and on the television. It is a miracle that you, too, were not taken ill." She crossed herself. "We must thank the blessed virgin."

"Yes, we must." Although he hadn't eaten a bite since yesterday's luncheon at the country club, he wasn't sure he could down a full breakfast, so to start with, he poured himself a cup of strong coffee. He knew it would be strong because that was the way he preferred his coffee and Ramona made sure things were done the way he wanted them done. "Has Señor Shea come down this morning?"

"Yes, he was down earlier, but went out. Carlos offered to drive him, but he took a taxi."

Miguel nodded. "Hmm… Yes, Dom is a very independent fellow."

"Will the *señorita* be joining you for breakfast?"

"No, she is still resting. Perhaps you would be kind enough to prepare a tray for her and I will take it up to her later."

"Yes, of course."

Only moments after Ramona disappeared into the kitchen, Miguel heard footsteps in the hallway. When he glanced up, he saw Dom Shea and Will Pierce.

"We came in the back way," Dom said, in English. "No one saw us except the servants. I told them that Will was an old buddy of mine from the States."

"Please, sit. Both of you. Have you had breakfast?" Miguel asked as he placed the cup and saucer on the table and pulled out his chair.

"Just coffee for me," Will said.

Dom poured two cups, added a dollop of cream to his and brought both cups to the table. After handing Will the cup of black coffee, Dom sat down and took a sip from his cup. "J.J. still in bed?"

"Yes, she was still resting when I came down a few minutes ago."

"I guess we should wait for her before Will gives you the results from the lab tests."

"I would prefer to know now," Miguel said.

Dom shrugged. "Sure thing. I'll relay the info to J.J. and you can fill in your people."

"My people?"

"Lopez and Aznar. I assume you plan to share the information with them."

"Yes, of course."

After Will joined them at the table, Miguel and Dom turned to him.

"The cocktail sauce was doctored with a non-lethal amount of dimethatate." Will took a sip of coffee. "If ingested in large doses, it's lethal. There was just enough mixed into the cocktail sauce to cause vomiting and diarrhea in anyone who ate a few teaspoons of the sauce."

"Apparently the goal was not to kill anyone," Dom said.

"And nothing was found in any of the other food?" Miguel asked.

"No, only in the cocktail sauce served with the boiled shrimp," Will said.

"Then whoever poisoned the sauce knew that I would not eat

any because it is a well-known fact that I have an aversion to shrimp." Miguel's worst fear concerning last night's near-tragedy had just been confirmed. "I was not the target. At least not the target of the poisoning."

"Just how many people know you won't eat shrimp?" Dom asked.

Miguel shrugged. "My family. My closest friends. A few colleagues. Enough people that it would be impossible to track down a traitor, if that is what you are thinking."

"Hm… Actually what I'm thinking is that you got hit with three warning messages in one day." Dom shook his head. "They wanted to make their point as quickly as possible, didn't they?"

"We have to assume that yesterday's three events were staged to get your attention and that they were just the prelude to bigger and more deadly incidents."

Will focused directly on Miguel. "You cannot allow them to frighten you into withdrawing from the presidential race."

"Spoken like a man who does not love my family and friends and loyal supporters as I do. You would be willing to shed innocent blood in order to see me become president." Miguel glowered at Pierce.

"Are you saying that they've already won?" Pierce asked. "A blown tire, a few harmless snakes at a luncheon and a couple of dozen people sick with what everyone assumes was food poisoning and you're ready to throw in the towel? I thought you were made of strong stuff, Ramirez. I had no idea you'd tuck tail and run at the first sign of trouble."

Before Miguel could form a reply in his mind, let alone utter a rebuttal, a feminine voice defended him. "Miguel Ramirez is not the kind of man to run from a fight," J.J. said as she entered the dining room. "But neither is he a man who is willing to risk the lives of others, to run roughshod over his people for his own selfish reasons."

"Well, what lit a fire in your belly, Agent Blair?" Will scrutinized J.J. closely as she walked over to the buffet table and poured herself a cup of coffee.

"You have no right to speak to Miguel the way you did," J.J. told the CIA agent. "This is his country and the people whose lives are at risk are his people. And it his decision and his alone whether to withdraw from the presidential race."

A moment of complete, stunned silence followed J.J.'s declaration. In that moment, Miguel sensed a deep emotional bond with Jennifer Blair, something unlike anything he had ever experienced with another person. After knowing him less than forty-eight hours, she understood who he was and what he felt.

In his peripheral vision, Miguel caught a questioning glance that Dom shot J.J., as if he were silently asking her what had brought about her staunch defense of a man neither of them really knew. But that was where Domingo Shea was wrong. He might not know Miguel, but J.J. did. He did not understand how it was possible for someone who had met him only the night before last to see inside his heart and mind so easily.

"Sorry." Pierce's one-word apology broke the awkward silence. "I'm used to dealing with jerks who respond better when they're on the defensive. But if you decide to continue with your candidacy, you will have our full backing and if necessary we can bring in more Dundee agents."

"To do what?" Dom asked. "It would take a small army to protect everyone who supports Ramirez."

"I was thinking more in terms of protecting those closest to him. His family and best friends," Pierce said.

"Before we start making plans on Miguel's behalf, perhaps we should find out what he intends to do." J.J. looked at Miguel, a softness in her gaze that told him she remembered those sweet, passionate moments early this morning.

"I will speak with Emilio and Dolores, with Roberto and Juan and Aunt Josephina, as well as the servants, especially Ramona and Carlos, who have been with me for many years." Miguel would not continue his candidacy unless those dearest to him were willing to risk their lives for the Nationalist cause.

"If they tell you that they do not want you to give in to threats, even threats against them, then you won't quit, is that right?" Pierce asked.

Miguel thought about Dolores, a very pregnant Dolores. How could he ask her to risk not only her life, but the life of her unborn child?

J.J. reached out and laid her hand over Miguel's where it rested on the table. "You should send Dolores away from Nava, perhaps even out of the country, until after the election. The Dundee agency can provide her with a personal bodyguard."

Miguel turned his hand over and clasped J.J.'s small, delicate hand in his. It was as if she had read his mind, as if she knew his thoughts. She understood that his first concern was for his cousin, who was like a sister to him.

"You do realize that since everyone in Mocorito believes you to be my fiancée, you, too, could be in grave danger? Perhaps in more danger than Dolores."

"That may be true, but I am also a professional, a highly trained bodyguard," J.J. told him. "I know how to take care of myself, as well as others."

Only when Dom Shea cleared his throat did Miguel realize that he and J.J. had been sitting there holding hands, staring into each other's eyes and speaking to each other as if they were alone.

J.J. eased her hand from his grasp a couple of seconds before Ramona walked into the dining room carrying a silver tray. She took one look at J.J. and paused, then came straight to her, set the tray in front of her and removed the linen cloth covering the food.

"Señor Ramirez asked me to prepare a breakfast tray for you, *señorita,*" Ramona told her. "He intended to bring it upstairs to you himself." The housekeeper smiled warmly at J.J.

"Thank you, Ramona," J.J. said in Spanish. "Miguel is very thoughtful, is he not?"

"Oh, yes, *señorita,* he is the most thoughtful man I know." Ramona blushed. "He will be a good husband."

Yes, he will. Had that been only an instant thought or a heartfelt knowledge? J.J. asked herself. Here she was once again buying into the fiancée fantasy, something she had to stop doing.

"Ramona, will you ask all the servants to come into my study in half an hour?" Miguel asked the housekeeper. "I need to discuss something with all of you."

"Do you want Carlos, too? And Pedro, the gardener?"

"Yes, everyone. Please."

Ramona scurried to do his bidding.

Miguel shoved back his chair and stood. "If you will excuse me, I wish to move forward with my plan to speak to the servants and my family and close friends. I intend to do that this morning. I am going to telephone Roberto and Emilio and Juan right now."

"You haven't eaten anything since lunch yesterday," J.J. reminded him. "Can't the calls wait until you've had breakfast?"

Will rose from his seat. "I should be going. I'll be in touch soon." He looked at Dom. "Contact me when a decision has been made and we'll proceed from there."

Dom stood. "Let me walk you out."

Once Dom and Will left the dining room, Miguel turned to J.J. "I will eat if you will eat. Then we will go into my den and I will telephone my family and friends. I cannot make this decision alone, as you so wisely pointed out to me last night."

"I will not be sent away!" Dolores Lopez planted her hands on her hips and glared back and forth from her husband to her cousin.

"*Querida,* you must go," Emilio told her. "Miguel cannot continue in his bid for the presidency unless you cooperate with us. He will do nothing to endanger your life and the life of our child." Emilio tenderly patted his wife's protruding belly.

"I agree," Roberto added. "Once Padilla's people realize their scare tactics are not working, they could very easily target those of us closest to Miguel."

"If that is true, then how can I leave you behind, Emilio?" She looked pleadingly at her husband. "And you Miguel?"

"You will do what you know you must," J.J. said, hoping she could persuade Dolores to do the sensible thing.

"Are you leaving, also, Jennifer?" Dolores asked. "No, you are not. You are staying with your man, not deserting him when he needs you."

"But I am not pregnant," J.J. said. "By staying, I am not risking the life of my child."

Dolores frowned, but she did not continue to argue. She sat there, on the sofa in the living room, and thought for several minutes before replying. "I will leave Nava, but I do not want to leave Mocorito. Send me, with the bodyguard you wish to hire, to Buenaventura. And no one except Emilio will know exactly where in Buenaventura I am. Will that be acceptable?"

A collective sigh of relief reverberated throughout the room.

By early afternoon the decision had been made that Miguel would not withdraw from the presidential race. And plans had been made to send Dolores to the northern seacoast village of Buenaventura with a Dundee bodyguard. J.J. wondered if, when Sawyer McNamara had told Lucie Evans he was sending her to Mocorito to guard Miguel's cousin, she had pointed out to him that she spoke only "tourist" Spanish. If she had, knowing Sawyer, he'd probably sent along a Learn Spanish Overnight CD and companion workbook on the flight with her from Atlanta to Caracas.

Chuckling softly to herself, J.J. didn't hear the door to the bedroom suite open. When she sensed someone in the room with her, she whirled around, prepared to defend herself. Then she saw Miguel and immediately relaxed.

"You were so deep in thought that you did not hear me, did you?" he asked.

"You caught me falling down on the job."

"What an odd expression. You Americans say the strangest things."

"Yes, I suppose we do."

"What did you find so amusing in your thoughts?"

J.J. smiled. "Just thinking about Lucie Evans, the agent my boss is sending to guard Dolores."

"There is something amusing about Señorita Evans?"

"No, not really. It's just that she and our boss, Sawyer Mc-Namara, have this ongoing feud and have had for as long as I've worked at the Dundee Agency. They cannot be in the same room together for more than two minutes without arguing."

"They have never been lovers?" Miguel asked.

"No. At least not as far as anyone knows. They were both FBI agents before they came to work for Dundee. We figure something must have happened between them way back when."

"Way back when?"

"Back when they worked for the Bureau. Two people don't dislike each other that much without a reason."

"You disliked me before you even met me, did you not?" Miguel walked toward her and looked down at the chaise lounge where she sat. Without even asking her, he sat down beside her.

She sucked in a deep breath, wishing there was room on the chaise for her to scoot away from him, so that his arm wouldn't brush up against hers.

"I drew some conclusions from the information I was given about you," she admitted.

"Was the information accurate?"

"Yes, it seems to have been."

"And were your conclusions also accurate?"

"Partially."

"Only partially? What have you discovered that tells you you misjudged me?"

"Fishing for compliments?"

He threw up his hands expressively. "Another silly Americanism."

"You *are* the old-fashioned, macho type. But I don't believe you separate women into only two categories—lady or whore."

"You forget there are also the nuns," he said.

She smiled. "Yes, of course. I'd forgotten about the nuns."

"What else?" he asked, as eagerly as a child.

"You genuinely care about people. Not just your family and friends, but everyone in Mocorito. The things you say come from your heart. They're not just rhetoric, not just campaign psychobabble."

"Psychobabble?"

"Another Americanism," she told him.

"Ah."

"You didn't like me when Dom and I first arrived. Were you wrong about me?"

"Partially."

She laughed.

"You are every bit the strong, independent woman I believed you to be, but you are not a man-hater. There is a softer, very feminine side to you." He lifted his hand to her face and cupped her chin between his thumb and forefinger. "For the right man, you would make the perfect wife."

J.J.'s heartbeat accelerated. Not again. Don't overreact to a simple compliment. He wasn't implying that he is Mr. Right.

"Do you enjoy the ballet?" Miguel asked.

"Huh?" Slightly startled when he changed the subject so quickly, she shook her head.

"Juan and Aunt Josephina have asked us to join them tonight at the ballet and for dinner afterward. I accepted on our behalf. That meets with your approval?"

"As your fiancée, yes, that meets with my approval," J.J. said. "However, as your bodyguard, I have to tell you that from now on, do not make any plans without checking with me first."

The corners of Miguel's sensuous mouth lifted in a hint of a smile. "That man—your future husband—he will have his hands filled keeping you in line."

J.J. laughed. "He will have his hands *full* keeping me in line," she corrected him.

His gaze traveled over her intimately, pausing on her breasts. "Yes, he will have his hands full."

An undeniable current of awareness passed between them, the sexual tension vibrating like a live wire.

J.J. jumped up off the chaise. "I need to find something appropriate to wear to the ballet."

"An evening gown," Miguel told her. "And be sure to wear the diamond necklace and earrings."

"I have only two evening gowns," J.J. said. "One is purple and one is teal. Would you like to choose which one I should wear?"

"Wear the purple one."

"Are you sure? Don't you want to see the gowns?"

"Teal is a dark bluish green, yes?"

"Yes."

"It is not the color for you. Wear the purple one. It will complement your beautiful violet eyes and flawless skin." When she just stood there smiling at him like an idiot, he said, "I should give you some privacy while you bathe and prepare for this evening."

When he headed toward the door, she called, "Miguel?"

"Yes?"

"Who else knows—other than Juan and his aunt—that we will be attending the ballet tonight?"

"Who else? Emilio, Roberto, Ramona and of course, Carlos. Why do you ask?" He shook his head. "No, do not think it. Not one of them would betray me. They are loyal to me and to the Nationalist Party."

"Then nothing bad should happen tonight, should it? Your enemies don't know where you will be this evening, therefore they can hardly plan a strike of some kind against you."

"I will not live my life in fear. And I will not distrust people who have always been loyal to me."

Miguel did not sound entirely certain in his convictions.

Chapter 10

Miguel had tried his best for many years to appreciate the ballet, but tonight was no different from the other times he had pretended to enjoy himself. Perhaps his lack of appreciation for both ballet and opera came from having been reared as a peasant, growing up with native music and dance, both vibrantly alive to him in a way that the more refined arts were not. He preferred a good soccer game or a bullfight or the racetrack in Colima, events he had attended as a boy with his grandfather, cousins and neighbors. He liked guitar music and songs sung in Spanish, with gusto and heart.

Just from looking at Jennifer, he could not tell if she was as bored as he and if she, too, wished they were somewhere else. Preferably alone together. Her placid expression gave away nothing, but she seemed to be totally absorbed in the performance.

With Juan and Aunt Josephina, there was no doubt. Both loved the ballet and the opera and often invited Miguel to go with them. Usually he came up with a good excuse to decline, but occasionally he accepted out of love for them. He enjoyed their company, although more so at other functions. And dinner tonight would more than make up for the time he felt was wasted at the ballet. Both Juan and his aunt were delightful dinner companions and always chose excellent restaurants. One of their favorites—where they would dine tonight—was Maria Bonita, where the colorful atmosphere and live music was almost more delectable than the delicious, authentic Mocoritian food.

If he could endure a few more minutes of this torture, they could escape to Miguel's waiting limousine and go directly to Maria Bonita. Good wine, good food and good friends. And a beautiful woman at his side. What more could a man ask for and not be considered selfish and ungrateful?

He glanced at his fiancée. No, not his fiancée, only the woman masquerading as his fiancée. Why was it, he wondered, that it was so easy to think of Jennifer as his betrothed? It was not as if she were perfectly suited for the job of First Lady or a perfect match for him. Indeed they were too much alike, both forceful and aggressive. And passionate about the things that mattered to them. He had always pictured himself married to a gentle, demure woman who looked to him for guidance in everything, from her choice in clothes to the way in which they would rear their children. Although capable of playing the part, Jennifer was not that woman.

His gaze traveled over her appreciatively. Her beauty took his breath away. Tonight she out-dazzled every woman there. The bodice of her purple silk gown crisscrossed over her breasts and hugged her tiny waist, then flowed downward, caressing her hips and swaying at her ankles as she walked. The diamonds he had given her sparkled at her ears and neck, their beauty mere accents to hers.

He reached over and grasped her hand resting in her lap. She entwined her fingers with his, but didn't look his way. Leaning toward her, he brought his mouth to her ear and whispered, "I hate the ballet."

She smiled, then moved her head, inadvertently brushing her cheek against his lips. A jolt of sexual energy shot through him. Perhaps she had intended to arouse him? The little tease. She would flirt with him in a place where he could do little about it. But later…ah, yes, later.

They held hands until the end of the performance, then she pulled free and applauded along with the rest of the audience. Miguel clapped half-heartedly and smiled when the house lights came up and Aunt Josephina, who sat to his right, patted him on the arm and asked how he'd enjoyed the performance.

"Very much," he lied. "As always."

Her broad grin told him that on some occasions, it was not a sin to lie. Especially when the lie spared a kind old woman's feelings.

As the foursome made their way out of the Nava Civic Center, Miguel spoke to numerous people, but did his best to avoid being waylaid by anyone who would demand more than a moment of his time. This evening was not about politics; it was about relaxation and camaraderie with friends.

Once outside, while they waited for their limousine—only one in a long line of limos—Jennifer pulled the purple shawl that matched her gown up and around her shoulders.

"Are you cold?" Miguel put his arm around her shoulders and brought her up against him.

"No, not really. But the wind is a bit chilly."

"We should not have to wait long. I believe our car is fourth in line."

"Do you really hate the ballet?" she asked in a hushed whisper as she leaned her head closer.

He glanced over at Aunt Josephina, who was chattering away with the couple behind them. And although Juan appeared to be listening to the conversation, Miguel knew his friend's mind had wandered off somewhere. He'd seen that look in Juan's eyes before and it usually meant he was thinking of a woman.

"Yes," Miguel admitted. "I fear that I have very plebeian tastes in entertainment. I prefer soccer games and bullfights and horse races. And watching movies. I especially like the old American gangster movies with Edward G. Robinson and James Cagney."

"I'm not surprised that you like sports, even something as bloody as a bullfight, but I never pegged you for an old-movie buff. I used to watch those old gangster movies with my dad when I was a little girl."

The smile vanished from her face, replaced by a wistful, bittersweet expression. Why did thinking of her father make her sad? he wondered. "Your father is still alive, is he not?"

Her smile returned, but it was a sarcastic smirk. "Oh, yes, General Rudd Blair is very much alive and quite well. His life couldn't be better. He recently remarried, for the second time since his divorce from my mother. And to a woman only five years older than I am. Or at least that's what I hear. But what makes his life truly worth living is the fact that my eighteen-year-old half-brother has just graduated from military school and even though I don't know for sure, my bet is that he's already been accepted at West Point."

"You do not have a close relationship with your father now?"

"Close? No, not for years and years." Probably without even realizing it, she changed from Spanish to English when she said, "Well, actually, we were probably never close, except in my mind."

"Was this rift between the two of you your choice or his?" Miguel asked, in English, then thought perhaps he should not probe deeper into a subject that might be painful for her.

"I'd say it was mutual. He never did have much use for me because I was just a girl. But I wised up. I finally realized that no matter what I did—even joining the army straight out of college—I would never be the one thing he wanted most."

Miguel kept silent, having no need to ask what her father had wanted most. What a foolish man this General Rudd Blair must be to not appreciate having a daughter such as Jennifer.

"He had a son and that's all he ever wanted. As far as he was concerned, my mother and I were simply mistakes in his past."

"Idiota!"

"Yes, you're right, he is an idiot." Jennifer laughed, the sound genuine.

Miguel loved her laughter. He would very much like to fill her life with such joy that she would laugh often and live well. She needed the right man to show her what a priceless treasure she was, a man capable of loving his daughters as much as his sons and taking as much pride in them, also.

"Is that your car, Miguel?" Aunt Josephina asked.

"Yes, I believe it is," he replied. "Are we all ready for a fabulous meal at Maria Bonita?"

"You will simply adore Maria Bonita," Juan told Jennifer. "It is one of my favorite restaurants, perhaps my very favorite."

Carlos pulled the limo to the curb, hopped out and opened the back door. After everyone else was safely inside and out of earshot, Miguel pulled Carlos aside and asked, "You did not leave the car unattended, did you? Not even for a few minutes?"

"No, Señor Ramirez, I have stayed with the car every moment."

"When we arrive at Maria Bonita, I will stay with the car while you take a break, if you would like."

"Thank you. All I require is a few moments, sir."

"You understand why I—"

"Yes, yes. Someone could tamper with the car—the engine, the gas tank or even place a bomb. I understand and I stay vigilant at all times."

The wharfs along the coast of Colima were dotted with numerous bars. Seedy, dangerous hellholes from the looks of them. What better place to meet an agent working undercover without anyone recognizing either of you or giving a damn who you were. The minute Dom entered Pepe's, loud music and even louder customer clatter engulfed him. As he moved deeper into this filthy den of iniquity, searching for Vic Noble, the stench of body odor and the haze of cigarette and cigar smoke assailed him. After searching for several minutes, he spotted Vic at a back corner table, a scantily clad *señorita* standing at his side, rubbing his shoulder and giving him a glimpse of her ample breasts as she leaned over him.

"Mind if I join you?" Dom asked in English.

Vic shoved the bosomy woman aside and gestured to the wooden chair across the table from him. The dismissed lady grumbled loudly in Spanish, most of her words a combination of curses, as she walked away to seek other prey.

Dom sat. He eyed the half-filled shot glass in front of Vic. "Tequila?"

"Want one?"

"Nope."

"Pierce is at the bar now, getting a bottle for the three of us."

"Will Pierce is sitting in on this meeting?"

Vic nodded. "Our government is going to want to know what I found out."

"And what would that be?"

"Wait for Pierce," Vic said. "But I'll tell you right now that once the big boys in D.C. hear about this, they will move heaven and earth to get Ramirez elected."

Pierce made his way through a bevy of client-seeking prostitutes and a couple of staggering drunks, barely managing to keep hold of the bottle of tequila and the two shot glasses he held.

When he reached their table, he slammed the bottle and glasses down, then yanked out a chair beside Vic, turned it backward and straddled the seat with his long legs. "Lovely place you chose for our meeting."

"Thanks," Vic said. "I thought the two of you would appreciate the decor and the atmosphere."

"So, what's this important information you've unearthed?" Dom asked.

Pierce removed the screw-on cap from the cheap tequila and

poured the liquor into the two empty shot glasses, then added enough to Vic's glass to fill it.

Vic leaned over the table and said in a low voice. "If the current president is reelected, he and his people have big plans for Mocorito."

"What sort of big plans?" Pierce asked.

"The kind that involves taking over the military and local law-enforcement agencies nationwide."

"That sounds like the current el presidente has plans for a dictatorship instead of a democracy." Dom rested his elbows on the table as he cupped his fingers together.

"Bingo. Give the man a cigar." Vic turned to Pierce. "Padilla has some rich and powerful supporters, but most of them aren't aware of his plans to return the country to a dictatorship. One of his most loyal followers, a man who is using his money and influence to help Padilla, is Diego Fernandez, Ramirez's half-brother."

"That's not a surprise," Pierce said.

"Fernandez is being kept in the dark about the president's plans for the future. He's being easily manipulated because his hatred for Ramirez has blinded him to the truth."

"Are you defending Fernandez?" Dom asked.

"Nope. Not me. Just stating facts. If Fernandez could be convinced that he's being played for a fool, then he might turn against Padilla."

"And just who is going to convince him?" Pierce scanned the bar, especially the tables nearest them.

"I'd say nobody here speaks enough English to understand anything we've said," Vic told them. "Besides, the music is so damn loud, I can barely hear myself think."

"What if we could place this information in the hands of Fernandez's sister, Seina?" Dom suggested. "If we were one hundred percent sure we can trust Dr. Esteban, he could be given the information and we could ask him to feed it to his lady love."

"Do we trust Esteban without reservations?" Vic looked at Pierce.

"Probably not. I'm not sure it would be wise to trust Esteban or Lopez or Aznar. We are almost certain that one of those three could be a traitor."

"Almost certain? Could be?" Vic's brow furrowed. "I haven't dug up any dirt on Esteban, at least so far. His only sin seems to be having clandestine meetings with Seina Fernandez."

"Then you think we should trust him with the information and ask him to pass it along to Señorita Fernandez?" Pierce glowered at Vic.

"I think Dom should talk it over with Ramirez," Vic said, "and if he says do it, then we do it."

"Ramirez is too close to Esteban to be able to—"

Dom interrupted Pierce in mid sentence. "It's Ramirez's frigging country, not yours or mine. I think he has more right than you do to make decisions that will affect not only him personally, but his fellow countrymen."

Vic coughed, barely suppressing a grin.

"Yeah, you're right," Pierce said. "Sometimes I just need to be reminded that I'm not always right."

The tension between Pierce and Dom subsided. The three men lifted their shot glasses and each took a hefty swig of the tequila.

Maria Bonita reminded J.J. of an upscale Mocoritian home, lavished with handmade tiles and what appeared to be miles of decorative wrought-iron. A mariachi band played traditional music and a dance floor was available. Not only did the members of the band dress in native costumes, but so did the waiters and waitresses. J.J. decided within minutes after their arrival that the food at this restaurant could not possibly surpass the incredible ambience.

Apparently Miguel was well-known here because the staff kowtowed to him as if he were already the president. Other customers waylaid him as their party passed by, everyone wanting to speak to him, shake his hand, kiss his cheek and wish him well. And as his fiancée, the attention spread to her.

Overwhelmed by the enthusiastic adoration showered on them, J.J. didn't realize that the maître d' was escorting them through the building, which was, in fact, an eighteenth-century hacienda, and out onto an enclosed patio. Their table for four was one of six tables placed around a central fountain.

"This place is unbelievable," J.J. said in English.

"What did she say?" Aunt Josephina asked as she was seated.

"Oh, forgive me," J.J. apologized in Spanish. "I was so impressed with this place that I reverted to my native tongue."

"It is perfectly understandable, my dear Jennifer." Aunt Josephina patted J.J.'s hand. "Maria Bonita has that effect on almost everyone the first time they come here."

No sooner had Miguel and Juan taken their seats than a small, bearded man wearing what J.J. thought were the clothes of a cook—or in this case, a chef—came to their table and suddenly burst into song. Totally surprised by the man's actions, J.J. gasped. Then, as she listened to him sing the romantic Latin ballad with such tenderness, she smiled at Miguel when he took her hand into his, showing her the appropriate affection a man would show his fiancée in a public place. No more. No less. After the little man sang two more ballads, he bowed, turned around and walked away.

"Who was that?" J.J. asked.

"That is Rolando," Miguel told her. "He is one of the chefs here at Maria Bonita, but he once had aspirations of being a singer. Since he is half owner of the restaurant, he performs for the customers."

"Especially customers he is fond of, as he is Miguel," Aunt Josephina said.

For a brief period of time, J.J. almost forgot why she was here in Mocorito and that she was not really Miguel's beloved fiancée. The wine was sheer perfection, the dinner conversation entertaining and the food was to die for. She ordered the *boquinete Dulce Vita,* which consisted of white snapper stuffed with shrimp and mushrooms and baked in a golden puff pastry. Sighing after finishing almost every bite, she shook her head when Miguel suggested dessert.

"But you must try the coconut ice cream," Juan said. "They top it with Kahlua." Laughing, he winked at her.

She had decided earlier that she liked Aunt Josephina very much and just this very second she decided she liked Juan, too, because she thought he was a genuinely nice person. Even though in her line of work, it paid to be suspicious of everyone, she wondered if she couldn't mark Dr. Juan Esteban off her list of possible traitors.

"I would love to try the coconut ice cream," J.J. said, "but I honestly don't think I can eat another bite."

"I will order the dessert." Miguel smiled at her. "And we will share it."

Flutters rippled through her stomach and trickled along her nerve endings. She longed to share more than dessert with Miguel.

"And we must order coffee, too." Aunt Josephina glanced at the waiter, but like a well-brought-up lady of her day, she did not place the order.

Miguel ordered three servings of the coconut ice cream with Kahlua, and freshly brewed coffee for four.

As they waited for dessert and chatted pleasantly, Juan suddenly went silent and turned quite pale. J.J. followed his line of vision to where the maître d' was seating a party of three on the far side of the patio. From the strong family resemblance the two women and one man shared, she assumed they were a mother, her son and her daughter. The mother was tall and thin, with a regal air about her that proclaimed she found most people far inferior to her. The son was also tall and quite handsome, with wavy black hair and a thin mustache, reminiscent of old Latin movie stars. The daughter was a few inches shorter than the mother and far prettier, with a round, soft face and bright black eyes.

Without realizing she had spoken aloud, J.J. asked, "Who are they?"

Juan did not answer, but Miguel turned his head so that he could catch a glimpse of whoever Juan was staring at so intensely. Miguel's face turned ashen.

"That is my father's widow," Miguel said. "And his legitimate son and daughter."

She heard and understood the bitterness in Miguel's voice. Even though she was her father's legitimate child, she felt every bit as much a bastard as Miguel did. She knew what it was like to be the unwanted, the cast-aside, the unloved.

"Perhaps we should leave," Juan said.

"No!" Miguel shook his head. "If they are offended by my presence, let them leave."

When J.J. reached out to grasp Miguel's hand, he snatched it away, withdrawing from her. Oh, God, how terrible this is for him, how raw his emotions must be. If only he would accept her comfort.

"The *señora* is showing her age," Aunt Josephina said. "She looks terrible. Not that Carlotta was ever a beautiful woman. Ah, but your mother, Miguel, she was beautiful." Josephina reached out and patted J.J.'s hand. "Luz Ramirez was as beautiful as you are, dear girl."

Miguel looked at Juan's aunt and smiled. "I forget that you knew my mother, that she and my grandmother worked in your home."

"They have seen us," Juan said. "Diego is glaring at us and his mother is—"

"Dance with me." J.J. scooted back her chair, stood and held her hand out to Miguel.

He stared at her with a questioning look in his golden eyes. Then without uttering a word, he stood, took her hand and led her from the patio, into the hacienda and onto the dance floor.

Apparently the band was taking a break because the music came from a single musician, a pianist who was playing a soft and romantic tune. Miguel took J.J. into his arms and they joined the other five couples on the dance floor.

"You are very good at reading me, *querida*." Miguel rubbed his cheek against hers as he held her close, but not too close. After all, they were in public. "You seem to know what I need before I do."

"Then you did need rescuing, didn't you? Juan and his aunt were making much too much over the arrival of the Fernandez family when you would have preferred ignoring them, as they have done you your whole life."

Miguel slowed, bringing them almost to a standstill, and gazed into her eyes. "How is it that you know me so well?"

"I honestly don't understand it myself," she admitted. "It's odd, but I feel as if I've known you forever."

"It is not odd at all, my sweet Jennifer. I feel the same. As if perhaps in some other life you and I were soul mates."

Yes, that was it. Soul mates. Never in a million years would she have thought she'd use that term to describe her relationship with any man, least of all a Latin lover who was "all man," to the nth degree.

Perhaps we are soul mates in this lifetime, too, she wanted to say, but didn't. Eternal soul mates fated to be together.

Seina excused herself to go to the ladies' room, hoping that Juan would follow her discreetly so they could have a few precious moments together. Stolen moments. She waited outside in the corridor that led to both the ladies' room and the men's room, feeling certain that Juan would show up at any moment. She waited and waited. Five minutes. Ten minutes. Had he not seen her leave her table? Did he not know that she expected him to come to her?

Finally giving up, she started to return to the patio. Then there he was, coming toward her. The joy of her heart. The love of her life.

She rushed to him. He stopped several feet from her. Then she, too, paused.

"I wish I could touch you," she said.

"Seina, please. What if someone were to overhear you?"

"You were at the Civic Center tonight, weren't you?" she asked. "I thought I caught a glimpse of you."

"I was not aware that your family was attending the ballet tonight."

"They did not see Miguel at the ballet. And if they had known he was dining here at Maria Bonita, they would have made reservations elsewhere."

"Your mother and brother hate Miguel and because he is my good friend, they probably hate me, too. That is if they even know who I am."

"Yes, you are right." Oh, my darling Juan, you have no idea how much my brother hates Miguel or to what lengths he is willing to go to prevent him from being elected president of Mocorito.

"You should go back to your table," Juan told her.

"We must find a way to be together again. Soon. I will make an appointment—"

"No." He shook his head. "I cannot allow things to continue. It is unfair to both of us."

In her peripheral vision, Seina caught a glimpse of her mother coming down the corridor. Oh, merciful God, her mother must not catch her with Juan. "Go to the men's room now. My mother is directly behind us."

Juan did as she had told him to do only seconds before her mother approached her. "Is everything all right? You have been gone such a long time, I was beginning to worry."

"Everything is fine, Mother." Seina managed a weak smile. "I am sorry if I worried you. I was on my way back to the table."

"We are no longer on the patio," Carlotta said. "Once I saw *that man* sitting across from us with his friends, I lost my appetite. To think that they allow his kind in a respectable place like this." She made a sound of utter disgust.

"Are we going home?" Seina asked.

"No, certainly not. Diego asked the maître d' to move us to a table inside, and, knowing who we are, he requested that another party exchange tables with us."

So like her mother and brother not to consider the inconvenience of their request for the waiters or for the other guests. "Then we are staying?"

"Of course we are staying. You do not think for one minute that I would allow the likes of Miguel Ramirez to force me to leave one of my favorite restaurants, do you?"

"No, Mother."

Taking Seina's arm and leading her down the corridor, Carlotta asked, "You were not speaking to that man, were you?"

"What man?"

"That Dr. Esteban. I saw him, you know. I thought there for a moment that he had paused to speak to you. He and his aunt have aligned themselves with the Nationalists, despite the fact that at one time Josephina Santiago was considered a lady of some standing in Nava."

"I have heard that Dr. Esteban is a brilliant physician and a good man."

Carlotta stopped and stared speculatively at Seina. "You heard this at the hospital, no doubt, when you have visited your doctor there."

"Yes."

"If he ever tries to make your acquaintance, you are to make sure he understands that you know of his association with Miguel Ramirez and that your family highly disapproves of that despicable man."

"Yes, Mother."

As Carlotta led Seina through the restaurant toward their table, they came face to face with Juan, his aunt, Miguel and his American fiancée. Apparently, they were leaving Maria Bonita.

Carlotta froze to the spot.

"Good evening, *señora* and *señorita*." Miguel looked Carlotta square in the eyes.

She lifted her head, huffed indignantly and marched away.

"Good evening, Señor Ramirez," Seina said. "Please excuse my mother's rudeness, but…"

"We understand," Juan said, then ushered his party hurriedly through the restaurant.

What a perfectly horrible moment, J.J. thought, as they made their escape. Perhaps it was understandable that Cesar Fernandez's widow had hated Luz Ramirez and her illegitimate son, but it was hardly fair to blame Miguel for the sins of his parents.

The night air seemed cooler than when they had arrived, so when Miguel lifted her shawl up and around her shoulders, she smiled and thanked him.

"I don't understand why Carlos isn't bringing the car," Miguel said. "Surely he must see us from where he is parked."

"Perhaps he has fallen asleep," Aunt Josephina suggested.

"Why don't we just walk across the street instead of waiting for him," J.J. said.

"I believe we shall have to," Miguel told her. "Apparently he is not aware that we are ready to leave."

When they approached the limousine, an ominous feeling hit J.J. immediately. "Wait!"

The other three paused on the sidewalk and stared at her.

"What is wrong?" Miguel asked.

"I'm not sure. Why don't y'all wait here and let me check things out?"

Miguel glowered at her. "Certainly not! If you believe something is not quite right, then I shall go—"

"We'll go together!" Dammit, she kept forgetting that she

wasn't supposed to identify herself as Miguel's bodyguard. Her taking charge would be seen as highly inappropriate.

"Very well."

"What is it?" Aunt Josephina asked. "What is wrong?"

"You two stay here," Miguel said to Juan and his aunt.

"Oh my. Shouldn't Jennifer stay here with me and Juan go with—"

Leaving Aunt Josephina still talking, Miguel and J.J. rushed over to the limo and inspected it from hood to trunk. She saw nothing unusual, nothing out of place. Not at first. The only illumination on this dark night came from two streetlights on either end of the block. On closer inspection, J.J. noticed what she thought might be drops of blood on the pavement outside the driver's door.

"Unless you want them to see me draw my gun, then get behind me," J.J. said as she opened her purse and removed the Beretta.

Placing his body directly behind J.J.'s, Miguel blocked her from the others. Holding the handgun in one hand, she reached out with the other and opened the limousine door. Her pulse raced. The moment the door came open, Carlos fell out, head first, his barely recognizable face covered with blood.

Chapter 11

J.J. and Miguel spent over three hours at the police station, explaining several times the details of their evening before, during and after their discovery of Carlos's body. Juan and his aunt gave their statements, then were allowed to leave. The old woman had been nearly hysterical at the scene, but had calmed to a dazed stupor by the time she signed her statement and kissed J.J. on both cheeks before allowing her nephew to escort her outside to their waiting taxi.

When the police had questioned J.J. about the Beretta 950 Jet-fire automatic she had in her purse, Miguel answered for her.

"The gun is mine," he'd said. "It is registered to me. As you well know, my life has been threatened, so we go nowhere without a weapon. The small pistol was easily concealed in my fiancée's purse."

Since Carlos had not been shot, there was really no reason for the police to question them any further about a registered weapon. So, by the time Roberto arrived to chauffeur them home,

Lieutenant Garcia had already thanked them for their cooperation and had given Miguel his condolences before asking if Miguel preferred to inform Carlos's family of his death himself.

"Yes, I will go tonight and tell his family. He has two children who live with his parents here in Nava."

"Very well, Señor Ramirez. Please tell them that we will notify them after the autopsy as to when they may claim the body."

"Please, notify me also." Miguel closed his eyes. J.J. understood the pain was almost more than he could bear. "I will handle the funeral arrangements for the family."

"Yes, of course, Señor Ramirez."

A light rain fell softly against the sidewalk and street when they left the police station. Roberto snapped open a large umbrella and held it over them as they walked to his car. Miguel opened the front passenger door of the Mercedes and helped J.J. inside, then slid in beside her. Roberto got behind the wheel and once everyone had their seatbelts fastened, he started the engine and backed out of the parking space.

For what seemed like hours, but was probably less than five minutes, they sat there in the front seat in silence.

Roberto focused on the road ahead of them and when the rain grew heavier, he turned on the windshield wipers. Miguel kept his arm draped around J.J.'s shoulders and she gladly rested her head against him, thankful for the warm strength of his large body. She could only imagine how Miguel felt, knowing that he blamed himself for Carlos's brutal murder. Miguel's chauffeur had not been shot or stabbed, not given a quick death. No, the poor man had been beaten unmercifully—probably with tire irons, the police had surmised. His skull had been crushed, his nose and cheekbones broken, as well as both arms and both legs.

"You will have to give me directions," Roberto said, breaking the mournful silence. "I do not know where—"

"Carlos came from my old neighborhood," Miguel said. "The Aguilar barrio. Take the turnoff on Carillo Avenue, go four blocks and take a right onto Santa Fe. Carlos's parents live in a second-floor apartment at 107 Santa Fe."

"When we get there, if you would rather, I can go in and speak to Carlos's father," Roberto said.

"No, I will speak to Carlos's parents. He was my chauffeur and faithful friend for many years and he was killed because of me. His parents have a right to know this."

J.J. gasped. "You can't say that to his parents. No, Miguel. You mustn't."

"No, not tonight. Tonight, I will tell them only that he is dead, that he was murdered. That alone will be more than they can deal with right now."

She clutched his hand in hers and held it fiercely. "I'll go with you to speak to his parents."

"That will not be necessary."

"I'll go with you."

He didn't reply, just squeezed her hand and tightened his hold around her shoulders.

During the past forty-eight hours, her latest Dundee assignment had transformed from what she had thought would be nothing more than bodyguard duty—protecting a South American political candidate—to an imminent love affair with both a man and his country. Miguel's devotion to and love for his family, friends and employees was contagious. Sitting there snuggled against him, her hand in his, she felt what he felt, experienced every emotion as if it were happening inside her. The strong bond between her and Miguel could not be explained, not in terms that anyone could understand. She didn't even understand it herself.

Two hours later, at three in the morning, Roberto dropped them off at Miguel's home. He offered to come in and stay, but Miguel had dismissed him, telling him to get some rest because the days ahead would be difficult for all of them.

When they reached the front door, it sprang wide open and

there in the foyer stood Ramona and Dom. Ramona's eyes were red and swollen and even now they glistened with fresh tears. Dom looked J.J. over and then glanced at Miguel.

"We need to talk," Dom said in English.

"Can it wait until morning?" J.J. asked. "Miguel is exhausted. We have just come from Carlos's parents' home."

"Señor Ramirez, our poor Carlos," Ramona said in Spanish.

Miguel opened his arms and hugged Ramona as she wept on his shoulder.

Dom pulled J.J. aside. "I met up with Vic and Will Pierce tonight over in Colima. Vic has unearthed some pretty nasty info and the sooner Miguel knows, the better."

"Unless there is something he can do about it right now, I don't want you burdening him with anything else. He's fast reaching the breaking point. You know he blames himself for Carlos's murder."

"I feel for the guy." When J.J. gave him a cynical look, he said, "I mean it. He's being put in a challenging situation to which there are no easy solutions. And what I have to tell him will only complicate matters more."

"What is it? Tell me and if I think he needs to know, I'll tell him."

Dom shook his head. "Sorry, but I'm telling Ramirez tonight."

"No."

"Yes, J.J., I am. He needs to know."

"What do I need to know?" Miguel asked.

J.J. jerked around at the sound of his voice and glanced behind him, searching for the housekeeper. "Where is Ramona?"

"I sent her to bed." He grabbed J.J.'s arm. "Why are you two arguing?" Keeping a tight hold on her arm, Miguel glared at Dom. "Tell me now what it is that you think I need to know."

"It can wait until later," J.J. said. "After you've had some rest."

"We have another Dundee agent here in Mocorito," Dom said and even though J.J. shot him with a condemning glare, he continued. "He's a former CIA operative, with connections here in your country. He has found out something you need to know before you make any future decisions about whether or not to withdraw from the current presidential race."

"After what happened to Carlos tonight, I have no choice but to reconsider my candidacy," Miguel said.

"The decisions you make in the next few days will also decide the future of Mocorito." Dom huffed loudly. "I hate to lay this on you after what just happened to Carlos, but I don't want you making any decisions without having all the facts."

"Just say whatever it is you have to say." Miguel kept his gaze focused on Dom as he eased his hand down J.J.'s arm and clasped her hand in his.

She knew as surely as she knew her own name that Miguel was holding on to her not only for her support, but to draw strength from her. Helpmates. Soul mates.

"Upon his reelection, Hector Padilla and his goon squad plan to take over the military and every law-enforcement agency in Mocorito," Dom said. "The Federalists plan to turn your country back into a dictatorship, even if it means civil war."

J.J. caught her shocked gasp seconds before it escaped her mouth. *Please, dear God, no!* First she sensed Miguel's horror and then she saw it on his face.

"And your half-brother, Diego Fernandez, is helping Padilla," Dom added. "But he has no idea what they are planning. They're using his hatred for you to gain his support, especially his financial support."

"You were right," Miguel said. "I needed to know this and I needed to know it now. Padilla has declared war on me and is willing to kill those who are close to me.

"And now I learn that if I withdraw from the presidential race in order to ensure that others won't die because of me, the Federalists will try to return Mocorito to a dictatorship and possibly throw the country into civil war, where thousands may die."

"You're in what we Americans call a no-win situation." Dom bit down on his bottom lip as he hazarded a glance at J.J.

"Later today, I will have a meeting with Emilio and Roberto and the leaders of the Nationalist Party." Miguel closed his eyes and groaned. "This is not a decision I can make alone."

"I realize I can't tell you what to do, but I'm going to give you some advice," Dom said. When Miguel simply stared at him, he continued. "It's almost a certainty that you have a traitor in your camp, someone who knows every move you make and is in on every decision. I don't think you can afford to trust anyone. Not Dr. Esteban. Not Roberto Aznar." Dom hesitated. "Not even Emilio Lopez."

Miguel glowered at Dom, his golden-brown eyes filled with anger. "You are telling me that I should not trust my closest friends, men who are like brothers to me? You want me to make a life-and-death decision for my country…for my people, without the advice and input of the three men I trust most in this world?"

"One of those men does not deserve your trust," Dom told him.

J.J. tugged on Miguel's arm. "You need rest. We can discuss this more later, after you've had a few hours of sleep."

Miguel nodded. And without saying a word he allowed her to lead him up the stairs and straight to his bedroom suite. After kicking off her heels and tossing her shawl into the nearest chair, she helped him out of his tuxedo jacket and then loosened and removed his tie. When she started to unbutton his shirt, he grabbed her hands and brought them to his lips. After kissing her knuckles, he whispered against her folded hands. "What am I going to do?"

"You are going to rest," she told him as she pulled her hands free and undid the top three buttons on his pleated-front shirt, then she removed his gold cuff links and laid them on the coffee table.

"How can I rest, knowing what I know?"

She turned him around as easily as if he'd been a child and herded him into his bedroom, not bothering to turn out the lights in the sitting room or turn them on in the bedroom. She led him over to his bed, shoved him down on the edge, then knelt at his feet and removed his shoes and socks. Reaching behind him, she yanked the coverlet, blanket and sheet down enough to reveal the big feather pillows.

"Lie down. Right now."

When she walked away, he called after her, "Where are you going?"

"I'll be right back. I just want to get out of this dress."

He scooted up in the bed and laid his head on one of the pillows, then closed his eyes. "After you do that, would you…would you lie down with me?"

"Yes." She had given the answer no thought. There was no need. Miguel was not asking her for sex, not propositioning her. She understood what he wanted, what he needed.

Once in the bathroom, she undressed hurriedly, removing everything, down to her silk panties, then she grabbed her robe from the wall hook where she'd left it, put it on and rushed back into the bedroom. Miguel lay there in the dark, not even a glimmer of moonlight to illuminate his face, only the faint glow from the lights still burning in the sitting room. At first she thought— hoped—he had fallen asleep. But when she neared the bed, he opened his eyes. Eyes like those of a jungle cat.

"I usually sleep well on nights when it rains," he said. "I enjoy the sound of raindrops hitting the roof, pouring down onto the earth."

J.J. went around to the other side of the bed and lay down alongside Miguel, a good three feet separating their bodies.

He turned and held out his hand across the smooth cotton sheet. Without a moment's hesitation, she closed the space between them and when she did, he pulled her into his arms and held her as if she was his lifeline, as if without her, he would perish.

His lips pressed against her forehead. Tender, sweet kisses. She wrapped one arm around him and cuddled as close as humanly possible.

"I have been placed in an unbearable position." His warm breathed fanned the curls she had pushed behind her ear. "No matter what I do, my decision will cost the lives of innocent people."

She kissed his cheek. "Hush, *querido,* hush. This problem cannot be solved right now."

"I fear it cannot be solved at all."

She lay there in his arms for quite some time, neither of them speaking, only listening to the rain and to each other's slow, steady breathing.

Suddenly Miguel sat straight up in bed, his body taut, his hands balled into fists. She sat up beside him.

"Miguel?"

"I am such a fool. I truly believed that I could offer Mocorito a future of prosperity, with equal rights for all citizens. I have been so full of myself, so certain that I and I alone was destined to lead my people into the twenty-first century."

His body trembled. Just a slight tremor, but visible even in the semidark. Oh, God, the pain inside him is ripping him apart.

J.J. wrapped her arms around him. "Don't do this to yourself. Please. Miguel. *Querido.*"

He fell into her arms and rested his head against her breasts. It was then that she felt the dampness of his tears as they moistened her chest where her robe had fallen open.

As she held him, she caressed his head and rubbed his back. Stroking him. Comforting him.

Loving him.

Seina was awakened by the ringing telephone. When she flipped on her bedside lamp and glanced at the clock, she saw that it was nearly five-thirty. Who would be calling this early in the morning? She rose from her bed and put on her robe, then slipped out of her room and down the hall. When she neared Diego's bedroom, she heard him talking. Without knocking, she opened the door and walked in on him.

He sat on the edge of his bed, his hair mussed, his eyes bleary.

"Why was I not notified before now? What? I don't care what she told you, she is like a member of my family, my sister's best friend."

"What is it?" Seina rushed to Diego. "Has something happened to Gala?"

He held up a his hand, issuing a halt gesture. Seina stopped cold.

"Señorita Hernandez's mother is dead and her father is remarried and lives in Buenaventura. I will notify him that she has been in an accident. And my sister and I will be at the hospital this morning."

"What happened?" Seina pleaded for more information.

"Spare no expense on her behalf," Diego said. "Our family will, naturally, pay for everything." He replaced the receiver and turned to Seina, holding his hand out to her.

She grabbed his hand and sat down on the bed beside him. "Tell me."

"Seina was in an automobile accident the night before last and was taken to St. Augustine's. She had no identification on her, no driver's license, no car registration. That foolish, foolish woman. When she recovered consciousness, she refused to talk to anyone, but one of the nurses managed to pry your name from her."

"I'm going to dress now and go straight to the hospital." Seina jumped up.

"Wait and I will go with you."

She glared at her brother. "Why? You do not care for Gala. If you did, you would not treat her as you do."

"What are you talking about? Of course I care for Gala."

"Liar."

Diego stared at her, a look of utter shock on his face.

"I know," Seina said.

"You know what?"

"I know that you forced her to take poison to Anton Casimiro's party so that someone could use it to make Miguel Ramirez's friends and political supporters sick. I know that you are helping President Padilla to undermine Miguel's bid for the presidency by using whatever unscrupulous means you believe necessary."

"How do you know—"

"I overheard you talking to Gala. I know she left our home drunk and frightened. Because of you."

Diego grabbed Seina by the shoulders. "You have to believe me when I say that I did not wish any harm to come to her."

"That is the problem—I do not believe you." She jerked loose from his tenacious hold. "Who are you? I do not know you. You are not the brother I have known and loved all my life. You have allowed your hatred for our brother—yes, our brother, our father's other son—to turn you into a monster. The old Diego helped Gala when she was in trouble. He kept her out of prison and paid for her stay in a rehabilitation center. He might have been a bit cocky and self-absorbed, but he had a good heart."

"Seina, I…I…"

She glared at him.

"I do not know what to say."

"Tell me it is not too late to save your soul."

He hung his head. In shame? She prayed with all her heart that her brother was still capable of feeling shame.

"I am going to take a shower, then dress and drive to St. Augustine's," she told him. "And I am quite certain that Seina will not want to see you. I am not even sure she will want to see me."

J.J. awoke slowly, languidly, her body warm, her limbs relaxed. She felt something touch her neck. Gentle strokes of a fingertip. Her eyelids fluttered.

"Mmm…mmm…" she opened her eyes and looked at Miguel

who lay beside her, staring at her as he ran his index finger down her throat, stopping just short of delving between her breasts.

She smiled at him. "What time is it?"

"Almost six."

She nodded. "How long have you been awake?"

"About fifteen minutes. I have been lying here looking at you."

Her smiled widened. "Have you?"

"I went to sleep in your arms, didn't I?"

"Yes."

He knew that she knew he had cried in her arms before he had fallen asleep. There was no need to mention it, to discuss it. It was a fact only the two of them shared. Now and forever.

"Thank you, Jennifer."

She reached out and cradled his cheek with the palm of her hand. "I want to do everything that I can to help you. These next few days will not be easy for you. You can depend on me to—"

He pulled away from her, sat up and then turned his back on her as he settled on the edge of the bed and slumped his shoulders.

"Miguel?"

"I want you to go back to America."

"What?"

"I want you to take the first flight out of Nava today."

She tossed back the covers and crawled over behind him, then wrapped her arms around him and laid her head on his back. "Don't talk foolishness," she said in English. "I won't leave you. Not now when you need me more than ever. I thought…I mean…after last night."

He shot up off the bed. She caught herself before falling flat on her face.

With his back to her, he said, "Instead of sleeping, I should have made love to you. You were so willing to do anything to make me feel better. Poor Miguel. He is falling apart. Let me comfort him. Let me show him how strong I am."

She got out of bed, but didn't go to him, just stared at his back. "I know what you're trying to do and it's not going to work."

"I am trying to tell you that I don't want you here, that I don't need you, that I want you to go away. You are only a woman and women have no purpose except—"

"Nice try, but it didn't work." She walked across the room and paused behind him. "There's no point in your trying to think of more ways to insult me or hurt my feelings. I'm not buying your mean macho act. You're afraid that if I stay here, I'll be in more danger than you are. You're concerned that the people who killed Carlos might come after me."

She placed her hand in the center of his back. His muscles tensed.

"Miguel, I'm not leaving you."

He turned and looked deeply into her eyes. "If only you were carrying my child as Dolores is carrying Emilio's child, you would go away, as she did, to protect the baby."

Tears sprang into J.J.'s eyes. "Dammit, you've made me cry."

He grabbed her and held her so tightly she could barely breathe and when she lifted her face to him, he lowered his head and kissed her. After he had thoroughly ravaged her mouth and they were both breathless, he ended the kiss and pressed his forehead against hers.

"What am I going to do with you?"

"You're going to let me stay here in Nava with you and help you through the days and nights ahead."

"Yes, *querida,* God forgive me, but that is exactly what I am going to do."

Chapter 12

J.J. clung to Miguel, knowing there was nowhere else on earth she would rather be than right here, with him, in his arms. But the logical part of her brain kept trying to get through to her, warning her that she was setting herself up for a fall. She and Miguel were caught up in a fantasy. A dangerous fantasy that could cost them dearly on a personal level when reality finally slapped them in the face with the hard, cold facts. No matter how sexually attracted they were to each other, no matter how strongly they felt the soul-deep connection that made no sense to either of them, the truth of the matter was that they had known each other for less than seventy-two hours. A bodyguard assignment that should have remained impersonal had altered drastically, metamorphosing into a grand passion.

But this isn't real, that nagging inner voice told her. You are not Miguel Ramirez's fiancée. You two are not in love with each other. And you have no future together.

As if he felt her uncertainty, Miguel eased his tenacious hold on her and lifted his head from where his cheek had been pressed against hers. For a split second she thought about holding on to him, clinging to him with every ounce of her strength, but instead she met his questioning gaze head-on.

"I very much want to make love to you," he said, his voice husky with emotion.

"I know. It's what I want, too…"

"But?"

"But if we make love, I'm very much afraid that I'll fall madly in love with you. And I cannot allow that to happen."

"Jennifer…" He closed his eyes for a moment.

"Please, help me to be strong. I cannot fight you and myself at the same time."

He ran his hands down her arms, then released her. She shivered uncontrollably for half a second, then took a deep breath and stepped backward, putting a couple of inches between their heated bodies.

He studied her intently, silently, as if he were trying to read her mind. Or look into her heart. "At another time, in another place…"

She offered him a fragile smile. "Yes, I know."

"I want you to be safe," he told her. "You should leave Mocorito as soon as possible. As my fiancée—even my fake fiancée—you could become a target. I could not bear it if anything happened to you."

"And if I leave and you are killed because I wasn't here to protect you, how do you think I will feel? I'm a highly trained professional who was assigned the job of protecting you. I understand your reasons for wanting me to leave, but—"

"No arguments." Shaking his head, he groaned. "Domingo Shea can take over as my personal bodyguard. I believe the time for pretense is over. I can no longer allow my ego to dictate my actions."

"I agree that you shouldn't hide the fact that you have skilled professionals protecting you. If you announce that I am not your fiancée, but your bodyguard—"

"I don't think that it would matter, not at this point," he told her. "It is obvious to everyone that we have feelings for each other. You will not be safe here in Mocorito. There is every chance that they will target you, just as they might target Emilio or Juan or the others closest to me.

"I will make no announcements about you or Dom. You will leave Mocorito for your own safety and for my peace of mind. And when Dom takes over and it becomes apparent that he is guarding me, I will say that yes, my cousin is now my personal bodyguard, that it is what he does for a living back home in Miami."

"You're going to downplay the fact. And you're going to keep up the pretense, at least in part."

"Yes. There will be time enough to admit the entire truth, later, after… After you are safely back in the United States and after the election is over."

"I don't want to leave you." She gazed at him pleadingly. "But you are the boss. If you choose to send me away…"

He caressed her cheek tenderly. "If circumstances were different…"

She sighed heavily. "I won't leave today, but I will go, if that's what you want. We can discuss the details later. Your first concern today is to make a decision about your candidacy. And you must make that decision without sharing the damning information about Hector Padilla with your closest advisors."

"Do you believe, as Dom does, that one of them is a traitor?"

"Yes, I do. We know you have a traitor among your closest friends, someone who is privy to all your secrets, all your decisions. Who else could it be if it is not Roberto or Emilio or perhaps Juan?"

"You spent the evening with Juan and Aunt Josephina. Do you honestly think Juan is capable of betrayal? He is a kind, gentle man who has dedicated his life to helping others."

"I know. I like Juan very much. And I adore his aunt. My gut instincts tell me that Juan is just what he appears to be and he would die before he would betray you."

"And yet you still think I should not share the information about Padilla's diabolical plot with Juan?"

"Oh, Miguel...I think the wisest course of action is to tell no one."

Seina Fernandez had packed a suitcase and taken it with her when she left home. Her plan was first to visit Gala in the hospital and promise her that Diego would never threaten her again; then she would go to Juan and tell him that she was cutting all ties to her family, that she wanted to be with him, to marry him and spend the rest of her life as his wife. In all honesty, she was scared to death and uncertain. When Diego and their mother discovered what she had done, they would be furious. And they would do all within their power to bring her back into the family fold. But she could not return to that house. Not ever again. Her mother would force her to marry a man she did not love, caring nothing for her happiness. And Diego had become a criminal, a man so filled with hatred that he could not see that the vile emotion was destroying him.

Seina hesitated before knocking on Gala's hospital-room door. She would not blame her friend if she did not want to see her. After all, she had overheard Gala's conversation with Diego two nights ago and she had done nothing to intervene at the time. In a way, she was as much to blame for Gala's automobile accident as Diego was. If only she had not cowered in the dark, afraid to make her presence known.

"Yes?" Gala said.

Seina opened the door and peeked in, gasping when she saw Gala's badly bruised face and her arm, apparently broken, in a sling. "May I come in?"

"Seina? Oh, God, Seina, I could have killed myself and the

driver of the other car. I am such a worthless piece of trash. How can you want to be my friend?"

Seina walked into the room, closed the door behind her and marched straight to Gala's side. Seeing the tears streaming down Gala's cheeks, Seina retrieved a tissue from the box on the bedside table, then reached down and wiped away her friend's tears.

"Everything will be all right." Seina grasped Gala's hand. "I know what has been going on with you and Diego. I overheard the two of you talking the other night. I—I confronted him this morning and I warned him that I will not tolerate him using you in such a shameful fashion."

Gala's eyes widened in shock. "You know? You heard? Oh, God! Oh, God…I am so sorry…"

Seina wrapped her arms carefully around her friend and stroked her head gently. "I am the one who is sorry. I am sorry that I have been so weak and foolishly naive. If I had acted sooner, I could have spared you this pain."

With her good arm clinging to Seina, Gala asked, "What has given you the courage to defy Diego? I have never seen you like this—so determined, so independent."

"It is time I grew up, is it not? I can no longer blame my mother and my brother for not allowing me to be the person I want to be or to live the life I want. From now on, no one makes my decisions for me."

"Diego will never allow you—"

"Diego cannot hurt you again. Nor will he interfere in my plans."

"You—you're going to blackmail him with what you heard us talking about the other night, aren't you?"

"I hope that will not be necessary," Seina said. "I pray that my brother will see the error of his ways before it is too late for him."

When J.J. and Miguel went downstairs, Roberto and Emilio were waiting for them in Miguel's study. The moment they saw J.J., they asked to speak to him privately.

"I have no secrets from Jennifer," Miguel said.

Roberto and Emilio exchanged anxious looks.

"Have you forgotten that she is an employee, an American bodyguard forced on you by her government?" Emilio asked, his gaze raking contemptuously over J.J.

"Never speak about Jennifer in such a way ever again," Miguel warned his friend.

"See, I told you that he had become besotted with her!" Roberto spat out the sentence, then threw his arms up in disgust.

"Carlos was murdered. Everyone in my employ, every friend, every supporter could well be in mortal danger." Miguel glared back and forth from one man to the other. "And your greatest concern this morning is my personal relationship with Jennifer?"

"I beg your forgiveness," Roberto said. "But Emilio and I…we believe that this woman has too much influence over you, that you are listening to her instead of to us. We are your closest friends, your staunchest supporters, but it seems that you trust a woman you barely know more than you do us."

"Has she bewitched you with her talented lovemaking?" Emilio asked. "Has she castrated the great Miguel Cesar Ramirez?"

Miguel's face flushed and his eyes glistened with barely suppressed anger as he clenched his jaw and knotted his hands into fists. She could almost hear him mentally counting to ten. Didn't Emilio realize that he had waved a red flag in front of a raging bull?

"How dare you!"

Both Roberto and Emilio took several steps backward, closer to the door.

J.J. knew that now was not the time for her to say or do anything.

"Leave me!" Miguel roared in a voice that brooked no opposition.

Like frightened mice scurrying from a menacing cat, both men practically ran from the room. Miguel clenched and unclenched his fisted hands as he walked to the windows overlooking the front of the house. J.J. remained silent and unmoving. He stood by the windows for several minutes, then turned around and focused on her.

"If you wish, I will make them apologize to you."

"Oh, Miguel, don't worry about what they said. It doesn't matter."

"It matters to me. You are—" He halted for a moment, as if considering his words carefully. "You are important to me. While you are living in my house, you are under my protection."

The corners of her mouth lifted as she shook her head. "Remember I am supposed to be your protector."

"You are, *querida,* you are."

Juan had seriously considered having Carmen tell Seina that he could not see her today, that she should leave his office and never return. But he did not have the strength to turn her away. Despite what he kept telling her—that they should stop seeing each other—he lived for the stolen moments they shared. Just a glimpse of her, a word or two spoken between them, would sustain him for days.

How could he have allowed himself to fall in love with a patient? And not just any patient, but with a woman who was betrothed to another man, a woman who was a member of the wealthy and powerful Fernandez family?

The moment he opened the door to his private office, Seina jumped up from her chair and rushed into his arms, giving him no time to prepare himself. He wrapped his arms around her and held her trembling body.

"Juan, my dearest, darling Juan."

"What has happened?" he asked. "What is wrong? You are shivering."

"I have left home," she told him. "I packed a bag and left. No matter what you say, I will not go back."

"I don't understand. How could you—"

She placed her hand over his mouth. "If you do not want me,

if you cannot take me in, then I will make other arrangements. If necessary, I will stay with Gala when she gets out of the hospital."

Juan grabbed Seina by the shoulders and shook her gently. "Stop jabbering nonsense and tell me what is going on."

She jerked away from him, stomped her foot and shook her fists at him. "Humph! Have you not been listening to me? I have left my mother's house and I have no intention of ever returning."

"You are giving up everything to be with me?" He stared at her, an incredulous feeling overwhelming him. "I cannot allow you to do that."

"You do not understand, Juan." She planted her hands on her hips. "It is not your decision to make. It is mine. I refuse to live in the house of a woman who would force me to marry a man I do not love and with a brother who has become a stranger to me."

"Seina…*querida*…what has come over you? You do not sound like yourself."

"Good. I do not wish to sound like a frightened little girl any longer. I want to sound like a woman who knows her mind and has come to claim her man."

"Claim her…do you mean me?"

She marched over to him, grabbed his face between her palms and kissed him passionately. When he lost his breath completely, she released him and smiled. "I want you to make love to me, Juan Esteban. And I want you to marry me. I leave it up to you which you want to do first."

He stared at her, his eyes bulging, his mouth agape.

"But while you are thinking it over and deciding, I want you to take me to see Miguel. Right this minute. I have much to tell him. I must warn him about Diego."

Emilio approached Miguel while he was alone in the courtyard. Miguel had needed time alone to think, without any distractions. He knew what must be done, the only real choice he had, had ever had. If he could survive the upcoming days and weeks until he was elected president, he would then face his guilt and anguish. Others might die, as Carlos had died, their lives, as his, sacrificed for the greater good. And a part of Miguel would never completely forgive himself, but it was a burden that he must bear to save his country.

"Miguel, may I speak to you?" Emilio asked.

Keeping his back turned to his oldest and dearest friend, Miguel replied, "If you have news of Dolores, then I wish to hear it. Otherwise…"

"I am deeply sorry," Emilio said. "Forgive me for the things I said to you, the disrespectful way I spoke about Señorita Blair. I spoke without thinking."

"I accept your apology only if you will go to Jennifer and apologize to her, also."

"I have already spoken with her and begged her forgiveness."

Miguel turned and faced his friend. "I want no derision in my camp, no squabbles among my people. I need you, Emilio, to support me, to be loyal to me, to—"

"Miguel, you must know that I would die for you, for the cause we both have fought for all our lives. I want to rid Mocorito of men like Hector Padilla once and for all."

There should be no doubts in Miguel's mind, no uncertainty over the issue of trust. He would stake his life on this man's loyalty. But could he stake the future of the nation on his belief in Emilio?

"Has Roberto left?" Miguel asked.

"Yes, he stormed out of here very angry. But he will be back. You know what a temper he has. Once he has cooled off, he will return and apologize."

"Yes, of course he will. We are all hot-headed Latins, are we not?" Miguel reached over and draped his arm around Miguel's shoulders. "We huff and shout and snort and puff out our manly chests in a show of strength. But Emilio, in the end, there can be only one leader, one man who must make the hard decisions and live with the choices he makes."

Emilio nodded. "Yes, you are right. And we all know that you, Miguel, are that man. That leader."

Ramona rushed out onto the patio, wiping her hands off on her white apron as she approached. "Señor Ramirez, you have guests."

"Guests?" Miguel asked.

"Yes. Dr. Esteban is here and he has brought a lady with him."

"What lady?" Emilio questioned.

"A very pretty young lady. He introduced her to Señorita Blair and they are sitting in the front parlor now, talking and waiting for you."

"Damn it, woman, who did Juan bring with him?" Emilio glowered at Ramona.

"Señorita Seina Fernandez."

Diego had two-dozen roses delivered to Gala Hernandez's hospital room and signed the card simply, Carlotta, Seina and Diego. His sister had been right about him caring little what happened to Gala. In truth, he did not care. But he also did not wish her harm, did not want her to die. Yes, he had seen her as only a tool, to use for whatever purposes that suited him. But it was not as if she was a respectable young lady, as if she was truly worthy of the friendship Seina bestowed upon her.

As he drove along the boulevard leading to the presidential palace in the heart of Nava, he struggled with his conscience. A conscience that he had conveniently misplaced for quite some time.

Was Seina right about him? Had he become a monster?

No! He had not. He was only a man willing to bend the rules, to manipulate others, to use some unscrupulous methods to achieve the results he desired. Was he really so different from most men? His wealth and power gave him the means by which to exert influence over the politics in his country. His backing and the backing of other wealthy men such as he could practically ensure a candidate's success. But in recent years, since Miguel Ramirez had become the people's champion, the once weak Nationalist Party had tripled in size and now threatened the Federalist Party in a way his father's generation could never have imagined.

What would dear papá think about his bastard son running for president? He would not have been able to back him publicly, but would he, in secret, have cheered Miguel on, even taken pride in his victory, if he won the election?

But he will not win this election. Surely Ramirez must see that it is in the best interests of his people to withdraw his candidacy. Now that Ramirez's chauffeur had been killed.

Diego shuddered at the thought of how the man had died. The newspaper had reported that he'd been beaten to death.

Have you sunk so low that you now condone murder? he asked himself.

Scare tactics were one thing, but murdering people was not something with which he wanted to be involved. When two people had been killed during the assassination attempt on Ramirez—an assassination attempt not designed to kill, only to frighten—Hector Padilla had sworn to Diego that the deaths of the two other men had been accidental. Now he wondered if Hector had lied to him.

The guards at the palace knew Diego on sight and always opened the gates for him and spoke to him with respect. Today was no different, although Hector was not expecting him. He parked his car in the usual place, reserved for special visitors. As he did on most visits, he entered the palace through a side door to which he'd been given a key by President Padilla himself.

Once inside the palace, facing the narrow corridor that led, the long way around, to the president's office, Diego removed his sunglasses and slipped them into the inside pocket of his sports coat. He ran into several lowly staff members, who either spoke or nodded. No one thought there was anything unusual about him being here today since he was a frequent visitor.

When he neared the rear entrance to Hector's private office, which was kept locked and to which only Hector had a key, Diego paused as he saw the president open the door, search right and left, and then quickly usher three men into his office. What were General Blanco and Secretary of Defense, Arlo Gonzalez, doing going into Hector's office, along with the grandson of former dictator, Felipe Menendez?

Slinking into a corner behind a large pillar, Diego hid from their view. Felipe Menendez's wife and children had been exiled from Mocorito after the dictator's execution many years ago. But ten years later, after they swore their allegiance to the new democracy, Menendez's son and daughter had been allowed to return. Felipe III, the old reprobate's only grandson, a wealthy playboy with whom Diego had attended private school, was an arrogant hothead, known for his radical political views.

It was a well-known fact that Felipe Menendez III supported a small band of extremists who wanted the government returned to the old dictatorship.

Why would Hector give such a man a private audience? Why meet with him at all? But an even better question would be, why had Hector included Menendez in what appeared to be a secret meeting with the country's two most powerful Federalists?

Chapter 13

Miguel had assured Emilio that Juan and Seina had come here today on a personal matter, not anything that would concern him. Since Miguel actually had no idea why Juan had brought his half-sister to his home, he had lied to Emilio, who had excused himself saying he had business to attend to at campaign headquarters. But it had been obvious that his feelings were hurt because he had not been invited to stay. Miguel wondered if the rift his own distrust had created between them could ever be mended completely. What if, when the traitor's identity was discovered, it turned out not to be Emilio, as Miguel felt certain would happen? Could his oldest and dearest friend ever understand why he had shut him out? And would Dolores ever forgive him?

When Miguel entered the living room, Juan rose to his feet, a nervous look in his eyes. "Seina has left her mother's home. She will not be returning."

Miguel simply nodded, puzzled by Seina Fernandez's unexpected appearance in his home and not understanding exactly what either he or Juan had to do with the fact that she had run away from home. It was not as if she were a child. She was a woman of twenty-four.

"Seina and Juan are in love," J.J. explained. "Seina's mother intended to force her to marry another man."

Miguel's eyes grew wide with utter surprise as he looked quizzically at Juan. "You and Seina? When did this happen? You have never mentioned the fact that you even knew her and now you come to me and tell me that the two of you are in love and she has run away from home."

There had been a time when his friends had not kept secrets from him. Nor he from them.

"Six months ago I was ill." Seina's gaze pinpointed Miguel. "Juan took over several cases for my regular doctor when he had a personal emergency and that is how Juan and I met."

Miguel glowered at Juan. "She was your patient?"

"Don't be angry with Juan," Seina said. "He tried to tell me that many young women get crushes on their doctors, but I knew it was more than a crush. I knew I was in love with him, so I have been pursuing him…secretly…for months now."

"Mother of God!" Miguel muttered under his breath. There would be no good time to hear this news, but why now, when all hell had broken loose and he was facing a crisis of conscience?

"I have invited your sister to stay here with us," J.J. said.

"You what?" Miguel snapped around and glowered at her. "How could you—"

"I declined the offer," Seina said. "It was most gracious of your fiancée, Miguel, but I will be staying with Juan's aunt until we are married."

"Married?" Miguel rubbed his forehead. "Do you think for one minute that your brother will allow you to marry Juan?"

"I am of age. I have a legal right to marry whomever I please." Seina stared defiantly at Miguel. "And I am not worried about Diego interfering."

"You're not? May I ask why not?"

"Miguel, Seina has something to tell you about Diego," Juan said. "And you must listen and not lose your temper."

J.J. stood up beside Miguel and placed her hand on his arm, whether to caution him to remain calm or to assure him of her support, he wasn't sure. Perhaps both.

Juan sat down on the sofa beside Seina and put his arm around her shoulders. "Tell him."

Seina nodded. "I have only recently learned that Diego blackmailed my friend Gala Hernandez and forced her to do something she did not want to do."

"Gala Hernandez?" Miguel mulled over the name. An image of the woman's body flashed through his mind, then her face.

"She was the woman at the country club who flirted with you," J.J. told him. "And then she showed up again at Anton Casimiro's dinner party. I can't believe you could have forgotten the beautiful woman who flirted outrageously with you."

"Diego made her do it," Seina said. "He encouraged her to try to start an affair with Miguel so that he could use her to gain inside information about him."

"I remember Gala." Miguel smiled. "But she failed in her attempts to distract me from Jennifer, so Diego's plan failed."

"That's not all," Juan said.

"Diego made her carry a vial of some kind of poison to the party at Señor Casimiro's," Seina told them.

"So she is the one who poisoned the cocktail sauce?" Somehow this news did not surprise Miguel in the least. He had distrusted Señorita Hernandez almost from the moment they met. And the fact that his half-brother had provided her with the poison that had made more than a dozen people ill did not shock Miguel, either.

"Gala did not put the poison in the food herself. She simply smuggled in the poison. Someone else took it from her purse and mixed it with the food."

"Who?" Miguel demanded.

"I do not know. I swear." Seina wrung her hands together.

Miguel nodded as he digested this information. This meant that among Anton's guests that night there had been another Nationalist supporter. A spy? An undercover agent? A traitor? "I am not surprised that your brother would do anything to stop me from being elected president. He has made it no secret that he supports Hector Padilla with his money and influence. But unless you have some kind of proof that Diego was behind the poisoning, then the police can do nothing."

"The police!" Seina gasped. "No, please, give Diego a chance to…to…" she struggled for the right word. "If you had known Diego before…before he learned that we had an illegitimate half-brother and before he came under President Padilla's influence, you would know he was not a bad man, not a man capable of harming others."

"But now he is involved with murderers, with people willing to kill countless innocent people to—" Only when J.J. squeezed his arm, did Miguel realize he had been on the verge of sharing secret information. Hector Padilla's plot to return Mocorito to a dictatorship was not something Miguel could share with anyone else. That type of news could easily tip the scales and send the country into civil unrest, which was something he wanted to avoid at all costs. If he could be elected president, then he would put a stop to Padilla's plans.

"I cannot believe Diego had any part in the attempt on your life," Seina said.

"Two men died that day and only last night my chauffeur was brutally beaten to death," Miguel told her. "If Diego is taking orders from Hector Padilla, then he may well be an accessory to murder."

Seina hung her head and wept. Juan frowned at Miguel.

J.J. pulled Miguel aside, out into the foyer. "Do you really want to take your anger out on Seina? She did a very brave thing today. She defied her mother and her brother. She is, in essence, giving up the only life she has ever known for the man she loves. And she is reaching out to you, her brother. She wants your help. She needs you. Are you going to turn your back on her?"

"This is the worst possible time for something like this to have happened. I have the fate of my country in my hands and I must—"

She took his hands in hers, turned them palms up and said, "You must do what is right. Offer her your support."

Miguel closed his eyes and nodded. When he reopened them, J.J. was smiling at him.

"You knew when you asked her to stay, she would decline the offer, didn't you?" he asked. "You simply wanted to show my sister that she is welcome in my home. Such diplomacy, *querida*. And such kindness."

"We should handle this problem, now, then move on to the next one," J.J. said.

"Yes, yes. One problem at a time."

Together, hand-in-hand, they returned to the living room.

"Seina, you and Juan have my blessings and my complete support. Mine and Jennifer's," Miguel told his sister. "It would be my honor for you to stay here in my home and be under my protection, if things were different. But at this time, the lives of those closest to me are in danger from my enemies. I fear you would not be safe here."

Seina's eyes filled with fresh tears, but these were tears of joy. A warm smile spread across her damp face. "I will stay with Juan's aunt Josephina, but I am very grateful that you would—" her voice cracked with emotion.

"We should go now." Juan urged Seina to stand. "I will take you to my aunt's and then I must return to the hospital."

"Of course." Seina offered Miguel and J.J. a grateful smile.

"Juan, I would like a moment with you before you leave," Miguel said, then glanced at J.J. "Jennifer, perhaps you will show my sister the garden."

"Yes, of course." J.J. motioned to Seina. "If you'll come with me, we'll leave the gentlemen to discuss business."

As soon as the ladies were out of earshot, Miguel closed the pocket doors and turned to Juan. "I have decided to ask Mario Lamas to allot me fifteen minutes of airtime this evening in order for me to speak to the people of Mocorito on national television." Miguel reached out and clasped Juan's shoulder. "I want the people to know that I will not—that I cannot!—withdraw from the presidential race. No matter what."

"I had thought perhaps, after Carlos was murdered… But no, no, you are right, Miguel." Juan grabbed Miguel's hand and held it tightly. "If the Federalists are capable of poisoning people, of murder, of attempted assassination, then who is to say what else they are capable of doing. You are a brave man, my friend, to risk everything for this country of ours that you love so much. And you are very fortunate to have found a woman such as Jennifer, who is willing to stand by you and help you fight for what you believe in."

J.J. lifted the black lace shawl over her head as she entered St. Ignacio's Cathedral with Miguel that afternoon. They entered the church alone, after driving here in Miguel's antique Aston-Martin. Dom Shea had followed them in a rental car and he was now parked across the street, guarding the front entrance to the building. The centuries-old cathedral, with its stained-glass windows, statues of numerous saints, the Blessed Virgin and Jesus Christ and the fretwork rising from the walls to form arches across the three-story ceiling, resembled the interiors of numerous age-old churches across Mexico and South America. The utter silence within added to the atmosphere of deep spirituality that prevailed within these holy walls.

J.J. sat with Miguel as he prayed. She admired his deep faith in a higher power. It was to his credit that though he was a modern man, as he thought of himself, self-sufficient and powerful, he still believed in the miracle of prayer.

Facing a terrible dilemma, he had made a gut-wrenching decision. How did a man such as Miguel—an honorable man who loved his country and wanted the best for his people—live with the knowledge that he held the fate of millions in his hands?

As the moments passed, one quickly after the other, J.J. felt an overwhelming need to share in this moment with Miguel, to make some requests of her own.

Help him. Please help him. He is not asking anything for himself. Only for his people. Protect him and protect them from the evil threatening this nation. And let me do what is right, whatever will help Miguel the most.

After they'd spent nearly an hour in the cathedral, they walked outside, hand-in-hand, into the warm sunlight of an autumn afternoon in Nava. On the surface, this city, like the entire country, was an island paradise. But men's greed for power and wealth had once chained this country in bondage. Set free only in the latter half of the twentieth century, Mocorito now faced a return to slavery under an uncaring taskmaster.

Miguel Cesar Ramirez stood alone, his country's savior.

"This evening I will make an announcement on television to the people of my country," Miguel said as they walked toward his car.

J.J. knew without asking what he planned to tell the citizens of Mocorito.

"I want you there with me tonight."

"I'll be right at your side."

"And tomorrow morning, I want you to leave Mocorito."

"No, Miguel. I want—"

He opened the car door for her and when she whirled around to face him, he looked her right in the eyes and said, "If you truly wish to help me, you will go back to America."

She searched his face, studying his expression. Knowing what was in his heart, she realized she had only one real choice. "All right. I'll make arrangements to fly to Caracas in the morning and then on to the United States."

He helped her into the Aston-Martin, then rounded the hood and got in on the other side. "I will telephone Roberto and Emilio and ask them to meet us at campaign headquarters. I have already told Juan what I plan to do and I must tell the others."

"They will support your decision."

"Will they? Even not knowing the real threat that Hector Padilla poses to Mocorito?"

"Yes, even not knowing that if Padilla is reelected he plans to replace democracy with a dictatorship, they will support your decision not to back down, not to allow the Federalists to intimidate you."

Miguel started the car and eased out into the street. "We have only a few hours this afternoon and then tonight to be together." Increasing speed, Miguel zigzagged the little sports car through afternoon traffic, Dom just barely keeping up with them as he followed in the rental car.

J.J. didn't respond. She understood what he meant and knew, in that moment, that no matter what happened tomorrow, next week or next year, this afternoon and tonight she would be, in every sense of the word, Miguel Ramirez's woman.

As Diego drove through the gates, disregarding the guards who waved at him as he left the palace grounds, he could think of nothing except what he had overheard as he had hidden in the room behind Hector Padilla's office.

A plot to overthrow the democratic government and replace it with a dictatorship within weeks of Hector's reelection!

He had been played for a fool! Used as a tool to further a cause he did not believe in and would never willingly have supported. Hector had even mentioned him by name when he spoke to the other men, laughing about how easily Diego could be manipulated.

Diego Fernandez's hatred for his half-brother has blinded him to everything else, Hector had said. *His stupidity has worked greatly to my advantage.*

What was he going to do? He had broken the law, had taken part in criminal activities on behalf of the Federalist Party, had even blackmailed his sister's best friend. He could hardly go to the police, could he?

You can go to Ramirez, an inner voice told him. Go to him and tell him what Hector has planned.

The thought of joining forces with his father's bastard son sickened Diego. He hated Miguel Ramirez as much as he hated admitting he had been wrong. But it was that very hatred that had made him so easily manipulated by that son of a bitch Padilla.

He had to do something to stop Hector and his ungodly band of supporters. And he had to do something soon.

Think about what can be done. Consider all your options. There must be a way that you can do what must be done without destroying your own life.

In three hours they would go to the television station for Miguel to give his address to the nation. Everything had been done to prepare for those fifteen minutes when candidate Ramirez would tell the people of Mocorito that no power on earth could make him withdraw from the presidential race. J.J. had read his speech and wept, knowing what this decision had cost him on a purely personal level. If his life, his future alone was at stake, he would have walked away with many regrets. But understanding fully the enormous impact on the nation if he protected only those closest to him, he had done the only thing he could have done. He had chosen to save Mocorito.

Due to impending rain showers, possibly even a tropical storm brewing off the coast, the humidity had risen gradually during the day, and now dampness hung in the air like an invisible mist. J.J. removed her suit and hung it in the closet, then took off her shoes. Perspiration dotted her forehead and trickled between her breasts. On their ride home from campaign headquarters, with the top down on Miguel's car, J.J. had gotten hot and only now, after ten minutes in the air-conditioned coolness of the house, had she begun to cool off. A little.

But in another sense she was still hot. Burning hot. There was a fire of passion blazing inside her. She and Miguel had a few precious hours to be together this afternoon and then again to-night. Tomorrow morning, she would take a ten o'clock flight from Mocorito to Caracas, and there board the Dundee jet for a flight home. Dom and Vic would remain in Mocorito, Dom as Miguel's bodyguard and Vic continuing to work undercover in conjunction with Will Pierce and the CIA.

"Jennifer?" Miguel called to her from the bedroom.

She walked out of the huge closet/dressing-room area, then halted in the doorway when she saw Miguel standing by the French doors overlooking the courtyard.

He had stripped off his shoes, socks and white shirt, and wore only his black dress slacks. His shoulders were broad, his back wide, his skin a polished bronze shimmering with perspiration in the shadowy light of the overcast afternoon.

Why was it that she felt her entire life—all thirty years—had been bringing her to this point in time, to this one cloudy, gray day in a country half a world away from home, with a man she had known only a few days?

"It is going to rain. Soon." Keeping his back to her, he spoke quietly, a hushed tone to his deep voice. "The wind is blowing very hard now."

Oh, Miguel, Miguel.

She walked across the room. Slowly. Her heart beating fast, her pulse racing. Everything feminine within her vibrated with a hunger she had never known, with a need to love and be loved in the most basic way a man and a woman can exchange that primitive emotion.

Why doesn't he turn around and hold out his arms to me? Why isn't he telling me how much he wants me?

When she came up behind him, she thought surely he would

turn and embrace her. She stood there for several strained moments. Then unable to bear another moment without his touch, she went to him, pressed herself against his back and reached her arms around him. His muscles went taut.

"Make love with me, Miguel," she whispered as she laid her head on the back of his shoulder.

He sucked in a deep breath, then released it as he turned and took her into his arms. He held her there, close to him, embracing her, one big hand resting across her spine, the other cupping her hip. His mouth raked across her temple and came to rest against her ear.

"You will not regret giving yourself to me, *querida?*" he asked, as if his life depended on her answer.

"Oh, Miguel. No. Never."

He grasped her shoulders and forced her to face him. With his fingers biting into her flesh, he said, "This will change nothing. You will leave Nava in the morning. You understand, yes?"

"Yes, I understand." She would leave tomorrow morning. She would get on the plane to Caracas, but she would leave behind her heart. And if he honestly thought that their becoming lovers would change nothing, then he was seriously mistaken. It would change everything.

The tension in his grasp lessened gradually as he lowered his head and brought their lips together. His arms encompassed her again, a forceful yet gentle embrace that claimed her as surely as if he had branded her. She had never before wanted to belong to a man. Body and soul. But she longed to belong to Miguel, in every possible way. And she wanted him to be hers and hers alone. His devouring kiss told her how much he wanted her, how hungry he was for her, as she was for him. But there was a gentleness in the kiss and in the way he held her, as if he wanted her to know that he cherished her, that she was precious to him.

"I ache for you," he said as his lips lifted from hers, then quickly made their way down her throat.

She ran her hands over his naked back, raking her fingernails over his hot, damp flesh. "I ache for you, too." She pulled away, just enough to gain access to his chest. While he threaded his fingers through her hair, she spread kisses from collarbone to collarbone, then went lower to flick her tongue over first one and then the other of his tiny male nipples.

Miguel arched his back and moaned, deep and low, the sound guttural, like that of an animal.

Spurred on by his arousal bulging just below his waist, J.J. dropped to her knees and unzipped his slacks, then eased them and his black briefs down his hips until his jutting sex popped up in front of her. Powerful and pulsating, he was a temptation she could not resist. J.J. caressed him with her fingers and sighed when he growled his satisfaction. Taking the next step immediately, she ran the tip of her tongue down and back up, then repeated the process, tormenting him with a promise of fulfillment. She played with him, taking him into her mouth as he held her head in place, encouraging her eager lips and tongue to pleasure him.

Lost in the frenzy of giving him what he needed, J.J. became unbearably aroused, her femininity dripping with moisture, her nipples peaked and aching. Unexpectedly, Miguel eased himself from her mouth, then reached down and brought her up off her knees. Breathless and dazed with desire, she stared at him.

Smiling devilishly, he swooped her up into his arms and carried her to his bed. He placed her on her feet, then reached down to grasp the hem of her silk slip. When he maneuvered the slip up her thighs and over her hips, she lifted her arms into the air, assisting him in undressing her. She stood there on wobbly legs, wearing her white lace bra, bikini panties, silk stockings and garter belt. While she stared pleadingly into his dark eyes, begging him silently to end this torture, he touched her in the center of her chest, between her breasts, with the tip of his index finger, pushing her down onto the edge of the bed.

She sat there, tingling from head to toe, her feminine core

clenching and unclenching with anticipation, as he knelt in front of her. First he undid the tabs on her garter belt, one by one, releasing their hold on her silk stockings. Then he lifted her right leg and slowly peeled off the first stocking, his hands gently seductive. After he rolled the first stocking below her knee, he painted a trail of damp kisses across the top of her thigh. She gasped. What a marvelous sensation. As he took the stocking down her calf, over her ankle and off her foot, his lips followed his hands. He lifted her foot and kissed each toe.

"Such a small, delicate foot," he said before placing it on the floor and turning to her other leg.

He repeated the process of removing her stocking from the left leg. By the time he tossed that stocking on the floor atop the other one, J.J. was quivering, every nerve in her body alert.

She held her breath when he looked at her breasts with longing and only after he unhooked her lace bra and brought the straps down her shoulders, did she breathe again. Her naked breasts rose and fell, the nipples tight and hard.

"Beautiful. Very beautiful."

He lifted her breasts in his palms, then covered them and squeezed tenderly. When his fingertips circled her areola, she thought she would die. Then when she whimpered, he gave her what she wanted. He flicked her nipples with his thumbs and that action released a firestorm of pure sensation inside her. She cried out.

"Did I hurt you?" he asked, concern in his golden-brown eyes.

"No, no. Please, please, don't stop."

He tormented her nipples, with his thumb and forefinger. Then while he pinched one aching point, he brought his mouth down over the other and suckled her until she thought she wouldn't be able to bear another minute of such intense pleasure.

Keening, the sound vibrating in her throat, she tossed back her head and thrust her breasts forward. Miguel rose up over her and then turned her in the bed until she lay flat on her back. Looking up at him, she opened her mouth with silent awe.

"You're beautiful, too," she told him. "Very beautiful."

And very large and very aroused.

Smiling at her compliment, he hooked his fingers inside her panties and pulled them down over her hips. When he stopped and nuzzled her mound with his mouth, her hips lifted of their own volition. As soon as he threw her panties on the floor, he joined her on the bed.

They gazed into each other's eyes, the tension between them electric. His eyes still on hers, he mounted her, delving deep with the first lunge, taking her completely, filling her to the hilt. For half a second she felt stretched beyond her limits, but her body soon adjusted to accommodate him and then she simply felt complete.

And so the dance began, Miguel setting the rhythm. Deep, slow thrusts that made her body sing. She couldn't get close enough, couldn't touch him enough, kiss him enough, say his name enough. He was on her, around her, inside her and yet she wanted more of him. She wanted her flesh and bones to melt into his.

He whispered dark, erotic words and phrases, moaning his desire and his intentions against her breasts. Suddenly he increased the tempo. Fast, hard jabs. J.J. shuddered, her core tightened, preparing for release.

She clung to him, encouraging him with every breath, every movement, every moaned sigh. She repeated his name over and over again, like a worshipful chant. Her climax hit her, releasing the spring on her tightly wound sex, allowing her to come apart completely. She cried and gasped and dug her nails into his back.

And then he jackhammered into her, giving her a second orgasm when he came. He roared out his pleasure, the sound rumbling from deep inside him. And then, after the aftershocks had rippled through them, he fell to one side and stared up at the ceiling, his breathing hard and fast.

She lay beside him. Sated. Spent. Deliriously happy. And totally, irrevocably in love.

Chapter 14

Dom sat with J.J., off camera, in a small, crowded room, as they waited for the moment the on-air commercial would conclude and the cameras would turn to Miguel. More nervous than she could remember ever being, J.J. had clasped and unclasped her hands a half-dozen times. She had rubbed her palms up and down her dress slacks until she feared she had thinned the gabardine. And she had glanced at the oval utility clock on the wall every two minutes. When she tapped one foot up and down, Dom reached over and placed his hand on her knee. She stopped immediately.

"You're making me nervous, honey," Dom said. "Calm down. He'll be all right."

Leaning toward Dom, she spoke in English as quietly as possible, hoping not to be overheard. "No, he won't be all right. He's aware that by swearing he will run for president, no matter what, he might be condemning other people like Carlos to death."

With so many supporters around them—everyone from Roberto and Emilio to Juan, Aunt Josephina and Seina—J.J. felt suffocated. And muffled. She couldn't say what she wanted to say to Dom, couldn't vent her frustration and anger at the top of her lungs. If only she could scream. Just once.

Dom took her hand and gave it a good squeeze, then released it. "God forbid anyone should think I'm flirting with my cousin's fiancée."

"Yes, God forbid." Knowing he had hoped to gain a smile from her, J.J. failed him. The best she could do was to stop frowning for a brief moment.

"You've gotten in over your head on this one, haven't you?" Dom said.

She pinned him with a be-quiet glare. "You have no idea," she whispered. Both Roberto and Emilio spoke some English and although both men knew who she really was, she didn't want to share her private feelings with either of them.

Lowering his voice, Dom said, "I never in a million years thought you'd fall for a guy like Ramirez."

J.J.'s mouth curved into a self-deprecating half smile. Thinking what a fool she must seem to Dom, she replied, "I didn't see it coming. It caught me totally unaware. Attraction is one thing, but…"

"You're in love with him." Dom looked at her, sympathy in his black eyes.

She didn't respond. She didn't need to.

"It is time." Emilio signaled to the group by fluttering his hands. "Quiet everyone. The future president of Mocorito is about to speak to us."

J.J. said so softly she wasn't sure Dom heard her, "Take care of him when I'm gone."

Dom mouthed the words. "I promise."

Mario Lamas, the Nationalist Party sympathizing owner of Nava's television station faced the in-house and at-home audience. First he cleared his throat. Then in a loud, distinct voice he announced that tonight Miguel Cesar Ramirez would be speaking to the people, speaking to them from his heart. Mario went on to praise Miguel, to recount his humble beginnings and brag about him as a teacher might a favorite student. As Mario's introduction continued, J.J.'s thoughts escaped from this place, from this moment in time, to the most glorious two hours of her life. Two hours spent with Miguel in his bedroom suite, shut off from the rest of the world. For those one hundred and twenty minutes, she had been in heaven. The heaven she and Miguel had created together.

These next fifteen minutes would be pure hell for Miguel and if they were that agonizing to him, then they would be to her. His pain was her pain. But once the deed was done, once he had made his stand, drawn his line in the sand, there would be no turning back. All they could do was wait for Hector Padilla and his Federalist cohorts to make their next move. Her instincts told her that they would strike again and soon. Another murder? The death of someone else near and dear to Miguel? But when would it happen? And to whom?

Hating the helpless feeling of knowing there was nothing she could do to prevent another tragedy, J.J. stood and paced around the room. As she passed by Aunt Josephina and Seina, the two women flanking Juan, she offered them a weak smile, doing her best to reassure them that all was well. What a damn lie!

This small room at the studio was filled with people who loved, admired and respected Miguel. Having realized upon their arrival tonight what a perfect time this would be to kill those closest to Miguel in one fell swoop, she and Dom had thoroughly searched this room and then Dom had excused himself and gone over every inch of the television station.

"Mind if I take a couple of your security guards with me to check things out?" Dom had asked Mario. "I just want to make sure my cousin is safe tonight for the broadcast."

Mario had not only given Dom his permission, he'd sent four security guards with him and given them orders to follow Señor Shea's every command.

"Best I can tell, this whole place is clean," Dom had told her. "If the bad guys are planning something, I don't think they're going to blow this place sky-high. At least not tonight."

"They must know what Miguel plans to say tonight. Whoever the traitor in Miguel's camp is, he or she must already have shared the information with Padilla."

"You said he—or she. Do you think the traitor could be female?"

"I don't know. If it is, we can rule out Dolores, of course. So that leaves only Ramona and Aunt Josephina and both of them seem devoted to Miguel."

The moment Miguel appeared on screen, everyone congregated in the small room at the station broke out in applause. J.J. clapped the longest and the loudest, a part of her wanting to whistle and stomp her feet and shout, "Viva Ramirez! Viva el presidente."

God, what love could do to a woman!

From the very second Miguel spoke his first word, J.J. kept her gaze focused on the television screen mounted on the wall. He looked so handsome. He had chosen his suit, she his shirt and tie. Clasping her hands in her lap to prevent them from trembling nervously, she recalled buttoning his pale blue shirt and wrapping the gray, navy and white striped tie around his neck, then tying it. He had kept kissing her while she knotted his tie and she had laughed as she struggled to keep her mind on the job at hand. What she had truly wanted, just as he had, was to go back to bed and make love again.

Tonight, she told herself. Tonight when this is over, when we go home, when we are alone in his bedroom suite. They would make love all night long.

And in the morning she would leave. Tonight might well be the last time she would see Miguel, the last time they would be together. Neither of them knew what the future would hold.

Diego sat in front of the television in the wood-paneled study of his father's home. Even though his mother now owned this fine house, which would one day be his, he would always think of it as his father's home. Reminders of Cesar Fernandez were in every room. Diego's mother had altered nothing since her husband's death. His favorite pipes remained on the desk in this room and the smell of his tobacco still permeated the upholstery and drapes. The liquor cabinet contained his preferred liquors and every article of clothing he had owned remained in the closets and chests upstairs. An oil painting of Cesar in his youth hung over the fireplace here in the den and another of him, in his prime, hung over the mantel in the front parlor. And Diego's mother kept her wedding photograph of a smiling young couple in a silver frame on her bedside table.

As Diego downed another swig of his father's aged brandy, he wondered how a man who had been loved so devotedly by a woman such as Carlotta could have lowered himself to sleep with the likes of Luz Ramirez, a gutter whore from the Aguilar barrio.

Looking at Ramirez on the television screen, Diego saw his father's fine features. The nose, the mouth, the bone structure identical to their father's. Yes, damn it—their father. Miguel looked far more like Cesar than either Diego or Seina. Diego had been told by many people that he was a cross between his parents. And who had not heard numerous times that Seina was the image of her grandmother Fernandez, for whom she had been named.

"I have come to you tonight to pledge my life to you, the people of Mocorito," Miguel Ramirez said.

Diego lifted his glass and saluted him.

The man had the eyes of a jungle cat. Yellow-brown. Cunning. Dangerous.

When Diego had arrived home today, his mother had met him at the door, ranting and raving about Seina having packed a bag and left home. He had done his best to soothe his mother and assure her that, in time, Seina would come to her senses and re-

turn home. He knew better. His sister would never return home.
And it was all his fault. His evil deeds had run her off.

"Everyone in Mocorito is aware that my chauffeur was murdered, but what you do not know is that threats have been made
against others, against those closest to me," Miguel said. "I have
no proof against anyone. We do not know who killed Carlos or
who might perpetrate other crimes against my family, my friends
and my supporters.

"But I say to you—and to them—if their purpose is to force
me to withdraw my candidacy, then they have failed. I will continue campaigning, continue seeking your vote. No matter what
happens, I promise I will give you, the good people of Mocorito, the choice between two candidates. Between Hector Padilla
and Miguel Cesar Ramirez!"

"And I'm going to vote for you, you bastard," Diego saluted
Miguel a second time with his now nearly empty glass of brandy.
"If you live to election day."

Hector Padilla seethed as he listened to Miguel Ramirez address the people of Mocorito. Damn fool, Hector thought. Or was
the man a heartless bastard? Yes, that was how they should play
this. The man was willing to let innocent people die, murdered
by some unknown madman intent on keeping Ramirez from becoming president. Of course he would do nothing himself, say
nothing. But his publicity people could spin an ugly little tale and
share it with the newspapers, as well as broadcast it from person
to person, like juicy gossip.

He had ordered the chauffeur's death, had even specified that
he wanted it to be particularly bloody. But three deaths had obviously not been enough to convince Ramirez that he should do
the right thing. Perhaps another death would be necessary. A
fourth death, even closer to home.

Such a pity that Miguel had feelings for his pretty little American bodyguard. It would be doubly tragic when she was struck

down. The country would mourn for Miguel and he would be devastated. Then, if he insisted on continuing his candidacy, the people would know him for the heartless bastard he was. How could he put his own ambition above the lives of others?

There would be some within his circle, fellow Federalists, who would protest another killing, the ones who had cried over the deaths of the first three people. But they were weak men who could not be told the truth. Men like Diego Fernandez.

A brilliant idea formed in Hector's mind. He snapped his fingers, then laughed. But of course. He would send an expert marksman and tell him to aim at Ramirez and when his little bodyguard got in the way, to shoot her.

Diego could not complain if the target had been Ramirez. He hated his half-brother and probably longed to see him dead. He knew what he would say to Diego.

Too bad that the phony fiancée had gotten in the way.

Diego was gullible enough to buy that explanation. And Ramirez would be destroyed, knowing she had given her life to save him.

The moment Miguel entered the small room at the studio, his friends surrounded him, patting him on the back, congratulating him on a fine speech, telling him how brave and fearless he was. Did they not understand that because they were here, supporting him, loving him, cheering him on, that they were in danger, that their very lives were at stake?

Trying his best to act appreciatively as he made his way through the well-wishers, Miguel sought the one person who understood him, the one person who knew what tonight's speech had cost him. Where was she?

And then he saw her, coming through the crowd, coming straight to him. Their gazes met and locked. He moved away from Roberto, who had been shaking his hand, and met Jennifer in the middle of the room. Surrounded by his supporters, Miguel reached out and pulled Jennifer into his arms. She hugged him fiercely and laid her head on his chest. A re-sounding cheer rose from the group. Jennifer lifted her head and looked around them, then gazed up at him and smiled. Tears filled her beautiful violet-blue eyes and cascaded down her alabaster cheeks.

All he wanted now was to take this woman home, to go upstairs to his room with her and close out the whole world for the rest of the night.

As if she had read his thoughts, she stood on tiptoe and whispered in his ear. "We can't leave yet. All the workers from campaign headquarters are outside in the parking lot, along with a large group of your supporters. You'll have to put in an appearance."

"You, *querida,* are a very understanding fiancée."

She clasped his hand. "I'm ready to face the crowd when you are."

Dom came up on the other side of Miguel as they approached the front entrance of the television studio. Although it was unlikely he would be targeted, judging by recent events, his bodyguards would be stupid to take any chances with his life.

If only each person in his entourage had their own personal bodyguard. If only he could ensure their safety. Tonight. Tomorrow. And in the days ahead.

He could not provide everyone who supported him, who worked tirelessly for his cause, a personal bodyguard, but he could see that Emilio, Roberto, Juan and Aunt Josephina had protection. And even his sister, Seina, now that she had publicly claimed him. They were the people most likely to become targets. Later tonight, he would speak with J.J. and Dom about making arrangements to call in more agents.

With his senses at full alert, Miguel exited the studio, and with his arm around Jennifer and Dom practically attached to his other side, he marched across the street.

Followed by the group who had come from inside the studio, Miguel made his way to the parking lot where an enormous crowd waited. The moment they saw him, they cheered and began rushing toward him.

Dom Shea cursed under his breath.

Jennifer clutched Miguel's arm to halt him. "This is bad," she said. "If they overrun us, there will be no way we can protect you."

Yanking away from her, thinking fast on his feet and yet not considering all the risks, Miguel crawled up into the bed of a parked pickup truck and lifted his arms in a gesture that requested his supporters to cease and desist. Within seconds, Jennifer and Dom had joined him in the truck bed, followed shortly by Emilio and Roberto.

"You're an easy target up here," Jennifer told him. "You can't stay here."

"Only for a few minutes. Just until I speak to these people and give them a few minutes of my time. That's all they want."

He motioned for the cheers and shouts to stop, but it took a good three or four minutes before anyone could hear him over the noise. Finally, he managed to make himself heard. He said a few words of thanks and asked for their continued support. Then, when J.J. and Dom escorted him down from the truck bed, the applause started anew. He wrapped his arm around Jennifer's shoulders and together they headed straight for Dom's rental car. Several people followed them, mostly his closest friends. He shook hands with Emilio and Roberto again, then hugged Aunt Josephina and held out his hand to Seina and when she placed her hand in his, he lifted it to his lips and kissed it.

"Thank you for being here tonight," he said.

"You're welcome, Miguel."

He then shook hands with Juan. "I will depend on you to take good care of my little sister."

"I vow to you that her happiness means more to me than anything else."

Miguel turned around and, with his arm still draped across J.J.'s shoulders, they walked toward Dom's car. Suddenly, before

Miguel had any idea what was happening, Dom barreled into him, knocking both him and J.J. to the ground. J.J. rose up quickly and threw her body over Miguel's.

Reaching out, he grabbed her shoulders and began rolling her over to his side. He would not allow her to die for him. He would not!

The sound of a rifle shot was almost muffled by frightened screams as people ran in every direction.

J.J. gasped. Once.

With his weapon drawn and his gaze scanning the area, Dom hovered over them. "Are either of you hit?"

"I am fine," Miguel replied, then looked over at J.J.

When she stared at him, her face chalk-white, he saw the pain in her eyes.

"Jennifer? J.J.?" he cried her name as he ran his hands over her body.

She groaned. He withdrew his hand from her side. His fingers dripped with blood. Jennifer's blood.

Chapter 15

Miguel paced the floor, like a caged tiger, his teeth bared, his claws ready to rip apart the first person who dared to cross him. Dom had tried to help him moments after the shooting, but Miguel had clung to J.J. as if he thought letting go of her would mean her death. Then later, Dom had tried to persuade Miguel to allow the paramedics to take J.J. from him, but to no avail. In the end, Juan Esteban had worked out a compromise that Miguel had agreed to reluctantly—they had allowed him to sit at her side in the ambulance. Dom had driven directly behind them, all the way to St. Augustine's, praying as hard as he'd ever prayed in his life. When he'd been a navy SEAL, he'd seen comrades killed, their heads blown off, their guts hanging out. But he'd never gotten used to the sight of death, the loss of a human life. Since going to work at the Dundee Agency, he had been faced with the injury of a fellow agent a couple of times. Both had survived.

As they waited now for word on J.J.'s condition, he knew what

Miguel was thinking and understood part of what he was feeling. He was thinking how small and delicate J.J. had looked lying there on the street, blood covering her beige jacket. He was thinking that if the bullet had hit a couple of inches over, he would be the one in the operating room right now.

Dom loved J.J. like a little sister. He liked to kid her, enjoyed how she could take a practical joke and the fact that she always understood that his ribald sense of humor held no prejudice or malice. In many ways, he knew J.J. far better than Miguel Ramirez did. At least he'd known her a lot longer. But he wasn't in love with J.J. and he suspected that Miguel was. If he wasn't a man in love, he sure as hell was giving a good imitation of one tonight.

Miguel had been inconsolable and unreachable after they had arrived at the hospital and the attendants had wheeled J.J. directly into an elevator to take her to the operating room. He had bellowed like a wounded bull when they'd told him that he could not go with her. If it had not been for Dr. Esteban finally being able to calm Miguel, the security officers would have taken him into custody.

Juan's aunt had arrived with Seina Fernandez, both of them having ridden to the hospital with Emilio. Roberto had come separately, two campaign staff members with him. The ten-by-twelve waiting room was filled to capacity and to a person, they had each tried to talk to Miguel, to reassure him, to give him hope. He had not responded to anyone, ignoring them as if he were deaf, dumb and blind. Part of the time, he paced the floor, looking neither right nor left, but straight down, as if he found the floor utterly fascinating. The rest of the time he stood and stared out the windows into the dark night. About an hour ago, it had started raining, and just now Dom saw streaks of lightning crackling through the black sky.

They had been waiting for three hours—the longest three hours of Dom's life. When he'd first arrived, he'd stayed outside long enough to call Vic and tell him what had happened. Vic had made him promise to call him once J.J. came out of surgery.

"She'll pull through," Vic had said. "She may look like a fragile china doll, but our little J.J. is as tough as nails."

He'd been acquainted with Vic long enough to realize the guy didn't make friends easily. He was a loner and although everyone at Dundee liked and respected him, no one could say they really knew him. J.J. had come closer than anyone to breaking through that impregnable wall surrounding Vic Noble, probably because she wasn't intimidated by him. God knew most women were. Intimidated and attracted. Vic had that mysterious Clint Eastwood gunslinger thing going for him that kept other men at arm's length and intrigued women.

"If she dies, so help me God…" Vic had left the rest unsaid. But Dom hadn't needed to hear the words to know what Vic meant. If J.J. died, there would be no place on earth for those responsible to hide.

But J.J. was not going to die. Dr. Esteban had told them that the bullet had entered her right side and his guess was that it was lodged in the lower rib cage.

"I don't believe the bullet hit any vital organs," Juan had told Miguel. "But we won't know the extent of the damage until we operate. Much depends upon the type of bullet that was used."

At seventeen minutes past eleven, Dr. Esteban, wearing green surgery scrubs, appeared in the waiting-room doorway. A hushed silence fell over the room. Miguel paused in his relentless pacing, looked at Juan and froze to the spot.

Juan walked toward Miguel and when he was within a couple of feet, he paused and said, "She came through surgery quite well. We removed the bullet. There was no injury to any vital organs. She is resting comfortably in recovery and we will move her to intensive care shortly."

"She will live?" Miguel asked.

"Yes," Juan replied. "Barring any complications, she should

recover fully in a few weeks and she should be able to travel in four or five days."

"I want to see her," Miguel said.

"She won't know you are there. She hasn't come out from under the anesthesia yet and when she does, we will keep her heavily sedated for the next eight to twelve hours."

"She will know I am there," Miguel said.

"It is highly irregular," Juan told him. "Family is usually permitted only brief visits with a patient in the intensive care."

"Make arrangements for me to stay with her."

Juan sighed heavily, then nodded before patting Miguel on the shoulder. "Stay here. I will send someone for you very soon."

When Dr. Esteban left without saying a word to anyone else, and apparently no one was brave enough to face Miguel, Dom made the first move. He walked over to Miguel and paused at his side where he still stood in the middle of the room.

"When she comes to, don't start babbling a lot of nonsense about this being your fault," Dom said in English. "That's not what she'll want to hear."

Miguel didn't reply.

Dom lowered his voice. "The way she'll see it is that she was doing her job. Her first instinct was to protect you."

"Yes, I know." Still Miguel did not look at Dom

"When you're thinking a little more rationally, we'll talk. Until then keep one thing in mind—you might not have been the target."

Miguel snapped his head around and glared at Dom.

When J.J. awoke, groggy and confused, she glanced around the room and realized she was in the hospital. Then she saw Miguel, sitting at her bedside, his head bowed, his eyes closed. Was he sleeping?

What happened? her dazed mind asked. Then slowly, bit by bit, she recalled the events of last evening. The crowds. The cheers. Miguel and she walking toward Dom's rental car. Dom knocking them off their feet. Her instincts taking over as she sought to shield Miguel with her own body.

Had that happened only this past evening? Just how long had she been in the hospital? She opened her mouth and tried to speak, but she couldn't manage to make a sound other than a gurgling gasp.

Miguel's eyelids flew open instantly and he came up out of his chair and hovered over her. "Jennifer? *Querida?*"

She tried to smile at him, but she wasn't sure whether she did or not. Then she tried to lift her hand, but couldn't do it. What was wrong with her? Why was she so weak?

Miguel grasped her hand tenderly and lifted it to hold over his heart. "Don't try to talk. Just rest, *querida.*"

She moaned, wanting desperately to communicate with him.

"Are you in pain?" he asked, his voice edged with near panic.

She managed to shake her head. She was uncomfortable, but not really in pain. I must be drugged, she thought. Doped up on some heavy-duty pain killers.

She tried to speak again and this time managed to say one word. "Miguel."

"Yes, I'm here." He kissed her hand, then placed it down by her side and leaned over to kiss her forehead.

"What happened?" she asked.

"Do you not remember?"

"Some." Then she recalled the searing pain hitting her in the side. "Was I shot?"

"Yes, you...you were shot."

"Am I going to be all right?"

He nodded. Tears pooled in his eyes.

"Is everyone else all right? You? Dom?"

"No one else was harmed. Only you." Frowning as if he were in immeasurable pain, Miguel momentarily closed his eyes.

"I guess I can't leave Mocorito now, can I?"

Caressing her face and looking at her with concern, he said,

"You should never have come here in the first place. If I had known… I would die before I would put your life in danger."

"I know that." She felt herself fading, as if this brief conversation had sapped all her strength

"We have talked too much already," Miguel said. "You must rest. No more talk."

"Stay with me."

"I won't leave you. I promise.

She sighed, then closed her eyes. "I love you."

The last thing she heard before she fell asleep was Miguel saying in an anguished voice, *"Querida…querida."*

Miguel spent forty-eight hours in the hospital, sleeping very little, eating only when Ramona came with food from home and threatened him with bodily harm if he did not eat. When Jennifer began staying awake for long periods of time, after that first night and day, she'd told him to go home and shower and shave, but he had refused. Then this morning, when a stranger arrived at the hospital and Dom Shea had brought the man in to see J.J., she had told Dom to take Miguel home.

"This is Geoff Monday," Dom had introduced the burly Brit, a rugged blond with bulging muscles and a friendly grin. "He will stay here and guard J.J. while you and I go back to your house."

Miguel had not wanted to leave, but J.J. had insisted, so, to please her, he acquiesced, promising to return in a few hours.

No sooner had he and Dom exited the hospital than a horde of reporters swarmed down on them. Behind the reporters, countless people carrying signs and shouting for justice crammed the parking lot and the street.

"What's going on?" Miguel asked.

"It started yesterday," Dom said. "These are your people, Ramirez. The citizens of Nava, up in arms over the second attempt on your life. They blame the Federalists and some have out-and-out accused President Padilla of plotting your death."

"Why did no one tell me what was happening? We cannot have rioting in the streets."

"Emilio and Roberto wanted to tell you, but I warned them that you had enough to deal with and that you'd find out soon enough. Besides, I don't think there's much you can do about it. You can hardly tell these people that they're wrong, that their president is innocent."

"I am surprised that Padilla hasn't sent out army troops to suppress the protests." Miguel stood on the sidewalk, Dom at his side, while the hospital security just barely managed to keep the reporters at bay.

"So far, these protests have been peaceful," Dom said. "But I doubt they'll stay that way. I think you'll have to make a statement to the press right now. If nothing else tell them your fiancée is recovering nicely, that the police have not caught the shooter and you will have more to say later today."

"Yes, you are right about what I must do, what I must say. And later, when I have had time to think, I must come up with a way to defuse this ticking time bomb."

Miguel then spoke to the reporters, making the brief statement that Dom had outlined for him.

"Okay, now that you've temporarily taken care of that problem, let's get out of here," Dom told him.

"How do we do that?"

As if on cue, the roar of a big black Hummer alerted the crowd to get out of the way or be plowed down in the monster vehicle's path.

"What—?" The one questioning word was all Miguel said before Dom grabbed his arm and, shoving through the reporters, raced with him to the Hummer.

Once safe inside, Dom said, "Vic Noble sent some of his friends to pick us up."

J.J. awoke later that afternoon, feeling more human than she'd felt since the shooting. She figured Juan Esteban had lowered the dosage of her pain medication, which had helped her not only to stay awake, but also to be at least partially alert. She hated that woozy, drugged feeling, that sense of not being fully in control of her mind or body.

Geoff Monday had been in and out of her room all day. Every time a nurse came in for whatever reason, they had asked him to step outside. She had been bathed, fed, prodded and poked. Although she knew the nurses checked her vital signs only at regular intervals, she felt as if they were doing it every hour on the hour. How on earth did anyone get any rest while they were in the hospital?

When a pair of nurses shooed Geoff out, he smiled, shrugged and left willingly. But when they wheeled her hospital bed out into the hall, he stopped them immediately. They explained in rapid Spanish that they were taking J.J. down for some X-rays.

"My Spanish is a little rusty," Geoff admitted as he kept his big, meaty hand planted on the foot of J.J.'s bed, effectively blocking the path. "Did they say something about some X-rays?"

"They're taking me downstairs for some X-rays," J.J. told him. "I'm not sure why, but I suppose it's simply hospital procedure. Apparently, Juan Esteban issued the order."

"I'll ride down in the elevator with you," Geoff said.

"I'll tell them that my friend will be going with us." She then turned to the two nurses and spoke to them in Spanish.

They both nodded and smiled, so Geoff moved out of the way and followed them to the service elevator. With one nurse at the head of her bed and the other at the foot, they maneuvered the bed into the elevator, then one of the nurses hopped out of the elevator in front of Geoff while the other one hit the down button.

"What's going on?" J.J. demanded half a second before the nurse covered her face with a foul-smelling rag.

Dom received a frantic call on his cell phone from Geoff Monday, who referred to himself by every conceivable name in the book for allowing J.J. to be snapped up right under his nose. Almost simultaneously, Miguel's cell phone rang.

"Answer it!" Dom shouted. "J.J.'s been kidnapped.

Chapter 16

Miguel's heart stopped for a moment, a part of him dying on the spot. That brief hesitation gained him another shout from Domingo Shea.

"Answer the goddamn phone."

With robotic movements, Miguel removed his cell phone from his belt clip, flipped it open and placed it to his ear. "Yes, this is Miguel Ramirez."

"Are you missing a wounded fiancée?" the obviously disguised voice asked.

"Where is she? What have you done with her?"

Dom clamped his hand down on Miguel's shoulder and gave him a look that told him not to panic, to stay calm.

Laughter. He heard the person on the other end of the phone laughing. When he found this person, he would rip out his heart.

"She is well. For now," the voice said. "Whether she lives or dies depends on you."

"What do you want?" Miguel asked, his heartbeat thundering in his ears.

"We want you to make another appearance on television. Call your friend Mario Lamas and arrange for another national broadcast."

"I can do that," Miguel said. "What am I supposed to announce?" He knew, but he had to hear the words said aloud, the demand made.

"If you wish to save Señorita Blair's life, you will withdraw from the presidential race. Make up any reason you choose to tell the citizens of Mocorito. If you do not do as we request, your American fiancée—" the man chuckled "—will die and her blood will be on your hands."

"I understand."

"You have until five o'clock today to speak to the people of Mocorito."

"And if I do as you request, you will release Jennifer unharmed?"

"Yes, of course."

The line went suddenly dead. Miguel gripped the phone with white-knuckled rage. He turned to Dom Shea. "They say they will kill her, if I don't—" He looked at his cell phone. "I have to call Mario Lamas and make arrangements for a few moments of air time."

"Tell me what the hell he said to you."

Miguel shook his head. "It does not matter. I know what I must do."

Dom grabbed Miguel's shoulders and shook him. The two men faced off, like two warriors preparing for hand-to-hand combat. "Don't try to handle this alone. Don't go all power-hungry on me. For God's sake, it's J.J.'s life that's at stake here."

Bristling, every muscle in his body taut, Miguel said," Do you think I do not know what is at stake?"

"Yeah, sure you do. Just fill me in," Dom told him. "You're not going to play God where J.J. is concerned. You're not making any decisions on your own. Do you understand?"

"They will kill her if I do not withdraw from the presidential race. There, I've said it. Does that change anything? No, it does not." He shrugged off Dom's hold and lifted his cell phone. "I must contact Mario and—"

Dom grabbed Miguel's wrist, effectively stopping him from making the call. "Hold on."

"I have only until five o'clock." Miguel glanced at his wrist-watch. "It is now two-thirty."

"What proof did they give you that they have J.J.?"

"She is missing, is she not? Was she not kidnapped from the hospital, despite one of your Dundee agents being there to protect her?"

"There's no reason for you to go off half-cocked. You need to slow down and think. What assurance did they give that, if they actually have J.J., they will release her unharmed when you publicly announce your withdrawal from the race?"

An overpowering sense of total deflation hit Miguel, as if all the wind had been knocked out of him. "They gave me no proof that they have her and I have only one man's word that she will be released unharmed if I do as they say."

Dom squeezed Miguel's wrist, then released him. "Call Mario and ask for air time at four-fifty. Tell him to make some public service announcements, starting immediately, that Miguel Ramirez will again speak to the people of Mocorito. At four-fifty this afternoon. That will buy us some time."

"What can we do in two hours and fifteen minutes?"

"We can turn this city upside down and right side out and if we're lucky we'll find her. If not, then you'll go on TV."

J.J. came to in a darkened room, the smell of fish and seawater strong. If she had to venture a guess as to where her kidnappers had taken her, she'd say it was somewhere near the waterfront. And since she seriously doubted that they were keeping her in any of the luxurious condos and cottages with ocean views in Nava, that probably meant she was in Colima. Like Ebano, Colima was little more than a suburb of Nava, but much less upscale than Ebano.

J.J.'s side ached something awful, the pain bearable, but for how long? She'd been kept on painkillers for days now, but she didn't know how long it had been since her last injection because she had no idea what time it was. Dim light came through the row of small, high windows near the top of the twenty-foot wall. That meant it wasn't nighttime yet.

When she tried to move, she realized her wrists were tied to the wooden arm rests on either side of the chair in which she sat. And her ankles were bound together.

While she was still trying to get her bearings and figure out what, if anything, she could do, a door on the far side of the room swung open, ushering in a bit more light which outlined the tall, menacing figure standing in the doorway.

"Good afternoon, Señorita Blair," the familiar voice said to her in Spanish.

When he walked into the room and came closer, close enough for her to see his face, she looked him right in the eye and said, "So it is you who are the traitor."

Diego went to the palace when Hector summoned him, and he sat there with the president and the secretary of state while Hector explained to Diego that some loyal Federalists had whisked Señorita Blair from her hospital room.

"She is being held now—quite safe you understand—in Colima, at the old abandoned Cristobal canning plant on the waterfront." Hector had smirked, thinking he was placating Diego by sharing every tidbit of information with him. "Since the assassination attempt several evenings ago went awry, our supporters were forced to improvise."

"If Ramirez withdraws his candidacy, you will free Señorita Blair?" Diego asked, doing his best to not appear at all concerned.

"Certainly. Of course."

Diego knew the man was lying to him. Lying now as he had been doing for the past year. He had flattered Diego, praised him and used his hatred for his half-brother to bring out the very worst in him. The dark, demonic side that lived deep inside every man.

"I know you have been concerned, my friend, about recent events." Hector Padilla looked remorseful, as if he truly regretted the horrible things that had been happening. "I, more than anyone, long for peace. But often the price of peace is the lives of innocent people. You understand, Diego, a man of your intelligence."

Diego nodded. "Yes, I understand, el presidente."

"Good. Good. Now that this is settled, come, join us for a late lunch. And tonight come back to the palace. I believe we will have much to celebrate then."

"Regrettably I must decline the offer of lunch. My mother is greatly concerned about my young sister who has left home. It is a family crisis and I must do what I can to help my poor mother and bring my sister back to her family."

"Yes, yes, of course." Hector rose from his chair and patted Diego on the back as he walked him to the door. "Be sure to watch television this afternoon at four-fifty. That bastard brother of yours will once again address the nation. But this time he will be saying what we want to hear."

At four-fifteen, just as Miguel and Dom entered Mario Lamas's office at the television station, Dom's cell phone rang.

"I cannot believe this has happened," Mario said. "There must be another way to handle this. You cannot withdraw from the presidential race."

Dom stepped outside into the hallway to answer his cell phone. Miguel prayed that the call was news about Jennifer.

Geoff Monday had joined Vic Noble, who had in turn called in Will Pierce and every contact either man had in Mocorito had been assigned the job of finding out where J.J. Blair had been taken. So far, not one lead had panned out. Time was running out. In thirty minutes, he would have to make the most difficult speech of his life. He had truly believed that he would always put Mocorito first, above everything and everyone. Had he not been willing to risk the lives of his family and friends in order to save his beloved country? How was it that now he planned to forsake every pledge he had made to his people in order to possibly save one woman?

Jennifer.

Dom came back into the office, a look of disappointment on his face. He glanced at Miguel and shook his head.

"If I refuse to do as the kidnappers asked, they will kill Jennifer," Miguel said to Mario.

"You are being asked to choose between the woman you love and the country—the people—that you love." Mario shook his head. "No man should be asked to make such a choice."

"You know what J.J. would tell you to do, don't you?" Dom said in English, knowing Mario would not understand him.

Dom Shea's words fell on deaf ears.

"And I wish I had the strength to do what she would want," Miguel said. "But I do not. I cannot let them kill her."

"Damn it, man, don't you know that no matter what you do, they're going to kill her."

No! He could not bear to hear the truth. And he knew, in his heart, that what Dom had been trying to tell him for the past couple of hours was the truth. No matter what he did, unless they could find J.J. soon, she would die.

If she were not already dead.

And if she could make the decision for him, she would tell him not to give in to threats, to tell her kidnappers to go to hell. She would expect him to stay in the presidential race and win.

Suddenly Miguel's cell phone rang. All three of them stared at the phone clipped to his belt. With a slightly unsteady hand, Miguel removed the phone, flipped it open and took a deep breath.

"This is Miguel Ramirez."

Silence.

"Who is this?"

Silence.

"Is someone there?"

"This is Diego Fernandez."

Miguel swallowed hard. "What do you want?"

"I realize you have no reason to believe me, no reason to trust me. If I were in your shoes, I would not trust you."

"What are you talking about?"

"I know where Señorita Blair is being held."

Miguel's heart stopped. "Why have you called? To torment me? I am here at the television station right now, preparing to announce my withdrawal from the presidential race at approximately four-fifty. What more can Hector Padilla ask of me?"

"To hell with Padilla," Diego said. "I am asking you not to withdraw from the race. And I am telling you that if you come now, you can save the American woman. I can tell you where she is."

"Why should I believe you?" Miguel's pulse raced, his heartbeat accelerated alarmingly. "Why would you want to help me?"

Mario's eyes widened inquiringly. Dom Shea came over and mouthed, "Who is it?" as he narrowed his gaze and frowned at Miguel.

"When you are elected president, I want a full pardon for any crimes I may have committed, in ignorance, on behalf of President Padilla," Diego said."

"If I swear to give you what you ask for—"

"I am only a few yards away from where she is being held," Diego told him. "Give me your solemn vow that you will pardon me unconditionally and I will tell you where she is."

"I swear to you, Diego Fernandez, that when I, Miguel Cesar Ramirez, am elected president of Mocorito, I will pardon you for any and all crimes."

"Come to Colima," Diego said. "They are holding her at the old Cristobal canning plant on the waterfront."

The line went dead. Miguel closed his cell phone, then faced Dom as his mind went into overdrive trying to figure out what had just happened.

"She's in Colima," Miguel said.

"What the hell was that all about?" Dom asked. "You were swearing some kind of oath to your half-brother?"

"Mario, go on television at four-fifty and tell the people that Miguel Ramirez will speak to them shortly, that his car has been held up by the thousands of supporters who are lining the streets and blocking traffic."

"Yes, Miguel." With a stunned look in his eyes, Mario nodded.

Miguel headed for the door, calling out to Dom without slowing down. "Let's go. I know where they're holding J.J."

Following behind Miguel as he ran down the corridor, Dom called out, "How do you know that Diego Fernandez isn't sending you off on a wild goose chase?"

"Why would he try to stop me from publicly withdrawing from the presidential race?"

"Hell if I know."

Dom kept pace with Miguel as he shoved open the front door and pushed his way through the horde of supporters who descended upon them.

Once they finally made it to Dom's rental car, Miguel held out his hand. "Give me the keys. I will drive. I know where we are going."

Dom tossed Miguel the keys, then rounded the trunk and got in on the passenger side. Miguel revved the motor, backed the car out of the parking slot and nearly ran over several people blocking the street.

"Call Vic Noble and Will Pierce," Miguel said. "Tell them to meet us in Colima as soon as possible."

Dom started dialing his cell phone immediately. "Exactly where in Colima do you want them to meet us?"

"On the waterfront. At the old Cristobal canning plant."

Chapter 17

When he was a child, Miguel had come to Colima often with his grandfather and they had sat for hours fishing off the pier. Sometimes his grandfather's old friends would drop by and bring a bottle of tequila or some domestic beer and the men would reminisce about when they were young. Without fail, a man named Joaquin would recall one of his amorous moments with this or that young lady and Miguel's grandfather would have to remind him that there was a child listening.

Joaquin would always rub Miguel's head, mussing his hair, and say, "Someday this one will be quite the man with the ladies."

"Miguel will have more important things to do with his life than charm the ladies," his grandfather had said.

The others would laugh and ask what could possibly be more important.

The memory filled Miguel's mind as he parked the rental car in the middle of the desolate street in Colima.

Dom glanced over at him and asked, "Is this it?"

"No, the old canning plant is up at the end of the block." He pointed the direction. "I think it best if we walk the rest of the way. I have no idea exactly where Diego is waiting for us."

"*If* he's waiting for us."

When Miguel got out of the car, Dom followed him.

Glancing over his shoulder as he headed up the street, Miguel replied, "You think we could be walking into a trap, don't you?"

"Anything is possible. We need to be prepared." Dom patted his hip where his holster was attached to his belt, then paused, bent down and hiked up his pants leg. There attached to his thigh was a small holster containing a 25-caliber pistol, at most four inches long. He withdrew the automatic and held it out to Miguel.

"Take this and keep it on you," Dom said. "It's loaded. It holds a six-shot magazine and it's a single action."

Miguel paused, turned and took the gun. After looking it over, he pocketed the pistol and continued walking. Since every building within a two-block area was empty, some in crumbled ruins, others dilapidated and on the verge of ruin, it was highly unlikely they would run into anyone. When they neared the end of the deserted street, Miguel paused and scanned the area around him, carefully looking and listening.

"You stay here. I'll go the rest of the way alone," Miguel said. "If Diego is here and he was telling me the truth—"

"There you go again, playing God, issuing orders and thinking you have to do this alone."

"If Diego did set us up, there is no sense in both of us taking a chance, is there? If you hear gunfire, feel free to come to my rescue. Besides, if Diego was being honest with me, then J.J. is in that building and we're probably going to need backup. You should wait here for Will Pierce and the other Dundee agents."

"Nice try," Dom said. "But I'm not buying. We've come this far together, we'll go the rest of the way side by side."

Miguel would have argued, but time was of the essence. "If

Diego is waiting for us, he is probably in the alley between these two buildings."

Alert to every sound, prepared to act on a moment's notice, they crept down the shadowy alleyway between the old canning plant and the three-story brick building beside it. Halfway down the alley, Miguel caught a glimpse of a man's silhouette slinking along the wall, then disappearing into an alcove.

Miguel glanced at Dom, who nodded and drew his 9 mm. They found Diego Fernandez pressed up against a closed door in the alcove. Miguel grabbed his half-brother by the lapels of his tailor-made sports jacket and yanked him out into the alley.

"Where is she?" Miguel demanded.

"In there." Diego nodded toward the canning plant. "I'm not sure exactly where."

"If you're lying to me, I'll kill you," Miguel told him.

"If she's not here, then Hector Padilla lied to me," Diego said, pulling away from Miguel. "He's the one who told me where they are keeping her."

"Why should we believe you?" Dom asked.

"Because I can go in there and take Miguel—or you—straight to her, past any guards. Everyone knows that I am a close friend of el presidente's."

"Yeah, so we've heard," Dom said. "So why change horses in midstream?"

"What?" Diego stared at Dom quizzically.

"He is asking why, if you are such good friends with Hector Padilla, would you help me, a man you profess to hate?"

"I do despise you, Ramirez," Diego admitted. "But President Padilla has proven that he is not my friend. I hate him far more than I do you."

Miguel had to trust his gut instincts because there was no time for second-guessing. And his gut instincts told him that Diego was telling him the truth. He turned to Dom and said, "I will go with Diego. You stay here and wait for the others."

"What others?" Diego asked.

"You did not think we would come here without arranging for backup, did you?" Miguel's gaze clashed with his half-brother's.

"Very wise of you." Diego nodded.

Dom grabbed Miguel's arm. "I don't think you should—"

"I have to be the one," Miguel said. "Put yourself in my place. If she was your woman…"

Dom huffed out an exasperated breath. "Okay. Okay." He let go of Miguel's arm. "You two go in first, but if I hear one gunshot or get a gut feeling things are going down all wrong, I'll be a one-man cavalry to the rescue. And the minute the others show up, we're coming in."

Miguel patted Dom on the shoulder, then turned to Diego and said, "I am ready."

The pain in J.J.'s side had grown progressively worse, but she hoped it was now about as bad as it was going to get. She figured she'd been here a couple of hours or close to it, since coming out of her drugged stupor. The outside light spilling through the high windows had begun to fade, which told her the sun would soon be setting. So far, she had seen only three men. Two goons that she pegged as flunkies and a third man who had ordered the other two outside to act as guard dogs.

"I will keep Señorita Blair company until after the broadcast," he had told the others. "El presidente will telephone me personally when the time comes."

"What broadcast?" she had asked.

He had smiled wickedly, and she wondered why she had never noticed that evil glint in his eyes before now. "Miguel will make an announcement withdrawing from the presidential race at four-fifty this afternoon." He had glanced at his wristwatch. "In approximately three minutes."

"Miguel will never—"

"He will do it to save your life."

"No, he won't," she'd argued. "Miguel knows that I would not want him to sacrifice the future of his country to save me." She had glowered at her captor, the man Miguel had called a friend. "Besides, he knows better than to trust his enemies. He knows I will be murdered regardless of what he does."

"Love is blind, is it not, *señorita?*"

If she had thought talking to this man, reasoning with him, would do any good, she would have talked her head off, but she knew he would show her no mercy. No matter what Miguel did, whether he withdrew from the presidential race or not, his dear and trusted friend, Roberto Aznar, was going to kill her. And she suddenly realized that the son of a bitch would enjoy killing her, would take pleasure in destroying someone who meant so very much to Miguel. How he must hate Miguel. But why?

A loud knock sounded on the closed door.

"Señor?" one of the guards called out. "You have a visitor. Someone sent from el presidente himself. He wishes to see the *señorita.*"

"Perhaps Miguel has already made the announcement," Roberto said as he walked toward the door.

When he opened it, J.J. strained to see who their visitor was. But before she caught a glimpse of the new arrival, Roberto laughed and shook the man's hands.

"Come in, Señor Fernandez, come in."

"President Padilla has sent me to watch the execution," the man said. "He thought perhaps seeing you kill Ramirez's American whore would amuse me."

When Roberto returned to the room, the other man came with him. She recognized him instantly. Diego Fernandez!

"How do you plan to kill her?" Diego asked as he looked her over contemptuously.

"I'm going to slit her lovely little throat." Roberto walked over to the chair in which he'd been sitting, reached down beside it and picked up a long, leather sheath. He removed a knife with a gleaming twelve-inch blade.

"Why do you hate Miguel so much?" The question popped out of J.J.'s mouth before she realized she's spoken.

Roberto glared at her. "Are you speaking to me or to Señor Fernandez?"

"To you, you damn Benedict Arnold. I know why Fernandez hates Miguel."

"Americans have such a strange way of speaking, do they not?" Diego chuckled, then glanced at her.

What was that odd look Diego Fernandez just gave her? Had she imagined it? Or had he actually tried to communicate to her with that peculiar expression?

"You, Diego, hate Miguel because he is your father's bastard son," she said.

"I hate him for that, yes." Diego swooped down on her, his face right up in hers. "And I hate him for believing he, the son of a harlot, has a right to be president of my country." Eye-to-eye, his warm breath on her face, Diego whispered, "Be prepared."

Be prepared for what? For Roberto killing her? No, that wasn't it. He would have shouted his comment from the rooftops if he hadn't wanted her alone to hear it. God, this didn't make any sense. If she didn't know better, she'd swear that Diego Fernandez intended to try to help her.

He rolled his eyes and tilted his head backward ever so slightly as he backed away from her, then turned to Roberto, chuckling in a good-natured, buddy-to-buddy manner.

"I am also curious, Aznar, as to why you hate my bastard half-brother. The whole world believes you are his good friend."

J.J. glanced toward the closed door, wondering if Diego had been trying to signal her to expect someone to come through that door.

Was she losing her mind? Had she become delusional? What made her think that Diego Fernandez would help her, that it was even remotely possible he had brought help?

"I hate Miguel because he is a fool." Roberto placed the knife on the chair. "When we first became friends, I knew he would one day run this country, but what I did not realize was that he actually meant all the things he said, that the promises he made the people were actually vows he took seriously. He wants this country to be a great democracy, with equal rights for all. Even women." He glared at J.J. "He would make all people equal under the law."

"And that is not what you want, is it?" J.J. asked.

"I want money and power. I believed that Miguel was the man who could give me these things, that they were the things he wanted. But I was wrong. I thought as he gained more power, he would realize how foolish his lofty ideas were, but he did not. He was not the man I thought he would become. I now know that only Hector Padilla can give me what I want."

Diego placed his hand on Roberto's shoulder and led him away from J.J. "You did bring a bottle of wine, did you not, my friend, to celebrate later?"

"No, but I can send one of the men to a nearby cantina to pick up a bottle."

He's taking Roberto's attention away from me, J.J. thought, and he is physically moving him as far away from me as possible. Was she right about Diego or was this simply wishful thinking on her part?

Suddenly the outer door burst open. She caught a glimpse of Miguel as he stormed in, Dom Shea and several other men behind him. Roberto whirled around and knocked Diego aside, grabbed the deadly knife off the chair and lunged toward her. As he came down over her, aiming the knife directly at her heart, a single shot rang out. The bullet hit Roberto in the back of his head. Blood suddenly shot everywhere, spraying the floor and the walls and raining down on J.J. She clenched her jaws tightly to keep from screaming. As Roberto's body dropped to the dirt floor, the twelve-inch blade fell from his hand and landed on the ground only seconds before he did.

Miguel rushed to her, dropped on his knees and looked at her, relief in his eyes. Without saying a word, he untied her hands and then her feet.

"How—how did you find me?" she asked as Miguel lifted her into his arms and carried her toward the door.

"Diego Fernandez led us to you," Miguel told her.

She caught a glimpse of Dom Shea, Vic Noble and Will Pierce as Miguel carried her through the door and out onto the wharf. Several other men stood around watching over the two bodies lying at their feet. The two guards who had held her prisoner were also dead.

"Why would Diego help you?" she asked.

"Hush, *querida,*" Miguel said. "Stop asking me questions. I was half out of my mind, thinking I might have already lost you. Then I find you alive and I am forced to kill Roberto, a man who had been my friend…a man I thought had been my friend."

Miguel kept walking as he talked, carrying her down a long, shadowy alley, while the others followed. "Roberto was a traitor. He would have murdered you. And the brother who has hated me, who has plotted and worked against me, helped me. I owe him your life.

"I was prepared to go before the people this afternoon to withdraw from the presidential race—for you. To save you because I would rather die myself, would rather see the whole world destroyed than to lose you. What kind of president would be willing to sacrifice a nation to save one woman?"

J.J. winced as pain shot through her side when she lifted her arm and draped it around Miguel's neck. She laid her head on his shoulder and said softly, "You wanted to sacrifice Mocorito to save me, possibly even believed you would do it, but when the moment came, you would have made the right decision. You would have done what you knew I wanted you to do, what I would have expected from the man I admire and respect…and love."

"Damn you, Jennifer." He marched out into the street and straight to Dom's rental car. "I am taking you back to the hospital and I am not leaving your side until you are well enough for me to put you on a plane back to America."

"Whatever you say, Miguel." She closed her eyes and smiled. If he thought he was going to pack her off back to Atlanta, then he had another thought coming. Surely he didn't believe that after she had come this close to death and now knew beyond a shadow of a doubt how he truly felt about her, that she would ever leave him. When she recovered and was released from the hospital, she had no intention of going anywhere, except straight to the presidential palace with Miguel when he won the election.

Chapter 18

T̲rue to his word, Miguel had stayed at the hospital day and night for the next seventy-two hours—except for some sort of secret mission that had taken him away for an hour yesterday. Then this morning, Juan Esteban had arranged for a private-duty nurse for J.J. so that she could be sent home. Home to Miguel's house, not home to Atlanta. She suspected that the hospital staff had begged Juan to find a way to remove Miguel from the premises because not only had he guarded J.J. like a hawk, questioning everyone about everything they did, even tasting her food to make sure it wasn't poisoned, but he also told the nurses that he would check J.J.'s vital signs himself.

So, here she was wearing a yellow silk nightgown, lying in the middle of Miguel's king-size bed and propped into a sitting position with six feather pillows. Her gunshot wound was healing nicely and although it would leave an ugly scar, Juan had assured her the scar could be all but erased with plastic surgery. Ramona had been fussing over her like a mother hen, bringing her more food than she could eat in two days, let alone at one meal. Aunt Josephina and Seina had sent Nurse Orlando downstairs and told her to take a long break. They chatted away with J.J. while they arranged the three dozen floral arrangements that had been brought upstairs, placing half in the sitting room and the other half in the bedroom so that J.J. could see and enjoy them from her bed. She was told that another three dozen decorated every room in the house and Miguel had ordered that any others that arrived today be sent to St. Augustine's.

The three women had shooed Miguel downstairs, where "the men" were waiting for him. He had gone, if somewhat reluctantly. J.J. suspected that "the men" consisted of two Dundee agents, one CIA agent and Emilio Lopez. And perhaps even Diego Fernandez. She had tried to bring up Diego's name several times while she'd been in the hospital and every time, Miguel had told her that they would discuss his half-brother later.

"Will you two stop fussing," J.J. said. "Come over and sit and tell me what's going on." She patted the bed.

Aunt Josephina and Seina glanced at each other.

"Perhaps we should go," Seina said. "You need to rest. Miguel cautioned us not to let you overtire yourself."

"You two are not going anywhere. Something is going on and I want to know exactly what it is."

Aunt Josephina smiled guilelessly. "Whatever do you think we could possibly know, my dear Jennifer? We are only women. You do not think the men would share any information with us."

"Cut the bull, Aunt Josephina." J.J. couldn't help laughing when the old woman's mouth fell open. "Come on. Woman-to-woman. Miguel won't tell me anything. He just keeps saying that everything is fine, that I should not worry. And Dom and Vic haven't even been allowed to do more than say hi and bye to me in the past three days."

Seina sighed. Aunt Josephina glanced at the closed door.

"Hector Padilla has been arrested," Seina said, practically

whispering. "Only this morning. He was caught trying to escape from Nava."

"What?" Of all the things she had expected to hear, this wasn't one of them.

"My brother, Diego, went on television with Miguel yesterday and told the people what President Padilla had been doing and that he planned, when he was reelected, to overthrow the government and form a new dictatorship." Seina sat down on the edge of the bed. "As soon as they knew that President Padilla had lost Diego's support and the support of all the other important families in Nava, his own cabinet members turned against him and agreed to testify in court about what they knew."

"Holy sh—" Why hadn't Miguel shared all this incredible news with her? "So this means that Miguel will become president by default, right?"

Aunt Josephina shook her head. "No, no. Our Miguel insists that the Federalist Party choose another candidate. He says it is the only fair thing to do."

J.J. smiled. "Our Miguel would say that wouldn't he? That man has to be the most honorable, most noble man on God's green earth."

"Today I am proud of both my brothers," Seina said, but she had a bittersweet expression on her face. "Diego is not a bad man and in the end, he did what was right."

"He saved my life," J.J. told her. "You know that don't you?"

"Yes, I know, but he—he bargained with Miguel for your life."

"What do you mean?" J.J. asked.

"Miguel does not want her upset," Aunt Josephina said.

"I'm not upset." J.J. reached out for Seina's hand.

Miguel's young half-sister grasped her hand and looked at her pleadingly. "Diego did many bad things for Hector Padilla and he did them because he hated Miguel."

"That's not exactly a surprise to me."

"When Diego learned where you were being held, he used that information to force Miguel to agree to pardon him for all of his crimes once Miguel is elected president."

"Oh, I see. So, Diego won't be punished for anything he did, is that it?"

"Yes, that is correct. Of course, he did not have to agree to testify against President Padilla nor did he have to contact all his friends and associates, many fellow Federalists, and tell them the truth about the president, but he did. And he went on television with Miguel and—"

J.J. squeezed Seina's hand. "It's all right. You don't have to keep defending Diego. He's not exactly my favorite person, but regardless of why he did it, his actions did save my life."

"You are very generous," Seina said, her eyes misty with tears.

"So, what is the meeting downstairs all about and why all the secrecy?"

Seina looked to Aunt Josephina, as if asking for permission to speak. But before the old woman could approve or disapprove, a female voice called out from the sitting room.

"Where is everyone?" Dolores Lopez came waddling into the bedroom, Lucie Evans directly behind her. "So here you all are." Dolores came straight over to the bed, sat on the opposite side from Seina and leaned over enough so that she could wrap her arms around J.J. "You look well for a lady who was shot less than a week ago. How good it is to see you recovering so nicely."

Surprised—no shocked—by Dolores's conciliatory manner, J.J. hugged Miguel's cousin and said, "It's good to see you, too."

Nailing Seina with her sharp gaze, Dolores said, "And you must be Miguel's half-sister. I hear you are going to marry Juan. He is a good man. You are very lucky."

"Yes, I know," Seina said shyly.

"Thank God this nightmare is over and we can return to our normal lives." Dolores waved her hand at Lucie, who rolled her eyes and came over to help Dolores to her feet. "Thank you. I am so fat I cannot get up out of a chair on my own these days."

Lucie looked down at J.J. "How are you…really?"

"I'm fine. Really."

"Perhaps we should all go into the sitting room and leave these old friends alone," Dolores said. "Come, Aunt Josephina. You must tell me about the plans for Juan and Seina's wedding."

As soon as they were alone, Lucie sat on the side of the bed. "Sawyer is sending the Dundee jet to Nava tomorrow to pick us all up. When he called to tell me to bring Señora Lopez home today, he asked me to find out if you'll need for him to send either a doctor or a nurse for you. I told him I'd call him back once I spoke to you."

"I will not require a doctor or a nurse."

"Are you sure?"

"I'm very sure. You see, Lucie, I'm not going back to America with the rest of you."

Lucie widened her eyes. "You're not? Mind telling me why?"

"I'm going to stay in Mocorito with Miguel."

Lucie frowned. "Has he asked you to stay?"

"No, not yet, but he will."

"Oh, honey, he may not. I mean, after all, it's not as if you were his real fiancée. You came here on an assignment and under a tropical moon, with a handsome Latin lover charming your pants off, you could easily have misinterpreted passion for love."

"I didn't misinterpret anything." J.J. studied Lucie's expression. "Spill the beans. What are you not telling me?"

"You don't know that yesterday when Miguel and Diego Fernandez appeared on television together that Miguel confessed that you were not really his fiancée, that you came to Mocorito to work as his bodyguard. He said something to the effect that you had gone above and beyond your duty as his protector."

J.J. couldn't speak, couldn't think. God, she could barely breathe. Finally she managed one word. "Oh."

"Damn, J.J., I'm sorry."

J.J. waved her hand in an it's-all-right gesture. Tears lodged in her throat, threatening to choke her. Why would Miguel have confessed to everyone that their engagement wasn't real if he planned to marry her?

He doesn't plan to marry you, that pesky inner voice told her.

"Men can be such pigs," Lucie said. "They screw you one night and the next morning, they can't remember your name."

"Miguel isn't like that. He's not."

Lucie reached over and hugged J.J. "You're really in love with the guy, aren't you?"

"You have no idea," J.J. said as she laid her head on Lucie's shoulder and cried. Damn it, she didn't cry. Not ever. Crying was for sissies. Well, hell, she was a woman, wasn't she? Couldn't a woman cry and not be seen as weak? Especially a woman with a broken heart.

"I better get downstairs and let the men know they can't make all the decisions without me." Lucie took hold of J.J.'s shoulders and helped her sit back against the pillows. "Dom and Vic and Will Pierce are helping Señor Ramirez and his people tie up all the loose ends. You know, cross all the t's and dot all the i's. When President Padilla and his cohorts go on trial, nobody wants them getting away with anything. Our country wants Padilla and his friends to spend the rest of their lives locked up."

"So that's what the big powwow is all about, huh?"

"That's it."

"Would you tell Aunt Josephina and Seina that I'm taking a nap and I do not wish to be disturbed."

"Sure thing," Lucie said as she headed for the door. "I'll catch you later."

J.J. hadn't realized that she had actually fallen asleep until something woke her. What was that tickling her cheek? It felt like her hair was being blown against her face. She opened her eyes, but the room lay in semidarkness. How long had she been asleep? She rolled over from her uninjured side to her back and looked up into a pair of golden-brown eyes. Miguel! He was lying beside her, propped up on his elbow, gazing down at her and blowing softly against her ear.

"Miguel?"

"Yes, *querida.*"

How dare he call her *querida!* "What time is it?"

"It is past seven in the evening. You have missed dinner. I can have Ramona bring up a tray—"

"No, that won't be necessary. I'm not hungry."

"Are you thirsty?" he asked. "Would you like some water or tea or a cola or—"

"No, nothing, thank you." She couldn't bring herself to break eye contact, but damn it, looking at him was tearing her apart inside. "Are Lucie and the others still here?"

"No, they have all gone to their hotel."

"Even Dom?"

"Yes, even Dom."

"Lucie told me that Sawyer McNamara is sending the Dundee jet in the morning to pick everyone up," she said.

"Yes, I know."

"He offered to send along a doctor or a nurse for me."

"That was very kind of him."

J.J. nodded.

"But of course you told Señorita Evans to tell Señor McNamara that you did not require the services of either a doctor or a nurse, did you not?"

"Yes, I did, but—"

"Juan tells me that you should be fully recovered by election day," Miguel said.

And where would she be on election day, the day Miguel became the president of Mocorito? In her apartment in Atlanta? Visiting her mother in Mobile?

"You are very quiet, *querida*. Are you all right?"

"Stop calling me *querida*."

He looked at her questioningly. "Jennifer…J.J., what is wrong? You seem upset. If someone has said or done anything to upset you, please tell me and I will deal with them."

"Stop pretending with me," J.J. told him. "I know. Do you hear me—I know. Lucie told me."

"Señorita Evans told you what?"

"That when you and Diego made your eventful TV appearance yesterday, you confessed to the people of Mocorito that I am not really your fiancée, that I'm nothing but your bodyguard."

Miguel laughed. Damn him, he laughed.

"Yes, I told the people the truth. There was no longer any reason to keep up the pretense, no reason to continue living a lie."

"Of course not."

"*Querida,* I want—"

J.J. shoved on his chest trying to push him away from her. "Stop calling me *querida*. I'm not your darling. I'm not anything to you."

He grasped her shoulders and held her gently but forcefully. "Jennifer Joy Blair, you are my darling, my *querida*. You are everything to me. How could you not know this? I love you. I love you more than anything, even more than Mocorito."

J.J. didn't know if she was more stunned by Miguel's confession or by her own stupidity. "I am an idiot, aren't I?"

"No, you are the woman I love, the woman I want to be my wife, the mother of my children, the first lady of Mocorito." He reached in his pocket and pulled out her engagement ring. "They had to take off all your jewelry when you were in the hospital. If you would prefer to choose a different ring, I will understand."

She grabbed the ring and put it on the third finger of her left hand. "This ring is perfect. And this time it really is my engagement ring." She threw her arms around his neck and hugged him, then kissed him on both cheeks, on his forehead and finally his mouth. "You confessed the truth to your people because you didn't want to start our marriage with a lie."

"You know me so well."

He kissed her and within minutes passion flared between them. When she accidentally grazed her bandaged side against his belt, she whimpered. Miguel pulled away from her.

"I hurt you. Forgive me. I should go now and—"

She grabbed him by the front of his shirt. "You aren't going anywhere. Take off your clothes and get in bed with me right now."

"Jennifer, you are still recovering from being shot. I will sleep in another bedroom."

"I don't want you sleeping in another bedroom. I want you to sleep here with me and hold me in your arms all night."

"You wish to torture me?"

She laughed. "Well, actually, I want you to make love to me."

"No, *querida,* you are not well enough for lovemaking."

"I'm not strong enough for anything vigorous, but if you do all the work and I just lie here and enjoy it…"

He pressed her gently back against the pillows, then leaned over her, bracing himself with his elbows on either side of her. "You are a wicked, wicked woman tempting me this way."

"For goodness sakes, shut up, and kiss me again, will you?"

He did as she requested. He kissed her. And kissed her again. And soon there was not one inch of body that he had not kissed— except the small, thick square of gauze covering her healing wound, which he circled lovingly with his fingertip.

She lay there, naked and aroused, allowing him to worship her body, to touch and kiss and lick and soothe until she was half out of her mind with desire. He spread her legs and ran his tongue up and down and then back up each inner thigh. He nuzzled her mound, then separated her intimate lips and made love to her with his mouth. When she came, she cried out his name, telling him how much she loved him.

As the aftershocks of her release rippled through her, he

moved up beside her, kissed her lips and eased her gently over onto her good side.

"Yes?" he asked, as he pressed his erection against her buttocks. "I will be very careful not to hurt you."

"Yes," she told him. "Yes, yes, yes."

Yes to his lovemaking, to the sweet joining of their bodies. And yes to the love he offered her and she returned to him with equal passion and devotion. Yes to a future together as man and wife. And yes to all the joys and sorrows, all the triumphs and disappointments, to every moment, every hour, every day, every year they would share for the rest of their lives.

Epilogue

Today the Ramirez family gathered their friends together at the presidential palace for a double celebration. Miguel had just been elected to his third term as el presidente. And he and J.J. had been married for eight years. They had married on election day, in the church in the Aguilar barrio where Miguel had been christened, with only a handful of their loved ones there. Several months later, after the inauguration, J.J.'s mother and step-father had flown in from Mobile and hosted a lavish reception at the palace.

Dolores waddled toward J.J., a wide smile on her full face. She was expecting her third child, another boy the doctors had told her, which made Emilio exceedingly happy.

"Are you sure you want to do this?" Dolores asked. "Four more years of this insanity. I do not know how you do it, Jennifer. Being Miguel's constant helpmate, serving on a hundred different committees, hosting endless social events and somehow managing to win Mother of the Year awards."

J.J. slipped her arm around Miguel's waist and hugged him to her. "I can do all this because I have such a good husband. He somehow not only manages to run this country, but he finds the time to be a loving, attentive husband and a hands-on father."

Ramona brought the children in to say good-night to their parents. Dolores and Emilio's two strapping boys, young Emilio, the image of his mother, would soon turn eight and four year-old Dario, the little mischief maker, resembled his father. Behind the two Lopez boys came three adorable little girls. Six-year-old Carlotta Josephina Esteban ran straight to her proud papa's arms. The spoiled only child was not only lovely but had a winning personality.

Not allowing their young cousin to outdo them, seven-year-old twins, Luz and Lenore, named for their grandmothers, rushed straight to their father. He gathered them up in his arms and placed one on each hip. They looked a great deal like J.J., both petite and raved-haired, but they had inherited their father's golden eyes. Then last but not least three-year-old Cesar escaped from Ramona and ran to his father, grabbing Miguel around the leg. Curly-haired and chubby, his blue-violet eyes gazed up adoringly at his papa.

"We are richly blessed," Aunt Josephina said. "Three happy marriages, six perfect children—" she eyed Dolores's protruding belly "—soon to be seven. And a democratic nation in which to raise the next generation."

J.J. walked over to Seina's side and put her arm around her sister-in-law, then gave her a hug. She understood the momentary sadness in Seina's eyes, a sadness that soon vanished. Carlotta Fernandez had never forgiven her daughter for marrying Juan and befriending her half-brother. And although she occasionally saw Diego and his wife, their relationship had never quite recovered. So the people gathered here this evening had become Seina's new family, as they had become J.J.'s.

Her father had died last spring. A heart attack at the age of sixty-six. Miguel had gone with her to his funeral to pay her last respects to a man who had never loved or respected her. And he had held her in his arms while she wept that night and many nights afterward. But in the end, the most precious solace he had given her had been the joy of watching him with his own two daughters, whom he not only loved as dearly as he did his son, but of whom he was every bit as proud.

Tears misted J.J.'s eyes as she laughed when Miguel tumbled onto the floor and took all three of their children with him. He tickled them, then hugged them and kissed them good-night before turning them back over to Ramona.

"Your mother and I will come upstairs in a few minutes to tuck each of you in," Miguel promised them and they knew, even at their tender ages that their father never made promises he did not keep.

After Ramona had ushered the band of wild little heathens out of the room, Miguel came over and slipped his arm around J.J.'s waist. "Family and friends, feel free to stay up as late as you wish, continue the party until dawn. But my wife and I are going up to say good-night to our children and then we are turning in for the evening."

He then urged J.J. into movement and led her into the hallway. As soon as they were alone for half a minute, he pulled her into his arms and kissed her.

"And after we say good-night to our children, Señora Ramirez, the president would like to see you alone in his bedroom. I believe he intends to make love to you. Does his request meet with your approval?"

She wrapped her arms around his neck, stood on tiptoe and rubbed herself against him seductively. *"Sí, sí, el presidente. Sí, sí."*

* * * * *

HER ROYAL BODYGUARD

BY
JOYCE SULLIVAN

Like most little girls, **Joyce Sullivan** entertained a secret desire to be a princess. Princesses, she was sure, did not have freckles. She grew up in Lakeside, California, and often visited La Jolla, where this story is set.

A former private investigator, Joyce has a bachelor's degree in criminal justice. She credits her lawyer mother with instilling in her a love of reading and solving mysteries. The Lakeside library was their favourite destination.

Joyce currently resides with her own French prince and two teenagers in a Georgian home with an English garden and a secret garden in Quebec, Canada. You can write to her and visit her website at www.joycesullivan.com

To Julie, Lauren, Elise, Christine, Aubree,
Isabelle, Lysanne, Sophie and Gabrielle.
The princesses in my life.

Acknowledgements

My heartfelt thanks to my editor Stacy Boyd,
and to the following generous people who
came to the rescue with this book:
Ottomar Adamitz, Claire Fried Huffaker,
Teresa Eckford, Dr Stephen W MacLean,
Jake Gravelle, Jeannie Danyiel,
T Lorraine Vassalo, Rickey R Mallory and
Judy McAnerin.

Prologue

Sophia Kenilworth couldn't put off the inevitable for too much longer. She'd lied to her daughter, Charlotte Aurora, about her birth, about her father and about her heritage. She'd have to tell Rory the truth soon, before her twenty-third birthday when that despicable marriage treaty would come into effect.

Her source in Estaire had informed Sophia that her former stepson, Prince Olivier, and his wife, Princess Penelope, were still childless after three years of marriage. Despite rumors that they'd been consulting with fertility specialists, there had been no announcement of a pregnancy that might save Rory from an arranged marriage to a crown prince.

Sophia was no fool. She knew Prince Olivier was as much a martinet as his father, Prince August, had been—always placing the principality and what was best for Estaire above the needs of his own child's happiness. Sophia's deceased ex-husband had viewed the treaty as a brilliant political and economic move that would settle a three-hundred-year-old feud with the neighboring country of Ducharme and ensure that Estaire had a suitable heir apparent in the event that his son Prince Olivier was unable to provide one.

With no sign of an heir on the horizon, Sophia knew it was futile to hold out hope that Prince Olivier would rescind the contract. During her two-year marriage to Prince Olivier's father, Sophia had become well-versed in the stifling complexities and obligations of royal life. But that damn marriage treaty had been the breaking point of her tolerance.

Sophia had cried, ranted and threatened divorce for months. She couldn't believe that her beloved prince, who'd chosen her—an American bride without a family trust fund or an ounce of nobility in her veins—had heartlessly consigned his daughter to a loveless marriage.

But at least she'd succeeded in giving Rory a normal childhood away from the spotlight in exchange for the sacrifice Prince August expected his daughter to make for her country. Under the terms of the separation agreement, Sophia had no obligation to tell Rory of her birthright until her twenty-third birthday. If Rory happened to fall in love and marry in the meantime, well then, *c'est la vie.*

Sophia frowned worriedly and stirred her tea. Unfortunately, Rory wasn't seeing anyone, despite Sophia's urgings that she go out more often.

Sophia consoled herself with the knowledge that she had done her best to prepare Rory for the future that awaited her. She'd encouraged her daughter's love of knowledge and had given her a broad range of experiences. She'd insisted Rory study French and had carefully chosen the small private college that would encourage Rory to find her strengths.

And Sophia would be there to guide her daughter through the transition to palace life. Provided, of course, that Rory forgave her for keeping this secret.

With a shaking hand, Sophia carried her mug of raspberry tea out to the cliff-side garden of their La Jolla home that overlooked the Pacific Ocean. The water was lazy this afternoon, the waves jiggling and lifting like huge rolls of blue-green gelatin topped with whipped cream. Surfers in wet suits bobbed among the waves.

Sophia settled into the wooden swing that perched on an outcropping of sandstone at the rear of the sun-drenched garden. It was Rory's favorite place to dream and read, with the world and the ocean at her feet.

Sophia kicked the swing into motion. How was she supposed to tell Rory she was a princess? Or explain that her father had betrothed her to a prince?

Sophia never had time to find the right words. With a sickening lurch, the cliff beneath the swing gave way. Crying out in horror, she plummeted to the rocky beach below.

La Jolla Woman Killed in Fall.

The ten-day-old newspaper headline made the reader's pulse thrum with excitement. Was Princess Charlotte Aurora dead? There was mention of a cliff and a swing. This had to be it. The reader eagerly devoured the details: "Neptune Place…erosion…the dangers of building homes on cretaceous sandstone along the California coast… The victim was pronounced dead on arrival."

Dead. For the paltry sum of one hundred thousand American dollars.

There was no mention that foul play was suspected.

The thrill of having successfully gotten away with murder buzzed in the reader's brain like the finest champagne. Prince Laurent would not be marrying Princess Charlotte Aurora after all.

Slowly, as if relishing the last bites of a delectable meal, the reader read the final sentence of the article. *The victim was identified as Sophia Kenilworth.*

No! This could not be! The reader gouged the newsprint with the ornate silver-plated letter opener from the desk. The wrong woman had died. Princess Charlotte Aurora still lived.

Chapter One

Eight Months Later

It was her first birthday without her mother.

Rory Kenilworth felt the raw ache of loss squeeze her throat as she stuck a birthday candle in her morning cranberry muffin—just as her mother, Sophia, would have done.

She was *not* going to cry.

She sniffled. Okay, maybe she was. *I miss you, Mom. I wish you were here singing off-key and giving me a birthday card announcing this year's bonding adventure.*

Her mother's birthday presents had always taken the form of memorable moments spent together rather than the exchange of material objects—a trip to Egypt to see the Great Pyramids of Giza, an Alaskan cruise, backpacking in the Grand Canyon, a tour of Thailand. Rory's favorite had been the trip to Prince Edward Island to see Green Gables—the home of Anne Shirley, one of her favorite fictional heroines, who had the enviable ability to express herself in a way that Rory rarely had the confidence to mimic.

Even the less agreeable aspects of those birthday adventures, such as having a fifty-five-pound pack strapped to her back, her fear of horses or her tendency to get motion sickness, couldn't dampen her fond memories today.

Following in the footsteps of tradition, Rory lit the candle and stared into the leaping yellow flame.

Tears collided in her throat.

"'Happy birthday to me,'" she sang quietly. "'Happy birthday to me—'" She broke off with a choked sob as pink wax dribbled down the candle onto her muffin.

Rory covered her mouth with her hand and blinked rapidly to stem the tears stinging her eyes. She could hear the echo of her mother's soft alto singing in her ears. See her mother's proud smile.

Rory was not going to fall apart. She could share her birthday with her mother in spirit. She sighed, causing the candle to flicker. Okay, what to wish for?

Usually she wished to meet her father, but since that hadn't happened on her twenty-two previous birthdays and she hadn't found any information about him in her mother's belongings after her death, Rory wasn't going to waste her wish again. If she could have anything in the world it would be to have her mother back.

But wishing wouldn't make that happen.

She frowned. How about the miracle loss of ten pounds in a single day?

Those kinds of diet never lasted.

A good hair day?

She grabbed a fistful of amber curls. Another miracle request that had no chance of ever coming true.

How about someone tall, dark and handsome who had read the classics?

Hmm…now *that* had potential. She rolled her eyes

heavenward and laughed. "Bet you never thought I'd make a wish like that, Mom." But then, she'd never been lonely while her mother was alive. Her mother had been her best friend, as well as her parent and her only family.

Rory upgraded her wish to a tall, handsome male under thirty-five who knew that the classics referred to literature, not cartoons featuring a smart-aleck rabbit or a roadrunner, and blew out the candle.

The doorbell chimed over the muffled roar of the surf.

"Okay, that was freaky." Rory ran her fingers through the riotous curls that slipped out from her ponytail no matter how hard she tried to contain them and tightened the belt of her mother's red silk kimono that she'd donned over her sleep shirt. Not for a moment did she really think she'd find a tall, dark and handsome man on her doorstep at 8:27 a.m. on a Saturday morning, but it was *her birthday* and she was keeping her options open.

Her stomach lurched as she peered through the glass door and recognized the sleek silver bob and Ann Taylor wardrobe of her mother's steel-magnolia lawyer, Marta Ishling.

Was it a coincidence that Marta had chosen today to drop by? She opened the door. "Marta, this is a surprise."

The lawyer's surgically perfected face stretched into a taut smile as she held up the briefcase clutched in a manicured hand. "Happy Birthday, Rory! I'm here this morning at your mother's behest. May I come in?"

Rory's hand faltered on the doorknob. A fresh spate of tears stung her eyes like dust. "Of course. Can I offer you some coffee or a glass of orange juice?"

"No, thank you, dear. Perhaps later, after we talk."

Rory stepped back to let the lawyer enter, her palms damp and her stomach churning. Marta's heels clicked on the marble slabs that formed a compass on the floor of the foyer as she crossed to the sunset-red-inspired great room. She settled on one of the white ultramodern sofas.

Rory sank into a nearby armchair and tried not to appear anxious as Marta laid her briefcase on the bubble-glass coffee table from which a bronze mermaid arose.

"I confess I feel somewhat like a fairy godmother this morning." Marta laughed as she removed a black portfolio embossed with an unusual seal from her briefcase. She held the portfolio on her lap as if guarding its contents. "How much did your mother tell you about your father, Rory?"

This was about her father? Curiosity tingled in Rory's chest. "Not much. I know he was a European businessman."

Marta arched a thinly plucked brow. "That's an interesting way of describing your father's occupation. Your father was August Frederick Louis Karl Valcourt, the tenth ruling prince of Estaire, a small European principality located along the Rhine. Your mother was the prince's second wife for just over two years. You were the only child of the marriage."

Rory gaped at the lawyer, stubbing her toe on the coffee table as her knee jerked in reaction. Valcourt was the name on her birth certificate, though she'd never used it. She rubbed her toe. "My father was a prince?"

"Yes, and you're a princess. Her Serene Highness, Charlotte Aurora, Princess of Estaire, first in line to the throne." Marta beamed, preening.

"The throne?" Rory felt dazed. She'd imagined

many things about her father, but not this! Why hadn't her mother said anything? Her fragile self-esteem immediately provided the most logical answer. Her father hadn't wanted her, of course. "You said my father *was* a prince?"

Compassion softened Marta's hazel eyes. "I'm afraid he died seven years ago. But you *do* have an older half brother, Prince Olivier, who is currently ruling Estaire. He is Prince August's child by his first marriage."

Rory's crushing disappointment over the loss of her father warred with the elation of discovering she had a brother. An older brother! She'd always wanted a sibling.

Her mother's lawyer studied her. "Your brother has arrived from Estaire for your birthday and wishes to meet you for dinner tonight. He's sending a car at seven."

"Tonight?" she squeaked. "But…I need time to prepare. I don't have a thing to wear, and look at my hair!"

"You'll do fine," Marta said.

Panic broadsided Rory. "Why didn't you tell me any of this after my mother died?"

"Under the terms of your parents' separation agreement, you were not to be informed of your birthright until your twenty-third birthday when it was expected that you would assume certain responsibilities. Your father left you a five-million-dollar trust fund that will provide you with a generous allowance as of today. You'll find documents concerning the trust fund and the first monthly check in the portfolio, plus some photos your mother intended to give to you on this occasion."

Rory nodded, her knees shaking. She and her mother had been comfortably well-off, but five million dollars! She struggled to think through the layers of shock numbing her brain. Something Marta had said had raised a red flag.

"What do you mean 'certain responsibilities'?"

Marta's smile faded a notch. "Your brother will explain that to you this evening." She handed Rory the portfolio. "I'll leave you to look at this in private. Call me on my cell phone if you have any questions. Happy Birthday, Princess Charlotte Aurora."

Princess Charlotte Aurora.

Rory nearly fell out of her chair. "Wait! What do I do? Should I curtsy? Should I address him as Your Highness? How do I act?"

But Marta just waved as she left.

Rory's mouth opened and closed in soundless protest. This had to be a mistake. She could *not* be a princess. She had her life all planned out. She was going to open a children's bookstore and marry a nice handsome man who loved literature as much as she did. They'd have four children in a house overflowing with books, a dog and her cat, Brontë.

Unease furrowed her brow. She hadn't liked the sound of her parents' separation agreement that Marta had mentioned. It sounded like a contract. And most contracts, she knew from the business course she'd taken, were difficult to break.

Was that why her mother hadn't told her about her father?

Rory felt sick to her stomach. She and her mother had always been close. Having this news dropped in her lap mere months after her mother's death felt like a betrayal. Her mother had been the one person she'd trusted most in her life to be honest with her. Why had Sophia lied to her?

Hoping to find answers, Rory opened the portfolio.

Papers, documents and photographs tumbled onto the coffee table.

But Rory only had eyes for one photograph. Tears blurred her vision. She'd waited a lifetime to see the handsome blond man wearing regal gold robes and a ruby-studded crown. The father who hadn't wanted her until now.

"Hi, Dad. Your timing sucks."

BY THE TIME the doorbell rang punctually at 7:00 p.m., Rory had drawn blood with her toenail clippers as she'd trimmed her nails, ripped two pairs of nylons and decided to do without them, and rejected as impractical the possibility of disguising herself as a paper bag princess. There wasn't a shopping bag large enough to contain the volume of her hair.

She stared at herself in the full-length mirror, her stomach churning with doubts. The dress she'd bought looked great, thanks to the cleavage that came courtesy of a water-filled bra that her personal shopper had convinced her to purchase. She just hadn't realized in the dressing room that the dress would be so snug across her backside or that the narrow skirt that was so slimming would be so difficult to walk in. But the gorgeous fabric made her feel special.

She might even order champagne to celebrate the gift of a newfound brother and drown out the wounded, angry voice in her head that kept asking why her mother had never told her the truth about her father or her heritage. The French and English newspaper articles she'd found in the portfolio along with her parents' wedding pictures had only told her that her parents had had a whirlwind romance. There were no details about their divorce.

The doorbell rang again. Rory reached for her mother's black evening bag. It looked hideously conspicuous against the brilliant orange tones of the gown. Whoever said black went with everything was wrong.

She teetered toward the foyer in her high heels, feeling more awkward than elegant. Why had she believed the sales clerk's promise that strappy sandals were sexy? She felt strappy enough, but not the least bit sexy.

The bell rang a third time before she could reach the door. "Coming," she called out, hurrying forward. To her dismay, she heard fabric rip.

She looked down. The right side seam of the skirt had torn a good two inches. The doorbell chimed impatiently, accompanied by an authoritative knock. No time for needle and thread, she needed duct tape. Shuffling to the kitchen, she scavenged some duct tape from the junk drawer and repaired the torn seam. Praying that her hair still looked decent, she finally jerked open her front door, blowing at a curl that flopped over her left eye.

The man waiting on her doorstep, whom she presumed was her half brother's chauffeur, was her birthday-wish fantasy come to life. Tall enough to be imposing, he fit the image of the dark hero in every romantic novel she'd devoured in her youth. Dark brows winged over eyes that were full of intelligence and capable of great arrogance. The refined strength in his full lips and aquiline nose made her shiver with appreciation.

Though broad in his shoulders and obviously athletic, she had a feeling this man had cracked the spines of dozens of books in his lifetime. Hundreds even.

He did not, however, look friendly. She tucked the curl away from her eye. Did her hair look worse than she'd originally diagnosed? With the duct tape rubbing against her leg and the water-filled chambers of her bra pressing against her breasts, she felt like a fraud. And she suspected this man knew it.

PRINCE LAURENT OF DUCHARME rarely found himself rendered speechless. His first glimpse of Princess Charlotte Aurora was one of those rare moments. By the time she'd opened the door, he'd been about to summon Heinrich, his bodyguard, fearful that she had come to harm.

Mein Gott, what was she wearing?

With her outrageously brilliant dress in three varying shades of orange clinging to her generous curves and her golden skin dewy with heat, she looked aflame.

And that hair. Amber curls corkscrewed in wild abandon around her head and shoulders, seizing him with an insane desire to catch one in his palm.

Feeling aflame himself, Laurent searched inward for the control he had mastered as a young boy while he took in the ripe, golden cleavage that should only be revealed to her husband on their wedding night. *To him.*

Sharp talons of frustration and grief curled into his heart. His first—and only—love might have deliberately ended her life three years ago because he was honor bound to marry the woman standing in front of him.

The never-ending questions about Marielle's death had been the reason he was embarking on this charade of posing as his own deputy secretary. He would never be convinced that she'd died by her own hand, no matter how deeply he'd hurt her that night by breaking off their relationship. Marielle had had too much self-esteem to dabble in recreational drugs.

No, Laurent was convinced that someone had slipped

her the drugs and that her death had darker political roots; to ensure his infatuation with her wouldn't threaten the marriage treaty between Estaire and Ducharme, or to implicate him in her death and cause a scandal that might induce Prince Olivier to rescind the treaty. Laurent was determined to keep his presence in California and his identity a secret to protect Charlotte Aurora. He would never forgive himself for failing to protect Marielle.

"I'm sorry I'm late," Princess Charlotte Aurora said, her cheeks pinking becomingly.

"No need to apologize, Your Serene Highness," he said with a formal bow. "Allow me to introduce myself. I am Sebastian Guimond. I hold the position of deputy secretary. Prince Olivier dispatched me to escort you to his hotel. The car is waiting out front."

"Pleased to meet you, Mr. Guimond."

Her eyes were an unusual shade of violet blue, like the hyacinths—a gift from the Netherlands—that bloomed in the spring in the royal gardens of Ducharme.

The fate of two countries and the resolution of a three-hundred-year-old feud hung in the balance of his union with this woman. Three hundred years earlier Charlotte Aurora's ancestors had purchased land from a bankrupt member of his family and had formed the country of Estaire. That land had previously been under Falkenberg rule for four centuries.

Laurent's father and Charlotte Aurora's father had hoped that the marriage treaty would put an end to the feud between their two countries and improve economic and diplomatic relations. But now that Prince Olivier had confided to Laurent that his passion for mountain biking had rendered him sterile, the treaty would change Estaire's history. The tiny principality would one day return to Falkenberg rule under the reign of Laurent's firstborn son.

With rumors of Prince Olivier's infertility circulating in the tabloids, Laurent feared that Princess Charlotte Aurora's timely reappearance and the announcement of their engagement would be greeted with suspicion and resistance.

Laurent and Olivier were both agreed that they had to protect Charlotte Aurora from possible threats against her life and prepare her for the future that lay ahead of her.

Laurent remembered his role and cleared his throat, disconcerted by the vulnerability gleaming in Princess Charlotte Aurora's blue eyes. She wore very little makeup, applied inexpertly, not that she needed much with her flawless skin. "Permit me to say you look lovely, madame."

While he'd hoped to put her at ease, his compliment appeared to make her more nervous.

"Thank you." Ducking her head, she lifted her skirt with one hand, wrinkling the delicate fabric as she stepped timidly onto the cobbled front stoop, closing the door behind her. She dug her house key out of her evening bag with shaking hands, then promptly dropped it at her feet.

"Allow me, madame."

Laurent gallantly pretended not to notice her clumsiness. When he bent to retrieve her keys, he noted that her toes were as erotically golden as the rest of her, and one of them was encircled with an inscribed gold band.

He locked her door, then offered her his arm, first checking with Heinrich to ensure it was safe to proceed to the car. Heinrich signaled that all was clear. As they walked down the cobblestone path, Laurent felt the quivering of Charlotte Aurora's fingers on the sleeve of his jacket. Fresh doubts overtook him as he tried to imagine sharing his life with this awkward creature. His stomach tensed at the thought of those amber curls tumbling across the cool linens of his bed. Curling around his fingers.

She was not as polished nor as sophisticated as he had hoped. She moved unsteadily in her shoes as if walking on ice. He would have his work cut out for him training her to be a proper princess to her people, and his.

Prince Olivier had informed him that the princess had been unaware of her title and her heritage until this morning. No doubt it had come as a shock, he thought with a large measure of sympathy. He could only imagine what her reaction to the news of their arranged marriage might be. He'd been spoon-fed the importance of their betrothal along with his morning porridge.

"Who's that?" the princess whispered timidly when she saw Heinrich. At six-three, Heinrich was solid imposing muscle. His head, which Heinrich kept razored in a brush cut, reminded Laurent of a boulder.

"That's Heinrich. One of the prince's bodyguards," he said simply. "Your brother wanted you to have protection."

Heinrich opened the rear door of the limo for them. Although Heinrich's vigilant presence drew unnecessary attention, Laurent was not taking any chances with his princess's safety. There was too much at stake. A second car containing four other bodyguards would follow them at a discreet distance.

As Princess Charlotte Aurora endeavored to seat her royal person, an awkward movement to be sure in that tight-fitting gown, Prince Laurent heard the ominous tearing of fabric.

"Shoot!" A deep flush spread from the princess's face to her generous cleavage as she gazed in dismay at the damage to her gown. A slit the width of his hand revealed the delicate shape of her ankle. And there appeared to be a peculiar object dangling from the hem of her gown. Prince Laurent saw no need to embarrass her further by drawing her attention to it.

The sheen of tears dampened her eyes. He touched her arm in the lightest of caresses and attempted to salvage her pride, remembering the many occasions in his life when he'd felt suffocated by his title and his duties and wished he were anyone but a crown prince. "Take me at my word, madame. You look so radiant in that gown, no one will be paying attention to the hem."

"Really?" A tremulous smile budded on her lips. A smile so filled with naiveté that he feared the machinations and the frustrations of life in the royal court would destroy her fragile confidence in a week's time, if not sooner. Her mother hadn't lasted more than two years in Estaire.

"Indeed," he assured her, catching the tropical scent of her hair—coconut, mangoes and pineapple. "You will be dining privately with your half brother in his suite."

"Well, in that case…" To his amazement she leaned over and removed what appeared to be some form of shiny adhesive tape from the hem of her skirt. Then she grasped the torn edges of her skirt and ripped it up to a point just below her knee. She peered up at him through her lashes. "Now I'll be able to walk without breaking my leg."

Prince Laurent should have been appalled by her lack

of decorum—a princess tearing off her clothing in the back seat of an automobile…and in full view of the hired chauffeur whose integrity could no doubt be sold to the highest bidder. This was exactly the kind of situation that made salacious headlines in the press. But oddly, he felt like laughing. She was such a study in contrasts. Her forthright ingenuousness and the provocative glimpse of her tanned calf were a fascinating combination.

His princess possessed lovely legs.

As he walked around the limo he visualized her golden legs twined tightly around his hips. Her belly swelling with his heir and their children playing in the palace garden. He deliberately set his jaw as his body betrayed him by reacting against his wishes to the images filling his mind. Images that both tempted and tortured him.

His mouth pressed into a thin line. He would do his duty to his country and marry Charlotte Aurora. He would produce an heir. But he would never love her.

Not the way he'd loved Marielle. Or his mother had foolishly loved his father.

He of all people knew love had no place in a royal marriage.

Chapter Two

Rory's heart was locked in her throat by the time they arrived at the Hotel Del Coronado. The San Diego hotel on North Island had a long history of receiving royalty, including King Edward VIII who'd met Wallis Warfield Simpson here, the divorcée whom he'd loved so much that he'd abdicated the throne of England to marry her.

From the curve of the Coronado Bridge, Rory saw the majestic hotel lit up for the evening. Its distinctive turrets traced in white lights resembled diamond-studded crowns. A shiver worked over her skin.

Overwhelmed by Sebastian Guimond's commanding presence and the prospect of meeting her brother—a prince!—for the first time, she nervously soaked up every word as the handsome deputy secretary instructed her how to properly address the prince.

"Okay, I curtsy and call him Your Serene Highness. After that I address him as sir or monsieur—unless we're alone. Then I can call him by his first name. But I never call him Olivier in public," she repeated.

"Excellent."

Her knees trembled as the limo pulled up at a rear entrance to the hotel. The steely strength of Sebastian's fingers was the only thing holding her up as they stepped out of the limo and were instantly surrounded by several dark-suited men.

Rory felt as if she were in the middle of a cloak-and-dagger movie.

"More bodyguards?" she murmured to Sebastian.

He gave her an enigmatic smile. "Protection against the paparazzi and other undesirables. You will become accustomed to it. Keep moving inside the building. You are at your most vulnerable in those few exposed seconds whenever you are arriving or departing from a vehicle."

Vulnerable to what? Rory wanted to ask. Not to mention, what were other undesirables? But they were quickly ushered into an elevator and she felt too self-conscious to say anything that could be overheard by the bodyguards. Anxiety and anticipation multiplied inside her. She was about to meet her brother!

The elevator doors finally slid open with a soft ping, and she and Sebastian were whisked down a corridor.

"Smile, madame," Sebastian commanded as he escorted her into a luxuriously appointed suite. The sensual charm of his German-accented British English raised goose bumps on her arms. "You are Princess Charlotte Aurora of Estaire, and *that* is a great deal to smile about."

She shot him an uneasy glance. "Easy for you to say. You're not trapped in strappy sandals."

"Pardon?"

"Never mind." She forced an obedient smile and prayed her brother would like her. The presence of the grim-faced security guards was unnerving. Two of them took up posts outside the door of the suite. But Heinrich and two other merry men accompanied them inside. She

didn't think she'd ever become accustomed to being surrounded by guards.

Sebastian bowed to her. "I will leave you now. The
prince will be joining you momentarily. *Bonne soirée.*"

Rory wanted to plead with him not to leave, but there
was something buried in the recesses of his intelligent
eyes—a level of expectation—that made her draw a
deep breath and square her shoulders. She glanced
pointedly at the bodyguards. "Are you taking Heinrich
and his merry men with you? I don't want an audience
for my first meeting with my brother. There aren't any
'undesirables' here."

Sebastian hesitated, then he said something in French
to the bodyguards. They followed him down a hallway,
but Rory had a feeling they wouldn't be far away. She
shuddered. Being surrounded by bodyguards didn't look
like a fun way to live.

"Charlotte Aurora."

Rory whirled around, joy and uncertainty bubbling
into her heart as she came face-to-face with her brother.
He looked older than his thirty-two years. She could
immediately see the resemblance to their father's picture
in the angular shape of his jaw, the slight flare to his
nostrils and his thinning blond hair. His eyes were a
paler blue than hers. In his finely cut black tux, he was
a model of decorum and perfection—the antithesis of
her.

She curtsied inexpertly. "Your Serene Highness."

"Olivier," he corrected her kindly, his accent distinctively French. "We are alone, *ma petite soeur.*"

Rory understood his French, *little sister.*

A faint smile curved the serious line of his mouth as
he took her hand and kissed her on both cheeks. "I was

nine years old when you were born. Your hair is much as I remembered it.''

She resisted the urge to hug him, not knowing whether it would be considered a breach of protocol. ''I'm so happy to meet you! I've always wanted a brother or a sister—I just assumed I'd be younger when I got one.'' Rory knew she was gushing, but she couldn't stop. She had a big brother, and he wasn't acting as if he disliked her on sight.

Her brother bowed slightly, formally. ''I agree, it has been too long. I understand your dear mother passed quite recently. I am sorry for your loss. I remember her well.''

Rory's grief surged within her like a wave about to crest. She closed her eyes, blocking the picture that wanted to form in her mind and replacing it with a pleasanter image of her mother strolling along the beach at sunset, the foam-tipped arcs of the waves lapping upon the shore and erasing her footsteps.

She hugged herself. ''What happened between them?'' she bluntly asked Olivier. ''Why didn't they stay together?''

He waved his hand in a regal dismissive gesture.

''I will endeavor to answer your questions while we dine, *ma petite soeur*. But first, some champagne. It is your birthday—a reason to celebrate.''

She hadn't noticed the bottle of champagne on ice in a silver bucket. Easing herself onto the sofa in the ridiculous dress, she hid her evening bag behind a pillow and watched in a haze of happiness and awe as her newfound brother popped the cork from the bottle, then pressed a crystal flute bubbling with champagne into her hand.

He raised his own glass to hers. *"Bonne fête,* Charlotte Aurora. And welcome to the Valcourt family."

Rory awkwardly clinked glasses with him. She was so happy she forgot to tell him she preferred being called Rory. She took a sip of the golden liquid and felt the bubbles dance over her tongue and swirl in her belly.

Olivier set aside his glass and produced a box covered in royal-blue velvet from the breast pocket of his tuxedo jacket. An insignia in gold and red thread—identical to the crest she'd seen on the portfolio—was stitched into the velvet. "This is for you. A gift from our father. It originally belonged to his great-grandmother, Princess Anne of Greece, who wore it on her wedding day. He had it redesigned especially for you for your twenty-third birthday."

He had? Rory was moved beyond words. The idea that her father had given any thought to her feelings or needs was alien to her. A child's wish that never came true. Until now. Her heart tapped a nervous rhythm like a finger on a pane of glass as she fumbled to open the box.

Oh, my word. The delicate necklace of diamonds with a heart-shaped diamond pendant was exquisite. Rory forgot how to breathe.

Olivier lifted the necklace from its velvet bed. "The heart was part of the original necklace. The twenty-two diamonds on either side were added to signify each year he thought of you, waiting for you to turn twenty-three."

A painful lump formed in Rory's chest. "Th-thank you," she blubbered, self-consciously aware of how awful she looked when she cried. But she couldn't help it. She was a princess and she had a brother, and the necklace was proof that her father hadn't conveniently forgotten about her existence. She held still, lifting her wayward hair off her neck while Olivier fastened the necklace around her throat.

He stood back and looked at her with a measuring gaze that gleamed with approval. "*Magnifique!* Now you look like a princess."

He held out his arm to her, "Come, *ma petite soeur,* your birthday feast awaits."

"HAPPY BIRTHDAY TO ME," Rory sang to herself, hiding a tiny hiccup behind her hand. After sipping two glasses of champagne and a glass of white wine, she was feeling completely pleased with herself and less conscious of the rigid formality of the wait staff and the bodyguards in her brother's suite. Under Olivier's questioning she had already confided that she had attained a bachelor of arts in the humanities from Sarah Lawrence College. She'd told him she was working in a bookstore to learn the business so she could achieve her lifelong dream of opening a children's bookstore once she had found the perfect location and formed a business plan.

"You promised you would tell me about my parents," she reminded him as the appetizer course of pan-seared sea scallops was cleared from the table and the entrée served. "The newspaper articles my mother left me said that they met at a European trade convention."

"That is correct. I believe our father was fascinated by your mother's business acumen, as well as her beauty. At the time, Estaire's economy was struggling. During her first visit to the palace, your mother suggested we entice Hollywood producers to use Estaire's fortress city of Auvergne and the surrounding country-side to film period pieces. The movie industry is now our second major industry after tourism."

Rory glowed with pride. "That sounds like my mother—she was always able to see possibilities no one else could see. She worked as a trendsetter for a department store, traveling the world for the latest fads in home decor."

"I'm not surprised. I remember when she moved into the palace she was eager to redecorate."

"She hated antiques."

Her brother looked up from his plate of grilled pacific swordfish, amusement lighting his pale blue eyes. "I remember that, as well. She created a furor when she suggested commissioning a new set of china for the palace. The plates were to be an appalling shade of yellow stamped with a red crown. She did not succeed in her request."

Rory tucked some stray curls behind her ear, feeling slightly defensive and ill at ease. She suspected that the plates her mother had wanted to replace were dreadfully ugly and still in use. "My mother's lawyer told me they were only married two years. What happened?"

"Your mother left when you were eight months old, citing irreconcilable differences. She was perhaps too American. Too independent. She wasn't accepting of our ways."

Rory flushed, not too giddy to hear the note of censure in his voice. She toyed with a spear of asparagus and wished Sebastian hadn't abandoned her so quickly. She still hadn't decided what color his eyes were. Could intelligence be considered a color? Maybe she shouldn't have drunk so much. Or eaten so many scallops. "What ways?"

"To marry into a royal family involves great personal sacrifice, a willingness to put the needs of one's country above one's own personal needs."

Rory stole another glance toward the bodyguards hovering in the hall. Her mother had been a creative and fiercely independent woman. She'd probably hated being hemmed in by guards and rigid rules. "So it was more than yellow china?"

Olivier nodded. "Much more, Charlotte Aurora." A haunting sadness touched his aristocratic features. He placed his fork on his plate. "A disagreement over the path of your future led to your parents' separation and divorce."

"My future?" Rory frowned. Her brain was muddled from the effects of the alcohol. "I don't understand."

"I've known my duty and my destiny from the time I was a toddler. My only desire has been to carry out my responsibilities to Estaire to the best of my abilities. Unfortunately, I have failed in one regard. Princess Penelope and I have been married three years. Recently we have learned that I am incapable of fathering children and that I can not provide Estaire with an heir to the throne."

Rory was at a true loss for words. She found her older brother intimidating, but she could see that his admission caused him great pain. She reached out and touched his arm, not caring if it broke some rigid protocol. "I'm so sorry."

He looked at her fingers, but instead of reprimanding her as she expected, he covered her fingers with his own. "Just as my destiny was predetermined for me, so was yours." The gesture brought tears to her eyes. Olivier squeezed her fingers, then removed a folded sheet of paper from a pocket of his tuxedo jacket. "I don't suppose you read French?"

"Not well," she admitted with a hiccup. "My mother and I traveled to France occasionally and she insisted I study French in college, but all I can do is find chicken on a menu and read street signs."

Olivier showed her the document. "This is a photocopy of a marriage treaty. Shortly after your birth, our father entered into negotiations with King Wilhelm of Ducharme, the ruling prince of the neighboring country. He promised your hand in marriage to Ducharme's Crown Prince Laurent. It was a political move to encourage trade and cooperation between both countries. And it was hoped that the marriage would put to rest the ill feelings of a three-hundred-year feud over the purchase of land from a member of the Falkenberg family, which became the country of Estaire. The Falkenbergs are the royal family of Ducharme. They did not take kindly to having a sizable portion of their country sold beneath their noses."

Rory tried to make sense of the piece of paper and the story her brother was telling her. In a way it sounded like a fairy tale, but she didn't think she was going to like the ending. In fact, her stomach felt queasy.

"Your mother left your father when she found out about the treaty," Olivier continued gently. "She brought you back to America with her. Our father allowed you to leave with her on the condition that you return to Estaire on your twenty-third birthday to assume your title and your responsibilities to your country and to marry Prince Laurent."

Rory stared at him, horrified. The father she'd fantasized about, made innumerable excuses for and dreamed she'd someday meet had bartered her away as if she were a piece of property. Her stomach dipped and rolled.

"That's sick!" she exclaimed, indignant. "It's so medieval. No wonder my mother left him." And no wonder her mother had kept the secret to herself all these years. Her mother had been a shrewd businesswoman, and she'd bargained for her daughter's life. Well, her childhood anyway.

Rory didn't know who to be more angry with. Her father or her mother. The elegantly papered walls of the suite seemed to close in on her; the candles burning on the table seemed suffocatingly warm. "I don't want to be a princess. I can't marry a prince. What if I refuse?"

"Then you place the future of the Valcourt family's rule of Estaire at great risk. You are the heir apparent. If you resign all rights to succession then the principality would revert back to France upon my death—unless you have a child who can be appointed as the heir. I would ask you to consider that decision carefully. Prince Laurent is an honorable man, who, like me, has been raised to assume the responsibilities of his position. He is as devoted to the well-being of Ducharme as I am to Estaire. Your firstborn son, or a daughter in the absence of a son, will one day rule both countries."

Rory gulped. Put that way it made her personal wishes seem childish and insignificant. Had her mother really expected her to go through with this wedding? Why, then, had she told Rory that she wanted her to marry for love?

Rory was royally confused. "I don't know anything about being a princess. Women more qualified than me have tried and were terribly unhappy—look at Princess Diana and Fergie!"

"I have taken that into consideration, as has your fiancé." Olivier lowered his gaze. "You've already met Sebastian Guimond. He is Prince Laurent's deputy secretary. He will train you in royal protocol and etiquette. When we feel you are ready to embrace your duties, we will make a formal announcement of your impending nuptials.''

Sebastian was her royal fiancé's secretary?

Rory lurched to her feet. She needed some air and a powder room. She was never, ever, ever going to make a wish on a birthday candle again. ''S'cuse me.''

Olivier tried to stop her, ''I know this must come as a surprise, but you have a duty to your country…''

She tuned him out as she ran toward a door she hoped would lead to a powder room. A bodyguard was hot on her trail. Her stomach had coiled into a monstrous cobra that was rearing its ugly head. She yanked open the door and ran full tilt into Sebastian Guimond.

She had the fleeting sensation of being captured and held against his solid chest by arms that were strong and unexpectedly comforting. He smelled wonderful—an erotic combination of wool, linen, sandalwood and warm male flesh.

She lifted her eyes to his face. She hoped that he would tell her that this was all a sick joke. Her parents would never force her to marry a stranger.

Sebastian's eyes, she finally noted, were black as ink on a page and as bluntly revealing. His gaze summed her up and found her lacking.

Something rebellious rose in Rory. All those years of feeling that if she were only prettier or smarter, her father would have wanted to love her. To be with her. Her silent entreaty turned to a mutinous glare. Then, she clutched her stomach and threw up on Sebastian's shoes.

THE PRINCESS'S HOUSE was silent and dark, the incessant pounding of the surf outside the only pulse of life.

The hit man toured the vast shadowed rooms, seeking to redeem himself for failing to kill her and earn the rest of his reward. There was a security alarm system, but the princess had not activated it before she'd left. He nearly jumped out of his skin when a black cat with yellow-green eyes wove around his ankles, meowing raucously.

He kicked the annoying creature away from him, hard enough that it struck the wall with a howl and slunk into the shadows. He only had a few hours to accomplish his task before Princess Charlotte Aurora returned. A few precious hours to arrange her death.

Chapter Three

Rory splashed cold water on her face and groaned at her reflection in the powder room mirror. Her non-smear mascara had smeared, and her hair resembled a clump of snarled wool.

She'd never been so embarrassed in her life. She'd ruined Sebastian's expensive leather shoes. He'd behaved like a perfect gentleman, whisking a pristine handkerchief from his pocket to offer her, one arm curling around her waist as he ushered her to a powder room. He'd dispatched a maid to her aid who'd provided her with a robe, a toothbrush and toothpaste. Rory accepted the maid's offerings, then sent her away. She wanted to wallow in her misery alone.

Some birthday. The dress she'd bought to give herself confidence was as ruined as her pride. She'd completely humiliated herself. Olivier was no doubt shaking his head, regretting that she'd ever been born. She couldn't imagine what Sebastian Guimond was thinking. Yes, she could.

Well, she thought mutinously, rubbing at the mascara smears on her cheek with a facecloth. She hadn't asked to be a princess. *Mom, why didn't you tell me? Why did*

I have to find out like this? Why couldn't you have let me meet my father at least once?

A discreet knock sounded on the door. Probably the maid again. Rory gave an exasperated sigh. "Please leave me alone. I told you I'm fine."

She just needed a few minutes to work up the courage to face the carefully disguised censure in her brother's and Sebastian Guimond's expressions.

A knock sounded on the door again. This one imperious in manner. "It's Sebastian. You will open the door, Your Serene Highness."

Something in his tone warned her she could not refuse. Rory took one look at the pink splotches on her face from her vigorous rubbing and threw the facecloth into the sink. What was the use? No amount of scrubbing would turn her into an elegant, composed princess. Not when she was wearing a bathrobe over a phony water-filled bra.

She yanked the bathroom door open. "Yes?"

He looked so arrestingly debonair, perfectly groomed without a hair out of place, his feet shod in a pair of glistening black leather shoes that seemed identical to the pair she had ruined.

Her heart thudded with uncertainty. His inky-black eyes raked over her, as if taking in every curve beneath the robe's soft material and counting every pink splotch on her face. "We will begin our lessons now, madame."

Before she could protest, he entered the powder room, closing the door behind him. She instinctively took a step back as his imposing presence filled the small room.

Rory flushed red with acute embarrassment. He exuded a dangerous aura of power and savoir faire. She didn't like the hard glint in his eyes as if he'd accepted an impossible challenge.

She hiked her chin a notch and glared at him. "Don't take this the wrong way, but no thanks. If you'll just call me a taxi, I'll see myself home."

"You will do no such thing." His eyes softened with what might have been compassion. "You will be living in distinguished circles. You will meet presidents, kings, prime ministers and their representatives. Their staffs will do their utmost to see to your comfort and security. And the first lesson you must learn is how to conduct yourself when the unexpected happens and things go wrong. No matter how awkward the moment, you ignore the gaffe and continue as if nothing has occurred."

His voice hardened. "Princess Charlotte Aurora of Estaire does not leave a dinner half-clothed with her head down. The lady's maid is well trained. I suggest you make wise use of her services. You will hand her your soiled gown to be properly cleaned and request her to have something in the same size sent up from the hotel's boutique. You will allow her to offer you some cosmetics and assistance with your hair. When you are presentable, you will make a simple apology to Prince Olivier and inform him that you are not feeling well. Then I will escort you home. Is that understood?"

Rory braced her hands on her hips. "No, I don't understand any of this! Do you think I asked to be lied to my entire life? I didn't even know my father was a prince until this morning—and I found that out from my mother's lawyer." Her chin wobbled. "Frankly, I don't want to be told the proper way to act by a big intimidating male secretary who—" She stopped before she could say he made her insides tremble like the aftershocks of an earthquake. Oh, God, this was embarrassing!

She yanked her gaze from Sebastian's shocked expression. The diamonds around her throat winked back at her in the mirror.

Grief prickled like needles in her throat. She touched the heart-shaped stone with a tentative finger. Was the necklace proof her father had missed her over the years?

"Did my father really have this necklace made for me?" she demanded. "Or is it some trick that my brother and Prince Laurent dreamed up to get me to do what they want?"

Sebastian frowned, the guarded fierceness of his dark eyes sending a warning rippling through her.

Oh, God. Were her brother and Prince Laurent trying to manipulate her? Bitter disappointment seeded in her breast. Was it too much to expect her brother to want an honest, loving relationship with her?

Sebastian stepped toward her, dwarfing her with his size, yet his eyes warmed with a protective compassionate air that made her want to seek the fortress of his arms again. "You are wise not to be so trusting, Princess. Palace life has its share of machinations to be sure. There are always factions who would seek out a royal's vulnerabilities and use them for their own purposes. I can assure you that Prince Laurent has the highest of intentions for this marriage. While I owe my allegiance to him, you have my word that my only purpose is to assist you in fulfilling your destiny."

He touched the heart-shaped pendant with a long supple finger. The moisture in her mouth evaporated and her stomach twisted and clenched like clay being kneaded.

She licked her dry lips as she noted the dusting of

dark hair on his fingers. She'd never noticed that a man could have sexy, arrogant fingers. Sebastian wasn't wearing a wedding band. Did that mean he wasn't married?

"As for the necklace," Sebastian continued in his German-accented English, "I am not personally aware of its history, but there are ways to obtain information. Discreetly, of course."

Rory's eyes widened. "You would do that for me?"

Determination settled on his handsome features. "That, and more, madame. Prince Laurent would trust no other with your concerns. Can you not do the same?"

Prince Laurent. Her fiancé.

Rory's face flamed at the reminder. Could she really trust Sebastian? Whether she was being played for a fool or not, the unanswered questions she had about her father lay in Estaire. As did the possibility of a relationship with her brother, Olivier. Could she completely turn her back on what they offered? Would she be a coward if she didn't even try? What would her mother say?

Knowing her mother's aversion for confrontation, Rory suspected her mother had hoped to avoid the whole sticky situation until the last possible moment, then tell Rory she was capable of making her own choices. When Rory was twelve, she'd found a bag of feminine products on her bed along with a magazine article describing how to use them. There'd been no embarrassing mother-daughter talk.

Anger and confusion battered Rory's emotions. She had no intention of rushing into a marriage to a stranger. She retreated two steps from Sebastian's disturbing presence to regain her equilibrium. Her fingers curled into her damp palms. "I would appreciate it if you could find out about the necklace, but let's get one thing straight. You can teach me how to be a princess, but you can tell your prince that I won't be marrying him unless he meets my standards.''

Sebastian's nostrils flared. ''Indeed,'' he said, a trace of wry amusement curving his lips. ''I will convey the message. And I look forward to discovering what standards those might be.'' With a slight bow, he left her.

Rory sagged against the sink. She'd insulted his prince and made him angry. Well, that was too damn bad.

''HOW IS SHE?'' Prince Olivier inquired, tapping his fingers worriedly on the arm of a gold brocade wing chair as Prince Laurent strode into the suite's sitting room.

Laurent flashed his future brother-in-law a confident smile. ''Nothing a good night's sleep and some aspirin won't cure. She'll be joining us shortly.''

But inwardly he was concerned about Charlotte Aurora. Turning her into a proper princess would not be what Americans termed a walk in the park.

The princess could barely walk in the shoes she was wearing. And he found her refusal to marry him unless he measured up to her standards preposterous. Americans placed far too much emphasis on the romance and completely ignored the more practical issues of sharing a life together.

Charlotte Aurora's mother had disgraced herself and made a public fool of her husband when she'd ended their marriage. Laurent's commitment to Charlotte Aurora would be built on honor and mutual trust and the devotion of duty to both their countries. Members of the Falkenberg royal family did not divorce, nor did they attract scandal.

Laurent routinely used his influence and contacts in the media to maintain a low profile in the press. He exercised discretion in his intimate relationships. But evading the paparazzi and overzealous fans was no easy feat.

Last year a fashion designer he'd dated had stopped seeing him after she was attacked in the ladies' room of a bar by an obsessed woman wielding a knife. Fortunately Nathalie suffered only a mild cut to her arm and Laurent had managed to whisk her to a hospital without making headlines. But he hadn't been so fortunate after Marielle's death. His name and his heart had been trampled in the press after she'd died at a party on her family's yacht.

While the authorities had concluded that her drug overdose was accidental, the gossip rags had pumped out rumors that Marielle had committed suicide after a violent argument with him. There were rumors she'd been pregnant with his child. Other articles had claimed he'd given her the drugs. The facts feeding the articles supposedly originated from an unnamed source inside the palace, but neither Laurent nor the palace press office had been able to identify this mysterious source.

Tension tightened Laurent's body. Losing Marielle and coping with her death had been the most devastating experience of his life. He'd loved Marielle the way his mother had loved his father. As if she were a rare treasure that had been entrusted to him. But Laurent had taken to heart the last conversation he'd had with his mother before her death from renal cancer when he was sixteen. His mother had tearfully confided that her deepest regret was falling in love with her husband. She would have spared herself much suffering over King

Wilhelm's lifelong affair with his mistress if she had kept her heart intact.

Laurent had known about his father's mistress. In fact, upon his entry to puberty, his father had detailed what was expected of him, including the advisability of keeping affairs private.

Laurent had always known that Marielle could never be his wife. Nor would she have been happy relegated to the role of his mistress. The heiress to a shipping fortune, she could have had any man in the world. As soon as he'd realized she was assuming he would propose, he'd told her about the marriage treaty and explained his duty to his country.

Laurent took a chair opposite Olivier.

Olivier sighed, frowning. "I'm not sure what I expected, *mon ami,* but she is so young."

Laurent understood Olivier's sigh. He knew well the mantle of responsibility that rested on his shoulders to ensure his country had a suitable heir. Despite the rivalry between their countries, he considered Olivier to be an honorable man and a strong ally. Although Olivier had been two years ahead of Laurent at Oxford, they'd traveled in the same royal Euro brat pack, partying on yachts, in castles and in ski chalets across the continent.

Doubts registered in Olivier's eyes. "Sophia should have told Charlotte Aurora about the treaty years ago. Today was too much of a shock for her."

"I'm afraid it will be the first of many shocks she'll have to deal with," Laurent said, alluding to the numerous precautions he and Prince Olivier had taken to travel to California in secret to prepare the princess for her future and to keep her safe from any political cells who might wish to prevent the marriage from taking place.

Laurent didn't plan to reveal his true identity to Charlotte Aurora until he judged she was ready to meet her fiancé and discuss the complexities their marriage would entail. "We have to prepare her to cope with the public and the media and to recognize the risks to her personal safety—"

"At the moment I think I'm my own worst enemy," Charlotte Aurora said, interrupting them.

Laurent rose, pleased that the princess had accepted his instructions and joined them so expediently. She looked presentable—and demure—in a simple black dress that shadowed her curves and rhinestone-studded sandals. Instead of repairing her makeup, she'd scrubbed her face and tied her hair into a knot at her nape.

She clutched her evening bag, and to Laurent's consternation, he noted that she'd removed the necklace. Her eyes carried the hint of a rebellious streak. She'd carried out his order just so far.

Still, she'd made a beginning. And the fact that she'd removed the necklace suggested she was not going to let herself be vulnerable to lies. He approved.

And he planned to continue earning her trust even though he wasn't yet ready to tell her his real identity.

Her gaze raked past him as she looked at her brother. Rarely had Laurent been so ignored. He felt a rather primitive desire to fist his hand in her hair and loosen the knot. To spread the abundance of amber curls out about her shoulders and whisper in her ear that she was far more entrancing that way. Earthy. Sensual.

"I'm sorry to end the evening so soon, Olivier," she said softly. "But I need some time to digest all this. Thank you for the dinner—and for coming all this way to meet me." Moisture misted in her hyacinth-blue eyes, and her sincerity and vulnerability etched a mark on

Laurent's heart. He couldn't imagine what his life would have been like had he been denied a relationship with his father. "I really am so glad to have a brother."

"*Bonne nuit,* Charlotte Aurora." Olivier kissed her on both cheeks. "We'll talk again tomorrow, *oui?*"

Her head jerked up. Her face reddened as she stammered, "I don't mean to be rude, but I prefer Rory. No one has ever called me Charlotte Aurora."

Rory? Laurent frowned, imagining the undignified headlines the press could create with her nickname.

"*Non?* That is what I called you, *ma petite soeur.* You were named after your grandmother, Queen Charlotte. She was a very fine woman. Aurora was your mother's contribution. It came from a storybook. I remember Sophia holding you in the nursery and telling me the story of a sleeping princess with several fairy godmothers."

Charlotte inelegantly sniffed back tears. "The story was *Sleeping Beauty.*"

Olivier patted her shoulder. "When you come to Estaire I will show you a portrait of your grandmother. You resemble her."

"Really?"

"Indeed," Olivier assured her. "There are many things I wish to share with you about our family and Estaire."

Laurent experienced a cinching tightness in his chest at the wistful yearning in Charlotte Aurora's tone. What had her mother been thinking to deprive Charlotte Aurora of her heritage for all these years? Instead, Sophia had encouraged her daughter to dream of fairy tales. Sophia had enjoyed her fairy-tale wedding to Prince August, but she had run the moment she was faced with the daunting responsibilities of royal life. Only time would reveal if her daughter was cut from the same cloth.

At least the princess hadn't immediately objected to the idea of visiting Estaire to learn about her family.

Olivier nodded. ''With your permission, I would like to continue calling you Charlotte Aurora.''

''Of c-course.''

''*Bien.* You rest now. Sebastian will see you home. And, *ma petite soeur,* you must be very careful to keep this news to yourself until you are ready to accept your duties as a princess. The press can be relentless in their pursuit of a story. You must learn to be guarded about your personal life and your activities.''

''Are you kidding? My lips are sealed. No one would believe me, anyway.''

''With your permission, I would like to assign you a team of bodyguards.''

''No,'' Charlotte Aurora said firmly.

''It is for your protection,'' Olivier insisted. ''Being a royal makes you a target. I'm concerned that there may be some resistance to your marriage to Prince Laurent.''

''Well, it's nice to know I'm not the only one who has concerns about the wisdom of the arrangement. But my answer is still no. I've had enough shocks for one day without suddenly taking on two stern-faced room-mates.''

She marched toward Laurent, her sandals slapping ominously against her heels and a glint of hostility embedded in her eyes. ''I'm ready when you are.''

Laurent bowed to Olivier. ''Your Serene Highness.''

He felt the stiffening of the princess's body as he politely took her elbow. He suspected it would be a very long walk in the park.

RORY BRIEFLY CONTEMPLATED ways to ditch Sebastian as they stepped into the hallway with Heinrich, the stony-faced human tank. She didn't know where the other bodyguards had gone. She'd much prefer to take a cab home alone than to put up with Sebastian's arrogant, disturbing presence one second longer than necessary. But his strong, uncompromising fingers cupped her elbow, preventing her from dashing into the elevator without him. Her skin resonated with his touch like a single clear note picked out on a piano keyboard. Every nerve of her body was attuned to the slowly fading sound and made her feet forget where to put themselves.

She jerked her arm free of his grasp, then almost wished she hadn't when the sensation abruptly ceased, leaving her feeling unbalanced and disoriented. Any thought of running away fled when Sebastian studied her with the inky-black fires of his eyes carefully banked and his firm, sexy lips pursed thoughtfully. A shiver inched in slow motion through her limbs.

"You're angry," he commented. "It shows."

"Well, duh! My whole life has been mapped out for me without my consent. Wouldn't you be angry?"

His eyes gleamed with faint amusement. "Duh?" Rory almost giggled at the sound of the word in his odd accent.

"This is a strange American word. As for your question, madame, I would be honored to be in your position where my actions could positively impact so many lives. I would consider it a privilege."

"Then, *you* marry Prince Laurent and spend the rest of your life surrounded by bodyguards," she snapped. "I have plans for my life that don't include becoming a princess."

Sebastian raised an eyebrow and regarded her dubiously.

"What do these plans for your life include?"

Rory suspected he was mocking her, but she wasn't sure. She narrowed her gaze on him. "It's none of your business."

"If it concerns your reasons for not wishing to marry Prince Laurent, then it is most certainly my business."

Rory swallowed hard and wished he would stop looking at her so intensely.

She wet her lips and told him her plan to open a children's bookstore. She expected him to peer down his arrogant nose at her and assume a patronizing smile. But he didn't laugh at her.

"So you are interested in literature and education and promoting literacy. I applaud you, madame. That is a very noble endeavor. Think what you could do on a grander scale to further those worthy causes. That is what I meant about positively affecting lives. Prince Laurent shares those interests, as well. He believes a society is formed on the education of its children. Ignore the needs of children and society suffers for it."

Rory eyed Sebastian suspiciously. Was he telling her what he wished her to believe? Or was it the truth?

Sebastian lowered his head over hers. "What other dreams do you have, Your Serene Highness?" he asked, his rich husky voice filtering into her ears like a caress. He touched her cheek with the back of two fingers. "Do you want a partner? A companion? Children? That is what Prince Laurent desires."

Rory disentangled herself from the disturbing touch of his hand. She knew exactly what she wanted. Someone who thought she was the center of his universe, who loved her unconditionally. "What about love?" she challenged him.

"Love?" He spat the word back at her. "You Americans talk of love and the importance of it, yet your divorce rate suggests you discard it at the first hint of incompatibility. Prince Laurent does not so easily disregard his promises or his responsibilities." He glanced down the hallway as a door opened. A middle-aged man in a navy suit stepped out into the hallway and gave them an interested glance. Rory noticed Heinrich close ranks in front of them and keep a trained eye on the man. Did the bodyguard really think the man with the bad comb-over might pose a threat to them?

Rory glanced back at Sebastian. He was smiling at her.

"Prince Laurent would most certainly not approve of my discussing him in such a venue. You make me forget myself."

"I do?" Her heart spun dizzily in her chest. She told herself it must have been a mistranslation. He couldn't have intended it to come out the way it had sounded. Not for a moment did she believe that Sebastian felt anything toward her more flattering than disdain. He was her supposed fiancé's deputy secretary. She'd never met another man like him. One who fascinated her as much as he did, whose touch set her nerves jangling with warnings and fantasies and whose dark, disapproving eyes instilled her with a curious desire to earn his approval.

Sebastian took her arm again, and Rory's hypersensitive nerves reacted like wind chimes caught in a breeze, twirling and playing out a melodious song that echoed through her bones. Rory attributed it to the combined effects of the champagne and the wine she'd drunk.

He smiled down at her, a smile that made him seem younger. Less intimidating. "You do not appear so angry now. That is good. You never know when the paparazzi might take an unflattering photo and create an unflattering story to accompany it. You must learn to conceal your emotions."

Rory sighed as he guided her toward the elevator. The navy-suited man who'd arrived before them was holding the elevator for them. Heinrich entered the elevator first, positioning himself between them and the man. Rory wondered if the bodyguard truly thought that harmless-looking man would pull a knife or a gun on them. "Give it up, Sebastian. This is as good as I—"

The toe of her beach sandal wedged in the crack between the floor and the elevator cage.

"—get," she huffed, bruising her toes as she pitched forward.

She cried out, accidentally smacking the gentleman in the face with her purse as she tried to catch her balance and keep from landing nose-first on the elevator floor. The man reached toward her. Heinrich grabbed him.

Rory could see the headlines: Clumsy Princess Assaults Man and Breaks Toe in Elevator Incident.

Fortunately, an arm that felt like iron clamped around her waist and stopped her inches from disaster. "Oomph!" she exhaled.

Sebastian helped her to her feet. "Are you all right?"

Rory wanted to snap that she obviously wasn't—her toes were shrieking with pain. But before she could complain, she noticed Heinrich had the poor man pressed up against the elevator wall, his forearm burrowed into the man's throat. Her purse print was clearly visible on the shocked gentleman's face.

She was mortified. "Heinrich, let him go! I'm so sorry, mister! I didn't mean to strike you. It was an accident. I tripped."

"No harm done, young lady," the man gasped. Alcohol oozed from his breath. Rory wondered if Heinrich had smelled the alcohol in the hallway. "What are you, a pop star or something? I'm having a party in my suite tomorrow night. You're welcome to come."

"The lady says no, thank you," Heinrich said, reluctantly releasing his hold on the man.

The bodyguard extracted her sandal from the gap and passed it to her. The toe strap had torn off and rhinestones dribbled forlornly onto the floor.

Rory felt as pathetic and tawdry as the ruined sandal. Heinrich pushed the button for the lobby. Rory's stomach lurched all the way down with the elevator's descent. She couldn't look at Sebastian, but she felt the humiliation of his nearness and the wrath of that iron-hard arm still circling her waist. Even the refined scent of him—wool, linen and sandalwood—rebuked her.

Mindful of Sebastian's warning about the paparazzi, Rory jerked free of Sebastian's grasp and hobbled out of the elevator to the limo as gracefully as possible.

She ducked into the limo's secluded rear seat. It wasn't a closet to hide in, but it would do.

Clenching her ruined sandal and her purse in her lap, she braced herself for another lecture as Sebastian slid onto the spacious black leather seat beside her.

But Rory was in no mood to talk. She threatened him with the sandal. "*Do not* say a word."

NOT SINCE MARIELLE'S DEATH had Laurent been at such a loss for words. How could one articulate Princess Charlotte Aurora's predisposition for faux pas? He ignored the sandal she was brandishing like a dagger and withdrew a handkerchief from the breast pocket of his blazer. "Your foot is bleeding."

"It is not."

He illuminated the lights in the rear compartment. "I suppose that's not blood on the carpet, either."

He heard her small sigh of surrender. "When I wake up tomorrow, will this be a bad dream?"

He found himself smiling. Gently. The day—especially this evening—had the makings of a nightmare. She looked so out of sorts brandishing that sandal that he couldn't bring himself to offer more constructive criticism. He gestured for her to lift her foot, so he could bandage it.

"It hasn't been all bad," he mused as she offered her foot up for examination. "You've discovered who you really are. Some people spend all their lives without accomplishing that feat."

"I already knew who I was. Who I *am*," she groused.

He raised an eyebrow as he gently took her narrow foot between his hands. It was an exceptional foot; finely arched, the skin golden and smooth. The toes perfectly formed and unvarnished. She'd cut the tip of her big toe. She winced as he dabbed at the wound. "Perhaps I misinterpreted the expression on your face when Prince Olivier confided that you resembled your grandmother."

"Ouch!" She attempted to pull her foot away. Laurent held it firmly, curiously aware of the intimacy between them. Of the tempting golden curve of her calf. Of the sweet mermaid scent of her hair. Of the lights shimmering on the mirrored surface of the bay beneath the Coronado Bridge and the salty tang of the ocean permeating the air.

"I'm sorry. I didn't mean to hurt you."

Her chin jutted up. "The fact that I resemble a grandmother I never knew doesn't have anything to do with who I am. I want to know who my father was. What's wrong with that?"

"You don't see a connection between who your father is and who you are?"

Her foot tensed in his hands. He sensed the resistance building in her and knew she wasn't going to admit to any such thing. "What's the connection between you and your father?" she asked.

Laurent paused for an instant, considering. "He's my teacher. I see myself as the continuation of everything he taught me."

"What does your father do?"

Laurent debated how to best answer the question. "He's one of King Wilhelm's most trusted advisors."

"He's still living, then?" Envy traced her tone.

"Yes."

Charlotte Aurora tilted her head against the leather headrest, her hair cascading over her shoulder in a fragrant waterfall of curls. Her lashes slowly lifted and her eyes pierced him. "Was it your choice to follow in his footsteps or was the decision made for you?"

Laurent avoided her gaze and stared down at her slender foot. "Both. We always have a choice to act or not to act." He deftly tied his handkerchief around her toe.

Charlotte wiggled her foot free and stretched her leg out like a sleek golden cat desiring to be stroked. She eyed the neatly folded bandage critically. "Do you always do everything so perfectly?"

"I suppose so. It's how I've been taught."

"By your father?"

Laurent shrugged and extinguished the overhead

light, cloaking them in shadows. "My father is often too…busy. I've been taught by many people." For some peculiar reason he was certain that he would remember this odd conversation for the rest of his life. He felt as if he'd revealed more to this woman he was fated to marry than he'd ever revealed to anyone before. Even Marielle.

He realized how freeing it was to be Sebastian Guimond and not Prince Laurent. He felt light, as if the world were a simple place and not complicated by his responsibilities of being a crown prince. If only that feeling could last.

Her hand crept onto his on the seat, fragile and trusting. "I'm sorry."

Laurent was puzzled. "Sorry? Whatever for?"

"That your father was too busy. At least you know him."

Laurent squeezed her fingers, not knowing how to reply.

She sighed. "I wasn't cut out to be a princess, Sebastian. Tonight was proof of that. Why don't you give me a call if an opening comes available for a court jester?"

He lifted her hand to his mouth and pressed a kiss on the back. A tremor rippled to his soul at the exquisite softness of her skin and the knowledge that his behavior was entirely inappropriate for a deputy secretary toward a royal. But tonight had been an extraordinary night.

"As I recall," he said softly, "Cinderella arrived home without one of her shoes and riding a very large squash."

"It was a pumpkin, not a squash."

"The point is, she wasn't a princess to begin with,

but she still went to the ball. All I can ask is that you choose to try. The future will take care of itself.''

He heard a quiet sniff. Was she crying?

He couldn't be sure, but he continued to hold her hand until the limo pulled into her driveway.

"I'll escort you inside," he offered. "Walking will be difficult on those cobblestones with only one shoe." The roar of the surf thrummed in his ears.

Down the street Laurent heard a car door slam and an engine start. Heinrich was aware of the other vehicle, too. Laurent knew that the bodyguard would wait until he received the all-clear signal from the detail in the car following them before he'd assist the princess out of the limo.

It was all clear. Heinrich opened the door for the princess and Laurent scooped Charlotte Aurora up in his arms.

It seemed a surprisingly natural gesture.

"What are you doing?" she yelped in surprise.

"Carrying you," he murmured against the fragrant cloud of her hair as her soft curves grudgingly relaxed against his chest. "I don't wish you to injure yourself further. This seemed the safest option."

"Oh. I thought that might be the bodyguard's job."

A smile flickered to Laurent's lips. "I outrank him." True, his princess was far from what he had expected. But his heart pounded with a curious combination of wonder and desire as he carried her up the cobblestone path that curved through lush, blooming shrubbery to the striking stained-glass front door with its unusual pattern of flowing water. Her home was distinctive—as if it had artistically evolved from its coastal setting—an architectural triumph of gray weathered shingles and beams, stone and stained glass.

"Pass me your key," he ordered brusquely.

Charlotte dutifully dug the key out of her purse. "I can unlock the door. I think I can do that without creating another disaster." Proving her words, she slid the key into the dead bolt lock and opened the door.

Laurent shouldered the door open and entered the darkened foyer. "Where's the light switch?"

"On the wall to the right."

He turned and nudged the stained-glass door with his foot. The door closed with a solid thud, shuddering in its frame. A split second later something struck him from behind and glass shattered all around them.

Chapter Four

Laurent fell to the floor, shielding Charlotte Aurora with his body.

Had they been shot at?

He couldn't tell in the dark. Piercing arrows of pain in his shoulders led him to fear he'd been hit. His heartbeat thundered in his ears. Where was the shooter now? He had to protect Charlotte Aurora.

She was Estaire's only heir. If Laurent were killed, he had a younger brother who could rule Ducharme.

He ran his fingers over her, checking for signs of injury. Relief surged in his heart when he felt the rise of her chest. Good, she was breathing.

"Are you all right?" he demanded harshly. "Heinrich!" Where was the bodyguard? Had he been shot, too?

"I can't breathe," she responded in a strangled tone. "You're crushing me—"

The door to the house burst open. Laurent saw the imposing broad-shouldered silhouette of a man holding a gun. Heinrich.

Gott sei Dank! Thank God. "Watch out, Heinrich," he warned in a low tone. "There's a shooter. I've been hit."

"Stay down, sir." Heinrich ordered him, conducting a physical sweep of the darkened foyer.

Laurent couldn't have risen if he tried. He was aware of the excruciating darts of pain in his back and the inviting softness of Charlotte Aurora's body beneath him.

Heinrich moved stealthily to check the rest of the house. Laurent could hear him issuing instructions, via the communications headset he wore, to the team of bodyguards who'd followed them back to the princess's home.

Charlotte Aurora's fingers curled against his cheek. Her voice trembled. "Sebastian, have you been shot?"

"Nowhere vital, Princess. I fear you will not escape your lessons that easily."

Her laugh sounded suspiciously like a sob. She wiggled beneath him, making him acutely aware of her enticing curves. "Let me up. You're hurt. You need an ambulance."

"I cannot do that, madame. My duty is to protect your person and your safety above my own. The shooter may still be present."

She shoved at him, and he heard the fear in her voice. "Don't be ridiculous! You might be seriously wounded! Get off me right now!"

Laurent groaned as pain arced through him. "I've never been more serious in my life, Princess. Humor me."

He gripped her hair in his fingers, holding her fast. Holding on to his future.

His mind raced with questions. Had someone followed him and Prince Olivier to California despite the security measures they'd taken to avoid the possibility of leaks? Had the threat to Charlotte Aurora originated from an Estairian faction or from within Ducharme?

The lights suddenly blazed on in the living room off the foyer. "It's all clear," Heinrich said. "There's no one in the house. Or outside."

Laurent blinked, taking in his surroundings as light filtered into the foyer. Shards of glass lay scattered across the inlaid compass pattern in the marble floor. Charlotte Aurora's eyes were frightened blue pools in her delicate face. She pointed at the ceiling.

"Oh, my God, Sebastian. The ceiling fixture fell. That's what hit you."

Laurent's breath whooshed out in a grateful sigh. It was a light fixture, not an assassin's bullet. "I'll take your word for it." He gritted his teeth against the pain and eased his weight off Charlotte Aurora so she could scramble out from beneath him.

"Heinrich, please carry the princess to the other room. She only has one shoe. She'll cut herself again."

The princess crouched beside him. Her fingers lightly stroked his hair. "Don't you dare touch me, Heinrich. Call an ambulance. Sebastian has glass embedded in his back."

"No," Laurent countermanded her. He shot a look at Heinrich, who looked uncomfortable at the conflicting orders. "How bad does it look, Heinrich?"

"Tweezers and rubbing alcohol should take care of it."

"Do you have tweezers and rubbing alcohol?" Laurent asked Charlotte Aurora.

Her mouth dropped open in disbelief. "Yes, but you can't be serious. Does Heinrich have a medical degree?"

Laurent gave her a crooked pain-filled grin. "I

thought we had previously established that I am always exceedingly serious. Heinrich is trained in first aid and I trust his judgment. Please, bring the items. I have no wish to go to a hospital where it might draw attention that a Ducharmian official is in San Diego.''

Her reluctance to forgo an ambulance was stamped clearly on her face. Laurent was oddly pleased by her concern and by the trembling touch of her fingers at his temple. Perhaps she was not as immune to him as he believed. ''Please, Princess, there is nothing to be gained by taking such a risk.''

''All right,'' she finally acquiesced. ''But I'm going on record that I disagree. I'll be back in a minute.''

Laurent watched as the bodyguard carried her down the hallway. When Heinrich returned, he retrieved the light fixture's hardware from the glass-strewn floor and peered up at the wiring at the ceiling.

Laurent knew exactly what he was thinking.

''Do you think it was an accident?'' he said.

The burly bodyguard shook his head. ''I'm not an expert, sir. But *ja,* it looks suspicious.''

RORY WAS SHAKING as she searched the bathroom for the first-aid kit. It was a miracle Sebastian hadn't been killed. What would have happened if she'd arrived home alone and the chandelier had hit her? Was it even an accident?

Heinrich and his band of merry men were making her see death threats around every turn. Her hands trembled as she grabbed cotton balls and tweezers. Sebastian had been sure she'd been shot at. He'd been willing to die for her. He'd protected her with his own body. Had he anticipated that something like this might happen? Was that why her brother had wanted to assign her a team of bodyguards?

Rory suddenly viewed her brother's tactfully worded warning about resistance to her marriage to Prince Laurent in a whole new light. This arranged marriage was supposed to mend a feud that was three hundred years old. Three hundred years was a long time to hold a grudge.

She tried to tell herself that she was being ridiculous. She was in no danger. The chandelier's falling was an unfortunate accident—just like the tragic accident that had killed her mother. She thanked God that Sebastian had been there to protect her tonight. With the exception of her mother, no one had ever treated Rory as if she were special and needed protection. Or said she was beautiful as if they really meant it.

She reminded herself that it was Sebastian's job. But it didn't matter. From the moment she'd met him, she'd felt an awareness burrow under her skin like a cactus needle, invisible to the eye but impossible to ignore.

She closed the cupboard door and hurried out of the bathroom. She knew she shouldn't be entertaining these feelings for Sebastian. Not when she was officially engaged to his employer. Treaty or no treaty, she and Sebastian were from different worlds.

Rory scrounged two plastic bowls from the kitchen and hobbled back to the foyer in a pair of slippers.

Sebastian lay on his stomach on the white leather ottoman in the great room. The bodyguard had moved a floor lamp so that it shone on the deputy secretary's back like an operating room light. Rory's stomach knotted in dismay at the bits of crystal piercing his blazer.

"Oh, Sebastian, this doesn't look good."

She dumped the first-aid supplies onto the coffee table. The plastic bowls bounced to the floor. She hurriedly picked them up.

Sebastian turned his head toward her, his dark eyes soothing her. "Charlotte, it's all right. I promise I'm not going to expire."

Charlotte. He'd called her Charlotte, not Charlotte Aurora, not madame or Your Serene Highness. So, the man was capable of the occasional blunder in protocol. That, or he was in great pain.

Rory decided it was probably the latter and quickly splashed some rubbing alcohol into one of the bowls. "If I find one piece of glass that looks deep we're going to a hospital. I took a wilderness first-aid course once, and I'm not going to run the risk of you bleeding to death if an artery's been punctured. I don't care who you are."

"Why would you take a wilderness first-aid course?" Sebastian asked, his dark eyes on her face.

"My mother made me. We were going backpacking in the Grand Canyon."

Sebastian muttered something in German. One of the words sounded like mother. Rory sterilized both pairs of tweezers in the rubbing alcohol, then handed one pair to the bodyguard. "Let's pick out the glass first, then we'll remove his clothes and disinfect the cuts."

Rory pinched a piece of crystal between the tips of her tweezers. Oh, God, she'd never liked blood. "This might hurt," she warned.

"It will hurt much worse if you *don't* remove it."

Rory eased the shard of glass from his skin and dropped it in the second bowl. A dot of blood seeped through the black wool of his coat. Sebastian muttered more German under his breath. By the time she and the bodyguard had removed all the bits of glass, she'd realized he was reciting something, *"'Und das hat mit ihrem Singen die Lorelei getan.'"*

Lorelei? Why did that name sound vaguely familiar?

"There. Can you take off your jacket and your shirt?"

Sebastian sat up gingerly, his mouth so compressed that she saw a white ring around his lips. She helped ease his coat off, experiencing a peculiar urge to hug the finely tailored garment to her breast. It was warm and smelled of his luxuriously male scent, and blood.

When she moved to help him with his tie, his dark eyes bore into her, carrying a warning. "I can manage, madame."

Okay, they were back to that again. She was not a virgin, but she had never witnessed firsthand a man of Sebastian's caliber remove his clothing. He tugged free his tie with mastered grace and made rapid work of the buttons.

Her breath caught in her throat as he eased the black silk shirt off his shoulders. Muscles that the exquisite cut of his clothes had only hinted at were revealed in their finest glory. Rory had always found the descriptions of the male body in books more fascinating than the real chests she saw at the beach. But Sebastian's chest completely captured her attention. An inky patch of hair matted his chest with an air of mystery, tempting her fingers to explore the flat dusky nipples and the springy, curling hair. His skin was lightly tanned, the ridges of muscles and ribs as sculpted and defined as ridges in the sand at low tide.

Below his left pectoral she saw a four-inch-long horizontal scar. And another puckered scar beside the sexy trail of hair that dipped past his navel.

Her mouth turned as dry as a Santa Ana wind with

lust, embarrassment and concern. Had he received those scars while protecting his prince? God, she hoped not. An image of Sebastian being attacked rose in her mind. She stared at the shards of broken glass on the foyer floor that had been her mother's treasured sea-spray chandelier. Was this what her life was slated to be like? One narrow escape from harm after another?

Prince Laurent had trusted Sebastian to protect her. For the first time, Rory considered the kind of man Prince Laurent might be. She knew he was educated, noble and considerate. Would she like him? Would she love him?

"Turn around," she ordered Sebastian. "Please," she added more gently. Her heart winced at the bleeding cuts marring his beautiful shoulders. She dabbed at the cuts with alcohol-soaked cotton balls, searching for pieces of glass they may have missed. Sebastian's shoulders twitched at the sting of the alcohol.

It was all she could do not to cry out or press tiny comforting kisses near the worst of the wounds, but she knew Sebastian would be affronted...especially if she kissed him. Not that she would.

How could she go from disliking him to wanting to comfort him in the course of a few hours? Her only explanation was the champagne and the wine she'd drunk.

She sneaked a sideways glance at Heinrich to see if he was as appalled as she was by Sebastian's injuries. The gruff, unsmiling bodyguard gave her a discreet nod. At least none of the cuts necessitated an emergency room visit.

Sebastian sucked in a breath as she wiped another cut.

"Almost finished. You just need some bandages and a clean shirt. I can loan you a T-shirt." Rory and Heinrich taped at least a dozen bandages and several large gauze pads to Sebastian's back.

Rory excused herself to find Sebastian a T-shirt. When she returned, Heinrich was sweeping up the last of the shattered crystal chandelier shards with a broom and dust pan and depositing them in a double-thickness garbage bag, and Sebastian was fitting the dented metal frame of the light fixture into another bag. They were talking in German. Judging by their stubborn expressions and their curt tones, Sebastian and Heinrich were arguing.

Heinrich shrugged his shoulders. *"War das ein Unfall? Oder vielleicht ein Mordversuch?"*

Mordversuch? The word reminded Rory of the word in French for death. Murder.

She hesitated in the hallway. Did they think someone was trying to kill her? Or was she just being paranoid?

Why did Sebastian look so disapproving? Did Sebastian and Heinrich think she would be an embarrassment to Prince Laurent? An embarrassment to their country? Tonight had been a complete disaster.

Rory felt a void open up inside her. She was eight years old again with skinned knees, and no one wanted to pick her for their dodge ball team because she was such a klutz.

She swallowed hard, battling confusion, anger and the deeply rooted childhood hurt that her father hadn't thought his daughter worthy of his time and his love. She'd told Olivier and Sebastian she wasn't princess material, and Sebastian had responded that all he asked was that she try. He'd sounded so sincere. On some elemental level she couldn't fully explain, she'd wanted to trust him. Wanted to believe him.

Rory cleared her throat. She wanted the day to finally

be over and Sebastian gone from her house so she could crawl into bed and try to make sense out of the unexpected turn her life had taken. Try to figure out what she wanted.

"Thanks for cleaning up the mess." She tossed the black T-shirt she'd found in her drawer to Sebastian, knowing that it would annoy him.

He caught the shirt easily with his left hand, his intelligent dark eyes telling her he knew that she was deliberately baiting him. "Thank you."

He pulled the T-shirt on over his head without so much as ruffling his hair. The soft cotton fabric stretched taut over his chest and biceps. He tucked his ruined shirt and jacket in the garbage bag with the light fixture.

"Heinrich, if you will be so kind as to leave us a moment. I will join you outside momentarily." He gestured toward the garbage bags. "Take this with you."

"Leave it. I'll take it out in the morning," Rory objected, but Heinrich followed Sebastian's orders.

Her insides quivered and trepidation raced over her skin like the trace of a feather as the bodyguard left. Sebastian stepped toward her, his jaw locked tight and his inky eyes unfathomable in their intent. He touched her chin with his thumb, his voice surprising her with its gentleness. "Will you be all right here alone?"

"Yes, of course I will," she said waspishly. "I'm not a helpless female. Besides, I need time to think."

He nodded. "Good night then, Princess. I hope you remember this day fondly for the rest of your life."

He was kidding, wasn't he? But no, she saw that he wasn't. His eyes dropped to her lips and for the craziest moment Rory thought he was considering kissing her. Her pulse kicked up into a frenzied state of alarm.

She waited expectantly. "Oh!" A soft sigh—half disappointment, half relief—escaped from her lungs when his strong fingers encircled her hand instead and he brushed a warm, electrifying kiss over her fingers.

"Happy birthday," he murmured huskily. He didn't immediately let go of her hand.

Rory forgot about the gaffes she'd made this evening. The warmth of Sebastian's fingers, his imposing presence and the secrets banked in his eyes held her spellbound. How could the closeness of a man's mouth be so distracting?

She inhaled, feeling her ribs expand at the swift intake of oxygen filling her lungs. She held up a finger. "Promise me one *little* thing before you go?"

One corner of Sebastian's mouth quirked. A skeptical line creased his cheek. "Just one?" he teased.

Rory blinked, flustered. Was he flirting with her?

"Put your mind at ease, madame. I will inquire at the hotel for a doctor to make what you Americans call a house call."

She smiled gratefully up at him. Even though she was wearing a pair of fuzzy yellow smiley-faced slippers and a water-filled bra, she felt more confident. More beautiful. "Wise decision, because wilderness first aid is a far cry from medical school. But seriously, promise me you'll never call me Princess Charlotte Aurora when we're alone. I'm not going to be able to do this if I lose myself."

She saw the objections mount in his eyes, but she wasn't up for another protocol lecture tonight.

"I can't, Sebastian. I won't," she said mulishly.

To her relief, he nodded solemnly and squeezed her hand. "*À demain,* Rory. Tomorrow is a new beginning."

Rory. One tiny victory in a day marked by mishaps. She'd settle for that. "*À demain,* Sebastian."

Rory closed the door after him, taking care to throw the dead bolt and set the security alarm. It couldn't hurt to be a little bit more conscious about safety. She usually only set the alarm when she was working.

On the abalone-inlaid table near the front door she noticed the ruined beach sandal resting beside her black evening bag. A tiny band of rhinestones hung precariously by a thread from the sandal. Had Sebastian left it there?

Rory reached for the broom that Heinrich had leaned against the wall to give the floor another sweep. She didn't want Brontë, her cat, to get a sliver in her paw. Her gaze shot back to the beach sandal. Funny, this wasn't how she remembered Cinderella turning out.

BRONTË'S PLAINTIVE CRIES roused Rory just before noon. The wooden shutters in her room were closed against the bright glare of the California sunlight. Rory blinked in the shadowy interior of her room, trying to orient herself as the whole embarrassing sequence of her birthday played through her mind like a half-baked comedy. The visit from her mother's lawyer. Meeting her brother. The gift from her father. Had she really thrown up on Sebastian's shoes?

Yes, she must have. Her stomach still felt unsteady, and a headache buzzed in her brain. Her fingers curled into the sheets as she remembered the way Sebastian had shielded her from flying glass last night. She yanked the sheet up over her head. Had he debated kissing her when he'd said good-night? Or was that only a fanciful flight of her imagination?

Brontë meowed again, the sound oddly muffled.

Rory sighed. "Brontë? Here, kitty. Did I lock you out last night?" Her cat usually slept curled up at the foot of her bed. She lowered the sheet and checked the door. Bad move. Her brain sloshed inside her skull like the gyrations of a lava lamp.

The bedroom door was open.

Brontë meowed again. Her cry sounded closer. Maybe she'd trapped the cat in the closet when she'd gone hunting for a T-shirt for Sebastian.

Dragging herself out of bed, Rory slid open the white shuttered door to the closet. "Sorry, baby," she crooned. "I didn't mean to lock you in."

Rory waited for the black long-haired Persian to appear and twist around her ankles, seeking a good-morning petting. "Come on, girl. Don't be shy." But no cat. Rory climbed into the closet to make sure Brontë wasn't curled up in her dirty laundry hamper.

She stubbed her cut toe on a shoe. *Ouch.*

Brontë was not in the closet. Rory listened for cries. "Come on, girl. You've got to be somewhere. Did the glass falling scare you? Come on out. Everything's fine now."

Rory peered under the bed. The space was jammed with books and magazines she'd read but didn't have room for on her bookshelves. "Hey, Brontë, are you under there?"

"Me-ow."

"You are under there." Rory pulled out several stacks of books and lay belly down on the hardwood floor. Brontë's yellow-green eyes gleamed from a cavern of books beneath the center of the bed. She stretched out a hand, shoving piles of books aside to clear a path. "Here, kitty."

Brontë didn't move. There was a pitiful sound to her

cry that wasn't right. Rory forgot about her headache and her sore toe. "What is it, sweetie? Are you stuck?"

Rory debated shoving the bed to one side, but was worried she might inadvertently topple some books on her pet. Poor Brontë was obviously frightened enough.

Shoving books out of the way to make a narrow passage, Rory wriggled under the bed until her fingers finally found Brontë's sleek head.

"Meow," the cat cried piteously, licking Rory's fingers with her sandpaper tongue.

Rory scratched her beloved pet behind the ears and murmured coaxing words. Brontë started to purr but made no effort to move. Hooking her arm around her pet's body so she could draw her out gently, Rory scooted backward the way she'd come—and came to an abrupt, painful halt when her hair got caught in the metal frame supporting the mattress. She tried to pull her right arm up to free the snared lock, but the passageway she'd made through the books was too narrow. Her phone started to ring.

Her head jerked at the jangling, pulling her hair. "Ouch! I'm coming, hold your horses," she muttered at the phone as she tugged her head to one side, hoping to free herself. But she succeeded only in yanking her hair taut to the roots. "Ow!" The phone rang again, insistently.

Brontë wailed pitifully.

It was probably her brother, Olivier, calling to arrange another meeting. Or maybe Sebastian wanting to book a time for her princess lessons.

Rory's heart raced at the thought of facing Sebastian again after last night. Would she still feel that undertow of attraction to him today? Or had that been a byproduct of nerves and too much to drink?

Rory jerked at her hair again, trying to free herself and the cat and get to the phone. "It's okay, girl. Just another minute." Her eyes smarted as the hair pulled at her tender scalp. Damn, it was no use. She was stuck. She gave up and collapsed, sneezing at a dust bunny.

Why did these things always happen to her?

RORY WASN'T ANSWERING her phone. Laurent hung up when her voice mail came on, choosing not to leave a message. He'd try again in an hour. The princess had told him last night she'd needed time to think. Even though he'd instructed Heinrich to assign two body-guards to watch over her home last night, Laurent was worried.

Was she safe? She could have been killed or horribly wounded if the heavy chandelier had struck her. Laurent's back throbbed. The hotel's doctor had recommended X-rays to ensure that glass wasn't embedded under the skin, but Laurent had declined. The doctor stitched three of the wounds and put antibiotic ointment and bandages on the rest. He'd told Laurent he would have a few scars. Scars were the least of Laurent's concerns.

Ignoring the twinge of protest in his bruised shoulders, he clasped his hands behind his back and paced in front of the windows of his suite. A panoramic view of the Pacific Ocean stretched toward a horizon shrouded with haze. The sun was burning through a layer of cloud cover, and seagulls dived over the waves. What were the chances of a light fixture crashing to the floor like that? Was it a coincidence? Or had it been an attempt to kill the princess under the guise of an accident?

Laurent had immediately alerted Prince Olivier of the incident when he'd returned to the hotel.

Prince Olivier had been shocked and concerned. They'd discussed the possibility of moving Rory to the hotel or hiring female bodyguards to protect the princess twenty-four hours a day. Olivier had approved of Laurent's forethought in bringing the fixture back with him so they could have an electrician examine it for signs of tampering, which Laurent planned to accomplish today.

A discreet knock sounded on the door of his suite.

"Enter," he commanded.

"Good morning, Prince Laurent," his royal press secretary, Odette Schoenfeldt, said to him in German. "You wished to see me?"

"Yes." Laurent cast an appraising eye on Odette who looked cool and elegant in a pale-lavender suit that accentuated her willowy figure and her high cheekbones. Her ice-blond hair was twisted into a knot at her nape and her gray-green eyes held a measure of calm that Laurent always appreciated when chaos threatened. He gestured for her to be seated. She demurely crossed her legs at the ankles, the hem of her skirt short enough to be sexy, yet well within the confines of propriety.

Laurent had known Odette since they were children. Her family, with their blood ties to the royal houses of Greece, the Netherlands and Great Britain, had always been part of the Falkenberg royal circle. Laurent could not remember a birthday when Odette had not been present. He'd even kissed her once on one of her birthdays. He couldn't remember how old they'd been, but they were young enough to hide in a coat closet and she'd been wearing braces.

He trusted no other with the diplomacy of his mission to California. He was counting on Odette to assist him with tutoring Rory in how to act and dress the part of a princess and future queen. And to deal with the press.

"How are the arrangements coming along?" he asked her.

She smiled. "Nearly finished. I've booked a top Beverly Hills hairstylist and a makeup artist to give Princess Charlotte Aurora a complete makeover at a nearby spa—appointment time to be confirmed. They've both signed confidentiality agreements. And I'm negotiating with a Hollywood stylist to attend to her wardrobe. The press will go crazy when they discover they've had a princess living in their midst. We want her looking and feeling her best."

"What about the French and German lessons?"

"Handled. A tutor is on retainer."

"Excellent. There is one other small matter I would like you to attend to—immediately."

"Certainly, Prince Laurent."

He gave her an abbreviated account of the incident and showed her the skeleton of the light fixture that he'd salvaged. "I'm quite all right," he assured her when she paled. "But I would like you to find an electrician. Have him examine this for signs of tampering."

"Tampering?" Odette frowned delicately. "Are you suggesting someone tried to harm the princess?"

"We both know that there are factions within Estaire—and within Ducharme—that may be opposed to this marriage."

Reproach rose faintly in the calm gray-green wash of her eyes. "Why did you not inform me of this last night?"

"It was late. The princess was not injured and I was assured by the hotel management that the doctor who examined me is the soul of discretion."

"Very well, then." She rose and curtsied. "I will locate an electrician immediately." She slid the fixture back into the bag to take with her.

Laurent delayed her on her way out. "Odette, be careful. Don't mention this to anyone on Prince Olivier's staff. There may be a leak."

"Understood."

OOOMPH! RORY BRACED one arm on the floor and lifted herself onto her toes, taking the weight of the bed onto her back. All she had to do was lift the mattress and box spring high enough so that she could wiggle her right arm free and untangle her hair from the metal crosspiece supporting the box spring. She was never going to use the space beneath her bed for a bookcase again.

Brontë mewled as the box spring rose. Rory freed her right arm and tugged viciously at the lock of hair that was caught in the crosspiece, hearing strands break. But hey, at least she was free. She lowered the bed down, then hooked her arm around her pet and slid out the rest of the way. Brontë hissed and sank her claws into Rory's arm.

Rory felt sick to her stomach when she saw Brontë's right front paw. It was swollen and misshapen. Definitely broken.

Her phone rang again as she was rushing Brontë out the door to the cat hospital. Rory ignored the summons. She put Brontë's carrier in the back seat and revved up the engine. Being a princess would have to wait.

THE LISTENING DEVICE had been worth the investment. Prince Olivier's personal secretary, Renald Dartois, frowned with concern as he eavesdropped on the private conversation between Prince Laurent and his press secretary taking place in the suite across the hall. So, Prince Laurent feared a plot was afoot to kill his intended bride.

Renald was not surprised. Why should Estairians embrace as their princess an uncouth American who'd been raised on a beach and who clerked in a bookstore? Renald shuddered at the very idea. Equally appalling was the prospect of Estaire's return to Falkenberg rule after three centuries of independence.

Renald had been groomed all of his life for a position of importance in the palace. His mother had been a close friend of Prince August's first wife. When Renald had finished school with high marks, he'd been singled out for an entry position on Prince August's personal staff. While Renald had held the prince in the highest regard, the treaty he'd negotiated with King Wilhelm of Ducharme was proving as disastrous as his marriage to that hussy Sophia Kenilworth.

Estaire must remain under the rule of the Valcourt family. Despite Prince Olivier's fears that modern technology would not be able to help him father a child, Renald was confident that Prince Olivier and Princess Penelope would soon be the proud parents of a Valcourt heir. He had researched everything—including DNA. The clinic had provided him with detailed information about its procedures, and he knew exactly what to do if the first cycle failed to prove successful. DNA would prove the child was a Valcourt.

"I will locate an electrician immediately," he heard Odette Schoenfeldt assure Prince Laurent, followed by the sound of plastic being rumpled.

"Odette, be careful. Don't mention this to anyone on Prince Olivier's staff. There may be a leak."

Renald smiled to himself and hurried to the door to

his suite. He waited, listening. The door to Prince Laurent's suite opened and footsteps passed by his room. Renald eased the door open a crack. Odette was leaving. She was carrying a large green garbage bag.

He slipped into the hallway after her. He would make sure there was no evidence. Then he would call Princess Penelope in Estaire and ask for further instructions.

Chapter Five

It was late afternoon before Rory zipped into her driveway in her red convertible with Brontë in her animal carrier on the back seat. She'd bought a fish taco and a soda from a fast-food drive-through on the way home, but she was exhausted and worried sick over Brontë's broken paw and cracked rib. She'd thought her beloved pet might have fallen or been hit by a car, but the veterinarian believed Brontë had been kicked.

What kind of sick person kicked a cat?

Rory was furious. She hated to think one of her neighbors capable of such an act. It must have happened after she'd left for dinner because while she was dressing Brontë had been fine. The curious cat had jumped up onto Rory's dresser and attacked the tissue in the shoe box.

The more she considered the warning her brother had given her last night about keeping her princess status a secret, the more worried Rory became that Brontë's injuries had not come from a neighbor. What if someone had entered her house while she was out and had tampered with that light fixture? Rory planned to call an electrician to have a look at it first thing Monday morning.

She climbed out of the car and lifted Brontë's carrier from the back seat. Now that she was home she planned to make herself a cup of herbal tea and snuggle with Brontë on the kitchen windowseat. They could both have a snooze.

As she headed up the cobblestone walk, Rory paused. An eerie sensation prickled over her scalp and spread down her back. Her front door was standing open.

Had she forgotten to close it when she'd raced out of the house earlier? Or had an intruder broken in while she was gone? She'd been too worried about Brontë to bother setting the alarm.

And her birthday necklace was in her evening bag, in plain sight on the table near the door! Rory hurried forward. How could she have been so careless? She'd never forgive herself if the only gift she would ever receive from her father was stolen.

She'd almost reached the door when the distinctive double tap of hard-soled shoes on the marble floor in the foyer froze her in her tracks.

Oh, God, someone *was* in her house!

What should she do? Go next door and call the police?

She didn't have a cell phone; she didn't have anyone in her life whom she could call from the grocery store to ask if she should bring home milk or lunch meat. Clutching Brontë's carrier protectively, she backed down the walk. She'd cut through the shrubbery to the Krugers' house—

"Aaah!" Rory screamed, nearly dropping Brontë as a hawk-nosed, dark-suited man appeared in her doorway. His stone-cold eyes narrowed on her. Fear catapulted to her chest and hammered at her heart. Brontë hissed. The man could be one of her brother's bodyguards, but Rory wasn't taking any chances. For all she knew she was facing down the person who'd kicked her cat and had rigged that light fixture to kill her.

"Stay away from me," she warned, her voice shaking. "I've just called the police."

Her heel hit a stone as she retreated another step. She stumbled, but quickly regained her balance as a second man appeared in the doorway.

Sebastian.

Rory's body sagged with a different kind of unease. Sebastian looked as fierce as a warrior en route to the battlefield, his brows bold strokes of charcoal on the tense planes of his face.

Uh-oh, this wasn't good, she thought as his gaze swept over her. She flushed, remembering that she'd snatched her Hawaiian print capris and halter top from the floor before she'd dashed out of the house to the vet's. And she hadn't bothered to comb her hair or put on lipstick.

Her hair. Rory cringed. She'd driven with the top down on the convertible. Okay, she was not going to punish herself by picturing a mental image. Sebastian had no right to show up without calling first.

Suppressing a sigh of annoyance she marched toward him. "What are you doing in my house?"

Sebastian bowed to her. "Your Serene Highness. I was concerned about your welfare. I phoned several times—"

"So you just came dashing over with your bodyguards? Didn't it occur to you that I might not have felt like talking?" She rudely nudged him out of the way so she could enter her home. Why was he glowering at her? "What did you do, have your muscle men pick the lock?"

"No, I—the door was unlocked when I arrived." He glanced down at the carrier, his expression puzzled. "Someone saw you load a suitcase in your car and drive away like a madwoman this morning. I thought—" he faltered.

She glared at him. "You thought what, that I'd run away?"

He had the grace to look uncomfortable. "Quite honestly, yes."

Rory told herself that she shouldn't feel hurt. Sebastian was a stranger to her. His opinion was irrelevant. "Thanks for the vote of confidence, teacher."

"You evaded the two guards I'd posted on the house."

"You posted guards on the house when I specifically told you I didn't want them? I don't believe this!" Rory whirled away from him. Her purse slipped off her shoulder and slapped against her legs.

"It was necessary. For your protection."

"Argh!" Rory clenched her teeth and marched through the foyer to the kitchen, Brontë's carrier still in her arms. Oh, she knew exactly why he thought it was so necessary that she had protection! That little snippet of conversation she'd overheard last night between Heinrich and Sebastian was proof they thought someone was trying to kill her.

But first things first. She wanted to get Brontë settled on the windowseat. The vet had told her that her pet needed plenty of rest.

Heinrich was in the kitchen, studying her address book and her calendar, which he'd spread out on the soapstone-topped island. He jerked up guiltily.

"Don't mind me, Heinrich, you go right ahead and

invade my privacy," she snapped. "I've got nothing to hide." But apparently Sebastian and her brother did.

Sebastian dogged her into the kitchen. "Leave us, *bitte*," he said to Heinrich, snapping his fingers.

"That's a neat trick, Mr. Secretary. I'll have to try it. Snap my fingers and watch people disappear. Will it work on you?" She gently set Brontë's animal carrier on the cushioned windowseat and opened the door.

"Here, we go, girl. Home sweet home," she said, settling Brontë in her favorite sunny spot on the pillows. The cat purred contentedly and swished her tail.

"What happened to her?" Sebastian leaned over her shoulder. Rory inhaled the distinctively rich scent of sandalwood combining with his clothes, with him.

She swallowed hard and gazed out the window. A stiff breeze ruffled the broad fronds of the palm trees. A kidney-shaped pool, its form softened by silvery mounds of ornamental grasses, dwarf evergreens and flamingo-pink geraniums, was tucked close to the house in the cobbled rear courtyard. Beyond the pool, the exotic orange flowers of birds of paradise and sprays of blue plumbago created pockets of color against the glossy dark-green leaves of lemon, orange and grapefruit trees. Ruby-red impatiens blazed in the shelter of an enormous avocado tree.

Rory let her gaze travel to the spot at the back of the garden where her swing had once stood.

"Rory?" Sebastian prodded gently, his fingers brushing her bare shoulder.

Her heart pulsed with an acknowledgment of him that was overwhelming. Her gaze remained rigidly fixed on the spot where her swing had once stood. The spot where her mother had died.

Hot, stinging tears blurred her vision. Rory told herself she was not going to cry. She was too angry and horrified by the suspicion that was fraying the edges of her control. She wanted to know the truth.

She rubbed Brontë behind the ears. "According to the vet she was kicked, Sebastian," she said tightly. "It happened last night—after I left for dinner. I think there was an intruder in my home who fiddled with the chandelier. That's really what my brother was trying to warn me about last night, isn't it? You're not just worried about the paparazzi. You think someone wants to kill me, which explains the bodyguards and sneaking into the hotel through the back entrance—and the tense words you had with Heinrich when you were cleaning up the glass. Admit it."

Her intelligence was commendable. He cupped her bowed shoulders. "It's a possibility," he admitted.

"Why?" she asked. "Because of the feud?" She tilted her head back, her fragrant curls tumbling over his hand, her blue eyes sharp. "Don't even think about lying to me, Sebastian."

Laurent was relieved to see the firmness surfacing through the wounded visage that her body language projected. "Ahh, the truth. 'It takes two to speak the truth—one to speak and another to hear,'" he quoted.

"That's Thoreau."

"Yes. For far too many years the people of Estaire and Ducharme have been unwilling to truly speak to one another, and to listen. They compete against each other in a world market rather than working together to foster opportunities that would benefit both countries. Had you grown up in Estaire, your marriage to Prince Laurent might have been viewed with more tolerance. A Romeo and Juliette story.

"But your long absence from Estaire and your

brother's inability to provide Estaire with an heir complicates matters considerably.''

Laurent allowed an amber curl to twine around his finger. "Estaire has been independent from Ducharme for three hundred years. I'm sure they view the prospect of being forced back under Falkenberg rule in much the same way that Americans would embrace the concept of accepting Queen Elizabeth as their sovereign.''

"What if I just refused to marry Prince Laurent?'' Rory asked. "The worst that could happen is he would be insulted and the feud would continue.''

Laurent frowned, but he didn't take her comment personally. One of his tasks was to teach her to evaluate the repercussions of her actions. "Your brother views this treaty as a means of preventing the worst from happening. If he were to die before you were properly trained to rule Estaire, your country could be plunged into political unrest. Prince Olivier has trained since birth to be a ruler. It would be strategic on his part to see you married to Prince Laurent who has been similarly trained.''

Tension bunched in her shoulders, giving away her emotions. "You don't think I can do it on my own?''

"It is too soon to tell, madame. It is a formidable undertaking.''

"Rory,'' she reminded him softly, her voice choked.

"Rory,'' he corrected. He caressed her shoulders, fighting the urge to hold her and reassure her that he would be with her every step along the way. She needed to find her own core strength, her own confidence. "You will have to win your people's hearts and earn their loyalty.''

"Provided someone doesn't kill me first.'' Her gaze

remained rigidly fixed on the horizon. Beneath her fingertips, her cat licked at the cast covering her paw.

"I will do everything in my power to keep you safe," Laurent promised, trying to interpret her thoughts. Was she scared? Would she run from her responsibilities as her mother had? He hoped she would commit herself to her duty, and to him.

"Then stop shielding me from the truth. Do you think whoever tried to kill me last night killed my mother?"

He stilled. Her mother? "What do you mean?"

"Didn't my brother tell you? She died eight months ago." Rory touched the windowpane. Laurent saw a tear course down her golden cheek. "Out there. On my swing. At the rear of the garden—overlooking the ocean. It was set back from the cliff by six or eight feet. It was my favorite place for dreaming and reading. My mother never sat there, but that day she did and—"

A shudder racked her thin shoulders. "The cliff gave way beneath her and she fell. The police said it was erosion, but now I don't know what to think. How could a swing be a murder weapon? But then I never thought of a light fixture as a weapon, either." She twisted around to look at him, the horror in her eyes reminding him of the sleepless nights he'd lain awake questioning Marielle's death. "Sebastian, do you know something I don't?"

"Mein Gott." His heart filling with compassion for her, Laurent lowered himself onto the windowseat and pillowed her head against his chest. The fragrant cloud of her hair tickled his nose.

She felt as soft and vulnerable as a child in his arms.

"I am so sorry. I was not made aware of this." But gut instinct was clamoring that it might have been staged—just like the light fixture that had fallen last night. No questions. Just another tragedy on the evening news. He had to protect Rory no matter what the cost.

Rory sniffed, her voice muffled against his shoulder. "Maybe my brother didn't know. Maybe my mother's lawyer didn't tell him." She choked back a sob. "I loved her so much. If she was killed, I want to know."

Laurent caressed her back. "I'll find out," he promised.

"Do you have evidence the fixture was tampered with?"

Laurent told her the truth. "I have someone looking into it. I'll inform you of the results." When the bodyguards had called to say that the princess had evaded them, his first priority had been to find her. He hadn't checked with Odette yet.

Guilt pricked his conscience that he was withholding his identity from her. But telling her now would only apply more pressure and make the situation more awkward. She had so much to learn before she could decide what was best for her, and for her country. And he hoped, too, that by then she would see what a partnership their marriage could be, based on common goals and concerns.

"Would it upset you too much to show me where the swing was located?"

She drew away from him, moisture glistening on her cheeks as she wiped at her face. "I can handle it. If someone killed my mother, I want them punished."

He handed her his handkerchief. "I'll get Heinrich. He trained with Interpol."

By the time he had returned to the kitchen with Heinrich, Rory had washed her face. A resolute air was stamped on her delicate features.

He remained close by her side as she unlocked the sliding glass door and walked out into the courtyard.

The blistering heat of the July afternoon seared his head and shimmered like stars on the surface of the pool. The surf clapped like sporadic applause as Rory silently led them to the back of the garden where the ocean and the sky merged into an enormous canvas of azure. The vegetation ended abruptly where soil became rock. Laurent's stomach knotted when he saw the jagged scar in the sandstone cliff that resembled a bite taken from a cookie.

Sunbathers dotted the boulder-dotted beach below, and Laurent prayed that her mother's end had been swift, without suffering. It could have been Rory.

Keeping a tight rein on his emotions, he cautiously took a step closer to the edge of the cliff.

But Rory restrained him, fear riddling her eyes. "Be careful," she pleaded.

Laurent tucked a stray curl behind her ear. Whether she knew it or not, they had a destiny together. "I promise. You wait here."

He joined Heinrich, who was examining the rock face below the edge of the break.

After a few moments Heinrich pointed out a horizontal gouge in the cliff about three meters down at one end of the bite mark. Then pointed to a similar gouge another meter below that. When Laurent looked carefully, he detected more gouges on the rock face at the other end of the bite mark.

Heinrich shook his head. "It's ingenious. A professional job. If I'm not mistaken, those are drill marks, though the stone is so crumbly you'd need to know what you were looking for to spot them. He probably lowered himself over the cliff with a rope attached to one of the trees in the garden and used a drill to start cracks along the section he wanted to fall off, then let gravity do the rest. The combination of her mother's weight and the vibrating motion of the swing probably set it off.''

''What do you mean 'a professional job'?'' Rory said from behind them. Despite the intense heat, she was shivering.

Heinrich deferred to Laurent.

Laurent had never felt so angry. So without power. First he had lost Marielle. He was not going to lose his princess. ''It is what you would call a hit man, madame. Someone was hired to do this.''

LAURENT STUDIED THE KNOBS on the gas range. He had never used a stove before, but Rory was huddled with her cat on the windowseat with a glazed look in her eyes. She needed a cup of tea. And he'd much prefer the bodyguards attend to their duties and keep his princess well protected.

He selected a knob. With a clicking sound, a flame appeared in the front left burner. He moved the kettle to that burner. Then he opened kitchen cupboards searching for a teacup and saucer. There were none. But he found some large mugs with ghastly surfboards and seagulls on them.

It was easier to locate a teaspoon, although the drawer in which it resided was in need of tidying. The kettle was whistling by the time he unearthed the tea bags in a canister on the counter. The princess most definitely needed a household staff, as well as a dresser and a lady's maid. Except that Laurent had no intention of allowing her to remain here. It was too dangerous.

He'd already notified Prince Olivier that the princess would be taking up residence in the hotel.

He poured water into the mug and added the tea bag. The scent of strawberries steamed from the mug. He had no idea what to do with the tea bag once he deemed the tea properly brewed. For lack of a better solution, he set it on the rim of the sink beside a bottle of vitamins. He had not seen any trays in the cupboards so he carried the tea to her on a sandwich plate.

"Drink this," he ordered.

Rory pulled herself out of her fog of grief and saw the mug of tea on the plate and the concern on Sebastian's darkly handsome face and felt less alone. She was still wrestling with shock and guilt that her mother had died in her place. She was shaking too much to drink the tea so she set it on the cushion beside her. "Thanks." Her hand sought the comforting sleek softness of Brontë's flank. "So, how do we go about finding out who killed my mother?"

Sebastian frowned at her disapprovingly. "*We* leave the matter in Heinrich's capable hands, because that is his job, and *we* begin the business of teaching you your duties, which is our job. Heinrich will make inquiries through the proper government channels and get a copy of the police report and request that experts examine the drill marks. There may be some evidence that he can connect to intelligence gathered by Estaire's or Ducharme's police agencies. In the meantime, our priority is to keep you safe. Your brother is making arrangements for you at the hotel. It's not safe for you here."

Rory dug in her heels. In the past thirty-six hours she'd experienced enough upheaval. Even though she was scared, she was not going to be chased out of her home. The hit man had worked his booby trap with the light fixture and was probably long gone by now. And if he decided to come back he'd be caught by Heinrich and his band of bodyguards, which suited Rory just fine.

"Well, you should have consulted me first. Brontë has a cracked rib and a broken leg. The vet told me she needs a tranquil environment to recuperate in. It would be too stressful to move her to an unfamiliar environment."

She'd annoyed him. Even though his face was carefully composed, she knew by the pulse that throbbed just above his starched collar that he expected her to do whatever he said. Too bad. She had a mind of her own.

"May I point out that the assassin may have rigged other booby traps."

"You think I haven't thought of that? I'm sure Heinrich is itching to search the house to find them—if he hasn't already. I'm *not* leaving."

Two indentations dug into the corners of his mouth. Rory sighed inwardly, wondering what it would be like to kiss the firmness of Sebastian's lips. Would he be as controlled as he appeared? Or was there a dark untamed passion lurking beneath the surface?

"Then you will consult with Heinrich to secure your residence and your person with suitable protection?"

"Just because I don't want to be run out of my home, it doesn't mean I'm stupid. It feels like I'm consigning myself to jail, but yes, I'll consent to some security. However, I'm not going to walk around in public surrounded by Heinrich's merry men. If I have to have bodyguards, I don't want them to look like undertakers." She reached for her mug of tea. "It would be nice if one of them was a woman."

Amusement—or it might have been respect—flickered warmly in his inky eyes. "Now that that is settled, I should like to discuss your schedule. With your permission, we will start our lessons first thing in the morning.''

She inhaled the soothing scent of strawberries from her mug. ''I'm sorry, you'll have to schedule the lessons for the afternoons. I work at the Book Nook weekday mornings.''

''Of course. You haven't had time to hand in your notice.''

Rory jerked her head up. Tea splashed over the rim of her mug and spotted her skirt. She rubbed at it. Fortunately, the multicolored Hawaiian print would hide the stain. ''Who said I was quitting?''

Sebastian bowed his dark head. ''My apologies. Given the circumstances, I assumed you would be handing in your notice. You have a great deal to learn and very little time. Your brother was hoping for a formal announcement of your engagement in the beginning of September, with the ceremony to be held in February. It's impossible to plan a royal wedding in under six months.''

September! Rory gulped. In six weeks she was going to be officially engaged to a stranger. Panic threaded through her. She thought she was going to hyperventilate. As if sensing her distress, Brontë lifted her head and meowed, What's up? as her yellow-green gaze met Rory's.

Rory put the mug out of spilling range and huddled over her cat, shutting Sebastian out. She'd never been in love. But she wanted love in her marriage. The kind of deep, lasting love that she'd read about in books. A love that was respectful, nourishing and passionate. Could she really give herself to Prince Laurent without that? She didn't even know what he looked like. Would she respect him?

"Rory?" Sebastian gently touched her hair.

Rory shivered as her scalp prickled with warmth. She resisted the urge to lean into his touch, to depend on his strength. He wanted her to marry his prince. "You can schedule the lesson for one-thirty. I...I'll let you know if I change my mind about quitting my job. Now, please, just leave me alone. Tell my brother I'll call him later." She wasn't quite ready to admit to herself—or to anyone else—that her life had unalterably changed.

HE LOUNGED BY THE POOL, the sun baking his skin and glinting off the gold medallion circling his throat, as if granting a benediction for a job well done. There had been no word yet on the news, but therein lay the brilliance of his work. The fatal accident could occur at any time. Science told him that the nuts he'd loosened on the chandelier wouldn't hold for long. The vibrations caused by the simple opening and closing of the door should be enough to jar them loose. Then, bye-bye princess.

The first few bugle notes of "Taps" on his cell phone broke into his soliloquy. He reached for the phone on the poolside table beside the piña colada he'd been sipping.

The caller's tone was icy. "I was under the impression I'd hired the best. I could forgive the first error. But once again the princess has escaped the tragic accident you'd planned for her. Need I remind you that you will not receive the remainder of your fee until the job is done."

"Chill. I *am* the best, which is why you have nothing to worry about. Do you think I only planted one booby trap? I always have a plan B. Even if she escaped being sliced to ribbons, it's only a matter of time until the princess closes her pretty blue eyes and never wakes up. You can bank on that."

Chapter Six

Rory felt a rush of homecoming as she slid the key into the lock of the Book Nook fifteen minutes before the store's opening. She glanced back anxiously over her shoulder.

Heinrich hadn't been able to supply her with a female bodyguard on such short notice, but the men assigned to her were wearing golf shirts and dress slacks. Franz, the hawk-nosed bodyguard, was feeding coins into the *USA TODAY* distribution box on the corner. The other bodyguard was parked in her red convertible across the street.

They had told her they would keep the bookstore under surveillance from different locations, occasionally entering the store to browse. If she left the store, they would discreetly appear. Heinrich had equipped her with a container of pepper spray that looked like a pen and a pretty little bracelet that had a panic button. All she had to do was press the button and they would come running.

It was a compromise she could live with. At least she wouldn't have them constantly hovering over her shoulder while she was waiting on customers.

The shop bell tinkled cheerily as she pushed the door

open and was instantly enveloped in the scent of books. Rory loved everything about the shop, from the cozy reading nook in the shop's front window to the white-painted custom-built shelves that lined the walls.

Rory locked the door behind her, flipped on the lights and went into the back office to plug the kettle in for a cup of pineapple Waikiki tea and to remove the cash for the till from the locked bottom drawer of the filing cabinet.

She hadn't slept well last night. She'd been too worried about Brontë and the announcement of her engagement in September. She hadn't felt hungry this morning so she'd taken a vitamin and brought a yogurt cup with her to work.

Monday mornings in the shop were traditionally quiet after the weekend rush. Her first task, once she'd hung the Open sign, was to tidy the shelves and stock any books that had arrived Friday afternoon, but Rory went to the travel section instead.

She selected the European travel guides and carried them to the front desk where she booted up the computer.

Time to do a little research on Estaire and Ducharme.

She looked up Estaire first.

It gave a brief account of the wealthy Austrian Prince Valcourt, who purchased the land from a bankrupt Falkenberg count in the 1700s and created the principality. The Falkenbergs had attempted to take back the land by force twice, but failed. It also described Estaire as a fairy-tale land of medieval castles, lush Rhine meadows and quaint villages. The capital city was Val des Monts. There was nothing about her father. They only mentioned that her brother Olivier was the ruling prince.

The books told her that Ducharme had a population

that was sixty percent German-speaking and forty percent French-speaking. The German population affectionately called it Liebenfels, meaning charming rock. The small kingdom had once been part of the Roman Empire and its history had been molded by the armies that had marched across it and by the treaties and alliances the powerful Falkenberg family had made with France, Spain, Prussia, Bohemia and the Netherlands in the seven hundred years of their rule.

Rory winced, wondering how many of those treaties had been marriage treaties. She rubbed her temple, feeling the beginning of a headache.

She snacked on the yogurt she'd brought for breakfast as she looked up Ducharme's official Web site on the Internet and clicked on an English version of the Web page. Pictures of cobbled streets, gracious fountains and mansions built by wealthy Renaissance burghers lined the top of the screen. She clicked on an inset picture of the royal palace Schloss Hohenheim, a magnificent blend of medieval and neo-Gothic architecture. The breath whooshed from her body.

Not in a million years could she imagine herself living there, much less sharing a bed with Prince Laurent.

She clicked on an inset picture of King Wilhelm—an imposing elderly man with iron-gray hair, black brows and a stern mustache. There were no pictures of Prince Laurent or other members of the royal family.

Next she tried an image search through Google. Over a dozen postage-stamp-size pictures appeared on the screen. Rory peered at the tiny pictures of the slender, dark-haired prince. Some were taken when he was a child, some were family groupings—the royal family of Ducharme she imagined—and some appeared to have been taken in his teen and adult years. She clicked on what she hoped was a recent photo to enlarge it. But the link took her to a page of German text and no picture. She tried the other images. The same thing happened. Frustrated, but determined not to be outsmarted by technology, Rory saved several of the pictures on the hard drive, then enlarged them on her own. Unfortunately, the photos were too grainy to tell whether her prince was totally hot or a total toad.

On a whim, she did a search on "Lorelei." A chill brushed her skin when she realized what Sebastian had been reciting while she'd picked slivers of glass from his back. He'd been reciting a German poem written by Heinrich Heine of the legendary Rhine mermaid Lorelei, who sat combing her hair on a high rock overlooking the Rhine near St. Goarshausen. Her beautiful song lured boats to their doom.

Did Sebastian think she was a mermaid who would lure his prince to his doom?

The bell on the door tinkled. Rory hit the close button and summoned a smile as a sunburned man in his twenties wearing board shorts and a navy tank top stepped into the shop. His streaked blond hair was parted in a ragged line, and the blunt ends swept his jaw. He wasn't one of her regular customers. She'd have remembered him.

"Hi, can I help you?"

His English was laced with a strong French accent. *"Allo, mademoiselle."* He leaned comfortably against the counter. "I need some books to read at the beach. Can you recommend something?"

"Fiction or nonfiction?" she asked.

His golden-brown eyes skimmed her with blatant interest, then grazed the travel books she'd spread out over the counter. "Fiction is more entertaining, *non?*"

"Okay, fiction. Do you like thrillers, mysteries, science fiction?"

"Something set in California."

"We have a shelf with works by local authors. There's a mystery set in a vineyard in the Napa Valley. And a thriller set in Los Angeles."

She showed him to the section displayed on a table near the door. "Are you a tourist?"

"Yes. A lonely tourist."

Rory flushed. Was he hitting on her? Maybe he meant bored. "You're never lonely when you have a book to read."

He selected several hardcovers off the shelf at random and handed them to her. "I'll take these."

"That was easy."

His lips twitched in a cocky grin. "I am that kind of guy. Easy."

Now Rory knew he was hitting on her. She scurried back to the cash desk to ring up the purchase, feeling flustered. He handed her a gold credit card. She quickly rang in the purchase and checked the name on the card: Claude Dupont.

La Jolla was a wealthy enclave. While many of the Book Nook's customers were well heeled and well traveled and of varying international backgrounds, the fact that Claude Dupont had a French accent put her mildly on edge. Was he from Estaire? Was he involved in a plot to kill her?

She felt the blood drain from her face. She practically thrust the bag of books at him, reddening when one of the books tumbled out onto the counter.

"I'm sorry." She clumsily jammed the book back into the bag, watching him closely. If he even looked at her suspiciously, she was pressing the panic button.

His fingers brushed hers as he took the bag from her. A ripple of uneasiness washed through her stomach.

"Are you free, *mademoiselle,* for dinner? I would very much like to get to know you better. In my country, we dream of California girls during the long winter."

Long winter? He must be French Canadian. Still, she wasn't interested in Claude's dreams. She just wanted him gone. "Sorry, I don't date strangers."

Claude propped an elbow on a travel book and gave her a cunning, pearly toothed smile. "Then it is very simple. I will make a point of becoming your friend."

She looked over in relief as the door signaled the arrival of another customer. It was Franz, checking on her. Good ol' Franz. Excellent timing.

Okay, maybe she was jumpier than she'd thought. Even though Sebastian had left a message on her answering machine that an electrician had found no evidence that her chandelier had been tampered with, she was grateful that he'd silkily maneuvered her into agreeing to the bodyguards.

Claude took one look at Franz's don't-mess-with-me expression and tapped two fingers to his forehead, saluting Rory. *"À bientôt, mademoiselle."*

Rory managed a tepid smile. *Don't count on it.*

"Are you all right, Your Serene Highness?" Franz inquired politely after Claude had gone.

"I'm fine," Rory lied, hugging herself. She turned back to her research. She didn't like this fear that Sebastian and Olivier had instilled in her. Was she destined to spend the rest of her life being afraid?

BETWEEN CUSTOMERS she printed off the information she'd found on the Internet about Estaire and Ducharme, including the lineage of the Valcourts back to the first prince of Estaire. She'd also found an article on the Falkenberg royal family, although it was in German. With the help of a German dictionary, she was attempting to translate it.

She wasn't making much progress.

She was happy to put it aside when one of her favorite customers dropped into the store at eleven-thirty. Stoop-shouldered, his skin freckled and weathered from the sun, Otto Gascon made a regular habit of dropping into the Book Nook to browse on Mondays and Thursdays before joining his cronies for lunch and an afternoon of chess.

Rory didn't know much about him except that he was in his seventies, retired and a widower. He lived in her neighborhood and she occasionally saw him walking on the beach or sitting on a bench with a plaid blanket covering his lap, reading a book.

His watery-gray eyes met hers warmly. His brow was damp with perspiration as he doffed his straw hat with a gnarled, blue-veined hand. "Good morning, young lady. You are looking hale and hearty. I've come about a book."

Rory laughed as he handed her a newspaper clipping from his wallet. Every week without fail, Otto brought in a review clipped from the book review section of the paper and requested a book. "I hope we have it."

She wasn't surprised to see he wanted a biography of a famous news anchor. Otto's reading tastes leaned toward biographies, travel, books about the world wars and the occasional political thriller. "We don't have it in stock yet, but it should be any day. I'll set one aside for you."

"Wonderful. I'll just browse in case something tempts me." He glanced down at the counter at the travel books and the German dictionary. "Are you planning a trip?"

"Actually, I'm trying to translate an article."

"Do you speak German?"

Rory grimaced. "No, that's what makes it hard."

"Perhaps I could help. I'm a little rusty, but I should be able to manage. My wife was from Germany."

"You never told me that." Rory slid the article toward him. "Would you?"

Otto nodded. "Ah, I see. It's an interesting choice in articles, although it's three years old. It's about King Wilhelm of Ducharme. He was asked when his son Prince Laurent, then twenty-seven, would succeed him to the throne. The king responded that he doesn't believe in making his son wait until his death, but that he would like to see his son married and settled with children before he assumes the responsibility."

Ice encased Rory's heart. Sebastian had told her about the feud, but he hadn't mentioned this.

Was Prince Laurent determined to marry her for altruistic reasons and the good of his country, or because his father was holding the treaty over his head and it was the only way he could get the crown?

Did it matter?

Otto peered at her. "May I ask what spurs your interest in Ducharme and King Wilhelm? Ducharme is a beautiful country. Excellent wines. Castles. The Rhine. Everything a young girl finds romantic."

"It's a long story, Otto."

"I'm retired, my dear. I have nothing but time."

Rory hesitated, tempted to confide in someone. She'd known Otto for years—well, for the two years she'd been working in the bookstore, anyway. But he wasn't a stranger. He was a neighbor, and the fact that he knew

German might prove helpful in figuring out what she was going to do about this marriage treaty. But her brother's warning about telling anyone of her new status made her hold back.

"I appreciate the offer, but I don't feel like talking about it today. Do you know anything else about the royal family of Ducharme?"

Otto frowned. "Well, the queen died years ago. Tragic. Some sort of illness. King Wilhelm never re-married. Prince Laurent has a reputation as a playboy. Lots of women. There's a younger brother, Prince Leopold, I think. He's a top-ranked soccer player."

So Prince Laurent was a playboy. Her brother thought she was going to marry a playboy?

Rory had heard enough. It was about time she asked Sebastian some serious questions about Prince Laurent.

FIVE MINUTES BEFORE her shift at the Book Nook ended, Rory received a call from Sebastian.

"Come out the rear exit when you're finished. The limo will be waiting."

More cloak-and-dagger stuff. Rory didn't bother asking about her car. She figured the bodyguards would take care of it. She'd planned to go to the bank after work with the check from her trust fund, but it would have to wait until tomorrow. "Will you be there, too?" she asked.

His voice was firm, reassuring. "Of course."

Hearing his voice, Rory realized how quickly she'd come to depend on him, and how disappointed she was that he'd only given her one side of the story about his prince. Still, what had she expected? He did work for Prince Laurent. "Good, because I have a bone to pick with you."

She hung up on him before he could respond.

Her knees trembling slightly and her fingers clutching the research she'd gathered, Rory walked out to the limo ten minutes later. Thank God nobody shot at her or pelted her with tomatoes.

She gave the bodyguard a nervous smile and slid into the limo's icy interior.

Rory took a deep breath. For the rest of her life, every time she smelled sandalwood or linen, she would think of Sebastian. His inky eyes compelled her to look at him as if he suspected the hurt she carried. He was so incredibly handsome. So incredibly what she wanted, so completely not what she was allowed to have. The ache in her heart grew.

Okay, be smart, she told herself. Keep it business.

He bowed his head, his tone perfectly composed. "Your Serene Highness."

"Sebastian." She plopped the stack of papers onto the perfectly creased oatmeal-colored linen stretched taut over his sleekly muscled thighs. He was wearing a snowy, crisp cotton shirt and a yellow silk tie that brought out the blackness of his eyes.

Laurent was instantly on guard. In her white gauzy sundress, Rory resembled a goddess on the warpath. Her skin glowed with a dewy sheen, and her blue eyes sparked with lightning. The discomfort of the stitches in his back was superseded by the taut reaction of his body to her beauty.

Holding himself in check, he examined the pile of documents. "Is this the bone you wanted to break?"

"Not break. Pick. You pick a bone. And yes, this is it," she snapped. "You neglected to tell me a few crucial pieces of information about Prince Laurent."

Laurent could think of only one crucial piece of information he'd left out. His real identity.

He read the top document. It was in German. Something she'd downloaded from the Internet. "You read this?"

"Well, duh! I used a dictionary. You didn't mention that King Wilhelm was holding this treaty over Prince Laurent's head. It says right there that the prince won't become king until he's married and has a family."

"You figured all that out with a dictionary? Impressive." He thumbed through the other documents, admiring her initiative and her thoroughness. She hadn't accepted anything that he and Prince Olivier had told her at face value. She'd researched Estaire and Ducharme. And him. At least there were no pictures of him, thanks to the foresight of the palace press office, which had posted notices that the sites were under maintenance.

"You didn't mention that Prince Laurent is a playboy, either. Do I strike you as the type of girl who would be happy married to a playboy?"

Laurent's conscience stirred, rumbled like a fabled beast with dark grasping tentacles. He could give her everything she had told him she wanted out of a marriage: a family, children, a partnership. Even the dog and the cat. "Is that what you think marriage is about—happiness?"

"No, I think marriage is about love. Commitment. What does a playboy know about love?"

Enough, Laurent thought. Love had destroyed his mother. It had destroyed Marielle. And it had nearly destroyed him.

"You shouldn't believe everything you read. The press wants to sell papers. People would rather read about the 'playboy prince' out on the town than the 'hardworking prince' who carries out his duties.''

''You didn't answer my question.''

Laurent's gaze was drawn to the haunting blueness of her eyes. To the hunger and vulnerability that lurked there. His jaw clenched. Rory was so naive. He didn't think he could bear it if their marriage destroyed her. He sought the right words. This was the lesson that would define their marriage and forge their relationship. ''I think the prince will commit every day of his life to this marriage. To your future together. To your children. He will be your partner in every sense of the word.''

''You didn't say anything about love.''

He didn't hesitate. ''No, I didn't. So very few royal marriages founded on love are successful. A royal marriage is a business partnership founded on mutual respect.''

''So, no hot sex?''

The question stunned him and fed an image of making love to her on the beach, her body soft and golden beneath him, her hair fanned over the wet sand, her enchanting white gauzy dress unbuttoned to her waist and the surf foaming at their joined hips. Laurent had never entertained such an uninhibited assignation, not when he knew the paparazzi could be lurking anywhere, hoping to make his private life next week's paycheck.

For the second time since he had met Rory, Laurent wished he wasn't a prince. He was enjoying the anonymity of reacting to her like an ordinary man. He was tempted to run a testing finger along the plump curve of her bottom lip and ask her what she meant by hot. But he knew she was goading him. Testing him.

He hid a smile at her cleverness. ''This would be one

aspect of your American upbringing that needs toning down.''

She folded her arms across her chest, the movement stretching the gauze fabric tight across her breasts. ''I'm not allowed to talk about sex? Or to have sex?''

Laurent felt uncomfortably hot under the collar—and under his briefs. She wasn't wearing a proper bra for the dress. The pert tips of her nipples and the shadows of her areolae were apparent. And distracting. The afternoon's lessons weren't beginning quite the way he'd planned.

''I believe I have made my point.''

She clapped her hands, twice. ''Very smooth, teacher. You appeared to answer the question and refrained from answering at the same time.''

He minutely adjusted the cuffs of his jacket. He easily commanded large audiences, and yet his control waffled precariously in her presence. ''Glad you were paying attention.''

''Oh, I'm paying attention. I'll be having sex with the prince, but only for procreating. And, by the way, my American ideals don't need toning down. Your medieval ideas need updating. No wonder my mother left my father.

''Oh, God, I can't believe I said that.'' Rory's throat swelled with tears. Her mother. Her quirky, vivacious mother, who could confidently choose the newest trends and yet never spoke about her personal feelings.

''Did your mother never talk to you about her marriage?''

She shook her head. ''Once when I really pushed the subject, she said they hadn't known each other well enough before they got married.'' And yet, her mother had never uttered a desire to marry again. She'd socialized, but rarely dated the same man more than a few times.

Was it an inborn reticence or had her mother's love for her husband never died? Had she held it all inside her, hoping that Prince August might see the error of his actions and return to her? Was that why her mother had told her she wanted Rory to marry for love? It occurred to her that her father had never remarried, either.

Rory sighed. She wondered if she would ever find any answers that would bring her peace. "I always thought my mother was my best friend. I thought I knew her better than anyone." Resentment crept from her heart to her voice. "Now I feel as if I didn't know her. How could she keep such a big secret from me? Everything I loved about her is colored by the lies she told me." It hurt.

Sebastian cupped her chin firmly, his intense inky gaze studying her. "What if the answer is very simple, and how do you Americans say...staring you in the face?"

"What do you mean?"

"What if she was trying to protect you?"

"FYI, I can take care of myself."

"FYI? What does that mean?" Sebastian asked her in a husky tone. A warm liquid rush, intoxicating as a fine liqueur, tingled through her body and spilled down to her belly, dangerous and exciting and inappropriate.

She had to remind herself that Sebastian was here on Prince Laurent's behalf, to convince her to go through with the marriage treaty.

Rory crossed her legs, the warmth gathering in her belly pulsed with awareness of Sebastian's closeness. Of the hard muscle beneath the armor of his exquisite suits. Of his scent. She thought it would be immensely satisfying to wrinkle his clothes while she had hot sex with him. Here in the back of the limo…just for the fun of it. She had to smile in irony. Yeah. When pigs could fly.

She cleared her throat. "FYI means 'for your information.'"

"I see." He quirked a brow. "Would you like to hear your schedule for the afternoon, FYI?"

He was teasing her, his German-accented English sexy in the extreme. Rory wondered whose brilliant idea it had been to send him to be her teacher. "Enlighten me. I hope you arranged for some of the lessons to be done at my house so I can keep an eye on Brontë."

"I have taken that into account. First, you will have lunch with your brother, followed by a palace protocol lesson. At two-thirty, you will meet with Prince Laurent's press secretary, your brother's personal secretary and a Hollywood stylist to consult on your image."

"My image?"

"Yes, how you are going to present yourself to the world—clothes, hair, comportment."

Rory squirmed. She knew exactly how she presented herself to the world. Bookish, klutzy and sincere. Obviously Sebastian and her brother didn't think she was up to snuff. But submitting to the lessons was her ticket to understanding her father and the world he'd inhabited. She might even meet people who had known her mother when she was Princess Sophia.

"Now, at 5:00 p.m.," Sebastian continued, "you will begin language studies. One hour of French, followed by one hour of German."

She hoped it wouldn't be too hard to learn how to order chicken from a menu in German.

"Then a brief course in table manners before you dress for dinner. Prince Olivier will join you."

Rory stared at Sebastian as if he'd asked her to fly to the moon. "I'm afraid takeout and an ocean view are all the hospitality I can provide at this late notice."

"Do not concern yourself with the meal, madame. The prince's staff will see to everything. You need only concentrate on your lessons."

"Well, we can skip the table manners. FYI, my mother showed me which fork and glass to use."

Sebastian shot her an unreadable look. "In Europe, the continental style is preferred. And you will need protocol instructions for state dinners."

"Believe it or not, I know the continental style is preferred." She performed a fair imitation of his accent. "My mother taught it to me on one of our trips to France." Rory had been thirteen. They'd made a game of it. Had her mother been preparing her for her future?

Rory sighed. She gazed out the window at the mustard, cream and salmon-colored stucco homes and the palm trees lining the streets. A young woman on in-line skates zipped down the sidewalk with the wind tousling her hair as if she didn't have a care in the world.

This was the only home she'd ever known. Sure, she and her mother had traveled, but Southern California was home.

Rory imagined sleeping in the castle where her father had been raised—and his ancestors before him.

Sebastian tapped her on the thigh. "A princess crosses her legs at the ankle only."

Rory suppressed a quiver at the touch of his fingers on her bare skin. She quickly uncrossed her legs. "You sound like my mother."

"A photographer likely earned a year's salary over a

scandalous photo of your mother's legs while she was married to your father. The paparazzi are infamous for climbing over walls, under tables, through windows to get a headline-grabbing photo.''

Rory's brain fed her an image of a famous photo taken of Lady Diana Spencer's legs. A photographer had coaxed her into posing for a photo. The sun was to her back, revealing her legs through her thin cotton skirt.

''Point taken.'' Rory had no desire whatsoever to make headlines doing anything stupid. ''How does Prince Laurent stand it? Photographers and journalists hovering around like vultures 24/7, waiting for the smallest mistake, the tiniest bit of scandal?''

An odd, sad look crossed Sebastian's face. ''Even after a lifetime, one never really gets used to it. And don't forget the political detractors, and—''

''And what? The assassins?'' A shiver flayed her spine. The world Sebastian painted of royal life was the extreme opposite of her common life. Marrying Prince Laurent seemed destined to make her unhappy and deny her the unconditional love of a husband.

Her heart clenched.

Was that a sacrifice she was truly willing to make?

CLAUDE DUPONT CURSED as he wove through traffic, trying to keep Princess Charlotte Aurora's limousine in sight.

He'd slammed the bag of books he'd purchased onto the hood of a parked car and hopped onto his motorcycle when he'd spotted the princess exit the back door of the book shop and climb into a waiting limousine.

He had missed his opportunity with her earlier. He

wouldn't miss another. Time was running out. Prince Laurent would press for a quick engagement, and Claude owed it to Marielle to stop the wedding from taking place.

Despite her doubts and uncertainties, Rory was delighted to have a brother. As Prince Olivier greeted her with a kiss on both cheeks, she gave him an impulsive hug.

When his arms slipped around her and hugged her back, Rory held on tight for a moment, regret filling her for the years they'd been strangers.

"*Ça va?*" her brother inquired. He studied her, his eyes reminding her of the pensive blue of the ocean at dusk. He was wearing slacks and a polo shirt and looked more like an ordinary big brother, caring and protective. She didn't even mind when he called her Charlotte Aurora. It gave her a sense of shared history.

He touched her chin. "You are frightened, *ma petite soeur*. I am very sorry about your mother. We will not allow whoever killed her to go unpunished. You have my word on that. But you must not let fear govern you.

"Just before I left for university *notre père* told me that I would encounter many people who, for one reason or another, might resent me for my birth. He warned me that if people who would be your enemy smell fear, it gives them power over you."

Rory swallowed the lump in her throat. "Are you afraid sometimes, Olivier?"

"Yes. My greatest fear is that I will not live up to my responsibilities." His face took on an ashen tinge. "Penelope is taking my inability to get her pregnant very hard. There is a fertility clinic she wants us to visit next week, to get another opinion."

"Will you go?"

"Of course."

"What is Penelope like? I looked up Estaire's Web site and saw pictures of you both. And of Estaire. Your wife is very beautiful."

"Beautiful and smart." Olivier guided her to a sofa. "She's British, the daughter of an earl. I met her at Oxford. She's a lawyer, an expert in international business. She is exceedingly good at winning a point."

Rory knew her brother considered Penelope's business experience a plus for Estaire. Had her father married her mother for similar reasons? "Are you in love with her?"

Her brother smiled wryly. "I assume this has something to do with the marriage treaty. When you are a royal, your first inclination is to be wary of anyone's intentions toward you. Penelope and I were honest about what we hoped to accomplish together. Since our marriage, she has devoted herself to Estaire, which makes me love her more every day. She is the best partner I could ever hope to find." Olivier met her gaze, his expression frank. "I think if you and Prince Laurent are honest with each other, you can come to an arrangement that will satisfy you both. He's a good man. I have a great deal of respect for him. And I have a great deal of respect for our father's judgment."

Unfortunately, Rory didn't share Olivier's opinion of

their father's judgment. "What was my father like?" she asked.

"Very disciplined. Very private. He didn't like to show weakness of any kind. He worked very hard to give his people a high standard of living, employment, good medical care, education. When he died, there was hardly a man, woman or child in Estaire who didn't attend his funeral."

"Except for me," Rory said, unable to keep the bitterness from creeping into her voice. "His own child."

Olivier tilted her chin up, apology in his tone. "He thought of you often. I found pictures of you in his wallet after he was gone."

Grief mixed with the bitterness that gnawed at her soul. Her father had carried her picture everywhere, and she hadn't even been allowed to know him. "Pictures?"

Olivier nodded. "Your mother sent them with annual reports of your progress, telling him about your birthday trips. Renald Dartois, my father's secretary, gave me the letters after my father died. I brought them with me because I thought you might like to have them. The trips were his gifts to you."

"They were?" Rory gave up any pretense of trying to hide the tears blurring her eyes.

"*Mais, oui.* You will meet Renald after lunch. He is my secretary now. We will ask him for the letters."

Rory sniffled and wiped the flood of tears from her cheeks. Why did she never have a tissue when she needed one? Olivier offered her a snowy handkerchief from his pocket. She took it gratefully.

"Did my mother know when he died?"

"Yes, but she chose not to attend the funeral. After that, she stopped sending the yearly updates."

Probably hoping Olivier would forget all about the

marriage treaty. Rory angrily wiped her tears. *You guessed wrong, Mom.*

RORY DIDN'T HAVE much appetite for the grilled mahi-mahi salad. She sipped a glass of iced tea and asked Olivier questions about his life. Her brother loved speed and the outdoors. He loved to ski, race power boats and mountain bike. She promised to teach him how to surf and to in-line skate.

After their lunch, Olivier introduced her to Renald Dartois, his private secretary. Rory judged Renald to be a few years older than her brother. He had a sharp, pointed face, his jaw outlined by a thin, meticulously trimmed beard and a haughty expression that made Rory feel as if she had dirt on her nose.

Her spine stiffened.

He was judging her on her mother's choices, not hers. But she wondered what her reception would be like from the rest of Prince Olivier's staff. Sebastian had told her she would need to win their hearts, and their loyalty. She could see that he was right.

"Renald, do you have the letters for the princess?"

Rory's fingers trembled as her brother's personal secretary offered her a portfolio from his briefcase.

"They are organized by date," he explained.

"Thank you. These letters mean a great deal to me."

"Renald will be escorting you home and giving you a lesson in palace protocol."

Rory felt alarmed by the prospect, then remembered what her brother had told her about not showing fear to her enemies. "Will Sebastian be coming?"

Sebastian had discreetly disappeared when they'd arrived back at the hotel. Somehow she felt safer when he was with her.

Her brother's personal secretary gave her a cold, polite smile as if he could read her thoughts. "He is already at your residence with the others. There were several tasks requiring his attention."

"Enjoy your lessons. I'll look forward to our dinner and tour of your home," Olivier said. "I have a golf game with representatives from the motion picture industry to discuss incentives to encourage their continued filming in Estaire."

Rory wished him good luck and allowed Renald Dartois and several bodyguards to escort her to the limousine. She bore Renald's continued disapproving silence until they reached the privacy of the limo. Then she decided she was going to take matters into her own hands and make conversation. She was not going to allow her brother's secretary to intimidate her. Besides, Renald had worked for her father, as well. And she ached to know whatever he could tell her.

She gripped the portfolio of letters in her lap, wishing she were alone so she could read them. "Prince Olivier told me that you were my father's personal secretary."

"I was privileged to serve him for the last three years before his death."

"You must have known him well."

"I'm afraid I cannot say, Your Serene Highness."

Can't? Or won't? Rory wondered. "Did my father and mother ever talk—or ever meet—after their divorce?"

Renald flushed from his angular cheeks to his thin pointy beard. "My apologies, madame, but I am not at liberty to divulge any details of my years of service with Prince August. As a member of the palace staff, I was required to sign a confidentiality agreement. The penalties are quite severe."

Rory found her face turning warm, as well. "But you gave my brother the letters after my father's death."

"As the new sovereign it was his decision whether Prince August's private letters should be preserved or destroyed."

And Olivier had chosen to give them to her. But she wondered uneasily if Renald's attitude was a reflection of her father's attitude toward her. "Well, I would like to learn more about my father and Estaire. May I have a biography of his life and a résumé of important dates in Estaire's history? I want to brush up on my facts."

His hazy blue eyes considered her thoughtfully. Something about his expression reminded her fleetingly of her brother, Olivier. "I have already provided this information to Odette Schoenfeldt, Prince Laurent's press secretary. You will meet her this afternoon."

Rory listened as Renald explained that when she returned to Estaire she would be assigned a suite of rooms in the palace and her own staff consisting of a personal secretary, a press secretary, a bodyguard, a butler, a dresser and a lady's maid.

Under consultation with Prince Olivier and Princess Penelope she would select a small number of public duties to ease her into her role as princess and introduce her to the people of Estaire. "Once the engagement is officially announced, we anticipate that your office will receive a large number of invitations and requests for appearances. Your personal secretary is to submit them to me for approval prior to accepting. I will coordinate any joint appearances with Prince Laurent through Sebastian Guimond."

Rory realized that Renald wielded a great deal of power in the palace with his weighty rubber stamp. By the time the limo finally squeezed into her driveway beside several vehicles, she was anxious to escape Renald's protocol instructions and his condescending reminders that she was not to embarrass the royal family under any circumstances.

Rory got the message. Renald considered her an embarrassment—a byproduct of her father's imprudent marriage to an American.

"Let me make myself very clear," she said as she waited for the bodyguard to open her door. "I may not fit your ideal of a proper Estairian princess, but I have no intention of embarrassing my brother or his wife—or embarrassing Estaire, as you so evidently appear to think I will. I had no input into the choices my parents made—I'm just trying to deal with the impact of them."

Renald's mouth thinned at her outburst. If he wasn't her enemy before, he definitely was now. He'd probably only send her to tea parties in nursing homes where she couldn't possibly say anything inappropriate. "With all due respect, madame, I am providing you with the necessary tools to smooth your reception in Estaire. Your mother disgraced Estaire and your father when she asked for a divorce and took you back to America. There are many who will remember…who thought her unworthy. Naturally, they will view your return with skepticism."

"Did the people of Estaire know about the marriage treaty?"

"Certainly not. A sovereign prince does not need to explain his decisions to his people or to anyone else."

Especially not to his wife or daughter, Rory thought bitterly. "So they judged her without knowing all the facts." As she said the words, Rory realized she was judging her mother's decision to keep her from her father without knowing all the facts, too. Maybe the letters her mother had sent to her father would help her understand what had motivated Sophia's actions.

The bodyguard opened her car door. "Thank you for the lesson, Renald. It's been enlightening."

Fuming, Rory wished she could be alone to decompress and read her mother's letters. But if the house was as crowded as the driveway, she wouldn't be given an opportunity to be alone. Not with Sebastian's lesson schedule.

And Brontë couldn't possibly be getting the rest and quiet she needed.

Rory shoved her house key into the lock. Or tried to, anyway. It didn't appear to fit anymore. Giving up in frustration, she rang the doorbell.

A butler opened the door. Her door.

There was a butler in her house. A proper English butler with a bald pate, papery skin and craggy salt-and-pepper eyebrows. Rory's temper shot up another notch. She'd given Sebastian permission to arrange her lessons and order dinner, not change her locks and hire a butler.

The butler bowed. "Welcome home, Your Serene Highness. My name is Pierce."

"Hi." Rory gaped at him, conscious that Renald was watching her every movement. Waiting for her to do something embarrassing. She was not going to give him the satisfaction. "Pleased to meet you, Pierce." She extended her hand.

Pierce looked at her hand as if he didn't know what to do with it, then shook it gallantly. Rory realized too late that she probably shouldn't have shaken hands with the hired help. However, this was America, and she'd shake hands with whomever she pleased.

"You are expected in the living room."

"Please show Mr. Dartois to the living room. I need a few moments to freshen up."

Ignoring whoever was in the great room, Rory went directly to the kitchen to check on Brontë. Three strangers had taken over her kitchen. One was chopping vegetables, one was making fresh pasta and the third was operating a food processor.

Brontë was not in her favorite spot on the windowseat. Rory seriously considered strangling Sebastian with her bare hands. She hadn't given him permission to invite all these people into her home. No doubt the noise and the strangers had sent Brontë into hiding—most likely in Rory's room.

Rory hurried down the hallway to her room and encountered another invasion into her personal space. Her closet doors were wide-open and three-quarters of her wardrobe had been thrown into two garbage cans. Someone had gone through her dresser drawers, as well.

Rory felt steam escape her ears. Sebastian was dead meat.

But she'd deal with him after she found her cat. She hid the portfolio containing her mother's letters under her pillow, then checked under the bed. "Are you under there, girl?"

There was no answer. Rory searched her bathroom next. She finally found Brontë curled up on the foot of the vibrant yellow silk throw that covered her mother's bed.

"There you are, kitty. Did you come in here to hide?"

Thank God nothing in this room appeared to have been disturbed. Before she'd left for work this morning she'd hidden her mother's evening bag, which contained her birthday necklace, between the folds of a blanket in her mother's closet. She scooped Brontë into her arms for a cuddle, then opened the closet to ensure the purse was still there.

She slipped her hand between the folds of a woven Mexican blanket. The purse was right where she'd left it. After work tomorrow she would put the necklace in a safe deposit box at the bank.

As she closed the closet door, she turned around to find Sebastian hovering in the doorway, a guilty expression making him look almost boyish. Less severe.

He should look guilty. Her house was overrun by strangers!

"My apologies. I didn't mean to disturb you," he said. "I wanted to ensure you found Brontë safe and sound. I carried her in here—away from distractions."

"Distractions?" Hysteria crept into her voice. "There are strangers inhabiting my kitchen and tossing out my clothes. And a butler answering my door!"

"They've all signed confidentiality agreements."

Rory rolled her eyes. "Oh, that makes it all better. Where did the butler come from?"

"He's part of your new household staff. We are still working on finding you a lady's maid."

"My household staff? I don't need a household staff. I'm only one person."

"You need to become accustomed to having a cook, a butler and a lady's maid. Consider it practical experience for your return to Estaire."

"Where are they supposed to sleep? Your bodyguards are already occupying the guest room."

"At their residences. They are day staff."

"And just when am I allowed to be alone with all these people around?"

His gaze grew troubled. "I am afraid, Your Serene

Highness, that you will find yourself far too alone in the days ahead.''

''What's that supposed to mean?'' Rory snuggled Brontë close to her, unsettled by Sebastian's troubled gaze. Was there something he wasn't telling her? Had they found another booby trap in the house? Or had Prince Laurent asked him to return to Ducharme?

''The most difficult aspect of accepting your title will be coping with the isolation from the public and from those within the intimate royal circle. Your position will forever define and change the way you are treated— even by your closest friends and family. I would be remiss in my duty if I did not adequately prepare you for that.''

Rory swallowed the lump in her throat that went down like a pinecone. Okay, that bit of insight was just as alarming as finding another booby trap. ''How does Prince Laurent deal with the isolation?''

Sebastian's rich voice gentled. ''He remembers how privileged he is. And he reads. Poetry, mostly. Goethe. Hugo. Longfellow. Byron.''

''Thoreau.''

He nodded, his dark eyes studying her intimately, unlocking the door to the private world inside her that was nourished by words. The world she'd never been able to share with anyone—until maybe now. ''Yes, Thoreau.''

A frisson of awareness danced through Rory, a kinetic connection with this man as if they were both plugged into the same channel. Both experiencing the push and pull of a growing attraction that swept her off her feet like an ocean swell. She didn't want the connection to be severed.

But Sebastian was the one man she could never have.

Falling in love with him would cause an even greater rift between Estaire and Ducharme. She could imagine the tabloid headlines: Princess Dumps Prince for His Secretary!

No she couldn't fall in love with Sebastian. Renald would surely consider a scandal of that magnitude embarrassing to the royal family.

Still, Rory took in the mouth-drying breadth of Sebastian's shoulders clad in charcoal-gray wool and the sensual firmness of his lips. She ached to feel his bare chest against hers and the strong sureness of his fingers around her waist. With a bittersweet smile she wondered if Sebastian was as indispensable to his prince as he was becoming to her.

"They are waiting for you, madame. I am curious to see you find yourself."

She flashed him a less-than-confident grin. "You and me both." Rory kissed Brontë. "You'd better stay here, girl. This could get ugly."

RORY TOOK ONE LOOK at the two women sifting through a rack of clothes with Renald in the great room and wanted to hurry back to her bedroom to change. Except, someone had thrown out her clothes.

One of the women was blond and reminded Rory of champagne in a slender crystal flute—refined, delicate. The other was ebony-haired, with vibrant velvet-brown eyes and tiny hands that moved expressively when she talked.

They turned curious eyes on Rory as Sebastian made introductions. The white-blonde was Prince Laurent's press secretary, Odette Schoenfeldt. Her English was flawless, her Continental accent charming and gracious. Rory had a sinking feeling she'd never live up to the press secretary's expectations. The brunette was Chandale Allard, a Hollywood stylist to the stars.

"You'll have to forgive me for raiding your closet," Chandale said, her tone cheerful and businesslike. "It's the only way I can research a new client, and there's a rush on this job. But you'll thank me in the end." She clapped her hands together, then made a circle in the air with her index finger. "Turn around for me."

Rory reluctantly followed orders, aware that Sebastian had taken a seat in a leather armchair to watch, keeping himself rigid so his wounded back didn't rest against the cushions. She could feel his eyes on her. Somehow it gave her courage. The truth was, when she finally met Prince Laurent she did want to look her best.

"Uh-huh. Show me your hands."

Rory held out her hands for inspection. She'd never been a girlie-girl or into doing her nails.

"Have you ever had a professional manicure or a pedicure?"

Rory flushed, feeling unfeminine. Unprincessish. "No."

"Do you use nail polish?"

"It's too much maintenance. The sea and the sand chip it right off."

"What about makeup?"

"Lip gloss and sunscreen—unless it's a special occasion."

Chandale nodded. "Walk across the room now. These are the type of clothes you would normally wear to work. Clothes you feel comfortable in?"

Rory studied the white sundress she'd worn to work. She'd bought it because she felt Bohemian in it. "Yes. The Book Nook is a casual environment." She walked toward the wall of windows that framed the ever-changing vista of the ocean. It was a beautiful after-noon—perfect southern California sunshine. Not a cloud in the sky. She paused in front of the picture window, caught up in the warmth of the sun cascading into the great room. The sand on the shoreline glistened like white lace against the indigo ruffled water.

She felt an urge to be out there in the surf, diving under the waves. She turned around, tripping on the edge of the zebra-striped area rug.

"Obviously a few lessons in deportment are in or-der," Renald said critically.

Odette bestowed Rory with an encouraging smile. "She is understandably nervous. A swan evolves from a cygnet with careful nurturing. With the proper clothes, the right makeup and some coaching, she is going to be gorgeous. The question is defining her image. Prince Laurent is one of the most eligible bachelors in the world. She will be a future queen. She must be seen as his equal in every way."

"She is a princess of Estaire first and foremost," Renald reminded her curtly.

"Naturally," Odette allowed. "I did not intend to suggest otherwise. The challenge lies in downplaying her Americanism and emphasizing her Estairian heri-tage. Prince Olivier and Princess Penelope are a modern couple—young, outgoing, professional, hardworking. She must complement that image, Chandale. The pol-ished long-lost daughter, returning to her country. It's such a shame she isn't more gainfully employed. There must be some sort of positive spin we can put on the book clerk job—"

Anger burst in a hot flash in Rory's chest. She won-dered if her mother been told to downplay her Ameri-canism. "Hey, people, I'm in the room. And I hope you're not suggesting there's anything wrong with working in a bookstore. Books educate minds. Where would society be without a record of its history? Or without new ideas, new experiences, new stories to entertain and teach us?''

Sebastian steepled his fingers together, his elbows braced on the chair arms. His firm lips twitched. ''I believe the princess has just given you your spin, Odette.''

Color stained Odette's pale cheeks. ''So it seems. Renald, perhaps we could involve her in literacy causes. Do you read French or German, Your Serene Highness?''

''A small amount of French,'' Rory admitted.

Odette shrugged. ''No matter. You will learn. In European schools, children learn two or three languages as a matter of course. Americans always seem to think the rest of the world should learn English to accommodate them.''

Rory bit the inside of her cheek and told herself that Odette was only trying to help her.

Odette's gaze traveled from the coffee table with the bronze dolphin sculpture leaping from its center to the clear acrylic shelves floating on the sunset-red walls that showcased the objets d'art her mother had collected. ''Your home suggests you have an interest in art.''

''That's my mother's doing. We traveled a great deal and she collected things wherever we went.''

''So you enjoy travel?''

Rory thought nostalgically of the trips she and her mother had shared. ''Yes.'' She wondered how her mother would have introduced this birthday adventure—happy birthday, Rory, you're going to princess boot camp! Even though she was still angry with her mother, she would give anything right now for one of her mom's hugs and an explanation. She hoped this image consulting would wind up shortly so she could read her mother's letters.

"Well, that is something at least," Renald said. "Her duties will require travel. Do you have other interests or hobbies that we can optimize?"

"I like to surf and in-line skate."

Rory could tell that answer went over big.

"Volunteer work?"

"I donate blood regularly."

Perspiration dotted Rory's upper lip even though the air-conditioning in the house was functioning. She felt as if she were being interviewed for a job and failing miserably. Odette and Renald continued to pepper her with questions until Sebastian turned to Chandale, who had been listening intently to the interrogation with her chin propped on a balled fist.

"What do you think?" he asked.

Chandale waved a hand as if she were a witch casting a magic spell. "I've heard and seen enough. It's time to try on some clothes and find her look."

Odette cleared her throat delicately. "What about her hair? Will it be a problem?"

Chandale sent Odette a patient look that made Rory feel she wasn't the only one sensing the press secretary's mild antagonism. "Not in the right hands. It will become her trademark."

A bubble of hysterical laughter formed in Rory's diaphragm. This, she had to see.

CLAUDE CRUISED PAST Princess Charlotte Aurora's house on his motorcycle, hoping to learn if the princess was still residing in her home. The number of vehicles jammed in the driveway gave him his answer. He also saw a bodyguard watching him.

Claude's lips thinned. Did Prince Laurent see the need to protect his princess?

Too little, too late, Laurent.

Was Laurent with the princess now? In the three years since his sister's death, Claude had been unable to get close enough to Laurent to perform the duty of a brother.

Claude revved the engine, the power of the motorcycle humming through his thighs and into the rest of his body. A smile warmed the emptiness inside him when he discovered a public beach access down the street. This could be the opportunity he had been waiting for.

He parked his bike beside a classic blue VW bug and removed his helmet. The princess's home was only four houses down. Claude could watch the princess's driveway from here if it weren't for the presence of an elderly man in a straw hat who was seated on one of two benches near the wooden staircase that led down to the beach.

The old man had a book in his lap and a thermos on the bench beside him. A pair of binoculars hung around his neck. He looked as if he planned to stay the afternoon.

Claude swore under his breath and removed a backpack from the saddlebag on his motorcycle. The backpack contained the handgun he'd purchased in a bar after his arrival in California a few days ago.

He concealed his eyes with a pair of sunglasses and gave the man a curt nod as he strode past him to the stairs.

Maybe he could find a way up to the princess's property from the beach. He had a score to settle with Laurent.

Chapter Eight

Laurent observed Rory's rebelliousness grow—a quiet storm that raged in her eyes and compressed her lips as each successive outfit was tried on, critiqued and accepted or rejected by Odette and Renald.

Laurent knew his princess would require up to four changes of clothing on her busiest days. Unfortunately, far too few outfits were making it onto the accepted list. Those that did were elegantly tailored suits with simple lines in understated colors that no one could possibly find fault with. A professional princess's wardrobe. Yet with each critical comment Rory seemed to shrink farther behind the clothes like a turtle withdrawing into its shell.

When a coral silk gown that displayed Rory's entrancing figure and brought out the first real smile of pleasure to her lips was rejected as being too showy, Laurent firmly put his foot down. "That gown is exquisite. Definitely that one for the engagement announcement."

"But, sir," Odette protested. "Don't you think a shade of blue that brings out her eyes would be more suitable for the official photograph?"

Laurent could tell exactly what Rory thought about that suggestion from the expressive tilt of her eyebrows.

"I agree with Mr. Guimond," Chandale said. "This one is stunning. The woman underneath is wearing the clothes, not the other way around."

Laurent felt a thrum of passion stir in his veins at Chandale's words. *The woman underneath.*

"She will have that one," he declared, admiring the lustrous coral tinge the vibrant dress coaxed into Rory's cheeks. He could imagine his sexy princess's golden skin shimmering with the heat of passion as this dress slid down her bare body. He would ensure she had delicate underwear that matched the dress. "A gift from her fiancé."

From me, he wanted to add as her hyacinth-blue eyes lifted to his, wide and wary, and her lips spread into a tremulous smile.

Laurent impatiently awaited the day when there would be no more secrets between them and he could claim those lips.

THE OLD MAN didn't leave his position on the bench until after the sun had set. Claude reached the summit of the wooden steps, relieved the way was clear at last. The cliffs had been too steep to climb up to the princess's property from the beach.

He had an alternate plan.

Checking that no one was watching in the darkness, he pulled himself over the vine-covered stucco wall that bordered the property nearest the beach access. He dropped down onto a low-growing succulent that made a peculiar popping sound as it crunched beneath his weight.

He froze, listening. His stomach growled. The granola bars he'd eaten on the beach hadn't been enough.

There were lights on inside the house. He took another step, wincing as the thick spears of iceplant popped beneath his feet. He swore silently, praying the sound could not be detected over the relentless pounding of the surf. His parents had endured enough pain over Marielle's death. He did not want them to see their last child in jail.

Cautiously Claude moved through the shrubbery toward the opposite fence. A climbing rose scratched his legs as he scaled the fence. This time he landed beside a swimming pool. He crept around the pool and into the next yard undetected, though he ripped his shorts on the metal pickets of a wrought-iron fence.

Princess Charlotte Aurora's house was next door. He could hear music playing in the backyard. Chopin, he thought. He concealed himself in the shrubbery and peered over the wall. A table was set for two in the courtyard beside a fountain. The gossamer tablecloth stirred in the faint breeze. Garlands of the same gossamer fabric and lights shaped like blue flowers were strung in the trees.

A bodyguard patrolled the courtyard. A second bodyguard stood on the side of the house near a rack that held two surfboards.

Claude's breath burned with a charge of adrenaline as he waited to be sure the guards hadn't seen him. He counted five people inside a room with bloodred walls. He recognized Marielle's friend, Odette Schoenfeldt, who had been at the yacht party the night Marielle died. Claude had heard she was working in the palace press office—some people had no loyalty.

The princess was speaking to Prince Laurent. She gazed up at the prince the same way Marielle had once looked at him. With love in her eyes.

Bitterness coated Claude's stomach like vinegar. Prince Laurent had deprived Marielle of her dreams.

He had deprived the Dupont family of a sister and a daughter.

He inched open the zipper of the backpack. The weight of the semiautomatic was heavy as he curled his palm around the handle and found the trigger.

He braced his shooting arm on the top of the stone wall and waited for Prince Laurent and Princess Charlotte Aurora to venture into the courtyard and into his line of sight.

The time of final reckoning had come.

"WE'LL TAKE OUR LEAVE NOW," Laurent told Rory, sending a nod in Heinrich's direction. "Heinrich just advised me your brother should be arriving any minute. How were the language lessons?"

"Bien. Recht Gutt." She rubbed her neck. "Exhausting, actually. I hope you aren't expecting great advances."

He arched a brow. "I am expecting your best."

A worried frown etched her forehead, and she glanced back toward Renald and Odette who were deep in conversation with Chandale.

"Will you think less of me if I confess that I hate the clothes? Well, most of them, anyway. I love the coral dress—and this one isn't bad."

Laurent felt a smile building inside him. The sultry copper and blue cocktail dress with the short hip-hugging skirt was much more than not bad. It made Rory look sexy and flirtatious and beautiful.

Acting on impulse, he took her hand. "Come outside a moment. I'm going to tell you a secret."

"What…?"

She giggled as he opened the patio doors and dragged her out into the courtyard. Laurent thought it the most entrancing sound he'd heard in ages. It made his chest hurt with the yearning to laugh with her. When was the last time he had truly laughed?

His princess was doing the most peculiar things to him. Like the mermaid Lorelei, she was entrancing him with her song and her beautiful hair. Luring him into danger.

But he told himself that he was wise enough to resist her allures and stay on solid ground.

He pulled her close, breathing deeply of the alluring tropical scent of her and wishing the candles and the music and the meal were for the two of them to share. There was still so much he wanted to learn about his princess if they were to be husband and wife. But she needed to bond with her brother first.

"I hate the clothes, too," he murmured in her ear.

Her eyes widened. "You do?"

"Unequivocally yes."

She laughed again. "Oh, Sebastian. I wish—" She paused, blushing furiously. "Do I have to wear them?"

Laurent couldn't resist touching her pink-tinged cheek. He traced the heated golden softness with his finger and tilted her face up to his. He had to fight to remind himself that he was her tutor, her mentor, not her lover. He took a deep breath.

"Renald and Odette have the best of intentions, but you will have to take some initiative and make their advice work for you. Choose things that make you feel like a princess and you'll always be appropriately attired."

"Are you sure I won't cause an international incident?"

He chuckled. "Perhaps a minor one. But it will be worth it to see you looking radiant."

She moistened her lips, and Laurent felt her pulse

quicken in the sensitive underside of her jaw. The music beckoned him to touch her, hold her. Make her his.

He reacted to the music. "Dance with me, Princess," he commanded.

She moved toward him shyly, her toes clumsily stepping on his. Her eyes implored Laurent's forgiveness, and embarrassment blossomed in her cheeks like a profusion of roses. If he lived forever he would never tire of watching the changing colors in her petal-soft cheeks.

He squeezed her fingers reassuringly. "It's a waltz. Very simple. Imagine we are skating on ice. That's what my mother taught me when I was twelve and taking my first lessons. Step, glide."

Rory stepped on his toe again. "I'm so sorry."

"You should be," he scolded her with mock severity. "Despite the fact that you are a princess, you must always allow your partner to lead. Relax. It's a beautiful evening. Pretend you are in-line skating."

Relax? He had to be kidding. Rory couldn't possibly relax. Sebastian was holding her, looking at her as if he thought she was beautiful. Special. Every nerve in her body recorded the overwhelming effects of his nearness: determining the precise degree of his heat; gauging the potent hardness of his body; and identifying the components of his sensual scent.

Her body melted into the steady warmth of his embrace. She had never felt so safe. So happy to be alive. She didn't want to ever meet Prince Laurent.

Sebastian's breath caressed her cheek, his lips precariously close to her own. For a tiny exhilarating second she let herself believe that he intended to kiss her. Instead, he twirled her away from him.

A sharp retort like the backfiring of a car split the night—followed by several others in rapid succession.

At first Rory thought it was fireworks.

Sebastian snatched her hand. He jerked her across his body and threw her toward the pool. He didn't let go. He fell into the water with her. Out of the corner of her eye she saw one of the bodyguards drawing his gun.

Then the water swallowed her up.

PANIC POUNDED in Rory's ears as she clung to Sebastian. The sky was as black as the lid of a coffin above them.

His face swam before her eyes, calm, resolute. His hands squeezed her shoulders, reassuring her that everything would be okay. But everything wasn't okay. Someone had shot at them! At her!

He kicked, pulling her with him. She came up gasping for air. Sebastian shielded her with his body near the edge of the pool.

"Are you hurt?" he whispered breathlessly.

"Sebastian, are you all right?" she demanded at the same time, running her fingers over his chest to ensure there were no bullet wounds. She checked the water for trickles of blood. She couldn't stand the thought of him taking a bullet for her.

Dying for her.

He cupped her nape with his hand. His lips brushed the damp hair from her temple and touched her skin in a fiercely tender kiss that chased the fear from her heart with an emotion so powerful that she trembled with the truth of it. She flattened her palm to his chest, seeking the solid hammering of his heartbeat through his damp shirt. Sebastian made her feel safe. Secure.

"Stay quiet, *mein Lorelei.* I am unharmed," he murmured in her ear.

She nodded dumbly in pure relief, her fingers latching on to his tie. She was not letting go of him.

His lips formed a wry smile. "When we are most afraid is when we must remain calm and think clearly. We must stay here and wait for instructions from the guards." His words belied the rapid beat of his heart and the dark fire in his eyes.

Rory started as the lights in the courtyard, the pool and inside the house were abruptly extinguished. Two bodyguards appeared at the pool's edge with their guns drawn and formed a human shield for them. Rory heard them speaking in low urgent tones into their headsets. Had they caught the shooter? Had anyone been hit?

"Hurry, now," Sebastian urged her. "Into the house." The five-hundred-dollar shoes that were so appropriate for dancing were treacherously slippery as she climbed out of the pool. Sebastian kept a protective arm around her as they raced the few yards to the patio doors.

He moved her briskly past the racks of clothes to the hallway where the catering staff and the others waited in the dark.

"What's happened, Sebastian?" Odette demanded in an imperious tone infused with fear. "We heard shots."

Rory was shivering. Her sopping-wet dress molded like a cold glove to her body as her eyes slowly adjusted to the darkness. But her trembling wasn't just from chill. Someone had tried to kill her—again.

Sebastian spoke calmly, soothingly. "We are safe, that is all that matters. Odette, I trust you will ensure that everything is under control. One of the neighbors may have called the police. The princess is soaked and needs to change out of her wet clothes."

Odette's shoulders snapped taut, her face pale, but her tone was brisk and businesslike again. "Understood, sir."

Renald stepped beside Odette. "I will assist Odette, sir. Prince Olivier has been diverted to the Hotel Del."

"Very good." Sebastian steered Rory past them to her bedroom. "This way, Your Serene Highness."

Serene, ha! Maybe once, when her life had been normal, back before she'd found out she was a princess. Except for some sullen door-slamming in her teens, Rory had never thrown a tantrum in her life. Much like her mother, whenever she was upset, Rory retreated to think until she'd regained her equilibrium.

But her life had disintegrated to a nightmare, and Rory was on the verge of a drama queen rant.

Too much had happened in the past few days.

Her mother—the person she'd trusted most in the world—had *lied* to her about her birth. A brother she'd just met expected her to marry a man she'd *never* met. And for the second time in three days, someone had tried to kill her.

Rory's stomach pitched. Oh, God, it was probably the same person who'd murdered her mother!

As if all that weren't enough to send her screaming into therapy, the most incredible man she'd ever known had just kissed her and was calmly leading her down the pitch-black hallway toward her bedroom so she could remove her wet clothes. She stamped her Manolo Blahnik-clad foot on the floor. Pain jarred through her ankle. "I am nowhere near being serene. Someone just tried to—"

He pressed a warning finger to her lips. "Hush!"

Rory did *not* want to hush. She felt an insane urge to nip at his finger. Or suckle it…just a little bit to see if any of this was real. What the heck, maybe she'd go for broke and plaster herself to his chest and kiss him. *Really* kiss him.

He pushed her into her room, his hand firmly at the base of her spine. "Don't turn on the light. We'll be visible to anyone lurking outside. Where's the bathroom? I'll get you some towels."

"Sebastian?" Her courage wavered. What if she kissed him and he didn't kiss her back?

Never in her life had Rory so desperately needed to hold on to someone. She reached for him in the dark, her fingers encountering soaked cotton and tiny wooden buttons. Her fingers found skin between the buttons. The scorching heat of his body seared her right down to the soles of her feet like hot sand on a ninety-degree afternoon.

Her voice trembled. "Thank you for saving me!"

Her lips tickled the stubble riding the edge of his jaw, her mouth feeling cold against the hardness of bone as her thumbs tried to ease his jacket off his shoulders. She rose onto her tiptoes, so she could find his mouth. She needed him. Needed his kiss.

He smelled so good, even with a dose of pool chlorine.

Her lips found the corner of his mouth. Found the firm warmth of a welcome.

Groaning, Sebastian gripped her shoulders. "I'm supposed to be helping you get your clothes off, madame."

Rory whimpered with need at the thought of him peeling this skimpy little dress from her breasts, from her hips. Her breasts ached, puckered with an overwhelming need for his touch. For hot, healing sex. She didn't care that the house was filled with people or that a hunt for a killer was going on outside. This moment and the way she felt about Sebastian were the only things that mattered.

Proving to herself that she hadn't imagined Sebastian's attraction to her was the only way she could stay sane.

"So, do it. Take my clothes off," she urged, inching his jacket off his shoulders. It fell to the floor with a wet plop. She reached for his tie. The muscles in his throat constricted.

He was going to argue with her. His fingers closed around hers, stopping her as she yanked the knot loose. "Princess... It is hardly appropriate—"

"Not Princess. Rory, or better yet, Lorelei." It was highly erotic knowing that he thought of her as his mermaid.

His enchantress.

Rory felt enchanted. Enchanted by the iron-hard feel of Sebastian's body, by the sexy spikes of damp black hair that curled toward his aristocratic forehead, and by the fierce smoldering heat in his inky eyes that suggested he wasn't nearly as composed as he pretended.

She pressed her pliant breasts into his chest, let him feel the sensitive nubs that craved his touch. His kiss.

He hitched in a breath. "Do you realize what you're saying? I work for—"

She yanked his head down with a sharp tug on his tie and closed her eyes. A sigh of pent-up satisfaction swelled in her throat as her mouth made bold, hungry contact with his. Desire tumbled through her in a kaleidoscope of colors. Red for passion. Black for intrigue. Yellow for the golden prisms that sparkled behind her eyelids like droplets of sun-kissed water. Dazzling blue for the depths of things to be explored. Green for the sense of coming home. And purple, purple for royalty.

His kiss was incredibly masculine, sensual and far too restrained. His hands hovered inches from her waist, his fingers splayed as if he desired to touch her but an invisible barrier prohibited it. She sensed him holding back, warring an ethical battle with his conscience even while his arousal pressed against her belly.

Though she was sopping wet, Rory felt moist heat slicken the most intimate part of her. She felt more powerful than she'd ever felt in her life. Unlike the men she'd dated in college, Sebastian wasn't a premed student or an accounting major looking for an easy score. He was a principled, well-educated man. And so incredibly sexy she wanted to rip the buttons off his exquisitely tailored shirt and shock his socks off.

She held on to his muscled shoulders for dear life, catapulted through the kiss as if she was surfing through the barrel of a wave, waiting to see if she'd emerge exhilarated and still standing, or be crushed.

Inexpertly she nibbled at the crease of his lips, imploring him to deepen the kiss, open the gate to the depths of Sebastian that she yearned to explore.

"Nein," he groaned, ruthlessly prying her from his body as if she were a barnacle glued to a ship's hull. "That did *not* just happen." His breath feathered hotly on her cheek, proving him a liar. She wanted to point out that he was breathing as raggedly as she.

His gaze avoided hers as he adjusted the cuffs of his shirt, an action that bordered on the ridiculous because she could hear the dripping of their clothes onto her red oak floors. She wished she'd torn his silly, officious buttons off. She'd like to hear him explain how that didn't happen!

The darkness cloaking the room like black chiffon veiled his expression. "You are distraught, madame."

His rejection crushed her. Wounded her in the same way that her mother's death had. Rory stood there in the shadows, hugging herself, wishing she was a Lorelei and a wave would come and sweep her away.

With heart-wrenching clarity she realized that it didn't matter if Sebastian cared about her, desired her. He was just like her father and her brother. He would always put his duty to his country above his personal feelings.

She'd embarrassed him and humiliated herself by acting upon what should never have been acknowledged. She hadn't taken into account his unwavering loyalty to his prince. Or the fact that he only cared about her because she would be his country's future queen.

Now she'd placed them both in an uncomfortable situation and proved herself unworthy of Prince Laurent in his eyes.

She struggled to find words to repair what couldn't be undone. To retain a strand of her dignity. "You're right, Sebastian. Someone just tried to kill me, and I don't know what I'm saying or doing."

Whirling away from him, she marched into the bathroom and slammed the door, locking it behind her. She leaned against the door, her heart aching with love and loss.

"Rory?" Sebastian knocked on the door, his voice impatient. "Please, let me in."

"No." Rory squeezed her eyes tight to hold back tears she was not going to let fall. She couldn't ever let Sebastian in, not where she wanted him to be.

"Go away. No more lessons, no more people." *No more kisses.* "I order you to go away."

Her teeth were chattering. She stepped inside the glass shower enclosure and turned the hot water on full blast. Then she peeled the wet dress from her body and kicked it from her. She'd never wear it again.

The hot water pummeled her chilled flesh, but even the driving heat couldn't erase the yearning for the forbidden touch of her prince's deputy secretary.

WHEN SHE EMERGED from the bathroom over an hour later, Rory was wrapped in a sky-blue fleece robe with cloud-shaped pockets. Her room was dark, and Sebastian was gone.

She tiptoed to her bedroom door and locked it. Then she quietly slid a chair beneath the knob for good measure. One of Heinrich's merry men could probably break the chair into matchsticks with one kick at the door, but it was the principle of the thing. She wanted a barricade from the chaos that had erupted in her life.

Since she didn't know if it was safe to turn on the lights, Rory collected pillows from her bed, a thick blue candle studded with seashells, a lighter and the portfolio containing her mother's letters and carried them into her closet. She made a cozy nest on the floor with pillows and set the candle in a safe spot where she couldn't possibly knock it over. Then she lit the candle and curled up with the letters. Brontë snuggled beside her, lending moral support.

The warm smell of candle wax and the coziness of the closet was comforting, intimate. Rory trembled as she started to read the first letter. Would her mother's letters give her a clue to her parents' relationship?

Cher August,
I have grown tired of living in hotels. I have bought a beach house with the vast Pacific Ocean at our back door. The ever-changing song of the surf drowns out the grief in my heart. But I am resolute in my decision. As intractable as you are in yours.

Charlotte Aurora—I call her Rory now—loves
the beach. She took her first steps in the sand. She
is fascinated by the shells and the kelp that wash
up along the shore. And she squeals with joy when
the waves tickle her toes. She is growing so fast—
without her father.

Is this really what you want?

Sophia

Rory studied three photographs that were paper
clipped to the letter. In one she was toddling across the
sand in a ruffled pink bathing suit, a yellow plastic sand
pail clutched in her fingers. In the second her mother
stood ankle deep in water, lifting Rory by the hands as
a wave washed over her toes.

The third photograph hit Rory straight in the heart. It
was a close-up of her and her mother taken beside the
magenta blooms of a bougainvillea. Rory's head was
nestled beneath her mother's chin. Sunlight highlighted
Sophia's short cap of curls with red fire as she stared
directly into the camera as if staring into her ex-
husband's eyes, her somber eyes silently asking why.

Tears traced Rory's cheek and splashed onto the sheet
of blue stationery. She saw the strength in the sorrowful,
stubborn tilt to her mother's chin. In the resolute firmness in her gaze. Yes, her mother had lied to her. But
she'd also taken a position based on her belief in what
was best for her child, and she was not going to back
down.

Rory read the next letter. It included a description of
her second birthday and a picture of her taken on
Santa's lap at Christmas. At the bottom of the letter her
mother had added a postscript:

It has been two years now—two irreplaceable years. How do you think your daughter will feel when she learns the truth? Will you expect her to love you? Will your people appreciate the sacrifice you have made?

The sacrifice. Was that how her father had viewed the treaty—as a personal sacrifice for the good of his country?

"I am keeping to the terms of the agreement," her mother added. "But I warn you, I am teaching your daughter to think for herself."

Rory discovered in the next letter that her father's response to her mother's last letter had been to initiate the birthday adventures. Her mother had included a photograph of Rory eating pancakes shaped like mouse ears and had thanked him for the birthday trip to Disneyworld.

After that, there were no further references to the bargain her parents had made. Rory sensed that her mother had given up hope of her father ever changing his mind about the treaty. The rest of Sophia's letters were no more than a curt account of Rory's activities.

There were sixteen letters in all. Just as her brother Olivier had told her, Sophia had stopped sending the yearly updates after her father's death.

Rory thumbed back through the letters and reread the postscript added to the second letter:

It has been two years now—two irreplaceable years. How do you think your daughter will feel when she learns the truth? Will you expect her to love you? Will your people appreciate the sacrifice you have made?

I am keeping to the terms of the agreement. But
I warn you, I am teaching your daughter to think
for herself.

Rory felt the tightly packed wad of emotions in her
chest loosen. She was still angry with her parents. Still
hurt and troubled that her mother had left her in the
vulnerable position of learning of her father and the
treaty from a lawyer rather than from her mother's lips.

But Rory saw from her mother's own hand how much
she had loved her. Her mother had protected her to the
best of her ability against the inevitable. That message
was clear in her mother's words. "I am keeping to the
terms of the agreement. But I warn you, I am teaching
your daughter to think for herself."

"You sure did, Mom," she whispered softly.
Odd...she realized that Sebastian—in his own way—
had told her the same thing when he'd coached her
about her wardrobe.

Sebastian. Pain pierced her heart as if pricked by a
needle.

Rory blew out the candle and hugged the letters to
her chest in the dark. She knew what she had to do.

Chapter Nine

Prince Olivier barged past Odette into Prince Laurent's suite as the hotel's doctor was departing.

"Prince Laurent is indispos—" Odette objected, trailing at Olivier's heels as if she were a Corgi sniffing an intruder.

She had summoned the hotel's doctor to ensure that Prince Laurent's unexpected plunge into the pool tonight had not caused further damage or harmed his stitches. The doctor had cleaned and rebandaged his wounds and cautioned him to be on the lookout for any signs of infection.

Prince Olivier dismissed Odette with a flick of his wrist. "He will see me. Leave us."

Odette curtsied in acquiescence, but her gray-green eyes met Laurent's gaze through her darkened lashes. "You will call me if you require anything further?"

Laurent found her uncharacteristic fussing touching, if unnecessary. *"Ja."* He eased a white terry bathrobe up over his shoulders and turned to face Prince Olivier, who was pacing in front of the drawn curtains, his hands clasped tightly behind his back. Prince Olivier was still dressed for dinner in a black tuxedo with a white silk scarf draped around his neck. His blond hair was ruffled and portended his mood.

"I just spoke to Heinrich. He informs me the assassin managed to escape. He's contacted the authorities to report the incident—discreetly, of course."

Laurent closed his eyes, hearing once again the popping sounds of the shots and the whine of bullets skimming past his ear. He saw the horror and awareness that had exploded in Rory's eyes as he'd pulled her into the pool. "It's a miracle she wasn't hit."

It was his duty to respect her, care for her and keep her safe. And he'd nearly failed. Not only that, but he realized, to his shame, that keeping his feelings for his bride-to-be in the proper perspective was proving more difficult than he had first imagined.

His heart still thundered in his chest like the deep resonant chimes of the grandfather clock in the Schloss. Rory had begged him to remove her dress and had savaged his mouth with fervent inexpert kisses.

He'd wanted to strip the damp knit from her body and fill his palms with the soft full warmth of her breasts.

He'd wanted to whisper poetic words to her as he slid inside her. He wanted to hear her scream his name when she shattered and found her fulfillment at his touch. He wanted to hear her beg him for it again.

She had been promised to a prince, and yet she desired *him*, Sebastian, the deputy secretary. The wonder of her innocent passion rattled every disciplined bone in his body and warned him that the box in which he caged his emotions had glass sides.

But he could not dishonor Rory by making love to her without first revealing his identity. There would be many nights after they were married when they could delight in hot consuming sex. His primary responsibility now was to prepare her for the role that awaited her. She had no idea of the pressure that would descend upon her sun-kissed shoulders once the paparazzi learned of her existence.

Laurent viewed the hours they were allowed to spend together without being hounded by flashbulbs and tele-photo lenses as a precious gift.

Prince Olivier halted in midstride. "Heinrich wants a police forensics team to search the grounds for evidence. I asked him to hold off until Charlotte Aurora has left for work. I don't wish to frighten her further." He lifted his head, his blue eyes stark. "There have been three attempts on her life including the unfortunate tragedy that killed her mother. My sister is clearly not safe here. We should return to Estaire immediately. She'll be safer in the palace. We have more guards. More resources to ensure her security."

Laurent hesitated. "Did you discuss that with her?"

"No. I'm told she has retired for the night."

Laurent thought of Rory battened down in her bath-room, keeping him and the world at bay. She had thrown him out after his rejection. Guilt festered in his stomach.

She was so vulnerable. All the more reason these lessons in protocol were so vital to her happiness and her survival.

"I agree she would be safer under your immediate protection," Laurent said. "But do you feel she is pre-pared for that step? It has only been a few days. If she is caged like a thrush her only focus will be to seek freedom. Far better to prop the door open and allow her to come and go and feather her nest of her own free will. Then she will sing."

Laurent told himself that was how he envisioned their marriage. Each of them able to come and go at their choosing, finding their strengths, rearing a family.

Prince Olivier resumed his pacing, the tails of his silk scarf fluttering. "What do you propose, then? The assassin has changed his tactics. This time he came within gunshot range."

"Perhaps. Or it was a different assailant." Laurent thought of the deranged woman who had stabbed his date in the ladies' room. He had no way of knowing if that incident was related to Marielle's overdose. "And how does that differ from what we face every day, *mon ami?* Weren't you assaulted by a pensioner's cane last year? And didn't Princess Penelope have a frightening encounter in a palace corridor with a footman who was armed with a knife?

"We place our trust in the experience of the good people who risk their lives for our safety. Charlotte Aurora needs to view that level of protection as something to be desired, not resented."

Prince Olivier pursed his lips thoughtfully. "You possess an annoying ability to be right."

Prince Laurent winced. He only hoped Rory would agree that he had made the right decision tonight when he'd prevented her kisses from getting out of hand.

AN ELECTRONIC RENDITION of "Taps" woke the hit man. He had been out on the job conducting surveillance. Gaining access into the princess's house again would be a challenge, considering all the firepower staked out on her property.

A challenge but not impossible. He was still confident his backup plan would succeed, but if not, he was already considering several new options. He wanted the second half of the hundred Gs. He fumbled around on the bedside table for his cell phone and hit the talk button. "Yeah?"

"What do you think you're doing? You nearly shot Prince Laurent last night!"

He sat up in bed, shaking the cobwebs from his sleep-fogged brain. "Shot? What are you talking about?"

"It's supposed to look like an accident, not an assassination!"

He was wide awake now. "What happened?"

He listened to the details of the shooting. That explained the firepower crawling around the shrubbery like ants swarming a picnic. "It wasn't me. I don't do guns. They leave too much evidence that can get you locked up. But I don't like the idea of another party invading my turf."

"If you had completed the job as contracted, we would not be having this conversation," his client reminded him.

"You wanted an accident. No evidence. Sometimes you have to be patient. It should be any day now."

"I don't care how she dies. I just want her buried."

"I'm on it." He turned the phone off and glanced at the clock. It was barely 5:00 a.m.

What the hell. Time for plan C. He climbed out of bed. The princess loved to surf. That had to be an accident waiting to happen.

THE COAST WAS CLEAR.

Sebastian would be furious, but Rory didn't care. Dressed in a purple rash guard and matching board shorts, she eased her teal, orchid-painted surfboard from the rack along the side of the house just before 6:00 a.m. and walked swiftly down the drive in her bare feet, stifling a cry of pain as a sharp stone bit into her tender insole.

She reached the end of the driveway and ducked down behind the stone wall bordering her yard when she heard one of the bodyguards exit her front door. He carried a stainless steel coffee mug.

She waited several long minutes until he continued his patrol of the grounds, then she ran down the sand-swept sidewalk toward the Windansea beach access. Cars jammed the tiny parking area.

After the search that had ensued last night for the shooter, she doubted anyone would be hanging out in her shrubbery, waiting for another opportunity to kill her. If the shooter had been caught, she hadn't been told. But then, she'd made it clear to Sebastian last night that she didn't want to be disturbed.

It was a small miracle that the police hadn't shown up asking questions. Any neighbors who'd heard the shots had probably erroneously assumed, like her, that the gunshots were test fireworks for the nightly show in Mission Bay.

The morning was overcast, the sun hiding behind opaque low clouds blanketing the coast. A perfect morning for burrowing under the covers and catching twenty minutes more sleep. But it was high tide and the waves were rolling in with glassy five- to six-feet faces on the sets. More than a dozen surfers were bobbing in the water. Windansea was one of La Jolla's favorite spots for surfers.

Rory trod down the stairs to the beach, the breeze tugging playfully at her ponytail. Huge sandstone boulders hunched over the white sand like beached whales providing private crannies for sunbathing. A hut roofed with palm fronds stood like a sentinel, waiting for the afternoon crowds. Rory filled her lungs with the damp briny air tainted with the tang of seaweed and board wax and felt perfectly safe. Free.

She needed to take back control of her life. She needed her worries to be lifted from her shoulders by the soothing swell of the ocean's currents. No one was going to attack her in broad daylight on a beach full of witnesses.

Rory reached the water's edge and paused a moment to attach the rainbow-striped surf leash around her right ankle. It prevented her from losing her board when she wiped out. Then she plunged into the chilly sixty-degree water, catching her breath as she was immediately submerged up to her thighs. The beach was steep at Windansea, creating a dangerous shorebreak surf that crashed hard at the shoreline—capable of causing serious injury to unsuspecting surfers and bathers. Sliding onto her board, she quickly reconnoitered her way past the shorebreak surf. Another glassy wave came at her, cresting with a white foamy lip. She took a deep breath and ducked under it. The wave pummeled over her like a steamroller.

Rory surfaced, laughter bubbling inside her. For the first time since her mother's lawyer had arrived on her doorstep, she felt like herself again. Dreamy, bookish Rory Kenilworth, a surf diva who loved the ocean. If only Renald and Odette could see her now.

She paddled hard toward the takeoff zone, riding the swells and judging the waves. The surfers who'd arrived before her were cued, defending their positions. There were rigid rules among surfers for taking off. She got into the lineup, her thoughts drifting to last night and what had happened between her and Sebastian.

Or what they'd both agreed had *not* happened. Her

cheeks burned with embarrassment. After reading her mother's letters, she'd made some decisions.

Sebastian had been right to prevent that kiss from going any further. She had been distraught—being shot at was a terrifying experience. She was grappling with too many changes forced upon her at once, and she had reached out to the one person who was offering advice and encouragement and a strong protective shoulder.

Sebastian was an incredibly handsome man. Intelligent and articulate. She'd have to be blind and deaf not to be attracted to him.

But no matter how tempted she was by his dark sexiness, she needed to keep an open mind about becoming a princess of Estaire and about this marriage treaty to Prince Laurent. Maybe, just maybe, she would want to rip the buttons off Prince Laurent's shirt. After all, she hadn't seen him yet.

No matter what happened, she was *not* going to continue to be bullied into living up to someone else's concept of who she should be. She needed to think for herself, like her mother and Sebastian had both said. Otherwise she could be in danger of losing herself.

Rory's turn at the takeoff zone arrived. She eyed the perfect wave coming in and started paddling hard. This was hers. And it was a beaut. She popped up on the board, leaning forward and maintaining her balance as the board shot along the curl. She felt powerful again. First thing after breakfast she was going to call Chandale and cancel the outfits that made her feel like a paper doll.

And she was going to be the soul of propriety in Sebastian's presence.

In her peripheral vision, Rory detected a blur of movement. A rogue surfer in a black wet suit cut across her path on a black short board with a row of shark's teeth painted across its curved tip.

Rory arced desperately, trying to avoid a collision and failed. Her board struck the black board and she wiped out, tumbling roughly into the water.

What did that idiot think he was doing horning in on *her* wave?

The wave crushed her. She tumbled around like a sock in a wash cycle, trying to determine which way was up. Something slammed her hard in the back, the impact forcing the air from her lungs. Her board? A rock? The other surfer? She wasn't sure. She needed a breath soon.

She started to swim toward the surface, but was stopped short by her leash. There were coral reefs in the water. The leash must have gotten caught on a reef.

She kicked hard, but the leash held her fast. Rory didn't waste time. She couldn't hold her breath much longer. She reached down to undo the leash around her ankle, when something smacked her broadside at her waist.

What the hell? God, she hoped it wasn't a shark!

She twisted around, relief sweeping through her as she saw the dark silhouette of a surfboard rocketing up toward the surface. The glimmer of gleaming white teeth told her it was the rogue surfer's board.

Had he gotten caught in the reef, too? What a jerk! This beach wasn't for novice surfers. The lifeguards weren't on duty until 9:00 a.m.

Rory quickly unfastened her leash. Kicking hard, she swam toward the surface. She'd check on the other surfer after she'd gotten some air. But she'd barely broken through and opened her mouth to suck in oxygen when another wave pounded her.

Silently swearing, Rory had to forget about the other surfer and worry about her own safety. Her chest burned from lack of oxygen.

She fought her way back to the surface, this time managing to catch a sufficient breath before ducking under another oncoming wave.

When her head poked free again beside a slimy patch of kelp, she scanned the water and the beach, looking for the other surfer and her board. Fortunately the rogue surfer was being helped out of the shorebreak by two of the Windansea rats. One of the local surfer rats gave the rogue a shove, ousting him from the beach. The rogue scrambled to his feet, his fists clenched, his blond hair hanging around his face like a string mop. Rory hoped there wasn't going to be a fight. The rats could be pretty territorial against aggressive outsiders.

A swell lifted her and she saw her board bobbing solo in the water thirty feet from her. She swam toward it. By the time she'd reached it, the other surfer had his board tucked under his arm and was swaggering off the beach.

Rory suppressed a shudder as she gazed at his stiff back and the hair stringing over his shoulders. Something about him seemed familiar. She didn't think she'd seen him at Windansea before, but she couldn't place him. She turned her board around and paddled back toward the takeoff zone. She wasn't coming in until she'd macked one good ride.

RORY CURLED UP on the windowseat beside Brontë, eating a breakfast of blueberry yogurt sprinkled with granola and slices of papaya and strawberries prepared by Alice, her new cook. The tiny Philippino woman had arrived with her own cooking pans and potted herbs, along with Pierce, the butler, while Rory had been surfing.

Sneaking back into the house this morning had not been as easy as sneaking out. One of Heinrich's merry men had caught her tiptoeing up the driveway. Remembering that she was taking control of her life, she'd wished him a good morning and told him the waves had been great.

He'd nodded politely, but she'd had the feeling that she'd never be able to sneak past him again. No problem. She'd realized last night when she'd asked Sebastian to leave that she could draw boundaries and establish rules.

She'd tried the same tactic on Pierce and Alice when she encountered them getting acquainted in the kitchen. She'd told them what she wanted for breakfast and where she usually took it, then went off to shower.

And here she was, dressed in a misty-blue sleeveless silk dress she'd found hanging on the clothes rack in the great room. It was more sophisticated than the clothes she normally wore to work, but she liked the shell-shaped lace overlays that added pizzazz to the skirt. And while she'd eyed the matching flirty square-heeled shoes with distrust, she'd tried them on and found them surprisingly comfortable.

Which reminded her that she still needed to call the Hollywood stylist at her hotel. Rory quickly finished her breakfast and did without her daily vitamin because the bottle wasn't on the counter where she normally kept it, then she asked Pierce to bring her the phone.

The stylist answered on the first ring.

Rory chased away the twinges of anxiety that hovered just below her breastbone. Her mother had never hesitated to be individualistic and to express her personality through her clothes, her home and her belongings. As a trendsetter, Sophia had sought out furniture and home accessories that would help other people define themselves.

Rory's voice wavered. "Chandale, this is Rory Kenilworth."

"Just the person I was thinking of!" Rory could picture Chandale's hands waving enthusiastically. "I've been on the phone all night talking with designers. I'm going to have some drawings and sample outfits for our meeting this afternoon. I think you're going to love them!"

Rory swallowed hard. She imagined a whole wardrobe of pastel suits and dresses with matching shoes and handbags. Maybe matching hats. She had to nip this in the bud! She told Chandale how she felt about the majority of yesterday's outfits. "I just don't think they're a reflection of me—although, I love the dress Sebastian Guimond picked out."

Heat flooded her belly at the thought of how Sebastian had looked at her when she'd modeled that dress. But it cooled when she realized that he had no doubt been seeing her with the idolatry of a subject fawning over the future queen of his country. He'd warned her that people would treat her differently because of her position. It hurt to discover that he was one of those people.

"Then we're on the same page!" Chandale said with a trill in her voice.

"We are?" Rory was confused.

"My thoughts were exactly the same, which is why I was on the phone all night. I see you in warmer, more vibrant colors. A modern princess who can surf the Internet and the ocean. We'll play up your natural beauty, your love for the outdoors and your love for the written word. No pretensions of grandeur—just an intelligent American girl discovering her roots. How does that sound?''

''Like you're a miracle worker and my new best friend.''

The stylist laughed. ''I'll see you this afternoon.''

Rory put down the phone and ran a hand down the curve of Brontë's sleek back. ''It's going to be an interesting day, girl,'' she whispered so Alice and Pierce wouldn't hear. ''Let's just hope it doesn't involve bullets.''

Brontë's purr sounded like a chuckle. Rory kissed her beloved pet behind the ears and checked her watch. She'd be late for work if she didn't hustle. She had no idea how Alice and Pierce were going to keep themselves occupied all day, much less who was paying them and how much, but she didn't have time to bog herself down with the details.

Rory brushed her teeth, then stopped in her mother's room to pick up the birthday necklace commissioned for her by her father. Sebastian hadn't yet told her if he'd found out anything about the necklace's making. Maybe it had slipped his mind with everything that had happened.

To her dismay, her mother's evening bag felt suspiciously light when she tugged it from the folds of the blanket. Had it felt that light when she'd hidden it?

Her heart knocking rapidly against her chest, she plucked out the velvet case and opened it.

The jewelry box was empty.

Rory sank onto her mother's bed. Someone had stolen her precious gift from her father.

How could she have been so careless? The necklace was the only gift from him.

No, that wasn't true, she told herself, pressing her fingers to her temples. She had the birthday adventures her father had picked out for her. That showed caring and thoughtfulness. And she had wonderful memories of those adventures, which could never be stolen.

She tried to think logically. Figure out who had taken the necklace. It was obviously valuable, but thanks to Sebastian's tutelage, she suspected its theft was purely political—a ploy to cast her in a poor light and create an atmosphere of distrust between the two countries when the theft was reported.

Although the necklace was a birthday gift, it was a signature piece that she would be expected to wear while performing certain official duties. The people of Estaire and her brother would be insulted by her carelessness. She could imagine the finger pointing that might take place between her brother's staff and Prince Laurent's staff if she brought up the theft.

She went back to her bedroom and checked her jewelry box to see if any other valuables were missing. Her mother's Rolex and her diamond pear-cut earrings were still nestled in their silk-lined compartments.

Rory did a head count of the people who'd been in her home yesterday. It was tempting to suspect Renald and Odette because they obviously didn't approve of her. But the fact that they held high positions of trust made their guilt unlikely. Her best guess was that one of the bodyguards had been bought. It was difficult to imagine Chandale, Pierce or one of the caterers taking the necklace. Sebastian, of course, had been in her home yesterday. But he was the only one she didn't suspect.

Her heart flinched with humiliation as she relived his

rejection of her last night. But not for a minute did she think he would betray her or act against the best interests of his country. He'd proven that when he'd refused her advances. His prince wanted this marriage. Ducharme had so much to gain.

Rory's skin grew clammy as she considered that the necklace might have been stolen on Sunday. She hadn't checked that it was in its box after she'd arrived back from the vet's and discovered Sebastian inside her home. He'd told her he'd found her door unlocked. Had the person who had rigged her chandelier returned? She'd left her evening bag within plain sight on the foyer table.

But now that she knew the necklace was gone, what was she going to do about it? Inform her brother? Inform Sebastian? Or keep quiet and hope the thief would give him or herself away?

Pierce tapped on her door and told her that the car was ready to take her to work.

"Coming." She returned the royal blue velvet case to its hiding place in her mother's closet, then grabbed her purse and double-checked that the check from her new trust fund was still safely inside. She knew exactly what to do with the money. But she'd have to ask Otto for a favor.

PRINCESS PENELOPE RECEIVED an update from her faithful spy as she lay in her silk dressing gown on the bed, resting before dressing for dinner. She'd had an exhausting day touring the children's hospital and hosting a luncheon to raise funds for new equipment.

Olivier had informed her that an assassin had fired at Charlotte Aurora minutes before he'd arrived at his sister's home for dinner. No one had been hurt, but the assassin had escaped.

Penelope's limbs turned to ice at the thought of what might have happened if Olivier had been present. Meeting the children today had been painful. All of them so beautiful and so vibrantly alive in the face of the terrible illnesses they were struggling to overcome. It had made her long for a Valcourt heir growing in her womb. A boy.

"Did the guards manage to get a description of the shooter?" she demanded. Olivier had not told her.

Renald sniffed disdainfully. "It was too dark."

Princess Penelope silently cursed the bodyguards' incompetence.

She rubbed her flat abdomen. She missed Olivier. Missed his smile and the adoration in his eyes when he tenderly made love to her. They had made so many plans together…she couldn't bear to think of Olivier placing Estaire's future in the hands of an *Americaine*— a Beach Boys' "California Girl," as Renald had described her.

Princess Penelope shuddered. At least Princess Charlotte Aurora was not illiterate—and an alliance with Ducharme would benefit Estaire.

But Charlotte Aurora was not taking away everything Princess Penelope had worked for. She and Olivier had tried hormonal therapies and artificial insemination. In vitro fertilization was their last hope to conceive a child. Renald had helped her research several clinics and their success rates. She'd finally chosen this clinic in France.

Princess Penelope pursed her mouth. "Prince Olivier's security must be your top priority, Renald. With this assassin roaming free, the prince could still be in danger. Our appointment at the clinic is next week." By autumn, she hoped the palace would be issuing an official announcement that Their Serene Highnesses were expecting a child.

"I understand."

"I know that you do, Renald." She thought of the stories Olivier had told her about Renald's parents. Dark and elegant with a body like a swan, Emilie Dartois had been a lady-in-waiting to Olivier's mother. She had dutifully nursed the princess during her last difficult pregnancy, which had ended sadly in the princess's—and the baby's—deaths. Emilie's husband had held a high position in the treasury. Renald was making that awkward transition from boy to man when his father died in a train accident on his way to Geneva. Prince August had taken a special interest in Renald after that. The prince had encouraged him in his studies and hand-picked him for service in the palace.

Gratitude touched her voice. "Your loyalty is a gift I cherish." Just as she would cherish a Valcourt heir.

STILL FRETTING about the theft of the necklace, Rory worked her shift at the Book Nook anxiously keeping one eye on the clock. She had her pepper spray and her panic button. And her bodyguards frequently checked on her.

With the exception of two phone calls, wrong numbers where the caller listened to her greeting then hung up, the morning passed uneventfully. Rory was relieved when Tom, the owner, arrived to take the afternoon shift. Tanned and fit in navy slacks and a yacht club shirt, Tom was lugging a bag of books in a Book Nook bag and had a fistful of mail.

"You look great today," her boss said, eyeing her new outfit. "Got a date for lunch?"

Rory blushed. "No."

Tom winked at her. "Keep wearing that dress and you will." He set the bag of books on the counter.

"Are you returning some purchases?" she asked.

"No, the mail carrier found these this morning when he was making his rounds." Tom emptied the bag.

Rory paused, staring at the titles, recalling the blond man with the French accent who'd bought them yesterday.

Unease shifted within her. He'd seemed more interested in hitting on her than buying books. It occurred to her that the rogue surfer on the beach this morning had been blond. Was it the same man? She shook herself. She was becoming paranoid. They had tourists in the store every day from all parts of the globe. But still. Maybe it wouldn't hurt to take note of his name. Run it by Heinrich.

"I remember the customer. He paid by credit card. I could look through yesterday's receipts if you like."

"That would be great," Tom said. "We'll leave the books here with his name on them, and if he doesn't claim them in a week, I'll credit his account."

Rory went into the office at the back and found the receipt with Claude Dupont's signature on it. She made a copy of it and tucked it inside her purse. Maybe Claude Dupont was an ordinary tourist and would come back to collect his books. But after the frightening attacks she'd experienced, she couldn't be too careful.

She wrote Dupont's name on a sticky note and left it with Tom. She slipped her sunglasses on as she stepped out into midday sunshine that was blindingly bright. Her bank was just on the corner.

Franz, her hawk-nosed bodyguard, escorted her into the bank while she made her transaction. When they exited, the other bodyguard was waiting for them at the curb behind the wheel of Rory's red Mercedes. The top of the convertible was up.

She hoped Sebastian would be meeting her at her home to continue her lessons. She wanted to ask him about the necklace and talk to Heinrich. But instead of heading toward Neptune Place, the bodyguard drove into La Jolla Shores past lushly landscaped Spanish-Craftsmen- and Mediterranean-style homes that sprawled luxuriously across the hill. He zipped up and down quiet residential streets at a speed more suitable to a freeway.

"Where are we going?" she asked Franz, who was routinely checking the side mirror to see if they were being followed.

"La Belleza. You have an appointment."

Rory knew the exclusive spa. Being pampered for the afternoon sounded less intimidating than trying on clothes or reciting German phrases. She caught her breath as the Mercedes pulled into a palm-lined, gated drive. An oval looking-glass was intricately worked into the massive brass-plated gates.

The bodyguard punched a code into a keypad and the gates automatically swung open. They drove into a slate courtyard. The spa was a majestic Italian-style villa, a graceful cream stucco building with arched windows and a double staircase that parted in a heart shape around a Venus de Milo fountain.

The interior of the spa possessed a timeless air with travertine floors and trompe l'oeil designs embellishing walls that were the faded, golden hue of late-afternoon sunshine. Cello music played in the background, and potted palms and stone urns massed with exotic flowers made Rory feel as if she'd entered a peaceful courtyard.

Odette rose from a tasseled chaise, where she'd been taking coffee in a porcelain cup with a palmetto design, to greet Rory. She looked elegant and princess perfect in a classic Chanel black-and-white silk dress. The publicist's gray-green eyes assessed Rory's misty-blue dress critically. She finally nodded approvingly. "Much better. I hope you're in the spirit to focus on details today. A princess needs to be impeccably groomed—hair, makeup, nails, legs." Odette paused a beat. "Eyebrows."

Rory's stomach churned. She'd rather be riding a wall of water or indulging herself in the latest hot read than be tortured with smelly color rinses, facials and tweezers. "I'm in," she said, defeated.

"Excellent." Odette gave Rory a reassuring smile that seemed forced. "By the end of the day you're going to walk out of here a new woman."

Rory thought of hot wax and shuddered.

ODETTE HADN'T EXAGGERATED.

Four hours later Rory stared at the miracle of her hair, dazed beyond words. Her amber curls had been hacked at, layered and conditioned into submission. Her hair now framed her face in striking silky ringlets that made her feel beautiful. Unique—just as Chandale had predicted.

She'd worried that the makeup artist would slather layers of color on her face and eyes, but the result was sparing and gave her skin a polished glow. Oh, this was much better than reading the latest antics of Janet Evanovich's female bounty hunter! Although, she was convinced the impeccable French manicure would be ruined the moment she hit the beach.

She met Odette's gaze in the mirror, awaiting her

verdict. Odette had sat in a chair all afternoon with her hands folded delicately in her lap and her legs crossed at the ankles, observing the transformation with a critical eye. Rory had taken advantage of the opportunity to ask the publicist questions about her life in the hopes of becoming more comfortable with her. Although Odette had chosen her words carefully because their conversation was being overheard, she had revealed that she was a career woman, single and still hoping to meet the right man, and that she'd known her employer most of her life. Their families had taken Mediterranean cruises and enjoyed ski holidays together.

Though Odette provided slim details, Rory realized from the affection that laced the publicist's voice why Prince Laurent had appointed her to the task force of transforming Rory into a princess. Odette was a trusted member of the royal family's inner circle. She understood what was fully at stake for the marriage and she was determined to ensure that Rory meet her high level of expectations.

Which made it seem all the more unlikely that Odette had stolen the necklace. It was more logical that opposition to the marriage would come from within Estaire.

Odette still hadn't said one word.

Rory nervously fingered one of her silky ringlets and wished she were sharing this moment with her mother. "What do you think?"

Odette rose gracefully from her chair, an enigmatic smile tracing her lips. To Rory's surprise, the blonde squeezed her shoulder in a sisterly overture. "I think your fiancé will find you irresistible."

"Thank you." A bubble of relief popped inside Rory at the high praise. She wiggled her newly polished toes and couldn't help wondering if Sebastian would approve of the dramatic change in her appearance, then told herself to stop. It wasn't Sebastian who needed to approve.

She would give Prince Laurent a fair chance—if it killed her. But it would be much easier if she at least had a mental image to connect to the sparse personal information she was learning about him.

"Do you have a picture of *him?*" she asked Odette, hoping she would be more sympathetic to her request than Sebastian had been. She understood why Sebastian wanted her to focus on her lessons, but then, he also seemed to think there was nothing wrong with expecting her to marry a perfect stranger out of a sense of duty to a father she'd never met. She hoped Odette, who was waiting for the right man to come along, would understand her curiosity.

Odette blanched and turned away to retrieve her purse from a marble-topped console. "The car is waiting. You have a fitting with the stylist next on your schedule. Then a deportment lesson."

Rory grabbed her own purse and thanked the makeup artist, who presented her with a goodie bag containing the cosmetics she'd purchased. Clutching the bag, Rory raced to catch up with Odette in the galleria outside their private salon. She laid a hand on her arm. "Please."

Odette paused, her gray-green eyes indicating she was mulling over Rory's request. "I'll see what I can do."

Chapter Ten

"Follow me, sir. The princess is in the midst of a deportment lesson."

Laurent followed Pierce to the great room at a clipped pace, anxious to reassure himself that his princess was okay. He and Prince Olivier had thought of little else but the princess's safety all day. The police had retrieved five bullets from tree trunks and the wall of Rory's home, as well as five bullet casings. And they had tracked the shooter's path through the neighboring yards where some fingerprints had been found on a wrought-iron fence. The police had obtained fingerprint samples from the bodyguards to eliminate the possibility that a guard had left the prints while pursuing the shooter.

Under Heinrich's recommendation they had moved up the defensive-driving course and self-defense lessons in the princess's schedule. Laurent also thought she should be instructed in how to fire a gun in the event she ever needed to pick one up to defend herself.

The butler announced his arrival. Laurent barely heard the butler's voice. The corners of the vibrant-red room blurred as if he were viewing them through the flicker of a gas flame as he laid eyes on the stunning young woman in the gossamer gold organza dress. She would grace his side for the rest of his life. She teetered across the room under Odette's coaching in a pair of spike heels like a gosling learning to walk.

Her hair. It had always entranced him, but now a surge of sexual need drove an impulse to catch a fistful of those curls as he brought his mouth down on her lush glossy lips. He had thought Rory beautiful before but now he found her—

Without conscious volition, he drew back a step as if some inner part of him instinctively recognized danger and urged him to retreat. But the draw of the sexual surge was as magnetic as the song of a siren to a doomed vessel.

His abdomen tensed as Rory met his gaze with wide, hyacinth eyes. Everything that had passed between them last night flashed in his heart as she hobbled unsteadily toward him. Laurent sensed disaster impending as her spike heels wobbled, but finally her delicate ankles straightened and she beamed at him.

Then she blushed.

Laurent remembered in vivid detail the feel of her wet, pliant body and the hungry softness of her mouth. She'd wanted him.

He trembled inside, unable to restrain the rampant erotic images filling his mind.

Stiffly he bowed to her, struggling to keep the distance and formality he'd been trained to maintain at all times. "Your Serene Highness. You are a sight to behold." He failed miserably at shutting out the images. He imagined peeling the filmy gold fabric from her beautiful breasts. He imagined the taste of her in his mouth.

"I'm flattered."

Laurent wanted the room cleared. He was iron hard with a need that demanded release.

Odette checked her diamond wristwatch. "We've nearly finished, Sebastian. Perhaps one more time across the room, madame? Imagine you are a ballet dancer and you are tapping your toes in front of you with each step. It's not a heel-toe motion as if you are wearing a sandal."

Rory shrugged. "Duty calls." She turned, wobbling precariously as she attempted to tap her toes as instructed.

Laurent feared for her ankles, but the sway of her sexy bottom as she strained to balance increased his desire.

"Perhaps we should consider a shoe with a lower heel," Odette murmured to Chandale. "She doesn't need the extra height."

Laurent discreetly shielded the front of his trousers with his hands as he observed Rory's progress. She was metamorphosing into a dazzling swan. "It will come," he assured both women confidently, even though he was sure his princess would always tread charmingly on his toes.

He glanced down at *her* toes, transfixed by the polished glow on her nails and by the tiny gold starfish that dangled from a chain circling her ankle.

His fingers craved to be as intimately close to her skin. "How is her wardrobe coming along?" he inquired in a passably neutral tone.

He sensed tension pass between Odette and Chandale.

Rory finished her walk without incident and propped her hands on her hips. A glow of pride illuminated her face. "It's in the works. I've made some choices that

I'm comfortable with, and Chandale has asked some designers to submit designs.''

Odette smoothed a finger along her brow as if smoothing away an imperfection in her makeup. Laurent knew that gesture well. His press secretary excelled at smoothing out problems before they snowballed into media crises. ''But of course they must meet with Sebastian's final approval for color and suitability,'' she said diplomatically, smiling at him for confirmation.

Laurent took the hint. Odette obviously perceived a problem with Rory's choices.

Rory pursed her glossy lips, and Laurent felt perspiration dampen his temples. ''I hardly think Sebastian's approval is required. The guidelines you and Renald provided me with were very clear. And you did say I would have an experienced lady's maid to help me make appropriate decisions.''

Odette smoothed her finger over her brow again.

While Laurent understood Odette's concerns, he was pleased to see his princess grasping the reins of her new role. ''As you wish, madame. If today's dress is any indication of your preferences, I'm confident you're on the right path. Now, if you ladies will excuse us, I am to escort Her Serene Highness to dinner with her brother.''

Even with Sebastian's praise washing over her, Rory knew she was going to break her neck in these shoes. Sebastian was looking at her as if she were a princess. And even though she worried she'd offended Odette, his display of confidence in her was worth the price.

Rory floated unsteadily in her shoes as Chandale handed her a gold-fringed silk shawl from a hanger and a gold dragonfly evening bag. She excused herself to powder her nose and rotate in front of a full-length mirror to ensure that all the details of her appearance were perfect and no embarrassing labels or price tags were showing as Odette had taught her in her deportment lesson. Odette had said that little trick would make her feel confident.

Looking at the stranger in the mirror, Rory did feel confident. Although she firmly told herself that she was going to give the marriage treaty due consideration, her heart was spinning around like a carnival ride at the prospect of being alone with Sebastian for a few minutes.

Take a deep breath. You're just nervous because you're going to ask him about the necklace, she told herself.

Liar, her reflection replied.

A balmy breeze tugged at her shawl and rippled through the trees, rattling palm fronds as Sebastian slowly escorted her out to the limo. Rory found it almost impossible to concentrate on tapping her toes when Sebastian's strong fingers were creating a disturbance on her elbow.

Determined to stay true to her mission, she broached the subject of the necklace as soon as they were settled in the buttery soft backseat of the limo. "So much has happened in the last few days, I haven't had a chance to ask you if you'd found out any information about my father's necklace."

"Forgive me, madame. I made some inquiries yesterday and received a fax at the hotel this afternoon. Apparently, your father commissioned the necklace from a Swiss jeweler ten years ago. Then the necklace was kept in storage with the crown jewels of Estaire."

"What's the jeweler's name?" she asked.

"I have it here." He passed her the fax. "I hope this

settles any doubts you may have about your brother's sincerity.''

Rory took the paper and wondered if she was making a mistake in not telling him what she intended to do with the information. But before she pointed an accusing finger and created a rift of suspicion between two already feuding countries, she needed substantial proof. ''Thank you.''

However, she saw no reason why she couldn't share her suspicions with him about the customer at the bookstore.

Haltingly, she told him about her encounter with the blond man with the French accent and how the bag of books he'd bought had been found in the street. ''I'm probably being paranoid, but I went surfing this morning and a blond man sideswiped me and knocked me off my board.'' She hesitated, not certain how much to tell Sebastian. A fierce glower was rising in his inky eyes. ''I can't be sure because I didn't get a good enough look at him, but he might be the same man.''

''Where were your bodyguards when this occurred?'' Sebastian asked in a low, dangerous tone that suggested heads were about to roll.

Rory gulped. No one was going to get fired because she'd chosen to ditch them. ''I didn't take them with me or tell them I was leaving. I wanted—I needed to be alone. This is all so overwhelming. I just needed some space. And when I'm on the water, I feel like I'm in control.''

Sebastian's eyes studied her face. Rory felt a chill, unable to guess what he was thinking. ''And were you in control when this man sideswiped you?'' he asked brusquely.

"Yes and no," she admitted. "I had trouble with my leash."

At his puzzled expression, she explained. "It's a cord that you attach to your ankle to keep you from losing your board. It got caught on something. When I was trying to release it, something bumped into me. The man—or his board—I'm not sure." Her voice trembled. "But I was scared and I was running out of air. By the time I was free, he was already being helped off the beach by the Windansea rats."

"Rats?"

"Local surfers. They're protective about people who horn in on their breaks without following proper etiquette."

"So someone else saw this man? Other witnesses?"

Rory knew he was thinking the man could be her assassin and that she was lucky she had survived without harm. "Yes. But I can do you one better than that." She whipped the copy of the sales receipt from her purse. "I know his name and I even have his credit card number."

"What is his name?"

"Claude Dupont."

To Rory's astonishment, Sebastian lifted a telephone and spoke to the driver. "Stop the car. Now!"

CLAUDE DUPONT. Marielle's brother. Laurent felt ill as the name wormed through him like a fatal poison.

Claude had been on the yacht the night Marielle had overdosed. Had he taken it upon himself to avenge his sister's suicide by attacking the women Laurent showed an interest in? Or was someone trying to pin Rory's murder on Dupont?

Laurent took the sales receipt from Rory's hand and

squeezed her chilled fingers. *Gott sei Dank!* Thank God
she had escaped harm this morning at the beach. He
would never forgive himself if he lost her. His princess
was becoming far more precious to him than he knew
was wise.

The rear door opened and Heinrich joined them on
the facing seat. *"Ja?"* he asked Laurent.

Laurent explained what had happened and showed
Heinrich the sales receipt with Dupont's signature on it.
If Heinrich immediately recognized the name, he was
too professional to give any indication of that in front
of Princess Charlotte Aurora.

"These books you mention. This Dupont touched
them?"

"Yes," Rory said. "We put them aside in case he
returns to the store for them."

Heinrich nodded. *"Gut.* His fingerprints will be on
these books. We can ask the police to compare them to
the fingerprints they found on the fence after the incident last night."

"The police?" Rory rounded on Laurent. Her voice
rose. "You called the police and they found fingerprints? And you didn't tell me?"

"It was not your concern. You have more important
matters requiring your attention."

"Someone is trying to kill me and you don't think I
want to know that some evidence was found? I'm not
a Barbie doll who can't think for herself. Granted, leaving the house this morning without protection was not
the smartest decision I've ever made, but I'm the one
who brought you this receipt. I want to be kept informed."

"You are not a Barbie doll, madame. I apologize if
I led you to believe that I considered your position or-

namental in nature. I'm afraid that threats to a member of a royal family are commonplace. Heinrich is working with the police to handle the matter as expediently as possible and to see that the perpetrator is identified and apprehended. Prince Olivier was informed immediately.''

"Well, that makes it all better—you told my brother! How patriarchal!'' Her blue eyes narrowed dangerously. "I think I need to have a talk with my brother, but I'm not finished with you."

Laurent's lips thinned. He did not need to defend his decisions to anyone except his father, the king.

Rory waggled a slender finger in front of his nose. "What happens on my property, to me, is *my* concern. This man killed my mother. I want to help."

He stared down his nose at her finger. His mother, in all her life, had never dared raise a finger or speak in such a manner to his father. "Your mother would wish to see you protected." He captured her finger. "As do I."

She gasped, her eyes widening as a frisson of awareness spontaneously combusted between them at his touch. She jerked her finger away, her eyes glittering with the brilliant fire of sapphires. "I'm not a child. I can protect myself."

Laurent dropped his hand to his thigh, his fingers clenched. She was not being reasonable. "You are made of flesh and blood. You could die and I would never be able to live with myself," he said far more harshly than he meant, his patience at an end. He was reminded that her mother with her romantic ideals of equality and love had not lasted more than two years in the Estairian court.

Even though his own mother had foolishly loved his

father and had suffered from his unfaithfulness, she'd at least fulfilled her duty.

But because he feared Rory might do something ill-advised like go off again without her bodyguards, he added, "I will refrain from going into specific details, but there have been two other incidents involving women whom Prince Laurent has seen socially."

Rory paled. "What? This has happened before?"

"It is difficult to determine if these events are related or coincidence. But one woman died under suspicious circumstances. Her last name was Dupont."

"Oh, my God!"

"We are not leaping to conclusions," Laurent reminded her. "We are going to let the experts handle the matter."

Heinrich nodded vigorously. "If I may, sir. If this credit card is legitimate, it may tell us a great deal about this Claude Dupont and where we can find him."

Rory frowned. "What do you mean *if* it's legitimate?"

"It could be a fake or a stolen identity," Heinrich explained. "Someone could be setting up Dupont.

"If I could obtain a picture of Claude Dupont, Your Serene Highness, could you assist me in showing it to the surfers who were at the beach this morning?"

"Of course."

"*Gut.* With your permission, then, I will accompany you to your place of work tomorrow to pick up these books and request the police run any prints they find through Interpol." Heinrich carefully removed a glass from the minibar and instructed Rory to grip it with her right hand so the police would be able to identify any fingerprints that might be hers. He preserved the glass in a motion-sickness bag, then repeated the procedure with Rory's left hand.

They were almost at the hotel. As the limo pulled up at the rear entrance, Laurent met Rory's defiant gaze and realized worriedly that his princess would not bow to his every command. He found her independent nature both a source of consternation and admiration. "Heinrich has suggested that you receive some immediate instruction in self-defense training. Are you amenable to that?"

"Of course," she said indignantly.

"Then you will begin tomorrow."

Laurent's chest tightened as he waited for the all-clear signal that it was safe to depart the vehicle. His fingers protectively circled Rory's elbow as he hustled her out of the limo and into the hotel. He saw the concentration in his princess's beautiful face as she struggled to walk with dignity in those shoes. Somehow he felt events were moving far beyond his control.

ODETTE DISCREETLY ENTERED the salon of Prince Laurent's suite and found him standing at the window, gazing out at the bay, his back to her. Only one lamp illuminated the salon, casting a puddle of light on the desk where he rigorously attended to his royal duties.

She hesitated to disturb him when he was seeking a moment of solitude from his work. He was stripped to the waist, a snifter of brandy clasped in his elegant fingers.

She trembled, her heart tightening with suppressed fury at the pale bandages gleaming against his bronzed skin. Twice in one week they had almost lost him—all because of this American princess.

She wondered if he was thinking of her now. Odette

knew her prince well. Knew that even though he fought
it, he desired Princess Charlotte Aurora. Perhaps was
even falling in love with her. Tonight, when he'd arrived
to escort her to dinner, he'd looked at her as if she were
the only woman in the room. Odette had only once before seen Laurent behave like this—with Marielle.

And he'd been oblivious then, too, to the ways that
women schemed. His precious Marielle had plotted behind his back. Just as Princess Charlotte Aurora
schemed now.

Odette knew where *her* loyalty lay. With Laurent.
"Am I intruding, *Königliche Hoheit,* Your Royal Highness?"

She saw the fatigue and the worry etched in his handsome features as he faced her. He took his duties so
seriously. She knew sometimes that he could not sleep
and spent lonely hours deep in thought or with his
books.

"Not at all," he said. "I assume this concerns Princess Charlotte Aurora's wardrobe?" He held up a hand.
"She will learn best from her own mistakes."

Odette smiled softly. He possessed all the qualities of
a great king: wisdom, compassion, strength. "*Nein,* that
is not what brings me here. But I will hold your phi-
losophy in mind." She stepped farther into the richly
furnished room. Prince Laurent set down his snifter of
brandy and reached for his black silk dressing robe,
draped over the back of the desk chair.

"*Bitte,* don't trouble yourself," she bade him. "I
know the stitches in your back pain you. We are alone."

"*Danke.*" He left the robe on the back of the chair.

"The Princess asked me today if I could give her a
picture of you. I was not sure how to respond."

His noble brow furrowed. "How did you reply?"

"I told her that I would see what I could do."

"She is curious. If her curiosity is satisfied she will concentrate more on her lessons. Give her a photo of my brother Leopold."

"You're sure? If I may speak freely, she does not strike me as a woman who appreciates dishonesty."

She felt a prick of alarm when his shoulders stiffened. Had she gone too far in questioning his judgment? The lines furrowed deeper in the corners of his mouth, and his jaw set with false conviction. "She will understand my reasons. She is not ready to meet her fiancé face-to-face."

"As you wish." Odette wished him good-night and left him to his solitude. Men were such fools.

RENALD JERKED AWAKE at the sound of Odette Schoenfeldt's voice on the sensitive listening device. He checked his watch. What was she doing in Prince Laurent's private rooms at one o'clock in the morning? Was the playboy prince sleeping with his press secretary?

Renald thought that little suspicion might well come in handy. He noted the date and the hour. Leaked to the right tabloids, this information could fuel a rat's nest of allegations that might make Princess Charlotte Aurora and Prince Olivier reconsider the wisdom of this marriage.

CLAUDE DUPONT was a desperate man on a mission. It was 3:00 a.m., and the shops of La Jolla Cove were darkened, the streets deserted beneath a crescent moon dangling high in the star-studded sky.

The ocean, obscured by the shops, rumbled and sighed as his deck shoes slapped on the pavement.

He had tried to make contact with Princess Charlotte

Aurora three times now. Tried to save her from Prince Laurent. But there had been no mention in the media of a man being shot or fatally wounded on Neptune Place.

He'd missed his opportunity and nearly got caught. He'd failed Marielle again. Just as he'd failed to listen to his sister that night on the yacht. He'd been too pre-occupied with finding a girl to share his bed, and he'd seen Marielle go off with a girlfriend. She'd had a shoulder to cry on. He'd thought she would be okay.

Remorse weighed on his chest and shoulders. For three years he'd wished he could relive that night.

He reached the door to the Book Nook and slid an envelope into the brass mail slot.

This had to work. He couldn't allow the marriage to take place.

RORY WENT TO BED angry and couldn't sleep. Her dinner with her brother was strained. Like Sebastian, her brother, Olivier, seemed to be living in the Dark Ages and actually thought he had a right to make decisions for her. He'd given her a brotherly kiss and suggested they learn to understand each other's ways.

"One is not right and the other wrong, *ma petite soeur*. They are just different." Then he'd explained that according to the laws of Estaire, she must seek his permission in writing to take on public duties, to marry, to divorce and to resign all rights to the succession of the throne.

Rory tossed and turned over the injustice of it until Brontë mewled with concern and hobbled over the sheets to nest herself against Rory's stomach. She buried her fingers into her pet's silken fur. "Sorry to bother you, girl."

Brontë grumbled throatily as if saying, "Pet me and I'll forgive you."

Rory debated finding a pen and paper and resigning her claim to succession of the throne of Estaire right now. Her mother had been murdered and someone was trying to kill her. Sebastian had as much as told her that even if the police caught her mother's killer, there would always be other threats. What kind of life was that?

It was the life she would have known if her parents hadn't separated, she thought miserably. She'd have been raised with the responsibility of knowing she might one day rule Estaire. Or be expected to make a sacrifice for her country by making a politically strategic marriage.

Rory hugged Brontë, feeling more pressure than she'd ever known.

RORY HAD EXPECTED Heinrich to accompany her to work in the morning, but not Sebastian. Funny, how she could be annoyed as hell with him and still find him drop-dead gorgeous. He wore a perfectly tailored black suit that fit him like a delectable coating of dark chocolate. His shirt was a dazzling white and his burgundy-and-black silk tie was a power statement.

He looked hot. Hard and composed, not a care evident in his aristocratic features as he greeted her cordially. She wanted to pull him into the shower, suit and all.

After her sleepless night, she wasn't in the mood to be reminded that her feelings for Sebastian were inappropriate. He was Prince Laurent's deputy secretary. She groaned inwardly as the rich timbre of his voice bewitched every hormone in her body with a desire to run her fingers through his thick dark hair.

She'd done her best to apply her makeup as she'd been instructed yesterday, but her eyes looked puffy and she wasn't satisfied with the results. At least Pierce and Alice had reorganized the kitchen cupboards yesterday and found her vitamins. She'd dutifully eaten the breakfast Alice had prepared, even though she wasn't hungry, and swallowed a vitamin.

How could Sebastian behave as if nothing was wrong? She felt as if she had just lost her new best friend. At least Heinrich had encouraging news to share, though his expression was guarded. Rory assumed there was a rule against smiling on duty.

"Dupont's credit card seems to be legitimate, and the police are checking with hotels in the area. I have been promised a copy of his passport photo today or tomorrow at the latest."

As the bodyguard preceded them to the limo, Rory whispered pointedly to Sebastian, "I'm glad someone around here is respecting my desire to be treated like an equal."

Sebastian speared her with a harsh look that jolted her to her soul. He opened his mouth to say something, then snapped it shut, a muscle flexing visibly in his jaw.

She wanted to apologize. Deep in her heart she knew he was being a gentleman and pretending that nothing awkward had happened between them. But she was hurt and confused and she'd wanted to rumple him. She'd never met a man who'd affected her this way.

A strained silence stretched between them in the car. She wanted to tell him about her mother's letters to her father and somehow regain that same level of intimacy they'd shared last night before he'd kissed her and called her his Lorelei, but she knew it wouldn't be wise.

She would follow his example and maintain a cordial distance between them. Maybe if she could convince him to show her a picture of Prince Laurent, she could replace Sebastian's face and body with the image of the man she was destined to marry.

When the limo pulled up outside the Book Nook, Rory hoped that Sebastian would stay in the car, but he stepped out onto the curb as if the world were at his command.

She sighed and dug her keys out of her purse.

She unlocked the door. The bell jingled merrily as she shoved the door open. She bent down to pick up a large manila envelope on the floor.

Rory flipped the envelope over, expecting to see a postage stamp. Someone had printed with a black marker: ''For Your Info.'' That was odd. Rory hit the light switch, flooding the shop with light.

''Where are the books?'' Heinrich asked.

''There, right behind the counter.''

Sebastian followed Heinrich, his hands clasped behind him as he paused to peer more closely at a book display.

Rory smiled. You could always tell a book lover. She slid a finger underneath the gummed flap and tore open the envelope. It contained newspaper clippings. For a moment she thought of Otto Gascon. He was always bringing in book reviews.

But these weren't book reviews. Rory's heart froze as she looked at the top clipping and saw the photograph. Sebastian's handsome face was captured in profile—each aristocratic line edged with light, his gaze hooded as he lifted the hand of a beautiful brunette to his lips. The brunette smiled demurely up at him as if she had a secret, her almond-shaped eyes clearly adoring.

The headline read: Crown Prince Implicated in Lover's Death.

Rory forced her gaze to the caption beneath the photograph. Her frozen heart thunked to her toes and broke. The couple in the photograph were identified as Prince Laurent of Ducharme and Marielle Dupont.

Her fingers crumpled the clippings as she swallowed the bitter truth. Sebastian wasn't the deputy secretary. He was her prince.

And he'd lied to her.

Chapter Eleven

Rory trembled with shock.

Discovering that Sebastian was the prince she was destined to marry should have been wonderful news. She was halfway in love with him and she knew that he desired her.

But he had deliberately misrepresented himself and not told her who he was. And he had been in love with Marielle Dupont.

Rory ignored the shard of pain that had lodged in her breast at the first sight of the headline. Maybe there was a reasonable explanation for Sebastian/Laurent's actions.

She scanned the opening paragraphs of the article:

Weeks after shipping heiress Marielle Dupont, 25, was found dead on her family's yacht after consuming an overdose of the drug popularly known as Ecstasy, authorities are still closemouthed about what role Crown Prince Laurent of Ducharme may have played in his lover's death.

The couple had been dating three years, leading gossip rags to speculate that a royal marriage might be in the offing for Ducharme's playboy prince.

Rumors abound that Prince Laurent supplied Ms. Dupont with the drugs. Witnesses attending the party on the yacht the night Marielle Dupont died claim that the couple had been involved in a lover's spat earlier in the evening and Prince Laurent left suddenly. One witness, who requested her name be withheld, suggested Marielle Dupont had committed suicide because she'd learned the prince was seeing another woman.

Rory peeked at the headlines of the other articles. They speculated on whether Marielle Dupont's death was an accident, a suicide or manslaughter.

She'd read enough. Her fingers were devoid of feeling. "Heinrich, could you please wait outside? I need a moment alone with *Prince Laurent*. Several moments, in fact. You have time to go for coffee."

Sebastian's, or rather, Laurent's head snapped up as he swiveled around and pegged her with a steely gaze. He swore under his breath in German. "Rory—"

She held up a hand, stopping him. "Please."

Rory followed Heinrich to the door on rubbery sea legs and locked it after him, checking to make sure the closed sign was facing out. Not that it mattered. Heinrich stood sentinel in front of the door, blocking the sign with his massive body. She glanced back at Laurent and her stomach lurched.

Oh, God, she wasn't sure she wanted to have this conversation. He looked so intimidating. She wasn't sure she wanted answers to the wariness that streaked his inky eyes like jagged flashes of lightning.

Then she remembered that although he was a prince, he was still a man.

He ran his thumb along his jaw. "How did you know?"

"These." She fanned out the articles. "They were in the envelope at the door. They're articles about Marielle Dupont's death. There's a picture of the two of you together. Someone obviously believed they contained information I needed to know." She laughed uneasily. "They were right."

"Claude, no doubt." Laurent blinked. Rory recognized it for a wince of pain—an attempt to maintain rigid control of his emotions. "We had words at Marielle's funeral, but he was grieving. I didn't take them seriously."

Rory rattled the articles warningly. "I'm waiting for an explanation as to why you lied to me."

He took a step toward her.

"I would really prefer you stay where you are," Rory said, her voice shaking. "Now, enlighten me."

He sighed and Rory felt a deep penetrating chill as if the California sun would never warm her again. "Much of it you already know. Your brother and I were concerned about your safety in light of the treaty. Marielle's death was very odd. She did not abuse her body with drugs."

"The article says you'd had an argument that night."

He nodded, his eyes stark with grief. "I severed our relationship. She was beginning to have expectations that I knew I could never fulfill. It wasn't fair to let her hope that I would propose. I told her I was already betrothed. I felt she deserved to know the truth."

Rory stared at him in disbelief. "You loved her and you ended your relationship, anyway?"

"Yes."

"But you loved her," she protested.

He swallowed, his posture as inflexible as a bronze statue. "Love has little to do with a royal marriage."

Ah, yes. Duty. Rory finally understood. He'd severed his relationship with Marielle out of duty. And he intended to go through with the marriage treaty with her out of the same sense of duty.

She felt sick. "The article suggests she may have committed suicide."

"Newspaper and magazine articles suggest many things. Marielle was understandably upset, but I don't believe she would take drugs—or deliberately commit suicide."

"What do you think happened that night?"

"I think someone put the Ecstasy in her drink without her knowledge."

Rory hugged herself. "Why?"

"Either one of my own countrymen viewed her as a threat to my commitment to the treaty or an Estairian wished to discredit me in your brother's eyes and hoped that he would call off our marriage. I had no proof—only suspicions. But my suspicions grew last year when a fashion designer whom I was dating was assaulted by a woman with a knife in the ladies' room of a club we were visiting. Fortunately Nathalie did not suffer serious injury, but her attacker was never caught."

"Oh, my God!"

His eyes bored into her, fiercely determined. Primal. "You could see why I was concerned for your safety. Olivier and I thought it would be safer if I traveled to meet you as part of his staff. We kept our plans as secret as possible, but obviously there is a leak in our security."

Rory decided now was not the time to mention the theft of the necklace. She wanted to know the whole truth first. "That still doesn't explain why you passed yourself off as your deputy secretary."

"I should think that would be obvious."

"Humor me. Spell it out."

He inclined his proud head. "You'd just discovered that you had a brother and a family history of which you were unaware. I thought it more important for you to establish a relationship with him and gain confidence in your status as a princess. You were under enough pressure without the added stress of being courted by a fiancé." He moved toward her, his eyes softening. "And while I had not anticipated this benefit, meeting you as Sebastian has allowed us to know each other as individuals. That is the basis of any partnership."

Rory held her ground. "I would think honesty is the foundation of any partnership," she said flatly.

"I had every intention of telling you when I felt you were ready." His tone gentled with the intimacy that she'd longed for this morning when he'd greeted her. "And I assure you that I have answered the questions you have posed to me about Prince Laurent with the utmost honesty. You know me as no one else ever has."

"But I said things… I did things—" She halted abruptly, blushing, as she remembered the way she'd begged him to take off her clothes and make love to her.

Huskiness seeped into his European accent. "I found nothing you said or did in any way offensive, Lorelei."

Lorelei. Goose bumps rasped over her arms. Laurent's gaze swept to her mouth as if he intended to kiss her.

She stepped back. He was two yards from her, but that was two yards too close. It was hard to think rationally when her heart was fluttering as if it wanted to escape her rib cage. She wet her lips, hungry for the taste of his mouth and the feel of his arms around her.

But no, she couldn't forget that he'd given up the woman he'd loved because of his obligation to marry her. Did she really want to give her heart to a man who didn't believe love had a place in their marriage?

"Somehow I'm not comforted being compared to a siren who lures men to their doom."

He chuckled.

It was the most dangerous sound Rory had ever heard.

"Ah, but you do lure me with your mind—and your body—and I am helpless to resist."

Her scalp prickled. A bonfire of warmth ignited in her belly, threatening her resolve. But misgivings crowded her heart. He was attracted to her. But he would never allow himself to love her, just as he'd never allowed himself a future with Marielle. She knew his duty to his crown would always guide his actions.

Could she really spend the rest of her life with a man who would never love her?

FOR THREE DAYS, Rory felt the tension crackle between her and Laurent. Now that his secret was out, she addressed him formally in front of the staff, though he had asked her to continue calling him Sebastian, which was his second name, in the few moments when they were alone. Just as she had asked him to call her Rory to remember who she was, he'd told her that he felt the same need to be called Sebastian.

She suspected it was a trick to court her. He needed this marriage. His father had been quoted as saying that he would not allow his son to take over the monarchy until he was married and settled with children.

But as angry as Rory was at Laurent for lying to her,

for arrogantly making decisions on her behalf, a part of her craved to know him more intimately. Craved to share his pain and the inner workings of his mind. Craved to call him by a name that no one else had the privilege to use—especially not Marielle.

It ate at her that Laurent had loved the shipping heiress. She'd read the articles in the envelope many times over. Heinrich had wanted to check them for fingerprints, but Rory only gave him the envelope.

Heinrich had a passport photo of Claude Dupont. His hair was cut short, but Rory was sure it was the same man who'd entered her store. She'd gone down to the beach with Heinrich on Thursday morning and showed the photo to the two Windansea rats who'd ousted the rogue surfer from the beach. The rats thought it could be the same man, but weren't one hundred percent certain.

Rory hoped the police would find where Claude Dupont was staying and arrest him soon. Even when she'd been down at the beach with Heinrich, she'd felt as if someone was watching her.

Working at the Book Nook on Thursday had been so nerve-racking that she'd handed in her notice, effective immediately, at the end of her shift. She'd told Tom that she'd learned she had a brother in Europe and she was going to meet him. But the truth was, she felt like a sitting duck in the store and she was terrified an innocent customer might get hurt in the crossfire.

She still hadn't told her brother or Laurent about the necklace. She'd hoped to enlist Otto's assistance in purchasing an exact replica on Thursday when he came into the bookstore, but Franz was in the store when Otto arrived and she couldn't talk privately. She'd have to figure out another way to talk to Otto.

So instead of working on Friday, Rory took self-defense lessons in the morning, learning how to evade grabs and block blows with her arms until her bones throbbed and her skin bore bruises. She spent the afternoon at a firing range learning how to fire an assortment of loaded guns. She learned how to hold her body in the Weaver stance and verify if a firearm had a safety before she pulled the trigger. But she couldn't even hit the target. The noise and the smell of gunpowder made her sick. She hoped she would never have to shoot someone.

That night Heinrich informed her that the police had lifted fingerprints from the envelope that matched the fingerprints they had found on her neighbor's fence after the shooting. Unfortunately, Interpol didn't have Claude Dupont's fingerprints on file. But the police had issued a warrant for Claude's arrest.

Saturday morning she was given a break from her lessons. She took Olivier and their entourage of bodyguards skating at Mission Beach. It was fun. She bought her new sister-in-law a California bikini with a matching sarong, board shorts and a T-shirt for Olivier, and muscle shirts for the bodyguards. Spending the morning laughing with Olivier made her realize how much they'd missed out on over the years. She was reluctant to see him go on Wednesday, but she didn't want him to miss his appointment at the fertility clinic.

Once her brother left, she'd be alone with Laurent. Would he court her? Or would he continue to maintain his distance? He'd held himself aloof the past three days.

Rory endured more self-defense lessons on Saturday afternoon. Her arms were black-and-blue, and she tripped herself more frequently than she tripped her at-

tacker, but Heinrich was relentless. With enough prac-
tice, he assured her the movements would become in-
stinctive and she would feel more sure of herself.

That night Rory had a nightmare. Someone grabbed
her by the shoulder during a walkabout. Without thinking, she gripped her attacker's arm and slammed them
onto the hard sidewalk, only to realize she'd assaulted
an arthritic elderly woman wanting an autograph.

By 5:30 a.m. Sunday, she was wide awake and dread-
ing the defensive-driving lessons on her schedule for
this morning. She had images of crashing the car. She
wished she could go surfing, but with Claude Dupont
still at large, she settled for fifty laps in the pool. She
was taking her vitamin with a glass of orange juice
when Pierce announced that Prince Laurent had arrived.

Rory told herself to breathe and went into the great
room. She hadn't seen Laurent yesterday.

She greedily took in his appearance. For the first time
since they'd met, Prince Laurent was dressed casually
in jeans and a navy-blue polo shirt. But even beneath
the casual clothes she sensed his rigid control.

Her heart jolted with uncertainty as she met his inky
gaze. "I wasn't expecting you this morning."

"Since I'll be staying with you for a few weeks, I
thought I might benefit from the instruction, too."

"A few weeks?" This was the first she'd heard of it.

"You still have much to learn. And I had hoped that
we could spend more time together. I would like to see
more of your home through your eyes. Just as I hope to
show you more of my home."

Rory wondered how his words could melt her de-
fenses as if she were made of wax. He was offering her
a partnership built on mutual understanding and respect.
It was the most irresistible offer she'd ever been made.

Without realizing it, Laurent was giving her glimpses into his mind, into his heart, into his soul. It wasn't nearly enough. She wanted so much more from him. But she foolishly let herself hope this might be a beginning.

THIS WAS INSANE. Rory sat behind the wheel of the Beemer and waited for the next simulation to begin. The driving school had a test area that was similar to a movie set. Building facades lined a Main Street that was several blocks long. There were signal intersections and four-way stops, parking lots, even a highway and something called a skid pad.

Rory felt strangely shaky. They'd begun the lesson with how to get into her vehicle. The most vulnerable time for a carjacking was upon entering or leaving a car. When she'd climbed into her assigned car, a man had risen out of the back seat and pressed a phony gun to her head.

And some people thought being a princess was all about wearing a tiara.

In the second lesson, a car bumped her rear bumper when she was driving down a side street. Her heart jumped at the unexpected impact. Instead of stopping, she drove to the phony town's police department and earned high praise for avoiding being the victim of a bump and rob.

In the last simulation a car had come up close behind her, weaving dangerously. She'd pulled over to let the car pass, but the instructor told her via the headset she wore that she should have made a right turn as soon as possible to get out of harm's way.

Rory closed her eyes, overwhelmed by fatigue. Having cars come at her from all directions and attackers popping out of the back seat was unnerving and exhausting.

A peculiar pressure built in her chest as the instructor told her to turn onto the test highway and accelerate to forty miles per hour.

God, what next?

Rory soon discovered what came next.

A car approached her on the highway test strip from the opposite direction. To her dismay, the car crossed the center line and barreled toward her.

Rory jerked the wheel to the right to avoid a collision, but her fingers weren't functioning properly.

"That's it," she heard the instructor coach her in her ear. "Pull off the road steadily without losing control—"

"I can't—" Rory experienced sheer horror as her body quit obeying her brain. She couldn't brake. Her mind went black as the BMW swerved out of control and started to roll.

"RORY!" LAURENT'S HEART pitched in horror as her car went off the pavement and flipped over in slow motion, raising a cloud of dust. Once. Twice.

He heard the ominous crunch of steel and crackling glass and saw smoke billow from the engine.

"Call an ambulance!" He ran toward the car, praying it wouldn't explode. It came to a groaning stop on its roof, its wheels spinning crazily in the air. They had to get her out of there.

The track's techs beat him to the car with a stretcher. They had the door open. Rory hung like a rag doll from her seat belt, pinned in place by the airbag. Her eyes were closed. Blood trickled down her left arm and dripped from her fingers.

The techs eased her out of the car and laid her on the stretcher. Laurent helped them carry her a safe distance from the vehicle.

A tech leaned over her. ''She's not breathing.''

Laurent squeezed her lifeless hand as one of the techs began artificial respiration. ''Breathe, Lorelei. We are not finished yet.''

The techs exchanged worried looks. Tears slid onto Laurent's cheeks. ''Stay with me, Lorelei. I can't lose you, too.'' He pressed her hand to his mouth and kissed it, tasting her blood on his lips.

He saw Marielle's body in a satin-lined coffin.

Not again. Please, not again.

Chapter Twelve

Laurent rode in the ambulance with Rory to the hospital, the sirens clamoring in his ears. He reluctantly surrendered her into the care of the emergency room personnel, demanding that she receive the best care available. The top specialists. Whatever was required. Cost was no object. And he insisted that Heinrich remain with her for protection.

A nurse gave him forms to fill out. He did his best, but he didn't know her medical history or whether she was on any medications. He'd clenched the pen so tightly it snapped in his grip.

He and Olivier had pushed her too hard, expected too much. They should have waited to tell her about the marriage treaty until after she'd grown accustomed to the shock of learning she was a princess. It was too much pressure. Although how else would they have explained the threats to her life?

When Olivier rushed into the waiting room accompanied by Renald and two bodyguards half an hour later, there was still no news from the doctors. Olivier was pale beneath his tan. "*Qu'est-ce qui se passe?* What's happening? I want to see her."

Laurent massaged the tight muscles in his neck. "I haven't been told anything."

"She is breathing on her own, *non?*"

Laurent shared the stark fear he saw in Olivier's eyes. "I don't know."

Olivier frowned and wiped his face with his hand in an impatient gesture. "You said she lost control of the car? I should never have allowed her to take such a course. It was too dangerous—"

"Sebastian Guimond?"

"Yes?" Laurent, Olivier and Renald turned simultaneously. A doctor, finally!

The doctor eyed the three men. "Are you family?"

Laurent took charge. "I am Ms. Kenilworth's fiancé and this is her brother. Mr. Dartois is a family retainer."

"She's very lucky to be alive. She's alert and breathing on her own."

Relief sapped the strength from Laurent's body.

Rory was alive!

"She says she blacked out while she was driving," the doctor continued. "We're running some tests. We suspect she may have overdosed on narcotics as her pupils were very small when she arrived. Other than the scalp laceration, there are no other internal injuries to cause her to be unconscious. Has she taken any medications this morning? Or eaten anything?"

Laurent was stunned. Drugs again? He instructed Renald to call the house and ask the servants what Rory had eaten.

Renald discreetly stepped away to make the call.

"We're running some tests," the doctor continued. "We've stitched up the head wound. The stitches will need to be removed in about a week."

"May we take her home soon?" Olivier asked.

The doctor hesitated. "We'd prefer to observe her overnight to make sure she has no other injuries."

Renald returned. "Ms. Kenilworth had a glass of orange juice, two slices of whole wheat toast and a vitamin this morning. She takes a vitamin every morning. Pierce didn't know if it was important, but he felt he should mention that Ms. Kenilworth noticed the bottle was missing after the dinner party the other night. He found it in a kitchen cupboard after a thorough search."

Laurent knew Olivier was thinking the same thing he was. The vitamins had been tampered with. It wasn't safe for Rory to remain in her home.

The doctor frowned. "I'd like to see this bottle of vitamins."

Renald nodded. "I'll have it delivered immediately."

"May we see her?" Laurent demanded, unable to control his anxiety.

"Of course. Only two of you, for a few minutes."

They followed the doctor into an exam room. Heinrich stood guard at the foot of Rory's bed.

"Tu m'as fait peur, ma petite soeur," Olivier scolded gently, approaching Rory's hospital gurney. He kissed her affectionately. "You gave us a scare. But Laurent assures me the car looks worse."

Rory laughed, the sound of her laughter immediately lifting Laurent's spirits. "Is he here?"

"Where else would I be?" Chaotic emotion stirred in his chest at his first sight of her.

Her blue eyes were enormous in her pale face. She looked frail, her body tucked beneath a yellow blanket. Her amber curls fanned over the white pillow and a bandage was taped to her left temple. The nurse had not done a proper job of cleaning the blood from her face.

Laurent threaded his fingers through hers as he tenderly kissed her brow.

Rory caught her lower lip between her teeth. Tears swam in her eyes. "I was so scared I was going to die! The doctor said I'd been drugged. But how?"

Laurent gathered her in his arms and inhaled the sweet scent of her hair. She was shaking. "We think it was your vitamins."

His throat ached. Despite all the security precautions and the bodyguards, he'd failed to keep her safe. Cold dread surfaced in his thoughts like scum on a pond. The killer wouldn't stop until Rory was dead. If he didn't call off the marriage treaty, his princess might die.

But Laurent couldn't bring himself to say the words that would sever their relationship, and his reasons had nothing to do with politics or the feud. His father had not raised him to be a servant to fear. Even though he knew that Prince Olivier would ensure that Rory received the highest level of protection, Laurent couldn't walk away from his sense of personal obligation to her. "We're relocating you and Brontë to other quarters until this person is caught. And we're not accepting any objections. You are outvoted two to one. Is that clear?"

Rory recognized a command when she heard one. She withdrew from the comforting strength of Laurent's shoulder. The shaking stopped when he held her. He gave her a strength she'd never known she possessed. "Absolutely clear," she stated quietly. "But my vote is the only one that counts."

She looked from Laurent to her brother and set her chin mulishly. Her head hurt, her body throbbed and she felt nauseous, but she was determined. Someone close to her brother or to Laurent had stolen her necklace and was probably in league with her assassin. Rory preferred to catch the mole on her own turf. "I'm not going to be chased out of my home."

Her gaze shifted to Heinrich. "Throw out everything consumable in the house—medicines, food, even the cleaning supplies and paper products. And search every square inch of the place for more booby traps. I want everything in the house cleaned—from the doorknobs down to the last spoon. Whoever is trying to kill me is obviously very clever."

As soon as she was released, Rory was going to see Otto. He was fluent in French and German. He could help her purchase a copy of the necklace from the Swiss jeweller. Then she would set her own trap.

RORY HAD TO WAIT until Tuesday morning to execute her plan. She'd been released from the hospital Monday morning and had spent the day resting and supervising Pierce and Alice as they carried out her orders to thoroughly cleanse her home, room by room.

Her blood tests had shown traces of opiates. The hospital lab had examined her vitamins for the presence of opiates but came up empty. Heinrich wasn't surprised. He didn't think a professional hit man would leave evidence behind. The doctor had told him that a large dose of morphine hidden in a gel capsule would be strong enough to make her lose consciousness.

Rory was glad for another reprieve from her lessons—even if only for a day. Her temple was swollen and her stitches still throbbed. Laurent and Olivier had hovered over her protectively, the two of them making a tour of the house and grounds with Heinrich. Rory felt guilty for plotting to deceive them. But she didn't change her mind.

When Laurent arrived Tuesday morning to review her

schedule for the day, she told him that she would like to skip her French lesson to go and buy her brother a painting of La Jolla as a parting gift, since he was leaving the next day.

Laurent was hesitant. ''I'll grant your request and advise Heinrich of the change in plans. In future, you might wish to give your staff more advance notice. The French tutor will be compensated for the inconvenience.''

''I'm sorry,'' Rory said, uncomfortably meeting his gaze. ''I only thought of it this morning.''

His inky eyes narrowed on her, warm and appraising. ''I'm glad you're forming ties to your brother. Would you mind if I accompanied you? I would like to select something that will remind you of home when you visit me at Schloss Hohenheim.'' His palm cupped her cheek, and Rory's world tilted off centre as he claimed a whisper-soft kiss from her lips. ''I want you to know there is a place for you there.''

Goose bumps tingled over her suddenly hot skin like the sparks from a brushfire. How could one gentle kiss from this man who had deceived her be so incredibly erotic?

Even though a cautious voice inside her warned against letting herself be seduced, Rory touched her fingers to his firm mouth, delighting in being able to touch him like this. ''Are you courting me, Sebastian?'' she asked warily.

He smiled down at her, a confident male smile that made her heart race. ''That was most assuredly not courting.'' He touched his tongue to her fingertips and nibbled gently. ''Nor was that courting,'' he murmured against her fingers.

His strong hands slid around her waist and tugged her

toward him until her pelvis was cradled against the hardness of his body and the ridge of his arousal. His eyes twinkled with virile amusement. "When I am courting you, my princess, you will have no doubt as to my intentions."

To her shock, he kissed her again. This time coaxing her mouth open with a mastery that had her sighing in surrender. His kiss took her in the most sensual way Rory had ever known. His tongue seduced her, teased her, gratified her. She clung to his shoulders as his hands cupped her bottom and fitted her more closely, more exquisitely against his arousal.

Rory gasped, gripped by a need so strong she forgot they were in her great room and anyone could walk in.

Until someone did walk in. Odette.

"My apologies. Excuse me," Odette murmured.

Rory nearly slid to the floor in a lump of rampaging hormones as Laurent reluctantly broke the kiss and released her. Odette looked as mortified as Rory felt.

While Prince Laurent explained the schedule change to Odette, Rory informed Heinrich that she and Prince Laurent were going into the cove on an errand.

There's no turning back now, she told herself, suppressing guilt as they got into the limo. Heinrich took the front passenger seat beside the driver.

Still dazed and sexually charged from Laurent's unexpected kiss, Rory jumped when Laurent took her hand and stroked the pulse point in her wrist with his thumb.

He frowned. "You're nervous of me, yes?"

Rory shook her head. "No. I mean, yes. Maybe."

He tucked a curl behind her ear, making her shiver in reaction. "I'm sorry we were interrupted. I look forward to the time when there will be no interruptions. I find you very beautiful, *mein* Lorelei."

Heat rushed up Rory's neck to her face. He'd used that name for her again. She imagined what it would be like to have him naked, inside her. Her pulse throbbed against his thumb. She had no doubt that he would be an experienced lover. But would he be restrained with her in bed?

Rory was a mass of unsettled nerves by the time they arrived at the gallery on Prospect Street.

She gave herself a pep talk. She could do this. She pasted on a smile as they entered the swank interior. "I'm sure we'll both find something here," she told Laurent confidently. "This was my mother's favorite gallery."

Joffre Wells, the gallery's owner, greeted them with a gentlemanly Southern accent that made Rory think of antebellum mansions and private country clubs. Rory explained what they were looking for, and Joffre immediately guided them toward a collection of oil seascapes.

Rory picked out an oil painting of Windansea Beach for her brother while Laurent chose a large seascape of the ocean at dawn. "Someday I will make love to you at dawn," he whispered silkily in her ear as they proceeded to the cash register.

Stunned by his promise, Rory dropped her purse on the floor, then bumped heads with Laurent as they both bent to retrieve it.

Knowing she had to act now, Rory paid for her purchase and excused herself to use the ladies' room while Laurent paid for his painting. As she had expected, Heinrich shadowed her to the rear of the gallery. Her heart thundering rapidly, Rory entered the bathroom and spent a few moments examining the double-hung window with its Cubist-inspired stained-glass panes over

the toilet. It unlocked easily. She anxiously waited another minute, then flushed the toilet and opened the
door.

She gestured furtively at Heinrich, feeling her face
heat with embarrassment. "I'm having a female problem. I need tampons." She handed him twenty dollars.
"There's a drugstore down the street, would you
mind?"

Heinrich reluctantly took the money. His thick neck
reddened. "I will send Franz."

She smiled in genuine relief. "Thank you!"

Rory didn't have a second to lose. She turned the tap
on to mask sounds and opened the window. Then she
contorted herself like a pretzel and dropped to the
ground behind a Dumpster.

Now came the tricky part. Prospect Street curved into
Prospect Place, which was crowded with little bou-
tiques, international shops, restaurants and retail outlets.
There were plenty of nooks and crannies and arcades
where she could hide. Rory figured that as soon as Heinrich realized she was gone, he'd concentrate his search
for her in that area.

Resisting the urge to look over her shoulder, she
walked to the Cave Store on Cave Street where tourists
paid a fee to climb down 145 steps to the famous Sunny
Jim Cave. She'd call a taxi from the store.

The place had a laid-back atmosphere and tempted
tourists to comb the shelves for starfish, sand dollars,
pink murex, tiger cowries and other shells after viewing
the cave. Rory ducked behind a postcard rack and studied the street through the window to make sure she
wasn't being followed. She breathed a sigh of relief.
There was no sign of the limo or her bodyguards. She
was alone.

HE HAD HER. Claude couldn't believe his good fortune. Because of the heightened security around the princess, he had not ventured onto her street in the past few days. Instead he had noted that the cross streets that led to her neighborhood intersected with La Jolla Boulevard, a main arterial route. He'd taken to sitting outside a little pizza shop on La Jolla Boulevard, reading the newspaper and keeping an eye out for her limo or her car.

He had finally spotted the limo this morning and had jumped onto his motorcycle to follow it. He was disappointed when Prince Laurent exited the limo with Princess Charlotte Aurora outside the gallery. He had hoped that the newspaper clippings would have been enough for the princess to send Prince Laurent packing.

Apparently not.

But Claude still had the gun.

He'd taken up a position in the shade of a magnolia tree and was debating the risks of shooting Prince Laurent on a public street when he'd glanced into his side mirror and saw the princess crossing the street behind him. Opportunity had knocked again and Claude was driving through full throttle.

He parked outside the Cave Store and bided his time.

THREE MINUTES AFTER he had dispatched Franz to the drugstore, Heinrich noticed that the sound of the water running in the bathroom was too constant. He knocked on the door. No man felt at ease dealing with a woman's monthly female problems. "Franz will return shortly, madame," he said.

There was no reply.

Heinrich tried the door. It was locked, but he defeated it with a tool from the pick set he carried.

As he feared, the bathroom was empty. The princess

had run away. For the first time since his appointment as Prince Laurent's royal protection officer, Heinrich feared his position was in jeopardy.

OTTO'S HOUSE was a board-and-batten bungalow painted a soft, silvery sage. The shrubs and grass had the well-tended look of being painstakingly trimmed by hand. A car was in the driveway, giving Rory hope that Otto was at home. She walked up the cement driveway and smiled at Otto's next-door neighbour, an elderly woman in a peacock-blue muumuu, who was carrying a poodle to her car.

"Don't bother ringing the bell," the woman said, depositing her poodle and her handbag on the passenger seat. "Otto's showing his nephew the garden around back. He never hears the doorbell. Just go through the gate."

Rory thanked the woman, but she hesitated as she reached the gate. Otto had company and she didn't want to intrude. Maybe they could arrange to meet later in the day.

She opened the cedar gate and walked down a flagstone path edged with variegated hostas and pink-plumed astilbe. She could hear low voices speaking in French.

As she rounded the corner of the house, Rory spotted Otto and his nephew. Their backs were to her as they stood examining a waterfall feature in the small garden. Otto's nephew wore a flint-gray suit.

Rory was about to call a greeting when the nephew turned his head toward Otto and she saw him in profile.

Her heart jolted in instant recognition of the thin beard that framed his angular jaw. Instinctively she dropped to her knees behind the arching branches of a plumbago. She'd been wrong to come here. The world of political intrigue was small and very treacherous. Otto's nephew was her brother's secretary: Renald Dartois.

Chapter Thirteen

Rory had run away.

Laurent's despair and guilt increased as the minutes ticked by and Heinrich and Franz failed to find her. She'd been under so much pressure. He'd seen the fear in her eyes when she'd lain in that hospital bed after the accident. He understood her need to escape. Laurent had often felt the same.

But Rory was out there alone, unprotected, and there was a killer after her. Laurent had to find her.

He turned to the owner of the art gallery. "Ms. Kenilworth has experienced emotional episodes since her mother's tragic death. I'm afraid our visit here today may have triggered one. She told me that this gallery was her mother's favorite. I'm not sure where she has gone—perhaps to a place where she feels close to her mother. I wonder if I might trouble you to call the taxi-cab company and inquire if anyone matching her description has been picked up in this area in the last hour."

"Of course, sir," Joffre replied. Laurent had no doubt that the gallery owner would be able to get the information out of the taxi company. Laurent had just purchased a thirty-five-thousand-dollar painting. "You might wish to tell the taxi company that there will be a substantial reward for the information," he added. "It is very important that I find her before she hurts herself."

After fifteen minutes of phone negotiations, Joffre gave Laurent an address on Playa del Norte Street and directions. "The driver remembered that his fare had a bandage."

Laurent tipped Joffre one thousand dollars in cash and raced to the limo. He didn't know why Rory would go to this address. He just hoped his Lorelei was safe.

"I CANNOT ALLOW ESTAIRE to fall into Ducharme's hands, *mon oncle,*" Rory heard Renald tell Otto as she was trying to extricate herself from the plumbago branches. She froze in her movements. Was Renald about to confess he'd hired the assassin? Was Otto involved, as well?

"You have met Princess Charlotte Aurora," Renald continued dismissively. "She is not our future."

Otto folded his arms over his chest, his head bent over a flower bed. "I see. And you believe that you have the right to change history? How is it that you are so confident that only you know what is best for Estaire? What of Prince Olivier? It is his decision is it not?"

"*Pfft!* Olivier is weak. He does not consider all his options. You have been in America twenty years. You do not know the full situation, *mon oncle.*"

"But I do know the princess. Perhaps you need to take the time to know her. You have the same father."

The same father? Nausea swirled in Rory's stomach. *She had another brother!* She thought of all the years that she'd seen Otto nearby in the neighborhood. Had he been spying on her and her mother all these years?

"You are not listening, old man. If Olivier cannot father an heir, then your great-nephew—with our flesh and blood—will one day rule Estaire!"

"How do you propose to achieve that?"

"I'll be accompanying Olivier tomorrow. He and Princess Penelope have an appointment at an in vitro fertilization clinic Thursday morning. I am hopeful that this clinic will aid them in their desire to have an heir. If not, I intend to assist the process. The one advantage of being my older brother's secretary is that I am often entrusted to handle errands of the most delicate nature."

Rory was frozen in place, her legs falling asleep. She couldn't believe what she was hearing. She was afraid to leave.

Otto slowly toured the perennial border, stopping before a Victorian gazing ball. Rory hoped he couldn't see her hunched behind the shrub in the ball's reflective surface. "Prince August was very good to you. And this is the way you repay him? By scheming to lay claim to the throne and hiding your identity from your own brother?"

Renald shrugged, his face stony with resentment. "Prince August had no compunctions about luring my mother into his bed. She was married. The end justifies the means."

"That's what Émilie thought when she embarked on an affair with Prince August after his wife died. She wanted to give her husband the one thing he desired most—a child. Émilie did not tell Prince August the truth until after her husband's death—she thought you needed a father's guidance. Prince August never should have told you the truth."

Rory had heard more than enough. Renald hadn't said that he'd hired the assassin, but she was willing to bet

he had stolen her necklace because he believed her unworthy of it. She willed feeling back into her legs as
she inched backward along the walkway on her
haunches. Pins and needles stabbed her numb feet. She
bumped into an iron shepherd's hook that suspended
ceramic wind chimes.

"What was that?" she heard Renald say. "Are you
expecting someone?"

Otto's answer was lost to her.

Rory grasped the shepherd's hook and tried to stand.
Pain shot up her legs as her blood rushed back to
cramped limbs.

Fear scattered through her like a deck of cards tossed
to the ground. She'd managed to stumble to the gate
when she heard Renald cry out, "Princess!"

Rory ran down the driveway toward the street. She
needed help.

The man came out of nowhere. His arm circled her
throat, choking off her breath. She smelled the sweat of
his body and his mouthwash-tainted breath as he jabbed
the gun roughly into her bruised temple and whispered
into her ear, "It's time we had a talk, Princess."

RORY GRABBED THE ARM choking her, but it felt as inflexible as a steel bar. What was she going to do now?

"Don't scream. I just want to talk."

"Let go of me!" she gasped, twisting her neck an
inch so she could see him. She saw long, blond hair and
a sunburned nose. Claude Dupont. He dragged her into
the deep shadows beneath the umbrella of a catalpa tree.

Had Renald seen Claude grab her? Even if he had,
he was more likely rubbing his hands together with glee
than rushing to her aid.

She was on her own. Rory forced herself to relax.

Struggling would only enrage Claude further. She tried to assess her surroundings. Maybe a neighbor would notice she was being held against her will. "You're Marielle's brother. I'm so sorry about your sister."

She cried out as the barrel of the gun thrust against her bandaged temple.

Anger reverberated from his hard-muscled body. "She died because of you—because of him. She didn't want to live without him." His voice choked with grief. "She told me that Laurent dumped her, and I let her cry on her girlfriend's shoulder instead of mine! I should have stayed with her!"

Even though she was terrified, Rory felt enormous sympathy for his pain. She'd give anything if she could turn back the clock and prevent her mother from sitting in the swing that day. "Is that why you left me the clippings? You hoped that I would think he had caused her to kill herself and I would refuse to marry him?"

"I couldn't let you marry him. He was Marielle's."

Tears choked her at the truth of Claude's statement. Laurent *was* Marielle's. She'd seen the sadness in his eyes and heard the deep regret when he spoke of her.

"He still loves her. Misses her," she admitted painfully. "You shot at us the other night."

"I wanted to kill him. He doesn't deserve to live."

Rory swallowed hard. "You stabbed Laurent's date in the bathroom, didn't you?" Claude wouldn't let any woman take his sister's place. "How will you justify killing me?"

"I'm—" Claude broke off at the sound of tires squealing around the street corner. Rory prayed that it was a police car and this would all end peacefully. But it was a limo. Oh, God! As it rocked to a halt outside

Otto's house she spotted Heinrich in the front passenger seat.

Had Heinrich seen her? She saw his hand reach inside his suit jacket for his gun.

The front passenger door and the rear door flew open simultaneously. Heinrich braced himself behind the door for cover, his weapon drawn. "Release her, Dupont."

"Move a finger and she dies," Claude warned.

A cold blade of terror sliced through Rory as Laurent stepped out of the limo and away from the door. His jaw was set firmly and his inky eyes were calm and determined. He was unarmed.

Rory screamed. His face told her what he was going to do—nobly sacrifice his life for hers. She couldn't let him. "No, Laurent! Don't!"

"Claude," he said with quiet authority, "the princess has done you no harm. Killing her will not bring you peace. If it is retribution that you require, then punish me. I never wanted to hurt Marielle. I loved her, but I was not free to marry her and I respected her by telling her the truth. I bear the guilt of her death with me every day."

Claude's gun hand trembled.

Rory prayed that Laurent was reaching him. She had seen many sides of Laurent since she had met him, but the courage he displayed now, the dignity and the compassion that he offered Marielle's brother, made her realize how much she loved this honorable man. She knew she would always love him, whether he could give his heart to her or not.

Laurent took a cautious step forward. "Is this what you truly want, Claude? Your parents have lost one child. Consider the pain they will experience at losing their only son, too. No one has been harmed. It is not too late to stop yourself from traveling down the wrong path.''

''I do this for them.''

Rory was aware of the precise second when she knew Claude would shoot Laurent. Instinctively she curled her fingers into a fist and threw up her left arm, ramming her elbow into Claude's arm, hoping to knock the gun from his hand or at least deflect his aim. Pain jarred through her arm as she made contact. The gun went off.

Noise exploded in her ears.

Laurent launched himself toward them. Toward the gun. Her heart ricocheted in her breast as she rammed her right elbow back, intending to dig into Claude's ribs—only she hit him in the shoulder. He was falling and dragging her down with him. Had he shot himself?

Laurent went for the gun, deflecting it downward with one hand while his other hand grasped Claude's wrist and twisted it inward. Rory tried to squirm away. Claude was on top of her. The gun discharged again, and Rory panicked. Was Laurent hit?

Suddenly she was jerked up and tossed out of harm's way.

She landed on the grass with a *whoof,* the air knocked from her lungs. Laurent had twisted Claude's arm behind his back and had him pinned facedown.

The gun lay on the grass. Heinrich started for it, but Renald, suddenly appearing with the shepherd's hook in hand, beat him to it. Otto hurried toward Renald.

Rory screamed, ''Stop him. Stop Renald! He's my brother, and he wants to kill me!''

Renald's fingers curled around the gun. His frank blue eyes—a deeper blue than Olivier's—met hers. ''*Non,* little sister. I helped save you. I tripped Dupont with this hook.''

"He did. I saw him," Otto insisted.

Heinrich grimly leveled his weapon at Renald's chest. "*Ja.* We'll debate it once you put the gun down."

Police sirens wailed in the distance like the insistent screeching of gulls.

Renald released the gun—and the hook—and rose stiffly. Rory saw shame and contrition in Otto's age-spotted face. She hugged her knees tightly to her chest and told herself she was not going to throw up. Laurent had Claude subdued and no one appeared to be wounded.

She was overwhelmed. She had no idea what the truth was anymore. Who had hired the assassin? Who had stolen her necklace? Who could she believe? She pillowed her head on her knees and studied Laurent's grief-stricken face.

She felt ten years older.

LAURENT KEPT HIS ARM anchored around Rory as she answered the police detective's questions in the living room of the house on Playa del Norte Street. Concerned that the press would have a field day with this story if any details leaked, Laurent had summoned Odette to manage the media. He'd also called Prince Olivier. Renald's uncle Otto brought in chairs from the kitchen.

Rory had told the police that Claude had confessed to attempting to kill Laurent on Monday night. Laurent could feel her trembling. She'd been so brave. He'd come so close to losing her. He was still not past the shock of seeing Claude Dupont holding a gun to her head.

Nor the shock of discovering that Renald Dartois was Rory's and Prince Olivier's half brother. To Laurent's consternation, Rory had explained that the diamond necklace she'd received as a gift from her father had been stolen from her home a week ago when she had begun her princess lessons. Suspecting that the thief might be working with the assassin, she'd decided to contact Otto who was fluent in German and French to help her order a copy of the necklace that she could use to trick the thief into revealing him or herself.

"Why did you not mention any of this to me or to your brother?" Laurent demanded testily.

"Because the thief was obviously a trusted member of the staff of one of you." She leveled her gaze on Renald. "I didn't want to create an atmosphere of distrust. To report the theft would have been playing into his hands."

Sweat glistened on Renald's angular features. "I did not take the necklace. Nor did I hire anyone to kill the princess. I have been a loyal servant to the Valcourt family—and to Estaire—all of my life. I have been loyal to you, Olivier. And I realized when Claude Dupont seized the princess that I could be loyal to her, even if it meant that Estaire might one day return to Falkenberg rule."

Olivier drummed his fingers upon his thigh, obviously agitated. "All these years we have worked together. Why did you not tell me you were my brother?"

Renald lowered his head shamefully. "Your father did not wish to dishonor my mother's reputation or his own. You were his legitimate heir. It was enough that he wanted me in the palace with him and that I knew the truth."

Olivier clasped Renald's shoulder. "It's important to me, and I believe it's important to Charlotte Aurora that we know we have a brother. My father was a rigid man. Too rigid, I think."

Rory felt her heart warm slightly for Renald. She knew exactly how it felt to have a parent who was supposed to love you make a decision that left you feeling as if you were inferior. Renald hadn't resented Olivier's position. He'd faithfully served his brother as his personal secretary. And although his back-up plan to ensure that Estaire had a Valcourt heir was misguided, it demonstrated a keen desire to protect the country that he loved.

Rory wouldn't reveal what she'd overheard. She'd grant him the dignity of confessing to Olivier in private.

She slipped from the buffering support of Laurent's arm and crossed the cozy living room to kiss Renald's cheek. Then she kissed Olivier. "I'm thrilled to have two brothers. You can take turns telling me what's best for me, and I can take turns telling you that I can figure it out for myself." Gratitude swelled in a hot lump in her throat. "But I appreciate the fact that you want to protect me."

Her remark won strained smiles from both Renald and Olivier. Laurent shifted awkwardly in his chair.

Rory sniffed, trying to pull herself together. Men were always so uncomfortable with emotion! Besides, she was not sure that Renald was completely trustworthy. "How did your uncle come to live in La Jolla?"

"I'll answer that," Otto volunteered from his chair near the entrance to the kitchen. "It was your father's doing, Princess. He wanted someone to keep an eye on your mother and you. I sent him monthly reports."

Rory thought of all the times she'd encountered Otto walking in the neighborhood or down at the beach, and his bi-weekly visits to the Book Nook. "All these years?"

Otto nodded, his watery gray eyes reflecting remorse.

"After his death I continued to give the reports to Renald. They were always glowing, Princess. Your father was very proud."

Yes, Rory thought wryly, considering the other meaning of the word. *Too proud to bend.* "Did my mother know?"

"I'm not sure."

Laurent addressed the police detectives. "Did Claude Dupont hire the assassin?"

"He may confess to it when we interrogate him," Detective Rodriguez, who seemed to be in charge, told her.

"If he'd hired a hit man, why would Claude try to shoot us, then?" Rory asked.

"Frustration, most likely. The accidents the hit man had arranged weren't achieving the desired results. Dupont was getting impatient. He wanted the job done and he didn't care about getting caught, which is why we found fingerprints on the fence and on the envelope."

"Do you think Claude stole my necklace, too?"

Detective Rodriguez shook his head. "No. My guess is it was the hit man. This kind of killer searches a home thoroughly looking for opportunities." He checked his notes. "You told me the necklace was stolen on Sunday while you took your cat to the vet. Or sometime on Monday when the house was overrun by assorted staff."

"Could the hit man be a bodyguard, Heinrich?" Laurent asked gravely.

"Anything is possible if one is offered enough money," Heinrich admitted. "I will make some enquiries."

"I do not believe the stylist is involved," Odette contributed from her post near the living room window where she was monitoring the activity in the street. "I accompanied her at all times. No one is to be left alone with a royal family member's personal belongings. Ms. Allard's references are impeccable.''

Detective Rodriguez noted the information. ''We'll need contact info for the catering company and the butler. We'll check them out.''

Renald produced a personal digital assistant from the pocket of his gray suit. ''I have the information here.''

Rory's heart pinched at the prospect that the grandfatherly butler could be the hit man. ''Pierce is the one who located my vitamins after I couldn't find them.''

''Dupont's been sloppy. We may find something to link us to the hit man once we discover where he's been holing up,'' Detective Rodriguez said confidently.

Laurent rose and took Rory's hand. ''You're staying at the hotel until the assassin is arrested. No arguments.''

Rory caved beneath the concern rife in his eyes and the tantalizing promise of protection in his strong fingers. The same fingers that had stripped a loaded gun from a crazed man's hand. When Laurent looked at her like she was his princess, she wanted to be near him tonight and always.

Even if her heart whispered that he didn't love her.

AFTER THE POLICE were finished with their questions, Rory, Laurent and Olivier were escorted to waiting limos with their heads covered to avoid the cameras. To satisfy the journalists lusting for a story, Detective Rodriguez made a brief statement. Then Otto was interviewed about the gunman's identity, but claimed he had never met the man. He referred to Rory as a friend who had dropped by, but refused to give her name.

Rory gratefully accepted the room that was prepared

for her in her brother's suite. She spent the rest of the day talking privately with Olivier and Renald. Although she still felt miles apart from their world, a fragile bond was forming between them, a sense of belonging that she hoped would grow stronger once she visited Estaire. They had an early dinner as her brothers were taking a private jet the next morning. Over dessert, Rory was relieved when Renald put down his fork and told Olivier of his plan to ensure that Princess Penelope gave birth to an heir.

Olivier's shock was apparent. "You would have done that for us?"

Renald nodded. "I would have considered it my duty. I will understand if you wish me to resign my position."

Olivier sighed. "I will need to give the matter more thought. In fact, I am beginning to reevaluate several of our father's decisions." He paused, his gaze resting pensively on Rory, "Including the marriage treaty with Ducharme. There is no question that the union would be beneficial. But if it alienates one further from one's family, I am not convinced that it is worth the sacrifice."

Rory's heart started to thud. She couldn't believe what she'd just heard. "Really?" she squeaked.

Olivier covered her hand with his. "I do not wish to deprive you of your right to choose your destiny, *ma petite soeur*. If something were to happen to me, I am confident that Renald would assist you in every way possible."

Renald smiled cautiously. "You can count on it."

Rory tried to grasp the thought that she could walk away from Laurent now if she wished. It was the only thing she'd wanted since she'd found out about the ridiculous treaty. But things had changed. Her heart had changed. Did she want to walk away? Could she?

She thought of how she felt when he held her and the way his inky gaze probed her to her soul, stirring up desires. "I'm not sure," she admitted honestly.

"*Bon.* Then I suggest you take time to know your heart. I can reschedule my appointment at the clinic and stay a few days longer until the police arrest this assassin. Or Renald can remain here with you."

"No! This appointment is too important to reschedule and I think you and Renald have a lot to discuss. I'll be fine with Laurent and Heinrich's men."

"All right, then. We will talk again of your feelings for Prince Laurent when you come to Estaire."

Rory forced a smile. Her feelings for Laurent were exactly what she was afraid of.

LAURENT FELT RATTLED about spending an evening alone with his princess. It was their first date, and he wanted it to be an evening that they would remember for the rest of their lives. He wanted to distract her from the fact that the police had not identified or arrested the assassin.

Although the police were strenuously investigating and conducting interviews, Claude Dupont had hired a lawyer and was not talking. The police had not yet discovered where he had been staying.

Rory had awakened early this morning to wish her brothers a safe flight, but Laurent had noticed she'd been subdued during her German lessons and her clothing fittings. He wondered if she was missing her brothers—or feeling trapped in her position, trapped with him.

Whenever their gazes met, he felt the strong pull of

a current, drawing him to her. He wanted their first dinner alone to be as intimate as the conversations they had shared when she thought he was Sebastian Guimond. With the assassin still at large he was reluctant to put Rory at risk by venturing outside the hotel. Instead he had made arrangements with the hotel staff for a private dinner.

Nerves lodged in his stomach as he presented himself at the princess's suite at 7:00 p.m. He had forgone a suit in favor of black trousers and a black knit shirt. He had told Rory that dinner would be informal. He nodded at the bodyguard posted outside the princess's suite.

Chandale Allard opened the door, beaming. "Good evening, sir. The princess will be right out." Her hands spread in front of her. "Prepare to be blown away."

Laurent raised his eyebrows. Americans had such peculiar expressions. "Blown away?"

"She looks incredible."

"Ahh." Laurent stepped into the suite. The last thing he desired was to be reminded that his princess affected his control like no other woman on earth.

Despite the stylist's warning, every muscle in his body ached with a need for release when his princess emerged from the hallway into the salon. She was half-clothed. She wore a virginal, white cotton crocheted top that bared her golden shoulders and her midriff and a white flirty skirt of a diaphanous material that made his fingers itch to peel it up over her thighs and explore her gorgeous body. Delicate sandals accented the slender beauty of her feet, and a fine gold chain studded with seed pearls circled one ankle.

Her eyes were as blue as the mysteries of the ocean, hiding her thoughts, but the hesitancy in her step and the blush of uncertainty in her cheeks was his complete undoing.

He was Crown Prince Laurent Sebastian Wilhelm of Ducharme, and he wanted to be on his knees before this woman, touching, tasting, granting her pleasures that made her tremble.

But they were only supposed to have dinner.

The scented sweetness of her hair enveloped him, sending a fierce hunger pounding to his groin as he kissed her forehead. "Words fail me at your beauty, Princess."

Her eyes leveled on him, frank and clear with a feminine power that made his heart pause. "Not Princess… Rory."

And Laurent knew that he was in more danger than he had ever been in. He knew why his mother had regretted falling in love with his father. He found himself on an emotional precipice and battled for the strength and the wisdom to keep a calm head. "I've been looking forward to this all day," he said, placing his hand lightly on the small of her back and guiding her to the door.

Her skin was temptation tenfold, so satiny soft he imagined it would taste like sun-warmed honey.

They stepped out into the hallway, and he guided her to the right, instead of across the hall.

Rory had intuitively known, from the moment her gaze had met Laurent's in her suite, that they were going to make love tonight. He'd looked at her as if he wanted her naked. Her breasts ached for his touch. Her body was already craving the hardness of his muscled chest and thighs.

"We aren't dining in your suite?" she asked as they walked toward the end of the hallway where she saw Heinrich standing in front of a door.

Laurent ducked his head, his voice caressing her ear. "I have a surprise. For you."

Warmth stole over her. "What kind of a surprise?"

Heinrich opened the door for them.

Rory caught her breath. She was being swept into a fantasy. The balcony doors facing the ocean were opened wide, and a gentle salt-laced breeze stirred the yards and yards of sheer white fabric draped sensuously over wooden Morrocan screens that concealed the room's formal wallpapered walls.

Rose petals and white lily-shaped candles floated in a brass tub nestled in a bed of sand in the open doorway. More candles glowed from tall brass lanterns with ruby-red glass lenses. On the floor was a bamboo mat on which a gold-silk-covered chaise was piled with luxurious pillows in bright sari fabrics of cerise, cobalt and celadon. Two red silk ottomans were placed beside a low table offering platters of cheese, pâté, fruits and other delicacies.

"I couldn't take you to the beach, so I brought the beach to us, *mein* Lorelei," he murmured to her.

"Oh, Sebastian!" Rory turned and Laurent's lips were on hers, hot, demanding and reckless. His fingers splayed through her hair, angling her mouth to fit his. This was a passionate, uncontrolled side of him that made her want to wrap her body around him now and agonize over the decision later. He felt so strong, so powerful.

She ran her hands over his chest. Then, needing to feel his hot smooth flesh, she yanked his shirt from his trousers and explored the rigid muscles of his abdomen.

Laurent groaned and deepened the kiss. Rory joyously continued her exploration, finding the flat circles of his nipples.

She smiled into the kiss as his hands moved from her hair to her breasts to the bared flesh of her midriff. The heat of his palms sent her senses skyrocketing into meltdown mode as he traced her ribs. When his thumbs finally brushed her swollen nipples through her lace bra, Rory whimpered with an urgency that left her thong panties damp with anticipation.

He eased her bra and the cotton fabric aside and suckled her breast, increasing the budding tension locked inside her. The tension built to an exquisite height as he devotedly caressed her other breast with his tongue. "I'm courting you, *mein* Lorelei," he whispered against her damp areola. His warm breath made her shiver with delight.

Rory made a unilateral decision that he was overdressed for the occasion. "I'm courting you, too, Sebastian. You need a wardrobe change."

She tore at his belt, then unzipped his zipper and freed his arousal from a pair of black briefs. The steely soft strength of him in her hand filled her with new love for this man. Laurent could be hard and inflexible, but gentle and sensitive at the same time.

She wanted him, wanted his love more than anything she'd ever wanted in her life. When she was in his arms, her father's abandonment and her mother's lies didn't matter. She felt healed. And she wanted to heal him from his own heartaches.

Laurent broke the kiss. With a fluid motion he pulled off his shirt and divested himself of his shoes and other clothes. His naked body was shockingly beautiful. He was at his most vulnerable—scars and all.

He took her hand and placed it on his chest where she could feel the racing thrum of his heartbeat. "I offer you my devotion and my passion, *mein* Lorelei. And my solemn word that I will treat you always with respect.''

She moistened her lips. ''Does that mean you still won't take off my clothes?''

He muttered an oath in German and picked her up, depositing her in a heap on the chaise. His lips curved with amusement. ''If madame would like her clothes removed, I am her humble servant.''

Rory's heart leaped as he joined her on the chaise.

Laying astride her, he hitched her top up over her breasts and laved her, his tongue tracing a damp path to her belly.

Rory dug her fingers into his hair and squirmed impatiently. ''I thought you were taking my clothes off.''

''All in due time. A man doesn't gorge himself at a feast, he takes his time and savors each bite.'' His tongue dipped into her belly button and a shudder of delight ripped through her. ''You see? I can taste you here. And here.''

His lips and his tongue moved seductively lower. Rory arched her hips toward him, greedily accepting his caresses.

He eased up her skirt as if peeling back the petals of a flower. He ran an appreciative finger over the thin strip of silk that covered her femininity, rubbing her through the fabric. Rory writhed at the incredibly erotic friction. He kissed her inner thigh, then kissed the damp fabric.

Her body quivered. ''Sebastian, please!''

He obligingly moved the tiny band aside, and the rasp of his tongue sent her over the edge. Only, the pleasure didn't stop. He kissed her and caressed her with his clever fingers while she shuddered and cried out his name. She was barely cognizant when he stripped her of her panties and her skirt, and slipped her top over her head.

Time shifted around her. She was only aware that as lovely as this pleasure was, she needed to hold him inside her to fully express the love she felt. She urged him between her parted thighs.

He slid into her, filling her body. Her heart soared at the communion of their souls. He started to move, murmuring words in German she didn't understand, but she knew they were beautiful and they were about her. His handsome features were fixed in concentration. Rory met his every thrust eagerly. Willingly.

The pleasure became too much, and her world fragmented like a wave crushing down on her. She felt Laurent buck inside her as he reached his own climax. She held him tightly into her body. "I love you, Sebastian!"

Laurent collapsed on top of his princess, breathing raggedly, holding himself back. Her words of love rang in his ears, reaching a deep part of him that hadn't been touched by anything in much too long. But he was unable to answer. He saw his mother's face, heard her grief.

He cradled Rory's face in his hands, kissing her delicate brows, her adorable nose and her golden rosy cheeks. "You are so beautiful, *mein* Lorelei," he told her over and over again. But he couldn't look her in her eyes, and he couldn't bring himself to say the words he knew she waited to hear. Duty came before everything, even love.

Chapter Fourteen

Rory stole out of the suite at six o'clock in the morning. Laurent was deeply asleep. They had made love three times, each time more incredible than the previous. They had lain on the chaise naked, eating and laughing. She felt sated and pleasantly sore, but a growing unease nagged her.

Even when she had rolled over on top of him and ridden him until he'd thrown his head into the pillows and buried his hands in her hair as he begged her never to stop, he had not whispered a word of love.

Maybe it's too soon, she thought, blushing as she nodded at the bodyguard who was on duty in the hall-way.

Maybe she was only kidding herself, an inner voice warned. Maybe he would only ever love Marielle.

To her surprise, Odette was sitting at the desk in her suite's salon, her head bent over the black leather portfolio that no doubt contained Rory's schedule for the next few days. A cup of coffee was at her elbow.

She lifted her head as Rory entered, a stiff, cautious smile spread on her coral-pink lips. "Good morning, Your Serene Highness. How was your evening?"

Rory was aware that her hair was a mess and her

clothes were wrinkled. She wanted a bath and a long nap and some time to think about what had happened between her and Laurent. "Eventful. I'm exhausted."

Odette demurely lowered her eyes to her schedule. "You have an elocution lesson at nine-thirty, followed by a French lesson at eleven. Will you be all right or would you like me to rearrange your schedule?"

Rory was tempted to cancel, but she remembered what Laurent had told her about inconveniencing the staff with last-minute schedule changes. "No, I'll be fine. Just make sure I'm awake by nine."

"Very good. Pleasant dreams, madame."

Rory was almost to her room when it occurred to her that Odette must have known Marielle. She doubled back to the salon, hoping to ask Odette about Laurent's relationship with the heiress, but Odette was on her cell phone.

"I've just reviewed the princess's schedule with her. Everything's continuing as planned…"

Rory told herself she'd ask the press secretary later.

TALKING INTO A MICROPHONE to an empty conference room on three hours of sleep was not a good way to begin the day.

Rory had never liked public speaking. The thought that she would be required to make speeches at public engagements was way beyond her comfort zone. She struggled with the mike for over an hour, trying to read the speech that Odette had prepared and master the art of making eye contact while appearing relaxed and sincere. To her frustration, the elocution teacher Odette had hired reminded her every few minutes to put her mouth closer to the mike or to speak up. Or not to slouch.

By the tenth rehearsal, Rory was ready to tear up the index cards. Her throat was bone dry.

Odette brought her a glass of water and told her she was doing fine. Rory took a grateful sip of the water and put it on the shelf inside the podium. Then she began the speech one more time from the beginning. "Good afternoon, ladies and gentlemen. It is a great privilege to—"

"Confidence. Acknowledge the audience," the elocutionist called from the center of the room.

Rory gave the podium a kick and felt a trickle of water dribble down her knee. Great.

Odette placed her hand over the mike. "Why don't you take a break and finish your water while I have a word with Ms. Johnson about your next lesson."

Rory glanced down. She'd spilled half the water. She drank what was left, then snagged several tissues from her purse and mopped up the mess.

Fortunately, Odette was walking the elocution teacher to the exit. Rory grabbed her purse to tell Odette she wasn't up for a French lesson.

As Rory caught up with Odette near the exit, the press secretary took a call on her cell phone. Odette signaled Franz at the entrance to the conference room. She spoke urgently to the bodyguard.

Shock telegraphed in the blonde's pale features, warned Rory that something was wrong. "What is it?"

"That was Heinrich. Prince Laurent went down to the hotel's jewelry store, and he was shot at close range."

"Shot? Close range? Is he—" Rory's heart sped up, and she had trouble getting a full breath. "Is he all right?"

They'd just made love all night, and now she faced the terrifying possibility of losing him.

Odette slipped a supportive arm around Rory's waist. "Come with me! The bodyguard's gone to get a car. They've taken Laurent to Mercy Hospital."

Rory needed no further urging.

"He's strong. We are not going to lose him," Odette told Rory comfortingly as they hurried out the lobby entrance. A limo pulled up to the curb, and Rory numbly clambered into the back seat.

Odette picked up the phone and told the driver their destination. "Don't waste any time!"

Rory couldn't believe this was happening. A heaviness descended upon her, weighing her down. She closed her eyes, digging deep inside herself for strength. For courage. She could hear Laurent calling her his Lorelei and telling her she was beautiful. A tear slid onto her cheek. They were supposed to have forever together. She wanted to experience the joy of knowing that he loved her. "Who did it? Did they catch him?" she asked, biting back a sob.

Odette patted her hand. "Heinrich didn't say."

Rory silently urged the limo to go faster. It seemed to take forever to drive over the Coronado Bridge. She expected the limo to head north on Interstate 5, but when the driver headed south toward National City she snatched up the phone. "You're going the wrong way—"

Suddenly her arm felt too heavy and it wasn't working right. The phone slipped from her fingers and tumbled to the floor. Her eyelids drooped. She felt odd, drowsy and incredibly tired—like the day she'd passed out during her defensive driving lessons. Had she been drugged again?

Odette serenely bent to retrieve the phone. "Don't worry, Princess. The driver knows where he's going."

Her foggy brain registered a note of triumph in Odette's tone. Oh, no. The water! Odette had drugged her!

Fighting to stay conscious, Rory fell across Odette while reaching for the button that controlled the privacy screen. She had to alert Franz. The screen slid down a few inches. But the front passenger seat was empty.

"Help!" she screamed to the driver.

Odette straightened, squishing Rory against the back of the seat. Then Odette grabbed her arm and yanked her down onto the floor of the limo.

Rory flopped like a dead fish. Odette smiled coldly, not an elegant blond hair out of place. Her gray-green eyes gleamed. "Meet the man who is going to kill you, Princess."

Rory blinked blearily at the press secretary. The drug was too strong. It was overtaking her. The stories Odette had told her of her childhood in the palace jumbled together in Rory's mind along with something Claude had said about the night Marielle had died. Claude had thought Marielle was okay because she was with a girl-friend. Rory had a sick, queasy feeling the shoulder Marielle had cried on was Odette's. She licked her lips. "You killed Marielle."

"Of course I did," Odette replied smugly. "She was planning to trick Laurent into marrying her by getting pregnant. I couldn't let that happen. Laurent kissed me when I was thirteen, and that's when I knew I was des-tined to be his princess. With you finally dead, he'll be free to follow his heart. He will realize that his true princess has always been beneath his nose."

"You stabbed the fashion designer, too?"

Odette shrugged. "He was sleeping with her."

Rory couldn't keep her eyelids open any longer. Regret that she couldn't protect Laurent from Odette's scheming flooded her heart. "He might marry you, but he'll never let himself love you," she mumbled as she lost consciousness.

RORY HAD LEFT HIS BED this morning without waking him. Laurent sat at his desk unable to concentrate, knowing the reason she'd left.

His head jerked up as Heinrich entered the salon accompanied by Franz. Heinrich's face was bone white. His dark eyes carried news Laurent knew he did not want to hear.

"It's Fraulein Schoenfeldt and the princess. They have been lured out of the hotel on false pretenses."

Franz flexed his shoulders, shame reddening his tight jaw. "Fraulein Schoenfeldt received a call she believed was from Heinrich. She was told that you had been shot and were taken to the hospital. She ordered me to get the car."

Disbelief echoed in Laurent's heart. The assassin was still at large. "Can you not call the driver?"

"He's not answering his phone."

Laurent glanced at his watch, horror growing inside him. "When did this happen?"

"It's been seventeen minutes since they were last seen by a doorman. Detective Rodriguez is en route," Heinrich reported solemnly. "They are putting out an APB for the vehicle, and Rodriguez is requesting the assistance of a police chopper." A flush crept over Heinrich's collar. "Sir, if you will forgive me for the impropriety, I fitted the princess's handbags with tracking devices last night. She had already breached her personal protection measures twice. After what happened with Dupont yesterday, I felt the measure justifiable with the assassin still at large.''

Laurent gripped Heinrich's shoulders. They'd address the privacy violation later. "Can you track her now?"

"*Ja.* If she has her handbag. I would prefer you—"

Laurent cut him off. "I am coming with you."

RORY HOVERED between consciousness and unconsciousness. She felt the hot July sun on her face as she was dragged out of the limo and heaved unceremoniously onto the padded floor of a delivery van. Her bones jarred with the impact. Why were people always tossing her around?

She flexed her fingers. She was too weak to move. But at least she was awake after a fashion. Maybe the drug was wearing off. She heard voices: Odette's and a man's.

"What do we do now?" Odette asked.

"I've found the perfect place to dump her. The police will be looking for the limousine. This will buy us time to get out of the area. I'll drop you off near a gas station on the way to El Centro. The police will believe I intended to dump her in the desert. You pretend you escaped, and I'll expect my final payment within two business days—along with a bonus for the chauffeur. He won't be talking."

Rory kept her eyes closed as they climbed into the van. They crossed her arms mummy-like over her chest, then tore a strip of duct tape and stuck it on her mouth.

"One more thing," Odette said. Rory felt her nemesis attach something around her neck. Her birthday necklace!

"Roll her up now," the hit man directed.

No! It took all Rory's self-control not to scream when she realized what they were doing. Claustrophic panic rioted through her as they rolled her up in a scratchy rug. She couldn't move, could hardly breathe. The sound of more strips of duct tape being torn almost made her sob.

The hit man bound the rug snugly around her with the tape. "That should keep her quiet. She won't last longer than an hour or two in this heat once we leave her in the Dumpster. Best thing is, they'll never find her body."

"Clever man. A garbage dump seems fitting for a trashy American princess. What about her purse?"

"Tuck it inside the carpet with her. I don't want any evidence left lying around."

Rory felt tears of gratitude as her purse was wedged into the roll above her head.

She waited until the van pulled onto the road, then she concentrated on the painstaking task of inching a hand up over her face toward her purse. A princess wouldn't be caught dead without certain essentials.

THE POLICE HELICOPTER had spotted a limousine parked behind an abandoned building two blocks ahead. Laurent sat in an unmarked police car as it raced through the streets of National City with its lights flashing, watching a blipping dot move on a computer screen. He prayed they would find his princess and his press secretary in time.

Detective Rodriguez radioed dispatch for an ambulance. Laurent's stomach felt as if it were being pummeled to dust. "But the dot is still moving east," he protested.

"We'll check the limo first. He may have left Odette there and switched vehicles," Heinrich explained. "We approach Odette with caution. I am finding it suspicious that she mistook someone else's voice for mine."

"I am wondering the same thing," Laurent admitted. "Could it have been a tape recording? She was distraught."

"But to dispatch Franz to get a car?"

Laurent stabbed his hair with his fingers as Detective Rodriguez gunned the police car through an intersection and wove through midday traffic at breakneck speed. "I keep thinking about the theft of the princess's necklace. You know, Odette was on the yacht the night Marielle died. She was a great comfort to me during that time. I secured her a position in the palace press office shortly thereafter and she has done her best to become indispensable to me. I am beginning to see, Heinrich, that we are sometimes blind to the secret ambitions of those around us."

The cruiser whipped into the parking lot of an out-of-business furniture store and drove around to the back of the drab building. Laurent's heart jammed in his throat as the police car screeched to a halt beside the limo.

Laurent and Heinrich bolted out of the car with Detective Rodriguez and his partner.

"There's no one inside the limo," Rodriguez shouted, trying the driver's side door. It was unlocked.

"Pop the trunk," his partner suggested.

Detective Rodriguez worked the trunk lever.

His partner swore. "There's someone in here."

Odette? Rory? Laurent forced himself to remain strong as he looked at the body in the trunk. It was the chauffeur, with a clear plastic bag sealed over his head.

He was dead.

Chapter Fifteen

Princess Charlotte Aurora, contortionist, Rory thought with pride as she squeezed her right hand up past her head toward her purse. She was never going to deride herself for her natural clumsiness. If she hadn't spilled the drugged water, she'd still be unconscious or maybe even dead.

Odette and the hit man were not engaging in chitchat. So far Rory had succeeded in peeling the duct tape from her mouth. Although she was suffocatingly hot and terrified, a sense of calm pervaded her. The night on her patio when Claude Dupont had shot at her and Laurent, Laurent had shown her by example to keep a cool head under fire.

Rory was taking that lesson to heart. She was not powerless. She was a princess of Estaire.

Odette and the man driving the van had killed her mother, and Rory was determined to survive her ordeal to see justice done. Her fingers were damp with sweat as she fumbled with the clasp of her purse. It finally opened.

Sweat pearled on her upper lip as she slid her hand into the purse and found the pepper spray pen that Heinrich had given her.

It took four attempts to flick the cap off the pepper spray with her thumb. Her fingers were so sweaty!

Rory stretched her arm as close to the end of the carpet roll as possible and attuned her senses to the movement of the van. Were they in street traffic or on the highway? Heinrich had warned her that a person's reaction to cayenne pepper spray would be immediate and severe. She didn't want to cause a highway pile up.

Unfortunately the van seemed to be moving smoothly with only the occasional tap on the brakes. She guessed they were on Highway 94 headed east.

"How much longer?" Odette demanded in a strained tone.

"Relax. We're right on schedule. Damn!" The hit man slammed suddenly on the brakes. Rory, bundled in the rug, slid a half-dozen inches closer to the front seats. "Geez, people don't know how to drive. Come on, asshole—" He hit the brakes again.

Rory felt the van's deceleration. She had to act now. Praying for deliverance, she took a deep breath, closed her eyes tight and pressed the button of the pepper spray.

THE TRAFFIC PARTED ahead of them like a school of fish avoiding a predator. They had been joined by several other police cars. Overhead, a police helicopter hovered.

"We're drawing nearer," Heinrich announced. "Just up ahead. The dot shows them merging onto the other highway."

"Watch for a truck or a van with dark windows," Detective Rodriguez said. "Once he sees us, he'll make a run for it."

Up ahead Laurent spotted the sudden erratic movement of a white van. It veered into another lane, side-swiping a silver sedan. "There, the white van!"

The silver sedan changed lanes to pull over to the shoulder of the highway.

The white van came to a halt, and the driver and passenger doors flew open. A blonde in a pastel-blue suit staggered out of the passenger side. She was bent over double, clutching her face. "That's Odette."

To Laurent's shock, the male driver reeled blindly away from the van and was struck by a semitrailer that was braking to avoid him. The man bounced off the truck as if he were made of rubber and landed on the asphalt.

There was no sign of Rory.

Pandemonium reigned. The police cars boxed in the scene and officers spilled out, headed toward Odette and the hit man. Detective Rodriguez tried to hold Laurent back, but he broke free of the detective's hold. The police were shouting warnings about approaching the van, but Laurent ignored them. An officer opened the rear of the van.

"Mein Gott!" Laurent stared in stupefaction at the roll of carpeting, pain tearing his heart. Were they too late?

He heard muffled coughing. "Help! Please, help me!"

"Lorelei, we're here," he shouted, coughing, his eyes tearing up as he helped the officer pull her out of the van. The officer cut the tape that bound the rug. And there was his princess, red-faced and rumpled, and very much alive.

Her beautiful blue eyes opened, filling with tears as he gathered her into his arms.

She buried her face into his shoulder. "That's no way to travel." Then she threw up all over his shoes.

RORY HUDDLED on the floor of Laurent's suite, the balcony doors flung open to the ocean, letting the sound of the surf soothe her.

After a quick trip to the emergency room, she'd returned to the hotel under police escort. Somehow the media had caught wind of her parentage and her title and Laurent's identity, and they had staked out the hotel's entrances. News footage of the accident scene was being broadcast on every station.

The intrusive glare of the cameras had been alarming. She'd been grateful for the protective strength of Laurent's arm. He'd insisted that she stay in his suite. She'd bathed and he'd joined her in the steamy water. He'd washed her hair and they'd made tender, gentle love. Then he'd carried her to bed and held her until she'd fallen asleep. But he didn't tell her he loved her, and although Rory needed to say the words to him as much as she needed to hear them, she bit them back.

A handful of stars shone in a sky that reminded her of the inky depths of Laurent's eyes. It was two o'clock in the morning. The ceaseless energy of the water called to her, tossing answers to her unspoken worries.

Rory had lit a white pillar candle for her mother and wore her birthday necklace in quiet celebration.

Odette was in jail and the hit man was dead. The police had identified him as Elmer Nash. They were searching his home in Long Beach for evidence of his crimes. Rory felt no sorrow for him. Fortunately, the driver of the silver sedan had not suffered any injuries in the collision.

"Mom, I'm okay," she whispered to the ocean's

sympathetic ears. "I survived. And I understand why you left Dad and you couldn't go back. You were right."

"Lorelei?"

Rory turned. Laurent stood in the shadows in a pair of black silk pajama bottoms. His beautiful chest was bare, the muscles gleaming in the flickering candlelight. Her throat ached with love and regret.

She patted the floor beside her. "Come join me."

His lips brushed her hair as he nestled beside her and circled her waist with his arms. "Could you not sleep?"

"No. There's too much to think about."

"You handled yourself magnificently today."

She squeezed his hard thigh. "I had an exemplary teacher. You saved me today."

He shook his head. "Heinrich deserves the honors although he broke several rules with his tracking device."

"I'm naming my firstborn son after Heinrich, but you were the one who taught me not to let fear overtake me."

"I'm flattered."

She leaned her shoulder into his chest and felt the steadying pound of his heartbeat. "I've made a few other decisions." She hesitated. "I'm meeting Olivier and Renald in France on Saturday. I'll be going to Estaire with them. I think it's time Princess Charlotte Aurora returned to her birthplace and faced up to her responsibilities."

"If that is what you wish, my princess."

She lifted her face and admired his dark profile and the tautness of his supple lips. "Do you love me, Sebastian?"

He stiffened, his features wary. "We have talked

about this before. Love serves very little purpose in a royal—"

"Marriage," she finished for him. "I know. I am prepared to make many sacrifices for Estaire, but the one thing I will not sacrifice is the right to be loved by a man of my own choosing. I love you, Sebastian. Not your crown." She touched his firm chin. She would miss not having children who bore his aristocratic features.

"I value your friendship and these moments we have spent together more than you'll ever know, but I can't devote my life to a partner who withholds his love from me." She sniffled, trying to retain her dignity. "I'll be asking Olivier formally in writing to release me from the terms of the treaty. I thought you deserved to hear it from me first. I hope that working together as colleagues we can bring an end to the feud between our countries."

Laurent nodded. He swallowed hard, but he didn't say anything. Frankly, Rory hadn't expected a response. She knew him so well. Her heart ached for his pain, his loneliness, his loss.

She kissed him lightly on the lips, then blew out the candle and walked away. Sometimes a woman needed to take a stand for what she believed in, even at the risk of losing the man she loved.

THE HEADLINES MOCKED HIM. Laurent wished Heinrich would quit leaving the damn tabloids all over his quarters. For the past six weeks, Laurent had found the newspapers and magazines left in chairs, on tables, even in his private car. It was damn irritating to be constantly reminded that he had been royally dumped.

Princess Spurns Royal Proposal. Prince Ducharme

Has No Heart. Princess Takes Palace by Storm. The Real Reason Rory Dumped Her Prince. Royal Love Triangle.

The flood of bad press had renewed the feud between Estaire and Ducharme. The world seemed to be cheering that Princess Rory refused to enter a loveless marriage.

Laurent was not cheering. He was spending long hours working or trying to find enrichment in books that no longer satisfied him as they once did. His pride was bruised, and his father had scolded him for bungling the treaty and allowing the situation to escalate into a full-blown scandal. The Schoenfeldt family had left Ducharme in disgrace, creating yet another flurry of headlines.

No matter how frequently Laurent tossed the tabloids in the rubbish bin, they resurfaced in another location to taunt him. On the one hand Laurent was incredibly proud that Rory was spreading her wings and proving that she could handle her royal responsibilities with confidence and wit. She'd even successfully ridden out the inevitable rumors questioning her legitimacy.

But he was disturbed to see her smiling picture in the paper at a Paris nightclub with a movie star. Did she really think some poorly shaven actor would know the first thing about raising an heir to the throne?

With each passing day Laurent felt an ache swell beneath his bruised pride—an ache for his beautiful Lorelei. He missed their stimulating conversations and her adorable faux pas. And the softness in her voice when she called him Sebastian. He missed her riotous curls and the impetuous unchecked heat that made him feel so incredibly alive when he touched her. When he kissed her.

He missed *her*. The isolation of his position had never

seemed so unbearable. Rory had opened up his emotions like a gutted fish, leaving him with his innards exposed.

Yet, what was he going to do about it?

With a sigh, Laurent helped himself to a brandy from the bar in his private quarters and sank down into his favorite club chair. To his irritation a newspaper had been tucked between the arm of the chair and the seat cushion. Laurent removed the newspaper with a grimace.

The front page headline pushed him beyond restraint: Princess Pregnant with Prince's Love Child.

Laurent swallowed the brandy in one gulp. There was rarely any truth in these trumped-up stories, but it was time to reopen negotiations.

''MESDAMES ET MESSIEURS, it is with great pleasure that I present my sister, Her Serene Highness, Charlotte Aurora, Princess of Estaire,'' Prince Olivier announced to the guests and dignitaries gathered in the palace ballroom.

Rory beamed and held her head high as she made her grand entrance into the ballroom amid applause in the stunning orange gown that Laurent had picked out for her all those weeks ago. Olivier kissed her, as did her newly pregnant sister-in-law Penelope.

The silver-and-blue rococo ballroom shimmered with light and mirrors and crystal. In well-rehearsed French, Rory told the invited guests how happy she was to be home after living abroad for so many years and that she was honored to serve Estaire and its citizens.

Despite the difficulties of learning what her new position entailed, Rory loved Estaire with its hillsides dotted with wild poppies and daisies and the vineyards of

Riesling grapes sloping down to the ancient village of Auvergne on the banks of the Rhine.

Renald winked at her from the sidelines. In the past eight weeks, Renald had decided that he would like to continue in his position as his brother's personal secretary, and he did not wish to bring scandal upon his mother's name by making the facts of his birth public.

Rory and Olivier had accepted his decision, but had made it clear that they considered him a brother in every way.

Rory's heart froze when she realized who was standing beside him. Laurent.

No, not just Laurent. It was Prince Laurent in formal ceremonial dress of black tailcoat, white piqué waistcoat and tie. He looked even more handsome than he did in her dreams, his inky eyes shielding mysteries that her heart still ached to share. She wasn't over him yet. Like her mother, she'd probably never get over the man she loved.

"*Mesdames et messieurs,* if you would indulge me for a special presentation." Olivier gestured regally. "His Royal Highness, Crown Prince Laurent of Ducharme."

Rory's pulse fluttered and her knees trembled as Laurent made his way up to the dais where she stood with her brother and sister-in-law. She watched him warily.

He acknowledged Olivier and Penelope, then he went down on one knee before Rory. Gasps filled the ballroom.

Her face turned scarlet and her heart plummeted to her stomach as Laurent kissed her gloved hand. Was he going to offer her a public apology?

Her knees threatened to buckle from the warmth of his fingers.

"My darling, Lorelei," he said in his rich clear voice. "I've come here this evening to beg your forgiveness for my arrogance. You offered me the gifts of your love and friendship and demanded the same in return. In my arrogance I thought our union would better withstand the pressures of our positions if we didn't bring false expectations of love into the equation. But there is nothing false about my feelings for you, *mein* Lorelei. I love you, not as a crown prince, but as a man who wants a cherished partner to share his joys and sorrows with. I want your beautiful face to light my days and your wise words to comfort me and make me laugh. I offer you my heart and my devotion with my two hands." His voice shook, and Rory saw tears in his eyes.

That set her off. She started to sniffle.

Laurent smiled at her, his handsome face softening with love. "Will you honor me by agreeing to be my wife?"

Rory beamed at hearing the words she'd longed to hear. "It's hard to resist a man who can admit when he's wrong. I love you, Sebastian. Yes, I'll marry you."

He removed a diamond ring from his pocket and slid it over her gloved finger. "This was my mother's ring." Then he rose and kissed her. The room exploded with applause.

"Champagne!" Olivier ordered.

Laurent laughed, joy dancing in his heart and in his soul. He had never been happier in his life.

Rory was breathless. "What made you change your mind?"

He told her about the newspapers Heinrich kept leaving for him to find. "I read one that suggested you were pregnant with our child."

Her beautiful blue eyes widened. "Is that what your proposal was about? Some kind of misguided duty because you think I might be pregnant?"

He pressed a finger over her lips, unable to keep from smiling. "Shh, *mein* Lorelei. Allow me to finish."

Rory stopped talking, but her eyes sparked her opinion.

"The newspaper article made me think about my mother and the legacy she passed on to me. She spent most of her life pining for my father's love and never having the courage to ask for what she wanted and to expect it as a right. I realized I didn't want to spend my life like that. Life can be very lonely when you do not have love."

The wariness faded from his princess's eyes as Laurent kissed her, losing himself in the lure of her sweet lips.

Love was much headier than the power of the monarchy.

PROTECTING THE PRINCESS

BY
CARLA CASSIDY

Carla Cassidy is an award-winning author who has written over fifty books. In 1998, she won a Career Achievement Award for Best Innovative Series from *Romantic Times*.

Carla believes the only thing better than curling up with a good book to read is sitting down at the computer with a good story to write. She's looking forward to writing many more books and bringing hours of pleasure to readers.

Prologue

The explosion of gunfire shattered the beauty of the California spring morning. Screams rent the air as people dove for cover or ran blindly in terror.

It happened so quickly she didn't have a chance to do anything but react. Princess Anna Johansson and her father, King Bjorn Johansson had just retrieved their baggage and been heading out of the Los Angeles airport to hail a cab when a pair of men opened fire.

The air filled with the acrid smoke of danger. A panicked crowd jostled Anna away from the scene as they pushed and shoved to escape. She dropped her suitcase in an effort to stay on her feet as the people went wild.

She held tightly to her purse and small overnight bag despite the press of the bodies against her.

Panic choked her as she lost sight of her father in the resulting chaos. What was happening? Had he been shot? How had they been found? They had been traveling under different names, had changed planes twice in the past twenty-four hours. How had the rebels known where they were?

Anna managed to slip out of the crowd that carried her away and crouch behind a stack of luggage. She tried to see what was happening, tried to catch sight of her father.

Her heart thundered. She had to go back. She had to find her father. But fear kept her momentarily rooted in place. What if they'd killed him? Grief ripped through her, but it was a grief that couldn't be sustained beneath the weight of cold, stark fear.

What if the gunmen were still around the area? They wouldn't be satisfied just killing her father. As his only heir, she was a liability.

Her heart continued its rapid beat as she tried to make sense of what had just occurred. She'd thought when they reached the United States they'd be safe. They had been so careful with their travel plans.

Roused from their beds two nights prior to the sound of gunfire and explosions, they'd learned from loyal palace staff members that rebels had taken over the small island kingdom.

Their lives in danger, they'd been hustled away

from the palace and into hiding until arrangements had been made to get them out of the country.

At this moment none of that mattered. What mattered was finding her father and getting them both to someplace safe. But, where was safe? And where was her father?

Taking a deep breath as she left the cover of the luggage stack, she tried to head back in the direction where she and her father had been separated, but was halted by police before she could even get close to the area.

There was no way she could speak to the authorities. She was traveling with false identification. She had no idea what might happen if she was detained. Her father had warned her that there would be danger until he could speak with the appropriate people and request some sort of temporary asylum. She had no idea who she could trust.

Think. She had to think. Turning away from the police line, she inhaled several more deep breaths in an attempt to still the racing of her heart. Her father had planned for the possibility of trouble.

Aware that her life could still be in danger, she hailed a cab and slid into the back seat.

"Take me to the nearest hotel," she said to the driver, then slumped back in the seat to catch her breath. The past forty-eight hours had been terrifying and apparently the danger wasn't behind her yet.

She wouldn't actually check in to a hotel, but she

could sit in the lobby to take a few minutes to bring her nerves under control and hopefully catch a news report to see exactly what had happened.

Digging into her purse, she withdrew the business card her father had handed her just before their plane had landed. "If there is trouble…" he'd said. "If we get separated for any reason, you go here."

He'd handed her the little white card that read "Wild West Protective Services." She had noted the address in Cotter Creek, Oklahoma, and several telephone numbers as he'd added. "These people will protect you and I will join you there as soon as it is possible."

She held the card tightly between her fingers and stared at it. Wild West Protective Services. She had no desire to go to Cotter Creek, Oklahoma, but knew she had no other choice.

She was in a strange country, with nothing more than what was contained in her purse and small overnight bag. Separated from her father, she would only be able to rejoin him if she got to Cotter Creek and utilized the services of these Wild West bodyguards.

She only prayed that the attack hadn't left her father dead and that the assassins wouldn't find her before her father did.

Chapter 1

"You must protect me." The voice belonged to the attractive blonde who flew through the open door of the Wild West Protective Services office.

Slamming the door, she locked it, then leaned against it as if to bar the hounds of hell from bursting through behind her.

Tanner West had just been about to leave the office for the day, but a burst of adrenaline drove all thoughts of home out of his head. Unsure of what was going on, he grabbed the 9 mm gun that was never far from his reach.

"Protect you from who?" Unceremoniously pushing her aside, he was fully aware that a lock on a door wouldn't keep out somebody determined to get in.

"You don't have to get physical," the blonde exclaimed, apparently offended by his actions.

He ignored her protest as he peered out the window. Nothing. He saw nobody on the street who looked like any kind of a threat. "What am I looking for?" he asked. "Who is after you? A crazy husband? A jealous boyfriend? A homicidal boss?"

"Rebel assassins."

He whirled from the window to stare at her, wondering if perhaps she was pulling his leg.

Rebel assassins in Cotter Creek?

She was a stranger to him. In a town the size of Cotter Creek, Oklahoma, he knew almost everyone and he'd never seen her before in his life. She was the type of woman he'd remember. "Rebel assassins?"

She nodded and dropped the small overnight bag she'd carried in to the floor. "Although I'm hoping I lost them after the shoot-out at the airport in Los Angeles."

Tanner felt as if he'd been thrust into the middle of a movie and had no idea of the beginning so couldn't begin to guess at the ending. Was the pretty blonde in front of him in need of some kind of protection or was she in the throes of some paranoid delusion?

"Maybe we should start at the beginning," he said, gesturing her toward the chair in front of the reception desk.

"I'm Tanner West, CEO of Wild West Protective Services." She sat in the chair and he moved to sit behind the desk—setting his gun next to him where it could be grabbed in a split second if needed. He took advantage of the moment to look at her more closely.

Her features were dainty. Her eyes a clear blue and her hair long and golden. Just looking at her caused the slightest rise in his pulse. She was one knockout.

"My father sent me here. Six nights ago rebel forces took over our palace and we fled our country and got on a plane for the United States. My father told me on the flight that if there was trouble, if for some reason we got separated, I was to come here to Cotter Creek and seek your aid. Obviously there was trouble, otherwise I wouldn't be here now. My father instructed me to come here and said you'd take care of things until he could arrive here, as well."

As his sense of urgency fled an edge of impatience took its place. He was no more clear now about what was going on than he'd been moments before when she'd first burst through the office door.

"Are you going to tell me who you are? Who your father is?" he asked, unable to keep the impatience from his voice.

Her startling blue eyes flashed with what appeared to be a touch of impatience of her own and her dainty chin rose slightly. "I am Princess Anna Johansson from the Island of Niflheim."

Tanner sat straighter in his chair, a new urgency

slicing through him. "Your father is King Bjorn?" Tanner had met the king of the small Scandinavian country two months before at a fund-raiser in Washington, D.C. At that time the king had mentioned having a twenty-five-year-old daughter. "Where is your father now?"

Her eyes darkened. "I don't know. We got separated at the airport in Los Angeles. Gunmen were waiting for us when we walked out of the exit to find ground transportation. The only thing I know for sure is that he wasn't shot. The news reports right after the incident indicated, thankfully, that nobody had been hurt but the suspects had gotten away."

She had a smoky kind of voice, a smooth alto that under other circumstances he might have found sexy as hell. But sex was the last thing on his mind at this moment.

He'd caught a bit of a newscast concerning the shooting at LAX and now wished he'd paid more attention, because it appeared that he'd just been handed the biggest protection assignment of his career. An assignment that would solidify Wild West Protective Services as the premier agency to call when trouble came knocking.

He and his father had been following the news report on the coup, although the information coming out of the small country had been sketchy. He hadn't realized until this moment that the incident at the airport and the coup in Niflheim were related, as the reporters had apparently not realized that King Bjorn and his daughter had been in the airport melee.

If her story was true, and he had no reason to doubt it, then the most urgent need was to get her to a safe location.

He stood and grabbed his black Stetson cowboy hat from the top of the file cabinet. "Come on. We've got to get you out of here."

She got up from the chair, her gaze focused upward on his hat as a tiny frown appeared across her forehead. "Are you a cowboy?"

She said the word with the same inflection she might have used to say "ax murderer." "Among other things," he answered. "We need to go." He had no idea what problem she might have with cowboys, but he didn't have time for it right now. His initial thought was to get her someplace safe immediately.

"Where are you taking me?" She leaned down to pick up the small overnight bag, then held it out for him to carry.

He grabbed the bag and headed for the front door. "To the ranch."

"The ranch?" She halted all forward movement, a new frown tugging together her pale, perfectly arched eyebrows. "Oh, that won't do. I don't do ranches. Surely there's a nice hotel here in town. What I'd really like is a long massage. The past two days on that bus were an absolute nightmare."

Tanner stared at her in disbelief. She'd just told him

that rebel assassins were after her, and she was worried about whether she could get a massage or not. He recognized at that moment that the princess might be pretty and sexy as all get-out, but she just might be trouble, as well.

"Look, lady, right now my goal is to get you someplace safe. You might have to skip a massage or two to stay alive."

Her vivid blue eyes narrowed. "There's no reason to use that tone of voice with me, Mr. West."

Tanner bit back his aggravation. "Your father sent you here for safekeeping and until I have a better idea of what's going on, the safest place for you to be is at the family ranch." He wasn't about to let her screw this up for him by making unrealistic demands.

He moved to the door, unlocked it and eased it open, his gun once again in hand. He simply didn't have enough information yet to know how imminent the danger might be for her.

The late-afternoon April sun shone on the quiet streets of the small town. Two women walked at a leisurely pace up the sidewalk and old man Thompson sat in a wooden chair outside his barbershop waiting for customers. There was nothing to indicate assassins lying in wait.

However, assassins could mean a sniper on the top of a building, an explosive lobbed at his truck, a shadowy figure in a doorway waiting for the perfect shot.

He turned back to look at her, unable to help noticing how the fine silk blouse clung to her breasts and the long navy skirt hugged lush curves. Even with the frown tugging at her features she was stunning. The momentary lapse into pure male thoughts irritated him.

"My truck is parked directly out front. We're going to walk out together and you're going to get into the passenger seat as quickly as you can."

There seemed to be a touch of mutiny in her eyes, but she nodded curtly and joined him at the door. Tanner was unsure exactly what to make of the princess, but he knew his job, and that was to assure her safety. He'd get a better handle on her and the entire situation once he got her to the safety of the ranch.

He set her overnight bag just outside the door. "To the passenger side," he murmured as he wrapped her in his arms and led her out of the door. He felt her stiffen, as if she found his closeness offensive, but he didn't care. He had no idea what they might be up against, so he used his body as armor for hers as they headed toward his truck.

"I think you might be overreacting, Mr. West," she said stiffly as they moved forward together in an awkward kind of dance.

"It's your life, Princess. Would you prefer I overreact or underreact?" he asked curtly. "I'm just doing my job."

He could smell her perfume, a spicy, exotic scent that matched the smoky tones of her voice. Her body radiated warmth and the curve of her buttocks was against his legs as they moved. He felt a stir deep inside his gut, a slight rise in his pulse that both surprised and increased his irritation.

It was a relief to get her into the truck. He hurried back to the door of the office to lock it and to retrieve her bag, knowing he couldn't relax until she was safely ensconced at the ranch.

He needed to find out everything that had happened in the small country. He had to quickly learn about the coup and the escape of King Bjorn and his daughter. He needed to learn as much as he could to do his job to the best of his ability.

The fact that King Bjorn had sent his daughter to Wild West Protective Services filled him with enormous pride and a sense of responsibility that was weighty. Of course, he shouldn't be surprised that the king had sent her to them for safekeeping. After all, years ago Tanner's father, Red West, had saved the king's life.

A real, honest-to-goodness princess. She was the first royalty to come to them for protection. It was an enormous boon for the company, a huge coup for him.

He didn't have enough facts yet to know exactly what was going on, but one thing was certain; failure would put the family business and reputation on the line.

But, more than that, if what she said was true and

assassins were after her, then failure could mean the death of the pretty young woman who had placed her life in his hands.

Anna couldn't believe it. She couldn't believe her father had sent her to this man, to this place. As she'd sat on the bus that had carried her from California and into this land of dust and cows, she'd been horrified.

She couldn't believe her father had sent her to a…a cowboy for protection. Anna knew all about American cowboys, having seen a couple of Western movies. She knew they loved their horses, drank too much whiskey, ate beans out of a can and often threw their women over their shoulders like sacks of potatoes.

She watched as Tanner West strode around the front of the truck to get to the driver's door. His worn jeans hugged the long length of his legs and the cotton shirt he wore with the sleeves rolled up to the elbows exposed lean, muscled forearms.

There was something about the tall, broad-shouldered man that had instantly put her on edge. Maybe it was the calculating light in his dark green eyes, or the stern lines of his face, a face both handsome and hard. Or maybe it was because she'd known him only minutes and already he had manhandled her more than anyone else had in her life.

As he got in behind the wheel he seemed to fill the interior of the truck with a taut energy. He placed his gun between them on the seat, then started the engine and backed out of the parking space.

"This ranch of yours? Does it have amenities?" she asked.

He turned his head and cast her a quick glance, his eyes almost hidden by the low cast of the rim of his hat. "Do you mean, do we have electricity and running water? Shucks, Princess, you're in luck. We even installed indoor plumbing not long ago."

She flushed, recognizing the slight bite of sarcasm in his deep voice. "Good," she said with a forced lightness in her tone. "I wasn't sure what to expect."

"You can probably expect that things at the ranch won't be up to your usual style of life, but we'll do our best to make sure that you're comfortable for the time that you're here."

"*We?* There are other people who live on this ranch of yours?"

Despite the fact that she wasn't thrilled at the prospect of spending any length of time at a ranch, she felt herself start to relax. This would be the last place on earth any of the rebel assassins would think to look for her. They would probably check out her ritzy vacation destinations first—Miami or Vegas or New York City.

"Lots of people live on the ranch," he said in answer to her question. "It's a big spread. Besides all the men who work for us, there's my father and the rest of the family and our housekeeper, Smokey. Although right now it's just my father and Smokey. Everyone else is out on assignments."

"You have lots of bodyguards who work for you?"

"It varies at any given time."

She studied him while his focus was fixed out the window and on the road. He looked so hard, as rugged as the scenery flashing by.

There were starbursts of lines at the corners of his eyes, lines she had a feeling hadn't been created by laughter. His jaw was lean and taut and already showing the bluish black hue of a five o'clock shadow. The black hat covered much of his dark hair, but from what she'd seen of it when he'd been hatless, it was thick and had just a hint of curl.

There was nothing soft about his body, either. As he'd hovered around her on the walk to the truck, she'd felt the hardness of muscle, the heat of his body and, to her surprise and dismay, she'd found his nearness just a little bit exciting.

She thought of the bodyguards who had been assigned to her in Niflheim. They had been professionals who had adhered to a strict dress code and who had always been deferential to her wants and needs. None of them would have ever shoved her aside without apology or taken liberties by nearly smothering her with their bodies.

This man, this Tanner West, didn't look like a professional bodyguard, nor did he look like the CEO of a business. He looked like a cowboy.

"My father will expect you to assign your best bodyguard to me," she said.

"I wouldn't have it any other way," he replied in his smooth, deep voice.

Satisfied for the moment, she looked out the window and frowned at the vast expanse of nothing but plains. Occasionally a house would appear tucked between pastures and wheat fields, but the general feeling she got as she gazed out the window was one of isolation and loneliness, of civilization gone.

"This is horrible," she murmured to herself. If she'd had anything in her wallet besides a handful of credit cards, she would have run. She would have escaped this place and this man and headed for real civilization.

"Excuse me?"

She turned to look at him. "This place. It's so…so barren."

"First trip to the United States?"

"No. I travel to the States frequently. New York City is one of my favorite places in the world to visit."

"We don't have much in common with New York City," he replied.

She frowned and stared out the window once again. "I can see that. What do people do out here?"

"They live. They work. They raise families and live a simple, productive life. I'm sure it all seems quite alien to you."

She shot him a sharp glance, and met his quick

gaze. His dark green eyes were fathomless, making it impossible to discern if he'd intended to insult her or not. She decided to give him the benefit of the doubt. She suspected most cowboys were probably rough around the edges and short on social skills. He'd certainly already shown himself to be short of social skills.

Surely the man he assigned to her would be more civilized, much more understanding and respectful of her position and accustomed lifestyle.

Surely whoever was assigned to guard her wouldn't have a hard glint in his eyes or a mouth that looked as if it had never curved up in a smile. Surely he wouldn't have the subtle arrogance she sensed in Mr. Tanner West.

I will not be intimidated by a cowboy, she told herself. Even if that cowboy wore his jeans better than any man she'd ever seen.

"You don't have an accent," he said, breaking the uncomfortable silence.

"My nanny was American. My teachers were Americans. My father thought it important that I speak English flawlessly, without any discernible accent."

Once again silence fell between them.

He turned down a dusty two-lane road with bumps as big as the suitcases she'd been forced to leave behind at the Los Angeles airport.

Within minutes a sprawling ranch house came into view. Anna sat up straighter in the seat as he turned into the driveway. Apparently this was to be the place where she would spend her time until her father showed up or contacted her with new plans.

The house itself was neat, painted a pristine white with black shutters and trim. Colorful spring flowers bedecked the sidewalk that led up to the front door. It didn't look as bad as she'd initially expected, and for that she was grateful.

In the distance were dozens of other buildings and there were cows in a nearby pasture, their heads raised as if watching their arrival.

He parked the truck in front of the house then turned to face her. "We'll get you settled in, let you clean up, then I'll have more questions for you."

His gaze was cool, with a flinty hardness that for some reason set her pulse racing. She was accustomed to men looking at her with a certain deference and respect. She saw neither in his eyes.

"Fine. All I want right now is a place to freshen up. When will I meet the person assigned to guard me?" she asked.

"You said you wanted the best."

"I insist on it," she replied firmly.

"Then you've already met him." His eyes, those impenetrable eyes, locked with hers. "I'm the best there is. You'll be my responsibility for the duration of the time that you're here." He opened the truck door, but still held her gaze. "We'll get you settled in, I'll do a little research, then I'll go over the rules with you."

He got out of the truck, but she remained seated for a long moment. Rules? She couldn't remember the last time she'd had rules for anything. What possible rules could he attempt to impose on her?

With any luck her father would arrive soon and the threat against them would be resolved. She had a feeling she and the handsome cowboy in the tight jeans weren't going to last long together at all.

Chapter 2

In Tanner's line of work it was important that he be a good judge of character. He had to be, to work with people as closely as he did. It had taken him all of two minutes to recognize that the princess was probably spoiled and more than a bit willful.

Niflheim was a wealthy country, and the personal wealth of King Bjorn was enormous. Tanner could be certain that Princess Anna was accustomed to a life of luxury.

Control. He had decided it was best to establish who was in control from the very beginning with the lovely princess.

He'd learned through his years in the business that

good protection wasn't possible if the agent wasn't in complete control of the potential victim. He hadn't become one of the best at this by accident.

Although officially he worked for his client in the protection business, it would only work if the client listened to him. He had to be the one in control.

Tanner retrieved her small overnight bag from the back of the pickup, then waited for her to get out of the truck. As he waited, he tried to remember everything he knew about Princess Anna Johansson of Niflheim, but nothing concrete came to mind. He was familiar with the country and with the king, but he knew nothing about the woman now in his keeping.

He'd have to do a thorough Internet search to see what he could find out about his newest assignment. He also needed to find out exactly what had happened in Niflheim and at LAX.

More than anything, it was imperative that he calculate the risk to her and establish a plan for her protection.

She got out of the truck and joined him on the sidewalk, looking none too pleased with him or the place where she found herself.

He didn't care about her happiness—he'd see to her basic creature comforts—but his main concern was to keep her alive. That's all that was important to him.

She swept past him with the imperial walk of a queen, head held high and small feet moving in purposeful strides. When she reached the front door she turned back to him, her eyes once again flashing with impatience. "Are you coming, Mr. West? I'm eager to get settled in."

He bit back a retort, joined her at the door and opened it to allow her entry. As always a sense of welcome engulfed him as he walked into the house where he'd been born and had lived most of his life.

He didn't live here in the main house anymore. Three years ago he had moved to the smaller three-bedroom house that had been the original homestead on the property when his father had bought the land years earlier.

This evening he'd move back into the main house to guard the princess 24/7.

The scent of cooking beef drifted from the kitchen. Nobody met them at the door, not that Tanner expected anyone. Smokey would be busy in the kitchen finishing up the dinner preparations and his father was probably out in the back working in the garden that had become an obsession in the past couple of years since he'd decided to semiretire from the family business.

"I'll take you to the room where you'll be staying," he said to Anna. She followed him down the long hallway that led off the entry.

When Tanner's father, Red, had married, he'd dreamed of lots of children and had built the house with a large brood in mind. The house boasted five bedrooms, four bathrooms and a dining area that could seat more than a dozen. It was perfect for a family that boasted six children.

The only people now living in the house on a regular basis were Tanner's father, Tanner's sister, Meredith, and Smokey Johnson, the cook and housekeeper.

He led Anna to what was now one of the guest rooms, a pleasant room decorated in greens and pinks with its own private bath. He set her overnight bag on the bed then turned to look at her.

She stood just inside the doorway, her gaze taking in the surroundings. She finally caught his gaze and nodded slightly, her blue eyes cool. "This will be fine for the brief time I'll be here. If you'll excuse me, I'd like to freshen up."

"You'll find everything you need in the bathroom. Dinner is in the dining room in half an hour. Don't be late." With these words he turned and left the room.

He went outside and around to the back of the house, where his father stood watering the large garden plot. Redmond West was a big man, tall with broad shoulders. He'd always been a dynamic man, but in the past couple of years he'd mellowed significantly.

A severe case of arthritis had forced Red to leave the business he loved and he'd taken to gardening as a way to pass some of the hours of the days.

Tanner quickly filled his dad in on what had transpired at the office and about their new houseguest. Red had been concerned about the king and his daugh-

ter when the reports of a coup had begun to trickle in
to the national news. All of the reports had indicated
the king had gone into hiding, but Red had feared
them dead. He was glad to hear that King Bjorn and
his daughter had escaped the country, but upset to
hear about the attack at the airport, which indicated
they were certainly not out of danger. Tanner then
went back into the house, to the study, and sat at the
desk where a computer was on and ready for his use.
Before he began his Internet search, he used his cell
phone to call two men who worked for him, arranging for them to take up guard positions at the front and
back of the house. It was just a precaution.

He used the Internet often for keeping up on the
news. The first thing he needed to do was to check any
and all stories concerning the coup in Niflheim. It
took him only minutes to learn what he needed.

The reports were sketchy and not filled with much
information other than the fact that insurgents, after
months of political unrest, had taken over the palace.
According to the news report the king and his daughter had gone into hiding.

He learned that there were two factions, a left wing
and a right wing, each attempting to gain control of
the country. Early reports were that the left-wing rad-
icals led by a man named Swensen had pulled off the
coup.

He also checked out the news about the shooting
at the airport, disappointed that the last news report

indicated that authorities had no idea what had prompted the attack or who had committed it. Because nobody had been killed, Tanner had a feeling this particular incident would fade quickly, would be shoved aside in favor of other crimes in the city.

He'd have to get more information from Anna. He needed to understand what was happening in the country and why the rebels would want her dead. She was gone from the country, so why the need for assassins?

Typing in Anna's name, he thought of the woman who was his newest assignment. Although she had full, inviting lips, there was a petulance to them that set him on edge.

As the search engine pulled up a long list of sites, he began to read the stories generated by the lovely princess.

She made the society pages frequently. Details of her jet-set lifestyle made good gossip fodder. There were pictures, as well, grainy photos of her modeling designer clothing, drinking Dom Perignon in a trendy London club and sunbathing on a yacht in the Caribbean.

He leaned back in his chair and studied one of the photos. In this particular picture she was on the dance floor in a Miami club. Her short dress exposed long, shapely legs and her head was thrown back in laughter.

Tanner knew the type. In his years in the protective services industry, he'd seen up close and personal the self-indulgent, lazy lifestyles of young men and women who had too much money and expected special treatment as their due.

After dinner he'd learn more important facts from her, facts that might help keep her alive.

He reared back in his chair, his thoughts racing. It had been almost twenty years before that his father had worked briefly for King Bjorn. The two men hadn't been in contact for years.

When Tanner had met the king at the fund-raiser in Washington he hadn't been working for the king. He couldn't see how anyone could make a connection between Wild West Protective Service and the king of Niflheim. Surely she was safe here…for the moment.

He shut off the computer and left the study, at the same time checking his wristwatch.

Life in the West household ran on a routine that was rigid yet comfortable. Dinner would be served in ten minutes and he needed to let Anna know that tardiness wasn't acceptable.

This wasn't a five-star restaurant where she could order up room service when she decided she was hungry. He didn't care what her life was like in her world. She was in his world now.

He knocked on the closed bedroom door and waited for a response. After several moments she opened the door. "Yes?" She eyed him as if he were a gnat buzzing irritably around her head.

Although she was fully dressed in the same clothes

she'd been wearing, her hair was wet and she smelled like soap, letting him know she'd used the past fifteen minutes to take a quick shower.

"Dinner will be served in five minutes. If you aren't at the table, you won't eat." He realized he sounded too abrupt, almost rude. Something about this woman set his teeth on edge. "Smokey, our cook, always has dinner ready at five-thirty," he said in an attempt to temper his abruptness.

"Then I'll be in the dining area at five-thirty." She closed the door.

Tanner sucked in a deep breath. He'd been with the woman only a little over an hour and already his irritation level had increased tenfold.

You're a professional, he reminded himself as he wandered through the great room and toward the dining room. You've worked with difficult clients before.

But none of those past clients had that silky blond hair. None of his past clients had lips that looked as if they needed to be kissed—badly.

Irritation surged up inside him and he pushed those particular thoughts aside. She was obviously spoiled, self-indulgent and demanding, negative traits certainly tempered any attraction he might feel toward her.

At five-thirty Tanner sat next to his father at the table as Smokey began to serve the evening meal. "Is the princess going to eat?" Smokey asked, his grizzly gray brows rising on his wrinkled forehead. Nobody knew Smokey's age, which he indicated was older than dirt. The old man had been the real head of the household for years.

"I have no idea what her plans are," Tanner replied as he served himself a large bowl of the beef stew. He'd told her what time dinner was served. Beyond that he had no responsibility as to whether she ate or not.

At exactly five thirty-five she entered the dining room.

"I'm sorry if I'm late," she said, although Tanner didn't think she sounded sorry at all. He wondered if perhaps her choosing to be late was a subtle form of control.

Red immediately stood and held out his hand to her. "Welcome to our home, Princess Anna. I'm Redmond West, Tanner's father and founder of Wild West Protective Services. Most folks around these parts call me Red."

"It's nice to meet you, Red. And please, just call me Anna."

"Anna it is," Red replied.

"Just Anna it has to be," Tanner said. "The last thing we want to do is let people know we have Princess Anna Johansson staying here. From now on everyone calls her Anna."

"Of course," she agreed. She smiled at Red as he held out her chair at the table.

It was the first real smile Tanner had seen on her face and it was magnificent. As her lips curved upward in the gesture all trace of petulance was gone and a warm sparkle lit her blue eyes.

The smile stirred Tanner on some base level that was distinctly uncomfortable and he looked down at his plate until she was settled in at the table.

Smokey entered from the kitchen carrying a platter of cornbread. "I see you made it in time," he said to Anna without preamble. "I hope you don't expect me to do no fancy cooking just for you. I only know one way to cook and that's plain, hearty food."

"I'm sure your cooking will be just fine," Anna said stiffly. "Besides, I don't expect to be here longer than a day, maybe two at the most. I can tolerate anything for that length of time."

Smokey snorted, slammed the platter of corn bread in front of her, then turned and disappeared back into the kitchen, which was his kingdom where he was the undisputed king.

"Don't let Smokey intimidate you," Red said. "He's all bark, but he doesn't bite hard."

"Help yourself," Tanner said, gesturing to the bowls and the stew. If she were waiting to be served, she'd have a long time to wait. "After dinner you and I need to talk."

She frowned, obviously not pleased at the prospect. "I can't imagine what we have to talk about. I've told you what happened and why I'm here. All you have to do is keep me safe until my father arrives, and I have every confidence in your ability."

"Tanner likes to cross his *t*'s and dot his *i*'s," Red said. "You might as well have a talk with him. He's a stubborn cuss and likes things done his own way." Red's voice was full of affection for his eldest son.

Anna's gaze met Tanner's and in those pretty eyes he saw a touch of calculation and more than a whisper of challenge. "All right, if you think it's absolutely necessary," she agreed.

"You know, I worked for your father many years ago," Red said as he passed her the butter.

"Really?"

"It was a long time ago, not long after your father first became king. I was in the process of building Wild West Protection Services and I'd managed to make some connections with some important people."

A wave of affection filled Tanner as he listened to his father talk. "Your father had planned a trip to New York, but he'd received information that one of his trusted bodyguards was a traitor." Red's voice was lively, his gaze fond as he eyed Anna from across the table. "King Bjorn contacted me and asked me to fly to Niflheim and accompany him on his journey. It was the biggest assignment of my career. I had to protect him not only from outside threats, but also from a potential inside threat."

"You must have been successful," she said.

Red nodded. "I managed to ferret out the traitor and keep your father safe for two weeks."

"That explains to me why my father sent me

here," she said. A frown appeared across her forehead. "Is it possible the rebels would guess that I'd be sent here?"

"I've thought about that," Tanner said. "I don't think so. As Dad said, it was years ago that he worked for your father and there has been no contact between them since then. I think you're safe here for now."

The rest of the meal consisted of good food and long, uncomfortable silences that nobody seemed inclined to fill. Tanner found himself casting surreptitious glances at her, noticing that while she ate most of the vegetables in the stew she didn't eat a lot of the beef.

He also couldn't help but notice she had the softest looking skin he'd ever seen, that her eyes were the blue of a cloudless Oklahoma sky and she had charming dimples that flashed occasionally in her cheeks.

He also saw that she had the hands of a woman who'd never worked a day in her life, soft hands with sculptured nails painted a pearly pink.

She'd made it clear she didn't want to have any sort of discussion with him, but Tanner was a thorough man and this was perhaps the biggest assignment of his career.

Whether she was under his protection for an hour or a week, he wouldn't be satisfied until he'd delved into the issues that had brought her here and had a profile of the group of men who apparently wanted her dead.

* * *

The meal had been horribly uncomfortable for Anna. The men had been quiet and she'd been aware that she was completely out of her element.

Throughout the tense meal, she'd found herself casting sly glances at Tanner. She found his face intriguing with its lean lines and firm square jaw. There seemed to be nothing soft about him. He was all broad shoulders and lean muscle and cold eyes.

Every moment she spent in his company only made her sorry she'd come to him in the first place. If circumstances were different there was no way she'd be here in the company of a rude cook and an arrogant cowboy bodyguard. The only one who had shown her any respect, any consideration at all, was Tanner's father.

The fear that had gripped her in those moments at the airport in California had long passed. She felt completely safe here. She didn't feel quite as safe after dinner as she followed Tanner into the study.

She had no idea what he thought they needed to talk about. She was beyond tired having slept little in the past three days. The meal had only served to deepen her exhaustion.

He closed the door behind them, then turned to face her and gestured her toward the chair in front of the desk. She didn't sit. As long as he was standing, she would stand.

She looked around the room with interest, noticing that one wall was covered with pictures. She walked closer, recognizing photos of both Red and Tanner. There were five more pictures, four men and one woman. "Are these the agents that work for you?" she asked.

"Yes and no. They are agents, but they're also my brothers and my sister." He moved to stand next to her and pointed to each photo. "My sister is Meredith and my brothers are Zack, Clay, Joshua and Dalton."

She could smell him, that scent of sunshine and male. She also thought she could feel his body heat radiating out to envelope her.

She focused her concentration on the photos and away from him. They were a handsome family, all of them dark-haired and with the same piercing green eyes that Tanner possessed. As much as she hated to admit it, she found Tanner the most attractive of them all. "You're the eldest?" she guessed.

He nodded. "Joshua is the youngest. He's twenty-five and I'm the oldest at thirty-five. The others are scattered in between."

"And your mother?"

"Is dead," he said flatly. "Now, can we get started?" He stepped away from her and to his desk.

She wanted to tell him she was sorry about his mother. She wondered when she had died, how old had Tanner been when she'd passed away.

Anna had lost her mother when she'd been twelve and her death had left a hole in her heart and a deep abiding loneliness that had never mended.

However the expression on Tanner's face seemed to forbid any kind of sympathy, so she swallowed whatever she might have said.

She didn't sit, but remained standing and looked at the rest of the photos that decorated the wall. "These other places, they're also offices for your business?"

"Satellite offices," he replied. "Wild West Protective Services has recently opened offices in San Diego and Miami. We're hoping to open an office soon in New York." There was an undeniable ring of pride in his voice.

"How did you get started in this?"

"My father started the business years ago when he was a young man."

"And what kind of clients do you have?"

"All kinds of people from all walks of life, although much of our business comes from high-profile people—politicians, dignitaries, athletes, even a rock star or two."

It was obvious Wild West Protective Services wasn't the rinky-dink operation she'd thought when she'd first burst through the doors of the office. "Why in Cotter Creek?"

"Dad originally began in Hollywood. He was in Special Forces, and when he left the service he wasn't sure what he wanted to do, so he went to Hollywood and began working as a stuntman. It didn't take long for him to realize there was a growing need for protection for some of the stars. He began the business there, but when he decided it was time to start a family he moved the business and his new wife out here to Cotter Creek." His eyes flashed darkly. "I've answered enough of your questions. Now it's time for you to answer some of mine."

She sighed and nodded, fighting off an overwhelming weariness. "What do you need to know?"

He sat behind the desk and pulled a notepad from a drawer, then focused his gaze on her.

He was a handsome devil, she thought. His gaze held no hint of any real friendliness and she held his stare boldly and wondered what he'd look like if he smiled.

Would a smile crinkle those fine lines next to his eyes? Would a smile ease the harshness of his features into something even more handsome? She decided she didn't care. She just wanted to get this over with and retreat to the privacy of her room.

"Who are the rebels who took over the palace?" he asked.

She blinked in surprise. "I don't know…just rebels… men who obviously want my father out of power."

"Did they belong to a specific political group? Are they part of an organization of some kind?"

She leaned back in the chair. "What difference does it make? They took over the palace and now they're in control of the country." She fought a shudder as she remembered the night she'd been roused from her bed and told her life was in danger.

His mouth thinned and a muscle ticked in his jaw. "I'm not asking these questions just to be nosy. I need to know everything I can about these men. Surely you know something about the coup, something about the unrest that had to have been present before the takeover. After all, we're talking about your homeland."

There was definite censure in his voice and she sat up and straightened her shoulders defensively. "Of course I knew there was unrest."

"But perhaps you were too busy traveling, sunbathing on yachts and clubbing until dawn to pay much attention to things back home." His voice was low and smooth, but it shot a hot burst of anger through her.

"What's the matter, Mr. West—jealous? I doubt if common cowboys have many opportunities to sun on yachts or go clubbing."

His eyes glittered with a dangerous light and his lips curved upward in a smile that wasn't particularly pleasant. "Trust me, Princess. I might be a cowboy, but there's nothing common about me."

She sighed impatiently. "Are you always this rude to clients?" She didn't wait for him to reply, but instead stood. "If all you intend to do is bait me, then I think I'll call it a night."

"Please." The muscle in his jaw ticked faster. "I apologize. This is important."

She hesitated, torn between wanting to run to her room and hide and the desire to show him she could take whatever he wanted to dish out. The latter won and she returned to the chair.

He gave a deep sigh and raked a hand through his hair. "Let me explain something to you," he said once she was seated. "One of the first things I do is create a profile on whomever is after my client. From the profile I try to figure out what might be the potential threat."

Anna sighed wearily. "I just think this is all unnecessary. I'm sure my father will be here in a day or so and there's no possible way the rebels could know I'm here. I wasn't even sure I'd come here when I left California. I'm sure there's no danger for me here."

"We can't know that for sure," he countered. "We can't know that unless I can identify the rebel forces, find out what kind of communication they have, what kind of technology they possess."

Again he surprised her. "I didn't know bodyguards concerned themselves with these kinds of things," she said slowly.

"Maybe others don't, but Wild West Protective Services is one of the best. Why do you think your father sent you here?"

"To punish me," she muttered under her breath.

He leaned forward in his chair, ignoring her reply. "I'll ask you again—what can you tell me about the rebel forces that took over the palace in Niflheim?"

She frowned thoughtfully, reluctantly admitting to herself that she hadn't paid much attention to such things. But, she certainly didn't intend to admit it out loud to him.

"The unrest in Niflheim wasn't something new, but in the past couple of months it has become much more intense. There were some people who believed it was time for the monarchy to fall and a new kind of government to take its place. The rebels who took over the palace want a parliamentary kind of government."

"And what does your father think?"

"I don't know for sure. My father doesn't confide in me about such matters." She could tell by his narrowed eyes that her answer didn't please him.

"According to the news reports the country is now in the hands of these rebels. They have what they want. Why would they want you and your father dead?"

"I don't know for sure. Maybe they're afraid my father will rally his supporters and attempt to reclaim the country. My father is not a man without loyal supporters. Maybe they're afraid that they'll never really have control unless we're in a position to never return."

He leaned forward, his gaze hard and focused. "Are these rebels organized? Is there a leader of their forces? Did you ever hear your father mention the names of these men?" The questions hit her like bullets.

"No...I don't know." Why hadn't she paid more attention to what was happening around her in Niflheim? "There was a group my father was concerned about, a radical group...but I can't remember their name." Exhaustion overwhelmed her and once again she stood. "I'm tired. I can't think anymore. We'll finish this tomorrow when I've rested."

"I certainly don't want to push you too hard," he said, an edge of coolness to his voice.

"You don't like me very much, do you?" she asked.

His gaze shifted away from her. "It doesn't matter whether I like you or not," he replied.

"If it's any consolation to you, I don't like you very much, either." She exited the office, breathing easier the minute she was out of his presence.

One thing was certain. He'd been right when he'd said that he wasn't a common cowboy. Tanner West was far more than that. It had been obvious from the story told by the photos on the wall in the office that Wild West Protective Services wasn't just a small family operation. It had also been obvious by the questions Tanner had wanted answered that he possessed a keen intelligence.

Smart and handsome, and something about him put her on edge, made her feel both vulnerable and defensive. She entered the bedroom where she would be staying and walked to the window.

Outside the sun had dipped below the horizon and darkness had begun to claim the sky. From this vantage point she could see nothing but pasture for as far as the eye could see.

A well of loneliness filled her. It wasn't a new emotion, but it had never been as intense as it was at this moment. She was stuck in a place she didn't want to be with an arrogant, hateful man who obviously didn't like her. She didn't want to be here but was powerless to go anywhere else.

She walked over to the bed and sat on the edge, pulling her overnight bag closer. She felt as if she'd been thrust into a horrid nightmare. As if the coup hadn't been bad enough, she now had to contend with Tanner West until her father arrived.

She opened the bag and withdrew the velvet pouch inside. Her fingers trembled slightly as she opened the pouch and withdrew the jeweled crown. It wasn't a large crown, but it held an array of flawless rubies, emeralds and diamonds.

Placing it on the top of her head, she leaned back against the pillows on the bed. She was Princess Anna Johansson of Niflheim and she wasn't about to let some arrogant cowboy bodyguard boss her around.

She pulled the crown from her head, once again filled with an overwhelming sense of loneliness. She hoped her father came for her soon and she could get back to her life of friends and parties and pleasures, a lifestyle that had always managed to keep that aching loneliness at bay.

Chapter 3

Tanner sat at the kitchen table reading through the information he'd printed off the Internet the night before. He'd worked long past midnight, searching obscure sites and trying to find whatever he could about Niflheim and the social unrest that had plagued the country.

He'd discovered that John Swenson, the leader of the left faction, had control of the palace but did not have control of the countryside and nobody seemed willing to guess who would eventually win total control.

He also tried to find out where King Bjorn was now, but he was unsuccessful. It was as if the king had

dropped off the face of the earth following the shooting at LAX.

It was now just after ten. Breakfast had come and
gone hours ago and still Anna hadn't put in an appearance. Not that he was surprised. She was probably accustomed to sleeping late, breakfasting in bed,
personal servants and social assistants.

While she slept the day away, he'd been busy. He'd
gone to his own place and packed a bag, then had moved
into the room next to hers. For the duration of her stay
here, he'd be here, as well. He'd also arranged for four
trusted ranch hands to work eight-hour shifts as guards
on the house, then be replaced by new, fresh men.

The rest of the morning he'd spent on the computer
printing off anything and everything he'd missed the
night before that pertained to the small Scandinavian
Island of Niflheim and the shoot-out at LAX.

It would have been nice if Anna had been able to
answer more of his questions the night before. But, he
supposed it had been too much to expect that the jet-
setting princess would have any clue about what might
have been going on in her own country. It was hard to
be in touch with the people's needs when you were
partying until dawn and shopping until you dropped.

"You want anything before I head to the laundry
room?" Smokey asked from behind Tanner.

"No thanks, I'm fine," he replied.

"You suppose that woman will ever make it to a
meal on time?"

Tanner turned in his chair and grinned at Smokey. "Who knows what that woman is going to do?"

"She's a pretty little thing even if she isn't worth a hill of beans," Smokey replied as he washed a coffee cup in the sink, then placed it in the dish drainer to dry.

"Is this where I come to be served breakfast?" Anna appeared in the kitchen doorway.

Smokey snorted. "I cook breakfast once a day, serve it at dawn. If you snooze, you lose. I ain't going to start changing my ways just because there's a princess in the house." With another snort, Smokey disappeared out the back door.

"My goodness, this house is full of disagreeable men," she said as she came into the kitchen and sat on the chair across from Tanner.

Tanner bit back the sharp reply that leaped to his tongue. He didn't want to start the day with a battle. "Smokey really isn't so disagreeable. I told you before, we have a routine in the house, a routine that was initially set up the year my mother died and Smokey wound up as cook and housekeeper. With six kids there had to be routines and rules. One of the cardinal rules of the house is if you aren't at the table when a meal is served, then you don't eat."

"All right, so breakfast is at dawn. What time is dawn?"

He eyed her narrowly, unsure if she was being sarcastic or not. She appeared to be quite serious. "Around six. Would you like a cup of coffee?"

She nodded and he got up from the table and went to a nearby cabinet to retrieve a mug. "If you want breakfast, I could probably rustle you up something," he offered grudgingly.

"Heavens, no. I wouldn't want to put anyone out. Coffee is fine."

"I guess you slept well," he said.

"Like a log. I hadn't slept much since the scene at the airport. I just got a few catnaps on the bus ride here. I was really exhausted. How old were you when your mother died?"

He blinked at the quick change in topic, then hesitated, unsure why she felt compelled to know this personal history of his. "Ten," he finally answered, realizing it might build some trust between them. "Cream or sugar?"

"No, black is fine."

He set the cup in front of her, then returned to his chair. "I was twelve when I lost my mother," she said. "I think it was the worst thing that's ever happened to me."

She took a sip of the coffee, eyeing him over the rim of the cup. "She had breast cancer and it wasn't caught soon enough. She went far too quickly. What about your mother? How did she die?"

"She was murdered."

Anna gasped and placed a hand on his forearm. "I'm so sorry," she exclaimed, her blue eyes radiating a compassion that surprised him. "That must have been horrible for you...for all of you."

Her hand felt dainty and warm on his bare skin. He moved his arm from beneath her hand, finding her touch far too appealing. "It was a long time ago," he said.

He picked up one of the pieces of paper in front of him and pretended to study it as she drank her coffee and stared out the window as if lost in her own thoughts.

She'd surprised him with that burst of sympathy that seemed at odds with the woman she'd shown herself to be in the short time he'd known her.

He stared at the paper and thought about his mother. It had been twenty-five years ago that his mother had been murdered on her way home from town. Twenty-five years ago and still Tanner felt the rip in his heart.

The night that her body had been found sprawled next to her car had been the only time Tanner had ever seen his father weep. That night had changed Tanner's life forever.

"The mist," Anna said suddenly, looking at him as if she'd surprised herself.

"Pardon me?"

She frowned and stared down into her coffee mug. "In Scandinavian mythology before Creation there were two places. Muspellsheim—"

"The land of fire," he said. Her gaze shot back at him and surprise once again lit her eyes. She was probably shocked that a stupid cowpoke would know such a thing. In truth yesterday he wouldn't have known about the myth, but his reading that morning had enlightened him.

"That's right. Muspellsheim was the land of fire and Niflheim was the land of ice and mist."

"Is there a reason for you mentioning this?" he asked, wondering where she was going. "Or is it that you just think I need a mythology lesson?"

"Yes...I mean no. The radical group—they call themselves something of the mist. Warriors of the Mist or Men of the Mist, or something like that. It just popped into my head." She looked inordinately pleased with herself.

"Good," Tanner said. "Maybe with that much information I can find out more about them. I already tried to find what I could on John Swenson, who apparently leads the rebels. But I couldn't find any information on him or his group."

"Did you find out anything about my father? Where he is now? If he's all right?"

He shook his head, wishing he had news for her. "Nothing. We can only assume that he's been taken into some sort of protective custody and will contact us when he can.

"Betrayed? What do you mean?" She wrapped her slender fingers around the coffee mug as if she needed to hang on to something concrete to hear what he had to say.

"There's no way assassins could have been waiting for you at the airport without knowing specifically what flight you and your father were on. They'd have to have known the time of your arrival and where you'd exit the airport, to lie in wait for you."

Her eyes grew wider with each word he spoke. "I hadn't thought about that," she said in a low, troubled voice.

"Who knew your flight information besides you and your father?"

"I don't know." She took a sip of the coffee, that charming frown back between her brows. "I don't know how the arrangements were made."

How could a twenty-five-year-old woman be so clueless, so uninformed about the forces that were driving her life? He couldn't imagine not being in control of his own destiny.

She raised her chin. "I can't imagine that anyone would betray us. I can't imagine anyone who was close enough to us could be capable of doing something like that."

"There's no other explanation for those men to have been at the airport at the right time, at the right exit."

He sighed and raked a hand through his hair impatiently. "Okay, then I'll see what I can dig up on this group of the mist or whatever."

"While you're doing that, I have some things to take care of myself."

Tanner eyed her warily. "Like what?"

"Hopefully there is a car that will be at my disposal while I'm here. If not, I can call a car service."

A car service in Cotter Creek? She'd have as much luck looking for an ocean in Oklahoma. The princess had no idea how normal people lived, he thought.

"One way or another I simply must go into town," she continued. "As you can see, I'm wearing the same clothes I've worn since my arrival in Los Angeles. I definitely need to do some shopping and I thought perhaps I'd get lunch while I was out."

Any modicum of amusement at her ignorance of a small town disappeared as he stared at her, for a moment at a complete loss for words.

"Are you insane?" he finally managed to exclaim.

She sat back in the chair, obviously offended. "Of course I'm not insane."

"Well, you aren't going anywhere." He stood. The abrupt motion sent his chair skittering backward along the wooden floor. "Especially not alone. What do you think this is? Some sort of vacation?"

She stood, as well, her blue eyes flashing with anger. "Of course not, but I think you're forgetting something, Mr. West. I'm your client, not your prisoner, and you can't stop me from going wherever I want." There was an edge of haughtiness in her voice coupled with more than a measure of stubborn resolve.

She turned to leave the room, but in three long strides he caught her by the arm, whirled her around and pulled her up against him.

"Listen, lady, I've worked my ass off for the last fifteen years to give this company the reputation of one that doesn't make mistakes. I'm not about to let you be my first mistake. If you're my client, then start acting like it instead of acting like a spoiled brat."

She gasped and her face paled. "Let go of me. How dare you speak to me that way." Her voice trembled and he released her, fully expecting her to run and lock herself in her room or some other such dramatic nonsense. He half expected her to yell, "Off with his head!"

Instead she straightened her shoulders and stood her ground. "I need some clothes and some personal items. If you don't want me to go to town by myself, then you take me or you send somebody to get the things I need." Her voice was deceptively calm.

The burst of anger that had exploded between them had astonished Tanner and he took a moment to intake a deep breath and steady himself.

The small overnight bag she'd brought with her hadn't been big enough to carry more than a few personal toiletry items. He reluctantly had to admit that she probably needed some clothes, especially if she was going to be on the ranch for any length of time. His sister Meredith's clothes wouldn't work, as Meredith was considerably taller that Anna.

"Be ready in fifteen minutes and I'll drive you into town to get what you need," he said against his better judgment. At least if he took her, he could control where she went and who got next to her.

"I'll be ready." She turned and started to leave the kitchen, but paused and turned back to face him. "And don't think for one minute you're going to throw me over your shoulder." She whirled around once again and stomped off in the direction of her bedroom.

Tanner stared after her, wondering what in the hell that meant. He took another deep breath and sank into a chair at the kitchen table once again. He couldn't remember the last time a woman had so riled him. And that anger had ignited so quickly.

What was it about her that had managed to push him over the edge of control? Tanner rarely lost his temper, but in the space of a few minutes she'd managed to make him lose all control.

Maybe it was the fact that she'd slept so late, or that she'd entered the kitchen apparently expecting somebody to serve her breakfast. Maybe it was the highfalutin tone in her voice.

It wasn't just the anger that had exploded so fast between them that had surprised him. He'd been shocked by the instantaneous streak of desire that had gripped him as he'd yanked her up tight against him.

Somewhere in the back of his mind, even though he'd been irritated with her, he'd registered the soft press of her breasts against his chest. His mind had heeded her scent, that provocative spicy fragrance that had been in his head since the moment she'd first walked into his office.

He didn't particularly like her. He certainly saw

nothing in her to respect or admire. But apparently that didn't matter to his body, for it had responded to her nearness with an intensity that had shocked him.

On some base perverse level he wanted her. And that was absolutely unacceptable. One of the worst things he could do as a bodyguard was get personally involved with a client.

Part of the problem was that Tanner couldn't remember the last time he'd been so attracted to a woman. For the last couple of years his work had consumed him. When this assignment was over, maybe he'd take a little time to attend to his personal life.

In the meantime, if what Anna believed was correct, then her father should show up here any day, any minute, for that matter, and that was just fine with Tanner.

The sooner he got rid of her, the better.

Anna stood in the bedroom, heart pounding in an unsteady rhythm. Tanner West was the most arrogant, aggravating and bossy man she'd ever met.

She grabbed her hairbrush from the dresser and dragged it through her hair, her thoughts still focused on Tanner and the scene they'd just had.

With a single glance of those wicked green eyes of his he could manage to make her feel stupid. And she wasn't stupid. Still, it wasn't the spat they'd just had that had shaken her.

What made her feel slightly unsteady, a little bit

breathless, was that moment when he'd yanked her up against him and that stern mouth of his had been mere inches from hers. She'd had an overwhelming impulse to kiss him, to see if those lips of his were softer than they looked. She'd wanted his eyes to flame with something other than cold disdain.

That impulse to kiss him irritated her more than his bossiness, more than the fact that he could make her feel stupid.

"Ouch," she muttered as she pulled her hair. She set the brush down and applied a touch of pink lipstick, dabbed some powder on her nose.

She had a feeling Tanner West was a man who was accustomed to people jumping when he spoke. Well, she didn't jump for any man, especially not a dusty cowboy.

She refused to allow Tanner to ruin her day with his ill temper. She was looking forward to going into town, eager to buy some clothing and burn the ones she'd been wearing for too long. At least the little trip would be something to do, a way to pass a couple of hours.

Aware that Tanner had said to be ready in fifteen minutes and that he was a man who obviously worshiped the clock, she left her room and went in search of him. She found him in the kitchen talking to his father.

"Good morning, Anna." Red offered her a warm smile. How did such a nice man get a son like Tanner? she wondered.

"Good morning, Mr. West," she replied.

"Please, I told you yesterday at dinner to call me Red."

"Then Red it is." She smiled at him. He was really quite nice. He was easy to see where Tanner got his height and broad shoulders for his father has the same attributes. Unlike Tanner, Red's eyes were blue, but the shape of their faces was the same, with the strength of a firm jaw and chiseled features.

"You might want to keep an eye on the sky," Red said. "The weatherman is calling for some strong storms moving in sometime this afternoon."

"Then we'd better get started," Tanner said, his voice brusque.

"We'll see you later, Red," she said, then hurried to follow Tanner's long strides as he walked toward the door.

Minutes later she was back in the dusty black pickup with Tanner behind the wheel. "Do you have bad storms here?" she asked once they were on their way.

"Sometimes."

"I've never liked storms," she said more to herself than to him. It had been storming the night her mother had died. She remembered that night as if it had happened yesterday. The storm had raged at the windows while inside her mother had finally given up her fight with the illness that had tormented her. Since that night rainstorms had always brought with them a sense of dread and loss for Anna.

"Before we get into town I want to go over the rules with you," he said.

She shoved her painful thoughts away and raised an eyebrow. "There are rules for going into town?"

He cast her a quick glance beneath the rim of his hat. "There are rules for everything you do while you're under my protection."

She released an audible sigh. "I'm not accustomed to rules."

"Get accustomed."

"Fine, tell me your rules, then I'll tell you some rules of my own." She intended to try to be as pleasant as possible for the duration of having to suffer his company.

"I'm not thrilled to be making this trip."

"Yes, I have that impression."

"I'll take you to a store where you should be able to get everything you need, but rule number one is that you don't leave my side…not for an instant. If anyone asks, and they probably will, your name is Anne Jones and you're a friend of mine from New York."

"Won't that make people suspicious?"

"What do you mean?" he asked.

"The fact that you have a friend."

A muscle ticked in his jaw, letting her know she'd scored a small point. "I was on assignment in New York last month," he said. "If anyone asks. That's when we met each other. The second rule is that once we're out in public you understand that you could be at risk. If I ask you to do anything, you comply immediately. You don't hesitate and you don't ask questions, you just do what I tell you to do."

She slid him a sideways glance. "You like that, don't you?"

"What?"

"You like having people who ask how high when you tell them to jump."

"Don't be ridiculous. I'm just doing my job."

"Is that it?"

"For now."

"Okay, now here are my rules." She sat up straighter in the seat. "When we're out in public you treat me with respect and you stop looking at me like I'm stupid, because I'm not."

"I never said you were stupid," he countered. "Is that it?"

"No, I have one more." She saw his fingers tighten around the steering wheel. "You have to get me something to eat while we're out. I missed breakfast and I have a feeling we won't make lunch and that means that cranky old cook of yours won't feed me again until dinnertime."

A whisper of a smile curved his lips, softening his features and sending an unexpected curl of heat through her stomach. "If Smokey heard you call him a 'cranky old cook' he'd tie you to Dante's horns."

"Who's Dante?"

"The biggest, meanest bull in the Midwest."

She noticed his hands had relaxed on the steering wheel. She turned her attention out the passenger window, wondering about that momentary surge of heat that had swept through her when he'd smiled.

Hunger, she decided. That had been a hunger pang, nothing more. She looked at him once again. "Smokey…how did he come to work for your family?"

"Smokey worked as my father's foreman. He took care of things on the ranch while Dad worked Wild West Protective Services," Tanner told her, then continued. "Two months before my mother's murder Smokey was thrown from a horse and trampled nearly to death." He shook his head. "My father always refers to that summer as the black summer."

"It must have been terrible," she said softly.

He gave a curt nod. "Anyway, with Mom's death and with Smokey no longer able to take care of the ranch work, Dad brought him into the house to help out. Smokey held us all together while we were growing up." His affection for the old man was obvious in his voice.

"Has he always been so…so…" She fought to find a word to describe Smokey.

"Yes," he replied. "Smokey has always been gruff and outspoken. But he also has a knack for organization, runs the house like a well-oiled machine and has a heart of gold."

She digested this information, unsure that she believed the crabby old man had a heart at all. "Your brothers and sister, do they all work for the agency?"

"All of them except Joshua. He left about a year ago and moved to New York City."

"Really? What does he do there?" She had a feeling she'd like the urban Joshua far better than she liked Tanner.

"He's a stockbroker." A wrinkle furrowed his brow.

"Where is everyone else?" she asked, curious about him and his family. As an only child Anna had always wondered what it would be like to have siblings.

The wrinkle disappeared from his forehead. "Right now we're all pretty well scattered to the wind. Zack is closest. He's on assignment in Oklahoma City. Clay is in New Orleans. Dalton is in Las Vegas and Meredith is down in Texas."

"You're close to all of them?"

He shot her a quick glance. "I'd die for any one of them."

A wave of longing stuck her as the familiar loneliness welled up inside her. She stuffed it down, refusing to allow it to take hold of her. "Tell me more about your family. What are they like? Are your brothers as mean and bossy as you are?"

Those green eyes splashed her with a look of cool mock indignation. "I'm not mean, except with people who force me to be."

She ignored his little dig. "Are your brothers and your sister as good as you are at this protection stuff?"

"No, but eventually they will be. I've answered enough of your questions. You talk too much."

"Just practicing a little civility, but I'm sure that's alien to you." She fell silent as she saw the small town of Cotter Creek in the distance.

She hadn't explored the town when she'd first arrived. She'd gotten off the bus and had gone directly to the offices of Wild West Protective Services.

As Tanner turned down what appeared to be the main street, she looked around with interest. They passed a post office, a bank and a grocery store.

The buildings looked ancient and were covered with the dust that seemed to be everywhere. Still, there was a certain charm in the stately old structures. Pots of bright-colored flowers decorated the front of many of the stores and awnings shielded the windows from the midday sun.

Tanner pulled up in front of a store with a pink awning and the words Betty's Boutique on the plate-glass window. A pleasant relief swept through her as she realized within minutes she would have new clothes to replace the ones she'd had on since the shooting at the airport in California.

Tanner cut the engine, unbuckled his seat belt and turned to look at her. "Okay, we go in, get what you need, then get out."

"Wait…I have a problem," she said as a sudden thought struck her.

"What?"

"I don't have any money. I spent my cash on the bus

ticket from California. I have a wallet full of credit cards but I have a feeling that's the last thing you'd want me to use."

"A credit card purchase would be an easy trail for somebody to follow," he said. "Don't worry about it. Get what you need and I'll charge it to our account."

"I'll pay you back," she assured him. "As soon as my father arrives, I'll see that you're paid back for any expense you have incurred."

"I'm not worried about it."

"I am. I don't want to owe you anything."

He nodded and together they got out of the truck.

She certainly hadn't expected designer fashions or a vast selection, but nothing had quite prepared her for Betty's Boutique.

The center of the store held racks that were filled with sturdy jeans and cotton shirts in all sizes. At the left of the store was a single rack of dresses, dresses that Anna could tell at a glance were like nothing she'd ever worn before.

"Morning, Tanner," a chirpy little voice called from the back of the store. The voice belonged to a plump, gray-haired woman who hurried toward them. "Don't see you in here too often." She gazed with open curiosity at Anna. "And who might this be?"

"Anne, this is Betty. She owns the store. Betty, this is Anne, she's a friend of mine from back east," Tanner said.

"I knew she wasn't from around here, not with

them fancy shoes." She pointed to Anna's dainty navy sling-back shoes.

"Actually, I'm from New York City," Anna said. "And it's nice to meet you, Betty."

Betty smiled at Anna, a sly smile. "Now I see why Tanner doesn't dally with any of the local women."

Anna sensed Tanner stiffening beside her. With impish mischief she smiled up at him and grabbed his arm. "He might not dally with the local women, but trust me, he dallies just fine. Don't you, darling?"

Tanner's arm was so rigid she felt that if she moved it just a little it would snap in two. A quick glance up at him let her know he was angry and eventually she'd pay, but at the moment she didn't care.

Betty released a high-pitched laugh, then winked at Anna. "I knew he probably had some pretty woman stashed somewhere. The rest of those West boys have always liked the women. Now, what can I do for you folks today?"

"I'm in need of some new clothing," Anna said as she released Tanner's arm.

"Ranch clothes," he said. Tanner placed an arm around her shoulder and smiled down at her, his eyes gleaming with what couldn't be mistaken for anything but payback. "My sweet Anne arrived with suitcases full of fancy designer things, but nothing strictly functional for mucking out stables and helping out around the place."

In that instant Anna saw her dreams of a couple of

sweet little dresses fly right out the window. She was unsure what "ranch clothes" were, but was certain she probably wouldn't like them.

"And boots," he added. "She definitely needs a pair of good, sturdy boots."

Half an hour later Anna stood in front of the counter and watched Betty ring up the purchases: three pairs of jeans, several T-shirts and short sleeved cotton shirts, and a pair of boots.

She'd picked out the boots herself, insisting on a red pair. Tanner and Betty had chosen the rest of the items. They'd even picked out a hat for her, a brown cowboy hat that she thought looked ridiculous on her head.

She had managed to snag two bras without a hint of lace on either one of them and several pairs of panties…no-nonsense white cotton. It had amused her that Tanner had looked distinctly uncomfortable as she'd made the underwear selection.

He might be the best bodyguard in the world, but he was obviously a man not comfortable with all things feminine and somehow that weakness made him less intimidating and more human.

They were just about to leave the store when he turned to her, a frown once again riding the center of his forehead. "We didn't get you nightclothes," he said. "Don't you need a gown or a pair of pajamas or something?"

With the knowledge of his discomfort in mind, she

smiled sweetly. "Oh no, that's not necessary. I always sleep in the nude." To her immense satisfaction his face blanched then filled with color as the muscle in his jaw ticked overtime.

Chapter 4

Tanner could have lived a long time without knowing that the princess slept in the nude. The minute the words left her mouth he'd been cursed with a vision that had sent his pulse rocketing and had dried every ounce of moisture from his mouth.

Shopping with her had been difficult enough. It had been obvious by the expression on her face that she hadn't been thrilled about the sturdy jeans and no-nonsense shirts he and Betty had chosen for her, although she proclaimed to adore the boots she'd picked out, a scarlet red pair embossed with flowers.

It had been particularly uncomfortable to watch her paw through the panties and bras, commenting that they were all so simple and plain. He had a feeling even simple and plain would look sexy on her.

He shifted the bag of her new clothes from one hand to the other, trying to think about something else.

She seemed to be holding no grudge after their spat in the kitchen earlier this morning. That surprised him. He'd thought she would be the type to pout and hold a grudge long after the fact.

He now stood outside the shop, waiting for Anna. He shifted from foot to foot, fighting a wave of impatience. Not all of the new purchases were in the bag. She'd insisted that she change into some of her new clothes before leaving the store.

Knowing that they'd been alone in the store with Betty, he'd decided to step outside to wait for her. He knew Betty kept the back door of the shop locked so the only way for anyone to get inside was through him, which wasn't going to happen unless he knew the person trying to enter posed no threat.

As he waited for her, he tried to shove the image of a naked Anna from his head and instead focus on his surroundings.

He knew this town and most of the people in it. He saw no strangers walking the streets, no reason to be concerned or alarmed for Anna's safety.

There seemed to be little chance that the assassins would guess that Anna would take a bus to a small Oklahoma town. He thought she was probably safe for the moment, but that didn't mean he intended to relax his vigil.

The gun tucked into the waistband of his jeans and hidden by the tails of his untucked shirt was a familiar companion, as was the knife strapped to his shin. He knew how to use both quite effectively and hoped he wouldn't have to while Anna was in his care.

"I look positively ridiculous."

He whirled around to see her standing in the doorway of the shop. Again his mouth went unaccountably dry and his pulse rate accelerated. The jeans fit her like a second skin, showing off her slender waist and clinging to her long legs.

The scarlet-red T-shirt matched her boots and the color enhanced her creamy complexion and blond hair. The shirt also pulled taut across her full breasts.

The cowboy hat sat on the very back of her head, looking as if it would slide off and to the ground, if she moved her head at all.

She didn't look ridiculous. She looked like a model that had stepped off the cover of a cowboy calendar. All she needed was a big horse and a lasso and she'd be every cowpoke's fantasy.

"You look fine. You now look like you belong in Cotter Creek," he replied, his voice sounding deeper than usual to his own ears.

"Now you're really scaring me," she said dryly.

He stepped closer to her and grabbed her hat,

adjusting it more on the crown on her head. "There. That's the way to wear a cowboy hat."

"Thanks, pardner," she drawled, her breath warm and sweet on his face. For a brief moment they remained mere inches from each other. Her scent surrounded him and he had the craziest impulse to press his mouth to hers. Her lips parted, as if in open invitation.

He jumped back from her, uncomfortable by their nearness and the crazy direction of his thoughts. What the hell was he thinking? "Where's your other things?" he asked, aware that she'd come out of the store empty-handed.

She waved her hands in dismissal. "I told Betty to throw them away. I certainly don't ever want to see that blouse and skirt again."

"She'll probably iron them up and hang them on a rack for resale. Not that people here have much use for designer clothes."

"If she can sell them, that's fine with me. I certainly don't want them anymore."

"Let's get these things in the truck."

"Lunch. You promised," she reminded him.

"I haven't forgotten," he replied. He really didn't like the idea of making her any more visible in the town. The less people who knew she was out at the ranch, the better.

But there were few secrets in Cotter Creek and Betty would probably already be buzzing to somebody about Tanner West's fancy big-city girlfriend. Trying to keep a secret was almost as impossible as having one in this small town.

It was easier to take her to lunch and to let people think she was a girlfriend visiting from out of town. Let people think he had nothing to hide. Besides, the lunch crowd was usually small and they should be able to eat and get out in a short period of time.

"We'll go to the café, but if I see somebody I don't recognize inside, we're going to head right back to the ranch," he explained as he stored her purchases inside the cab of his pickup.

She eyed him through narrowed eyelids. "You wouldn't pretend to see a stranger just to screw up lunch for me, would you?"

At first he assumed she was just giving him a hard time, but as he held her gaze he saw that she was serious. It surprised him, that she thought he would do something like that.

"Anna, you might not like me. You might think I'm bossy and controlling, but I wouldn't lie to you just to steal a little pleasure from you. Now, let's go get some lunch."

To his vast relief, she said nothing, but merely nodded, those big blue eyes of hers studying him as he led her toward the Sunny Side Up Café.

"The dining choices are limited here in Cotter Creek," he said as they crossed the street.

"Well, there's a surprise," she said, again that edge of dry humor in her tone.

He ignored her quip. "There's the café and a pizza place about four miles up the road just off the highway."

"Right now I'm so hungry you could just tie me up to Dante and I'd eat him," she said, and grinned up at him.

That grin filled her face with warm invitation and sparked her eyes and, for just a moment, she wasn't a princess with an attitude. She wasn't spoiled, lazy and demanding. She was just a very pretty young woman whose smile warmed him from the inside out.

Again he had a flash of a mental image of her naked in bed, her body sleep-warmed and her blond hair in tousled disarray.

She'd thrown him off balance almost from the get-go this morning, first irritating him to distraction with their argument, then flashing tantalizing glimpses of her sense of humor on the drive into town.

"Don't get too comfortable over lunch," he said gruffly. "I've got a lot of things to do when we get back to the ranch."

He was eager to get back to the computer. With the tidbit of information she'd told him earlier, that the rebels name had something to do with mist, he was hoping he could find something that would give him a handle on who he was dealing with.

While he worked on the computer she could surely

find something to do to entertain herself. He could use a little distance from her, at least until the thought of her naked body completely left his brain.

"Not much of a lunch crowd, is there?" she murmured as they walked into the Sunny Side Up. Two old-timers sat at the long counter that stretched along one wall and three middle-aged women sat at a table near the front of the café.

They were all familiar faces and Tanner felt himself relax a bit as he recognized the place held no obvious danger for a princess. He swept his hat off his head and she did the same.

"They do a good breakfast and dinner business, but at lunchtime most folks are too busy to have lunch out," he explained.

"Busy doing what?" she asked.

"Working. That's what most people do out here." He led her toward a table in the rear, where he could sit with his back to the wall and face the doorway.

He walked just behind her, trying not to notice how the tight jeans molded to her shapely backside. She sat across from him and immediately picked up one of the worn menus on the table.

"The rest rooms are down this hallway," he said, gesturing to the hallway next to their table. "Beyond the rest rooms is a back door." He spoke in a low voice. "If there's any problems and I tell you to run, you run out the back door and to the sheriff's office three doors down."

"I still don't think I'm in any danger here. Nobody in their right mind would look for me in a place like Cotter Creek."

That highbrow tone was back in her voice and he did his best to ignore it. "You're probably right, but I'm not willing to let down my guard until your father arrives and I know you're in good hands," he replied. "The reputation of my company rests on me keeping you safe."

"It's possible by the time we get back to the ranch he will have arrived. Then I won't need all the clothes and things you bought for me." She sounded pleased at this thought.

He shrugged and opened his menu. "I can always take them back." He'd like to take them all back right now and get bigger sizes for her.

As she studied the menu, Tanner scanned the interior of the café once again, then looked at his menu.

"Hey, Tanner."

He looked up to see Shelia Burnwell waving to him from the doorway. He nodded a hello.

"When are you going to get your old man to sell?" she asked.

"Won't happen in this lifetime."

She moved in displeasure and took a seat on the opposite side of the café.

"Who's that?" Anna asked curiously.

"A local Realtor. She's had her eye on our place for some time."

Their conversation was interrupted by the appearance of their waitress.

When the waitress left, Anna leaned back in the chair, looking pleased as punch to be someplace where someone worked.

"Tell me something, Tanner. Why don't you dally with any of the local women?" she asked, a mischievous twinkle in her eyes. "Are you gay?"

"Of course not," he exclaimed. The woman was impossible. She was not only spoiled, but far too outspoken for his taste. Most people didn't talk about their sexuality so openly.

"You know, it's nothing to be ashamed of if you are," she continued. She pulled a paper napkin from the container in the center of the table and spread it over her lap. "I know lots of gay men and I also know that men who are conflicted about it sometimes come off as overly macho and controlling."

"I'm not gay," he repeated tersely as he felt his irritation with her rising once again. "I just don't date much. I don't have time."

"Don't you ever want to get married? Have some children?"

"Sure, eventually that's what I want. When I think the time is right." In fact, over the course of the past year the desire had become more intense. He did want a family of his own, but only when he found the perfect woman who would accept his commitment to his job.

"I've been focused on building up the business since the time I was twenty years old," he explained. "That's taken up all my time and energy."

"You have to make time to have fun. It's what makes you a healthy, balanced person. You know what they say about all work and no play."

"Yeah. I wonder what they say about all play and no work," he said pointedly. The last thing he needed or wanted was a lecture about working from a woman who'd probably never done an honest day's work in her life.

Her delicate eyebrows pulled together as she frowned. "It's impossible to have any kind of a reasonable conversation with you, so I'm not even going to try anymore. You're an impossible man, Tanner West, and if I wasn't so hungry, I'd get up and leave right now."

At that moment the waitress appeared with their orders. Tanner tried to concentrate on his food and not on her. He hoped she was right. He hoped they returned to the ranch and her father was there waiting for her. She'd been in Tanner's care less than twenty-four hours and for some reason was burrowing into his skin like an irritating tick.

For the first time in his life he couldn't wait for an assignment to be over.

Respect had been Anna's birthright and something she'd never thought about much before. She'd commanded it without doing a thing, by merely being born into royalty. For most of her life people had fawned over her, talked to her with homage.

However, it was obvious that Tanner didn't respect her and it surprised her that she was bothered by it. He might be the CEO of a big company, but he was also obviously uncivilized and socially unpolished.

What did she care if some hard-ass cowboy body-guard didn't respect her? What difference did it make to her whether he liked her or not? He had a job to do and she was comfortable he'd do it to the best of his ability. That's all she should care about.

Besides, if she were very lucky she'd be leaving his ranch within the next twenty-four hours at the most. She'd be back enjoying her own life and far away from this man and this godforsaken countryside.

At last, that's what she wanted to believe, but she knew in her heart nothing would be the same in Nifl-heim. What was happening there? She regretted not being better informed about the political unrest that had exploded.

What about her friends and the palace staff? Were they safe? She had to believe they were, otherwise grief would consume her.

Her irritation with Tanner and the thought of home did nothing to staunch her appetite, and despite the ten-sion-filled silence between them, she enjoyed the cheeseburger and fries and chocolate shake she'd or-dered.

Tanner ate more quickly, finishing his meal before she was even half finished. He tapped his fingers on the tabletop, unconsciously signaling impatience, which only made her eat at a more leisurely pace.

"Ever hear of stopping to smell the roses?" she asked.

"I thought you weren't speaking to me," he replied as his fingers stopped their rapid tattoo.

"I wasn't. Now I am." She stabbed a French fry into a pool of ketchup, popped it into her mouth and chewed thoughtfully.

"Can I ask you something?"

"Sure." She ate another fry.

"This morning you said something about I'd better not throw you over my shoulder." A wrinkle furrowed his brow. "What was that all about?"

"I assumed it was a cowboy thing. I watched a Western one time and the cowboy got irritated with the woman and threw her over his shoulder. I just wanted to let you know I won't tolerate such behavior."

One of his dark brows rose. "You don't have to worry. In the movies the cowboy throws the woman he loves over his shoulder."

She paused with a French fry in midair. "I always wondered what happened after that," she mused. "I mean, where does he carry her off to and what do they do?"

He tapped his fingers once again on the tabletop. "It's the movies, who knows?"

She stabbed another fry into the ketchup, ignoring the edge of irritation in his voice. "Who's minding the office today while you're minding me?"

"I have a very efficient receptionist/secretary. Ida Marie will handle things at the office and call me if anything comes up. She's a good woman."

She eyed him curiously. "What makes her a good woman?"

He sat back in the booth. "What do you mean?"

"I mean, what qualities do you think make a woman a good woman?"

"This is a ridiculous conversation," he scoffed.

"It's called small talk. People often do it when they're sharing a meal. Come on, Tanner, pretend for a moment you're a civilized man."

She was aware of the fact that she baiting him and she wasn't sure why. Maybe because of his crack earlier about all play and no work. And maybe because she really wondered what kind of a woman a man like Tanner would respect.

"Ida Marie raised two children as a single parent," he said, apparently deciding to play along. "Before I hired her to work for me she'd done all kinds of jobs— waitressing, housecleaning—whatever it took to keep a roof over her kids' head and put food on their table."

"Is that all that you worship?" she asked. "Work?"

He eyed her with a deceptive laziness. "What do you worship, Anna?"

Before she could reply, the door to the café opened

and a tall, older man in a khaki uniform walked in. Instantly she saw Tanner's tension increase. The muscle in his jaw ticked and his body stiffened a bit.

"Afternoon, Tanner," the man said as he approached their table.

"Afternoon, Sheriff," he replied.

The sheriff swept his hat off his head to reveal a thick head of salt-and-pepper hair. He nodded to Anna. "Ma'am," he said, then looked at Tanner expectantly.

"Anne, this is Sheriff Jim Ramsey. Jim, this is Anne Jones, a friend of mine from New York City," Tanner said.

"New York. You're a long way from home, little lady." He looped his thumbs into his thick black belt and rested his arms on his protruding stomach as he eyed her with brown eyes filled with open curiosity.

"She's just visiting the family for several days," Tanner replied smoothly.

"I see." He looked from Tanner to Anna. "First time here in Cotter Creek?"

"Yes, first time," she replied.

He rocked back on his heels, his gaze returning to Tanner. "Not going to be any trouble, is there?" His gray eyebrows danced upward on his broad forehead.

"Not planning on any," Tanner replied.

"Good. Good. You know I like my town nice and quiet. Nice meeting you, Anne." He nodded to Tanner, then turned and headed toward the counter where he sat on one of the stools, his back to them.

Anna looked at Tanner curiously. There had been a subtle tension between the two men. "You don't like Sheriff Ramsey?" she asked softly.

He hesitated a moment, his eyes darkly shadowed and impossible to read. "He's all right. He and his men have worked with me on occasion. You ready to go?" He pulled his wallet from his pocket and placed several bills on the table.

She nodded and together they got up and left the café. "But, you don't really like him," she said, trying to understand the tension that had existed between the two men.

He frowned. "Sheriff Ramsey was the one who notified us of my mother's death," he said as they walked toward the pickup. "Of course, at that time he wasn't the sheriff, he was just a young deputy. He was the first one on the scene and, unfortunately didn't secure the area and evidence was compromised."

Anna wondered what it would be like to see on a daily basis the bearer of such bad news. "And that's why you don't really like him?"

He sucked in a deep breath and put his hat on his head, effectively shielding his eyes with the shadow of the brim. "It's not that I don't like him. The more successful we've become, the more concerned Jim had become about us bringing problems to Cotter Creek. But he can't really complain, we rarely bring trouble here. In fact, you're the first client we've had in a couple of years that is staying on the ranch."

They got in the truck and headed back to the ranch. Anna had a feeling this would be the last that she saw of the small town. If her father came for her this afternoon, they would leave immediately. If he didn't come for her immediately, she had a feeling Tanner wouldn't be eager to take her back to town no matter what she needed or wanted.

"When we get back to the house you'll need to find something to do while I spend a little time on the Internet," he said. "I want to see if I can find out something about a group called something of the Mist."

"I could help you," she said. The last thing she wanted was to be sent to her room like a recalcitrant child.

"You can help me by leaving me alone for an hour or two."

"And what am I supposed to do in that time?" she asked.

"I don't know…watch television, read a book. If you really get bored you could ask Smokey if there's something you can help him do with dinner preparations."

"It's bad enough I have to put up with your disrespect. I certainly don't intend to put up with that man's disagreeable nature," she exclaimed as she thought of the man who owned the kitchen.

"I need an hour, two at the most. Surely you can entertain yourself for that length of time."

"All right." She sighed. "I'll be a good girl and entertain myself while you work. But when you're finished, then you have to do something for me."

He released a sigh twice as long as hers. "What?"

She snapped a finger against the brim of her hat. "If I'm going to dress the part of a cowgirl, then the least you can do is show me around the ranch."

He raised a dark eyebrow. "You sure you want to do that? You're liable to get your boots dusty."

"I don't mind. I've never been on a ranch before and I'd like to see everything."

He frowned and didn't answer for a long moment. "All right, after I take care of my business, I'll give you a little tour of the place," he agreed.

The rest of the drive was accomplished in a silence that he didn't seem inclined to fill. Once again she found herself sneaking glances in his direction. Today he wore a short-sleeved, light blue shirt, the color transforming his eyes to a blue-green mix.

Anna had dated plenty of men, but none as handsome as Tanner and none who had the power with a mere glance of eyes or a curve of lips to accelerate her heartbeat and make her feel both excited and anxious at the same time.

Earlier, when he'd adjusted her hat, there had been a moment when she'd thought he was going to kiss her, when she'd wanted him to kiss her. But that was crazy. Why would she want a man who managed to make her feel both anxious and slightly inadequate to kiss her?

She didn't even know Tanner. He meant nothing to her, and as soon as her father came for her, he would be nothing more than a memory to store away forever.

They had just entered when Red came out of the study. "Anna, your father is on the phone."

She raced to the study and grabbed up the receiver. "Father!"

"Anna, my dear. I'm so glad you managed to get to safety. I was worried you'd not be able to handle yourself." His familiar voice filled the line and she closed her eyes as a wave of deep relief swept over her.

Even though the news sources had indicated that nobody had been hurt in the shoot-out in L.A., she'd needed to hear her father's voice. She'd needed to know for herself that he was truly all right.

"I'm here… I'm fine," she replied, aware that Tanner had entered the study and was standing just inside the doorway. She gripped the receiver tightly against her ear. "Where are you? What's happening? When are you coming here for me?"

"I need to speak with Tanner West, Anna."

"But Father—"

"Anna, this is important business. Don't you worry yourself. Everything will be just fine, but I need to speak to Mr. West right now." His voice was firm and sharp.

A burning sting of unexpected tears sprang to her eyes as she realized she'd been summarily dismissed. Without another word she handed the phone to Tanner and hurried from the study.

She went directly to her bedroom, needing a few minutes alone. Standing at the window, she stared outside where thick, heavy, dark gray clouds were gathering in the distance. It felt as if they were a reflection of the heavy grayness of her heart.

She adored her father and knew that he loved her, too, but this wasn't the first time he'd hurt her feelings. He rarely had time for her, but she'd always understood that he was an important man.

Still for most of her life he had dismissed her as a pretty, empty-headed bauble. The telephone conversation she'd just had with him had merely served to emphasize their relationship.

She'd been sheltered from the dark side of power, but she'd allowed it, and she had to take a certain amount of responsibility for not knowing what had been happening in Niflheim before the coup. She recognized now that knowledge was a good thing and if she'd really been a good princess she would have educated herself despite her father's sheltering ways.

Her father was a good man, but she had a feeling he'd been a king out of touch with what his people wanted, what they needed. She hoped he was doing some serious soul-searching that would result in making him a better king…if he got the opportunity to return to Niflheim.

The future loomed before her, dark and uncertain. What would become of her father if he couldn't go back to his country? Would he abdicate his throne and live the remainder of his life in hiding? What was her future? Would peace be returned to Niflheim? So many questions and so few answers.

A knock fell on her door. Quickly she wiped the tears that had gathered at her eyes and opened the door. Tanner eyed her closely. "Are you all right?" He shoved his hands into his pockets and looked ill at ease.

"Of course I'm all right," she said too quickly.

"Well, I have good news and bad news," he said. "The good news is your father is fine. The bad news is he wants you to remain here and it will be a week, possibly two, before he can come here to get you."

"A week or two?" She sank onto the edge of her bed.

"It looks like we're stuck here and we'll just have to make the best of the situation. I'm going to check out what I can find about those rebels. When I'm finished, I'll give you that tour we talked about."

"No, that's all right. I've changed my mind," she said. "I'd rather not get all dirty and icky." She thought she saw a shadow of disappointment in his eyes. She didn't care. She was everything he thought she was…a spoiled, lazy, overindulged young woman. "I'll just hang out here and do my nails or something until dinnertime."

"Fine. I'll see you at dinner." He closed the door, but not before she saw the disgust in his eyes.

Chapter 5

The thunder awakened him, but it was the scream that followed that shot him out of bed. He grabbed his gun from the nightstand and bolted toward the bedroom door.

It had been Anna's scream. And the fear that ripped through his veins was as electric as the lightning that flashed, illuminating the night sky.

As he left his room a hundred questions ran through his mind. Had he underestimated the enemy? Not taken the necessary security measures? The night-light burning in the hallway led him to her room.

He didn't bother to knock on her door, but rather threw it open and stepped inside with the gun in his hands and ready for business.

Lightning once again seared through the sky, its brilliance filling every corner of her room. In that flash of light he saw her. It was just a flicker of sight, but it was enough to freeze him in place as thunder boomed overhead.

She sat up in the bed and the sheet was at her waist, leaving her naked from that point up.

"Tanner," she gasped. Lightning flashed once again and this time he saw that she had grabbed the sheet up to her neck, hiding her nakedness from his eyes.

"Are you all right? I heard you scream." His voice sounded thick and strange to his own ears. That vision of her with her hair wild and tangled and her breasts bare was like a snapshot permanently burned into his brain.

"I—I had a nightmare and the thunder frightened me. I'm sorry. I didn't mean to disturb you."

She had no idea just how much she'd disturbed him. Thunder boomed again and a small cry escaped her. This time when lightning filled the room he saw her eyes, big and round and filled with fear.

"Get dressed and we'll get something to drink and wait for the storm to pass." He turned and headed for his own room, where he put his gun away and pulled on a pair of jeans over his boxers.

And tried to forget the picture of her naked in bed.

He was surprised that the scream hadn't awakened his father or Smokey, but as he walked through the great room toward the kitchen, nobody else stirred in the house.

What he needed was a shot of whiskey or something that would put a fire in his gut that had nothing to do with the one Princess Anna Johansson had lit inside him.

He poured a single glass of milk and set it at the table, then reached into the cabinet where he knew Smokey kept a bottle of whiskey hidden. He poured himself two fingers, then sat at the table to wait for her.

He'd seen little of her that evening. She'd come to the table for dinner and had been unusually quiet. Afterward she had immediately returned to her room.

He had the feeling that something about the phone call from her father had upset her, but the conversation had been so brief he couldn't imagine what had been said to upset her in such a short amount of time.

She was probably devastated to realize she was stuck here for a week or two and had spent that time in her room pouting like a child who hadn't gotten her way. She'd certainly made it clear that she didn't want to be here a moment longer than necessary.

He'd thought she was somehow needling him when she'd told him she slept in the nude, but he knew now she'd been telling him the truth. He turned the glass of whiskey in his hand, wondering how many of them he'd have to drink before that vision of her would blur in his head.

Unfortunately he couldn't afford to have as many as it would take to fuzz his thoughts. It never left his mind that he was on duty twenty-four hours a day.

"I'd rather have one of those than a glass of milk," she said as she entered the room. She gestured to the whiskey he held, then winced as another clap of thunder boomed overhead. She slid into a chair at the table and wrapped her arms around herself.

He nodded and got up to get her a glass. When he returned to the table he poured her a small amount of the amber liquid, then watched as she took a sip.

She was dressed in the same T-shirt and jeans she'd had on earlier in the day and he tried desperately to keep his gaze off her breasts, tried to forget their naked fullness with their dark pink centers.

"I'm sorry I screamed and woke you. It's not just the storm," she said, wrapping her slender fingers around the small glass in front of her. "It's the combination of the storm and the nightmare I was having about that day at the airport and the thunder boomed and in my dream it was a gun shooting and my father was shot and there was blood…." Her voice trailed off and she closed her eyes, as if to steady herself.

For the first time Tanner realized the trauma that she'd suffered in the days before she'd appeared on his doorstep.

She hadn't really talked about the terror of being roused out of sleep and taken away from home.

She hadn't really told him all about that moment in the airport when guns had blazed and bullets had flown. Whatever terror she'd felt had been hidden beneath a layer of attitude.

"It was just a dream," he said, recognizing that his words could do little to help with whatever was going on in her head.

"I know." She opened her eyes and he saw the glimmer of tears. "It was just so awful." She jumped as thunder once again boomed so loud that the windows rattled in their frames. "The thunder sounds like the guns that day at the airport."

She downed the liquor in one swallow and he followed her lead, downing his own as quickly. "You want to talk about it?" he asked, and poured them each another small shot.

She stared down into the glass and turned it slowly in her hands. "It had been such a long flight and my father and I were both exhausted." Her voice was soft and low. "We got off the plane and went to the baggage claim to get our bags."

She paused a moment and twirled her glass between her fingers, then continued. "We got our luggage and followed the signs for ground transportation and had just stepped outside of the airport when the gunmen began shooting."

Her eyes were haunted and she reached a trembling hand across the table toward him. He hesitated only a second, then grabbed her hand in his. So small, he thought. Her hand was so small and soft and trembling, and a fierce, unexpected protectiveness swelled up in his chest.

"Bullets seemed to come from every direction. I

don't know how they managed to miss me, miss my father. I don't know how the rebels didn't kill innocent people with their attack."

"Thank God they didn't."

She squeezed his hand and gave him a forced smile. "Yes, thank God for that. Have you ever been shot at?"

The question let him know she wanted a change of subject. "Once. A couple years ago."

"What happened?" She held his hand tight as if he were her lifeline through the storm and through the darkness of her memory.

"I was acting as a bodyguard for a businessman who had ticked off a nasty ex-con. We were getting into the car one morning and somebody took a shot. It shattered the windshield on the car, but missed us."

"Were you scared?" she asked.

"I'm not the kind of man who scares easily."

"So what happened?" she asked.

"The ex-con wasn't especially bright. Two witnesses saw him take the shot at us. He was arrested, and as far as I know is still in prison for attempted murder."

"You're very brave."

"No more than anyone else," he countered. He was feeling uncomfortable, aware that he was seeing a side to her that he hadn't seen before. It was a softer, more vulnerable side and it was far too appealing for his comfort.

"I was just doing what had to be done," he said gruffly, then pulled his hand from hers and drank the last of the whiskey in his glass.

"What did my father have to say to you?" she asked.

He leaned back in his chair and frowned thoughtfully. "Not a lot. We only spoke for a moment. But he did give me the name of the fanatical rebels...the Brotherhood of the Mist. I spent most of the evening on the Internet trying to find out something about them, but had no luck."

"At least you got that much. It's certainly more than he said to me." She looked down for a long moment, and when she looked back at him her eyes were filled with a soft vulnerability, a deep longing for something. It shook him.

"Your father...is he a good king?"

A tiny frown appeared between her eyebrows. "He's a good man and he wants what's best for the country, but I don't think he's been a man in touch with the people. I think he's ignored the fact that it's time for changes in Niflheim."

"Sounds to me like he can't ignore it any longer," he observed. "What do you want for your country?"

"Me?" She looked surprised, as if nobody had ever asked her opinion before. The frown deepened slightly. "I'm just hoping some sort of compromise can be reached that would allow my father a place and give the people what they want." She shrugged. "Where did you meet my father?"

"A couple of months ago we were both at a fund-raiser in Washington. We found ourselves standing next to each other while we waited to be seated for dinner. I told him about my business and he told me about his connection to my father. He also mentioned his daughter."

"That's surprising," she murmured so softly he wasn't sure he'd heard her correctly.

Again he was struck by how fragile she looked, how lost. "The storm has pretty well passed. You shouldn't have any problems sleeping for the rest of the night." He stood, feeling the need to escape her.

Anna with her pretty blue eyes and winsome smile. Anna with her soft skin and provocative scent. Anna with her full breasts and her bare flesh shining in that flash of lightning. She suddenly scared him more than any bullet he might have to dodge.

She downed her drink without blinking, then stood and carried her glass to the sink. When she turned to face him her eyelids were heavy and, with her tousled hair, she looked sexy as hell.

"Come on, it's late and going without sleep makes me cranky," he said.

"Everything makes you cranky," she replied.

He merely grunted, his blood pressure feeling dangerously high as he followed behind her to the bedrooms. She had a sexy sway to her hips that could torment a man to distraction.

She stopped at her bedroom door and turned to face him, her features illuminated by the night-light that burned in the hallway. "Thank you, Tanner. Thank you for distracting me through the storm."

"It's all part of the job," he said, trying desperately to keep everything on a professional basis. He started to walk away, but stopped as she called his name once again.

"The offer of the tour of the ranch, does it still stand?"

"Sure. We could do it tomorrow."

"I'd like that," she replied, then disappeared into the room and closed her door.

Tanner went to his bedroom, knowing that sleep would be a long time coming. He shucked off his jeans and got back into bed, adrenaline making relaxation impossible.

Thoughts of Anna filled his head, visions of her danced in front of his eyes. He had to remember that bad dreams and a thunderstorm had prompted the softness, the vulnerability, he'd seen moments before.

He had no doubt in his mind that when the sun was shining once again in the morning she'd return to being irritating, outspoken and demanding.

Now if he could just forget how she'd looked in bed.

The alarm clock went off and Anna groaned and threw a hand out to slap at the offending instrument.

She rolled over and sat up, eyeing the clock with malicious intent.

Five-thirty. In her real life she rarely got up before noon.

If she'd been home she would have awakened when she'd felt like it and rung for her personal maid and assistant. Astrid would have come into her bedroom carrying her breakfast on a tray and while Anna ate they would have talked about the plans for the day.

Her automatic response now was to fall back down and go back to sleep, but instead she got out of bed and headed for the shower, determined that she'd be at the table when breakfast was served.

As she stood beneath the spray of hot water, she thought of those moments she'd spent in the kitchen with Tanner the night before.

The storm had terrified her, but she'd been comforted by his calm, steady presence. She tried to forget the vision she'd had of him in that brief flash of lightning when he'd first entered her bedroom.

He'd been wearing only a pair of boxers and he'd stolen her breath away with his half-naked masculinity. She'd wanted to leap out of bed and into his arms. She'd wanted to feel his broad, muscled chest against her bare breasts. She'd wanted to stand up and pull him down on the bed with her.

It must have been the storm and her fear that had created such crazy feelings. She didn't need a man like Tanner in her life, at least not after the potential for danger had passed. She definitely didn't need too many mornings beginning before the crack of dawn.

She dressed and pulled her still damp hair together with a ribbon at the nape of her neck, then left her bedroom and headed for the dining room.

She was surprised to discover herself the first one there. As she stood hesitantly in the doorway, Smokey came in through the kitchen carrying a large platter of bacon and sausage.

"Well, well. Will wonders never cease?" he said as he set the platter on the table. "She's actually going to make a meal on time."

"Oh, stuff it in your ear, Smokey," she muttered, refusing to be intimidated by him.

One of his grizzled gray eyebrows shot up in surprise then a small smile curled one corner of his mouth. "Coffee's coming," he said, then returned to the kitchen.

Before Smokey returned with the coffee, Tanner entered the dining room, looking as crabby as a grizzly bear awakened from his winter's nap.

"Good morning," she said as she sat at her place at the table. "You look like you crawled out on the wrong side of the bed." She smiled at Red, who followed on his son's heels.

Tanner's scowl deepened and before he could say anything Smokey reentered with a pot of steaming coffee. He served Anna first, then Tanner, who threw himself into his chair at the table as if the entire world was an affront to him.

His foul mood didn't seem to ease with the meal. As Anna listened to Red tell her stories about past spring storms, Tanner nursed a cup of coffee, his eyes dark and fathomless.

"So, are we on for the tour of the ranch?" she asked, rising when breakfast was finished.

"I've got some work to catch up on this morning in the study. We'll take the tour after lunch." As he stood, it was obvious his tone of voice brooked no room for argument. "In the meantime, you can go back to bed or count your diamonds or do whatever princesses do in the mornings."

She had no idea what had caused his current mood but was aware that he was dismissing her, just like her father did so often. "A wonderful idea," she said airily. "I'll just crawl back into bed and catch up on my beauty sleep or maybe do my nails. It's a shame there isn't a spa nearby. I don't believe I've ever gone this long without a facial."

That telltale muscle ticked in his jaw. "Stay in the house, stay out of trouble and I'll see you at lunch," he said, then turned and left the dining room.

"He's got his britches twisted in a knot this morning, doesn't he?" Red said as he sipped his coffee.

Anna couldn't help but smile at Red's words. "I've never heard that particular expression before," she said, and once again sat at the table.

"I'd say in this instance it fits." Red shook his head and took another sip of his coffee.

"If I was to guess, he was born with his britches in a knot," she said.

Red grinned, then shook his head once again. "I keep telling him he needs to take some time off, have a vacation and forget the business for a while, but he doesn't listen to me."

"He strikes me as a man who doesn't listen to anyone," she replied.

"He's a tough one, all right. Always has been, even when he was young. But he's a good man. Wild West Protective Services enjoyed a good reputation and a certain amount of success while the kids were growing up, but it was Tanner who took the business by the horns and grew it into the multimillion dollar industry it has become." There was an undeniable ring of love and respect in Red's voice. "He's a successful man, but I think he's a lonely man."

If he's lonely, it's his own fault, Anna thought a few minutes later as she left the dining room. He was judgmental and overbearing. Was it any wonder he didn't have a woman in his life?

She walked to the window in the great room and peered outside. The sun was just peeking over the horizon, sending splashes of pinks and oranges across the sky. The beauty made her breath catch in her throat.

She opened the front door and stepped out onto the wide, wraparound porch, taking in the sweet-scented morning air as she watched the most beautiful sunrise she'd ever seen in her life. The colors were as bright, as pure, as any gemstone she'd ever seen.

Maybe this was why ranchers got up at such an ungodly hour, to enjoy this spectacle of nature. It was worth every minute of sleep she'd missed.

She saw several men walking in the distance and assumed they were hired help for the ranch. They waved and she waved back. Several horses danced in a fenced area, snorting and feisty as if the crisp morning air suited their fancy.

For the first time since arriving, she felt peace filter through her, a peace she couldn't remember feeling for a very long time.

What would it be like to live like this? To wake up every morning to a splendid sky and smell wind-sweetened air? To travel into town every day or two and eat at the café, know people by face and by name?

There was a silence to this life she'd never known before. Even now a stillness surrounded her. Would the quiet of this place calm her or drive her slowly insane? How did the people who lived here handle the quiet?

What was she thinking? This wasn't her life. This would never be her life. Her life was shopping and dancing and playing hostess for dignitaries visiting her country. She frowned. But at the moment she didn't have a country. Instead she had rebels who wanted her dead.

For the first time since the night she and her father

had been whisked out of the palace reality sank in and she realized she had no clue what the future held for her.

It was possible her father intended to see exactly what happened in the next week or two in Niflheim and would decide to make a stand to get his country back. It was also possible they would never return to Niflheim again.

It made her sad just a little, to realize that the thought of never returning to Niflheim didn't bother her too much. Although it was home, it had never really felt like home to her.

Troubled by the uncertainty of the future and her own thoughts, she turned and went back inside and to her room. She sat on her bed and wondered what the future held for her.

She stood and wandered around the room, wondering what women did to pass the time in a place like this? What was she going to do to pass her time here? Tanner certainly didn't seem inclined to entertain her and she'd rather die from boredom than attempt to make small talk with Smokey.

Red was the only person she might have sought out to pass the time, but he had indicated at breakfast that he was heading out for Oklahoma City to a horse auction and wouldn't be home until later in the evening.

By nine o'clock she was bored out of her head and went down the hallway to the study. She knew with the mood Tanner had been in earlier she was taking her life into her hands by disturbing him, but she wondered if he'd learned anything about the group of rebels who wanted her dead.

He looked up from his computer monitor as she entered the room, a frown creasing his forehead.

"Are you going to growl or bite at me?" she asked as she stood in the doorway.

He leaned back in his chair and raked a hand through his thick dark hair. "Depends. What do you want?"

"I'm not sure," she said, sliding into the chair opposite the desk. "I saw the sunrise earlier. Are they always so pretty here?"

The frown across his forehead disappeared. "If you think the sunrises are pretty you should see the stars at night."

"Maybe you'll show them to me some night?"

"Maybe," he replied, his eyes dark and guarded.

She sighed. "So what are you working on?"

He ran a hand across his lower jaw, the frown once again appearing in his forehead. "I spent most of yesterday evening and this morning trying to find out more information about the Brotherhood of the Mist."

"Have you had any luck?"

"No, but I'll tell you what I have discovered. There are hundreds of wacko subversive groups functioning in the world these days. There are religious, political, ecological groups working both inside and outside the law. What I'm not finding is anything new about the situation in Niflheim." He sighed in frustration.

"Why don't you knock off and take me on the tour

before lunch?" she suggested. "It's a beautiful morning, too pretty to be cooped up in here." He hesitated and she knew an automatic protest was about to make its way to his lips. "Come on, Tanner. All work and no play isn't healthy. Besides, don't you want me to say nice things about you and your business after I'm gone?"

"If you can say anything after you've left here, then I'd say I've done my job well," he countered. To her surprise he pushed away from the desk and stood. "All right. I guess I could use a break."

Minutes later with her new hat on her head, Anna followed Tanner out the front door. "There's no sign of the storm from last night," she said as they walked around the house and to the back.

"It was mostly lightning and thunder but very little rain," he replied, his own hat low on his forehead. She saw him nod to a man who stood on the far side of the porch. "So, what do you want to see?"

"Anything…everything," she replied, glad to be outside instead of cooped up in the house. "Is that man one of your employees?"

"Yeah, and there's another one at the back of the house. We'll have guards on the house as long as you're here."

This sobered her somewhat. She'd felt utterly safe here from the moment she'd arrived, but the knowledge that there were two men on guard duty reminded her that danger could find her.

"We'll start in the stables," he said. "Do you ride?"

"It's been years. My mother loved to ride and when I was little we'd often ride together. After her death my father sold all the horses." She remembered that day, with her heart still grieving for her mother, her beloved pony had been sold and taken away.

"Maybe while you're here we'll get you up on a horse again," he said.

"I'd love that."

They entered the stables and her nose was assailed by the scents of horse and leather and hay. They were greeted by soft whinnies and pawing from the stalls. Anna walked to the first stall and turned to face Tanner. "I'll ride this one," she said, indicating the large brown horse.

"Yeah, you'd last about a minute on his back." He pointed to the next stall. "If you ride, you'll ride Molly."

She stepped in front of the next stall to see a smaller brown horse with a white marking on her forehead. "Molly. Hey, pretty lady," she said, and rubbed her fingers over the horse's forehead. She turned back to Tanner to see him wearing a deep frown. "What's wrong?"

"Her stall. It needs mucking out."

"Mucking out? What does that mean?"

"The old bedding needs to be removed and new bedding put in."

"Then why don't you do it?" she asked.

He tipped his hat back from his forehead. "Why don't you?" he countered. His eyes glittered with challenge.

"You don't think I can?" She looked at the stall floor. It couldn't be that hard to remove the straw that was there and put down some new straw. He thought she couldn't do it. He thought she couldn't do anything.

He walked over to the wall and retrieved a pick and a shovel and returned to where she stood. He held out the tools, an amused grin on his face. "Princess, I don't think you'll last five minutes."

"Start your clock, pardner," she replied, and took the pick and shovel from him.

Chapter 6

Tanner almost felt guilty as he handed her a pick and a shovel, then moved Molly into an empty stall. Mucking out a stable was one of the nastiest jobs there was and certainly not work befitting a princess.

As he got a wheelbarrow to carry away the old bedding, he recognized that he'd baited her into this particular challenge because he'd been in a foul mood.

His mood had been the result of an endless night of tossing and turning and dreaming about a very naked Anna in his arms.

He'd been angry with her for being tempting and alluring and yet everything he did not want in a woman. This little challenge, which he was certain she would fail, would merely serve to prove to him that she was all wrong for him despite his intense physical desire for her.

He watched her start to work, wielding the pick with her slender arms. Her jeans pulled taut across her bottom as she bent over and he tried not to think about the fantasies he'd entertained the night before.

She flashed a glance at him and gave him a cocky smile. The light blue T-shirt she wore made the blue of her eyes all the more startling.

She could look cocky now, but she'd only been working for three minutes. He fully expected her within the next couple of minutes to stomp her foot and announce that she was finished, that this kind of physical labor was beneath her.

That kind of a reaction would make it easy for him to remember that she was nothing more than a spoiled, pampered princess who wouldn't know the pleasure of a day's work if her life depended on it.

"Had enough?" he asked as she dumped her third shovel full of old bedding into the wheelbarrow.

Her eyes sparked with stubbornness. "It's not finished, so neither am I." She got back to work.

Flies buzzed in the air and the temperature in the stable began to climb. She threw off her hat and he saw that dots of perspiration had appeared on her forehead. She didn't talk, which was a miracle in itself.

In the time they had spent together he'd found her

to be annoyingly chatty. But now it was as if the physical labor took too much out of her for her to work and carry on a conversation.

His guilt nearly choked him. What did he think he was doing letting her work like this? What kind of perverse notion had even led to this challenge?

"I could give you a hand," he offered, and reached for the shovel leaning against the stall.

She whirled around, wielding the pick like a weapon of mass destruction and glared at him. "Don't you dare touch that shovel. I don't want your help. I don't need your help." She set down the pick and grabbed the shovel and filled it once again.

"You'd love that, wouldn't you," she muttered under her breath. "You'd love it if I'd grab my crown and run to my room."

"Anna…"

"Don't 'Anna' me," she exclaimed. "I'm going to finish this work and in turn you're going take me for a horseback ride and you're going to sing a cowboy song and not think about work for at least an hour."

He grinned, amused by her list of demands. "If I were to sing a cowboy song you really would grab your crown and run to your room."

She leaned against the shovel, looking as charming as he'd ever seen her. Several pieces of straw clung to her hair and a smudge of dirt darkened one cheek. "That bad, huh?"

"Tone deaf," he replied. "Stone-cold tone deaf.

Anna, you've proved your point, there's no reason for you to finish this."

"I need to do this, Tanner." She frowned thoughtfully. "I'm not sure why, but I need to do it all by myself. But, I'm serious about that horseback ride."

"It's a deal," he agreed. "We'll ride right after lunch."

At heart he liked to think he was a gentleman, and standing around watching a woman work wasn't his idea of fun. He wasn't even sure now why he'd challenged her, what he'd hoped to prove.

She worked until she was half breathless and her arms trembled from over-exertion. Not a word of complaint spilled forth from her and Tanner felt a grudging admiration for her tenacity.

When she had the floor of the stall cleaned, he ignored her protests and helped her put down new bedding. When they were finished she leaned on the handle of the shovel and pushed a strand of her golden hair away from her glistening face.

"I can work," she said. "Nobody's ever expected me to before. Nobody has ever let me before." She leaned the shovel against the wall. "And now, I'm going to take a long hot shower before lunch."

He walked just behind her toward the house, wondering if he hadn't drastically underestimated her character. As she headed down the hallway toward her bedroom, he went into the kitchen where Smokey was busy with lunch preparations.

"You've been scarce this morning," Smokey said.

"I've been teaching Anna how to be a cowgirl."

Smokey snorted. "And next week you can teach me how to be king."

Tanner smiled wryly. "I think I'd have far more luck transforming Anna into a cowgirl than I could have trying to turn you into a king. She spent the morning mucking out a stall."

Smokey raised a grizzled eyebrow. "Maybe there's more fiber to the woman than I first thought. She's a feisty one, that's for sure. Damned if she didn't tell me to stick it in my ear this morning."

"Now that doesn't surprise me," Tanner replied. "She doesn't take any guff from anyone. Don't set the table for me and Anna for lunch," he said as an idea struck him.

"You're not eating?" Smokey asked.

"I promised her we'd take a horseback ride. I think I'll just throw a couple sandwiches in a bag and we'll have a picnic while we're out."

"A picnic?" Smokey looked at him as if he'd just grown a second head.

"Don't look at me as if I've lost my mind," he said irritably. "It's for her, not me. I'm just going along for the ride." Tanner walked over to the refrigerator and pulled it open.

"Go on, get out of here." Smokey flicked a dish-towel at him. "You want a picnic lunch, I'll make you one, but don't go pawing around in my refrigerator. I hate it when people paw around in my refrigerator."

Tanner started to reply but was interrupted as his cell phone rang.

"Tanner," he said into the small phone. It was his brother Zack checking in from his assignment in Oklahoma City.

He'd just finished up with the call when Anna entered the kitchen, bringing with her the clean scent of soap and shampoo and the spicy perfume he couldn't seem to get out of his head.

"You're going on a picnic," Smokey said to her.

She looked at Tanner for confirmation. "Really?" He nodded and delight lit her face. "A ride and a picnic? What a wonderful idea."

"Why don't you two go saddle up and I'll bring your lunch out to you," Smokey suggested, obviously eager to get them both out of his kitchen.

"If I'd known that my mucking out a stall would make you so agreeable I would have done it on the day I first arrived here," she said to Tanner as they headed back outside.

"I'm not a disagreeable man," he replied.

She grinned at him slyly. "No, you're quite agreeable when you get your own way and are in total control of things."

"Speaking of control, there are some things we need to go over before we take this ride."

She rolled her eyes. "Let me guess. Rules. Rules for trips into town, rules for eating lunch, rules for horseback riding. I suppose you even have rules when you make love to a woman."

"Don't be ridiculous," he replied. The woman was impossible. Just when he was feeling inclined to be kind to her, she managed to do or to say something to irritate him. After spending the night fantasizing about making love to her, the last thing he wanted to do was to talk about making love.

"I'll bet I know the rules already. Whatever happens, I do exactly what you tell me to do, exactly when you tell me to."

He nodded. "Hopefully these are rules that will keep you alive, Anna."

By the time he saddled up their two horses, Smokey brought them out their lunch. It took only minutes for Tanner to store the bottled water, fresh fruit and sandwiches in his saddlebag, then he watched as Anna mounted Molly.

She looked right on the back of a horse. However, Tanner had yet to see her in any position where she didn't look right. He frowned and mounted his own horse, a black, high-spirited gelding named Simon.

At least with them each on horseback he couldn't smell the provocative scent of her, couldn't see the silver flecks that made her blue eyes interesting as well as pretty.

"Where are we headed, pardner?" she drawled as if she'd been born and raised in Texas.

He couldn't help the smile that curved his lips. She

was irrepressible. "Just riding. No special destination." However, he didn't intend for them to go too far from the house.

Over the course of the past forty-eight hours he'd begun to think that she really might have lost her pursuers in Los Angeles, that she was safe here and he was baby-sitting more than protecting, waiting for her father to arrive.

Besides, there were plenty of ranch hands on the property and they would recognize any strangers that strayed onto the West land. He decided to keep the guards on the house. A short ride on the property should be fine.

Although Simon would have loved a swift gallop, Tanner kept tight control, forcing the gelding to a sedate walk. He had no idea what kind of riding skills Anna might possess and until he did know intended to take it nice and slow.

"Looks like you're going to meet another member of the West family," he said as they headed toward the pasture.

"Really? Who?"

"Zack. He called earlier to tell me that his client has released him and he's returning in the morning."

"What kind of an assignment was he on?"

"The kind we hate to take. A domestic case."

"Domestic case, what does that mean?"

"A husband and wife. The wife wanted a divorce, the husband didn't. It seems he has a temper. Zack was hired to keep an eye on the wife between the time the divorce papers were served to the husband and the trial date, which was today."

"And so the danger to the client is over?"

"She thinks so. Apparently her ex-husband has left town and so she's confident everything will be fine." What he didn't tell her was that there had been something in Zack's voice that had made him wonder if perhaps his brother had gotten a little too close to his client.

Always a mistake, he reminded himself.

As they headed down the lane she asked about the various outbuildings they passed. He explained what each building was and what it was used for. As they passed the original homestead, he told her that it was where he now lived.

"It's very nice," she said. "In fact, it's quite lovely."

"Thanks. I've put a lot of work into it." A sense of pride filled him as they rode past the attractive ranch house. "I've been updating it for the past couple of years…new wiring and new plumbing."

"How many bedrooms does it have?" she asked.

"Three."

"Big enough for a family. How many children do you want?"

"A boy and a girl would be nice." He tried not to notice how the sun sparkled on the ends of her hair beneath her hat. The golden strands seemed to beckon for his touch. "What about you?" he asked, trying to keep his mind focused on the conversation at hand.

"At least two…a boy and a girl. I wouldn't want to have an only child. It's far too lonely." Her expression darkened and she leaned forward to pat Molly's mane.

"From what I've seen of your life you didn't look too lonely to me. I'm sure you have lots of friends." He thought of the pictures of her surrounded by beautiful, wealthy people such as herself.

"Friends? I don't know if I had any or not. That's the problem with being a princess. When I told a joke, everyone laughed whether it was a good joke or not. When I had an idea, it was the best idea anyone ever had. When I wore a dress, everyone said it was the prettiest one in the room. Now I'm sure at one time or another I told a bad joke, had a bad idea and wore an ugly dress, but nobody would tell me because of my position, because of who I was. Were those people friends?"

It was a rhetorical question and he didn't even try to answer it. What surprised him was the touch of sadness he heard in her voice. "You tell a bad joke, don't expect me to laugh. You have a bad idea, I'll be the first one to tell you. You wear an ugly dress and I'm not taking you out in public."

She flashed him a smile, a beautiful, open smile that set a fire in the pit of his stomach. "Ah, he has a sense of humor after all."

Tanner returned her smile. It felt as if it had been years since he'd really smiled at anyone. Months of stress melted away from him. "Of course I have a sense of humor."

"You should show it more often," she exclaimed.

They rode in silence for a few minutes and Tanner felt himself relaxing with each step of the horse. Maybe he had been working too hard lately, not taking any time at all to just enjoy being alive.

"This was a good idea," he said. "I needed to get out and enjoy a ride."

"Do you ride every day?" she asked.

"I used to, but lately it seems there's too much work at the office to do." He'd noticed that she sat the saddle like a natural, that whatever training she'd had as a young girl was evident in the easy way she controlled Molly. "Feel like a run?" he asked.

She flashed another of her smiles. "Just lead the way, pardner."

With a touch of his heels and a loosening of the reins, Simon took off and Molly followed. As far as Tanner was concerned there was nothing more liberating than a run, with the sun warming his shoulders and the scent of pasture filling his lungs.

He kept the gelding reined in enough that Molly could stay abreast. The mare didn't have the long legs or the strength of his horse.

He tried without success to keep his gaze off Anna. The air had whipped color into her cheeks and the hair beneath her hat was tangled and wind-whipped. Her breasts moved up and down beneath her T-shirt as the horse ran.

The subtle embers of desire that had burned in his

stomach from the moment he'd first seen her burst into flames. If he'd been by himself, he would have urged Simon faster, as if to outrun an emotion he didn't want to feel.

Maybe what he felt in his the pit of his stomach nothing more than his appetite? He hoped whatever Smokey had packed for lunch sated that burning hunger.

The gallop invigorated Anna and reminded her of when she'd been little and she and her mother had ridden on the palace grounds. Her mother had been happiest, it seemed, when she'd been on the back of a horse. She'd given the gift of the love of riding to her daughter. Those childhood days had been the happiest Anna had ever known.

Funny that she'd felt almost happy when she'd been shoveling horse manure earlier. There had been a profound sense of accomplishment inside her when she'd finished the test and the fresh bedding had been put down. Who would have thought it?

She was a little bit disappointed when Tanner slowed once again and the horses fell into an easy side-by-side walk.

"I'd forgotten how much I love riding," she said, and tipped her face up toward the midday sun.

"It's one of the simple pleasures of life."

She turned her head to look at Tanner, wondering if he was digging at her once again. But he wasn't looking at her, rather he seemed to be scanning the area around them.

"Everything all right?" she asked, a touch of worry filtering through her.

His gaze flickered to her and he smiled. "Everything seems to be fine. You ready for lunch?"

Beneath the power of his easy smile her worry found no food to sustain it and disappeared. She shook her head. "Not yet. I'm enjoying the ride too much to stop."

For the next few minutes they rode in silence. It was a pleasant silence and Anna found herself looking at Tanner over and over again.

He fascinated her every bit as much as he irritated her. There was a steadiness about him that was comforting, a sense of purpose and drive that intrigued her. In the brief time she'd been in his care she'd come to trust him implicitly.

He'd surprised her the night before with his gentle understanding of her fear of the storm. She remembered the feel of his hand wrapped around hers. His hand had been warm and comforting as the thunder had roared overhead.

He sat tall in his saddle, like a man confident with who he was and how he was living his life. He seemed to know exactly where he was going in life. Unlike her. She had no idea what she was doing or where she was headed.

"It's so quiet out here," she said, needing, wanting

any kind of conversation to take her out of the doubts and worries her thoughts had produced. "That's one of the things I've noticed in the time I've been here."

"Quiet?" He tilted his head and gazed at her quizzically. His lips turned up at one corner in a half smile. "Maybe it's quiet to a woman who's accustomed to loud music and jet engines and the ring of cash registers, but it's not quiet to me. You just don't know how to listen. Tell me what you hear right now."

It was her turn to tilt her head and listen. Certainly there was no music, no ca-ching of a cash register and no traffic noise. "I hear the sounds of the horses' hooves…a bird singing somewhere nearby. A cow mooing." She was surprised at what she heard now that she was really listening.

"The sounds of nature, that's what you hear out here in God's country. Nothing artificial about it. You can hear nature at work. I don't think it's quiet. I think it sounds like home."

Sounds like home. What a nice way to think of it, she thought. When she thought of home no particular sounds came to mind except the silence of loneliness.

"You think your father will fight to get his country back?"

"I can only venture a guess," she said thoughtfully. "Even though the rebels appear to be in power at the moment, I'm not sure how long that power will last. My father was not a king without influence, without supporters."

"So tell me, how does a princess spend her days?" he asked as the horses continued to walk side by side.

She frowned thoughtfully before replying. "I know what you think…that I probably slept late, got breakfast in bed, spent the afternoon in a spa or shopping, then partied all night."

"So, tell me differently," he replied.

She straightened in the saddle and thrust her shoulders back, eyeing him from beneath the brim of her hat. "I can't. That's exactly the way I spent many of my days as a princess." She thought she saw a tinge of disappointment in his eyes. "I won't apologize for living out what was expected of me," she continued defensively. "There's no way you could understand my life."

"Why? Because I'm just a dumb cowboy?" There was an edge of defensiveness to his voice.

"I didn't say that."

"But secretly you think that," he said.

"Maybe I did the first time I saw you, but I know differently now. And why are you trying to pick a fight with me?" she asked with a flash of impatience. "You do one thing nice for me, arranging a ride and a picnic, and now you seem determined to ruin it by provoking me into an argument."

"I'm not—"

Whatever he had been about to say was lost beneath the sound of a loud crack.

Molly reared up on her hind legs with a frantic

whinny. Anna tried desperately to hang on as the horse reared again.

"Anna!"

She heard Tanner cry her name as she felt herself falling from the horse. She hit the ground with a painful thud, landing on her backside as the back of her head crashed on the hard earth.

Chapter 7

Tanner flew off Simon as Molly took off in a panicked run. Tanner didn't just crouch next to Anna—he threw his body over hers, his gun drawn and his gaze focused on the trees in the distance.

His heart thundered in his chest as he glanced at Anna, grateful to see her eyes open and looking at him. He'd been afraid she'd been hit when he'd seen her body fall like a rag doll from Molly's back.

"Are you all right?" he whispered. He didn't look down at her again but rather kept his attention riveted to the copse of trees.

"I—I think I'm okay. I hit my head…that's all. What…what happened?"

"Somebody took a shot at us. I think the bullet must have hit Molly."

"Oh, no. We have to find her." She pushed against his chest, but he remained flat against her, his weight making it impossible for her to move.

"We're not going anywhere until I'm certain whoever took that shot isn't waiting to take another one."

"But, Molly…"

"She'll head back to the stable."

Dammit, the trees were just thick enough to provide ample cover for a gunman. Was somebody still there waiting to take another shot at them? At Anna?

"They found me," she whispered, her terror obvious as her fingers clutched at his back.

"We don't know that." He shot a quick look at her. "You hear me? We don't know that for sure. It could have been a hunter." He said it for her benefit, but he knew it wasn't hunting season and nobody in their right mind would be hunting on West property.

"A hunter?" Hope lightened her voice. "What are we going to do?" she asked.

"We're going to wait." He kept his gaze on the trees, cursing himself for not sensing any danger. Even now he saw no hint of anyone hiding in the thick brush. No flash of color from clothing, no glint of a shotgun barrel peeking out. Nothing.

Minutes ticked by and Tanner remained on the ground, his body covering hers. As the initial wave of shock passed, he became acutely aware of every point of contact his body had with hers.

His chest mashed against her breasts, his groin against hers. Despite the reason for their present position, a crazy heat swept over him.

He ignored it and focused on the problem at hand. And the problem was he didn't know what they were up against. He had no idea if the shooter was still in the trees. He had no idea if there was more than one shooter. He just didn't know what in the hell they might be facing.

The fact that no other shots had followed confused him. The fact that they had missed Anna, who had been an upright target in the saddle, also confused him. An assassin rebel with a bad aim?

"Whoever was there, I don't think they're there any longer," he finally said.

"How do you know?" she asked.

"I don't know for sure, but Simon doesn't seem to be sensing anyone in the area."

The big horse stood grazing in the nearby distance. "So, how can we be sure?" Her voice was half breathless.

He looked down at her again. "I'm going to rise. If somebody is hiding in those trees and waiting to take a shot, they'll probably take a shot when I get up."

"Then don't get up," she replied in horror. Her arms tightened around him as if to keep him on top of her.

He offered her a tense smile. "We can't exactly stay here for the rest of our lives."

"I guess this means our picnic is off."

She was impossible. They'd just had a close encounter with a bullet and she was worried about a damned picnic. "I'd say that's the smallest of our problems."

She reached up with one hand and touched his cheek. "Be careful," she said.

In that instant, with her body warm beneath him and her eyes large and luminous, he wanted nothing more than to crash his mouth to hers, to taste those lips that had tormented him to distraction since the moment she'd charged into his office.

But he was her bodyguard, not her lover, and at the moment his job was to keep her protected from harm, harm that had come much too close for his comfort.

In one smooth movement he raised up into a crouch over her. "Stay down," he commanded, grateful that for once she didn't argue or make any movements to protest his command.

Muscles tensed with expectation, he slowly straightened to a standing position. Nothing. No shot, no sound. Nothing happened.

"Simon," he called softly, then whistled. The horse raised its head and whinnied, then ambled over to where he stood. He grabbed the reins and positioned the horse between Anna and the stand of trees.

At that moment the sound of hooves thundered against the earth. Burt Randall, one of the men who'd been on guard duty, came into view, riding fast toward them. He reined in as he reached them, his gaze dark, a line of worry deep across his forehead beneath his worn dark hat.

"You okay?" he asked.

"I think so. How did you know to come find us?" Tanner asked.

"Molly showed up at the stables. I knew the two of you had taken off earlier and something must have happened."

"Somebody took a shot at us," Tanner said. He leaned over and held out his hand to help Anna up careful to keep Simon as a barrier between her and the trees.

Burt touched the butt of the shotgun that lay across his lap. "Where did it come from?"

"Those trees." Tanner pointed.

"I'll go check it out."

Tanner nodded, knowing that the man could take care of himself. "I'm going to get Anna back to the house."

As Burt took off in the direction of the trees Tanner turned to Anna. "It should be safe for you to mount. Whoever was in those trees, if they're still there, they should be running to escape Burt." He motioned her to the horse's back.

She stepped into the stirrup and pulled herself up on Simon's back. Immediately Tanner mounted and, with his arms around her, urged Simon toward home.

She took her hat off and held it in front of her, then

leaned back against him. He wrapped one arm around her and held his gun in the other.

He was relatively certain the danger had passed, knew that Burt had his back. But with each step Simon took toward home, he relived that terrifying moment of watching Molly rear and Anna fall to the ground.

He'd feared she was dead. He'd been terrified that he'd screwed up and Anna had paid for his mistake with her life.

The ride had been foolish. He should have known better than to take her out in the open where she could be a potential target. He'd allowed himself a moment of softness and that moment had almost gotten her killed.

He could smell her hair, the clean scent of sunshine and shampoo. Her body was warm against his and despite all that had happened, she stirred him.

He tightened his arm around her, thinking of how close they had come to catastrophe, how close he had come to losing her. What had he been thinking? How could he have taken such a chance with her, especially not knowing what he was up against?

The stables came into view, but still his nerves felt strung as tight as he'd ever felt them. For now, she was safe, but a deep dread kept at bay any real feelings of relief.

"There won't be any more rides," he said as they dismounted. "In fact, I don't want you outside at all. I don't want you standing on the front porch, in the doorway or peeking out a window."

She eyed him solemnly. "So you don't think it was a hunter after all," she said.

He didn't hold her gaze, but instead led Simon to his stall. "I didn't say that," he replied. He didn't want to worry her, but in his gut he just couldn't believe that the shot was accidental.

"Then why are you saying that I have to stay inside?" She tossed her hat back on the top of her head and peered up at him. "Do you often have problems with hunters?"

"Never," he admitted truthfully as he secured the big gelding in his stall.

"Tanner West, I demand that you tell me what you're thinking," she exclaimed. "I have a right to know what you think."

He whirled around to look at her, his eyes narrowed as the emotions that had roared up inside him at the sight of her falling off the horse spun out of control. "That tone of voice might work on the servants you have back home, but it sure as hell doesn't work on me."

She bit her lip as a wash of pink filled her cheeks. "I'm sorry." She took a deep breath and stepped closer to him, so close he could smell the scent of her, see the silver flecks in her blue eyes. "Tanner, I trust you to tell me what's going on. I need you to be different from everyone else in my life and to tell me what's really going on. I need you to treat me like a competent woman, not like a pampered princess."

"You want me to treat you like a woman?" Somewhere in the back of his mind he knew he was out of control, but at the moment he didn't care.

He grabbed her by her upper arms and pulled her even closer to him. Her soft full lips that had tormented him since the moment he'd met her opened in surprise.

He gave himself no time to think, no time to question his own judgment. Instead, driven by a need more powerful than he'd ever known, he crashed his mouth to hers.

He'd known her lips would be soft. He hadn't expected the heat they contained, a heat that sucked him in, spinning his senses and threatening to buckle his knees.

She didn't fight him, but rather wound her arms around his neck and leaned into him, molding her body to his as she returned his kiss with fervor.

Her hat fell to the ground behind her as he tangled his hands in her hair and reveled in the feel of the soft, silky strands.

He wanted to pull her into a straw-filled stall and make love to her. He wanted to lose himself in the blue depths of her eyes, in the sweet fragrance of her, in the lush curves that confirmed she was, indeed, a woman.

But she was more than a woman. She was a princess. His client. His responsibility. He tore his mouth from hers and stepped back from her, unsure if he was angry at himself for crossing a line or at her for shoving him over that line.

"Get in the house," he ordered, trying not to notice that her lips were red from the kiss they'd shared.

She crossed her arms over her chest and eyed him with a touch of defiance. "I will not. Not until I make sure Molly is all right."

It surprised him, the fact that she'd even thought about the horse. But he needed to get her somewhere safe now. "I'll have somebody check her later. Right now we need to get you into the house immediately."

He took her by the upper arm and led her to the stable door. He paused there, not releasing her. The distance between the house and the stable appeared daunting. A lot of open ground to cover without any protection.

"Tanner, you're hurting me," she murmured. He realized in his urgency he'd been squeezing her arm.

He released her. "Stay here. I need to get Sam's attention." He stepped out of the stable and waved to the man standing on the end of the front porch. Sam Wilson, another valued ranch hand who was as good with his gun as he was with the cattle, caught his gesture and headed toward Tanner.

As Tanner waited his mind whirled. He needed to get Anna inside, into an interior room in the house. He had no idea who might be out there, waiting to take another shot, readying for some sort of attack.

"Are you all right, boss?" Sam asked as he reached Tanner.

"Somebody took a shot at us while we were riding.

Burt is out seeing what he can find, but we need to get Anna into the house. I need you to go back to the porch and cover us."

Sam nodded and turned on his heels. As he hurried back to the porch, Tanner could see him turning his head from side to side, assessing the area for an imminent threat.

When he reached the porch he raised his rifle to his shoulder and waited. Tanner turned back to Anna. Her eyes were huge, as if she just now fully understood the danger.

"We're going to walk toward the house," he said. "I'll be directly behind you, covering you like a shield. If anything happens, if you hear gunfire or if for some reason something happens to me, you run for Sam. He'll get you safely inside."

"Okay." Her pulse beat rapidly in the hollow of her throat, belying her calm reply.

"Ready?" Once again he took her arm. Together they left the shadows of the stable and walked out into the sunshine. Although there was some comfort in the fact that there would be few places between the house and the stables for anyone to hide, Tanner couldn't discount the use of weaponry that wouldn't need to put the shooter nearby.

Awkwardly he kept himself as close to Anna's back as he could, alternating between looking ahead and looking back. He didn't breathe a sigh of relief until they hit the porch and she disappeared into the house.

"Thanks, Sam," he said tersely.

Sam didn't lower his rifle. "Nobody is getting through me," he said with determination, displaying one of the reasons he was a trusted employee.

Tanner went inside, to see Anna standing just inside the living room. "Go to the study," he said. The study had no windows, and was an interior room that would be easier to defend if an attack should occur.

"What happens now?" she asked.

"I'm going to call Jim Ramsey and tell him what happened."

"You'll tell him who I am?" she asked as she sank onto the chair in front of the desk.

"No. The fewer people who know who you are, the better. All he needs to know is that somebody took a shot at us." Tanner had learned a long time ago that things went more smoothly if he kept in touch with the local authorities, but as far as he was concerned it was on a need to know basis. "I'll also double the guards around the house."

"What can I do?"

"Stay in here and out of the way," he said curtly. "I'll let you know when the sheriff arrives."

He met Smokey in the hallway and quickly filled the old man in on what had occurred. "I'll get my gun," Smokey said.

Tanner nodded. "Until we know what's going on it would be a good idea if everyone in the house is armed."

It took Tanner only a few minutes to rally more guards and get them stationed around the house. By the time he'd done that, Burt had arrived back at the house.

"I found a couple of cigarette butts just on the other side of the trees," Burt said.

Tanner frowned. "That implies somebody lying in wait. But there's no way anyone could have known I'd taken Anna out for a ride today. I didn't know myself until ten minutes before we went out." He leaned against one of the porch railings, staring out in the distance. "And something else that doesn't make sense is why there was only one shot. If it was some kind of rebel warrior, why not ten shots? Why not a hundred to see that the job got done?"

As he waited for the sheriff to arrive, his mind worked overtime. If the security of this location had been breached, then he needed to move Anna.

Dust in the distance drew his attention and tension ripped through him as he held his gun ready. He relaxed when the car came into view and he recognized it as his father returning from his trip to Oklahoma City.

By the time he'd filled his father in on what was going on, Sheriff Ramsey had arrived. He went back to the study to get Anna and found her sound asleep in the chair.

Oddly enough, he wasn't irritated. Rather he was surprised that she obviously trusted her safety to him enough that she could fall into a deep, easy sleep.

* * *

Anna awoke to a dark room. She sat up and gasped as muscles in her arms, her back and even her neck screamed in protest of any movement.

For a moment she was disoriented, then remembered. The gunshot. The danger. She was in the study and must have fallen asleep while waiting for the sheriff to arrive.

She stood and stretched, then checked the clock on the desk. Just after ten. She'd been asleep for several hours. Wondering what had happened while she'd slept, hunger pangs making her aware she'd missed dinner, she opened the door to the study. She nearly screamed in surprise as she saw Tanner seated in the hallway across from the room.

"You scared me to death," she exclaimed.

He rose to his full height, clad only in a pair of jeans. "Sorry. I was sitting here trying to decide if I should wake you up or just let you continue to sleep."

"I think if I wasn't hungry, I would have slept the night away in that chair."

"Come on, let's get you something to eat and I'll fill you in on what's happened while you slept."

She followed him through the darkened living room to the kitchen, aware that the tension that had emanated from him before seemed to be gone. "Did the sheriff come?" she asked as he gestured her into a chair at the table.

"Yeah, and he gave us some good news." He

opened the refrigerator door and she tried not to notice that he looked as if he'd recently stepped out of a shower. His hair was tousled and slightly damp, and it made her remember the kiss they had shared in the stable.

"What kind of good news?" She couldn't think about the kiss. What she needed to think about was the fact that she'd almost been killed this afternoon.

"The mystery of the gunshot has been solved."

She looked at him in surprise. "What do you mean?"

He didn't answer immediately, but took a moment to slap together a ham sandwich and place it on a paper plate. He set it down in front of her, then slid into the seat next to her.

"Jeffrey Canfield owns the ranch next to ours. Seems his grandson and a friend were out visiting him today. They snuck away from the house and onto our property and spent the afternoon smoking cigarettes and shooting at old tin cans. One of those shots found us."

"So, it wasn't any rebels." A rush of relief swept through her. She picked up the sandwich and took a bite.

"Jeffrey called and apologized, said he intended to tan the hides off the two boys, but I'm just glad to find out it was all an accident." His eyes were the dark green of forest moss, and his expression was serious. "But the same rules apply. I don't want you outside again. We took a chance today and it was foolish, damned foolish."

For some reason she got the impression he wasn't just talking about the horseback ride, but might just be talking about the kiss they had shared, as well.

She took another bite of her sandwich and chewed thoughtfully. It had been a little bit of madness, that kiss. She certainly had no desire to develop any real relationship with Tanner West. Her destiny was not on a ranch with a cowboy, although at the moment she didn't know what her destiny was.

Still, even knowing the kiss had been madness, she wanted a repeat of the insanity. For just that moment when he'd held her so close, when his lips had burned into hers, she'd felt alive for the first time in her life.

As she ate her sandwich he leaned back in his chair and gazed at her with eyes darkly shuttered. She wished she knew him well enough to guess at his thoughts. He looked half angry with her, but that wasn't unusual. Half the time she was around him he looked as if he were angry with her.

A wave of homesickness struck her and she pushed her half-eaten sandwich away, no longer hungry.

"What's wrong? You don't like the sandwich?"

"No, it's fine. I'm just not as hungry as I thought I was. Actually I was just struck by a wave of homesickness."

"Homesick for Niflheim or your lifestyle or what?"

She frowned thoughtfully. "I think I'm mostly homesick for Astrid."

One of his dark eyebrows shot up. "Astrid?"

"She was my personal assistant and maid and as close to a real friend as I had in my life. She'd bring me breakfast in the mornings and we'd talk about anything and everything. Have you learned anything about what happened to the palace staff since the coup?"

"No. I'm sorry."

"What about you, Tanner? Do you have friends?"

"Of course I have friends," he replied quickly, too quickly.

"Really? What are their names?"

He leaned forward, raking a hand through his dark hair. "This is a silly conversation. I have friends. I just don't have a lot of time to spend with them. None of them bring me breakfast in bed and chat about the party I attended the night before."

"Why do you have to do that? Why, when I ask you questions about yourself, do you always have to somehow turn them into an attack on me?"

He sat back once again and averted his gaze. "I wasn't aware that I do that."

"You do, and I'm growing weary of it."

His gaze shot back to her and she saw the narrowing of his eyes. She steeled herself for a retort. Instead he stood and grabbed her plate from the table. "It's late."

She got up from the table and winced as she felt a kink in her shoulder.

"What's wrong?"

"Nothing…I'm just a little sore, that's all." She reached up and touched her shoulder. "I'm not sure whether it's from all the shoveling I did this morning or from my contact with the ground when I fell off Molly."

He frowned, placed her plate in the sink, then walked over to her. "Stand still," he said as he moved behind her. He placed his hands on top of her shoulders and began to knead the muscles.

"Oh-h-h." A soft moan escaped her as his fingers worked the sore muscles, creating a combination of pleasure and exquisite pain. She dropped her chin to her chest to allow him better access.

He had big hands, and by touching her he sent the crazy heat cascading through her again. She knew it was strictly physical. She didn't know him well enough for it to be anything else, but whatever it was, it was wonderful.

"Hmm." Another moan escaped her, and what she wanted to do more than anything was turn around and place her hands on his broad, naked chest. She wanted to touch that wide expanse of tanned skin and muscle, feel the warmth of his skin beneath her fingertips. She wanted him to kiss her again, kiss her long and hard so she could forget everything, especially the danger she'd been reminded today that she was still in.

His ministrations had begun strong and sure, but

had softened, so that it almost felt as if he were caressing her shoulders rather than working out the kinks.

She moaned again and his hands suddenly fell away. She turned, and the look on his face made her breath catch in her chest. Shining from his eyes was a look of hunger. It was there only a moment, then gone.

He stepped back from her and shoved his hands into his pockets. "You might want to take a hot bath to get the rest of the kinks out." His voice was deeper, huskier than usual.

"I'll do that," she said, aware that her voice was more breathless than normal.

"And you'd better get back to bed. Breakfast comes early in the morning." There was a definite edge to his voice.

She stepped closer, reached out and placed a hand on his thick biceps. Just as she'd suspected, his skin was warm and smooth. "Thank you for the sandwich."

She knew she should drop her hand from his arm, but was reluctant to break the physical contact.

"No big deal. But if you don't stop touching me you might get more than you bargained for."

Her heart thrummed in excitement. So, he felt it, too, the crazy pull, the sizzling heat. "And that would be so bad?"

He plucked her hand from his arm. "Lady, that could be downright deadly for both of us." He inhaled a deep, audible breath. "Go to bed, Anna. Your father will be here in the next couple of days and then you can go back to living the lifestyle you had before coming to Cotter Creek."

Moments later, when she was back in her own bed, for the first time since arriving in Cotter Creek the thought of returning to her previous lifestyle didn't excite her but rather filled her with the familiar loneliness and a strange sense of dread.

Chapter 8

"Is Smokey in charge of changing the sheets on the beds?"

Tanner looked up from the computer to see Anna standing in the doorway of the study. It was after ten. She'd missed breakfast that morning and this was the first time he'd seen her since the night before.

He'd almost been glad he hadn't had to face her first thing this morning. Their middle-of-the-night conversation had disturbed him almost as much as the feel of her slender shoulders beneath his fingertips, almost as much as the silky softness of the ends of her hair against the backs of his hands, the scent of her that had whirled in his head.

"Yeah, Smokey is in charge of clean sheets," he replied, and got up from the desk.

"Don't bother yourself. I'll speak to Smokey about it." Whatever fire he'd seen in her eyes last night was gone, doused beneath a frostiness that was comforting to him.

He had no idea what had caused the distance in her eyes, the coolness in her voice, but he liked it far better than the fire of desire that had lit her eyes the night before.

"I need to take a break anyway," he replied. Besides, he wouldn't miss for the world the princess asking Smokey to change her sheets.

He followed her down the hallway toward the kitchen, trying not to look at the sway of her hips in the jeans that fit her as if she'd been born into them. But, she hadn't been born in denim. She'd been born with a crown on her head, he reminded himself.

Smokey was in the kitchen, cutting up vegetables for lunch. He looked up as they entered, a frown cutting into his forehead. "What is this? A convention of some kind in my kitchen? What do you want?"

"I was wondering when you'd be changing the sheets on my bed?" Anna asked. "It's been several days now. I'm accustomed to them being changed every other day."

Tanner held his breath as Smokey set down his paring knife and wiped his hands on a dish towel. The old man's eyes glittered with a light that Tanner remembered well from his youth, a light that had always made Tanner and the rest of his siblings make themselves scarce.

"You want to know when I'll be changing the sheets on your bed?" he asked.

Anna nodded slowly as if she was aware that she'd made a faux pas but didn't quite know what to do about it.

Smokey disappeared into the laundry room and returned a moment later with a set of clean sheets in his hands. He thrust them toward Anna. "This ain't no full-service hotel and I ain't your personal maid service. You want the sheets changed on your bed, you do it yourself."

Anna glared at Tanner, then at Smokey. "You cranky old toad. You don't have to be so hateful. All you had to do was explain it to me." She turned on her heels and, with all the dignity of a queen, exited the kitchen.

"She's a pain," Tanner said.

"I like her." Smokey looked up to meet Tanner's look of surprise. "Oh, she's spoiled all right, but she's got gumption. She just doesn't know our ways. Can't exactly fault her for being foreign. I 'spect if I went to Paris or some such a place the Frenchies wouldn't quite know what to make of me. I 'spect they wouldn't even know what to make of you."

Tanner grunted, not having a more intelligent reply. As he left the kitchen Smokey's words whirled in his head. Had he been too hard on Anna? Had he not taken into account the fact that she'd been unceremoniously thrust into a foreign lifestyle in a foreign country?

As he walked down the long hallway he heard muttered curses coming from her bedroom. He stepped into the doorway and peered inside to see her wrestling with the bottom fitted sheet. She got one corner beneath the mattress only to have an opposite corner pull free.

"Need some help?" The minute the words left his mouth he regretted them. He wasn't a nursemaid, for crying out loud. He was a bodyguard. Making beds for clients wasn't in his job description.

She looked up at him and blew a strand of her golden blond hair off her forehead. "There's some kind of a mistake. This damned sheet doesn't fit." She glared at him as if he were personally responsible for her being unable to get the sheet on the bed. "Smokey probably did this on purpose, gave me sheets that are too small. He obviously hates me and wants to see me sweat."

"He wouldn't do that. He likes you."

She stared at him with disbelief. "He does not. He's just like you. He thinks I'm stupid and shallow and spoiled." She sank to the edge of the bed. "I can speak five foreign languages, but I can't even get sheets on a bed."

She sounded and looked so miserable, his heart

constricted just a bit. "Why don't I help you with the bed?" he offered.

"If you help me, will you think I'm stupid?"

He smiled at her. "A woman who speaks five foreign languages can't be all that stupid."

She returned his smile and for just a moment there was no tension between them, no underlying friction of any kind. "I would appreciate some help," she finally said grudgingly.

"Come on, it's always easier when there's two people working at it."

It took them only minutes to get the sheets on the bed. As Tanner helped her, he remembered years ago when he'd helped his mother do the same task.

Elizabeth West had been a beautiful woman. Tanner could remember trips into town, where men hurried to nod hello or to open a door for her. Her black hair had been worn long and her eyes had been an emerald-green that had been both beautiful and startling.

"Tanner? Are you all right?"

Anna's voice startled him and he realized he'd been standing still, lost in the memories of boyhood long past. "Yeah, I'm fine. I was just thinking about my mother."

She sat on the edge of the bed once again and this time patted the spot next to her. "What was she like?"

He sank down beside her and for a moment allowed himself to fall back into memories of the woman who had given him birth, the woman who had loved him for the first ten years of his life.

"She was beautiful." Tanner rarely allowed himself the luxury of his memories, but he found himself allowing them now. "She had long dark hair and green eyes and a smile that warmed an entire room. She loved to laugh."

Anna leaned against him, her warmth welcoming. "She sounds like a wonderful person."

"She was. She was strong. Dad was gone a lot and Mom had all of us to contend with, often alone, but I don't ever remember hearing her complain. She loved Dad, loved being our mother, and it showed in everything she did."

"She would have been very proud of the man you've become," Anna said softly. "Your father loved her very much?"

"Very much. I don't think he ever stopped grieving for her." He turned to look at Anna. "I don't think any of us ever really stopped grieving her loss."

He stood abruptly, unwilling to entertain any more painful memories. "Let's get the bedspread on," he said. He walked over and grabbed the bedspread from the floor near the dresser, his gaze falling on a dark blue velvet pouch. "What is this?" he asked.

"My crown. Want to see it?"

He was surprised how much he didn't want to see a reminder of her position, but before he could reply, his cell phone rang.

He held up a finger to indicate she hold on a minute at the same time he answered the call. "Tanner," he said into the receiver.

"She's dead, Tanner. The son-of-a-bitch killed Melissa this morning. He shot her in her driveway then turned the gun on himself." Zack's voice reverberated with all-consuming rage and torment.

Tanner went cold. His breath whooshed out of him as if he'd been punched in the stomach. "Zack…where are you now? Are you still in Oklahoma City?"

"No. I'm an hour out of Cotter Creek." The emotion nearly made his brother's words indecipherable.

"Come straight to the house, Zack. You hear me? Come on in and we'll talk. Dammit," he exclaimed as the line went dead.

"What's wrong?" Anna asked.

"That was Zack. Apparently his client was killed this morning. Her ex-husband killed her, then killed himself."

"That poor woman."

He tugged a hand down his jaw. "Dammit! Zack didn't sound good." His stomach twisted in knots as he thought of his brother. "He got too close to her. I warned him that the first rule in being a good bodyguard was to keep emotional distance between yourself and the client. He didn't listen to me."

"Where's your brother now?"

"He's on his way home, said he was about an hour away. I've got to go speak with my father and Smokey. Will you be all right now?"

"Of course. Go take care of whatever you need to."

He turned and left the room, his thoughts racing. Maybe Zack hadn't been ready for this particular assignment. It had been too long an assignment. Zack had been gone nearly three months.

Zack couldn't blame himself, nor was this a company failure. The client had released Zack. Tanner needed his brother to understand that evil was often more patient than good, that if her ex-husband hadn't killed her today he might have killed her next week or next month or at any time in the future. Zack hadn't failed. He'd kept her from harm until she'd told Zack to go home.

Dammit. He should have sent somebody else, or taken care of it himself. Zack had always been the most emotional of his siblings. Tanner should have known this assignment wouldn't be good for him.

A mistake, and now Zack was hurting as Tanner had never heard him hurt before. Somehow, some way, Tanner had to figure out how to make it all okay.

He found Red weeding in the garden. "Dad, something's happened."

Red stood, the expression on his face letting Tanner know his father's arthritis was bothering him. "What's up?"

"Zack called. All he said was that he's on his way home and his former client was killed sometime this morning. He sounded bad, Dad. I think he got too close."

Red sighed heavily as the two headed back into the house. "We'll get through this, Tanner. We've gotten through worse."

Tanner nodded, wondering what he was going to say to his brother when he had a feeling he was perilously close to making the same mistake with his own client.

Anna sat on the end of the sofa in the great room thumbing through a magazine, aware of Tanner pacing back and forth in front of the windows that looked out to the front of the house.

It had been an hour since Zack had called and Tanner's worry, his tension, seemed big enough to fill the entire house. She wished she knew what to say, what to do to ease his worry, but she didn't have a clue how to help him through this.

Red sat in a nearby chair, staring down at a magazine, but he hadn't turned a page in the past fifteen minutes. Even Smokey occasionally came in from the kitchen to see if Zack had arrived yet.

There wasn't just tension in the room, there was an underlying sense of support, of love, that was almost palpable. It wasn't the first time in the three days that she had been here that she'd noticed the love that was contained within the walls of the house.

At each meal as Tanner and his father talked, Anna had sensed a deep connection between the two men. And whenever Tanner had mentioned one of his brothers or sister, his devotion had been evident in his tone of voice.

What must it be like to be part of such a big support system, to be a part of something so much bigger than one's self? Not as big as a country, which Anna had found impersonal and unfulfilling, but to be a piece of a family who cared about not only your failures, but your triumphs, as well.

She thought it must be an amazing feeling and it was one she hoped one day she would know.

Red stood and Tanner froze as the sound of the crunching of wheels on gravel came through the windows. "He's here," Tanner said softly, his gaze focused out the pane of glass.

Someplace deep inside her Anna knew she should probably retreat to her bedroom and leave this family alone to deal with the situation. She had a feeling there would be pieces to put back together and she really had no place in this family meeting.

But she didn't move from her perch on the sofa as she found herself drawn to the real lives of real people. She realized somehow, some way in the short span of time she'd been in the house, she'd come to care about these people and their lives.

She would have known Zack in a crowd of cowboys. The moment he walked through the front door, she was struck by his close resemblance to his older brother.

He was roughly the same height and body type. Although his hair was longer than Tanner's, it was the same rich dark color and his green eyes stamped him as one of the West children.

Under normal circumstances he was probably quite handsome, but at the moment his features were pulled taut and twisted with raw, naked emotion that was almost painful to see.

"Zackary." Red was the first one to greet him. He wrapped his arms around his son and gave him a bear hug. Zack stood perfectly still in the embrace, neither accepting nor rejecting.

As Red released his son, Tanner stepped toward his brother. "You okay?" he asked.

"Hell, no, I'm not okay." Zack's voice was thick with emotion. "I don't know if I'll ever be okay." He ripped a hand through his hair. "But I'll tell you this. I'm done. I'm finished with all this. I don't want to do this kind of work ever again."

"What do you mean?" Tanner's features pulled into a deep frown.

"What do you think it means? I quit. I don't want to work for you. I don't want to work for the agency anymore."

"That's ridiculous. For God's sake, Zack, give yourself some time." Tanner reached out and placed his hand on Zack's shoulder. "Don't make any decisions while you're upset. You don't want to leave the business. We need you."

Zack jerked away from his brother, his eyes dark

and his mouth a slash of despair. "You know what I need, Tanner? Right now, at this very moment, I need a big brother, not a boss. But I should have known not to expect that from you."

Before anyone could say another word Zack stormed back out the front door and slammed it shut behind him. For just a brief moment Tanner's features reflected a haggard vulnerability, a slicing pain that stole Anna's breath.

It was there only a moment, then gone, replaced by the stoic expression and dark gaze that was so familiar to her. Anna suddenly felt like the intruder she was and she quietly slipped away to her room.

She sat at the foot of her bed and thought about the scene she had just witnessed. What she had just seen was a slice of real life. What she had experienced the whole morning was a vignette of a family.

She'd felt the love and support of Tanner and his father for Zack. She'd felt their worry about him. And she'd seen how people who love one another could hurt and disappoint each other.

Real-life drama, unlike the superficial life she'd led had the capacity to hurt, but it also had the capacity to bring joy and to heal.

There was no way for her to imagine what Zack had been feeling after what he'd been through, but she couldn't forget that moment of stark expression on Tanner's face.

In that unguarded vulnerable moment, she'd seen

that Zack's words had cut him deep and she'd felt Tanner's pain resonating inside of her. It was a strange feeling, that of another's pain. It awed her and made her feel more real than she ever had in her life.

Lunch was difficult. Tension pulsed in the air. Red made small-talk with Anna, but she was acutely aware of Tanner's brooding silence, his dark gaze seemingly focused inward to a place where nobody could follow.

Dinner was a repeat of the uncomfortable lunch. Had Anna not spent the past several days in Tanner's company, she might have thought his dark eyes and tense facial muscles to be solely possessed by anger. But she knew in her heart that it wasn't just anger. It was pain.

That night as she lay in bed sleep remained elusive as she thought of Tanner and his brother. In that moment when Zack had turned angrily on his eldest brother, Tanner had looked as if he'd been slapped.

For the past couple of days Tanner had put his life on hold for her. He'd kept her safe and helped her through the terror of a thunderstorm, had even helped her make the bed where she now attempted to sleep. And now he was all alone in his room and in pain.

Without giving herself a second to think, she slid out of bed, pulled on a T-shirt and pair of jeans and left her room. She padded down the hallway to the room next door, wondering if he was already asleep.

It was possible he wouldn't want to see her, wouldn't want to talk to her. But it was also possible he just might need somebody at this moment. And it surprised her how much she wanted to be the person he needed.

His closed bedroom door should have warned her away, but it didn't. She knocked softly. There was no reply. She knocked again, then took a deep breath, twisted the knob and opened the door.

He stood next to the window, the dim lamp on the nightstand casting him in deep shadows. He wore only a pair of jeans slung low on his hips and his male scent filled the entire room.

He turned to face her. "What do you need, Anna?" His voice was just short of a bark.

For the first time since she'd left her bedroom she realized she had no idea why she was here, why she had felt compelled to come to him. "I'm not sure," she said honestly. "I thought maybe you might need something."

He took a step forward, leaving the shadows of the room behind him. Now she could see the darkness in his eyes, feel the dangerous energy that rolled off him. "You thought I might need something?" He took a step toward her and it wasn't just a feeling of danger that communicated itself to her, but rather a thrum of excitement, as well.

"And just what was it you thought I might need?" he asked as he took another step toward her.

Her mouth dried and her heart began to pound an unnatural rhythm. She was acutely conscious of the bed, mere inches from where she stood, the navy sheets rumpled and the depression of a head still evident on one of the pillows.

She wasn't sure what he needed, but her need for him washed over her. Seeing the way the lamplight played on his bare chest with his scent working its way into her very pores, she felt as if she'd needed him for weeks, months…years.

He dragged a hand through his hair. "Go back to bed, Anna," he said, his voice with a weary rough edge.

She knew she had two choices, to follow his command or to follow her heart. There was really no choice as far as she was concerned.

She took a step toward him. "I don't want to go back to bed. I want to be here with you."

His eyes narrowed and she felt the taut, powerful energy of him sweeping over her. She fought the shiver that tried to crawl up her spine, a shiver of delicious anticipation.

"If you don't leave now, this cowboy won't be responsible for the consequences." There was a distinct warning in his words, but there was also a flame in his eyes that warmed her from head to toe.

"I've never worried much about consequences," she said half breathlessly. "And in this particular case, it's the consequence that I want…that I need."

In three long strides he was in front of her and as he wrapped her in his arms and captured her mouth with his, she knew there was no going back.

Chapter 9

Tanner knew it was wrong. Someplace in the back of his mind as his arms filled with Anna, as his mouth plundered hers, he knew it was all wrong, but he had no intention of stopping.

The pain of Zack's words retreated as the heat of Anna's mouth suffused him. He knew the pain would return eventually, along with the guilt, but at the moment it was impossible for his mind to entertain anything but the scent and feel of the woman pressed intimately against him.

"Anna," he said as he pulled his mouth from hers. He stared down into her eyes, unsure what he wanted to say. He'd started to warn her that there would be no promises, no future just because of this one night.

But he suddenly recognized he didn't need to tell her that. She was a princess and in all probability the insurgents in her country would be silenced, peace would be restored and she'd return to resume her life. She wasn't about to throw all that away because of one night in bed with a cowboy bodyguard.

She was probably the safest woman he could have a physical relationship with, for she would expect and demand nothing in return.

"Don't talk, Tanner," she replied, her eyes shimmering and luminous. "Don't tell me all the reasons why I shouldn't be in here, why I shouldn't be with you. Just make love to me now."

He certainly hadn't needed any additional encouragement, but her words broke a dam inside him, a dam of want that had been building from the moment she had stormed through his office door.

He crashed his mouth to hers, at the same time his hands moved up beneath her T-shirt to touch the bare flesh of her smooth back. Her skin was like warm satin and electrified his fingertips.

There was nothing soft or hesitant in the way their mouths clung, in the battle of their tongues and the panting breathlessness that seemed to consume them. There was no gentle teasing, no hesitant exploration, only ravenous hunger and clawing need.

There was no bra to encumber him and the thought

of how close he was to feeling those breasts that he'd seen in the lightning nearly sent him spinning wildly out of control. He took several deep, steadying breaths as his hands crept around her and stopped just beneath the sweet swell of her full breasts. Even though he hadn't touched her intimately, he could see through her T-shirt that her nipples were erect as if eagerly anticipating his touch.

He needed to take a moment, wanted to slow down and to enjoy the journey as much as the final destination. Anna stirred him as he could never remember any woman doing before her.

Her hands sizzled against the skin on his chest and as she danced him toward the bed there was nothing he wanted more than to fall with her amid the tangled sheets and make fast, furious love to her. She seemed to want the same thing as her fingers moved to the first button of his fly and began to fumble to unfasten it. He grabbed her hands, recognizing that she was a woman accustomed to being in control and this time, with him, he intended to be in control.

She looked up at him, her eyes hungry and her lips slightly swollen and partly open as if to invite him to another kiss. "Let me," he said as he dropped her hands and instead reached for the button on her fly.

He'd expected an argument, but she surprised him by standing perfectly still as he unfastened the top button of her jeans. One by one he unbuttoned until there was nothing more to unfasten.

When he'd finished she shimmied her jeans to the floor and stepped out of them. Her body was still hidden from his view by the length of her shirt. He reached for the bottom of her top, but she stepped back from him.

"The lamp," she said in a faint whisper.

"I want it on." He reached out and dragged a finger down the side of her face. She closed her eyes for a moment as if finding his touch excruciatingly intense.

"I don't want to fumble around in the dark with you," he said, his voice a husky rasp. "I want to look at your face while I'm touching you, I want to see your eyes when I make love to you."

She opened her eyes, inhaled a tremulous breath and pulled her T-shirt over her head. She dropped it to the floor and stood naked and proud in front of him.

The sight of her stole his breath away. Her hips were curvy and her stomach was flat. Her smallish breasts begged to be touched. To him she was stunning…absolutely perfect.

As he tore off his jeans, she crawled beneath the sheets of the bed and when he joined her there he pulled her into his arms for a full-contact body embrace.

She felt just as she had in his dreams, soft and hot, eager and beyond tempting. Their mouths met once again as his hands found the fullness of her breasts and cupped them.

As his thumbs stroked across her nipples she released a low, deep moan. He tore his mouth from hers and looked down at her, saw the darkened irises of her eyes, eyes filled with a hunger that torched through him.

He could have taken her then, buried himself inside her and taken her in frantic need. But he didn't. He had no idea how many lovers she'd had before, but he wanted to make love to her better than any other man ever had. He wanted her to remember her cowboy lover long after she left Cotter Creek and him behind.

With this thought in mind, he began to explore her body inch by delectable inch. He stroked and kissed as she clutched at him and moaned her pleasure. Each moan shot through him like a jolt of electricity, moving him closer to his point of no return.

He stoked her at her center, using his fingers to drive her mindless. She moaned his name, and he loved the sound of it on her lips. Her hips moved against him in frantic need and he increased the pressure of his touch.

It took only moments for her to stiffen and cry out, a soft mewling cry as she shuddered her release.

He could wait no longer. He leaned over and ripped open the drawer of his nightstand. His fingers trembled as he clasped one of the foil packets. Hurry, his brain screamed as he ripped it open and quickly rolled on the condom. Need drove him into her, and as he buried himself in her sweet, wet warmth he lost all sense of himself.

Together their hips moved in unison as his mouth once again found hers. Faster and faster they moved, their mouths no longer capable of clinging to each other while their bodies moved in raging need.

He felt her stiffening again, watched her eyelids flutter and her eyes roll back and then close and knew she had once again found her release.

It was all he needed to let himself go.

Moments later they remained in each other's arms, and for the first time Tanner recognized how utterly foolish they had been giving in to the desire that had been pulsating between them for the past couple of days.

"Anna." He rose on one elbow and gazed at her.

She reached up and laid a gentle hand on the side of his face. She looked at him as if she could see all that lay inside him. "You need to talk?"

Her soft touch, her knowing eyes and the invitation to share scared the hell out of him. In a matter of days she'd be gone, back to her superficial life of leisure.

No matter what they had just shared physically, he didn't intend to share anything with her emotionally. There was no point to baring his soul.

"No. What I really need is to sleep."

He hadn't realized how gruff he'd sounded until she jerked her hand away from him as if he'd slapped her. With one graceful movement she slid from the bed and stood. "Then I guess I'd better let you get some sleep."

With the dignity of a queen, she grabbed her jeans

and T-shirt, then slid out of his bedroom door and shut it behind her.

Tanner leaned his head back against the pillow and closed his eyes even though he knew sleep would be a long time coming. He'd hurt her by sending her away so abruptly, but the last thing he wanted to do was to snuggle beneath warm, sex-scented sheets and share the secrets of his heart.

Still her natural empathy got to him. If she really had been the spoiled young woman he believed she was, then she wouldn't have noticed or cared that Zack's words had bothered him. But apparently she had noticed and she did care.

He found his thoughts drifting away from Anna and to his brother. Zack's words had stung more deeply than he'd believed possible. He'd needed a brother, not a boss, that's what Zack had said.

Tanner had been trying to be a brother. He couldn't help it that his concern had been not only for Zack but for how Zack's actions might affect the company. The company was built for the benefit of his siblings. Tanner had worked hard to make the company successful enough that hopefully his siblings would never have to worry about money.

Zack was a hell of a bodyguard, a huge asset to Wild West Protective Services. Tanner couldn't imagine his brother not working for the agency. Zack belonged with the agency and Tanner knew that better than anyone. He'd just been trying to make Zack see that point.

He turned to his side as his thoughts once again returned to Anna. Anna, the spoiled, jet-setting princess. Anna, with gold in her hair and challenge sparkling her eyes. Anna, with her satiny skin and throaty sighs.

He hoped her father arrived tomorrow and would take her away from here, back to the life where she belonged.

Yes, this night had been a mistake and would have never happened had he not been feeling vulnerable. It was a mistake that wouldn't ever happen again.

Tanner West was the most aggravating man she'd ever known in her entire life. He was driven, arrogant and far more complex than she'd realized.

Last night he'd made exquisite love to her and there had been a moment when she'd felt him open to her not only with his body but with his heart and soul, as well. There had been a moment when he'd looked into her eyes and she'd seen the man beneath and he'd taken her breath away.

Unfortunately he'd ruined everything by shutting down and turning off, by throwing her to the curb before her heartbeat had even returned to a normal rhythm.

This morning had been no better. He'd been cranky and distant, pacing the floor in the great room and studiously ignoring her.

She felt a bit cranky herself. There was only so many times she could thumb through a copy of

Ranch Living, only so many times she could stare out the window and only so much silence she could handle.

It was just before noon when desperation drove her into Smokey's lair, the kitchen. "What do you want?" He looked about as inviting as the act of shoving a size-five shoe onto a size-seven foot.

"I want to know what it is about living in the middle of nowhere that makes everyone so darned crabby." She pulled out a stool and sat at the counter where Smokey was cutting up vegetables.

"Who's crabby?"

She eyed him through narrowed eyes. "Oh, I forgot, you're the epitome of cheerful," she said dryly.

A whisper of a twinkle lit Smokey's eyes. "I am what I am, and I don't pretend to put on airs."

"Is that what you think I do? Put on airs?" She propped her elbow on the counter and placed her chin in her hand.

A full grin pulled Smokey's worn features upward. "I think you were probably born with airs, but that's not your fault. That's just a circumstance of birth."

She frowned thoughtfully. "Then why do I get the feeling he blames me for my circumstance of birth?"

Smokey shrugged. "If Tanner's got a problem with you it's not because of your birth, but maybe because of the choices you've made in your life."

He resumed cutting up cucumbers. "That man is hard on people, but not half as hard as he is on himself. He stopped being a kid, stopped having fun the day his mama died."

"But he was just a little boy," she exclaimed.

"That he was, but that day he shed boyhood and became a man." Smokey set the cucumbers aside and reached for several large tomatoes. "He wasn't just a ten-year-old boy, he was the eldest of six younguns who were all confused and scared and wanting their mama. Red wasn't no good. He fell into a hole of booze and grief. I wasn't much better. Them kids didn't know me very well and it was Tanner who held them all together."

Anna watched for a moment as Smokey expertly sliced and diced the tomatoes, her thoughts embracing the little boy Tanner had been. Her heart cried for the boy who had become a man too soon, raised by life tragedy.

"Tanner doesn't know nothin' but work." Smokey continued speaking in the rough-hewn voice that was oddly appealing. "Since he was a teenager he's been determined to build something secure for his family. That business is all he thinks about, all he cares about."

He turned from the counter and went to the refrigerator. He grabbed several green peppers from the bin then returned to the cutting board and cast her a sly look. "I think a woman like you might be good for him."

"A woman like me?"

He sliced into one of the green peppers, the pungent scent filling the air. "You know, a woman who

knows how to have fun…maybe a little too much fun."
Again he gazed at her with that sly glance.

Anna had never in her life felt the need to apologize or to defend her lifestyle, but she did now. She had the strongest desire to not only apologize but to vow to herself that somehow, some way when this was all over she'd change her life.

"Maybe you're right. Maybe I've had a little too much fun in my life." She thought of the traveling, the clubbing, the frantic kind of fun she'd had. It certainly hadn't brought her anything close to happiness.

The phone rang and Smokey ignored it. It rang only once then apparently was answered by either Tanner or his father. Smokey continued cutting the peppers. "Nothing wrong with fun, but everyone needs a little work in their life, too. Something that makes them feel good about themselves. A man like Tanner would be good for you, too."

She wanted to snort in derision, to protest long and loudly, but deep inside she couldn't fool herself into thinking that Tanner meant nothing to her.

She didn't sleep with men who meant nothing. Men who meant nothing didn't have the potential to hurt her and she thought Tanner possessed that potential.

"It would take a better woman than me to bring a little fun to Tanner's life," she finally exclaimed.

"I don't know about that. I never thought I'd see the day that he'd be standing in front of my refrigerator sorting through things for a picnic."

"A picnic we never got to enjoy," she said wistfully.

"Maybe there will be another time for a picnic," Smokey said.

"Maybe," she agreed, although she doubted it. She was aware that her days here were definitely limited. At any moment her father could arrive and take her away from this ranch where she hadn't wanted to be and now almost hated to leave. She frowned thoughtfully. When had that happened? When had this place begun to feel like home?

The phone rang again. It was not an unusual occurrence. Most mornings the phone rang often as Tanner's agents checked in with him for the day.

"Is there anything I can do to help with lunch?" she asked.

Smokey's gray eyebrows danced upward. "You show a lot of potential, young lady. If you want, you can get the dishes out to set the table." He motioned toward one of the cabinets.

Potential. Nobody had ever told her she had potential before. Smokey's words warmed her as she took the plates out of the cabinet and carried them into the dining room.

There had never been any expectations for her. She was the sum of her frivolity, encouraged to be carefree and superficial and utterly empty inside.

She'd just returned to the kitchen to retrieve the silverware when Tanner came in, his features as grim as she'd ever seen them.

"Something's happened," he said.

"What?" The tension rolling off him forced her heart to beat faster. She was vaguely aware of Smokey setting down his knife, his grizzly brows pulled together.

"Linda Wilcox was found unconscious in an alley this morning." Tanner and Smokey exchanged a glance. "She'd been hit over the head with something and left there."

"That's horrible," she exclaimed. "Was she a friend of yours?"

"Just an acquaintance," Tanner said.

"Why did he call you?" Smokey asked.

"He thought I might be interested."

"He calling everyone in town or did he have a specific reason for thinking you might be especially interested?" Smokey asked.

Tanner's gaze held Anna's and she felt as if the pit of her stomach hit the floor. "He thought we'd be especially interested."

"Why?" The single word crawled from Anna's throat.

"Linda has blond hair, kind of loose around her shoulders like yours. Sheriff Ramsey thought it was interesting that she was wearing your clothes, Anna. The clothes you left at Betty's Boutique."

Chapter 10

Tanner paced in front of the window, waiting for Jim Ramsey to arrive. Anna sat on the sofa, her face blanched of color as she watched him walk back and forth.

Over the years Tanner had worked on hundreds of assignments. He'd headed up protection for a rock star on a six-week tour, had guarded a priceless painting on display at a museum in Phoenix. He'd worked for politicians and businessmen, starlets and athletes, but he'd never had an assignment that worried him more than this one.

He couldn't get a handle on the bad guys, didn't understand them. Always before Tanner had relied on his instincts, but his instincts had been ominously silent on this particular assignment.

"It could just be some awful coincidence," Anna said tentatively, breaking in to his thoughts.

He stopped his pacing and turned to look at her once again. "Yeah, could be," he replied. But he didn't think so. There was a twist in his gut that made him fear it was something much worse than coincidence.

"Why is the sheriff coming to speak to us?" she asked, worry evident in her voice.

"I asked him to come out." Tanner tamped down his restless energy enough to sit next to her on the sofa. "I asked him to bring us the clothes Linda was wearing when she was attacked. I want to make sure they really are the ones you left at Betty's. Maybe she was wearing something similar and Betty got it wrong. If they are the clothes that belonged to you, then I want to go over them."

She frowned. "What do you mean, go over them? It was just a blouse and a long skirt. What's to go over?"

"I don't know. I just want to look at them." He needed to know if that skirt and blouse had somehow led to Linda's attack. He wasn't sure what he was looking for, but he wanted to see those articles of clothing.

Anna leaned into him, her warmth welcome despite his morning of regrets. "I hope Linda Wilcox was the victim of a random mugger. I hope she had a boyfriend who went crazy with jealousy. I hope anything explains what happened to her other than me being the cause of her pain."

He hadn't thought it possible that she would take some sort of personal responsibility for Linda's attack. He wrapped an arm around her shoulder and looked down into her troubled blue eyes. "Anna, you aren't responsible for what's happened. Whoever knocked Linda over the head is solely responsible for this."

"Yes, but if I hadn't come here…if I hadn't left those clothes at Betty's…"

He placed a finger against her soft, sweet lips. "If Betty hadn't resold them, if Linda hadn't bought them…if…if…if."

She grabbed his hand with both of hers and squeezed, her gaze vulnerable and unsure as it held his. Suddenly he felt like the biggest jerk on earth. He'd made love to her then had unceremoniously tossed her out of bed and had spent the morning subtly punishing her with his silence.

"Anna…about last night," he began, unsure what he intended to say but feeling as though he needed to say something.

"I wasn't exactly a gentleman and I apologize for being so brusque with you."

"Apology accepted," she said easily. She gazed at him with her clear, beautiful blue eyes and again he was surprised by the fact that she held no grudge.

"I just didn't want you to think that what happened…"

"Meant anything?" She raised one pale eyebrow. She offered him a faint smile. "The way I look at it we're both adults. There's been some kind of chemistry between us and last night we acted upon it. For as long as it lasted it was beautiful, but I wasn't expecting any hearts or flowers afterward, certainly not from a man like you. I'm just glad about one thing."

"What's that?"

Her dimples flashed. "At least you didn't tell me what to do or accuse me of breaking one of your rules."

His laughter surprised him, momentarily breaking the tension that had held him in its grip. The laughter felt good and he gazed at her almost gratefully. "I told you I didn't have any rules for lovemaking."

"Yes, but I wasn't sure I believed you."

Unfortunately the light moment between them lasted only a minute as the sound of gravel beneath car wheels drifted through the window.

He jumped up from the sofa and was at the front door as Jim Ramsey pulled his patrol car to a halt in the driveway. Once again the twist was in his gut as he watched the beefy man climb out of his car and head toward the porch.

Because it had been Jim Ramsey who had delivered the news of his mother's death, Tanner had never been able to completely separate Ramsey from his mother's murder. In his mind, the two were forever bound together in tragedy, even though Tanner knew it was irrational.

In Jim's hand he carried a brown bag that Tanner knew contained the clothes Linda Wilcox had been wearing before somebody slammed her over the head.

"Tanner." Jim greeted him with a grim smile. "You know I'm breaking about a hundred rules to bring you these clothes." He stepped through the door and nodded to Anna, then turned once again to Tanner. "You going to tell me what the hell is going on?"

Tanner hesitated a moment. Although he and Jim had always been civil to one another and there had been times in the past when Tanner had called on the sheriff to help him with a protection problem, Tanner had never felt any bond, no real connection to the man. He'd always felt that the sheriff helped not because he respected Tanner and the work they did, but merely because it was his job.

"Let me see what you've got and I'll tell you if anything is going on," he said. He gestured for the sheriff and Anna to follow him into the kitchen.

He didn't want to tell Ramsey any more than necessary. He still believed that Anna's safety depended on nobody knowing who she was.

He could tell Ramsey wasn't pleased with his answer, but the sheriff walked into the kitchen and set the bag on the table after giving a curt nod to Smokey.

"Where's your father?" he asked as he opened the bag.

"He drove into Oklahoma City this morning," Tanner replied. His father had left before dawn to see what he could find out about the murder of the woman Zack had been protecting.

Red wanted to talk to the authorities and to get the details of what had gone wrong. Tanner knew it was his father's attempt to find out something, anything, that would ease Zack's guilt and grief.

"What can you tell me about Linda's attack?" Tanner asked, aware of Anna moving closer to him as if needing him near as she heard the details.

"Mind if I sit?" Ramsey didn't wait for a reply, but pulled out a chair and eased down, the bag in front of him on the table. "Been a long day and it isn't even noon yet."

Anna sank into the chair across from him and Tanner wondered if it would have been better had she gone to her room and not been a part of any of this.

Sitting next to Ramsey, he reminded himself that she needed to be here. She needed to know what was going on. After all, it was her life, her safety they were concerned about.

"Early this morning Ted Miller went into the alley behind his feed store to empty some garbage cans. That's where he found Linda." Ramsey shook his head. "Like I told you on the phone, she'd been knocked pretty hard on the back of her head. She was unconscious when she was found, but she came to about an hour ago."

"Was she able to tell you who attacked her?" Tanner asked.

Jim frowned once again. "She doesn't know. She remembers going to Betty's and buying new clothes. She changed into them before she left the shop, then she went to the café for dinner. It was as she was walking home that somebody came up from behind and dragged her into the alley. It was dark, and she said whoever it was shined a flashlight in her face, cursed, then slammed her in the head and that's all she remembers."

"Any suspects?" Tanner was aware of Anna leaning forward, her eyes begging Ramsey to have a suspect in custody or at least somebody in mind.

"None." Ramsey's blunt features pulled together in a frown. "She's a nice young woman who doesn't seem to have an enemy in the world. No boyfriend in the picture at the moment, no old boyfriends that were threatening or seemed to be any kind of a problem. Why did you want me to bring her clothes?"

"I just want to look at them," Tanner said.

Ramsey's brown eyes held Tanner's gaze. "You got a reason you're willing to share?"

"I'll let you know if I find what I'm looking for."

Ramsey frowned, but he reluctantly reached his hand into the bag and withdrew the two articles of clothing. The first item he pulled out of the bag was a long navy skirt, the same one Anna had worn when she'd first come into Tanner's office, the same one she'd left at Betty's on the day they had bought her new clothing.

Tanner took the skirt and began to check every inch of it, feeling the fabric, staring at the detail of material and thread. He focused on finding something— anything—that would explain how it was possible that the rebels might have come to Cotter Creek and thought that Linda was the princess they sought.

"What are you looking for?" Anna asked.

"I'm not sure."

They were all silent as Tanner worked his fingers over every inch of the skirt. When he was finished he motioned for Jim to hand him the blouse.

The blouse was silk with large decorative buttons down the front and at each wrist. He was aware of the tense silence of the room as he worked the silk through his fingers, exploring the blouse inch by inch.

"Smokey, hand me a mallet, would you?" he asked when he was finished going over the material.

"What are you fixing to do?" Jim asked, a touch of worry in his voice.

"I'll show you." Tanner took the mallet, normally used to tenderize meat, and without warning smashed it against one of the buttons on the blouse.

"Tanner!" Anna exclaimed as the button was crushed into pieces. Jim said nothing and Tanner had a feeling the sheriff knew exactly what he was doing.

Systematically Tanner crushed every button down the front of the blouse, then moved to the two on the wrists. He found what he had suspected in the first wrist button and his pulse thundered in his veins.

"What's that?" Anna asked, staring at the tiny device that had been hidden inside the plump button.

Tanner held it up between his fingertips. "If I was to guess, I'd say this is some sort of tracking device. This is how they know you're here in Cotter Creek."

The afternoon took on a surreal quality for Anna. In the space of Tanner cracking open a button, everything had changed. She listened as he told Sheriff Ramsey her real identity and why she was here.

However, Tanner assured the sheriff things were under control and he didn't need Ramsey to do anything but keep his mouth shut about Anna's location. "It's a matter of life or death to the princess," he said.

After the sheriff left, Tanner, Smokey and Anna remained seated at the kitchen table as Tanner told Anna how everything had changed.

"Although they know you're in Cotter Creek, it's obvious by the attack on Linda that they aren't sure exactly where you are," he said.

"But it's just a matter of time," she said flatly.

He nodded, his eyes darkly hooded. "Unfortunately, we just ran out of time. If that tracking device was working when Jim arrived, then they will have tracked the blouse to this ranch. We need to make immediate adjustments."

"Like what?" There was no hint of the man who had made love to her the night before or the man who had laughed with her a little while ago. His green eyes were cold, calculating, and she felt his energy as if it were another human presence in the room.

"The first thing I'm going to do is triple the guards around the house. I want armed guards every ten feet around the perimeter. I'll also put some on the road coming up to the house. But the major difference is that you aren't going to be here."

Anna frowned. "But my father is expecting me to be here."

"You'll be here at the ranch, but you won't be here in this house."

She stared at him with wariness. "You aren't going to stick me in the stable, are you?" She'd hoped for a smile, but got none.

His jaw was tense, his lips a grim slash. "We'll move you after dark tonight. We'll move you to my place." He exchanged looks with Smokey. "Hopefully the guard presence on this house will work as a diversion. The rebels will assume you're in here because of the visibility of the guards."

He looked back at Anna. "The only way the rebels will know that you aren't in this house is if they come through my men." His jaw clenched tighter. "And that's not going to happen."

Anna fought against a shiver. For the past three days she'd felt utterly safe here at the ranch. She'd believed the rebels had had no idea where she was, no idea how to find her, but now she knew simply by looking into Tanner's bottle-green eyes that danger was near, far too near.

Tanner turned his attention to her once again. "Why don't you go pack your things? Smokey will find you a suitcase to use, and while you're doing that I'm going to make some phone calls."

The afternoon and evening alternated between flying too fast for thoughts and creeping by with excruciating slowness. Anna packed her things into a small suitcase, then returned to the living room to sit on the sofa and wait until dinner.

She was aware of men arriving and departing from Tanner's study, hard-looking men with rifles in hand and a grim purpose in their steps. Although they were all dressed like cowpokes, she knew they were much more than that. They were the men who would be on guard duty here at the house.

It was just after a quiet supper that Red returned from the city. Tanner took his father into the study and Anna knew he was filling Red in on what had occurred and the new plans Tanner had made.

As the two men remained locked in the study, Anna helped Smokey clear the table. "You doing okay?" Smokey asked.

"I'm fine. Why?"

"A princess helping to clear a table doesn't happen every day around here."

She flashed him a quick smile. "If you're nice to me, this princess might even help wash and dry the dishes." She grabbed the plates off the table and followed Smokey into the kitchen. "I kind of like doing this kind of work," she said. "Nobody has ever let me before."

"Any housework you want to do around here, you knock yourself out, ain't nobody going to tell you to stop," Smokey replied. She laughed and decided that Smokey had a certain charm all his own.

They finished clearing the table, then stood side by side at the sink as Smokey washed and Anna dried. "Have you ever been married, Smokey?"

"Nah, never could find a woman who'd put up with me for more than a minute or two. Besides, for a lot of years I was needed here. Still am, far as I know."

"Did you know Tanner's mother?" she asked.

"Sure. Everyone knew Elizabeth West." Smokey squirted more dish soap into the sinkful of water.

"What was she like?"

"She was a fine woman, always cooking pies for sick neighbors, taking baskets of goodies to the kids at the hospital. To look at her, you'd have thought she was one of those Hollywood types. She was Red's first protection assignment."

"Really?"

Smokey grabbed a dirty plate and sank it in the water. "She was making her second movie and Red was working on the set as a stunt man. Seems some wacko had taken a shine to her, was stalking her and scaring her. Red offered to work as her bodyguard and the rest, as they say, is history."

Anna found the information interesting. She'd just assumed that Tanner's mother had been born and raised in the small town with dreams no bigger than a house of her own and kids.

It intrigued her to know that Elizabeth had been a Hollywood starlet. She'd obviously had big dreams and, if she was making her second movie, a certain measure of success. But she'd left all that behind to marry Red and to move to Cotter Creek and have a house full of children.

"She didn't mind moving out here?"

"According to what Red told me, she would have moved to Alaska and lived in an igloo if it meant being with him and having her family. Those were her priorities, not the tinsel and glitz of Hollywood."

Elizabeth West had chosen the beauty of sunrises over the sparkle of jewels, the sound of childrens' laughter instead of the raucous music of a club. She'd chosen the love of one good man over the adulation of thousands of fans. She'd obviously been not only beautiful, but smart, as well.

She and Smokey had just finished with the dishes when Tanner came into the kitchen, his features still set in the grim lines that had taken up residence for most of the afternoon.

"We're all set," he said as he sank onto a chair. "I've got all the men I need. Now all we do is wait until dark, then we move."

She dried her hands on the dish towel, then joined him at the table. She wanted to touch him, to place her hand on his cheek, to lean her head against his chest to hear his heartbeat.

But she did none of these things. He looked forbidding, his features drawn tight, his eyes darker than she'd ever seen them. "I've got some questions for you," he said. "Tell me exactly what happened on the night of the coup in Niflheim."

"What do you mean?" she asked.

"You told me that you were awakened and hustled away from the palace. Who woke you up? Who picked out the clothes you put on? Who had access to your clothing?" The questions came from him fast and sharp.

She frowned, trying to remember that night when she'd been awakened with the news that her life was in danger. Had it been only a little more than a week ago? It felt as if at least two lifetimes had passed since that night.

"I was awakened by one of my bodyguards. He burst into my room and told me that the palace was about to be lost to the rebels and my father and I had to leave immediately. Astrid, my personal assistant and maid, came in right behind him. She got my clothes for me. She packed a couple of suitcases for me."

The sense of betrayal that swept through her cut deep and brought a small gasp to her lips. Tanner's eyes softened slightly as he continued to gaze at her. "You didn't pick out your own clothes? She got them for you?"

She nodded. "Astrid." The name fell from her lips softly as her heart constricted tightly. "I thought she was my friend. She was the one person in my life I thought I could trust. I thought she cared about me, but she betrayed me. She had to have known about the tracking devices, had to have known what clothes to pack."

"It's possible somebody else could have been responsible." he said. "Who knows how many of those little technical bugs might have been in your suitcases."

Again a weary sense of betrayal filled her heart. Political intrigue, betrayal by friends…why would anyone want to be a king or a princess? Why would anyone want to live a life of never knowing whom to trust, whom to depend on?

At least here and now, she knew she could trust Tanner. She knew she could depend on him no matter what happened. She leaned back in her seat and sighed. "Thank you, Tanner, for everything you're doing for me," she said.

His brooding eyes flashed with a touch of impatience. "I'm just doing my job."

His job. Yes, that's what she needed to remember.

Even though they had made love, she was nothing more than a job to him, an important job that if successful would earn Wild West Protective Services a sterling reputation and more success than Tanner could dream of.

Before anyone could say anything else the back door opened and Zack walked in. He nodded at Anna, then looked at his brother. "Heard there might be some trouble," he said.

Tanner stood. "Could be."

"Know what you're up against?"

"Don't have a clue," Tanner replied, his frustration evident in his voice.

"I'll stand guard duty. I'm not coming back to work for the agency, but I'll help protect what is ours," Zack said.

It was at that moment that Anna truly realized what was at risk. Her presence was threatening not only the lives of each and every person on the ranch, but the very ranch itself. The rebels could set off a bomb, toss a grenade or set a fire to the West family home.

These people were risking everything for her, and in that instant Anna realized she was precariously close to falling in love with Tanner West.

Chapter 11

Darkness didn't steal in gently, but seemed to drop like a blanket across the earth. Clouds obscured even the faintest moonlight, which suited Tanner's needs very well.

The darkness was their friend when it came to moving Anna from the big house into his home. Although the distance between the two structures wasn't that great, it was a distance where they would be vulnerable to a sniper's intent.

Finding the bug in the button of Anna's blouse had galvanized and recentered him. He was angry with himself for growing lax, for succumbing to Anna's charm and momentarily forgetting exactly what was at stake.

It was not only the reputation of the agency at risk if something should go wrong, but Anna's very life. Failure definitely wasn't an option.

It was just before ten when he and Anna prepared to leave the house. The guards were on duty, silent sentries watching for danger.

He turned to Anna, saw the slight tremble to her lips, the paleness of her skin. "It's going to be fine," he said. "All you need to do when we step outside is to hold my hand and keep quiet. You ready?"

She nodded and he grabbed her hand in one of his, her suitcase in the other. Together they walked out the front door then stepped off the porch and headed in the direction of his house. Her hand was cool in his and trembled slightly. The feel of it, so soft and yielding, swelled in his chest.

He told himself the overwhelming surge of emotion was because of the importance of the job he was doing. He tried to convince himself that his emotions had nothing to do with the softness of her skin or the sound of her laughter. It had nothing to do with the stubbornness he found oddly charming or the fact that over the past couple of days she'd even managed to win Smokey's affection.

When he'd walked into the kitchen just after supper and seen her standing at the sink helping Smokey finish up the dinner dishes, he'd been shocked. The princess was transforming right before his eyes, and it was a transformation that made both a feeling of satisfaction and discomfort sweep through him.

He focused on the here and now, his eyes quickly adjusting to the darkness. They didn't run, but walked at a fast pace, the light he'd left on in his living room shining like a beacon in the darkness that surrounded them. He knew the trees and brush around his place would hide the additional men he'd called on and some of Cotter Creek's finest.

True to his instructions, she said not a word, made not a sound, and he didn't breathe until they were safely inside the house and behind a closed, locked door.

He watched her as she looked around the living room with interest. "It's nice," she said.

"No, it isn't." He set her suitcase down and gazed at the room as if seeing it for the very first time. A couch, a chair, a coffee table and a television were the sum of the interior decorating.

It was a room without personality, without warmth or life. It was a perfect reflection of the man who lived here.

He frowned. Where had that thought come from? "I'll put you in the master bed and I'll sleep on the floor in there," he explained. "Even though there are three bedrooms, two of them are empty. I haven't gotten around to doing anything with them."

"I don't want to take your bed. I'll be happy to sleep on the floor," she replied.

"I'm on the floor," he said firmly. "That keeps me between you and the front door." He walked around the room, twisting the blinds closed on every window as she sank onto the sofa.

He hoped he hadn't made an error in not taking her off the ranch altogether, but this was familiar territory and there was a certain comfort, a certain security in knowing his surroundings.

He just hoped his little ploy worked and they would assume by the visible guards that she was in the main house. He had every confidence that the men guarding the main house could handle whatever might come their way. And if by chance their ploy didn't work, this house was guarded, as well.

Anna curled her feet beneath her, looking as if she belonged on the navy sofa. "So what happens now?"

"We wait. We see who shows up first, your father or the rebels. Want some coffee?"

"That sounds good. I'm certainly too wound up to go to bed."

He walked into the kitchen, twisted the blinds tightly closed, then set about making a pot of coffee. He had a feeling this was going to be the most difficult part of the assignment, being alone with her in his house for an undetermined amount of time.

Moments later he carried two cups of coffee into the living room and joined her on the sofa, making sure he kept as much distance as possible between them.

"Thank you," she said as he handed her one of the

cups. For a few minutes they sat in silence and sipped their coffees. Tanner tried to ignore the scent of her, a scent that had become as familiar as the smell of sunshine on the Oklahoma ground.

"I'll bet you'll be glad when this is all over," he said, finally breaking the silence between them.

She took another sip of the coffee and eyed him thoughtfully over the rim of the cup. "I'll be glad when the danger has passed."

"Can't wait to get back to shopping and yachting and doing all the things that princesses do?" He expected a sharp retort from her, but instead she shrugged her shoulders, looking small and vulnerable.

"I'm sure my father loves me in his own way," she said, and looked down into her cup. "But he's always dismissed me, had little expectations of me, and that's what I lived up to." She looked at Tanner once again. "And I've always had this terrible loneliness inside me, a loneliness I thought I could still by shopping and traveling and partying."

She uncurled her legs from beneath her and set her cup on the glass-topped coffee table. "I've had a lot of time to think in the past couple of days and whatever the future holds, I intend to make different choices concerning my lifestyle."

Tanner didn't want to hear this. He didn't want to think of her suffering loneliness, perhaps the same kind of loneliness that haunted him at odd hours of the day and night.

He also strangely didn't want to hear about her decision to make better choices in her life. He was afraid she might become in his mind a woman he could fall in love with.

He stood and picked up her cup from the coffee table. "It's getting late. We should get settled in for the night."

She frowned and didn't move from the sofa. "Do you realize almost every night I've been here you've sent me to bed like a child?"

"There's nothing wrong with structure in your life."

"Structure…rules…that's all you seem to know. I was trying to talk to you, to tell you how things have changed for me since I've been here. I was trying to share with you and all you can do is stick to the rules." Her chin rose in a touch of defiance. "Maybe I'm not sleepy yet."

He wasn't sure if she was trying to pick a fight or just being difficult in general. But the last thing he wanted was to sit around and listen to her talk about her transformation from spoiled willful princess to something else.

"I don't give a damn if you dance around in the bedroom until dawn. I don't care if you sit and make lists of all the things you're going to do when you leave here until the sun comes up. But right now I'm tired and it's time to go to bed."

He hadn't realized when it had happened, had no idea that somewhere in the course of the past few days he had gained the power to hurt her, but he had and hurt now shone from her eyes. It was there for just a moment, then masked beneath a facade of coolness as she stood.

"I apologize. I don't want to keep you from getting a good night's sleep. If you'll just show me to my room, I won't bother you for the rest of the night."

He picked up her suitcase and carried it into the master bedroom, trying not to feel guilty about shutting her down, shutting her up. He went to the two windows in the room and checked to make sure they were locked, then closed the blinds.

This room held no more personality than the living room. The bed was neatly made with a brown spread and a small lamp set on the nightstand. The dresser, a rich cherrywood, held nothing on its gleaming top. For some reason, the sight of the room that had been his for the past three years depressed him.

He placed her suitcase on the bed, then turned to look at her. "There's some new rules while we're here."

"What?" She sat on the bed and eyed him with a touch of weariness.

"First of all, we sleep with the bedroom door open. I need to be able to hear if anyone tries to break through any of the windows or if anything threatens us."

She nodded, her eyes more somber than they'd been moments before. "Second," he continued, "you don't go near the windows. Don't even open them a sliver to look outside. And last of all, no more sleeping in the nude. If anything happens in the middle of the night, we might have to make a run for it. I don't want you naked and running around for everyone to see."

"Is that it?"

"For now."

She reached behind her, grabbed one of the bed pillows and threw it to him with more force than necessary. "Fine, then get out of my bedroom long enough for me to get ready for bed."

He carried the pillow back into the living room and tossed it on the sofa, but sleep was the last thing on his mind. He'd needed to shut her down, had been afraid of what she might confess in her monologue of sharing her innermost thoughts. There was no telling what might come out of her mouth and he didn't want things more complicated than they already were.

As he walked around the interior of the house, double-checking that all the windows in each room were locked, he thought of his brother, Zack.

He had no idea exactly what had happened between Zack and his client in the three months that Zack had been on duty, but he'd seen the result. Zack had returned home a broken man because he'd allowed himself to get too close, to get emotionally involved.

Tanner absolutely refused to make the same mistake with Anna. No matter what happened, she wasn't meant for him. She was a princess, and despite her earlier words she would go back to being a princess once this was all over. One way or another, she would be out of his life, and he refused to put himself in a position to mourn her loss.

For three days they had been in his house, and the three days had been filled with stress as intense awareness of one another and a simmering tension grew by the moment.

Each night she slept in sheets that smelled of him, that clean male scent with a touch of the cologne he always wore. She'd burrow her head in the pillow and wonder why she had fallen in love with him. She fell asleep each night to the sound of him breathing as he lay on a bedroll on the floor. She suspected if he slept at all it was only briefly.

Despite the fact that he was bossy and a workaholic, in spite of the fact that he was reluctant to share meaningful pieces of himself, she loved him as she'd never loved a man before.

She wasn't sure when exactly she'd fallen in love with him, had no idea if there had been a single defining moment—she only knew what was in her heart.

There were moments when she felt his gaze on her, when she felt a connection with him that stole her breath away. There were moments when she saw a small smile begin to curve the corners of his mouth and she felt as if she'd been gifted with the riches of the world.

She loved the fact that he had worked so hard on behalf of his family, that his values were good even if he did need some balance.

She wanted him. She wanted him to sweep her up into his arms and make love to her through the long, lonely night. She wanted to feel his heartbeat against hers, to taste the heat of his kisses, to feel his big, strong hands against her skin.

But she had her pride and he had shown no indication, other than that whisper of hunger she occasionally saw flashing in his eyes, that he wanted a repeat of what they'd shared before.

While he'd spent his time pacing and brooding, she'd spent much of her time seated at the kitchen table playing hand after hand of solitaire with a deck of cards he'd found in one of the drawers.

It was now after dinner and Anna was once again at the kitchen table, the deck of cards in front of her. Tanner sat on the sofa, tension radiating from him to fill all the spaces of the house.

"I'm sick of solitaire," she announced. "Why don't you come over here and play a little poker with me?"

He raised a dark eyebrow. "Don't you realize all us cowboys are champions when it comes to poker playing?"

She grinned. "I'll bet you haven't played against a princess before."

She watched as he pulled himself up from the sofa and ambled toward the table, a lazy smile curving his lips. It was the first hint of a smile she'd seen from him since they'd come to his house and warmth cascaded through her at the sight.

He sat in the chair opposite hers and reached for the cards. Those wicked green eyes of his splashed her with heat. "So what are the stakes?"

Her heart beat a little faster. "Let's make it really interesting. How about some strip poker?" His eyebrows shot up and she saw the protest forming on his lips. Before he could voice it, she added, "What's wrong, Tanner? Afraid you'll lose?"

His eyes flashed with challenge and he reached for the deck of cards. She jumped up from the table. "Before we start, I need to do something. I'll be right back."

She went into her bedroom where she pulled on an extra T-shirt, two more socks and as a final thought stuck her crown on top of her head. There was no way she intended to be the first one naked.

When she returned to the table he grinned in obvious amusement. "Feeling a bit insecure, are we?"

She returned his grin, grateful for the break in the tension and stress. "Just hedging my bets." She grabbed the cards from him. "Five card stud, deuces wild. Ready to play?"

"Just a minute." He got up from the table and grabbed his cowboy hat and plopped it on his head.

"Just hedging my bets," he said as he sat once again. His eyes glittered with challenge. "Deal 'em, partner."

Within minutes she realized he was a tough adversary. She lost the first two hands, her extra socks. He lost the next and removed his hat, tossing it to the floor next to the table.

Back and forth they went for the next hour until she was down to her T-shirt and jeans. Her crown rested across the top of Tanner's boots, which sat just beside the table. He was shirtless and holding his cards close to his chest.

She had a pair of aces and a heart full of desire. She felt as if each hand they'd played had been a form of foreplay and her knees were weak with wanting him.

She knew he wanted her, too. She felt his desire radiating from him, saw it shining in his eyes. But he made no move to act on it. His eyes remained dark and he'd gotten more and more quiet as the game had gone on and articles of clothing had piled up.

"I'll see you," he said. "Read 'em and weep." He laid down his cards, showing a pair of queens.

Her aces beat his queens, but in the instant before she showed her hand, her mind raced. She wanted to make love with him again, but it was obvious he didn't intend to make any move to get her back into bed.

If she lost the hand, she'd literally lose her shirt. Would that be enough to make him lose control and shove him over the edge? Or was she imagining his desire for her because she wanted him so badly.

"You got me," she replied, and quickly added her cards to the discard pile. She stood and grabbed the bottom of her T-shirt, intent on pulling it over her head.

He jumped up from the table and grabbed her hands, halting her movement. "That's enough," he said. "We stop the game right now."

He stood so close to him she could see the tiny gold flecks in his green eyes, could feel the heat radiating off him as he held her hands tightly.

"I'm not playing a game anymore," she replied softly.

For a long moment they stood mere inches from each other, gazes locked as her heartbeat raced. His hands were hot on hers, as if he was consumed with fever.

With a muttered curse he pulled her to him, tangled his hands in her hair and took her mouth in a kiss that nearly buckled her knees.

The desire she'd thought she'd seen in his eyes was there in his kiss, in the way his hands gripped her hair, then slid down her back, pressing her close…closer against him.

It was silly, but she felt like crying as her love for him welled up and swelled in her chest. It wasn't just the fact that she loved the taste of his mouth or the way his hard body felt against hers. It wasn't merely that his touch electrified her.

When he was near, she didn't feel the loneliness that had always plagued her. She loved that he expected her to be a better woman than what she'd been. She loved him and she knew nothing in her life would ever be the same because of her love for him.

His mouth slid from hers and went to the hollow of her throat as his hands gripped her buttocks and pulled her more firmly against him.

She could feel his arousal and her ability to think edged away as she allowed herself to be overtaken by sheer physical pleasure.

"You make me crazy," he murmured against her ear. "You make me crazy with wanting you."

His words enflamed her.

"I'm crazy with wanting you," she gasped. "I haven't been able to think of anything else but being with you again."

His mouth claimed hers once again, making conversation impossible. Their tongues battled, dancing together in erotic play.

She wasn't sure how, didn't really remember walking the distance to the bedroom, but suddenly they were there, tearing off their clothes, then falling onto the bed and into each other's arms.

The urgency that had gripped him in the kitchen seemed to ebb as he began to stroke her skin. The darkness in the room made it impossible for her to see his face clearly, but she didn't need to see him.

She *saw* him through his touch as his hands cupped

her breasts and one of his legs rubbed against hers. She *saw* him in the kisses that scalded her lips with the fever of desire. She *saw* him in her soul, the man who held not just her safety in his hands, but her heart.

This time she helped him put on protection, loving the way he moaned at her intimate touch. When she was finished, his mouth moved down her throat, across her collarbone and to one of her nipples. She tangled her hands in his hair as he licked and teased the rigid peak. Shivers of delight worked up her spine at each touch of his mouth.

She felt fragile, as if every bone in her body had become soft and yielding. As his mouth moved from the underside of her breast down the flat of her abdomen, every nerve in her body sizzled with a growing tension that threatened to snap her in two.

His hands preceded his mouth, caressing her stomach, across her hips, then touching her softly at her center. She moaned his name with pleasure and thrust her hips upward to meet his intimate touch.

His ragged breathing filled the room along with her moans of pleasure as he stroked her and the tension inside her grew to unimaginable proportion.

Higher and higher he took her until there was nothing but his touch and her response. When she could go no higher, she went over the edge and crashed, shattering into a million pieces as she cried his name over and over again.

It was then, while she was weak and gasping, that

he moved back up her body and entered her. She wrapped her arms around his broad back and held him tight, wishing she could keep him this close to her forever.

She could feel his heartbeat thundering against hers as he remained unmoving for a long moment. His hands touched her on the sides of her face in a caress of infinite tenderness. The gesture brought tears to her eyes.

He filled up her body, but no more so than he filled up her heart. As he moved his hips against hers, stroking deep and slow, once again he swept her up to a dizzying height of pleasure.

"Anna," he whispered just before his lips claimed hers.

Her heart cried his name in return and then she was lost, beyond words, beyond thought, as he drove into her, bringing her to climax once again. He stiffened and moaned as he reached the pinnacle of his pleasure.

Moments later they remained tangled together amid the navy sheets, waiting for heartbeats to slow, for pulses to return to a more normal rate.

The tears that had filled her eyes earlier once again threatened. They were the physical expression of the emotions that burned inside her. Tears of joy. Tears of love.

He rolled her to her side and with one hand he stroked her hair. It seemed that she had been drifting all her life, seeking something…seeking someone.

She had degrees she hadn't used, skills and talents that had been thrown away by a life wasted in running away from herself.

In the brief time she'd been with Tanner and his family, she'd seen a different kind of life, one filled with love and respect, of work and self-fulfillment.

She realized she wanted to be a woman Tanner could respect, but more important she wanted to be a woman she could respect.

She looked at him, his features barely discernible in the near darkness of the room. There had been many times when she'd wondered what people did to fill the silences of the nights.

As she listened to the sound of Tanner's deep, even breathing, as she thought of the sweet words he'd murmured to her while he'd made love to her, she knew.

There was no silence for the people in Cotter Creek who spent their nights listening to their loved ones, comforted by the nearly inaudible sounds of hearts beating and love flourishing.

"You okay?" he asked, his voice a deep, soft whisper.

"I'm better than okay." Surely he loved her. Surely he couldn't make love to her as he did and not be in love with her. He couldn't look at her the way he did and not love her. "I've made some decisions."

He propped himself up on one elbow. "Decisions?"

"No matter what happens with my father in Niflheim, I'm not returning." The moment the words were spoken out loud she knew the rightness of her decision. "There's nothing for me there. There never has been anything there for me."

"So what will you do?" The questions seemed hesitant, as if he wasn't sure he wanted the answer.

"Arrange for citizenship, then maybe teach. I could teach a foreign language or economics. I think I'd like that…working with kids."

"Are you sure now is the best time to make life-changing decisions?" he asked. "I mean, you've been under a tremendous amount of stress and now might not be the best time to make those kinds of decisions."

"When is a good time?" she countered. She wished she could see his facial features better. "I've been unhappy for a long time. This week here has given me time to assess things, to figure out that going back to the same kind of lifestyle isn't going to make me happy."

His finger smoothed across her lips, the gesture as intimate as anything she had ever experienced. "You deserve happiness, Anna."

She held her breath, hoping…praying he would say something, anything that would indicate he hoped she'd spend her life with him.

He had to love her. He had to, because she couldn't imagine what she'd do if he didn't. *Tell him,* a little voice whispered inside her. *Tell him how you feel.*

Her heart pounded as the words formed on her lips. She had never wanted anything as much as she wanted Tanner's respect, his love.

"I love you, Tanner." The words that had beat in her heart spilled from her lips and she knew that by speaking them out loud she had crossed a line and couldn't go back.

I love you, Tanner." The words that she had been trying to avoid saying had slipped out and now that he'd

Chapter 12

"I love you, Tanner."

It wasn't just the words that sent a weighty dread through him, but the sweet yearning, the naked emotion that was in her voice as she'd spoken them.

This wasn't supposed to happen. She wasn't supposed to fall in love with him. Those four words that she'd spoken were words he'd never expected to hear from her, hadn't wanted to hear from her.

A mistake. He'd made mistake after mistake where she was concerned and now he had the difficult task of trying to straighten out the mess and it was the worst kind of mess, one of sheer, naked emotions.

He'd rather wrestle with a gunman or face a psycho with a knife than do what he had to do now. He'd rather cut off his right arm than see the hurt he knew was about to steal over her features.

"Anna," he began, and sat up, needing to get some distance from her. "You might think you're in love with me, but I'm sure you're mistaking love for other feelings."

She leaned over and turned on the lamp on the nightstand. He tried not to notice how beautiful she looked with her hair in disarray and her lips slightly swollen from his kisses. She looked soft and sexy, except for her eyes, which glittered with familiar challenge.

"So you know what's in my heart and you think I must be mistaken?" Without warning, she hit him in the chest with her fist. "You are the most irritating, aggravating man I've ever known. You are so arrogant you think you know what I'm thinking, what I'm feeling, and you don't."

"Whoa." He caught her fist before she could hit him again, then scrambled from the bed and grabbed his jeans from the floor.

As he pulled them on, he was aware of her staring at him and knew she was waiting for some sort of a response. But for a moment he couldn't speak around the lump that had risen in his throat.

He raked a hand through his hair, wondering how on earth he'd allowed things to get so out of control. He'd never had this problem before with any of his assignments, and he'd had plenty of assignments in the past where he'd worked with pretty women. For God's sake, he was supposed to be on twenty-four-hour watch. What had he been thinking? That he'd find the rebels in the sheets on the bed? She should be just like all the other jobs he'd worked, but she wasn't.

Anna was different. She'd been different from the moment she'd come through his office door. She challenged him, excited him in a way nobody had ever done before. She made him laugh and somehow made him feel more vulnerable than he'd ever felt in his life.

"Anna, I'm sure whatever you think you feel for me is all tied up with the uncertainty in your life right now, the fear of being hunted, our forced proximity to each other and maybe more than a little bit of boredom."

Her eyes narrowed. "You think I'm in love with you because I'm bored? That's a horrible thing to say."

He grimaced. "I think it's a combination of things that have you mistaken."

"I know you think I'm worthless, a piece of fluff who has never done anything productive in her life." Her voice trembled with the depth of her emotion. "And in some ways you're right. I have been spoiled, I am willful, but that doesn't mean I don't know what's in my heart. I love you, Tanner West, and that's something you can't be in control of. It's my feelings, my emotions, and you can't change them no matter how much you might want to."

Why was this so hard? he wondered. Why did his

heart feel so heavy, so utterly dead? Zack had made him feel bad, but this was worse…far worse. It seemed so wrong, to break her heart even while the scent of her still lingered on his skin, in his pores.

"I'm sorry if I led you on," he said softly, "if I made you think there was something more than a strong physical desire between us."

He grabbed his gun from the dresser where he'd placed it as they'd entered the room, then left the bedroom, needing space from her luminous, slightly accusing eyes, needing distance from the scent of her, the very sight of her.

But she gave him no distance. As he shoved the gun into the waistband of his jeans, she appeared in the bedroom doorway, once again dressed in her jeans and the light blue T-shirt that did dazzling things to her eyes.

He'd never seen her look so vulnerable. There was no hint of the willful princess now, no touch of haughty disdain. There was only a woman with all her emotions naked and bared for him to see.

"I know you feel something more for me than just physical desire," she said. "I've seen it in your eyes. I've seen tenderness…caring. You can pretend this has been just a job to you, but I think it's been something more. You can pretend you don't care about me at all, but I know differently." She took several steps toward him.

"Anna, you've only known me for a week. I know

it seems longer, but it's only been a short period of time. Love doesn't happen that fast." He fought the impulse to step back from her.

Her eyes flashed once again, this time with a touch of annoyance. "Really? Then you tell me, Tanner, how long does it take to fall in love? What are your rules when it comes to matters of the heart?"

"There are no rules…"

"Exactly."

He sucked in a deep breath, wishing he were anywhere but in this room with her, in this room breaking her heart into pieces. "Anna, you're a princess. I'm a cowboy. We're from two different worlds." He tried to reason with her.

"You know what I think? I think you're a cowboy with fences around your heart and if you'd just let them fall like I've done with the walls around mine then you'd see what you really feel for me."

"Please, don't make this difficult." Instantly he knew they were the wrong words to say.

Her back stiffened. "Don't worry, Tanner. I won't play the poor, pitiful wronged woman and make things uncomfortable for you. I just want you to understand one thing. I love you and I would have made a good partner for you."

God, he wanted her to stop. He didn't want to hear any more. Her words were killing him inch by inch, but he felt the least he could do for her was to allow her to get it all out. He'd messed up big-time with her and he owed her to at least listen to her.

Tears shone in her eyes as she held his gaze. "It might have taken me time to completely understand your way of life, but I've always been a quick study. And I'll tell you this, I would have brought you laughter and passion."

She strode across the room and grabbed her crown from where it lay on the top of his boots. "I would have given you a daughter who would have worn this when she played dress-up and a son who could have one day filled your boots."

She tossed the crown onto the sofa, tears now running down her cheeks. "I've spent most of my life running away from the loneliness that plagued me, jetting off here and there, shopping until I wanted to be sick because I didn't want to take a look at who I was and where I was going. Where are you going, Tanner? What are you running away from with your workaholic lifestyle? With your need to never get personally involved with anyone?"

"Enough," he exclaimed. He didn't want to hear any more. He didn't want to hear the hurt in her voice, feel the strange gnawing pain that tore through his gut.

Again he raked his hand through his hair and averted his gaze from her. "Look, I made a mistake. I should have never indulged in my desire for you. I should have maintained professional integrity and never allowed this to happen."

It wasn't so much a shadow as a slight displacement of light outside the window that caught his attention. Instantly a surge of adrenaline seared through him as he reached up and grabbed the gun from his waist-band.

"What are you going to do? Shoot me if I don't shut up?" she asked.

"I think there's somebody outside," he said in a deceptively calm, steady voice. "I want you to go to the bathroom, keep the light turned off and lock yourself inside. Do it now, Anna. No questions. Just do it and don't open the door again until you hear me…no matter what."

Already he was mentally far away from her and this room; focused instead on the knowledge that he was relatively certain there was somebody lurking just outside his house. None of his men would be walking so close to the house.

To his eternal gratefulness, she must have realized he was serious and wasn't just trying to change the subject. She didn't argue with him, but instead turned and hurried toward the bathroom.

Only when he heard the click of the lock did he quickly move through the house, turning off lights to even the odds with the darkness outside.

In each room after turning off the lights he crept to the windows and peeked through the slats of the blinds to see what might be out there. The half moon sent down just enough light to illuminate the landscape in ghostly hues.

There was nobody in the front of the house that he could see and he wondered if perhaps he had just imagined a presence. Had his mind conjured up a diversion from the painful conversation with Anna?

He got his answer when he peered through the windows of the master bedroom. There he saw the dark silhouette of a man running across the yard.

He quickly moved to the bedroom window on the east side of the house. Another tall, burly silhouette moved nearer the house.

At least two men. And they definitely weren't his men. If there were just two, he could take them. But he had no idea how many might be out there. Where were his men? Where were the cops?

While he had made love to Anna, a whole damn army could have surrounded the house. Dammit, another mistake he hoped he didn't have to pay for.

He grabbed his cell phone and punched in the number for the main house Smokey answered. "Something's going down," he said.

"Got it," Smokey replied, then clicked off. Tanner hung up as well, knowing that backup would be on the way. He still had no idea where the guards were that had been assigned on his place.

Just for his own information, he picked up the regular phone receiver.

Silence.

No dial tone.

Nothing. He wasn't surprised, but his heart still

pounded an unsteady rhythm. An attack was imminent. He knew it by the shadows moving around the house, the dead phone line and the instincts that now screamed of danger.

There was no way he intended to be in a defensive position, not knowing what had happened to the half-dozen men who were supposed to be stationed around the house. He grabbed a knife and a roll of duct tape and moved to the front door.

With grim intent he eased open the front door, looked outside, then locked and closed the door behind him and slid into the deepest shadows of the night.

For a moment he remained perfectly still, listening for sounds of movement, the crackle of branches, the whisper of footsteps against the grass. Before he moved he needed to make sure there was nobody nearby. He also hoped to hell that his own men didn't put a bullet through his brain by accident.

The house was surrounded by trees on three sides, and he knew if he could get into the cover of the trees he could get a better idea of how many men lurked around the perimeter of the house.

The immediate problem was getting to the cover of the trees. Between the house and the tree line there was about fifty yards where he would be visible and vulnerable should he be seen.

His heartbeat had slowed the moment he'd stepped outside. A calm, coolness swept through him, a feeling that was familiar and comforting.

Control. It was absolutely imperative that he maintain control and not allow any emotion to cloud his mind. Emotion got men killed.

He looked left, then right, his eyes adjusting to the near darkness of the night. He saw nothing, heard nobody, and with the stealth of a thief he crouched and moved fast toward the cover of the trees.

The grass was cool against his bare feet and he wished he'd taken a moment to pull on his boots. He hoped he didn't step on anything that would hobble him.

As he ran he tensed, as if expecting a warning shout from one rebel to another, or worse, a bullet in his back. He didn't take a breath until he'd reached the trees and leaned with his back against an ancient old oak.

He took in several deep breaths as his gaze scanned the area directly around him. His heart seemed to stop as he saw one of his men lying prone on the grass. Dead?

He crouched and ran to the man's side. Burt. Not dead, but unconscious. He'd been taken down with an obvious struggle and Tanner had a feeling that Burt wasn't the only man down. Somehow the rebels had managed to sneak up on the guards and take them down soundlessly, one by one.

He gazed back toward the house, fighting rage as he thought of his men. There...on the side of the house, a man stood near the window of one of the spare bedrooms. The faint moonlight glittered off the barrel of the gun he held as he crept closer to the window, apparently attempting to see inside.

These men had been sent to kill Anna. Tanner knew he had to take them on one by one to have any chance at all. With this in mind, he moved quickly across the lawn as the man lowered his gun to peer into the window.

Without boots and only in his bare feet, Tanner moved soundlessly against the thick, springy grass. He came up behind the man, wrapped a forearm around his neck and squeezed as tight as he could. He pulled tight, cutting off air.

A grunt escaped the man as he struggled against Tanner's hold. It took only seconds for Tanner to render the man unconscious.

As he slipped to the ground, Tanner quickly duct-taped his wrists and ankles, then slapped several pieces of the sticky tape over his mouth. He grabbed him by the feet and dragged him across the lawn and into the trees.

One down, and he had no idea how many were left. Where was his backup? At that moment he heard a grunt come from the trees nearby and he hoped the sound meant he was no longer battling alone.

Moving stealthily in a couched position he made his way through the trees. He knew the landscape as well as he knew his own name. That was his advantage as he stalked his prey through the woods.

There was little noise. The crickets and other insects were silent, as if sensing danger. The only sound was the faint slap of footsteps against grass and an occasional snap of a twig.

He followed the sounds until he spied his quarry, another burly male moving like a shadow in the night. He was moving toward the opposite side of the house from where Tanner had caught up with the other man.

Movement on his left made him jerk his head, and he saw Zack slicing through the trees with speed and agility, obviously tracking somebody.

Tanner looked back toward the house and froze. He'd momentarily lost sight of the man who had been near the house. His pulse raced as he tried to find the assassin.

He heard the bullet before he felt the impact. The faint puff of a gun with a silencer. The bullet ripped into the bark of a tree mere inches from his head. He threw himself to the ground.

Game on.

If he'd been coldly emotionless before, he was positively bloodless now. This was survival. Another bullet hit the tree just above where he lay on the ground. He rolled to the left, came up to his feet and ran for the cover of the nearest tree trunk.

The flash of the last shot had let him know where the enemy was hiding, and Tanner moved farther into the woods, hoping to come up behind the man.

Slowly and steadily he moved. He still had a visual of the shooter and knew from the way the man turned his head from side to side, gun pointed first one direction then another, that the man had lost sight of him.

He only hoped that while he was taking care of this threat some of the other men were watching the front of the house to assure nobody got inside. He was comforted only by the fact that if anyone tried to get into the bathroom where Anna was hiding, she'd scream bloody murder and alert him to her danger.

With the silence of a shadow Tanner moved toward the gunman, grateful when a cloud drifted in front of the moon, momentarily obscuring everything. He used the cover of the deep darkness to move closer.

When the cloud drifted away and moonlight once again filtered down, he found himself no more than twenty feet behind the gunman.

It would be easy to take a shot now, to eliminate the threat with a bullet, but he was afraid the sound of the gunshot would rally any others he might not have seen. He had no idea how many more might be hiding in the woods, concealed by the darkness.

He'd much prefer to take the man down soundlessly, as he had the first one. With this thought in mind, he crept closer, careful not to make a sound that would give away his position.

When he was close enough that he could smell the body odor emanating from the man, could hear his slightly raspy breaths, he lunged forward and knocked the gun from the man's hand.

Before he could get a choke hold around his neck, the man spun around and clipped Tanner in the jaw with his fist.

The blow landed squarely. Pain shot through the side of his head. He ignored the pain and thrust a fist into the man's stomach. The man gasped and stumbled backward. Tanner gave him no time to recover, but hit him again, this time with an uppercut that snapped his head upward.

The man lunged forward, swinging wildly, and again a fist clipped Tanner's jaw. With all the force his body could summon, Tanner threw a punch and connected once again with the man's stomach.

The man fell to the ground, grasping for the gun that had fallen into the grass. Tanner grabbed his feet to pull him away from the gun, then fell on top of him and wrapped his arm around his neck. As he pulled with his arm, he pushed at the back of the head with his other hand.

Unconsciousness came quickly. Gasping for breath, Tanner rose and bound the man's hands and feet with the duct tape. As he tore off a piece of the tape to slap across the man's mouth a roar split the night, a roar followed by the whoosh of flames.

He looked toward the house and in horror saw that

it appeared to be consumed by flames. Glass exploded outward from all the windows.

"Anna!" he screamed, and ran toward the inferno.

She heard the explosion, but remained in the bathroom, afraid to move, afraid to ignore Tanner's order that she remain in the bathroom until he returned for her.

She stood in the dark, in the tub, wondering what was happening. Other than the explosion, she'd heard not a sound since she'd run to hide. What had caused the loud blast? What was going on outside?

Tanner. Her heart cried out. Please, please, keep him safe. Please let him be okay. At least she hadn't heard any gunshots. That was something, wasn't it? At least she knew he probably hadn't been shot.

She stared in the direction of the locked door, able to see it only a little from the moonlight drifting in through the window high above the tub. She was afraid who might enter.

It took her a moment to realize she smelled something...something acrid...something burning. She heard the faint tinkle of glass breaking somewhere in the house. The smell grew stronger, more pronounced.

Smoke! It burned her eyes, tickled the back of her throat. She coughed. Once. Twice. A spasm of choking left her weakly leaning against the bathroom wall.

Needing light, she reached her hand out and flipped the switch, shocked to see the thick black smoke pouring into the room from under the door.

Fire! The house was on fire. She shoved a fist in her mouth to staunch the scream that threatened to escape. She had to get out. She couldn't wait for Tanner. It wouldn't take long for her to die from smoke inhalation.

She jumped out of the tub and grabbed hold of the doorknob. Instantly she yanked her hand back. Hot. The knob was like grabbing hold of a hot chunk of coal. She couldn't go out that way. Smoke poured in beneath the door, and she quickly wet a towel and shoved it against the door to stop the flow of smoke.

She stepped back into the tub and gazed at the window overhead. It was a small window, up high over the tub. She could grab the edge with her fingertips, but didn't think she'd be able to pull herself up and through.

She shrieked as the lights went off, leaving her only with a sliver of moonlight for light and the thickening smoke that made it difficult to breathe.

A fit of coughing sent her to her knees. Where was Tanner? Had the rebels killed him? A piercing pain shot through her at the thought. Please don't let him be dead, she mentally prayed as another coughing spasm overtook her.

She was losing it. She felt the blackness closing in. The air was too thick to breathe and she could barely keep her eyes open. In the faint moonlight the smoke thickened and boiled around her.

Let go, a little voice whispered in her head. *Just a few deep breaths and you'll go to sleep.*

Just her luck, to finally find the love she'd yearned for, then die when it was still fresh and new in her heart.

Just breathe, it will all be over soon. The little voice in her head was an irritating refrain. But she'd never been a quitter, and between sobs and coughs she slid from the tub and tried to find something she could use to break the window. If she could just get some air, she'd be fine.

Again the darkness threatened, but before it could claim her completely, the bathroom door burst open and Tanner came in. He said nothing, but pulled her from the floor and lifted her up over his shoulder and ran.

She was vaguely aware of the fire all around them, but all she could think about was the fact that Tanner had lied to her. He'd told her a cowboy threw a woman over his shoulder when he loved her. But he didn't love her. This was the last conscious thought she had.

Chapter 13

Anna awakened to the early-morning sun seeping softly through the window. She started to sit up, worried that she'd be late for breakfast and Smokey would give her attitude. But she wasn't at the ranch. She blinked and looked around, for a moment disoriented.

It was a hospital room. She didn't move as her mind raced. Why was she here? She didn't seem to be hurt, other than a bad sore throat.

The fire. The smoke. Her memory returned with a jolt. But she remembered nothing after Tanner breaking into the bathroom, nothing of how she had come to be here and what had happened.

She was alone in the room, although the door was

open and she saw that somebody was seated just outside. "Hello?" Her voice was husky and she winced,
wishing for a drink of water to ease the burning ache.

It was Tanner seated just outside her room. He
jumped up and walked in, the sight of him both joy-
ous and painful at the same time.

She was thrilled that he appeared to be all right, but
the sight of him reminded her of all that would never
be. She loved him and he didn't love her back.

"Hi." For the first time since she'd met him he
sounded hesitant...tentative, although his facial
expression was, as usual, inscrutable. "How are you
doing?"

"Thirsty," she croaked.

She watched as he poured her a glass of water from
a pitcher on the stand next to the bed. He stuck in a
straw then held the glass to her lips so she could take
a sip.

The cold water soothed the scratchiness of her
throat, but did nothing to ease the ache that filled her
heart. She needed something, anything, to take her
mind away from the memory of the painful conversation they'd had before he'd spied movement outside
the window.

She desperately wanted to think about anything other
than the fact that Tanner didn't love her, that there was
no future here for her with him. "What happened?" she
asked.

He pulled up a chair next to her bed and sat, his

gaze somber. For the first time she noticed the slight purple bruise that decorated his left jaw. "Looks like you lost the battle."

He reached up and touched his jaw, then shrugged. "Maybe lost the battle, but won the war. You should see the other guy." He leaned back in the chair. "There were three of them. I managed to take out two, but while I was fighting with the second man, a third somehow got to the front of the house and threw some sort of small bomb through the window. The explosion brought my men from the main house. They caught the third man and all three are now in custody down at the sheriff's office."

She struggled to sit up and he quickly jumped out of the chair to plump the pillow behind her. "Thanks," she murmured as he once again sat in the chair. "I know I'm in a hospital, but where?"

"Cotter Creek Memorial," he replied. A faint whisper of a smile curved the corners of his lips. "A big name for a small, twenty-bed facility."

She had a feeling he was hoping for a returning smile from her, but she simply couldn't summon one. "Why am I here? I don't seem to be hurt."

Any kind of a smile disappeared as a grim look thinned his lips. "You inhaled a lot of smoke. By the time I got you outside you were unconscious. You came around a bit in the ambulance that brought you here, but the doctor sedated you after you were breathing normally. He wanted to keep you overnight for observation."

She closed her eyes, remembering those moments when the bathroom had filled with choking smoke, the feel of the hot doorknob in her fingers, the absolute terror that had gripped her. If not for Tanner she would be dead.

She opened her eyes and gazed at him, wishing she could be the one to put soothing compresses against his bruised jaw, lay a cool hand across his weary-looking forehead.

"I know you were just doing your job, but thank you for saving my life."

"It's what I do," he replied, averting his gaze from hers.

She closed her eyes again, but only for a moment. As she thought of the consequence of that smoke, that heat, her eyelids popped open and she gasped. "Your home?" she asked, even though she was afraid she knew the answer.

"Was just a place of lumber and nails. It can all be rebuilt." His voice was steady, without emotion.

"Oh, Tanner. I'm so sorry." Tears burned at her eyes as she thought of the house he'd been working on for the past three years. Now, all gone, nothing but ash and memories.

"Hey, no tears allowed," he replied gently. "I was well aware of the risk I took when I brought you into the house."

"I'm sure you didn't expect your house to burn to the ground," she retorted.

"Anna, I'm just glad you're safe."

"Of course, I wouldn't want to be a blot on your perfect protection record." She hadn't meant the bitterness to creep into her voice, but it had.

He stood, his gaze drifting away from her face and toward the bank of windows. "I've got some good news for you. I heard from your father this morning. We've set up a meet early tomorrow."

"At the ranch?" she asked.

"No, the ranch has been compromised. We're meeting him twenty miles from here, at a small convenience store off the highway." His gaze found hers again. "Within twenty-four hours you'll be gone from this dusty little cowboy town and back to the lifestyle you were accustomed to living.

It was as if they hadn't had their conversation in bed the night before, the conversation where she'd told him of the changes she intended to make in her life.

Apparently he hadn't believed her. It didn't matter whether he did or not. She knew what she wanted to do, with or without Tanner West.

"When can I get out of here?" she asked.

"The doctor said he'd probably release you sometime this morning. I'll go see if I can find him and get some information for you."

He seemed relieved, relieved to leave the room, relieved that her father was coming and that his time with her was coming to an end.

As he left the room Anna turned her head toward

the window where the morning had brightened, portending a beautiful day.

Her last day in Cotter Creek.

Her last day with Tanner West.

She'd spent all the years since she'd turned eighteen running from the loneliness that had no name, the yearning for something nebulous and undefined.

Her loneliness now had a name...Tanner West. She knew he was exactly what she'd yearned for, what she'd wanted, needed in her life.

Unfortunately he didn't want or need her.

The doctor released Anna just before noon and the drive back to the ranch was a silent one. The past twelve hours had been the longest in Tanner's life.

When he'd seen the flames licking up to the sky and had known that Anna was inside the inferno, a desperation the likes of which he'd never known had flooded him. Both his father and Zack had tried to keep him from going inside the house, but no force on earth could have stopped him.

As the ranch hands wrestled the assassin to the ground, Tanner had broken away and run around the house to the back door. The fire had been intense, but thankfully had been mostly confined to the living room.

When he'd broken in the bathroom door and seen Anna on her hands and knees gasping for air, he'd felt as if he'd been unable to breathe.

Throughout the night as she had slept in the hospital room, he'd sat in a chair just outside her door, making sure that nothing and nobody could harm her.

Disaster had been so close…too close. He'd nearly lost her, and as he drove toward the ranch his mind played and replayed all the decisions he had made concerning her safety from the moment she'd charged into the office.

Had he made mistakes? Had he allowed his desire to be with Anna to cloud his judgment? He didn't know. The one thing he did know was that if they'd lingered in bed after making love, if he'd been 100 percent focused on her during the argument they'd had, he would have missed that shadow moving in front of the window. In all probability both of them would now be dead.

Even knowing he'd probably made mistakes, understanding that he'd crossed a boundary and had gotten too personally involved, he still wanted to take her in his arms and hold her tight. Even though he knew it was the worst possible thing to do, he wanted to wrap her in his arms and kiss the sadness from her lips.

Instead he tightened his hands on the steering wheel and scowled out the window, aware of her sad gaze lingering on him. Behind his truck was another vehicle holding two armed men in Tanner's employment. Even though they had successfully thwarted one attack, that didn't mean the danger had passed. Tanner hadn't been willing to take any chances. He'd had guards outside her hospital room and would have the house heavily guarded for the night.

"Did you have insurance on the house?" she asked, breaking the uncomfortable silence that had existed since the moment they'd gotten into his truck.

"Yeah. Don't worry about it. It will all be taken care of." He glanced over at her, noting that despite the trauma of the night's events, she looked lovely.

She was clad in a pair of sweatpants and a T-shirt that a nurse had offered her so she wouldn't have to go home in her smoky clothing. The sweatpants were too big and the T-shirt swam on her, but still she was as pretty as Tanner had ever seen her. So pretty it ached deep inside him.

It was a good thing her father would arrive tomorrow. It was the best thing for both of them. She might not realize it at the moment, but she needed something different than he could give her. She deserved more than he was willing to give.

He was relieved when the ranch house came into sight. He'd been afraid that at any moment she might want to resume the discussion they'd been having before all hell had broken loose. He didn't want to revisit it. There was nothing more to say between them except goodbye.

Red and Smokey came out to the front porch as if they'd been standing inside watching for their arrival.

Both men approached the passenger door as Tanner came to a stop.

"Come on, I got some herbal tea waiting for you," Smokey said.

"And I got some magazines for you at the grocery store, some of those fashion women-kind magazines so you can read and relax while you recover," Red added.

For moment Tanner thought she might burst into tears, but instead she pulled herself out of the car and with the dignity he'd come to expect from her, walked toward the house, flanked by the two older men.

Tanner saw with satisfaction that the house was surrounded by armed men. He'd arranged for additional men that morning, taking no chance that they wouldn't be prepared for another attack of some kind.

The air still held the faint tinge of smoke, a reminder of just how close he'd come to losing her last night. He was about to follow them inside when Zack called to him.

He and Zack had really not spoken much at all since the day Zack had returned from his assignment and as Zack approached him, Tanner felt his heart constrict with emotions too great to bear.

"You doing okay?" Zack asked. There was still a haunted look in his eyes and again Tanner wondered what had happened between his brother and the client who had been killed.

"I'm fine. What about you? We haven't really had a chance to talk."

Zack looked off in the distance, a frown creasing his forehead. "I love you, Tanner, but you aren't always the easiest man in the world to talk to."

Tanner shoved his hands into his pockets and sucked in a deep breath. "Why is that?"

Zack looked at him once again. "I'm not sure. Maybe it's because I get the feeling you never allow yourself to get personally involved in any situation. You don't give much of yourself and that makes it hard for anyone to want to give to you."

"I'm sorry." He didn't know what else to say.

Zack shrugged. "It's all right." He paused a long moment but Tanner had the feeling he wasn't finished speaking yet. "You look at her differently than I've ever seen you look at anyone." The words were soft and once again Zack averted his gaze from his brother's. "She looks at you the same way."

A knot formed in Tanner's chest. He wanted to protest, to tell his brother that he was mistaken, but he knew he'd only sound the fool. "She's leaving tomorrow." The knot expanded in his chest. "Her father's due to arrive sometime tomorrow morning."

"That's what I heard. How do you feel about that?"

Feel? How did he feel about it? He'd spent every moment since the phone call from King Bjorn trying not to think about it, not to feel at all. "It's time," he replied succinctly.

For a moment the two brothers remained side by side, staring off in the distance where Tanner's house was nothing more than a rubble of still smoldering ash and concrete.

"Did you love her?" Tanner asked abruptly.

Zack flashed him a quick glance, then returned his gaze to the distance. "Not like a lover. I loved her but not in a romantic way." He took a tremulous deep breath. "We became close as friends. Melissa was a wonderful woman and so easy to talk to. She told me about the heartache of her marriage and I found myself telling her all about my relationship with Jamie."

Jamie Coffer was a young woman Zack had dated nearly two years before. Everyone had just assumed the two of them would be married, but Jamie had left town and within months had married another man.

Tanner had no idea what had caused the breakup and until this moment hadn't realized that apparently the whole thing had left some deep scars on Zack's heart.

"I'm sorry, Zack." Zack turned to look at him once again. "I'm sorry if I haven't been the brother you needed." The words came with difficulty, but he knew they were words that needed to be said. "I always wanted to be there for you, for you and all the rest of us kids."

"I don't know if you've noticed or not, brother, but we're all grown up now. Maybe you need to ease up a little and figure out where you're going in your life."

Tanner frowned, realizing that Zack's words almost echoed what Anna had said to him the night before. Where was he going with his life? He was thirty-five years old and even though he'd told himself over and over again that he eventually wanted a wife and a family, he'd done nothing to take steps to achieve that particular goal.

"I'd better get inside to check on her highness," he finally said.

"Just one thing to think about," Zack said. "I think I'd rather take a chance at getting my heart broken than live the rest of my life with regrets. What about you?"

Tanner didn't reply, knew his brother expected no reply. Instead he turned and went into the house. Life seemed to have turned upside down.

Smokey was making herbal tea and his thirty-one-year-old brother seemed to be trying to give him advice. For the first time in his life Tanner felt as if he'd lost control and it scared him.

He found his father and Smokey in the kitchen with Anna, who was seated at the table, a cup of tea in front of her. Her face was pale, her eyes lifeless as she stared listlessly out the window.

Was it the trauma of the night's events that had sucked all the life, all the energy, from her? Or was it him? Surely it was the fact that she'd nearly lost her life to smoke inhalation and nothing more.

"I made some soup and sandwiches for lunch," Smokey said. "I figured we'd eat informally right here."

Another surprise. Smokey usually insisted on eating properly in the dining room. The old man smiled at Anna. "I made some special chicken soup. Nothing better for a sore throat no matter what made it sore in the first place."

Special tea...special soup. It appeared Anna had made an indelible mark on the heart of Smokey. Amazing, Tanner thought as he sat across from her at the table. How had a princess who had been in the house only a mere week managed to affect each and every person who lived here?

"I hate to be the bearer of more bad news," Red said as they began to eat lunch.

"What bad news?" Tanner asked.

"I heard that Gray Sampson died this morning."

Shock swept through Tanner. "How? What happened?"

"Seems he got thrown from his horse, hit his head on a rock and was killed."

"Damn, that's the second accidental death in the last couple of months." Tanner frowned. Two months ago Joe Wainfield had been killed in his field in a freak tractor accident.

"This Gray Sampson, he was a friend of yours?" Anna's features radiated concern as she gazed at him.

"He lives on a ranch on the north side of town. He was a respected rancher." Tanner looked down at his plate. He didn't want to see that caring in her eyes, that empathetic softness that threatened to pull him in.

She'd be gone tomorrow, Tanner told himself as he

ate. Then everything would get back to normal. He could get back to normal.

He needed to get back to the office, back to working long days so the nights seemed shorter. He needed to get back to focusing solely on the business, so there wouldn't be time to recognize and acknowledge his loneliness.

He was grateful when the meal was over and Anna retreated to her room for a nap. Red headed for the front door and Tanner remained at the kitchen table watching while Smokey cleared the dishes from lunch.

"You look like you sat on a thornbush," Smokey observed as he grabbed the plates in front of Tanner. "Something wrong?"

"Just wondering if the danger is over."

"Even if it's not, you've got enough men stationed around the house to stop any kind of attack that might come," Smokey said. "Besides, from what I heard, one of the half-dozen men Jim arrested last night is singing, and his tune is that there was just their team sent to assassinate the king and Anna."

"I hope he is singing a song of truth," Tanner replied dryly. "I won't relax until Anna and her father are far, far away from here." He stood. "I've got some work to do in the office. I'll be in there if anyone needs anything."

Smokey grunted and Tanner left the kitchen. As he sank down at the desk in the office, he felt a comforting familiarity wash over him. This was where he belonged, taking care of business, not thinking about the woman in the bedroom who had momentarily twisted his world upside down.

Within twenty-four hours she'd be gone and he tried to tell himself that was a good thing.

Chapter 14

Anna stood at her bedroom window for a last good-bye to the place where she'd come to love. The sun was just rising, painting the landscape in lush tones of pinks and oranges.

Although she was eager to see her father, her eagerness was tempered with the overwhelming grief that after today she would never see Tanner again. After today she'd never see his frowns, or the beauty of his smiles. She'd never again hear his smooth deep voice. She'd never again taste the passion of his kisses.

In her twenty-five years she'd dated enough men to recognize the man she wanted to spend the rest of her life with—the man who didn't want to spend his life with her.

Sleep had been elusive the night before. She'd tossed and turned, playing and replaying every moment she'd spent with Tanner. What she'd wanted to do was to sneak into his bedroom to make love with him one final time before they parted forever, but she'd been afraid that if she did that she'd never recover. It was difficult enough as it was.

She'd already packed what little she would take with her. She was taking only her small overnight bag, her red boots and the pair of jeans and T-shirt that she wore. The rest of the things Tanner had bought for her she was leaving behind…along with her heart.

"Anna, it's time to go." Tanner's voice spoke from the doorway.

She stood reluctantly and carried the overnight bag into the living room, dropped it on the floor, then went into the kitchen where Red and Smokey sat at the table.

"I want to thank you for your hospitality," she said to Red. "Thank you for opening your home to me during this difficult time."

Red jumped up out of his chair and took her hand in his. "It's been an honor, Anna. I'd forgotten how nice it was to have a female presence in the house." He dropped her hand with a sad smile.

She went over to where Smokey sat, looking as grumpy as she'd ever seen him. She didn't let his crabby look stop her from planting a fond kiss on his forehead. "Thank you, Smokey."

"For what?" He snorted. "I didn't do nothing special. I wouldn't even change your sheets on your bed for you."

She smiled at him, her heart feeling as if it was far too big for her chest. "You'll never know what you did for me." She looked at Red. "Neither of you will ever know just how much you have given me in the time I've been here." She felt tears burning too close to the surface. She swallowed hard against them.

"I just hope you find what you're looking for," Smokey said softly.

I did, she wanted to say. I did, but it didn't work out.

"We need to go," Tanner said, his voice tense.

Three guards awaited her on the porch and they surrounded her as she and Tanner made their way to his pickup truck.

She shouldn't be thinking of this as the end of something, but rather as the beginning…the beginning of a new life for her.

She should be excited and eagerly anticipating what the future might bring. But as she slid into the passenger seat her heart didn't feel the anticipation of new beginnings. It felt only the pain of the ending of something wonderful…magical.

As Tanner got behind the steering wheel, he checked his watch. "We're to meet your father in thirty minutes." He waited for a car to pull in front of him and behind him. Apparently he was still taking her safety very seriously.

"There was no way we could have your father meet us at the ranch," he said once they were on their way. "This location has been compromised. The convenience store where we're meeting him is off the beaten path and I've already sent three men ahead to secure the location before we arrive. I'm sure you're eager to see your father again."

She nodded, too heart weary to summon any kind of reply. Yes, she'd be glad to see her father again, but she wasn't returning to Niflheim anytime in the near future even if the unrest there was resolved. She couldn't return to the place that had never really been her home, a lifestyle that had only deepened the ache in her heart.

If she was certain about anything, it was that her future didn't include Niflheim.

They spent the rest of the short journey in silence. Anna felt too sick to speak, knowing that each and every mile took her closer to her final goodbye to Tanner.

They arrived at the convenience store ahead of King Bjorn. Tanner's men were already there, stationed around the perimeter. Anna unfastened her seat belt and realized she wanted to say goodbye to Tanner here and now, while they were alone.

"Tanner."

He turned to face her with those beautiful dark

green eyes and those strong, stern features that she'd grown to love. The corner of his mouth twitched, and with that slight tick of vulnerability she found the words she wanted, needed to say.

"I love you, Tanner. I won't say it again, because I've said it enough that I'd hoped you'd believe the words. But, there is something I want to tell you. During some talks with Smokey I was introduced to a very special woman."

He frowned with obvious confusion. "I don't understand."

She leaned toward him and saw the corner of his mouth twitch once again. "Smokey told me about a lovely woman, a strong woman who had the world by the tail. She might have become wealthy, she might have married royalty and become a princess or even a queen. She might have done all kinds of things to bring herself wealth and adulation, but she chose to marry the man she loved and have his children. Smokey told me about your mother, Tanner, and that's the kind of woman I hope to be."

There was a flash of genuine pain in his eyes. "Anna, for God's sake, don't make this any more difficult than it already is."

She leaned even closer and could smell him, that familiar scent of sunshine and wind, of faint cologne and male. God help her, but it smelled like home.

"I just needed to tell you one last thing," she continued. "If you don't love me, then you're doing the right thing by allowing me to leave here. But if you do love me, it would be a tragic mistake on your part to let me go."

At that moment two cars approached the convenience store and Anna knew her father had arrived. It was time to go.

The two cars pulled to a halt. The first men out of the car were armed and obviously there for protection. The third man out was Anna's father.

King Bjorn Johansson was a big man. Standing well over six feet tall, he had a broad girth that spoke of good living. Despite his large size, he carried himself with a regal grace and a commanding dignity.

Anna got out of Tanner's truck and flew to her father's arms, vaguely aware of another imposing man getting out of her father's car.

"Ah, my dear. I knew Mr. West would take good care of you," he said as he released her. "He's a man like his father." He smiled over her head at Tanner.

Tanner returned the smile with a respectful bow. "It will take years for me to be the man my father is."

"I understand there was trouble last night and you lost your home."

Anna felt herself lost as her father focused all his attention on Tanner. Her resolve to make a future all her own grew. She adored her father, but would she always be dismissed by him as something pretty and frivolous?

"A little trouble and nothing that insurance won't cover," Tanner replied as he gestured for the king to move inside the store. He wasn't comfortable standing out in the open despite the guards that surrounded them.

"Mr. West, may I introduce you to General Jorge Hauptman," King Bjorn said once they were inside the store. He gestured to the dignified man standing just behind him.

Anna watched as Tanner and general Hauptman shook hands. "Father, what is the news from Niflheim?" she asked.

"At this moment General Hauptman's troops are attempting to wrest control of the palace from the rebel forces who hold it."

"And you expect this to be successful?" Anna asked. Even though she had no intention of returning, her heart ached with the divisiveness that had ripped apart the small country.

General Hauptman nodded. "John Swenson and his Brotherhood of the Mist used surprise and an alarming lack of security to overwhelm the palace, much like what the terrorists did here in your country on 9/11. But the Brotherhood of the Mist is a small, rather disorganized group. We hope to have the palace back in our control by nightfall."

King Bjorn looked at Tanner. "General Hauptman and I have been at odds in the past. But he has agreed to work with me in a strong, unified front."

"Certainly the danger has not passed and will not be over even when we gain control of the palace," Hauptman added.

"But it's my country," King Bjorn said passionately. "And no matter what the dangers, it is where I belong."

"What about the men who were arrested here last night?" Tanner asked.

"They will be transported back to Niflheim to stand trail for treason. Unfortunately we have no way of knowing if there are others in the country. I would hope that after today you and your family will be safe."

"It's Anna's safety I'm concerned about," Tanner replied, but he kept his gaze focused on the king and not on Anna.

"Anna will have all the bodyguards she needs to assure her safety in Niflheim," he said. "As I said before, we're quite aware that dangerous times lie ahead and we will take the necessary precautions to ward off tragedy. We will not be caught unaware and unprepared again."

Anna said nothing, aware that now wasn't the time to tell her father that she had very different plans for herself. She had no intention of returning to Niflheim and living with armed guards." Surely a princess could find obscurity and happiness in the United States.

"And now we must be on our way," King Bjorn said.

"We have a flight to catch this afternoon and many plans to make in the meantime." He held out his hand to Tanner.

Anna watched the two men in her life shake hands, and again tears threatened to fall. Tanner—her heart cried—I don't want to say goodbye!

"Ready?" her father asked.

She nodded and picked up the overnight bag that Tanner had carried with him into the store. Flanked by bodyguards, she and her father and the general left the convenience store.

"Somebody want to tell me what's going on?" The ready voice belonged to the teenage male working the counter. His eyes were huge and his protruding Adam's apple danced up and down.

"Don't worry about it, kid," Tanner said, then turned his attention out the window.

His heart hurt as Anna's final private words to him went around and around in his head, mingling with Zack's advice about regrets.

He hadn't meant to fall in love with Anna. He hadn't meant to ever fall in love with anyone. Love hurt too much. He'd learned that lesson with his mother's death, and at that time he'd done exactly what Anna had accused him of doing...built fences around his heart.

But now, the fences were tumbling down and raw emotion swept through him. Would he be satisfied living forever with regrets or was he man enough to face his fear and go after what he wanted more than anything else in the world?

Anna. Her name cried out from his heart. Anna, with her flashing blue eyes and sparkling blond hair. Anna, with her sweet lips and womanly curves. She intoxicated him.

Anna, with her determination to be something more, with her sense of humor and warm laughter. She already held his heart in her hands. So, what was he waiting for?

He watched her get into the back seat of the second car with her father and energy ripped through him. He tore open the store's door and raced outside as the roar of their engines sounded.

"Wait!" He ran to the car that held the king and his daughter and pounded on the window. He saw Anna's face through the window, her eyes huge and her mouth forming an O of surprise. He ripped open her door and stared at her.

"Don't go." The words tore from his throat, a desperate plea like he'd never voiced before.

He'd expected her to bolt out of the car and into his arms, but instead she remained seated, staring at him with those gorgeous eyes. "Why not?" she asked. She waited only a moment, then continued. "You have to say the words, Tanner. I need to hear the words."

"I love you. I love you, Anna, and I can't imagine my life without you." Once the dam had burst, the words seemed to come without thought, driven out of him by sheer emotion. "I need you to make me laugh. I need you to remind me that there's more to life than work. Anna, I need you to help me be the man I want to be. And I'll help you be the woman you want to be."

Tears filled her eyes and for a dreadful moment he wondered if he was too late or if perhaps she'd realized her love for him wasn't real after all. "You heard what my father said. There might still be danger."

"Then I won't just be your husband—I'll be your lifetime bodyguard," he replied. His heart hammered as she leaned to the side and said something to her father. Then she turned back to Tanner, and in the smile she gave him he saw his future.

She stepped out of the car and set her overnight bag on the ground. He started to take her into his arms, needing her close, wanting to embrace her forever, but she held up a hand to stop him. "Throw me over your shoulder, Tanner."

"Excuse me?"

Her eyes flashed with the impatience he'd come to love. "You heard me—throw me over your shoulder."

"Why would you want me to do that?" he asked.

She smiled, her charming dimples flashing. "Because that's what cowboys do when they love a woman."

With a burst of laughter that seemed to fill his very soul, he grabbed her and lifted her over his shoulder, then bent and picked up her overnight case.

"She'll be in touch," he said to a surprised-looking but smiling King Bjorn, then turned to carry her to his pickup truck. The men who had been tapped for guard duty clapped and cheered, and in that sound Tanner heard his future calling.

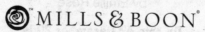

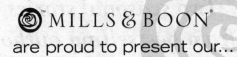

Two seasonal stories
from bestselling author
Diana Palmer

Featuring

Heart of Ice

and

Carrera's Bride

Available 4th December 2009

millsandboon.co.uk Community

Join Us!

The Community is the perfect place to meet and chat to kindred spirits who love books and reading as much as you do, but it's also the place to:

■ Get the inside scoop from authors about their latest books

■ Learn how to write a romance book with advice from our editors

■ Help us to continue publishing the best in women's fiction

■ Share your thoughts on the books we publish

■ Befriend other users

Forums: Interact with each other as well as authors, editors and a whole host of other users worldwide.

Blogs: Every registered community member has their own blog to tell the world what they're up to and what's on their mind.

Book Challenge: We're aiming to read 5,000 books and have joined forces with The Reading Agency in our inaugural Book Challenge.

Profile Page: Showcase yourself and keep a record of your recent community activity.

Social Networking: We've added buttons at the end of every post to share via digg, Facebook, Google, Yahoo, technorati and de.licio.us.

www.millsandboon.co.uk

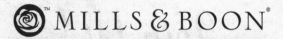